A

THOUSAND

FORESTS

IN

ONE

ACORN:

An

Anthology

of

Spanish-

Language

Fiction

A THOUSAND FORESTS IN ONE ACORN

AN ANTHOLOGY OF SPANISH-LANGUAGE FICTION

Valerie Miles

OPEN LETTER

LITERARY TRANSLATIONS FROM THE UNIVERSITY OF ROCHESTER

Originally punlished as *Mil Bosques en una bellota*
Copyright © 2012 by Valerie Miles

First edition, 2014
All rights reserved

Rights to individual pieces used with permission of original copyright holders.
Information on permissions for English translations can be found in the back.

Library of Congress Cataloging-in-Publication Data: Available upon request.
ISBN-13: 978-1-934824-91-7 / ISBN-10: 1-934824-91-7

*This anthology was made possible thanks to the generous support of the
Spain-USA Foundation and its SPAIN arts & culture program*

SPAIN/USA/
/ Foundation /

Printed on acid-free paper in the United States of America.

Text set in Caslon, a family of serif typefaces based on the designs of
William Caslon (1692–1766).

Design by N. J. Furl

Open Letter is the University of Rochester's nonprofit, literary translation press:
Lattimore Hall 411, Box 270082, Rochester, NY 14627

www.openletterbooks.org

TABLE OF CONTENTS

RETIRADO en la paz de estos desiertos,
con pocos, pero doctos libros juntos,
vivo en conversación con los difuntos,
y escucho con mis ojos a los muertos.

Si no siempre entendidos, siempre abiertos,
o enmiendan, o fecundan mis asuntos;
y en músicos callados contrapuntos
al sueño de la vida hablan despiertos.

Las grandes almas que la muerte ausenta,
de injuras de los años vengadora,
libra, ¡oh gran don Joseph!, docta la imprenta.

En fuga irrevocable huye la hora;
pero aquélla el mejor cálculo cuenta,
que en la lección y estudios nos mejora.

—FRANCISCO DE QUEVADO

PROLOGUE

One breezy August afternoon in the village of Cashiers, North Carolina, I accompanied my mother to the local library. Despite a population of some 200 souls, the library is impressive and well-sponsored by the families who spend their summers in the mountains. They had received donations of estate books as part of the civic tradition of raising funds for community projects and we went to browse through what was available. A book edited by Whit Burnett—idea by John Pen—caught my eye, titled *This Is My Best: Over 150 Self-Chosen and Complete Masterpieces, Together with Their Reasons for Their Selection*. As I flipped through the pages, I began to realize what an extraordinary piece of literary history it was. Published by Dial Press in 1942, the editor had asked the influential writers of the time to "edit their entire lifetime output to select the one unit which in their own, uninfluenced opinion represents their best creative moment. A book composed over many years, the focusing of many lifetime viewpoints, a public revelation of the private opinions of our best authors on how they look upon themselves, and what, in their writings, they most value."

The introduction explains that neither T. S. Eliot nor Gertrude Stein were able to contribute because they were in Europe (this was 1942). However, William Faulkner, Pearl Buck, Sinclair Lewis, Ernest Hemingway, Willa Cather, Theodore Dreiser, Wallace Stevens, Langston Hughes, a trove of writers, thinkers, poets and philosophers contributed by selecting their own favorite writing. Some took the exercise to be a form of torture, but made the effort. John Dos Passos wrote that "The pages in past books you remember so vividly as having turned out well have a way of going sour on you when you look them up again." Booth Tarkington considered that "There are few writers, and they are to be envied for their youth, who can be fond concerning works of their own construction already in cold print."

Others were quite pleased to be asked. William Saroyan boasted outright "I have little use for any other kind of writing, unless it is my own, in which case I am devoted to the stuff." Dorothy Parker, in pure Parkerian finesse, responded: "Now what is a writer to say about a sample of his own work? If he takes one course, he's simpering. If he goes the opposite way, he's Saroyan. It may be that I felt a certain maternal obligation to say a few words in its favor. Nobody else did."

I found it fascinating that Lillian Hellman contributed a piece from her trip to Valencia, circa 1937. "This part is about Spain during the Civil War. I hope these people are alive, that they will live to see a better day." And John Dewey, engaged in a study of Adolf Hitler's writing and speeches predicted Hitler's failure: "His views and his practice rest upon the lowest kind of estimate of the capacities of human nature. The moral source of his final defeat will be just this total lack of faith. For the foundation of a pacified and unified Europe is the discovery by European peoples of the true nature of the democratic ideal and of the democratic methods by which alone the ideal can be made effective." Seems like forever ago, although in historical terms this happened just yesterday.

I found the anthology captivating not only because of the peculiar historical context of the pieces chosen, which gives a panorama of American literature and thought at a crucial moment in time, but also because through comparing the voices of the writers presenting their own work, one glimpses the vast differences in styles and ways in which each one approached writing. Oddly, the more I spoke with friends about the find, the more I realized that in fact it was still available in many libraries both personal and public. Carlos Fuentes, upon receiving the invitation to this project, responded by saying that he was pleased to be a part of the Spanish language version, since it brought back happy memories of his own father's library.

•

Ralph Waldo Emerson wrote in his essay *History* that there is one mind common to all individual men and therefore the whole of history exists in one man, all of history lies folded into a single individual experience: "The creation of a thousand forests is in one acorn." He also wrote that "The fact narrated must correspond to something in me to be credible or intelligible. As we read, we must become Greeks, Romans, Turks, priest and king, martyr and executioner, must fasten these images to some reality in our secret experience." A little bit like taking a walk through Baudelaire's forest of symbols that nod to all men in understanding.

As an American who has spent half a life in Spain working in publishing, I had long specialized in providing authors in translation for a Spanish language audience. So I found the idea of putting together a Spanish language version of this anthology a fascinating proposal for a literary adventure through some of the most celebrated writing in the language during the second half of the twentieth century. To root out the acorn, the kernel, the driving obsession of a writer, of knowing what he or she, in the quiet of their study, considers the best representation of that obsession. To listen to the individual voices and fasten the images to some reality in my secret experience, walk among the nodding symbols; to be a lonely child growing up in Peru, a young man in Madrid whose lover dies in bed before they can consummate the act, a painter in Tahiti who finds inspiration on a stormy night, or a mother who chooses power over love for her son's future in a world of magical creatures. Perhaps, by living out these secret experiences, I might discover some occult map of the forest by its trees.

A Thousand Forests in One Acorn is much less ambitious in size and scope than Whit Burnett's original. I suppose it is fitting for the new century and much could be and is being written on the current state of attention spans. Here there are 28 writers and they are all narrators of fiction. It's worth noting that this in no way should be considered a canon, not even a personal one, but simply a selection of some of the important writers of the twentieth century who have been awarded prizes and widely acclaimed and celebrated in their countries. Space would never allow me to include all the writers whose work I admire and there are writers who would be considered more or less canonical who are not here, many of whom were invited but who were not able to participate—Gabriel García Márquez, Fernando del Paso, Fernando Vallejo, César Aira, José Emilio Pacheco, and William Opsina, among others. Sadly, others were invited whom we have lost before the process could begin, namely Guillermo Cabrera Infante and Daniel Sada. The late Carlos Fuentes was one of the last writers with whom I had the opportunity to work, his words having now passed into literary history.

By this I want to say that readers should not find scandal in the fact that one or another writer is not included since the selection openly assumes the multiple limitations of time and space, and the inevitable tendencies of a reader who is of the feminine sex, born in New York in 1963, who has had a more or less constant interest in Spanish language writing, and who has lived in Barcelona for the past 20 years. This is the work of an investigative reader, accompanied by the writers who have kindly allowed themselves to be carried away by the enthusiasm of a literary adventure. Here, the writers are the specialists in their own work, and my job as editor has been that of compiling the work chosen by the authors themselves.

Organized chronologically by age beginning with the Argentine writer Aurora Venturini, who received a prize from Borges as a girl and from young readers just recently, the anthology gathers the work of some of the best writers in the Spanish language of the second half of the twentieth century. The youngest writer included, Evelio Rosero, was born in 1958. The premise is that the younger the writer, the more difficult it is to think that they have already written their best pages. If the anthology is to comply with a function of being a historical document, at least the bulk of the writers should be able to choose something that might be considered the best writing of their entire career.

Each writer constitutes a chapter of their own, which is divided into three parts. The first part, titled "The Torture of Doctor Johnson" subjects the writer to the pain of selection alluded to earlier in this introduction by Dos Passos and Tarkington. Dr. Johnson wrote that "The man who is asked by an author what he thinks of his work is put to torture and is not obliged to speak the truth." So here it becomes even more torturous when it is the writer who must speak the truth about themselves and their own work. A few of the writers found it particularly troubling; Eduardo Mendoza, Rafael Sánchez Ferlosio, Hebe Uhart, Alberto Ruy Sánchez, but they were all good sports in the end, so much the better for us.

The second section is titled "In Conversation with the Dead," which comes from Quevedo's celebrated sonnet: *Retirado en la paz de estos desiertos / con pocos, pero doctos libros juntos / vivo en conversación con los difuntos / y escucho con mis ojos a los muertos.* This section gives us the opportunity to know more about the influences, the traditions of each author, about the departed friends— writers, thinkers, poets, philosophers—who have marked or impacted their work or whom they have read and reread and "converse" with creatively.

The third section is a coda meant to bring out some of the peculiarities of each writer's work and intentions since, as Katherine Anne Porter mentioned in the English version of the anthology: "an author's choice of his own work must always be decided by such private knowledge of the margin between intention and the accomplished fact." Here I nudge a little, ask a few more pesky questions to round out the information provided in the first and second sections.

Reading the series of presentations followed by the selections themselves, together in one volume, provides an interesting mirror to the events that shaped the authors' lives and how their writing was particularly affected, and consequently, the larger context of literature in the language. Blending the writers not by country but by chronology offers a sense of the march of literature on both continents, and follows the ebb and flow of the wider events both political and literary, the cultural traffic moving back and forth from each side of the Atlantic, the exiles and diasporas resulting from a century of turbulence. One can clearly see the devastating effects of the Franco regime, writers who had to exile or publish in other countries or self-censor, or who limited themselves to realism as the best means for denouncing the state of affairs at the time. Paris looms as more than a mere legend, here it is virtually a protagonist, a literary motherland for the lost tribe: the hub first for the Spanish writers seeking an atmosphere in which they could write, but also a city of refuge for Latin American writers fleeing instability or martial law during the '70s. William Faulkner looms large as, to quote Ishmael in *Moby-Dick*, "one grand hooded phantom, like a snow hill in the air." García Márquez invoked him as "maestro" when he received the Nobel Prize and Mario Vargas Llosa wrote that "Without the influence of Faulkner, Latin America would not have had the modern novel. The best writers read him and, like Carlos Fuentes and Juan Rulfo, Cortázar and Carpentier, Sabato and Roa Bastos, García Márquez and Onetti, knew how to take advantage of his teachings, like Faulkner himself took advantage of the technical mastery of James Joyce and the subtleties of Henry James, among others, to build his splendid narrative saga." He is one of the departed friends most cited, also by Ramón Pinilla, whose Getxo, an imaginary microcosm, can be seen as a Basque version of Yoknapatawpha.

Most of the conversations were done in person and I have very fond memories of the afternoon spent with Javier Marías in his home in Madrid, taking down books from the shelves of his library, looking up translations of Nabokov and searching for the origin of his "luna pulposa"; and of Antonio Muñoz Molina in a coffee shop on a very hot August afternoon, also in Madrid, talking about memory and literature and Mágina, how time in the south of Spain jumped a century in the year after Franco died. And the animated conversation with Ana María Matute in her home in Barcelona where we spoke about Medieval literature, Arthurian lore, the limits of realism, and the difficulties of having been an intelligent woman at a time when nice girls didn't go to college. Cristina Fernández Cubas, who met with me in one of her favorite spots in the Eixample, was a sparkling conversationalist, entertaining with delightful turns of phrase and a passionate defense of the short story, and Enrique Vila-Matas whose literary playfulness on the page is but a manifestation of the erudite writer. I strolled the Ramblas with Juan Goytisolo to buy a newspaper after spending some time chatting in the salon of Hotel Oriente, and had drinks with Carlos Fuentes in the Hotel Majestic, who spoke using his flawless English to honor the original anthology and his father's library. I spent an afternoon with Juan Marsé in his home remembering the original "Teresa in Paris" and wild Monte Carmelo back in the day, with Esther Tusquets talking about Virginia Woolf, shared 5 o'clock champagne (on more than one occasion) and secret milongas with Edgardo Cozarinsky, enjoyed a bookstore café with Abilio Estévez who recreated the nostalgia of his pre-exile times in Cuba, delighted in the cultivated exchanges at dinner and lunch with Jorge Edwards in Madrid and Mallorca, in tequilas and taxis with Alberto Ruy Sánchez in Mexico. There were many long and repeated conversations by telephone with Rafael Sánchez Ferlosio who started out gruff and imposing but who grew more and more endearing with every conversation. Ramiro Pinilla's delightful humbleness before his own monumental achievement and impressive command of American literature, and the list goes on.

As in Burnett's anthology in which Hemingway sent a note from Cuba asking to include the story *A Short Happy Life of Francis Macomber* instead of others that had been until then the fodder of all school children, so *A*

Thousand Forests in One Acorn has had some interesting surprise responses. For example, Mario Vargas Llosa chose a fragment of *The Way to Paradise* (*El paraíso en la otra esquina*) instead of *Conversation in the Cathedral* (*Conversación en la catedral*) or *The War of the End of the World* (*La guerra del fin del mundo*) as I or many others might have expected. Carlos Fuentes decided upon a fragment of *Terra Nostra* instead of something from his highly celebrated *The Death of Artemio Cruz* (*La muerte de Artemio Cruz*) or beloved *Aura*. Or the discovery that Vila Matas has a story in *Explorers of the Abyss* (*Exploradores del abismo*) that he considers to be highly representative of his deepest literary obsessions.

Four years of work and many hands went into this project. It has been a literary adventure to be sure and there are myriad interesting conclusions that can be drawn, and I suspect more than one occult map of the forest to be revealed for the discerning reader. But I will leave that to each individual to decipher according to his own secret experiences, to find the thousand forests in his own acorn. This is not meant to be a curated experience, but one of discovery and even self-discovery. The objective is to provide a direct connection between the reader and some of the writers who have left a mark on the history of literature in the Spanish language, who have played an essential role in painting with words and years of trade its many moods, its various colors, its diverse aspects, its rich landscape, its history, and tradition.

It would make me very pleased if some day far into the future, someone would donate a copy of this anthology to a local library, and perhaps thereby allow it to fall by chance into the hands of a reader who finds in it a pathway into the nodding forest of letters. My wish is that she enjoy this reading adventure through Spanish language literature at the hands of its writers and recognize that she has been touched by a project whose idea goes all the way back to New York in 1942 when T.S. Eliot and Gertrude Stein couldn't send their contributions for the U-boats.

Happy reading!

Valerie Miles

Barcelona, Spain
May 17, 2012

THOUSAND

FORESTS

IN ONE

ACORN

AN ANTHOLOGY OF SPANISH-LANGUAGE FICTION

AURORA
VENTURINI
(Argentina, 1922)

Aurora Venturini's career has been defined by the will of a long-distance runner. Born in 1922 in La Plata, Argentina, from a very young age she knew that her relationship with language was different, that she had a very special connection to it, and even as a child she took refuge in words and in reading.

The cousin of her paternal grandmother was none other than Giuseppe Tomasi di Lampedusa, the celebrated author of *The Leopard*. But the person who really served as her guide, in terms of writing and reading, was her grandfather, Juan Bautista Venturini, with whom she maintained a close relationship. As the years passed, his persistent influence would prove indispensable.

When she was nineteen, having recently earned her teaching certificate, Venturini starting working as a teacher to pay for her studies at Universidad Nacional de La Plata, where she was taking courses in Philosophy and Education Sciences. Seven years later, she had already published numerous books of poetry, and added a profoundly distinct voice to La Plata's literary history, augmenting its mythical status as "the city of poets." Critics have often praised her lyricism and the formal mastery of her poetry, displayed in titles like *Versos al recuerdo, El anticuario, Peregrino del aliento*. In 1948 her book of poetry *El solitario* won the Premio Iniciación, which the author accepted from the hands of Borges himself.

Even though the radical party reigned in her family, she became a supporter of the man running the country at the time: Juan Domingo Perón. Due to her political affiliation, before long, she began to write speeches for the wife of the governor of the province of Buenos Aires, Elena Caporale. Later on, Elena introduced her to Eva Perón—a woman who changed her life forever. Evita, whom she described as a "force of nature," enjoyed her company, her sense of humor, and her passion for the thought of Heraclitus. Evita makes frequent appearances in the work of the writer from La Plata.

In 1956, a year after the overthrow of Perón, Venturini left for Paris. She studied psychology at the Sorbonne and became a member of the "existential-ist group," beginning a period of great professional fecundity. She became friends with Jean-Paul Sartre, Simone de Beauvoir, Albert Camus, Eugène Ionesco, and Juliette Gréco. Aurora got married twice: the first time in 1956 to the judge Eduardo Varela and the second in 1993 to historian Fermín Chávez. She has translated and written critical essays on poets like Isidore Ducasse, Comte de Lautréamont, François Villon, and Arthur Rimbaud; her translations of the latter two won her the Iron Cross medal from the French government. She also published collections of short stories (*Carta a Zoraida*; *relatos para las tías viejas*), poetry (*Laúd, La trova, La Plata mon amour*), and traveled throughout much of Europe. In her short stories, the prose is intensely poetic, enriched by frequent autobiographical evocations, as stark as they are candid, and enriched too by the history and politics of those difficult years in Argentina, full of conflict, persecution, and flight.

When she returned to Argentina, she continued to write and publish with small, independent publishers. But recognition came to her in 2007. That year the Buenos Aires journal *Página/12* organized and presented the Premio Nueva Novela, and her book *Las primas* ended up winning. An unsettling story, the committee described it as "A unique novel, extreme, of disconcert-ing originality, that forces readers to ask themselves many questions books tend to ignore or carefully keep quiet." Convinced that new literature never depends on a writer's age but on the thirst for adventure a writer retains, Venturini accepted the award emulating Flaubert: "*Las primas* c'est moi."

THE ACORN

The Torture of Doctor Johnson

I think of the Golden Age playwrights and the surprising formal hybridity they managed. Lope de Vega, for example (along with many others), used the tragicomedy to convey his characters' development. I had those authors as a point of reference for this first chapter of my novel, *Las primas*. I explain what the family of the protagonist, Yuna, was like: what her mother did, what her cousins were like, her sister, her aunt Nené, and the art professor, whose role in the development of the story is crucial. Yuna's mother feels a profound detachment from her family in particular because her husband abandoned her with two very strange daughters. One is a handicapped girl, Betina, who's in a wheelchair. The other is Yuna, the narrator, who loves to paint. In this first part I tried to describe not only this girl's talent when she attends a fine arts school in La Plata, where she wins prizes at exhibitions, but also the astuteness of the professor. Yuna has trouble speaking, and since she can hardly read or write, she expresses herself through painting. She meets a professor who values her very highly and who tells her they're going to show her work first in Buenos Aires and then in Europe. He tells her they're going to travel and she jumps on the professor to kiss him and they fall over together. "No, Yuna, that's not done. Because men are fire and women straw and the devil comes along and blows."

In Conversation with the Dead

I feel very close to Dostoyevsky, who for me is the greatest writer ever, especially in *The Idiot*. And also Pasternak, whose work I enjoy immensely, and

Joyce, whose *Ulysses* I've read so many times. Incredible that everything takes place in one day. We're so dynamic, so full of internal monologues. And I can't forget Alberto Ponce de León; I often revisit his book, *Tiempo de muchachas*. I've also translated Villon, Rimbaud, the Comte de Lautréamont, and in Sicily I struck up a friendship with Quasimodo. Those are my literary dead. With respect to the others, to the dead in my family, the figure of my grandfather, Giovanni Battista, is very important. He was a wise man. He came to Argentina from Sicily, fleeing Garibaldi; he didn't want a united Italy. He was a person who never rested and who read a lot, especially Dante, Virgil, Petrarch. He would tell me: "If you ever write a sonnet, write it like Petrarch or don't bother." He arrived in 1860, started a family, and, on top of that, gave us the nostalgia that all children of immigrants share.

CODA

Before leaving for Paris, you received a prize from Borges's own hands, and later, when you were eighty-five, you won another award from young Argentine writers who considered you one of their own. Narratively, Paris was like an intermezzo between Buenos Aires and Buenos Aires.

I began writing here but I love Paris very much. It was the happiest time of my life, amazing to be in Paris at the height of existentialism. I entered university in 1942 and ended up with a doctorate in Philosophy and Education. Afterward, with the Revolución Libertadora in '55, I had to leave, and in Paris I specialized in psychology. The French authorities were good enough to give me citizenship and I was able to work. Nothing like what happened to me in Argentina after the fall of Perón, where I was attacked over and over. But no one remembers that and no one talks about it. Because people who went to war don't talk, the ones who talk are inventing, because if someone told what actually happened no one would think it was possible. But I went to Paris and that influenced me because I was with the greatest writers. I was with poets like Quasimodo, I took courses with Jean-Paul Sartre and Simone de Beauvoir, I was very close friends with Violette Leduc. We had such beautiful experiences, the nights we'd get together in the Latin Quarter.

And now, here, the "youth" prize for *Las primas* opened the door to many opportunities, the novel has been adapted for the theater several times and has been translated into many languages.

A THOUSAND FORESTS

FROM *LAS PRIMAS*
(THE COUSINS)
[A NOVEL]

A disabled childhood

My mom carried a pointer when she taught and wore a white dustcoat and she was very strict but she was a good teacher in a suburban school for not the brightest kids from middle class families on downward. The best one was the grocer's son Ruben Fiorlandi. My mom rapped the ones that acted up on their heads and sent them to the corner wearing the colored cardboard donkey ears. The misbehavior was rarely repeated. In my mom's opinion a little blood makes any lesson stick. The third graders called her the third grade miss but she was married to my father who left her and never performed the obligations of a *pater familiae*. She worked as a teacher in the mornings and came home at two in the afternoon where dinner would be waiting because our small dark housemaid Rufina did the cooking. I was sick of stew every day. A chicken coop clucked behind the house and in the yard squash sprouted miraculously and unruly golden sunflowers stretched from the earth to the heavens next to violets and stunted roses that gave that miserable heap its perfume and that's how we ate.

I never admitted that I learned to read time when I was twenty. That confession embarrasses and surprises me. It embarrasses and surprises me for reasons that you'll find out later and lots of questions come to mind. One I remember especially: What time is it? Honest truth I couldn't tell time and clocks frightened me just like the sound of my sister's wheelchair.

She was even more of an idiot than me but she could read the face of a clock even though she couldn't read a book. We weren't typical, never mind normal.

Vroom . . . vroom . . . vroom . . . murmured Betina my sister wheeling her misfortune around the garden and the stone courtyards. The vroom was usually wet with the idiot's drool. Poor Betina. Freak of nature. Poor me, another freak, and my mom weighed down by abandonment and by monsters even more so.

But everything in this awful world passes. That's why it doesn't make sense to dwell too much on anything or anyone.

Sometimes I think we're a dream or a nightmare relived day after day that at any second will stop that won't appear on the screen of the soul to torture us any more.

Betina suffers from a mental disorder

That was the psychologist's diagnosis. I don't know if that's all it was. My sister had a crooked spine, from behind in her chair she looked like a tiny hunchback with puny legs and massive arms. The old lady who came to darn the socks said that someone had done something to my mom during her pregnancies, the worst during the one with Betina.

I asked the unibrowed mustachioed lady psychologist what a mental disorder was.

She said it was related to the soul but that I wouldn't understand till I was older. But I supposed that the soul was something like a white sheet inside the body and that when it got stained people became idiots, Betina a lot and me a little.

I started noticing when Betina wheeled around the table with her vroom that she was dragging a little tail that stuck out through the back of the wheelchair seat and I told myself it had to be her soul coming untucked.

When I asked the psychologist this time if the soul had anything to do with being alive she said it did and even added that when it was missing people died and the soul went to heaven if it had been good and to hell if it had been bad.

Vroom . . . vroom . . . vroom her soul dragged more and had more gray stains every day and I decided that it wouldn't be long before it fell out and

Betina would be dead which didn't matter to me because she made me sick.

When it was time to eat, I had to feed my sister and on purpose I'd mistake the orifice and I'd put the spoon in her eye, in her ear, in her nose, before finally her cakehole. Ah . . . ah . . . ah . . . moaned the filthy creature.

I would grab her hair and put her face in her food and then she'd be quiet. Why did I have to pay for my parents' mistakes? I thought about stepping on the tail of her soul. The thing about hell stopped me.

Reading the catechism had burned the "thou shalt not kill" into me. But with every little bump today and again tomorrow, the tail grew and no one else saw. Only I did and I rejoiced.

The institutes for different students

I wheeled Betina to hers. Then I walked to the one for me. Betina's institute was for treating very serious cases. The pig-boy, puffy-faced, thick-lipped, and pointy-eared. He ate from a gold plate and drank his soup from a gold cup. He held the cup in his stubby cloven hooves and made a sound like a gush of water down a well and when he ate solids his jaw and ears moved and he couldn't chew with his canines, which jutted out like a wild boar. Once he looked at me. His tiny black beady eyes swimming in a pool of grease wouldn't look away and I stuck my tongue out and he roared and threw his dish. The attendants came and to control him they had to tie him up like an animal, which is what he was.

While I waited for Betina's class to end I'd wander around the corridors of that coven. I saw a priest come in followed by an acolyte. Someone had dropped their sheet, their soul. The priest was sprinkling water and saying if you have a soul may God receive you in his bosom.

Who or what was he talking to?

I got close and saw an important family from Adrogué. On a table there was a silk cloth and a cannelloni. If it hadn't been a cannelloni but something that a human womb had expelled the priest wouldn't have done a christening.

I asked a nurse who told me that every year a prominent family brought a cannelloni to baptize. That the doctor had urged them not to have any more children because it wasn't working. And that they'd said that because they were very Catholic they had to keep procreating. Even with my disability I could tell this was a nauseating situation but I couldn't say so. That night I was too sick to eat.

And my sister's soul got longer all the time. I was glad my dad had gone.

The development

Betina was eleven and I was twelve. Rufina said it's the age they'll start developing and I pictured something from inside coming out of me and I prayed to Santa Theresa that it wouldn't be cannelloni. I asked the psychologist if she thought I was developing and with a red face she suggested I ask my mom.

My mom got red in the face too and said that at a certain age girls stopped being girls and became young ladies. That was all she said and I was left in suspense.

I already said that I attended a handicapped school, less handicapped than Betina's. One girl said that she was developing. I couldn't tell any difference. She said that when it happens blood comes out between your legs for several days and that you don't have to take a bath and that you have to use a rag so your clothes don't get stained and be careful around boys so you don't end up pregnant.

That night I felt the place she'd said and couldn't sleep. But it wasn't damp so I could still talk to boys. When I was developed I'd never even look at a single boy if I didn't want to get pregnant and have a cannelloni or something like it.

Betina talked or blabbered and everyone understood. So it happened that one night during a family gathering that because of our manners they didn't let us come to, we ate alone and my sister started squawking like a trombone: *Mamá I'm bleeding from my cookie!* We were in the next room over from the dinner. A grandmother and two cousins came in.

I told my cousins to stay away from the blood because they could end up pregnant.

Everyone left in a huff and my mom gave us both the pointer.

At the institute I told them that Betina was developed even though she was younger than me. The teacher stopped me. The classroom is no place for immoral talk like that and she covered me with moral and civic lessons.

Everyone in the class was suddenly worried especially the girls who every so often felt for any possible dampness.

Just in case I stopped talking to the boys.

Margarita came in radiant one afternoon and said "it came" and we knew what she meant.

My sister left school in third grade. There wasn't any point. Actually for either of us there wasn't any point and I left in sixth grade. I did learn to read and write, but with terrible spelling, everything without an H because if you didn't pronounce it what was the point?

The psychologist said I had dyslexia. But she suggested I'd improve with practice and she forced me to do tongue twisters like María Chusena her shack she was thatching when along comes a thatcher who asks Miss Chusena your shack are you thatching or stocking the shacks dear my shack I'm not thatching nor shacks am I stocking only thatching the shack for María Chusena.

My mom watched me and when I couldn't untwist it she'd hit me over the head with the pointer. The psychologist made sure my mom wasn't there for María Chusena and I untwisted better because if my mom was there when I tried to finish María Chusena I'd make a mistake in my rush to avoid the pointer.

Betina wheeled around, vroom, opened her mouth and pointed into it because she was hungry.

I didn't want to eat at the table with Betina. It made me sick. She drank her soup straight from the dish without a spoon and scooped up the solids with her hands. She cried if I insisted on feeding her by putting the spoon in every orifice on her face.

They bought Betina a high chair with a tray attached and a hole in the seat to piss and defecate through. She'd get the urge in the middle of the meal. The smell made me vomit. My mom told me not to act so delicate or she'd send me to the lunatic asylum. I knew what the lunatic asylum was and from then on I ate my meals *perfumed* by my sister's feces and *misted* by her piss. When she farted I'd pinch her.

After dinner I'd go to the garden.

Rufina would disinfect Betina and sit her in her wheelchair. The idiot would nap with her head on her breast or *breasts* because now her clothes showed two very round and provocative bumps because she'd developed before me and even though she was a horror she was a young lady and from then Rufina had to change her rags every month and wash between her legs.

I took care of mine myself and I could tell that I was still skinny as a broomstick or like my mom's pointer because my breasts weren't growing. And like this the birthdays came and went, but I was taking a drawing and painting class and the teacher thought that I'd be an important visual artist because being half crazy I was drawing and painting like the extravagant visual artists of the day.

The art exhibition

The professor told me, Yuna—that's what they call me—your paintings should be part of an exhibition. One of them might even sell.

I was so overcome with happiness that I threw my whole body on the professor and attached myself to him with all four feet and legs and we fell together.

The professor said that I was really pretty, that when I grew up we'd get engaged, and that he'd teach me the most beautiful things like drawing and painting but not to tell anyone our secret which actually was his secret and I guessed that he meant another more important exhibition so I grabbed him and kissed him again. And he kissed me too, a blue-colored kiss that affected me in places that I won't name because it wouldn't be proper and so I grabbed a big canvas and without drawing I painted two mouths in red joined together, *inseparable, musical*, and two blue eyes above them crying tears of glass. Still on his knees, the professor kissed the painting and he was still there when I went home.

I told my mom about the exposition and because she didn't understand art she said that those shapeless blobs on my boards would make everyone at the fine art school laugh but if the professor wanted me to it didn't make any difference to her.

Two of them sold when I showed my pieces with some from other students. Too bad that one of them was the kisses. The professor christened it *First Love*. Which seemed fine to me. But I didn't completely understand the meaning.

Yuna is a prodigy the professor would say and I liked this so much that every time he said it I would stay after and throw myself on him. He never stopped me. But when my breasts came in he said not to jump on him because men are fire and women straw. I didn't understand. I stopped jumping.

The diploma

So when I was seventeen I got my diploma in painting and drawing from the fine arts school, but because of my dyslexia I'd never be able to teach classes or private lessons. When I could buy boards I kept painting because the paints were a gift from the professor who'd often visit us.

Betina and her vroom chair circled the professor until he was dizzy but my mom never left me alone with him and once she slapped me maybe because she saw us kiss but on the cheek not on the mouth like the movie stars on screen.

I was afraid she'd keep the professor away. But she didn't so long as we didn't go around kissing because if the devil put his tail in it and the professor put some other part of his male anatomy in mine I'd end up pregnant and the professor would never marry a disabled student.

Betina wheeled around more than ever when the professor came for my private lessons and examined the boards and canvases piled up along the wall intended for the art exhibition in Buenos Aires.

One time it got late and my mom invited him to dinner which he accepted. I trembled thinking of the disgusting sounds and emanations coming from the pile known as Betina. But as the captain commands, the sailor obeys.

Rufina had cooked cannelloni. And on top of that I remembered the cannelloni from the lunatic asylum. I wanted to paint to calm down. I painted a board that no one else understood. A cannelloni with eyes and a hand blessing it. *In mente* I whispered: if you have a soul may God receive you in his bosom . . .

The dinner

Rufina set the embroidered tablecloth that my mom kept away and the nice plates that she kept too. Whenever she set the table like that her eyes would mist over because they were wedding gifts. It must've been the memories of when her marriage unraveled and my dad gone. It never hurt me because I didn't love her.

Let her cry . . . my dad must have found someone better without a pointer. My dad must have had normal children not idiots like the ones she had and which were us.

In the middle of the table was a smart ceramic statuette of a pair of villagers embraced on a thicket under a willow. One day I'd paint what that scene made me feel because at seventeen every girl wants to be embraced in a thicket under a tree.

We ate on the fancy china because the everyday things were chipped and stained from use. The silverware was also the good ones that my mom was careful with because she said it was the set from her marriage. The crystal came out after several years away and looked like solid water. It didn't seem like the same stew dressed up in such luxury.

There was even sweet wine. Not the other kind because there wasn't money for it. In the water pitcher there was water, of course.

My mom sat down first at the head of the table and next to her the professor who arrived exactly on time and with candies.

Across from the professor, me, and next to me Betina.

My mom said first something to pick at. I wondered where she was keeping a pick and if that was some other kind of utensil we never saw it, but that wasn't what it was but actually some plates of salami and cheese with tiny swords in them.

My mom said serve yourselves and she put wine in the adults' glasses and water in mine and Betina's and when the bell rang and in came Aunt Nené my mom said it was the surprise she had for us.

Rufina went back and forth busily. Now Aunt Nené helped her.

The main dish arrived delivered by the hands of Nené. The same chicken stew as always but in a silver dish and dressed up with the vegetables that Nené brought it seemed like an offering to a king.

And so the meal began, each one as best they could. My mom watched us without her pointer but I knew she had it within reach under the table.

Betina struck a visible and frightening note. Brutish resonant belches chased by my mom's apologies that the poor thing at sixteen had the mental age of a four year old as a result of the disability according to the *tests* that they'd given her.

Aunt Nené concluded the melody with poor Clelia—that was my mom's name—two retards for daughters, and immediately stuffed a piece of breast meat in her letterbox-red mouth.

The professor said I wasn't retarded but a dreaming visual artist and that I was exhibiting paintings in Buenos Aires and that in the city I'd already sold two.

Aunt Nené

Aunt Nené painted too. She'd frame her canvases and hang them all over the walls of the house she lived in with her mother who was my grandmother and my mom's mother. Two paintings signed "Nené" hung in our house, portraits of ladies with perfectly black eyes, like cows, and these big faces that frightened me. One had a mustache. Nené said she liked being a portraitist and she said it to the professor who asked her where she'd studied the art of manipulating oils and the rest, she confessed that she was an amateur, that she didn't need anyone holding her hand because the pictures poured from her heart like water from a spring.

The professor didn't respond. Nené looked at one of my boards and said the lines didn't mean anything, that she didn't like the new painters and that once she'd laughed at Pettoruti's absurd cubism. The professor lurched and because he was looking at Nené's painting it collapsed onto the floor.

Then Aunt Nené said that my squiggles might make sense to me, what with my cognitive deficiencies, but can we even know what the handicapped think and feel, she said in the form of a question.

The professor insisted that I was the best student at the fine arts school, that I'd graduated and was going to exhibit soon, and Aunt Nené asked what must the other students be like and the situation started to sour.

My mom added that my painting was kids' stuff and it would soon pass.

The cow eyes Nené painted stared out at us from between the wood frame. Suddenly I said something that would earn me a few lashes later: It's like a cow is staring at me wondering if I'm going to eat her because this painting is boring like a cow face and ugly like an ugly woman's face.

Nené screeched like the monkey in the zoo and screamed how long was her sister going to put up with me and that it was about time they sent me to the loony bin.

The professor said his stomach hurt and please excuse him he had to go to the bathroom to vomit. I felt as happy as if they'd given me a prize at an exhibition.

Total silence until my mom told Nené that she'd overstepped and to remember that it made me feel good to paint those things on the boards and canvases that the professor gave me. Nené pounced like a wasp: can't you see that man looking at the girl with bad intentions, she said in the form of a question and my mom scolded her for her dirty mind and added that she agreed that such big eyes couldn't fit in any woman's face unless she *was* a cow.

I sensed that my mom accepted me and I held back a tear that was at the point of crashing to the ground because it would've been the most giant tear I'd ever cried since I could mostly understand the basics of conversations between so-called normal people like my mom and Nené were. The professor came back from vomiting and started saying something that she interrupted immediately, which was the following:

Miss, he began and she said that she didn't go by miss and he begged her pardon and added that a woman as pretty at her age could never be called miss and that he was sure her husband must be pleased to have a painter at his side and she informed him that she was separated because her ex's ordinary habits bothered her. The cultured and educated professor couldn't stop himself from saying that it seemed like no one in that house was ordinary.

My mom could tell that the spoiled dinner bothered everyone but Nené. She brought a tray and the champagne glasses. She'd kept the champagne to celebrate the fifteenth birthday of one of her daughters which were me and Betina but she hadn't opened it knowing that it didn't make sense when our mental age didn't keep pace with the hours and the days.

We went back to the table. Betina snoring, asleep in her chair. So ugly, so horrible, how could there be someone so ugly and horrible, buffalo head, moldy rag stink. Poor thing . . .

A toast to peace, Nené said, feigning intellectuality. And then she told the story of how her failed marriage weighed on her because of the guilt she owed to her lack of sexual education and sometimes she missed Sancho, which was the name of her ex.

She sat waiting for a question but no one asked her one so turning red she told how she spent the first night with her ravenous husband chasing her around the house and the marriage wasn't consummated and he left. It freaked him out.

She filled a second glass with champagne and her listeners' ears with the clarification that she was a married virgin, neither miss nor mistress or anything else and that was the reason she'd taken shelter in the art of painting.

The way my Aunt Nené was

She lived glued to her mother's skirts, who was my mom's mother too and also my grandmother and Betina's. Our grandmother's skirts were like a priest's habit and her shoes were like a man's and she wore her hair in a black bun because she didn't have any gray hair because her mother had been a native and the natives never went gray probably because they didn't think. My mom didn't have any gray hair just like grandmother but she did think.

Nené could play the guitar by ear and when she did she wore a white headband and she hated gringos. So many ideas spill out when I try to describe her, so many and so stupid but I have to remember I'm talking about a character.

She liked to go dating and would kiss boys nibbling on their lips, she had about eight hundred boyfriends but she kept her virginity to the point of fleeing her marriage bed from the court house and the white church.

In the early thirties an Italian carpenter fell for Nené. I remember what a good guy the carpenter was—tall, blonde, always scrubbed, and perfumed with scented water. He came courting to the door of grandmother's house which because it was just a neighborhood house wasn't much. But since no one in the family worked they had to get by with what Uncle Tito who worked in the papers sent them.

Aunt Nené let him kiss her however he wanted. But they didn't go any further because if she ever got married she wanted to be in a virgin state, which I didn't understand. By wearing a medallion of the Virgin I thought I'd be saved from anything very sinful you got from pregnancy. Maybe when she got married she'd have to take off the medallion so that the Virgin wouldn't see her, I don't know what kinds of things the Mother of God shouldn't be seeing. My head was full of enormous troubles that I poured out onto the boards which was how I painted a very thin delicate neck from which hung a chain for the Virgin of Luján, and coming from the shadows that I created by rubbing my finger over thick black strokes a huge man like the Basque milk-man who brought the milk and always complained "arrauia" or something like that and from his bulk poured liquids that drowned the delicate little neck and the Virgin wept. To simulate tears I painted red splashes of damage that pained the lily-white necked creature.

The Italian boyfriend finished the bedroom with good woods, the bed, and the night stands. Then he finished the furniture in the living room and other knickknacks required of a decent house. I knew because I listened at the door that Aunt Nené laughed at the gringo: does that wop think I'm going to marry him for his pasta? Once I told her: better pasta than drinking café con leche all day.

She told me I had to help her throw the Italian off and I answered that no, that wasn't right, no. She told me that my dad who was another gringo abandoned my mom. I asked her why she wasn't ashamed to be lying that way to a good man and she said that wop lowlifes weren't men and that night she left for Chascomús where one of her brothers lived, my uncle and my mom's brother.

I didn't hear anything else about that situation but Nené spent a year away from her maternal home out of fear that she'd bump into the Italian but I was happy to find out that he'd been disillusioned with Nené and had contracted marriage with a Genovese and that the woman was already pregnant and I thought that she wouldn't be able to keep wearing her medallion for the Virgin because of the contact with her husband that the Virgin wasn't supposed to see.

Soon after that Aunt Nené took up with an Argentine boyfriend from Córdoba. I liked hearing the lilt of his talk and I painted something along those lines.

With this boyfriend they sang and she played the guitar while a friend brewed the *mate*. It didn't last. This man didn't build furniture or anything. One afternoon in June when it darkens early he pressed her against a wall and she screamed like a morning rooster and the watchman came around the corner and pulled off the scoundrel—he had to peel him off because he was stuck to my aunt—and took him prisoner to the station.

It was a brief and scandalous romance. I think there were others, but from a distance, until Don Sancho showed up and conquered her.

I loved Don Sancho the Spanish republican because he looked like Don Quixote de la Mancha.

I had a hardcover book with an image of the Knight of Rocinante the horse and Sancho Panza, but my aunt's boyfriend didn't have a paunch, he was skinny as a rail and so well-spoken that I wanted them to come to our house, both of them, for tea and the cakes that the boyfriend brought. But I wasn't interested in the tea but in hearing the voice of Don Sancho. He told stories of his distant country which inspired me to paint and my ears overflowed with names of places like Paseo de la Infanta, Río Manzanares, and I imagined a girl in white holding a crown of flowers between her arms and the waters of the apple orchards loaded with dancing apples in the waves like the heads of cherubs which I painted.

Don Sancho gave me a fine porcelain doll that I was supposed to call Nené, the name of my aunt and his beloved girlfriend. My mom suggested that I was turning fourteen soon and that dolls wouldn't suit me anymore. I put her on my bed and at night we embraced.

I understood that my fate hung over a sad cloudscape of melancholy rain when my mom launched my doll Nené while shaking out the bed sheets, shattering her charms and leaving me with a fever that took a long time to subside. I grew after that illness. Something ruptured inside me hurt. Pieces of porcelain from my doll Nené stuck to my liver and caused a nervous hepatitis and on top of that I learned to cry.

And I cried when Nené left her husband Don Sancho. One day I asked her why she didn't fulfill her marriage vows. She answered that it wasn't right to discuss intimate matters with me because since I was her niece I owed her some respect that there'd be time later on for spicy and dirty things.

I said that her sister, my other aunt, did spicy and revolting things with her husband and she told me to keep my mouth shut.

Translated by Steve Dolph

WORK

1942, *Versos al recuerdo*, Talleres Gráficos Olivieri & Domínquez (poetry).

1948, *El anticuario*, Ediciones del Bosque (poetry).

1948, *Adiós desde la muerte*, Ediciones del Bosque (poetry).

1951, *El solitario*, Moreno (poetry).

1953, *Peregrino del aliento*, Moreno (poetry).

1955, *Lamentación mayor*, Colombo (poetry).

1959, *El ángel del espejo*, Municipalidad de La Plata (poetry).

1959, *Laúd*, Colombo (poetry).

1962, *La trova*, Colombo (poetry).

1962, *Panorama de afuera con gorriones*, University of Texas (poetry).

1963, *La pica de la Susona; leyenda andaluza*, Hojas del Simurg (stories).

1963, *Cuaderno de Angelina: relatos de infancia*, Municipalidad de la Plata (stories).

1963, *François Villon, raíz de iracunida; vida y pasión del juglar de Francia*, Colombo (essay).

1964, *Carta a Zoraida; relatos par alas tías viejas*, Colombo (stories).

1969, *Pogrom del cabecita negra*, Colombo (novel).

1974, *Jovita la osa*, A. Peña Lillo Editor (stories).

1974, *La Plata mon amour*, Pueblo Entero (novel).

1974, *Muerte del Lobizón y Pariciones*, Colombo (poetry).

1981, *Antología personal, 1940-1976*, Ramos Americana (miscellaneous).

1988, *Zingarella*, Botella al mar (stories).

1991, *Las Marías de Los Toldos*, Ediciones Theoria (novel).

1994, *Estos locos bajitos por los senderos de su educación*, Pueblo Entero (essay).

1994, *Poesía gauchipolítica federal*, Colección Estrella Federal (poetry).

1995, *Nicilina y las Meninas*, Pueblo Entero (poetry).

1997, *Hadas, brujas y señoritas*, Ediciones Theoria (stories).

1997, *45 poemas paleoperonistas*, Pueblo Entero (poetry).

1997, *Evita, mester de amor*, con Fermín Chávez, Pueblo Entero (poetry).

1998, *Me moriré en París, con aguacero*, Corregidor (novel).

1999, *Lieder*, Edicones Theoría (poetry).

1999, *Ponce de León y el fuego*, con Fermín Chávez, Corregidor (essay).

2001, *Alma y Sebastián*, Nueva Generación (stories).

2001, *Venid amada alma*, Ediciones Theoría (poetry).

2004, *Racconto*, Corregidor (poetry).

2005, *John W. Cooke*, Nueva Generación (essay).

2006, *Bruna Maura-Maura Bruna*, Nueva Generación (novel).

2007, *Al pez*, Libros El Búho (poetry).

2008, *Las primas*, Caballo de Troya (novel).

2011, *Nosotros, los Caserta*, Random House Mondadori (novel).

2012, *El marido de mi madrastra*, Random House Mondadori (stories).

2013, *Los rieles*, Random House Mondadori (novel).

•

AWARDS AND RECOGNITIONS

1948, Premio Iniciación for *El solitario*.

1958, French Iron Cross Award for her translations of François Villon and Rimbaud.

1966, Gran Premio de Honor Almafuerte.

1968, Premio Raúl Scalabrini Ortiz for *Pogrom de una cabecita negra*.

1969, Premio Domani for *Nosotros, los Caserta*.

1969, Premio Pirandello d'oro della Collegiatura di Cicilia for *Nosotros, los Caserta*.

2007, Premio de Nueva Novela Página/12 for *Las primas*.

2010, II Premio Otras Voces, Otros Ámbitos for *Las primas*.

RAMIRO
PINILLA
(Spain, 1923)

Ramiro Pinilla was born in 1923 in Bilbao, but the center of his life were the summers he spent in Arrigunaga—a beach on the Biscayan coast bathed in the waters of the Cantábrico—near the town of Gexto. In his recollections, those summers are perceived as the most beautiful of his childhood, when he enjoyed a limitless freedom. Then September would come and with it, the end of happiness: he had to make the trip back to Bilbao and get ready for the start of classes at a seminary. Left behind were the cliffs, the sea, life itself: the beach where, as Pinilla has stated many times, life on earth began.

Later on, now an adolescent, Pinilla discovered that writing was one of the things he liked doing more than anything. To write and to read writers like Charles Dickens and Henry David Thoreau, whose philosophy he identified with right away: like the author of *Walden*, he too dreamed of living apart from the world, surrounded by nature and far from civilization. He sailed on a trade ship for two years, acquiring a portable Underwood in the Canaries and began writing in earnest.

Back on land in 1944, under the pseudonym Romo P. Girca he published his first book: *El misterio de la pensión Florrie*, a detective novel inspired by another from that period: *Las siete llaves*. Some time later, he got an administrative job in the Municipal Gas Company, where he went in the mornings, and another job at a children's books publisher, where he spent his afternoons writing catch phrases for stickers. Already married and a father to three children, he would steal away for hours at a time to write.

And in that way, in seven months he wrote *Las ciegas hormigas*, which tells of the bravery and tenacity of Sabas Jáuregui and his family, who, on one stormy night, recover all the coal that a British vessel, run aground on the cliffs of the Cantábrico, had spilled on the rocks. An unadorned, deliberate,

and profound style, and an open structure, with divergent voices—these were
some of the reasons why in 1960 the novel won the Premio Nadal and, the
following year the Premio de la Crítica.

But Pinilla did not relish all the public exposure. He took the award money
and ended up building a small house near the Arrigunaga beach, he named
it "Walden" and he stayed there, away from commercial activity, publishing
with independent publishers and doing all kinds of jobs—from cultivating the
land to raising chickens and writing—to sustain a home and three children.

In 2004, the publication of the first volume of *Verdes valles, colinas rojas*
(a nearly 3,000 page trilogy, spanning from 1879 to the rise of the ETA and
examining the private and familial microcosms of a city much like Getxo)
situated him among the indispensible writers of Spanish literature. The novel
received the Premio Nacional de la Crítica, the Premio Nacional de Narrativa,
and the Premio Euskadi. Almost ninety years old, Ramiro Pinilla continues
to write and expand a body of work destined to become classic.

THE ACORN

The Torture of Doctor Johnson

If there's anything good in *Las ciegas hormigas*, it's this chapter. I wrote it more than fifty years ago, but I still remember what I thought when I finished it: why isn't the whole novel like this, and why won't most of what I write in the future be like this? It's the felicitous fusion of narrative language with what I hoped for and still hope for, that synthesis of rhythm, continual forward movement, ideas and more ideas, humor, expressive transparency, something like the inescapable music of a deceitfully playful Mozart that we get hopelessly hooked on. A passion for my creations? Maybe. But here the protagonists are sketched out for the entire novel, their courtship, as recounted by Josefa, establishes the roots of Sabas, whose epic downfall you can already imagine, along with Josefa's own unconditional surrender to Sabas's impossible stubbornness. Which buttons do you have to press to yield something like this? I have no idea.

In Conversation with the Dead

Las ciegas hormigas wouldn't have existed without Faulkner. Even the critics have said so. He taught me to put myself in another's place, which is to say, in a character's place. And in order to accomplish that you have to *show* them instead of simply *telling* about them. The divine law for a fiction writer is to *show*, not *tell*. García Márquez later taught me to be irreverent by using humor. To turn a story into pure musical rhythm. I wish I were still learning.

Coda

Does Faulkner's Yoknapatawpha serve as a model for your literary Getxo? Have you read a lot of American literature?

I spent my childhood and adolescence in Getxo, and those times were influenced by the coast, the sea, and the people who lived off the land, surviving by their own hands. I returned to that world when I wanted to novelize my epic conceptualization of the world. I found in the American writers what I hadn't found in European writers, at least not in the ones that Franco allowed us to read. When the Casa Americana Library opened in Bilbao around 1955, sponsored by the United States, I imagine, it brought fresh air, literature that was powerful, social, epic, and above all, free. Steinbeck, Faulkner, Hemingway, Santayana, Capote, Dos Passos . . . it was so unlike the generally placid European literature. It was a leap from one continent, with its obligations already met, to another that was at the height of expansion. Its literature breathed liberty. It was my new path.

A THOUSAND FORESTS

FROM *LAS CIEGAS HORMIGAS*
(THE BLIND ANTS)
[A NOVEL]

CHAPTER 21: JOSEFA

I still remember it well. The priest said, "Sabas, do you take this woman as your lawfully wedded wife?" And then, without even turning to me: "Josefa, do you want this man to take you as his lawfully wedded wife?"

That's what I heard, kneeling next to him, my hands and feet tied up without a rope, subjugated, defeated, and (why not?) devoted—perhaps not out of love, but controlled by some kind of irrational vertigo—furiously subdued, captured, and kidnapped while everyone watched impassively. No longer daring to rebel, even though I'd tried before, despite the fact that I'd known from the beginning it would all be useless, I contemplated what the priest had done, with his benevolent, distant face, loading the ship with cargo he wouldn't travel with, muttering the words, unrelenting, without looking into my eyes, which were desperately asking him, "Why don't you do something? Why don't you ask me, like all the other women, 'Josefa, do you take this man as your lawfully wedded husband?'"

He appeared one day in Berango, chewing on a piece of straw. Serious, skinny, calm, his hands in his pockets. All put together with his corduroy pants, white cotton socks, rubber-soled sandals, and checkered shirt. And an umbrella hanging on his arm.

It was a workday, a Monday, around twilight. I watched him from the garden plot my family had near the road. He was coming from Algorta, and his steps weren't quick, but they were steady, insistent, active, each one promising another. By the time I noticed him, he was already looking at me. The distance between us wasn't short, so he was able to stare at me for four or five minutes without appearing to, without even turning his head, chewing his piece of straw the whole time. When he reached a point where he had to turn his head, he stopped looking at me, walked past me, and continued down the road, and nobody would have said that he'd noticed me.

When I went back to hoeing, I realized who he was: Sabas Jáuregui, from the farm on the beach in Algorta, who'd lived alone ever since he found himself without a family. We all knew the story: a family of father, mother, and two sons, they were all very hardworking and had enough land to show it. Sabas's brother died, and father, mother, and Sabas took on the work; not long afterward, the mother died, and the two men kept going as well as they could, preparing the meals themselves. When his father died, Sabas was already prepared for it, and he took onto his shoulders the work that used to leave four people exhausted. And he lived there, abandoned near the edge of the beach, completing all the chores every day before going to bed, when he'd no longer hear the undertow scraping the rocks, like before, when all his family members were still alive and he was able to rest a while before sleep would take him. Now he fell asleep before he even had time to lift his second foot off the floor.

I saw him on rare occasions, when I went to that beach with my family to gather coked coal and I'd find him with a scythe cutting grass for the cows, or carrying manure from the stable to the garden, or I'd simply see smoke coming from the chimney and figure he was frying something for dinner.

The following Sunday, six days after I saw him on the road, I discovered him among the couples who were dancing on the pelota court to the shrill music playing on the loudspeakers. He was wearing twill pants, a wrinkled brown jacket, and a white shirt with the collar unbuttoned (no tie, of course). He searched for me specifically, among the dancing couples, and finally spotted me and came over to my group of friends, rigid and deliberate, looking up, walking and moving naturally, pretending he wasn't bothered by his shirt collar, which was stiff even though it wasn't buttoned: he'd probably put too much starch on it when he ironed it.

He stopped in front of me and, without moving his lips, without appearing to speak, even though his words didn't come out timid at all, but whole, determined, firm, said, "Would you like to dance with me?"

It would have been enough to say "would you like to dance?" or even simply "do you dance?" but he wanted to be very clear about the "with me," and
at that moment I had a vague feeling that I was starting to figure him out,
finding out what he was like, what he was proposing, how he would make it
happen, and even that he would win.

I said no, not because he seemed to be acting like a Don Juan (he could
have been: he sort of looked like one, and he was svelte, strong, rather handsome compared to the rest of those rough peasants), but because he didn't
even entertain any hope that I would dance with him; I even suspected
that he didn't want me to; his only intention was to make me start burning
through my supply of ammunition, knowing that one day it would run out
and I would be defenseless; that I had a certain number of vulnerable "noes"
in reserve (it didn't matter how many: he had enough patience to wait and
persevere). Because after that week, he started coming to Berango at least
twice a week: once on Sunday, at the dance, for me; and another day during
the workweek, to the milkman Benito's farm, for the cow.

Soon the whole town knew what he was up to. The cow he wanted
belonged to one of our neighbors: Benito, the milkman, who kept himself
afloat with the seven he fed (and milked) in the stable on his farm. My late
father and my mother used to say that it wasn't fair: the man already had six
cows, and on top of that, God gave him those inexhaustible udders that, to
everyone's astonishment, produced thirty liters of milk a day.

He wouldn't sell it, he wouldn't trade it, he wouldn't rent it, he would
hardly let anyone see it; he never had to say it for his neighbors and the
inhabitants of nearby towns to know it; it was something you understood if
you knew Benito (his whole life among cows and knowing everything there is
to know about them) and the cow. And if it didn't become a source of pride for
our town, that was because it apparently wasn't that even for Benito himself.
Distrusting, suspicious, alert, he knew a lot about things other than cows: he
knew that good things are covetable, and that even though he acquired his
treasure through the most legal and definitive way (Nature made the dona-
tion when one of his cows gave birth, a cow who, in turn, was the daughter of
another of Benito's properties, who, in turn . . .), he had a feeling that maybe
that block of legality and rights could crack: an error, a low blow, in the form
of a new municipal ordinance or a jealous complaint inventing a trivial offense

(witchcraft, even). The only thing Benito didn't take into account was the colossal tenacity of men, of one man.

He kept coming to find me every Sunday, in the middle of the dance, asking me the question, and I kept giving him the same answer. He never talked to any other girl: he arrived, he saw me, he asked me the question, I answered him, and he went away without tilting his head an inch, trying not to notice everyone looking at him, the slightly mocking looks (just barely, and surreptitiously: there was something about Sabas that commanded respect) from everyone who waited all week for that inevitable moment at the dance on the pelota court. After three months, we performed the scene to perfection, without error, everyone in their role, he in his and I in mine, and the people discussing whether our performance was better than the one last Sunday.

But then there was a small change, a tiny new development that broke the monotony of those three months. Sabas hadn't shown up at the dance yet that Sunday, and it was already dark out and the court lights were on. But then the lights suddenly went out and everything went dark. This happened frequently: the boys would cut the electricity and the girls would start screaming, and then you'd hear quick steps chasing others that were running away, and, every once in a while, you'd hear a slap in the face, and when the girls' protests turned serious the lights would come back on and reveal a scene of laughing, breathless, flushed faces, and more than one red cheek. It was one of those times, after three months, when, in total intentional darkness, I felt someone gently take my hand and encircle my waist; I never could have imagined a more delicate contact between a man and a woman. I wasn't frightened, despite the darkness, nor did I resist. The music had stopped too, since the electricity was out, but we started dancing, in the middle of that whirlwind of shouts, chases, and insults. An instant before he spoke (I'd just asked him who he was) I noticed that the hand holding mine wasn't just gentle, but also firm, and the arm around my waist was feathers and iron at the same time, and I felt like I was enclosed in something, a prisoner: it was a strange sensation, but not new, I realized as I remembered what I'd felt the first time Sabas had asked me to dance . . .

And then he spoke, before I could free myself from his arms, as soon as he realized that I'd recognized him.

"Wait," he said. "I wanted to tell you that my father left some nice tools in the attic and I've started building the bed and the wardrobe."

By the time the lights came on, he had left me, and he went away slowly through the boisterous crowd.

That same night, at dinner, I asked my father:

"Benito's cow . . . ?"

"What?" he asked, rolling his cigar.

"Is it possible that . . . that the man from Algorta . . . that Sabas, will get . . . ?"

"Benito said yesterday afternoon at La Venta that he was thinking seven cows might be too many for him . . ."

The only thing I asked for in my prayers was a little time to believe that nothing could possibly happen if I didn't want it to. But that oppression didn't abandon me, and I spent all my time thinking about it. I was already heading down a path that led to something I didn't want in my life. Whether I liked him or not wasn't important. Of course I liked him. (Sabas: young and virile, full of life, indefatigable, skilled, protective, able to rise from any difficult situation, determined, sufficiently attractive and desirable.) But that wasn't love, the love I'd dreamed of ever since the idea occurred to me, without understanding it at first. I'd only intuited it, having to believe that it must exist in relationships between men and women so that they would be more than just a series of unions like the ones between the male and female animals around me that I knew; that wasn't the love I longed for and that I wanted to be a part of more than anything. But that wasn't the reason either, since I could accept Sabas without distorting my intimate and unspoken desires, hidden then even to me; it was that I wasn't included in the situation. I was thrown into it violently, without remission, and the one who decided ought to have considered that, perhaps, I didn't want it; but he didn't, he simply wrapped me up in his irrational vertigo of invincible tenacity and turned me into a manageable, even tangible instrument, so that, at that moment, I didn't know if my desire to accept him was mine or if it also belonged to him and to that blind strength of his.

I searched for a solution and thought I'd found one when I thought that, up until then, my refusals hadn't been emphatic enough, and I tried to make them so. But he kept on, oblivious, going to the dance every Sunday (even though, after he told me about the furniture, he never asked me to dance again, not because he thought it was too ridiculous to keep doing it after three months of failure, but surely because he knew that the first phase was over, the first fortifications were destroyed, and it was time for another mode of attack). Desperate, I trusted in the ultimate "no," that of the church (I could already see myself there, kneeling next to him, kidnapped), trusting that the situation would give me strength. But when I started thinking about the cow, I knew that he had also rejected that extreme consolation.

The cow. I asked myself: what could be stronger: my will to resist, or Benito's repeated refusals to sell the cow? Because Sabas kept insisting, obstinately. He would show up at the milkman's farm once a week, or twice, talking to him about who knows what, trying to convince him or interest him in some sort of exchange or sale or promise; that's what we all thought; not a swindle: he wasn't capable of doing such a thing. Benito didn't even tell anyone at La Venta what Sabas talked to him about, nor how, nor what he promised or offered, as if he were ashamed of having to listen to him, of not being able to refuse him, of admitting he was defeated before he really was. And that's how I came to trust that cow with my salvation, believing that if he didn't get it, if the cow could convince me that he was vulnerable, that he could be defeated, there would be some hope for me.

Then, in May, the Catalan salesman came to town, with his two big suitcases covered in oilcloth, full of colorful fabrics, lace, buttons, and ribbons. He visited the town every year and stayed for a couple of months, not because he had enough customers there, but because he used it as a general headquarters, from which he would embark on one-, two-, or three-day trips to the other towns in the area, returning to his departure point to recover his strength in the station house, where he stayed, ate, and slept. Chubby, red-faced, always smiling, talkative, insincere, whose other life (the one he lived the remaining ten months of the year, in Barcelona) was a complete mystery to us, even though he talked about it excessively and frequently, and for that very reason we never believed a single word he said. Surely he was married with several children—even if we never saw a wedding ring (he must have carried it in his pocket, since when he said goodbye to his wife he would have to show it in its place, on his finger)—hoping in vain for an easy fling with a married woman or a single girl, making the stories he always told his friends back home true, for once.

I used him, to put it simply, because I wanted to make a decision too, rather than wait around for whatever was in store for me. Yes, I started going

out with him, shocking the town and my family, since everyone knew that no
girl would have done what I did, let herself be accompanied by that traveling stranger who was outside the circle of possible suitors for more than a
dozen reasons: among them, the certainty that he was foreign and untrust-
worthy, the probability that he was married, or at least had promises scattered throughout Cataluña. I used him. I needed a sort of shock treatment,
a flashy explosion, a storm that would raise the water levels and then change
course, altering what I thought was inevitable. And I wasn't disappointed
because, as far as I could tell, the only person who wasn't concerned about my
relationship with the Catalan salesman was him, Sabas, who kept coming to
Berango every Sunday (although, now, he had to wait for us to walk down
the road, when that man and I used to walk the same route all the couples in
town did, all the same places: the church portico, the rudimentary sidewalks,
and down the road a kilometer outside of town; when he saw us he'd stand
there staring at us, staring at me, rather, since there was no indication he
even saw the salesman, and he even waved at me slightly, serious, inscrutable,
infuriatingly tenacious, until we walked away, and I wouldn't see him again
until the following Sunday). I was counting on another source of strength,
the certainty that a girl's first kiss sealed something eternal, or at least lasting
until it became apparent that the man would refuse marriage or that he was
already married; and that, in any case, I could count on a period of precious
time, a pause, in which I could find whatever there was to find, that I would
make the most of it somehow, that at least Sabas couldn't enjoy it, and it
would be time that would go by uselessly, that would escape his immovable
plan of waiting, in which time was fundamental.

Then came July, and on the night of the 30th, when I was on my way home
with the donkey carrying grass for the only cow we had, I saw him on the
road, waiting for me. He moved only when I reached him, after the donkey
had passed him.

"Wait," he said, pulling a piece of straw from some brambles and starting
to crush it with his fingers. He'd positioned himself in the middle of the
road, so I was forced to stop. "I'm not upset. Listen. I need to talk to you.
Everything is already decided and we haven't even talked. I'll come get you
tomorrow and we'll go to the San Ignacio festival together."

When he finished speaking, he stuck the broken piece of straw in his
mouth and turned around, walking away silently in the dark.

I had made up my mind and I felt strong for the first time, bolstered by a single, unpleasant kiss from the Catalan salesman. But when I saw Sabas the next morning, coming down the road from Benito's farm, with the cow on a leash following behind him, walking slowly, without any hint of triumph on his face, stiff and serious, I understood that everything had been useless; all there was left to do was look at the sky where it touched the sea to know whether I should take an umbrella to the festival that afternoon.

I wanted to see the salesman and I went looking for him, but they told me he wouldn't be back until evening. Therefore, I couldn't tell him I was breaking up with him. And I waited for Sabas and he took me to Algorta, to the San Ignacio festival. I didn't know what was happening to me; I couldn't think, as if he'd already taken possession of me, even my inner self.

There he had me, not listening to him but just hearing him, forced to do so because I had two healthy ears and I was next to him (I still couldn't believe it), and not even the bedlam of the carousel, the stands selling churros, French fries, beer, and soda, the municipal band in their blue uniforms or, on their breaks, the shrill loudspeakers, managed to get between us, to interrupt his clipped sentences, through which I found out that the bed and the oak wardrobe were finished (he even described the carved decorations they had), and that the wedding date had been set—August 31st—so I wouldn't even get to have the engagement that every woman dreams of, with enough time and all the necessary formalities. He would yank me out of single life and, with no transition, I would be sharing a bed with him, captured, kidnapped, and, in a way, enslaved, since he also said it was a good date because then we could harvest the corn together in September. He would also be denying me a honeymoon, transplanting me in a single day from a single woman's house to a married woman's house, from the convent to the brothel, without the purification that the honeymoon trip means to every woman (the first night and the following nights, up to seven or fifteen—or even just the first—under a different sky, in a new room in a new city, far from our hometowns, with our nice new white clothing debuting that first night, so that we can more easily believe that we've entered a fantasy world, where not only everything is possible, but even logical and forgivable, including the obsession that has dominated us since we were thirteen or fifteen—sex); wanting to purify what needs purifying, since we were born pure in the moment the man and the woman, upon admiring one another, admired their unborn children, and the rest is superfluous. I wouldn't even get that.

We were sitting in the field near the fair, and it was getting dark. I stood up and said: "He hugged me and he kissed me. Are you upset?"

"It's alright," he said. "I was counting on that. But no more than that."

He was so confident about what he said, so sure of himself, foreseeing everything, domineering, with nearly enough power to pull the strings of everyone else's lives.

"Where are you going?" he asked.

But I was already running away from him, desperate, elbowing my way through the crowds, and probably sobbing. The whole way back to Berango, to the house where the Catalan salesman was staying—nearly an hour—I didn't once look behind me to see if he was following me. I climbed the stairs and knocked softly on his door (he lived in the loft, alone) and he opened the door and looked at me strangely, but then he smiled and his face suddenly turned repugnant. He moved to one side, inviting me to come in. But I didn't move. And then I looked behind me, though that wasn't exactly it: I looked at the stairs, then down, trying, at the same time, to hear something. He looked at me, looked at the stairs, looked at me again, and smiled, moving back to the center of the doorway.

"It's a shame he didn't follow you," he said, his little eyes smiling. "At the very least, you would have stepped inside the door and I would have closed it behind you. Even though that wouldn't change anything, since whatever you told him afterward couldn't be taken into consideration; he simply wouldn't have believed you; and whatever I told him—if you chose this approach—wouldn't matter either, because whatever a man says about such things, and certainly if he's a tramp, is just taken as bragging. He would have had to see it and then be sure he hadn't dreamed it. He needed to have followed you and seen it with his own eyes. Because a man who was capable of getting that cow from Benito, even if it cost all that money, is capable of disbelieving any sort of logic pertaining to men . . ."

So that was it. The cow. The reason I couldn't plan a honeymoon, not even a brief stay in San Sebastián. He had spent all his savings, figuring that in order to have a wife he could cut out a lot of things, including money, but if he wanted a cow, especially if it was like that cow, he had to pay for it.

And I stood there, in front of the open door, rigid, bewildered, once I'd understood that even if I took one step across that threshold and gained a power much stronger than a simple kiss to be able to resist him and—I imagined—defeat him, I wouldn't accomplish anything, since he was invincible. Not even by resorting to all that a woman is capable of giving up in order to get something, would I liberate myself from his stubbornness.

The traveler was still looking at me, and I lifted my head and, no longer using a casual tone with him, asked, "Do you happen to have a pattern for embroidering sheets with an interlocking J and S?"

Translated by Emily Davis

WORK

1944, *El misterio de la pensión Florrie*, Moderna (published under the pseudonym Romo P. Girca) (novel).

1957, *El ídolo*, El Mensajero del Corazón de Jesús (novel).

1961, *Las ciegas hormigas*, Destino (novel, new edition published by Tusquets,
2010).

1961, *El héroe del Tonkin*, Comisión Ejecutiva Proceso Canonización Beato
Valentín de Berrio Ochoa (biography).

1969, *En el tiempo de los tallos verdes*, Destino (novel).

1972, *Seno*, Planeta (novel).

1975, *El salto*, Marte (novel).

1975, *Recuerda, oh, recuerda*, Ediciones del Centro (stories).

1975, *Guía secreta de Vizcaya*, Al-Borak (monograph).

1977, *Antonio B... "el rojo," ciudadano de tercera*, Albia (novel reedited in 2007
by Tusquets with the title *Antonio B. el Ruso, ciudadano tecera*).

1977, *Primeras historias de la Guerra interminable*, Luis Haranburu (stories).

1978, *La gran Guerra de doña Toda*, Herriliburu, Ediciones Libropueblo
(novel).

1979, *Andanzas de Txiki Baskardo*, Herriliburu, Ediciones Libropueblo (novel).

1990, *Quince años*, Libros Pérgola (novel).

1997, *Huesos*, Bermingham (novel).

1998, *La estación de Getxo*, Asociación de Vecinos del Transporte (monograph).

2004, *Verdes valles, colinas rojas I. La tierra convulsa*, Tusquets (novel).

2005, *Verdes valles, colinas rojas II. Los cuerpos desnudos*, Tusquets (novel).

2005, *Verdes valles, colinas rojas III. Las cenizas del hierro*, Tusquets (novel).

2006, *La higuera*, Tusquets (novel).

2009, *Sólo un muerto más*, Tusquets (novel).

2011, *Los cuentos*, Tusquets (includes both of the volumes of stories *Recuerda,
oh, recuerda* and *Primeras historias de la Guerra interminable*, revised in their
final edition).

2012, *Aquella edad inolvidable*, Tusquets.

2013, *El cementerio vacío*, Tusquets.

•

AWARDS AND RECOGNITIONS

1957, Premio Mensajero (Messenger Prize) for *El ídolo*.

1960, Premio Nadal (Nadal Prize) for *Las ciegas hormigas*.

1961, Premio de la Crítica de narrativa castellana (Spanish Narrative Critics
Award) for *Las ciegas hormigas*.

1972, Finalist for Premio Planeta (Planeta Award) for *Seno*.

2004, Premio Euskadi de Novela (Euskadi Award for the Novel) for *Verdes
valles, colinas rojas I. La tierra convulsa*.

2005, Premio de la Crítica de narrativa castellana (Spanish Book Critics
Award) for *Verdes valles, colinas rojas III. Las cenizas del hierro*.

2006, Premio Nacional de Narrativa (National Book Award) for *Verdes valles,
colinas rojas III. Las cenizas del hierro*.

2013, Premio Euskadi de Novela (Euskadi Award for the Novel) for *Aquella
edad inolvidable*.

ANA
MARÍA
MATUTE
(Spain, 1926)

Ana María Matute was a very precocious writer. She was born in Barcelona on July 26, 1925 ("and not in 1926 as has been stubbornly insisted!") into a family belonging to the petite bourgeoisie. Her father, don Facundo Matute, had established an umbrella factory on n° 60 Calle Urgell. The business led to his taking frequent trips to around Europe, which he returned from with all kinds of fantastic stories and gifts for the little Ana María (like the doll Gorogó, that ended up a part of her extensive body of literary work). These first fantasies led her to write and illustrate her first story when she was only five years old, while she was recovering from a serious renal infection. When she was eight years old, she fell ill again and her parents decided to put her under the care of her grandparents in Mansilla de la Sierra. That picturesque Riojan location became the landscape of her childhood, and the memories of those years and those people would be captured in many of her works, especially in *Historias de la Artámila* (1961) and in *El río* (1963).

That world was broken by the explosion of the civil war, a few days before her eleventh birthday. The brutal aggression that this superimposed on her childhood memories is reflected most of all in her early books, whose protagonists are children with a vision of the world that makes a distinction between the real (adult) world and fantasy, which she depicts with great psychological subtlety.

Educated in a religious French high school, while earning her bachelor's, Ana María Matute broadened her academic formation by taking courses in music and painting, outlining what from that moment on would be her varied and intense intellectual activity. When she was seventeen she wrote her first novel, *Pequeño teatro*. She showed up at the Destino publishing house with the novel written in a notebook with a black oilcloth cover; Ignacio Agustí, the publishing director at the time, agreed, after several attempts, to meet with the young girl, and he suggested she type up the novel, and then he would read it. Two weeks later she submitted the typed ("at full speed!") novel as well as several stories that would be published in *Destino* magazine. In 1948, *Los Abel*, her second novel, was a finalist for the Premio Nadal (won by Miguel Delibes).

In 1952, Matute married Ramón Eugenio Goicoechea (alias "the specimen") and two years later her son Juan Pablo was born. Over the course of a decade, Matute became the breadwinner in the family with extraordinary literary production, and began winning important prizes like Premio Nadal, Premio Nacional de Literatura, and Premio Nacional de la Crítica. Leaving behind the realist vision of the literature of that time, she developed her own voice that moved between lyrical and sensorial, achieving a genuine mixture of social criticism and poetic message. As Pere Gimferrer has said of her: "She's unlike any other author. Some have said she's like Faulkner; actually it's really that her way of being unlike anyone else makes you think about the way Faulkner was unlike anyone else."

Her marriage fell apart in 1963 and Spanish law under Franco prohibited her from seeing her son, leaving her overcome with intense emotional suffering. She kept on writing anyway: *Los soldados lloran de noche* (1964) and the children's story "El polizón del Ulises" (1965) and she completed the trilogy that began with *Primera memoria*, which was followed by *Algunos muchachos* (1964) and *La trampa* (1969). In 1976, Ana María Matute was nominated for the Nobel Prize in Literature and in 1984 she won the Premio Nacional de Literatura Infantil for "Sólo un pie descalzo."

Then she met Julio Brocard, at whose side she lived several very happy years until he passed away the day she turned sixty-five. Once again, she kept on writing, aware that literature had been and would be "the savior lighthouse of many of her storms." In 1996, she published *Olvidado Rey Gudú* ("the book I wanted to write ever since I was a girl, all of my obsessions are in it"), one of her most celebrated novels that, along with *La torre vigía* and *Aranmanoth*, make up a trilogy about a medieval court, with which she shows her literary versatility once again. That same year she was made a member of the Real Academia Española de la Lengua, occupying seat K, becoming the third woman inducted into the institution in its long three-hundred year history. In 2010 she was the third woman in history to receive the Premio Cervantes.

Translated into more than twenty-three languages and invited to teach at universities such as University of Indiana, University of Oklahoma, and Boston University, today Ana María Matute is one of the most personal voices in contemporary literature.

THE ACORN

In my work the fantastic has all the intentionality of reality. The core of *Olvidado Rey Gudú* is when his mother, while he's still a boy, removes his capacity to love. She has been a victim of love, because in her lifetime she has only tried it with an old man. How does a thirteen-year-old girl fall in love with an old man? It turns out that what attracts her is a man with experience. And she pays dearly because the old man doesn't fall in love with her, she's the one who falls in love. And he treats her badly. She asks for it a little, it must be said, but in any case he treats her very badly. And so the only thing she wants is power. She hasn't been able to get it, but her son will become King. Why does the mother take away his capacity to love? Lust for power. Because she has already renounced everything. Then Prince Almíbar crosses her path and satisfies her physically but doesn't fill her spirit, her soul, because she has become a very ambitious person. That's why she does what she does to her son, so he'll never love. Because for her, love has been the source of everything bad. And her son must be a great king, a powerful man, what she had aspired to but failed at herself. To never love anyone. And she thinks she's doing him a favor because obviously, like most mothers, she loves her son. But it's a favor done for herself too, for her wounded pride, for her desires, her ambitions. It's a gift she gives herself. As I once said: "Love is a wonderful mistake."

IN CONVERSATION WITH THE DEAD

It's very difficult to explain, I'd need an entire book for that. The book I'm writing now is called *Diablos familiares*. That says it all. My dead are

48

my family demons. I belong to a generation in which "good" girls generally weren't allowed to study. I was forbidden to go to university, but now I have an honorary doctorate. I got revenge! And so I have been very much an autodidact. I've also had the great fortune of meeting many people who have taught me and from whom I've learned a great deal throughout my life. I've also been shaped by my reading, my passion for literature. But I would have loved to be able to study Philosophy and Letters. And now I'd like to study Mathematics because I see some very interesting connections to poetry and music and those are two things I like a lot. Poetry has always influenced me and I read it now more than ever. Although I also must confess that I love crime novels [she laughs]. And I'm passionate about history, especially the history of the Middle Ages. I've immersed myself in the Arthurian sagas, living absorbed in that period for years.

CODA

You refer to your generation as the "shadow children" and you explain how important fairy tales were for them, and the phrase "once upon a time." You started out writing social realism but over time you've shifted to the fantasy novel. Why?

Some women began to make significant inroads in literature in the postwar era. Carmen Laforet was the first, and although I'm often included in the same generation as her and Cela, she was older—I'm from the generation of the fifties. But it's not entirely true to say that I've switched from realism to fantasy. It is, but not entirely. My intended style of writing forms part of the magic, you understand, of the magic of literature, of literature as invention. So that has always existed in my books and stories. But you have to take into account the time in which I had to live and develop as a writer. It was the Francoist era. First, when I was eleven years old the civil war broke out right in front of me and after I was fourteen, in my adolescence, I lived through a very long postwar period. And that left a mark on all of us, marked us decisively. This explains why I had to find a lung to breathe and to fight this man and his system. *Pequeño tentro* or *Primaria memoria* are realist, but not entirely. There is always a more poetic part. I think that social realism really killed Spanish literature for a while and I wanted to get away from it. I didn't renounce my rebelliousness or my strong social criticism by writing literature instead of social reporting. I haven't limited myself to telling, to narrating. I imagine. I invent. In any case, I have traveled a lot and I've seen how women are treated in the world and I've come to the realization that it's not solely the heritage of Spain. But in a country like ours and at that time there were strong inherited prejudices.

Did this generation of "shadow children" lose their innocence because of what they saw so young?

I've known many people for whom it's not that they've lost it, it's that they never had it. But childhood is something that's never lost. Childhood leaves a mark. I've often stressed that childhood, the boy or girl that we were, is something we have inside forever and it's a very rich place for imagination and invention.

A THOUSAND FORESTS

FROM *OLVIDADO REY GUDÚ*
(THE FORGOTTEN KING GUDÚ)
[A NOVEL]

CHAPTER VIII: GUDÚ, KING

I.

Queen Ardid was not a timid woman. Since celebrating her spectacular and unusual marriage to the late King Volodioso at the age of seven, she proved that this virtue had not diminished during the six years of her confinement in the East Tower. On the contrary, she confirmed the resolve of her character and the cunning of her methods. She enjoyed the unconditional support of Almíbar and his small army led by Randal. The soldiers of Olar were willing to act on her behalf, even though the treatment they received was by no means equal to that given to Almíbar's men.

While the nobility were generally quite mortified by Volodioso's behavior—although they never dared openly express this mortification—they felt their hopes for war revive when they surmised that the future King Gudú was still very young and that, if they played their cards right, his mother's regency could be beneficial to them. And from the start Ardid did not waver for even a moment in showing herself to be benevolent and generous with them, and even went so far as to reinstate certain privileges and rights, which Volodioso had seized from them all at once. And so, the new stance, proclaimed with great solemnity by the interim Queen—which she would defend during the years of her rule as though it were as important as keeping the country at peace, without engaging in costly and senseless wars that would benefit no one—filled every spirit with a warm hope of well-being.

And while the seed of intrigue blossomed in many hearts—this was inevitable and normal—the development of this seed required years of contemplation, observation, and patience, which were essential for all. In turn,
the Queen did not dismiss the Counselor in any capacity—thus playing an
important card in her favor, for in addition to being brave and not in the
least bit timid, cunning was one of her primary characteristics. She showed
herself to be full of amity for that figure who, deep down, was repulsive
and ridiculous in equal measure. But she knew, as much from her Master's
teachings as from personal experience, that an alliance with the enemy, if it
did not solve the root of the problem, at least brought about a truce that was
clearly both beneficial and necessary. So to everyone's surprise, she did not
make Prince Almíbar her official Counselor or her husband—she had bitter experiences with marriage. Instead she simply gave him distinctions and
absolute power over such dealings as the exchange of goods in neighboring
countries. Similarly, she announced a friendlier relationship with the opulent
Kingdom of Leonia. She appointed Almíbar something akin to ambassador
of the Realm, since he was without a doubt a refined and charming man,
and women always—or almost always—tend to be vulnerable in negotiations
with people possessing such qualities. With that they all remained, for the
time being, happy and relieved, and, understandably, Count Tuso and his
protégé Ancio most of all. Their hopes of continuing their machinations were
renewed, and although Ancio was initially consumed by indignation, Tuso
advised patience and tact; and so he was placated little by little.

Demonstrating a magnanimity that left everyone amazed, the Queen
declared that she was putting her personal treasure—which she had slowly
and meticulously collected during her brief reign with Volodioso, who had
been extremely generous with her—at the service of the Realm. And the first
thing she did was to send Almíbar to negotiate trade with Leonia, with a
view toward general improvement.

The return of the first expedition from the island of coveted riches was
received with great delight, because, thanks to a highly favorable agreement
with the Queen of that picturesque southern land, Almíbar had brought very
fine goods, credit, countless rich fabrics, and other luxurious novelties that
filled the ladies, and more than one gentleman, with excitement and pleasure.
In this way, the Queen enjoyed the favor of the nobility, and then after ordering flour and wine to be distributed to the people, the jubilation spread, and

her name gained a certain popularity among the commoners as well, although in truth, with less trust than among the nobility.

Not content with all this and to further prove her magnanimity, she extravagantly worshipped the memory of her unkind husband. In the Monastery of the Abundios—to whom she also demonstrated a benevolence unprecedented in the Realm—she had an extraordinary Royal Cemetery constructed, where they buried him beneath his own stone effigy—she'd commissioned a sculptor from the Island of Leonia, where the arts flourished abundantly, according to Almíbar and his nostalgic wonder—in which in every light, he appeared younger and more dashing than he ever was. And he himself declared that, like any proud King, he should have an epithet describing his nature, so, from that moment on he was known as Volodioso I the Aggrandizer. And this made everyone feel, beyond any logical explanation, grander and richer. Everyone, that is, except the Wretched, because the Queen, in the magnificent beginning of her reign, forgot about them.

Once these issues were all resolved, the Queen settled comfortably into the South Wing, where she rested and rejuvenated her weary bones. She appointed Dolinda and Artisia duchesses, and then royal ladies-in-waiting, which, as was to be expected, pleased the girls greatly. Unfortunately, from that moment, they too forgot their relatives in the coal regions, the Wretched. In turn, they married two noblemen, twice their age, but also twice as rich.

And so, all these matters attended to, the time came for the Queen to gather together her advisors in a very private assembly to disclose to them something that had remained dormant in her mind and heart through her long years of thought and confinement.

Once they were gathered in her private chambers, the Sorcerer, the Goblin of the South, and the handsome Almíbar—although he was not essential, since in such circumstances he usually fell asleep: it was only a matter of courtesy—the Queen addressed her true—and perhaps her only—friends:

—Dear friends, the time has come to make an important decision regarding Gudú to emphatically and definitively secure the crown and the glory of the Realm for him. And as your lessons and my own experience have taught me, an essential condition has become very clear for endowing him with a unique virtue in this regard.

She was silent for a moment, one of her few weaknesses was a penchant for solemnity. Her friends listened attentively:

—My dear friends, she repeated, with her customary sweetness and strength, the matter is simple and complicated at the same time, and that is why I am in great need of your arts and wisdom. The decision is to, once and for all, render Gudú completely incapable of any form of love for others.

—Dear girl, the Sorcerer said, I do not wish to contradict you, since you know well my thoughts on this matter, but I think that you exaggerate your aversion to that impulse: no one knows better than you that it can yield as many delights as disasters. But rest assured that if we find a potion or something similar to achieve it, I can already tell you that it will not be perfect: one cannot remove the capacity to love partially, or that is to say, conditionally, but rather, if it is possible, it will have to be removed in all its forms.

—I know that, she said, patiently. I see no disadvantage.

—It's just, said the Goblin, that he will also be denied the capacity for friendship, and the capacity for any affection. And therefore, he will not love you either. I say this because you humans generally appreciate that sentiment, while in our species things work differently, dear girl, and it is my duty to warn you of this.

—I have already considered it, Ardid replied, this time forcefully and dispensing with any sweetness, which in the moment she considered superfluous. I have no objection to him not loving me: it is enough for Gudú that I love him.

They discussed the issue some more, but given Ardid's unwavering resolve, the Sorcerer and the Goblin agreed to study the matter with great caution and care. Almíbar had already fallen asleep, and might have missed the heart of the matter; in any case, he would have forgotten it. He forgot almost everything, except his love for Ardid, since it was so ingrained in him and had become rooted throughout his entire being in such a way that little space remained for other things.

Some time later, the Sorcerer and the Goblin informed the Queen of the fruits of their lengthy investigation. Ardid herself went to the dungeon where the old Master was so at ease. He had refused to occupy a more comfortable place, since for him there was no better spot in the Castle of Olar. The three, alone this time, gathered around a fire that reawakened ancient times in their hearts, when they hid in the ruins of the Castle of Ansélico. Finally, the two elders informed Ardid of the following:

—Indeed there exists the possibility of removing King Gudú's capacity to love. Just as we warned you, the procedure is extreme and total. If you persist in your plan, we must clarify several aspects of the matter. As you know, there is no sorcery, enchantment, or contract with the Higher Powers that is not subject to some requirement, which (depending on the circumstances) may or may not ultimately turn out to be counterproductive. In the case at hand, the detail or stipulation is that if a being's capacity to love is removed, the ability to weep is simultaneously taken from him.

—I see no disadvantage, she said. All the better: he will not know that humiliating sensation.

—True, said the Goblin, but there is a more complicated issue in this case that seems so simple: if for some strange or unexpected reason (which cannot be foreseen, as our powers are limited), the subject treated with such procedures were to one day shed a tear, not only he, but every place his feet had touched, and all those who had shared his existence, would disappear forever from Time and Earth, into Oblivion.

—But if you eliminate the capacity to love and with it the ability to weep . . . such a disappearance logically cannot occur.

—That's what I think, said the Sorcerer, but without much conviction.

—This is what everything would lead one to believe, if our investigation has not failed in its calculations, added the Goblin. But that clause is recorded in the Tractate: and if it appears there, there must exist some loophole which we may not be able to foresee.

—I see no logic in your fears, repeated Ardid, impatiently. You yourselves have said that the one entails the other: if he does not love, he shall not weep. If he does not weep, there is no cause for concern.

The Queen's two friends nodded in silence, but doubt—vague and remote, but doubt nonetheless—lingered in their eyes.

—Keep in mind, the Goblin finally said, that our power is not an absolute power. Not even safe from contamination do goblins have knowledge of All Possibilities. This is especially true in the state—although mild—of contamination in which I find myself. There is something, perhaps, that we have forgotten or failed to see.

They discussed the matter at great length, and at daybreak when it seemed to them that it was only a matter of human doubt rather than something probable, they reached an agreement to perform the delicate operation on the boy Gudú. And in the course of the discussion, they clarified some important details. The Queen noted that although Gudú would not love anyone, she could not deprive the King of attraction to the opposite sex, since he must have offspring and avoid the cursed question of succession, which had put the child's rights in such danger as well as, in the view of all, the Realm.

—Yes, this is possible, said the Goblin, after a brief consultation with the Sorcerer. Although it does not occur very often among humans, it can be arranged for him to lust after creatures of the opposite sex a great deal, without loving them in the least.

—And there's something else, said the Queen, and it's that we must prevent this attraction from controlling him. Keeping in mind his father's last passion, I think this can be as harmful as love itself.

—Very wise, said the Sorcerer. We will make it so no woman is capable of holding onto him for too long. Let us look into it, and we'll tell you the result of these inquiries later.

They soon returned to the Queen with the following news:

—Although it may seem strange, dear girl, this last bit is more difficult than any other. There are no recipes for it. But don't be alarmed: we have found a very clever and cunning solution, although the Goblin, in order to indulge you, may find himself in a difficult and unpleasant situation.

—Tell me at once. Ardid grew impatient.

—We have pondered the issue, coming to the conclusion that if we obtain a woman who takes thousands of different forms, who would be responsible for satisfying the carnal desires of the King, distracting him with each unique form, but only for a short time, it's clear that it won't be possible for the King to take a fancy to anyone. The wives he may have, of course, do not count, the old man clarified. With them, at any rate, he can do whatever he wants. We already know that they pose no danger to what concerns us.

—Of course, said the Queen, with a trace of sorrow or resentment. In the long term or the short, the wife negates herself. We are in agreement, for that negation there is no better prescription than marriage. But . . . where is this miraculous creature? I don't know anyone who meets these conditions. And even if they are met, years pass, and she who is fresh today, for all that she disguises herself, tomorrow will be old and lose all her appeal.

—I know of someone, dear girl, said the Goblin, who is spared from these miseries. Obviously, of course, she is not of your species.

—Well then, it doesn't work, said the Queen. A being that is not of the flesh does not attract the flesh.

—Leave it to me, said the Goblin, with a laugh that smelled too strongly of new wine, in the opinion of his two friends. Leave it to me: she must not be of the flesh, but she can take human form, when it suits her, although only for a short time. A short time is precisely what this is about, isn't it? As many human forms as she desires, and the most seductive, he made a condescending gesture. According to human standards, of course.

—Well then, be that as it may, attend to this creature as soon as possible.

—Here is the great sacrifice of our dear friend, said the Sorcerer with great sorrow. We are going to expose him to an encounter that he doesn't like at all and which he's been avoiding the entire time he's been contaminated: he must go in search of Ondina, she who lives at the bottom of the Lake. And while he maintains an excellent relationship with her, it is not so with her grandmother, the Great Lady. And the Great Lady, High and Most Pure Power par excellence, detests the contaminated. And to make matters worse, she dwells at the source of the Water, which she so wisely conducts.

—At the bottom of the Lake? Ardid marveled at such a significant revelation.

—Not at the bottom, thankfully, said the Goblin, taking a swig to lift his spirits. If that were the case, it could not be done. But yes, a little higher up, in the Cave of the Spring. And with luck, she won't happen to travel the watery paths to visit her granddaughter while I am talking with her.

Having said that, he drank more than usual, got almost scandalously drunk, and his nose took on a shade of such vivid crimson as had never been seen on him before. Which, as might be expected, filled his two friends with unease.

But the decision had already been made.

2.

Ondina of the Depths of the Lake had lived in the loveliest spot in the Lake of Disappearances for four-hundred-and-thirty years. Ondina was extraordinarily beautiful: smooth floating hair the color of seaweed coming down to her waist, large eyes ranging from the softest gold to dark green, as changeable as the light, and bluish-white skin. Her arms waved slowly between the deep roots of the plants, and her legs moved like the fins of a carp. A steady and shining smile, which transitioned from the pearlescent white of a shell to the liquid pink of a sunrise, floated across her lips. Any human would have felt a captivating desire to study her in all of her details—with the exception of her ears, which, like all of her kind, were long and pointed at the tips, although of a soft color between rose and gold.

Despite being the granddaughter of the Great Lady of the Lake, she did not possess a shred of her wisdom, not even a speck of the slightest intelligence—as often happens with water nymphs. On the contrary, she was so sweet and gentle, and exuded such innocence, that her profound stupidity could very well be mistaken for more poignant charm and enchantment. Like all water nymphs, she was exceedingly capricious, and her great whimsy was her Collection at the Bottom, where she had cultivated her garden of Intricate Greens with care. Ondina's collection consisted of an already considerable display of men, young and handsome, between fourteen and twenty years of age. She liked them so much that she would often drag them to the bottom, and there she preserved them, rosy and unharmed, thanks to the sap of the maraubina plant that grows once every three thousand years among the wellsprings. But soon she grew tired of them, and however much she adorned them with flowers from the lake and crowned their heads with all sorts of glittering stones, and caressed their hair, and kissed their cold lips, they said and did nothing; and so she always needed more and more young men to distract her with variety.

Every so often, cautiously approaching the shores of the Lake, she had seen how young peasant couples caressed and kissed one another, and it filled her with envy. She had confessed as much on more than one occasion to the goblins, who, out of pity, sometimes pushed men to the bottom. Among them was the Goblin of the South, to whom she had confided her wayward obsession. "This is foolishness," the goblins told her. "Choose a dolphin from those that roam the Southern coasts to take as your husband and stop this. Considering your youth, you can be forgiven, but tread carefully so your grandmother doesn't find out: she doesn't tolerate human contamination, and you can only play safely with the drowned." "That's what I'll do," she said then, contritely. "I promise not to forget." But since she was stupid to the most remote depths of her being, she not only forgot, but persisted in her foolish desire to receive caresses and kisses from a living man. "But what for?" the Goblin of the South asked her, who, after his libations had given him his post in the Castle, the Northern region of which grazed the waters of the rising Lake, had long conversations with her. "I see no reason." "Nor do I," responded Ondina. "I see no reason, but so it is."

This was the state of things when the Goblin opportunely remembered about her, her naïve nature and her foolish whimsy. This is how water nymphs were, it was said. He had met another, in the South, who had taken a fancy to donkeys, and also another, farther East, who had a penchant for red-bearded soldiers. Anything could be expected from a water nymph, except common sense.

He waited for a propitious night—that is to say, a night of a waxing moon—and burrowing into the recesses of the earth, he opened a passage to the Fountainhead of the Lake.

—It's been some time since you've come, Goblin of the South, said Ondina, who preferred him, without knowing it, for the whiff of humanity that was gradually consuming him. I want to show you the last one who entered. The Goblin of the Alamanita Region sent him to me, he's quite handsome. I have yet to tire of decorating him: look, I put seashells on his ears, bouquets of maraubina everywhere, and here, this pearl that an oyster from the Drango Sea gave me. What more can I do now, to keep from growing bored?

The Goblin thoughtfully studied the young man with dark hair and a golden complexion, fixed in an expression of terror—he hadn't had time to close his eyes. It seemed like the epitome of ugliness and absurdity to him, but he kept his opinions to himself, to better win over Ondina. He looked warily from side to side, and finally muttered:

—You're not expecting a visit from the Great Lady, right?

—Oh, no, she said. She's too busy preparing for the next thaw. She hasn't seen the last three, and although she doesn't like them very much, she tells me if I'm satisfied with drowned men, she has nothing to reproach me for.

—Well then, I've thought a lot about you, beauty, said the Goblin. And it so happens that we have found a solution, without you incurring the anger of your wonderful Grandmother who Inspires Such Respect from Me—he could only speak of her in capitalized words.

—Really? Ondina exclaimed, with great interest. Tell me, Goblin of the South.

—The thing that I'm offering you is an opportunity: we have found a potion that will allow you to take human form, for a short time—ten days, at most—without risk of contamination. Of course if you maintain this human form a single minute longer, you would be contaminated, and in such a dangerous way that there will be no remedy for it. But since you are fickle, as I see it, you are not going to spend more than two days entertaining human men, with whom you can cavort as you please during that time. And this way the danger will dissipate, to your great advantage: you can drink the elixir as many times as you'd like, and take, for ten days, the very useful figure of a woman (always different from the one before) . . . As I see it, you will enjoy nice things, and you will not get bored, which, through the past centuries, has never been said.

Ondina somersaulted twice in the water. It was her ultimate expression of glee, given that her smile was fixed.

—Quickly! she cried. And the surface of the Lake trembled suddenly, as if under a strong wind—quickly! Give me this potion!

—One moment, beauty, said the Goblin. Sorry to say it, but everything has its price.

—Tell me your conditions.

—Here it is: over the course of these delights, you'll enjoy the caresses and kisses and however much you like from as many young men as you see fit. But . . . —and here he picked his words very carefully—that's provided that you continue, time and again, to attract a certain man, who although in his day will be young and maybe even handsome, with time he will gradually become old and even ugly or repulsive. Only with this condition, under solemn oath, will I give you the potion.

—Alright, she said, it hardly matters. I will know exactly how to console myself with the others, for as long as the human race exists and produces such delightful creatures—and she pointed to the Garden of Drowned Youths.

—Very well. I will communicate your consent to the others involved, said the Goblin. And leaving her very excited, he returned from where he had come.

Queen Ardid was quite pleased to learn of this. Nevertheless, she said:

—My dear friend, are you sure Ondina will not grow tired of waiting for the promised potion? Keep in mind that many years have to pass until Gudú is of an age to appreciate her charms.

—Oh, dear girl, said the Goblin, what are a few years to those who live submerged for ages upon ages? Nothing, dear girl, nothing.

And he drank with gusto, still trembling, a big gulp of a certain light, rosy wine that he reserved for special occasions. The fear that the Great Lady inspired in him was comparable only to the affection he felt for Queen Ardid.

It was decided that since the birthday of the young King would take place in a few days, this would be the appropriate moment to perform the agreed upon procedures.

Gudú, meanwhile, roamed freely about the Castle without hindrance, quite oblivious to the plot being woven around him. His brother Predilecto followed him everywhere, and he took care of him with such tenderness and affection that Queen Ardid took notice. One day she called him aside. She felt an overwhelming affection for that boy, so different from his brothers, and said to him:

—Prince Predilecto, I have observed that you feel great tenderness for our beloved Lord and King.

—That's right, said the boy. In truth, he is the only one of all my brothers for whom I feel genuine affection . . . a true fraternal bond.

—From now on, said the Queen, I appoint you as his Protector and Guardian, because you do not ignore the many dangers lying in wait for my son in this Castle: in spite of all appearances to the contrary, not everything here is as it seems.

Predilecto kept silent, but the Queen did not fail to observe that a sadness, truly premature for his age, filled the boy's eyes.

—Come with me, she added. I want, from this day onward, for you to see in me the mother you have never known.

Saying this, she kissed him. And from the strong blush that spread over the boy, she realized how much happiness her words had stirred in him. "I have here," Ardid told herself, "someone who must not be conquered by fear, nor by force nor by greed; I have here someone who will only be conquered by love." And thinking this, she led him to her bedchamber. Then she opened a small chest, where she usually kept the few treasures she had left, and found at the bottom a small stone that, years ago—as a child—she had discovered on the riverbank. It was blue, smooth, and elongated, and it appeared to have been slit through the center by a sharp blade. That small stone had been the only plaything in her austere childhood. A small hole opened at its center: she had brought an eye close to it to peer through and look at the reflection of the sun on the sea, for many years. Perhaps for this reason, she kept it. And though at times she was tempted to throw it away, without knowing why, there it remained. She took it between her fingers very solemnly and told him:

—My son, this, so simple in appearance, is one of my most prized heirlooms . . . I'm giving it to you, to keep as proof of my affection and as a token of this pact.

With devotion and reverence that she never would have expected, Predilecto delicately took the cleaved stone, and kissing it, said:

—Thank you, my Lady. I swear on my life that I will never forget it. This stone will never leave my side, and I will respect this pact until the end of my days.

And leaving the Queen mute with bewilderment and some regret—albeit not for long—Prince Predilecto strung the stone—by that hole through which Ardid had in the past stared at the sea—on a gold chain, a gift from his father. And he displayed it on his chest forever, with the pride and love that others showed their highest honors.

"Truly," thought Ardid, when the boy disappeared from her view, "he is a naïve boy. It will be necessary to preserve this ingenuity, for as many years as possible." And unable to help it, she sighed to herself: "Poor Prince Predilecto."

But at once, more pressing concerns carried that sigh far away from her heart.

On Gudú's birthday, the Queen took him to her bedchamber, and sitting him on a stool, she gave him a drink from a large cup containing poppy diluted in a sweet drink of mead along with some mysterious ingredients. Once the child was asleep, she called for the Goblin and the Sorcerer. With utmost care they laid him down on the floor. They fanned the flames of the hearth, and when the fire turned the color of the sunset over the Lake, the Wizard pronounced the words of his ritual. Then the Goblin took the child's head with great tenderness, blew on his brow, and it opened with the delicacy and softness of a flower. He did the same over his chest, and when his heart emerged, the Sorcerer locked it up, with great skill, in a glass that was at once transparent and sturdy. The boy's brow displayed dreams of horses, a large sun, harsh and red, the clashing of swords and a poplar swaying in the breeze.

"Nothing dangerous," said the Goblin. "Tell me, we still have time, should we remove something more from him?: Intelligence? Innocence?" Suddenly the Queen felt a deep sorrow, and covering her eyes with her hands, burst into tears:

—Enough, she said, enough. That will do.

The Goblin blew on the child's brow and chest, which closed, seamlessly, and the fire went out on its own. An hourglass, on the hearth's ledge, slowly shed its golden rain.

As if seeing it for the first time, Ardid's eyes and thoughts traveled around the room. Through the window, and even through the stones, curtains, and walls of the Tower, the night, in all its fullness, reached her. It was a lovely night, which swelled with the slumber of some birds and the wakefulness of others. She seemed to even perceive the translucent quivering of the dragonflies over the stillness of the ponds. And down below, in the Lake of Disappearances, something or someone—Ardid partly knew, and partly guessed—skimmed the surface of its waters with invisible fingers. "How grand and mysterious, how tranquil and terrible a night can be . . ." she thought. Then she realized that her eyes were covered with a shining dampness that awoke distant memories. Achingly she broke away from that reverie, and turned back to her friends:

—The King is born, Ardid said, drying her tears. May we live to see his greatness! Wake him, and may all the bells of Olar ring at once.

And so it was done, and the King's birthday was celebrated with a pomp and splendor never before known.

Translated by Lisa Boscov-Ellen

WORK

1948, *Los Abel*, Destino (novel).

1953, *Fiesta al Noroeste (La Ronda y Los niños buenos)*, Afrodisio Aguado (novel).

1953, "La pequeña vida," Tecnos (story).

1954, *Pequeño teatro*, Planeta (novel).

1955, *Los cuentos vagabundos*, Ediciones G.P. (stories).

1956, *Los niños tontos*, Arión (stories).

1957, *El Tiempo*, Mateu (stories).

1957, "El país de la pizarra," Molino Carville (children's story).

1958, *Los hijos muertos*, Planeta (novel).

1960, *El saltamontes verde / El aprendiz*, Lumen (children's stories).

1960, "Paulina, el mundo y las estrellas," Garbo (children's story).

1960, *Primera memoria*, Destino (novel).

1961, *A la mitad del camino*, Rocas (stories).

1961, "Libro de juegos para los niños de los otros," Lumen (story and photography).

1961, *Tres y un sueño*, Destino (children's stories).

1961, *Historias de la Artámila*, Destino (stories).

1961, *El arrepentido*, Rocas (stories).

1962, *Caballito loco / Carnavalito*, Lumen (children's stories).

1963, *El río*, Argos (stories).

1964, *Los soldados lloran de noche*, Destino (novel).

1964, *Algunos muchachos*, Destino (novel).

1965, "El polizón de Ulises," Lumen (children's story).

1969, *La trampa*, Destino (novel).

1971, *La torre vigía*, Lumen (novel).

1971, *Obra completa*, Destino (anthology).

1983, "Sólo un pie descalzo," Lumen (story).

1990, *La virgen de Antioquía y otros relatos*, Mondadori (stories).

1991, *El árbol de oro y otros relatos*, Bruño (children's stories).

1991, "Sino espada," Compañía Europea de Comunicación e Información (story).

1993, *De ninguna parte y otros relatos*, Fundación Ferrocarriles Españoles (stories).

1993, *Luciérnagas*, Destino (novel).

1994, "La oveja negra," Destino (children's story).

1995, "El verdadero final de la bella durmiente," Lumen (children's story).

1995, *El árbol de oro y otros relatos*, Lumen (children's stories).

1996, *Olvidado Rey Gudú*, Espasa-Calpe (novel).

1997, *Casa de juegos prohibidos*, Espasa Calpe (stories).

1998, *Los de la tienda / El maestro / La brutalidad del mundo*, Plaza & Janés (stories).

2000, *Aranmanoth*, Espasa-Calpe (novel).

2000, *Todos mis cuentos*, Lumen (children's stories).

2002, *Cuentos de infancia*, Martínez Roca (children's stories).

2003, "Tolín," Iberautor (children's story).

2008, *Paraíso inhabitado*, Destino (novel).

2010, *La puerta de la luna*, Destino (stories and articles).

2011, *Las Artámilas*, Fondo de Cultura Económica (stories).

·

ENGLISH TRANSLATIONS

1989, *School of the Sun*, translated by Elaine Kerrigan, Colombia University Press (novel).

·

AWARDS AND RECOGNITIONS

1947, Finalist for the Premio Nadal for *Los Abel.*

1952, Premio Café Gijón de novela for *Fiesta al Noroeste.*

1954, Premio Planeta for *Pequeño teatro.*

1959, Premio Nadal for *Primera memoria.*

1959, Premio Nacional de Literatura for *Los hijos muertos.*

1959, Premio de la Crítica Narrativa Castellana for *Los hijos muertos.*

1965, Premio Lazarillo de Creación Literaria for "El polizón de Ulises."

1965, Premio Fastenrath for *Los soldados lloran de noche.*

1976, Children's Book of Interest from the Ministerio de Cultura for *Paulina.*

1984, Premio Nacional de Literatura Infantil y Juvenil for "Sólo un pie descalzo."

1995, Premio Cuidad de Barcelona for *El verdadero final de la bella durmiente.*

1997, Premio Ojo Crítico de Narrativa for *Olvidado Rey Gudú.*

1998, Named a Member of the Real Academia Española (seat K).

2001, Premio Ciudad de Alcalá Arts and Letters for her writing career.

2006, Internacional Terenci Moix Award for her literary work.

2007, Premio Nacional de las Letras Españolas for her body of work.

2008, Premio Extremadura a la Creación for best Literary Career of an Iberoamerican author.

2008, Premio Quijote de las Letras Españolas.

2010, Premio Lorenzo Luzuriaga de las Letras.

2010, Premio Averroes de Oro a las Bellas Letras.

2010, Premio Cervantes.

2011, Premio de la Crítica de la Feria del Libro de Bilbao.

2011, Honorary Doctorate from UIMP.

RAFAEL

SÁNCHEZ

FERLOSIO

(Spain, 1927)

Rafael Sánchez Ferlosio, the son of Rafael Sánchez Mazas—who was a writer too and a founding member of the Falange Española—and the Italian Liliana Ferlosio, was born in Rome on the fourth of December, 1927, where his father worked as a correspondent for the newspaper *ABC*. That was where he lived his first years.

Back in Spain, he enrolled in the Jesuit high school San José de Villafranca de los Barros. He started off taking preparatory courses to get into the Escuela de Arquitectura, but he ended up attending the department of Philosophy and Literature at the Universidad Complutense de Madrid and he even took some courses at Escuela Oficial de Cinematografía.

Though not a big fan of literary or intellectual groups, he ended up a member in the Círculo Lingüístico de Madrid along with Agustín García Calvo, Isabel Llácer, Carlos Piera, and Víctor Sánchez de Zavala, and he's considered one of the children of the war that ended up forming part of the generation of the middle of the century. In addition, along with Ignacio Aldecoa, Jesús Fernández Santos, Carmen Martín Gaite (to whom he would be married until 1970), and Alfonso Sastre, he participated in the creation and direction of *Revista Española*, which was as much a platform for that generation of writers, poets, and playwrights as it was a mouthpiece for up-and-coming Western literature: the still emerging work of Capote, of Zavattini (expertly translated by Sánchez Ferlosio[1]), or the first experiments of the *Nouveau Roman de l'école du Regard*.

Rafael Sánchez Ferlosio became known in 1951 with *Industrias y andanzas de Alfanhuí*, a bildungsroman on horses, somewhere between a picaresque

---

1 The little novel, which it would be inappropriate to call "neorealist," *Totó il buono de Cesare Zavattini* was the story from where Vittorio De Sica got the screenplay for *Miracolo a Milano*.

novel and magic realism, but true recognition come to him in 1955 for *El Jarama* (which would win him the Premio Nadal that same year and the Premio de la Critica the next one). Years later, he himself summarized that time: "first I made an incursion into 'prose,' or 'la bella pagina' (*Alfanhui*); then I wanted to have some fun with speech (*El Jarama*), and finally, after many years of grammar, I discovered the language."

Of course, after his incursion into the world of fiction writing, he rejected "the grotesque imposture of the literati," and dedicated the years that followed to the study of grammar. Seized by this passion, Sánchez Ferlosio would spend those years in a "graphomaniacal furor" in absolute silence in terms of publishing. As he once said, "I don't write with the immediate need to publish. I always say that I know how to knit, but I don't know how to make a sweater."

For reasons of mental health (grammar is tremendously obsessive), he returned to the publishing world (that doesn't publish) in 1974 with *Las semanas del jardín* (a title inspired by the novel that Cervantes never managed to write). The years that followed, he dedicated to his work as an essayist and in 1986 he returned to writing fiction with *El testimonio de Yarfoz*.

The largest part of his most recent work has centered around essays with titles like *Vendrán más años malos y nos harán más ciegos*, a collection of reflections and aphorisms that won him Premio Nacional de Ensayo and Premio Ciudad de Barcelona. Like a dyed-in-the-wool bellicose intellectual, he has freely proclaimed a total lack of influence from contemporary literature, similarly his complete repudiation of television, sports, and publicity. His darts have struck such figures as Ortega y Gasset, Julián Marías, Karl Popper, and García Lorca.

His agent, Carmen Balcells, once said of him that he has written two or three hundred times as many pages as he has published. Though the number is, perhaps, exaggerated, there is no doubt that Rafael Sánchez Ferlosio is an author as irrepressible as he is indispensable. With your permission . . .

THE ACORN

The Torture of Doctor Johnson

For many years I did no literary work, so I would have preferred to submit an essay or a fragment of an essay, but it would have been too long. So I selected a few paragraphs from my most recent novel, *El testimonio de Yarfoz*, which seemed to me the most ingenious and inventive. I picked them just because I like them and because they seem like a joyful creation, especially the part about the begging baboons; the part about the ramp is a bit tedious because it's difficult to describe.

In Conversation with the Dead

I'm not familiar with that Quevedo sonnet—I don't really like him as an author. I prefer the dead of my own family, of which there are many, but the authors who I would mention are not authors I read for pleasure, but rather read to use in essays. I'll mention several books that are, you might say, those I frequently reference. Almost all of them, oddly enough, are German. One is Austrian Karl Bühler, his *Sprachtheorie*, the *Theory of Language*, and the *Theory of Expression*. Another is Theordor Wiesengrund Adorno, all of his works except the one on Aesthetics, which is unintelligible. No one understands his Aesthetics. And also Max Weber, all of his work, especially *Economy and Society* and *The Sociologies of Religion*. Those two in particular. And maybe some other types of works as well, like a field study examining the practices of certain industrial workers and the way the parts and muscles of the human body, and its proper movements, compare with the violent and twisted movements that in some cases industrial-manual labor requires of them, but apparently they don't like field studies. It's odd, but the writers who interest me most are theorists.

Those are the authors who I consult and cite, among several others. The influence just comes about from consulting the text. If Adorno has something on what I'm looking for, well I go to the text, and there you go; or I transcribe it or cite it without transcribing it or paraphrase it, but it is always a conscious consultation, with one exception, employed all the time and unique for being a literary author, that is Franz Kafka, who seems to me the most extraordinary author of this century as well as many prior centuries.

Coda

Critics have said that you are "the twentieth century author with the greatest lexical richness and that you use the language with the greatest precision and meticulousness. That the breadth of your narrative register does not cease to amaze, from fantasy to the objectivity of El Jarama.*" All told, this precision has an impressionistic poetic and a symbolic strength. The fantastical world of prince Nébride comes to seem even more real than reality itself. In the beginning was the word. Could Yarfoz and prince Nébride be a sort of fantastical Don Quixote and Sancho Panza? Prince Nébride seems to be a character of uncertain destiny.*

The greatest lexical richness is false because what I have are prohibitions—self-prohibitions—and not a very broad vocabulary. For example, I can't say "efectuar." I never use the verb *efectuar* or the verb *realizar*. I always say "hacer" and I was greatly annoyed when I discovered that the verb *efectuar* was already in use in the sixteenth century. I am precise and meticulous in terms of description, but it's not richness of vocabulary. Sometimes I have a predilection for antiquated words—some—very few, but that's another story.

I don't now how to apply personality and fate to these characters, but they aren't characters of personality. They are characters of fate because they are part of a plot; here, for example, they are going into exile. They have personalities like everyone, but the manifestation of their personalities is not part of the plot. They have almost no personality, but they do have fate; things happen to them, they do things. So the previous comparison of Yarfoz and prince Nébride, because they are on horseback, is absolutely ridiculous, in the first place because Don Quixote and Sancho Panza are definitely characters of personality and all of *Quixote* is the manifestation of their personalities. Besides, mounts—the donkey and the horse—are subject to sumptuary norms of the time in which *Quixote* was written, perhaps they were in decline, but up until then the mount you rode was symbolic of your social status. It was prohibited for a peasant like Sancho Panza to ride a horse. Maybe already in the seventeenth century some peasants did because there were so many bandits who rode horses around the end of the sixteenth century and at the beginning of the seventeenth, but before then horses were status symbols, and the "nobleman" Alonso Quijano the Good had to ride a horse, as the word *caballero* (horseman) indicates. This is emphasized by, although I do not know until when, the fact that the mule was the mount of the clergy. The clerics rode mules, the caballeros rode horses, and peasants rode donkeys.

I could point out that the Christian interpreters of the Gospel say that Jesus Christ entered Jerusalem on a donkey because it was a humble mount. Out of humility. The donkey was the sumptuary mount as the victory song shows, the Song of Deborah (Judges 5:10). It was the mount of the most noble. There were seven white donkeys in the Song of Deborah. So, Jesus Christ entered Jerusalem to take power and the people sang to him "Hosanna, filio David" because "son of David" means "you are of the Jewish tribe" and a descendent of David and you are entering Jerusalem to retake the throne of David. This is the most modern interpretation that there is. It does not take heed of the mount. This is something I say to myself, it seems to me that it is a mount of the nobles and moreover what they sing is "son of David" meaning "king of the Jews." He was not coming to die. He was coming to triumph, not to triumph through death, which is a Christian solution, but to triumph as the king of Jerusalem. So, Nébride and Yarfoz both ride horses, but there are no great social divisions among the Grágidos. There was no triumph. It has not ended. Soon they lose importance because they die and the history of the Grágidos continues.

A THOUSAND FORESTS

from *El testimonio de Yarfoz*
(The Testimony of Yarfoz)
[a novel]

The Third Day of Nébride's Journey into Exile

Apart from the escorts provided by the king, our expedition was made up of ten horses: Nébride rode one, his wife Táiz another, on another rode Sorfos, and on a horse he had just been given by Mirigalla, rode Sebsidio; Fosco, the carpenter, and Anarino, his wife, rode their own horses, each carrying one of their children; on another rode Chano, Táiz's lady-in-waiting, on another Quiarces, the Atánida of Ebna, who had come along as the head of the household; on another was Nerigreo, the agronomist, and, finally, on the last horse, rode Vandren and myself; then came eight cargo mules and a mule driver, lent us by Mirigalla, who would return with the mule train. Only Fosco's children and Vandren were without their own mount, and the horse the king had gifted Sebsidio was far and away the best.

XXIX. The "Path of the Iscobascos" is described in the Grágidos as a passageway carved out of living rock, but we would never have been able to imagine the monumental construction we would encounter that morning. We had only traveled a distance of eight hundred horses—not along the path leading to the cliffs, but on a path running perpendicular to that one, heading west, through the lush coolness of cedars and yews—when turning to the south we saw the path start gradually to drop underground, as if burrowing into the rock. We descended to a point where the walls of rock flanking the path closed in a vault over our heads, forming an underground tunnel. My

sense of direction led me to believe that the mouth of the tunnel was perpendicular to the line of cliffs such that, if it continued in a straight line, inevitably there would be a light at the other end. But this was not the case; instead
it continued to drop, maintaining the same angle, through the heart of the
living rock, banking slowly to the right. It got so dark that our guide lit a
torch, by which light I saw the great craftsmanship of the stone carvers, no
hollows or protuberances, and I could see a channel, about a foot wide and a
foot deep along the right hand wall, coursing with clear, fast-moving water.
Soon, however, a light appeared and the tunnel opened into a room with a
circumference of at least two-hundred-and-fifty horses, positioned parallel to
the vertical face of the precipice that we had encountered days before. The
tunnel was the entryway to a ramp cut into the stone wall of the Meseged,
forming a sort of lateral groove, so that not only the floor was stone, but the
right-hand wall and the ceiling were stone as well; on the left, it was open to
the air, but a thick stone parapet came up to a safe height. It was a kind of
overlook cut into the wall but always descending, almost rectilinear, with only
a few protrusions and recessions in the hard stone wall. The channel of water
still coursed rapidly to our right. Soon we saw that at a distance of approxi-
mately one-hundred-and-fifty horses the ramp seemed to dead-end against a
wall, on a landing that was either wider than the path, or cut deeper into the
rock; but when we came up to the wall, we saw that at the landing another
tunnel opened into the rock; this second tunnel also curved, but not as sharply
as the first one, delving into the rock, and always descending, inscribing first
three quarters of a helicoid to a point where, turning back on itself, it rotated
a final quarter of a circle, arriving parallel to the cliff face once again, giving
way to another ramp, identical to the first, but the inverse of it because now
the stone was on our left and the emptiness on our right. Seeing this, we
understood, in essential terms, what the so-called "Path of Iscobascos" was: if
we had been able to look down at it from the plain, we would have seen a
succession of zigzagging ramps cut into the stone, mysteriously connected at
the ends by tunnels that penetrated the heart of the rock, always descending,
inverting and dropping to the next ramp, emerging parallel to the cliff face
thanks to the doubling back or inverse curvature of the last quarter of a circle.
In the end, the totality was not structurally different from a great spiral staircase, but one that had been pressed flat, except at its extremes, against a

single plane. The guide told us that the landings at the ends of the ramps, along with the square recesses that appeared here and there, greater in number all the time approaching the center, were pullouts for carts that crossed paths while descending and ascending, for resting mules, fixing malfunctions, or any other eventuality. Before long we saw water tanks, troughs, and even small gardens, jutting out over the luminous abyss. In places where the rock seemed unstable, the parapet extended in columns to the bridge that formed the ceiling, all of it carved out of living rock, not a single fabricated feature. Our admiration for that prodigious construction increased at each new ramp: I even thought I saw the melancholy dissipate in Nébride's eyes, replaced by a glow of joy for the past and excitement for great public works. At a particularly lush overhanging garden, on a landing significantly larger than all the others, uniquely adorned with a small columned vista, Nébride stood out like a white stone in the middle of the dense foliage. "Is there, perhaps, a tomb here?" he asked our guide. "Yes, there is a tomb. The tomb of master Susubruz, who built this ramp and oversaw its fifty-two year construction." The guide parted the foliage and showed us the tomb: the date read 317 of the Isobascos Era, which, accordingly, would mark the date of his death, the guide told us, less than one year after the completion of the ramp, corresponding to the year 232 of the Grágido-Atánida Era: the ramp of the Meseged was completed, then, some eighty years before the Barcial bridge. "So much glory," said Nébride, "has come to Grágidos and the Atánidas because of the bridge connecting the eastern and western sides of the Barcial, even though the two sides already communicated via raft; and here we have the Iscobascos and this astonishing ramp, which eighty years prior connected the north with the south, upper Barcial with lower Barcial—no other connection between them existed apart from the long circuitous route through the region of the Sovereign Villages or through the Llábrides Mountains—and yet they never received any great recognition for it. Then the guide detailed for us the characteristics of the ramp: the precipice was five hundred vertical units, and as the slope of the ramp was about eight percent, every hundred horses the drop was twelve vertical units,[2] such that, to cover the five hundred units of the drop, the total length of the ramp was four-thousand-one-hundred-and-sixty horses. It necessarily had to be supplied with water; this came

---

2   Each vertical unit equals 2/3 of a horse—measured lengthwise.

primarily from the stream that we had been seeing, but also from other springs that the carving of the rock had uncovered. It took a horse four to five hours to make the climb, it could take a cart fifteen to twenty hours, and men and animals had to be able to refresh themselves and to drink; so there were water tanks every six ramps, thirty-one in all; the water was also necessary to wash away excrement that was carried out through sewers to the cliff face. The excess water was used to vitalize the ramp with the cool, overhanging gardens that provided shade and moisture to the stone, burning in the midday sun. Water was such a necessity that when there was none, because of a problem at the source, cart drivers did not even attempt the climb, certain that at the very least their mules would perish, if not they themselves. Then we asked him about master Susubruz. The guide told us that he'd been the brother of the king's mother, and was only slightly older than his nephew. That he'd begun planning the ramp's construction even before his nephew took the throne. Some said he'd acted with excessive grace and flattery, hoping that when his nephew was king, he'd be allowed to carry out his project and that later on he'd take advantage of his nephew's youth to exert his influence. But this was untrue; he was never disloyal nor did he mistreat the king in any way. His whole life had been driven by the desire to build that ramp and his behavior had to be understood in light of that singular passion. But in truth the notion that his passion was such that it robbed him of all human tenderness was refuted by his assertion that the greatest undertaking in the world was not worth a single human life, and by his consequent instructions that absolutely all of the work be done from inside and from above, never allowing a single scaffolding to be lowered over the edge of the abyss. He even managed to irritate his workers with the extreme nature of his precautions. The Sea-bounds, who were much wealthier than the Iscobascos, had supposedly offered significant financial assistance for the project, which would have required of the Iscobascos essentially only a symbolic contribution, such that the project might be finished in one half or one quarter of the anticipated time. But the Iscobascos cared little for this sort of intrusion—although it would alleviate a sizable expenditure for such a poor and austere people—and Susubruz threatened once again to resign from overseeing the project. That's what he did whenever someone opposed him. And, of course, his departure had to be avoided at all costs; still, he was not always able to sway everyone with this threat, some quickly figured out what sort of thing would actually make him resign and when he was just posturing in order to get his way. The participation of the Sea-bounds would have actually caused Susubruz to abandon the project; so they had no choice but to reject the offer. The project, which lasted fifty-two years, ended without a single fatality and without any injuries more serious than a few men with hands or feet crushed by blocks of stone. Still, it was said, that in the last years of his life, already over eighty, his legs no longer permitting him to walk uphill and downhill, Susubruz commissioned a chair of wood and wicker in which, hanging from a rope and using a pulley, they raised and lowered him outside the parapet, suspended over the abyss, until on one occasion, seeing a strong wind lash him terrifyingly, scraping him and even causing his chair to slam into the rock wall, they'd had enough, and so they approached him claiming that he was not submitting himself to the same cautionary measures that he so harshly submitted the rest of them to, and he answered that the project could be finished perfectly without him and that he was old enough to be allowed certain whims and to satisfy them as he desired. To which the others were silent at first, but then someone even older than him said: "So you're just an old egoist, because you know that it will be a death you won't even feel, but it doesn't even occur to you to think about how unpleasant it would be for us to have to go recover your body, shattered in a thousand pieces on the rocks down below. We can have a couple strong youths here everyday to take you up and down on a stretcher as many times as you like, even though it won't be as much fun for you as the chair." And with these words he was convinced to stop using the chair and pulley. [. . .] Because of the nature of the project, master Susubruz was given the nickname "woodworm of the Meseged." When the guide stopped speaking, Nébride was thoughtful for a moment; then, removing a beautiful enamel pendant that he always wore around his neck, he said to the courtier: "Might I honor the memory of such a great man and great master, by leaving here, on his tomb, this pendant given to me by my grandfather Arriasco?" "Yes you may, and you can be sure that the Iscobascos will be grateful to you for the appreciation you have shown for such a deserving and so honorably remembered man." [. . .]

XXX. It took us more than four hours, allowing for several stops, to descend the four-hundred-thousand horses of the Meseged ramp that comprised the fifty vertical unit drop of the cliff-face. Before us now opened a desolate territory of scattered whitish deposits formed by the accumulation of detritus that came, mostly, from the Meseged itself, with erosion ditches running through it, converging in sandy ravines that dropped to the banks of the Barcial. Here the path was not at all firm or stable, almost annually it was worn down or washed away, if not erased, by waters that, without a solid bed to retain them, continued to flow torrentially for some time after a downpour ended. Our Iscobasco escorts did not want to return without first seeing us through that desert—which extended a length of some three thousand horses—and putting us on the road to Gromba Feceria. Of course, that stretch was not without frequent traffic, it led to the Iscobasco ramp, which was the obligatory route to the north, because to the right was the path of Atabates, a people that traders generally avoided. That desert itself was vaguely considered an Atabate territory, although that consideration meant nothing. The Atabates populated an area to our right, on both banks of the Barcial, with only messenger rafts to communicate between the two sides, occupying an area of five thousand horses, downriver from the waterfalls. The Atabates were the only people at the bottom of the Meseged not descended from the Sea-bounds, and their bodies were no different than ours, nor those of the Atánidas, nor the Iscobascos. At one time it was speculated that the Atabates were the forefathers of all peoples and that, having previously occupied the lower Barcial much farther downriver, they had been pushed back by the invasion of the Sea-bounds, sending off successive emigrations that had gone into the Contrarrío mountains on opposite ends of the Meseged, and later returned, on opposite sides of the Barcial, as the Grágidos and the Atánidas. That the Grágidos and the Atánidas had descended, on opposite sides, from the high valleys and their tributaries to arrive at the Barcial was a recognized fact; but that their previous origin had been a divergent emigration from the banks of the lower Barcial was the new—and, for me, the ludicrous—part of this theory. On the other hand, a different theory proposed the opposite, that is: that the Atabates came down from upper Barcial and were the only people to have gone around the Meseged to settle at the foot of the great waterfalls. But the truly inquisitive did not trust either of these ideas, since it has always been the jurists of Esteverna who have advocated this sort of hypothesis, using them to establish juridical theses, all of which provoke distrust among the rest of the people. The Barcial emerged from the waterfalls perpendicular to the Meseged and followed the path of the Atabates, but then it began meandering and curving to the west at an obtuse angle, and at the height of

Gromba Feceria it more or less came parallel to the ramp of the Iscobascos, such that our road to the city was perpendicular to the spot in the Meseged where we had emerged.

However, we would face a strange and profound sadness before leaving that desert and bidding farewell to our escorts. It was Vandren who, riding on the back of my horse, suddenly pointed out, on the profile of one of the whitish dunes, dappled with small dark shrubs, about five hundred paces away, the dark silhouettes of a pack of animals that I was unable to identify just then, running diagonally in the direction of the path, as if aiming to cross it up ahead of us. I didn't know how they'd spotted us or what imperative of their nature had made us their apparent object of interest. An erosion ditch hid them from our view for a few seconds, but soon they reappeared, closer and at the exact point where our eyes expected them; now everyone else was waiting for them too; I was able to identify them as a tribe of monkeys. There were no monkeys in our lands, and we did not suspect that they lived anywhere outside the remote jungles of the Barcial delta. Our guide noted our surprise and without waiting for our questions: "They are the begging baboons," he said, "you'll see when we get up to them." We had just arrived at the point of convergence. Now their group stood motionless, about ten or fifteen paces from the path, all of them facing us; there must have been about forty of them, males, females, and infants, horribly ragged, hairy and covered with scabs and filth; the largest male had come six or seven paces out in front of the others and, as soon as we stopped our horses, he broke into a feverish speech, garrulous, whining, gesticulating, more distorted than inarticulate and more discontinuous than articulate, but recalling without a doubt the intonations and sounds and inflection of human speech, above all in his mode of emphasis and the profiles of his elocution; who knows what infinite resolve had put the need in those eyelids covered with the whitish dust of the desert and in that red snout twisting imploringly, denying all the proud power and ferocity of those long baboon fangs; who knows what incomplete destiny had transformed those long and dark hands, born for pure and immediate prehension, identical to the primal appropriation, into instruments not made for gesturing, but for the gesture of a gesture, for the supplicating search for or simulation of a gesture. We were quiet, entranced, listening to him, just like his quiet, expectant tribe behind him, when the solitary motion of our second escort dismounting from his horse put an immediate end to his speech. His

stillness and that of the others was absolute. The Iscobasco untied a sack from
the back of his horse and carried it over, leaving it two paces from the largest
baboon who waited for the man to return to his horse and then quickly
approached the sack, expertly untied it, now emitting only the soft grunts
appropriate to his species, and then grabbed it by the bottom corners, and
with a single motion, dumped all its contents on the ground. In that same
instant, the whole tribe threw themselves on the crusts, chestnuts, carrots,
beans, apples, and, with total desperation and speed, but in almost total
silence, they devoured everything in a few seconds. Even before it was over,
Nébride had already turned his back on the spectacle and started riding off,
but he thought he heard Sorfos laughing behind him and he looked back to
see. The guides too prompted us to continue on our way, but I felt Vandren's
hands on top of mine, as if he wanted to detain the horse for another moment;
I couldn't look at his face to find out if his emotion and his interest came
from curiosity or trembling compassion. In the end, I brought my horse up
next to the guide's and asked him: "What was that?" "Those are the begging
baboons," he said, "animals who've suffered a long and sad history." He told
me that breed had previously only occupied the forests along the Barcial delta.
When a group of Sesemnesces farmers tried to colonize one of those areas,
the baboons had apparently ravaged their crops, which had been planted in an
area the baboons considered part of their own territory. Having no experience
hunting them and not feeling it right to start killing a breed of animal they
had never killed, and seeing that they were not unfriendly nor fearful, the
farmers opted—in their words—to make an agreement with them, to the
extent that you can talk about an "agreement" between men and animals, and
to teach them how to gather food in designated areas, showing them how to
maintain crops and take advantage of them. And that was the beginning of
their domesticity; they ended up moving into the villages and even became
laborers, thanks to their intelligence, in some collection jobs, in the use of
waterwheels, transporting loads, and in a great diversity of tasks, tasks more
diverse and difficult than those any other domestic animal, or all of them
combined, are capable of doing. But around nine years ago, a sudden flood
washed away the villages and drowned the majority of their inhabitants, while
the baboons, numbering close to one thousand, had almost all lived, because
they slept in trees and had superior survival skills. The survivors searched for
their village and could not find it, they called for their masters, they wept,

they grew desperate and ended up scattering. But a small group of some fifty or sixty found the eleven humans who survived the flood: two families and two men who had lost their families and joined the others. There was nothing left for the people to do there; they were too few to start over, and they had no desire to stay in that horrible place. So they left in search of a new life, but the monkeys did not abandon them; they went and begged in Sea-bound towns, but the people did not want them coming near the village with the monkeys because they claimed they carried diseases. To abandon the monkeys was unthinkable; they couldn't even fool one of those animals, how would they be able to fool forty or fifty of them? So they decided first to separate the women and children, one of them at a time, so that when they had gotten away they would reunite with their husbands, one at a time as well, so the baboons would not notice, assuming they would stay wherever the greatest number of humans stayed, wherever they thought the center was. But before putting this plan into practice, they discovered, by fortuitous circumstance, that for the baboons the center was one of the men, the oldest of the eleven, that it was to him they were fundamentally connected and they would not go anywhere unless he went as well. So his companions, the two families and the other man, parted ways with him amid many apologies. They showed him the great need they had—fearing for the children, condemned to a life of begging, expelled from everywhere—for him to stay with the monkeys, the pointlessness of sacrificing all of them, and a thousand other things, offering the final hope that he might manage to escape from the baboons too if he waited for the right moment, and with many blessings, they left in search of another life. The baboons remained impassive seeing them depart and gathered affectionately around their master and protector. It was this man who came to settle where the two paths leading to the ramp of the Iscobascos came together, hoping to beg, since the monkeys grew weaker every day—many had died already, although others had been born—and their appearance was totally repugnant, which would keep him from approaching any city or village with them, he feared too that they might go into the countryside and steal, and he would be the one captured and held responsible for any damage they caused and be beaten or pardoned for their thefts, since everyone knew the monkeys were with him. So, always accompanied by the monkeys, he approached travelers passing through the desert, and asked for alms for the monkeys and for himself, recounting his unfortunate story in words and with a voice more and more the same every day until he only told a single identical tale. And they said that he was totally deranged, because although what he said sounded clear and intelligible, he could not answer a single question posed to him; he seemed to be mute and deaf to everyone else. Because of this man the history of the begging baboons was known, but three years ago he had died of consumption and sickness. The baboons did not know how to leave that place and now they came out to the path on their own to beg, and the speech delivered by the oldest male of the tribe was nothing but an imitation of that man's tale, including his hand gestures, to the point where many heard that same tale or believed to recognize it perfectly in the senseless, inarticulate, and unintelligible harangue of the oldest baboon. At last the courtier told me how the Iscobascos, whenever they passed through that region, often remembered to carry provisions for those miserable animals, like the sack that he himself had brought on this occasion, although it wasn't always guaranteed that they would come out to the path, because during some periods, at the foot of the Meseged wall, where the great curtain of rain that ran down cliff face kept the slope permanently damp, there grew a few nutritious plants that the baboons knew how to identify and collect. But they would end up extinct, in spite of the babies that were born, because the land and conditions were not adequate for their lives, and even more so because, having shaped themselves according to the teachings of man, they'd become more like children, less able to fend for themselves. This oldest baboon that today asked for alms for his own, imitating the role and even the mannerisms of the man who he'd known as father and protector, would perhaps pass down, upon his death, his incongruous speech to the oldest male who would succeed him, and the begging and the reliance on the aid of strangers would be perpetuated among the baboons, undoubtedly, like a human condition from which they no longer knew how to return, with a great reduction in the use of their own unique faculties with which they would be able to survive and prosper. And if, for example, those unhappy creatures would just travel a distance of six thousand horses to the west, along the wall of the Meseged, they would come to the lush and ample walnut groves that extended to the regions of the Aldeas Soberanas, whose production the Atabates or the Aldeanos de Soberanía, in whose territories the forests grew, were unable to exhaust; but the baboons found themselves inevitably tied to the desert and the path where their master, or more precisely, their father had given them a way of life that, as precarious as it was, continued to constitute for them an inescapable condition.

Translated by Will Vanderhyden

WORK

1951, *Industrias y andanzas de Alfanhuí*, Talleres Gráficos Cies (novel).

1956, *El Jarama*, Destino (novel).

1961, "Y el corazón caliente" Destino (short story included in Destino's second edition of *Industrias y andanzas de Alfanhuí*).

1961, "Dientes, Pólvora, febrero" Destino (short story included in Destino's second edition of *Industrias y andanzas de Alfanhuí*).

1966, "Personas y animales en una fiesta de bautizo," in *Revista de Occidente* (essay).

1974, *Las semanas del jardín*, Mauricio d'Ors (essay).

1986, *Mientras no cambien los dioses, nada habrá cambiado*, Alianza (essay).

1986, *El testimonio de Yarfoz*, Alianza (novel).

1986, *Campo de Marte 1. El ejército nacional*, Alianza (essay).

1986, *La homilía del ratón*, El País (essay).

1992, *Ensayos y artículos I*, Destino (essay).

1992, *Ensayos y artículos II*, Destino (essay).

1993, *Vendrán más años malos y nos harán más ciegos*, Destino (essay).

1993, *Esas Yndias equivocadas y malditas*, Destino 1993 (essay).

2000, *El alma y la vergüenza*, Destino (essay).

2002, *La hija de la guerra y la madre de la patria*, Destino (essay).

2003, *Non Olet*, Destino (essay).

2005, *El Feco*, Destino, (stories and fragments).

2005, *Glosas castellanas y otros ensayos (diversiones)*, Fondo de Cultura Económica (essay).

2007, *Sobre la guerra*, Destino (essay).

2008, *God & Gun. Apuntes de polemología*, Destino (essay).

2009, *"Guapo" y sus isótopos*, Destino (essay).

ENGLISH TRANSLATIONS

1975, *Alfanhui: A translation with critical Introduction of Rafael Sanchez Ferlosio's Industrias y andanzas de Alfanhuí*, translated by Rafael Sánchez Ferlosio, Purdue University Press (novel and critical introduction).

2000, *The Adventures of the Ingenious Alfanhuí*, translated by Margaret Jull Costa and Rafael Sánchez Ferlosio, Dedalus (novel).

2005, *The River: El Jarama*, translated by Margaret Jull Costa, Dedalus (novel).

•

AWARDS AND RECOGNITIONS

1955, Premio Nadal for *El Jarama*.

1957, Premio de La Critica de Narrativa Castellana for *El Jarama*.

1983, Premio del Periodismo Francisco Cerecedo for his defense of freedom of expression.

1987, Finalist for the Premio Nacional de Narrativa for *El testimonio de Yarfoz*.

1991, Premio La Comunidad de Madrid.

1994, Premio Nacional de Ensayo for *Vendrán más años malos y nos harán más ciegos*.

1994, Premio Ciudad de Barcelona.

2002, Premio Mariano de Cavia, for his work as a journalist.

2003, Premio Extremadura a la Creación.

2004, Premio Cervantes.

2009, Premio Nacional de las Letras Españolas.

CARLOS
FUENTES
(Mexico, 1928)

The life of Carlos Fuentes could write itself on a world map. Born in 1928 in Panama City, where his father, a member of the Mexican diplomatic core, was assigned at the time. He received a cosmopolitan education, attending prestigious prep schools in Ecuador, Uruguay, Brazil, and Washington, D.C., where his family moved in 1933, contributing to his early bilingualism. During those years, his father Rafael and his mother Berta made sure that he spent all his summer vacations in Mexico, in the care of his grandmothers, to whom he owes his mother tongue and the first books he read. As he said on one occasion, "I learned to imagine Mexico before being a Mexican." After a few years, they left Washington, D.C., this time heading to Chile.

In 1944 they moved to Buenos Aires. The Nazi environment and the proliferation of anti-Semitic prejudices present in Argentine schools in those years prompted the young Fuentes—supported by his parents—to abandon his studies. Throughout his life, political and social engagement were to be fundamental characteristics of his intellectual trajectory: "What a writer can do politically he should also do as a citizen." Far from the classroom, the memory of those years nourished him, as well as his discovery of Borges and the tango.

At sixteen, Carlos Fuentes settled in Mexico, where he pursued his studies and maintained an active and sophisticated social life. Finishing his bachelor's, he debated between his passion and the duty to pursue a "healthy" university degree. In the end, he would follow the advice of Alfonso Reyes: "You should become a *lawyer*, an attorney; then, you'll be able to whatever you most enjoy, like I did." So, while finishing law school (and having spent two years in Europe taking classes in International Studies), he finally resolved to become a writer.

In 1954 he published his first book, *Los días enmascarados*, comprised of six fantastic stories. In the following years, he founded and edited the *Revista Mexicana de Literatura* with Emmanuel Carballo while finishing his novel *La región más transparente*, which was published in 1958 to great praise; the variety of resources the writer used to give voice to a whole society, to express the desires of its inhabitants, their thoughts, and their vices, were early indications that with time Carlos Fuentes would be one of the most recognized novelists of the Spanish language. Then he got married to Rita Macedo, one of Luis Buñuel's favorite actresses. It was actually in the decrepit mansion of the film producer Manuel Barbachano Ponce where Carlos Fuentes and Gabriel García Márquez—"there during the heat waves of 1961"—had their first encounter. The Mexican writer has since stated, "we were friends forever, to such an extent that I can mark out the stages of my life after my thirty-second year using the milestones of my friendship with Gabo."

"1962 was the fullest year of my life, when I best loved, wrote, struggled . . ." *Aura* and *La muerte de Artemio Cruz* appear, confirming Fuentes as one of the great literary voices of the moment, and around the same time, his first daughter, Cecilia (his *Fuentecita*), was born. A year later, Gallimard published *La región más transparente* (*La plus limpide région*), thus initiating a lasting relationship between Fuentes and Paris, where that same year he met Julio Cortázar, Mario Vargas Llosa, Juan Goytisolo, and Jorge Semprún. In the end he decided to take up residence in Europe (Rome, Paris, Venice, London), involving himself in the social movements alive throughout the continent at that time. After divorcing Rita Macedo, he married the renowned journalist Silvia Lemus, with whom he had two children, Carlos and Natasha (both sadly deceased). The family lived a constant coming and going between France and the United States, where the writer developed a prolific academic life. It was precisely his interest in language, in the American continent, that lead him to write his most ambitious project, *Terra nostra* (1975), "a response to the loss of the narrative subject, of the psychologically complete character, torn to shreds by the brutality of the twentieth century's heartless history." The book won the Premio Rómulo Gallegos in 1977, for many readers and critics it is considered one of the pillars of Latin American literature in the twentieth century.

In 1987 he won the Premio Cervantes and his writing continued to shift between channels of realism, fantasy, and the psychological perspective. All of his literary obsessions are melded together in *El naranjo, o los círculos del tiempo* (1993), a synthesis representative of his body of work in which he closes his narrative cycle "La edad del tiempo." Sadly, as the pages of this anthology were being finalized, Carlos Fuentes passed away in Mexico May 15, 2012. A few days before his death, the writer completed two posthumous works: *Federico en su balcón* and *Personas*. In 1994 his work had taken a turn with the publication of *Diana o la cazadora solitaria*. The book presents a loving relationship between the writer and the actress Jean Seberg, years after her death in Paris.

Now in the new century, his novels *Adán en Edén* (2009) and *Vlad* (2010) have come to expand a body of work capable of incorporating neologisms into a language that is always alive and colloquial, confirming Carlos Fuentes as one of the most important writers in all of his country's literature, able to continue enriching Mexican letters with the greatest resources of the European vanguards.

THE ACORN

The Torture of Doctor Johnson

I selected these fragments from *Terra Nostra* because they have the unfortunate habit of summarizing my approach to storytelling.

In Conversation with the Dead

My dead are all the ancestors I remember (very few) and all of those I am unable to recall (the immensity). I am who I am thanks to them. But in particular I cite my grandmothers. I will tell you why: when I was four I arrived in Washington, D.C. and went to public school and my parents demanded that every summer I go back to Mexico to stay with my grandmothers so that I wouldn't forget Spanish. So I owe the Spanish language to my grannies. One was from Veracruz, the other was from Sonora, two extremes of Mexico, and with very different personalities. My father's mother was German, she was very strict and very disciplined. Her husband became paralyzed and she set up a boarding house and every Sunday we would go to a pyramid. She collected pyramids so it was essential for my education, we went to the pyramids again and again and there are lots of pyramids in Mexico. She had a wonderful, severe personality. She didn't do jokes or anything of the sort. I revered her as I did my other grandmother who brought up her three daughters by becoming the cake-making teacher after her husband died. This great *repostería*. And then her old friend Alvaro Bregón became president of México—he had delivered milk to her when he was a little boy—and she asked him for a post in the ministry of education which was headed by the great Vasconcelos. So she became a school inspector. And then she married

92

off her three daughters and she was hell for her sons-in-law, whom she bailed out and corrected. One of them was a general and she said "you've only had battles with me, general, and you've lost them all." And to the others she would say "didn't they teach you manners at home?" She got along very well with my father, but she was like a bird that pecked at the greatness of the other men. But her daughters loved her as did her grandchildren, we were very close to her. She came from the north of Mexico, the mining town of Alamos and Mazatlán, the poet's city and had millions of memories. And she made me read, she made me read Eça de Queirós. When I went from childhood reading to adult reading she was with me and said that I had to read Eça de Queirós and that was very important. My other grandmother gave me books for children that were horrifying, they were all about murders and mutilations and abductions. They were called *Las tardes de la granja* and an old man called Palemon sat with children and told them these horrifying stories. So you see, these are two very important influences in my life, apart from many others, but I would like to choose these two. The grannies always stay with you, later you go to Faulkner.

CODA

Your life has brought you to live in many different countries and have to communicate in many different languages. How has that affected you as a writer?

I was very privileged in having that kind of childhood, living in Mexico and then in Chile and Argentina—so it was very broad. But I was also anchored in a very nationalist period of Mexican writing, when literature was considered national, and writers had to be national. I remember when Alfonso Reyes, our great polygraphist, was attacked by these nationalistic minions saying "you talk about Greece, why don't you talk about Mexico?" And it demonstrated that he also talked about Mexico, but that they hadn't read him. Now that has evaporated, it is no longer consequential. The younger generation of Mexican writers can write about Germany or Russia or whatever they feel with no obligation to the Mexican nation. But let's go beyond that, I think what you have are writers, you have Günter Grass, Nadine Gordimer, you have Juan Goytisolo or Philip Roth, who happen to write in this or that language or have this or that nationality but who are no longer simply a part of a nation-alistic canon. Thankfully, because it was very limiting and noxious I think. So I take pride in myself that, because of my upbringing, I was outside of that kind of nationalistic feeling. I got battered for it when I began writing, they said "Oh, he doesn't write about Mexico, he writes about witches and silly things" and then I wrote a very Mexican novel, the *La región más transparente*, and they said "Oh he only writes about Mexico because he doesn't know about anything else." What you learn with life is that you don't bother about what people say, you write for yourself and for your grandmothers wherever they are and don't worry a bit about the public's criticism. I feel extremely independent in that sense and very linked to friends of mine who are also writers and who are writers beyond their nationality and often their politics sometimes. I still admire Borges as a writer, for example.

You have been very generous to the younger generations, often providing means and refuge from when you were living in Paris through today.

Literature doesn't belong to anyone. We belong to a tradition. I think there's a very straight relationship between creation and tradition. You create in order to prolong the tradition and the tradition gives you the tools for the new creation. So that always puts you in a line with previous authors and coming authors. I think it may be egotistical in helping so many young authors because without them where would I be? I know so many figures who, because of their isolation, have disappeared and I really have a great admiration for many young writers and give them a hand if I can. In Paris in 1960 there were only four Mexican authors published, Mariano Azuela, *Los de abajo*, Octavio Paz, *El laberinto de la solidad*, Juan Rulfo, *Pedro Páramo* and myself. I went to the Paris bookfair two years ago, where Mexico was the guest of honor, and there were 42 Mexican authors published in France, and that doesn't include authors from the rest of Latin America. There are some 500 interesting writers in Latin America now, which is extraordinary. So what happened? First, we won independence from Spain so we had to cut everything that seemed Spanish. We had to imitate Europe and the United States, so we had a lot of realism, a lot of naturalism, a lot of Mexican *nanas* floating around. Then many events happened; there was Borges, I think Borges was very, very important in saying you could write whatever you want.

Anything that comes into your head, literature is open. Many people don't realize that he is a descendent of Machado de Assis. And then there was Carpentier and Lezama Lima and Onetti, who was very important, and then the younger writers Cortázar, García Márquez, Vargas Llosa, and myself. So the whole spectrum opened and each generation provided ten or twelve new writers. Besides, we felt we had the obligation to say what had not been said. Novels were prohibited by the Spanish crown during the time of the colonies, no novels were written. Then we had this imitative literature during the nineteenth century. So we had a lot of things to say that had not been said. We said it, so now the younger generation doesn't have that obligation and they write about what is happening today. You cannot classify them, you cannot say this is the subject matter, this is what they are representing. They are representing the variety of contemporary Latin American culture. Pablo Neruda told me that we all have an obligation to our peoples, we go around with the Mexican or the Chilean people on our backs and we must write for them because they have no other voice. Today that isn't true anymore. There is press, there is congress, there are political parties, there are unions, so now if you speak publicly it is because you want to, and not because you are obliged to do it. And you respect those people who don't speak in public. So it is a much more modern and creative setup where you are not constrained by dogma or by allegiances that are alien to literature.

A THOUSAND FORESTS

"Theater of Memory" from *Terra Nostra*
[a novel]

They left Spalato before the anticipated time. Three times Ludovico had returned alone to the beach; each time he found there, unerased, the gypsy's footprints. They traveled to Venice, a city where stone and water retain no trace of footsteps. In that place of mirages there is room for no phantom but time, and its traces are imperceptible; the lagoon would disappear without stone to reflect it and the stone without water in which to be reflected. Against this enchantment there is little the transitory bodies of men—solid or spectral, it is the same—can do. All Venice is a phantom: it issues no entry permits to other phantoms. There no one would recognize them as such, and so they would cease to be. No phantom exposes itself to such risk.

They found lodging in the ample solitudes of the island of La Giudecca; Ludovico felt reassured, being near the Hebraic traditions he had studied so thoroughly in Toledo, even though not sharing all their beliefs. The coins Celestina had sent by hand of the monk Simón had been exhausted in the last voyage; Ludovico inquired in the neighborhoods of the ancient Jewry where many refugees from Spain and Portugal had found asylum, as he now did, whether anyone had need of a translator; laughing, everyone recommended he cross the broad Vigano canal, disembark at San Basilio, walk along the estuaries of the shipwrights and sugar merchants, continue past the workshops of the waxworkers, cross the Ponte Foscarini, and ask for the house of a certain Maestro Valerio Camillo, between the River of San Barnaba and the Church of Santa Maria del Carmine, for it was widely known that no one in Venice had accumulated a greater number of ancient manuscripts than the said Dominie, whose windows even were blocked with parchments; at times papers fell into the street, where children made little boats of them and floated them in the canals, and great was the uproar when the meager, stuttering Maestro ran out to rescue the priceless documents, shouting at the top of his voice whether it were the destiny of Quintilian and Pliny the Elder to be soaked in canals and serve as a diversion for brainless little brats.

Ludovico found the described house without difficulty, but its doors and windows prevented the passage of either light or human; the residence of Donno Valerio Camillo was a paper fortress, mountains, walls, pillars and piles of exposed documents, folio piled upon folio, yellowed, teetering, held upright thanks only to the counterpressure of other stacks of paper.

Ludovico circled the building, looking for the house's garden. And, in fact, beside a small sotto portico facing the vast Campo Santa Margherita, extended a narrow iron railing worked in a series of three recurring heads: wolf, lion, and dog; fragrant vines trailed from the walls, and in the dark little garden stood an extremely thin man, the meagerness of his body disguised by the ample folds of a long, draped tunic, but the angularity of his face emphasized by a black hood—similar to those worn by executioners—that hid his head and ears, revealing only an eagle-like profile; he was occupied in training several ferocious mastiffs; he held a long stick on which were impaled pieces of raw meat; he teased the dogs, dangling it above their heads; the barking dogs leaped to snatch the prize, but at every leap the man placed his arm between the raw meat and the beasts' fangs, miraculously barely escaping being wounded; each time, with amazing swiftness, the frail, hooded Donno pulled back the arm grazed by the dogs, and stuttered: "Very well, very well, Biondino, Preziosa, very well, Pocogarbato, my flesh is the more savory, you know how I trust you, do not fail me, for at the hour of my death I shall be in no condition to discipline you."

Then he threw another piece of meat to the mastiffs and watched with delight as they devoured it, fighting among themselves to seize the best portions. When he saw Ludovico standing in the entrance to the garden, he rudely demanded whether he had so little interest in his life that he had to pry into the lives of others. Ludovico asked his pardon and explained that the motive for his visit was not gratuitous curiosity but the need for employment. He showed him a letter signed by the ancient of the Synagogue of the Passing, and after reading it Donno Valerio Camillo said: "Very well, very well, Monsignore Ludovicus. Although it would take many lifetimes to classify and translate the papers I have accumulated throughout my lifetime, we can do some small part, we can begin. Consider yourself employed—with two conditions. The first is that you never laugh at my stuttering. I shall explain the reason this once: my capacity for reading is infinitely superior to my capacity for speaking; I employ so much time reading that at times I completely forget how to speak; in any case, I read so rapidly that in compensation I trip and stumble as I speak. My thoughts are swifter than my words."

"And the second condition?"

The Maestro threw another scrap of meat to the mastiffs. "That if I die during the period of your service, you must be responsible to see that they not bury my body in holy ground, or throw it into the waters of this pestilent city, but instead lay my naked body here in my garden and loose the dogs to devour me. I have trained them to do this. They will be my tomb. There is none better or more honorable: matter to matter. I but follow the wise counsel of Cicero. If in spite of everything I am someday resurrected in my former body, it will not have been without first giving every digestive opportunity to the divine matter of the world."

Daily Ludovico presented himself at the house of Maestro Donno Valerio Camillo and daily the emaciated Venetian handed him ancient folios to be translated into the tongues of the various courts where, mysteriously, he hinted he would send his invention, along with all the authenticating documents of scientific proof.

Soon Ludovico became aware that everything he was translating from Greek and Latin into Tuscan, French, or Spanish possessed a common theme: memory. From Cicero, he translated the *De inventione*: "Prudence is the knowledge of good, of evil, and of that which is neither good nor evil. Its parts are: memory, intelligence, and pre-vision, or pre-sight. Memory is the faculty through which the mind recalls what was. Intelligence certifies what is. Pre-vision or pre-sight permits the mind to see that something is going to occur before it occurs." From Plato, the passages wherein Socrates speaks of memory as of a gift: it is the mother of the Muses, and in every soul there is one part of wax upon which are imprinted the seals of thought and perception. From Philostratus, the *Life of Apollonius of Tyana*: Euxenes asked Apollonius why, being a man of elevated thought, and expressing himself so clearly and swiftly, he had never written anything, and Apollonius answered him: "Because until now I have not practiced silence." From that moment he resolved to remain silent; he never spoke again, although his eyes and his mind absorbed every experience and stored it in his memory. Even after he was a hundred years old he had a better memory than Simonides himself, and he wrote a hymn in eulogy of memory, wherein he stated that all things are erased with time, but that time itself becomes ineradicable and eternal because of memory. And among the pages of St. Thomas Aquinas, he found this quotation underlined in red ink: "*Nihil potest homo intelligere sine phantasmate.*" Man can understand nothing without images. And images are phantoms.

In Pliny he read the amazing feats of memory of antiquity: Cyrus knew the names of all the soldiers in his army; Seneca the Elder could repeat two thousand names in the order they were communicated to him; Mithridates, King of Pontus, spoke the tongues of the twenty nations under his dominion; Metrodorus of Scepsis could repeat every conversation he had heard in his lifetime, in the exact original words; and Charmides the Greek knew by memory the content of all the books in his library, the greatest of his age. On the other hand, Themistocles refused to practice the art of memory, saying he preferred the science of forgetfulness to that of memory. And constantly, in all these manuscripts, appeared references to the poet Simonides, called the inventor of memory.

One day, many months after beginning his work, Ludovico dared ask the always silent Maestro Valerio Camillo the identity of that renowned poet Simonides. The Dominie looked at him, eyes flashing beneath heavy eyebrows. "I always knew you were curious. I told you so that first day."

"Do not judge my curiosity as vain, Maestro Valerio, now it is in your service."

"Search among my papers. If you do not know how to encounter what I myself found, I shall consider you are not as clever as I believed."

After which the agile, stammering, slight Maestro bounded across the room to an iron door he always kept closed, protected by chains and locks; he opened it with difficulty and disappeared behind it.

It took Ludovico almost a year, alternating translation with investigation, to locate a slim, brittle document in Greek wherein the narrator recounted the story of a poet of bad reputation, despised because he was the first to charge for writing, or even reading, his verses. His name was Simonides and he was a native of the island of Ceos. This said Simonides was invited one night to sing a poem in honor of a noble of Thessaly named Scopas. The wealthy Scopas had prepared a great banquet for the occasion. But the waggish Simonides, in addition to a eulogy in honor of his host, included in the poem a dithyramb to the legendary brothers, the Dioscuri, Castor and Pollux, both sons of Leda, the former by a swan and the latter by a god. Half mocking, half in earnest, Scopas told the poet when he had ended his recital that, since only half the panegyric had honored him, he would pay only half the agreed sum, and that he should collect the other half from the mythic twins.

Bested, Simonides sat down to eat, hoping to collect in food what the miserly Scopas had denied him in coin. But at that instant a messenger arrived and told the poet that two youths urgently sought him outside. With increasing bad humor, Simonides left his place at the banquet table and went out into the street, but found no one. As he turned to reenter the dining hall of Scopas he heard a fearful sound of falling masonry and cracking plaster; the roof of the house had collapsed. Everyone inside had been killed; the weight of the columns crushed all the guests at the banquet, and beneath the ruins it was impossible to identify anyone. The relatives of the dead arrived and wept when they were unable to recognize their loved ones lost among all those bodies crushed like insects, disfigured, their heads smashed in, their brains spilled out. Then Simonides pointed out to each kinsman which was his dead: the poet recalled the exact place each guest had occupied during the banquet.

Everyone marveled, for never before had anyone achieved a similar feat; and thus was invented the art of memory. Simonides voyaged to offer his thanks at the shrine of Castor and Pollux in Sparta. Through his mind, again and again, passed in perfect order the mocking, indifferent, scornful, ignorant faces of Scopas and his guests.

Ludovico showed this text to Valerio Camillo, and the Dominie nodded thoughtfully. Finally he said: "I congratulate you. Now you know how memory was invented and who invented it."

"But surely, Maestro, men have always remembered . . ."

"Of course, Monsignore Ludovicus; but the intent of memory was different. Simonides was the first to remember something besides the present and the remote as such, for before him memory was only an inventory of daily tasks, lists of cattle, utensils, slaves, cities, and houses, or a blurred nostalgia for past events and lost places: memory was *factum*, not *ars*. Simonides proposed something more: everything that men have been, everything they have said and done can be remembered, in perfect order and location; from then on, nothing had to be forgotten. Do you realize what that means? Before him, memory was a fortuitous fact: each person spontaneously remembered what he wished to or what he could remember; the poet opened the doors to scientific memory, independent of individual memories; he proposed memory as total knowledge of a total past. And since that memory was exercised in the present, it must also totally embrace the present so that, in the future, actuality is remembered past. To this goal many systems have been elaborated throughout the centuries. Memory sought assistance from places, images, taxonomy. From the memory of the present and the past, it progressed to an ambition to recall the future before it occurred, and this faculty was called pre-vision or pre-sight. Other men, more audacious than those preceding them, were inspired by the Jewish teachings of the Cabala, the Zohar, and the Sephirot to go further and to know the time of all times and the space of all spaces; the simultaneous memory of all hours and all places. I, monsignore, have gone still further. For me the memory of the eternity of times, which I already possess, is not sufficient, or the memory of the simultaneity of places, that I always knew . . ."

Ludovico told himself that Dominie Valerio Camillo was mad: he expected to find burial in the ferocious digestive system of mastiffs, and life in a memory that was not of here or some other place, or the sum of all spaces, or the memory of the past, present, and future, or the sum of all times. He aspired, perhaps, to the absolute, the vacuum. The Venetian's eyes glittered with malice as he observed the Spanish student. Then gently he took him by the arm and led him to the locked door. "You have never asked me what lies behind that door. Your intellectual curiosity has been more powerful than common curiosity, which you would judge disrespectful, personal, unwholesome. You have respected my secret. As a reward I am going to show you my invention."

Valerio Camillo inserted keys into the several locks, removed the chains, and opened the door. Ludovico followed down a dark musty passageway of dank brick where the only gleam came from the eyes of rats and the skin of lizards. They came to a second iron door. Valerio Camillo opened it and then closed it behind Ludovico. They stood in a silent white space of marble, illuminated by the light of the scrupulously clean stone, so marvelously joined that not even a suggestion of a line could be seen between the blocks of marble.

"No rat can enter here," laughed the Donno. And then, with great seriousness, he added, "I am the only one who has ever entered here. And now you, Monsignore Ludovicus, now you will know the Theater of Memory of Valerio Camillo."

The Maestro lightly pressed one of the marble blocks and a whole section of the wall opened like a door, swinging on invisible hinges. Stooping, the two men passed through; a low, lugubrious chant resounded in Ludovico's ears; they entered a corridor of wood that grew narrower with every step, until they emerged upon a tiny stage; a stage so small, in fact, that only Ludovico could stand upon it, while the Donno Valerio remained behind him, his dry hands resting upon the translator's shoulders, his eagle's face near Ludovico's ear, stuttering, his breath redolent of fish and garlic. "This is the Theater of Memory. Here roles are reversed. You, the only spectator, will occupy the stage. The performance will take place in the auditorium."

Enclosed within the wooden structure, the auditorium was formed of seven ascending, fan-shaped gradins sustained upon seven pillars; each gradin was of seven rows, but instead of seats Ludovico saw a succession of ornamental railings, similar to those guarding Valerio Camillo's garden facing the Campo Santa Margherita; the filigree of the figures on the railings was almost ethereal, so that each figure seemed to superimpose itself upon those in front of and behind it; the whole gave the impression of a fantastic hemicycle of transparent silk screens; Ludovico felt incapable of understanding the meaning of this vast inverted scenography where the sets were spectators and the spectator the theater's only actor.

The low chant of the passageway became a choir of a million voices joined, without words, in a single sustained ululation. "My theater rests upon seven pillars," the Venetian stammered, "like the house of Solomon. These columns represent the seven Sephirot of the supra-celestial world, which are the seven measures of the plots of the celestial and lower worlds and which contain all the possible ideas of all three worlds. Seven divinities preside over each of the seven gradins: look, Monsignore Ludovicus, at the representations on each of the first railings. They are Diana, Mercury, Venus, Apollo, Mars, Jupiter, and Saturn: the six planets and the central sun. And seven themes, each beneath the sign of a star, are represented on the seven rows of each gradin. They are the seven fundamental situations of humanity: the Cavern, the human reflection of the immutable essence of being and idea; Prometheus, who steals fire from the intelligence of the gods; the Banquet, the conviviality of men joined together in society; Mercury's sandals, symbols of human activity and labor; Europa and the Bull, love; and on the highest row, the Gorgons, who contemplate everything from on high; they have three bodies, but a single shared eye. And the only spectator—you—has a single body but possesses three souls, as stated in the Zohar. Three bodies and one eye; one body and three souls. And between these poles, all the possible combinations of the seven stars and the seven situations. Hermes Trismegistus has written wisely that he who knows how to join himself to this diversity of the unique will also be divine and will know all past, present, and future, and all the things that Heaven and earth contain."

Dominie Valerio, with increasing excitement, manipulated a series of cords, pulleys, and buttons behind Ludovico's back; successive sections of the auditorium were bathed in light; the figures seemed to acquire movement, to gain transparency, to combine with and blend into one another, to integrate into fleeting combinations and constantly transform their original silhouettes while at the same time never ceasing to be recognizable.

"What, to you, Monsignore Ludovicus, is the definition of an imperfect world?"

"Doubtless, a world in which things are lacking, an incomplete world . . ."

"My invention is founded upon precisely the opposite premise: the world is imperfect when we believe there is nothing lacking in it; the world is perfect when we know that something will always be missing from it. Will you admit, monsignore, that we can conceive of an ideal series of events that run parallel to the real series of events?"

"Yes; in Toledo I learned that all matter and all spirit project the aura of what they were and what they will be . . ."

"And what they might have been, monsignore, will you give no opportunity to what, not having been yesterday, probably will never be?"

"Each of us has asked himself at some moment of his existence, if we were given the grace of living our life over again would we live it the same way the second time?, what errors would we avoid, what omissions amend?, should I have told that woman, that night, that I loved her?, why did I not visit my father the day before his death?, would I again give that coin to the beggar who held out his hand to me at the entrance to the church?, how would we choose again among all the persons, occupations, profits, and ideas we must constantly elect?, for life is but an interminable selection between this and this and that, a perpetual choice, never freely decided, even when we believe it so, but determined by conditions others impose upon us: gods, judges, monarchs, slaves, fathers, mothers, children."

"Look; see upon the combined canvases of my theater the passage of the most absolute of memories: the memory of what could have been but was not; see it in its greatest and least important detail, in gestures not fulfilled, in words not spoken, in choices sacrificed, in decisions postponed, see Cicero's patient silence as he hears of Catiline's foolish plot, see how Calpurnia convinces Caesar not to attend the Senate on the Ides of March, see the defeat of the Greek army in Salamis, see the birth of the baby girl in a stable in Bethlehem in Palestine during the reign of Augustus, see the pardon Pilate grants the prophetess, and the death of Barabbas upon the cross, see how Socrates in his prison refuses the temptation of suicide, see how Odysseus dies, consumed by flames, within the wooden horse the clever Trojans set afire upon finding it outside the walls of the city, see the old age of Alexander of Macedonia, the silent vision of Homer; see—but do not speak of—the return of Helen to her home, Job's flight from his, Abel forgotten by his brother, Medea remembered by her husband, Antigone's submission to the law of the tyrant in exchange for peace in the kingdom, the success of Spartacus's rebellion, the sinking of Noah's ark, the return of Lucifer to his seat at the side of God, pardoned by divine decision; but see also the other possibility: an obedient Satan who renounces rebellion and remains in the original Heaven; look, watch as the Genoese Colombo sets out to seek the route to Cipango, the court of the Great Khan, by land, from West to East, on camelback; watch while my canvases whirl and blend and fade into one another, see the young shepherd, Oedipus, satisfied to live forever with his adoptive father, Polybus of Corinth, and see the solitude of Jocasta, the intangible anguish of a life she senses is incomplete, empty; only a sinful dream redeems it; no eyes will be put out, there will be no destiny, there will be no tragedy, and the Greek order will perish because it lacked the tragic transgression which, as it violates that order, restores and eternally revives it: the power of Rome did not subjugate the soul of Greece; Greece could be subjugated only by the absence of tragedy; look, Paris occupied by the Mohammedans, the victory and consecration of Pelagius in his dispute with Augustine, the cave of Plato inundated by the river of Heraclitus; look, the marriage of Dante and Beatrice, a book never written, an aged libertine and merchant of Assisi, and untouched walls never painted by Giotto, a Demosthenes who swallowed a pebble and died choking beside the sea. See the greatest and the least important detail, the beggar born in a Prince's cradle, the Prince in that of the beggar; the child who grew, dead upon birth; and the child who died, full-grown; the ugly woman, beautiful; the cripple, whole; the ignorant, learned; the sainted, perverse; the rich, poor; the warrior, a musician; the politician, a philosopher; one small turn of this great circle upon which my theater is seated is sufficient, the great plot woven by the three equilateral triangles within a circumference ruled by the multiple combinations of the seven stars, the three souls, the seven mutations, and the single eye: the waters of the Red Sea do not part, a young girl in Toledo does not know which she prefers of the seven identical columns of a church or the two identical chick-peas of her supper, Judas cannot be bribed, the boy who cried 'Wolf!' was never believed."

Panting, for a moment Donno Valerio fell silent and ceased to manipulate his cords and buttons. Then, more calmly, he asked Ludovico: "What will the Kings of this world pay me for this invention that would permit them to recall what could have been and was not?"

"Nothing, Maestro Valerio. For the only thing that interests them is what really is, and what will be."

Valerio Camillo's eyes glistened as never before, the only light in the suddenly darkened theater: "And it is not important to them, either, to know what never will be?"

"Perhaps, since that is a different manner of knowing what will be."

"You do not understand me, monsignore. The images of my theater bring together all the possibilities of the past, but they also represent all the opportunities of the future, for knowing what was not, we shall know what demands to be: what has not been, you have seen, is a latent event awaiting its moment to be, its second chance, the opportunity to live another life. History repeats itself only because we are unaware of the alternate possibility for each historic event: what that event could have been but was not. Knowing, we can insure that history does not repeat itself; that the alternate possibility is the one that occurs for the first time. The universe would achieve true equilibrium. This will be the culmination of my investigations: to combine the elements of my theater in such a manner that two different epochs fully coincide; for example, that what happened or did not happen in your Spanish fatherland in 1492, in 1520, or 1598, coincide exactly with what happens there in 1938, or 1975, or 1999. Then, and I am convinced of it, the space of that co-incidence will germinate, will accommodate the unfulfilled past that once lived and died there: this doubled time will demand that precise space in which to complete itself."

"And then, in accord with your theory, it will be imperfect."

"Perfection, monsignore, is death."

"But at least do you know the space where everything that did not happen awaits the co-incidence of two different times to be fulfilled?"

"I have just told you. Look again, monsignore; I shall turn the lights on again, place the figures in movement, combine spaces, that of your land, Spain, and that of an unknown world where Spain will destroy everything that previously existed in order to reproduce itself: a doubly immobile, doubly sterile, gestation, for in addition to what could have been—see those burning temples, see the eagles fall, see how the original inhabitants of the unknown lands are subjugated—your country, Spain, imposes another impossibility: that of itself, see the gates closing, the Jew expelled, the Moor persecuted, see how it hides itself in a mausoleum and from there governs in the name of death: purity of faith, purity of bloodlines, horror of the body, prohibition of thought, extermination of anything that cannot be understood. Look: centuries and centuries of living death, fear, silence, the cult of appearances, vacuity of substances, gestures of imbecilic honor, see them, the miserable realities, see them, hunger, poverty, injustice, ignorance: a naked empire that imagines itself clothed in golden robes. Look: there will never be in history, monsignore, nations more needful of a second opportunity to be what they were not than these that speak and that will speak your tongue, or peoples who for such lengthy periods store the possibilities of what they could have been had they not sacrificed the very reason for their being: impurity, the mixture of all bloods, all beliefs, all the spiritual impulses of a multitude of cultures. Only in Spain did the three peoples of the Book—Christians, Moors, and Jews—meet and flourish. As she mutilates their union, Spain mutilates herself and mutilates all she finds in her path. Will these lands have the second opportunity the first history will deny them?"

Before Ludovico's eyes, amid the screens and railings and lights and shadows of the gradins of this Theater of Memory of everything that was not but that could sometime have been, passed, in reverse, with the assurance it would be they he watched, animated, incomprehensible images, bearded warriors in iron cuirasses, tattered pennants, autos-da-fé, bewigged lords, dark men with enormous burdens on their backs, he heard speeches, proclamations, grandiloquent orators, and saw places and landscapes never before seen: strange temples devoured by the jungle, convents built like fortresses, rivers broad as seas, deserts poor as an outstretched hand, volcanoes higher than the stars, prairies devoured by the horizon, cities with iron-railed balconies, red-tile roofs, crumbling walls, immense cathedrals, towers of shattered glass, military men, their chests covered with medals and gold galloon, dusty feet pricked by thorns, emaciated children with swollen bellies, abundance by the side of hunger, a golden god seated upon a ragged beggar; mud and silver . . .

Again the lights died down. Ludovico did not dare ask Valerio Camillo how he controlled the illumination of the theater, how he projected or mounted or raised from nowhere these moving images through railings, upon screens, or what was the function of the cords he pulled, the buttons he pressed. He could imagine, yes, that the Dominie was capable of repeating the unspoken words of Medea, Cicero, or Dante through the simple expedient of reading lips: the understandable art of the stutterer.

Valerio Camillo said only: "I shall reveal my secrets to the Prince who will pay the highest price for my invention."

But again Ludovico doubted that any Prince would want to see face to face what was not, but wished to be. Politics was the art of the possible: neither the statue of Gomorrah nor the flight of Icarus.

Every night the translator returned to his miserable room on the long backbone of La Giudecca, resembling, in truth, the skeleton of a flounder, and there found his children engaged in their personal occupations. One would be wielding a wooden sword against the late-evening shadow projected onto the ancient walls of the Church of Santa Eufemia; another, wood shavings tangled in his golden hair, would be sawing, polishing, and varnishing shelves for the books and papers of Ludovico; the third would be sitting tailor-fashion in the doorway, contemplating the bare paving stones of the Campo Cosmo. Then the four would dine on fried seafood, beans, and mozzarella cheese. One night they were awakened by a desperate pounding. One of the boys opened the door. Gasping, his face caked with ashes, his clothing scorched, Dominie Valerio Camillo fell across the threshold. He stretched out his hands toward Ludovico and grasped his wrist with the fierce last strength of a dying man.

"Someone denounced me as a wizard," said the Donno without a trace of a stutter. "Someone slipped a letter into the stone mouth. They tried to take me prisoner. I resisted. I feared for my secrets. They set fire to my house. They prodded me with their blades, to subdue me. They wanted to enter the theater. They tried to break the chains. I fled. Monsignore Ludovicus: protect my invention. What a fool I was! I should have told you my true secrets. The theater lights. A deposit of magnetic carbons on the rooftop of the house. They attract and store the energy of lightning and the supercharged skies above the lagoon. I filter this energy through waterproof conductors, copper filaments and bulbs of the finest Venetian crystal. The buttons. They set some black boxes in motion. There are mercury-coated silk ribbons bearing the images of all the ages, miniatures I have painted, that increase in size as they are projected upon the gradins by a light behind the ribbons. A hypothesis, monsignore, only a hypothesis . . . you must prove it . . . save my invention . . . and remember your promise."

There, upon the brick floor, Donno Valerio died. Ludovico covered the body with a blanket. He asked the boys to hide the body in a boat and bring it the following day to the Dominie's house. Lodovico went to the Campo Santa Margherita that same afternoon. He found a black shell: the house burned, the documents burned. He made his way inside to the locked door. The mastiffs Biondino, Preziosa, and Pocogarbato were huddled there. He called them by name. They recognized him. He unlocked the chains with the Maestro's keys. He penetrated the passageways of the rats and lizards. He reached the marble chamber. He touched the invisible door and it swung open. He entered the narrow space of the stage. Darkness reigned. He pulled a cord. A brilliant light illuminated the figure of the three Gorgons with the single eye beneath the sign of Apollo. He pressed three buttons. On the screens and railings were projected three figures: his three sons. On the gradin of Venus, on the railing of love, the first son was a statue of stone. On the gradin of Saturn, on the railing of the Cave, the second son lay dead, his arms crossed upon his breast. On the gradin of Mars, on the railing of

Prometheus, the third, writhing, was bound to a rock, pecked by a falcon that was not devouring his liver but mutilating his arm.

As he turned to leave, Ludovico found himself face to face with his three sons. He whirled toward the auditorium of the theater; the shadows of his sons had disappeared. He looked back at the three boys. Had they seen what he had seen?

"We had to flee with the body of the Maestro," said the first.

"The Magistrati alla Bestemmia came in search of the fugitive," said the second.

"They threatened us; they know your connection with Valerio, Father," said the third.

They left the theater; they retraced their lost steps. Ludovico again chained and locked the door; from a burned-out window he threw the keys into the River of San Barnaba. They recovered the body of Valerio Camillo from the boat and carried it to the garden. Ludovico collected the mastiffs. They removed the clothing from the corpse. They laid it in the garden. More than ever, in death the Dominie, with his sharp profile and waxen flesh, resembled a frail young cardinal. Ludovico loosed the dogs. The bells chimed in the tall campanile of Santa Maria del Carmine.

Valerio Camillo had found his tomb.

Translated by Margaret Sayers Peden

•

"Confessions of a Confessor" from *Terra Nostra*
[a novel]

Up to now, Julián said to the Chronicler, that is what I know. No one knows the things I know, or knows things I do not know. I have been confessor to them all; believe only my version of events; listen to no other possible narrators. Celestina believed she knew everything and told everything, because with her lips she inherited memory and through them she thinks to transmit it. But she did not hear El Señor's daily confession before taking Communion, the details of the vanquished illusions of youth, the meaning of his penances in the chapel, his ascent up the stairway leading to the plain, the defiance of his listing of heresies, his relationship with our Señora, or his late passion for Inés. Furthermore, I heard the confessions of the Mad Lady, those of nuns and scrubbing maids; those of the Idiot and the dwarf before they were joined in matrimony and with my benediction wed; and those of the workmen. I heard Guzmán's confession; and if he believes that, in fleeing in search of the new world, he will leave behind the memory of his guilt, a great frustration awaits him. And I heard, my friend Chronicler, Ludovico's and Celestina's relations in El Señor's bedchamber: only I know the passageway that leads to the wall where hangs the King's ocher map; I pierced holes for my eyes and ears in the eyes of the Neptune that adorns it. Everyone who spoke there, everyone who thought aloud there, everyone who acted there, everyone who listened or was listened to there, gave me their secret voices, as I lent them my penitent ear, for often the confessor suffers more than the one who confesses; he relieves himself of a burden and the confessor assumes it.

Therefore, give no attention or credence to what others tell you, Julián continued, nor hold any faith in the simple and deceitful chronologies that are written about this epoch in an attempt to establish the logic of a perishable and linear history; true history is circular and eternal. You have seen: when she found him on the beach, the young Celestina did not tell all the truth to the pilgrim of the new world, so as not to distract him from his central purpose, which was to narrate before El Señor the dreamed existence of an unknown land beyond the sea; and even less, much less, was La Señora able to tell all the truth to the castaway called Juan when she took him to her bedchamber and there made love with him with such intense fury. How could Guzmán tell anyone except me—as the fires of the secret seal my lips—of his turbulent acts, the debates within his soul, and the designs of his life?, who but I could know, and keep secret, the ignominy of his drugging El Señor and setting the dogs on him?; he conceived of regicide, but he opted to kill our Señor not with a dagger, not with philters of lunacy, but by making potent his impotence, leading him step by step: the shattered mirror restored, pitchers filled after they were emptied, candles that grew taller as they were burned, the howling of the phantasmal dog, the commotion of the nuns in the chapel,

Bocanegra's death, the impossible passion with Inés, always greater and greater confrontations with what cannot be.

I kept everything secret, my candid friend, and if now I have told you everything, it is because my need to confess and do penance for the harm I have caused you supersedes all the vows of my priesthood. Including the secrets of the confessional. I am going far away. Someone must know these stories and write them. That is your vocation. Mine carries me to other places. But I do not want this story to be cut short, this hadith-novella, as you say it must be called in order to give to the tale the dignity the Arabic settlers in our peninsula gave to the communication of news. I give you, then, all the news I know—which is all the news—as I told you from the day you returned, exhausted, dressed as a beggar, your arm crippled from the fierce naval battle against the Turk. You saw things clearly, friend; your freedom was not given you in exchange for your meritorious performance in combat; but with only one good arm you were of little service on the galleys. You were abandoned on the Algerian coast and taken captive by the Arabs. They treated you well, but you, a Christian, fell in love with a beautiful Moorish girl, Zoraida, and she with you; you knew spring in autumn. Zoraida's father wished to separate her from you; you were abandoned on the Valencian coast by Algerian pirates and returned to prison in Alicante. That is where I went in search of you once I obtained the roll of those dead, wounded, and repatriated following the famous battle. With my facile hand it was no effort to feign El Señor's signature on your order of liberation, and even less to take advantage of Don Felipe's sleep to seal it with his ring. From the bold terraces of the muscatel, the almond, and the fig, through the vast garden of Valencia, through open land and rice fields I brought you here, disguised as a mendicant, up to the arid Castilian plain to this tower of the astronomer Toribio where the tasks of science and art can ward off, even if only momentarily, the ambush of madness, crime, injustice, and torment that seethes before our eyes. Here you have heard everything: all that happened before your arrival and after it, from Felipe's first crime to the last. I say, deluded creature that I am, that I am telling you the story so you will write it and thus, perhaps, his story will not be repeated. But history does repeat itself; that is the comedy and crime of history. Men learn nothing. Times change, scenes change, names change, but the passions are the same. Nevertheless, the enigma of the story I have told

you is that in repeating itself it does not end: see how many facets of this had-
ith, this novella, in spite of the appearance of conclusion, remain inconclusive,
latent, awaiting, perhaps, another time in which to reappear, another space in
which to germinate, another opportunity in which to manifest themselves,
other names to call themselves.

Celestina made a rendezvous with the pilgrim for a very distant date in
Paris, the last day of this millennium. How shall we put a period to this narration if we do not know what will happen then? That is why I have revealed
the secrets of the confessional to you, and only to you, because you write for
the future, because it does not matter to you what is said today concerning
your writing or the laughter your writing provokes: the day will come when
no one will laugh at you, but everyone will laugh at the Kings, Princes, and
prelates who today monopolize all homage and respect. Ludovico said that
one lifetime is not enough: one needs multiple existences to unify a personality. He also said other things that impressed me. He called immortal those
who reappear from time to time because they had more life than their own
death, but less time than their own life. He said that since a man or woman
can be several persons mentally, they can become several persons physically;
we are specters of time, and our present contains the aura of what we were
before and the aura of what we will become when we disappear. Don't you
see, Chronicler, my friend, how this argument coincides with El Señor's
repeated malediction in his testament, his bequest of a future of resurrections
that can be glimpsed only in forgotten pauses, in the orifices of time, in the
dark, empty minutes when the past tried to imagine the future, a blind, per-
tinacious, and painful return to the imagination of the future in the past as
the only future possible to this race and this land, Spain, and all the peoples
that descend from Spain?

I, Julián, friar and painter, I tell you that as the conflicting words of El
Señor and Ludovico blend together to offer us a new reason born of the
encounter of opposites, so in the same way are allied shadows and lights,
outline and volume, flat color and perspective on a canvas, and thus must be
allied in your book the real and the virtual, what was with what could have
been, and what is with what can be. Why would you tell us only what we
already know, without revealing what we still do not know? Why would you
describe to us only this time and this space without all the invisible times
and spaces our time contains?, why, in short, would you content yourself with

the painful dribble of the sequential when your pen offers you the fullness of the simultaneous? I choose my word well, Chronicler, and I say: content yourself. Discontented, you will aspire to simultaneity of times, spaces, and events, because men resign themselves to that patient dribble that drains their lives, they have scarcely forgotten their birth when it is time to confront their death; you, on the other hand, have decided to suffer, to fly in pursuit of the impossible on the wings of your unique freedom, that of your pen, though still bound to the earth by the chains of accursed reality that imprisons, reduces, weakens, and levels all things. Let us not complain, my friend; it is possible that without the ugly gravity of the real our dreams would lack weight, would be gratuitous, and thus of little worth and small conviction. Let us be grateful for this battle between imagination and reality that lends weight to fantasy and wing to facts, for the bird will not fly that does not encounter resistance from the air. But the earth would be converted into something less than air were it not constantly thought, dreamed, sung, written, sculpted, and painted. Listen to what my brother Toribio says: Mathematically, everyone's age is zero. The world dissolves when someone ceases to dream, to remember, to write. Time is the invention of personality. The spider, the hawk, the she-wolf, have no time.

To cease to remember. I fear sequential memory because it means duplicating the pain of time. To live it all, friend. To remember it all. But it is one thing to live, remembering everything, and something different to remember, living everything. Which road will you choose in order to complete this novella that I entrust to you today? I see you here, beside me, diviner of time, of the past and the present and the future, and I see how you are looking at me, reproaching me for the loose ends of this narration while I ask you to be grateful to me for the oblivion in which I left so many unfulfilled gestures, so many unspoken words . . . But I see that my wise warning does not satiate your thirst for prophecy: you ask yourself, what will be the future of the past?

For you, I have violated the secrets of the confessional. You will tell me that a secret is the same as death: the secret is a word and an event that have ceased to exist. Then, is all past secret and dead? No, is it not true?, because the remembered past is secret and living. And how can it be saved by memory and cease to be the past? By converting itself into the present. Then it is no longer the past. Then all true past is impenetrable secret and death. Do you wish that, having told you everything of the past I wish to rescue in order to convert it into present, I also tell you what must be secret and dead in order to continue to be the past? And all of it only to give to you what you yourself do not know: a story that will end in the future? Oh, my indiscreet scribe, that is why you ended up in a galley, unceasingly you confound reality with paper, just like the one-eyed magus whose quartered body was thrown into the waters of the Adriatic. Be grateful, I tell you, for loose ends; accept the truth spoken by the Mad Lady: every being has the right to carry a secret to the tomb; every narrator reserves to himself the privilege of not clarifying mysteries, so that they remain mysteries; and who is not pleased, let him demand his money . . .

Who said that? Who? Wait. One minute. He who would know more, let him loosen his purse strings . . . There are so many things I myself do not understand, my friend. For example I, as much as you, depend upon Ludovico and Celestina for an understanding of the story of the three youths . . . For me they were always three usurpers, three youths allied to frustrate El Señor's intent and prolong history beyond the limits of death and immobility indicated by the King; three heirs, three bastards, yes, even three founders, as Ludovico said, but, I swear to you, I never understood that story, those signs, clearly. I repeated to La Señora what Ludovico asked me: a blood-red cross upon the back, six toes on each foot, the kingdom of Rome still lives, Agrippa, his is the continuity of the original kingdoms, phrases, phrases I repeated without understanding, loose ends, accept them, be grateful for them, I tell you . . .

The three bottles? What did the three bottles contain? I do not know that either, I tell you, and he who would know more, let . . . Equality? You ask me for equality, then?, you accept not knowing the things I do not know, and ask only to know what I know, you permit me no secret, nothing I can take to the tomb except what, like you, I do not know?, that is the only agreement you will accept?, oh, my friend, that is the only way you will forgive me for having been the cause of your harm, the galleys, your certainty of death on the eve of the battle, your being crippled in it, your delivery to the Arabs, your prison in Alicante . . . only in that way?

I am going far away, my poor friend. I shall know nothing of what happens here. It is left in your hands, to your eyes and your ears, to continue the story of El Señor Don Felipe. Where I am going, little news will reach me. And certainly, less news, or none, will you have of me. I do not know if a new world exists. I know only what I imagine. I know only what I desire. As a consequence, it exists for me. I am an exasperated Christian. I wish to know, and if it exists, I wish to protect it, and if it does not exist, I wish to adopt it, a minimal community of people who live in harmony with nature, who own no property except those things shared by all: a new world, not because it was found anew, but because it is or it will be like that of the first Golden Age. Remember, my candid and culpable friend, everything I have told you and, with me, ask yourself, what blindness is this?, we call ourselves Christians but we live worse than brutish animals; and if we believe that this Christian doctrine is but a deceit, why do we not abandon it altogether? I am abandoning this palace; I am abandoning my friends, you, my brother Toribio; I am abandoning El Señor. I go with one who needs me more: Guzmán. It is true; do not look at me with such amazement. I know that I go in search of the happy Golden Age; I know that Guzmán goes, with great malice and covetousness, in search of sources of gold, and that his age in the new world will be an iron age, and worse; I know that I seek, tentatively, the restoration of true Christianity, while Guzmán seeks, with certainty, the instauration of fortunate Guzmánism. I am needed more there than here; there will be need of someone who will speak on behalf of the defeated, perpetuate their founding dreams, defend their lives, protect their labors, affirm that they are men with souls and not simple beasts of burden, watch for the continuity of beauty and the pleasure of a thousand small offices, and channel souls, for the glory of God, toward the construction of new temples, the astounding temples of the new world, a new flowering of a new art that will defeat forever the fixity of icons that reflects a truth revealed only once, and forever, and instead reveal a new knowledge that unfolds in every direction for every delectation, a circular encounter between what they know and what I know, a hybrid art, temples raised in the image and likeness of the paradise we all envision in our dreams: color and form will be liberated, expanded, and fructified in celestial domed ceilings of white grape clusters, polychrome vines, silver fruit, dusky angels, tile façades, altars of excessive golden foliage, images, yes, of the paradise shared by them and me, cathedrals for the future, the anonymous seed of rebellion, renovating imagination, constant and unfulfilled aspiration: a vast circle in perpetual movement, sweet friend, my white hands and their swarthy ones joined to do more, much more, than anything I could ever do in the old world, secretly painting culpable paintings to disturb the conscience of a King; hybrid temples of the new world, the solution of all our mute inheritances in one stone embrace: pyramid, church, mosque, and synagogue united in a single place: look at that wall of serpents, look at that transplanted arch, look at those Moorish tiles, look at those floors of sand.

There is no such place? No, my friend, there isn't if you look for it in space. Seek it, rather, in time: in the same future you will investigate in your exemplary—and thereby scandalous—novels. My white hands and their dark hands will juxtapose the simultaneous spaces of the old and the new worlds to create the promise of a different time. I shall assume, my sweet, bitter, lovable, desperate friend, the dreams dreamed and lost by Ludovico and Celestina, Pedro and Simón, on that long-ago afternoon on the beach of the Cabo de los Desastres. Without their knowing it, I shall also assume the dreams of El Señor and Guzmán, of the Comendador and the Inquisitor, for neither they nor we know what we do, only God, whose instruments we are. Guzmán will seek new countries in his desire for gold and riches; El Señor will accept events in order to transfer there the sins, the rigidity, and the will for extinction operating here, but God and I, your servant Julián, shall work together for the most exalted goals. My friend: will the new world truly be the new world where everything can be begun anew, man's entire history, without the burdens of our old errors? Shall we Europeans be worthy of our own Utopia?

Thus, I accept your proposition to teach by example: I shall arrive in the new world cleansed of culpable secrets and odious burdens. Let us be ignorant of the same things, you and I; let us know the same things; and he who wishes to know more, let him loosen his purse strings, and he who is not pleased with what I tell him, let him demand his money. That is what the jester with the broad bedaubed smile used to say when he entertained with his buffoonery in El Señor's castle, with the grimace of the dying day reflected in the twin orbs of eyes beneath a pointed cap pulled low on his brow; how would he not see the glances of carnal cupidity El Señor's father directed toward the beautiful child Isabel, come from England after her parents' death to find refuge and consolation by the side of her Spanish aunt and uncle: starched white petticoats, long corkscrew curls, Elizabeth, yes, that incontinent and whoring Prince desired her as a child, he who had raped every country girl in the district, taken all the honorable maids of his kingdoms by seignorial right, who was pursuing the girls of Flanders while in a latrine in the palace of Brabant his wife was giving birth to his son, our present Señor, he who had satiated his appetites with a she-wolf, scarcely had he seen the budding breasts and the down in the armpits of his English niece—after playing with her and offering her dolls and gifts, then breaking upon the floor the same dolls he had given her as a gift—when he surreptitiously deflowered her.

In whom was the young girl to confide but in the only man in that castle who, like her, played: the jester? But if she said nothing to me, I, who even then entertained her with my brushes and engravings and miniatures, found her weeping one day, and noted the swelling fullness of her belly and breasts, and she, weeping, told me she wept because for two months she had not bled.

I was shocked by the news: what was to be done with the young English girl who was gazed upon with eyes of love by the youthful heir Felipe, and who had committed the indiscretion—worse than the deed—of telling the truth to the most deceitful and disturbed of the courtiers, the jester of bitter features, a buffoon because in all his existence he found no cause for joy? It would be useless to tell the jester that I shared the secret and urge him to guard it. He would have placed a price on his silence, as in the end he did; an intriguer, but stupid, he told El Señor's father he knew the truth.

First our insatiable master ordered that the Princess Isabel be removed for seven months to the ancient castle in Tordesillas, there to receive a disciplined education in the arts of the court, to be accompanied only by a marshal, three duennas, a dozen halberdiers and the famous Jewish physician, the hump-backed Dr. José Luis Cuevas, brought from prison where he was expiating the unconfessed crime of boiling in oil six Christian children by the light of the moon, exactly as an ancestor of his had done with three royal Princes, for which the King of that time had ordered burned alive thirty thousand false converts in the plaza of Logroño. Cuevas was taken to Tordesillas with the promise of being exonerated if he fulfilled well his office in the somber castle, the ancient lodging of many mad royalty. Cuevas attended the birth; he marveled at the monstrous signs on the child and, laughing, said that he looked more like a son of his than of the beautiful young girl; he laughed for the last time: the halberdiers cut off his head in the very chamber of the birth, and they were at the point of doing the same to the newborn child, had not the young Isabel, clutching the child against her breast, defended him as a she-wolf defends her cub.

She said: "If you touch him, first I shall strangle him and then kill myself, and we shall see how you explain my death to your Señor. Your own death is hovering nearby. I know that as soon as we reach the castle, the Señor will

order you killed as he ordered the death of this poor Hebrew doctor, so that
no one can tell of what happened here. On the other hand, I have promised
before God and before man to keep eternal silence if the child leaves here
alive with me. Which will have the greater import, your word or mine?"

With this, the halberdiers fled, for well they knew the violent disposi-
tion of El Señor's father, and they did not doubt the words of Isabel, who
returned to the castle with two of the duennas, while another, with the marshal, carried the child by a different route. Warned by my young mistress of
the approximate dates of events, I had circled about the palace of Tordesillas
for several days prior to the birth, and cloaked, wearing the hat and clothing
of a highwayman, I assaulted the duenna and the marshal, galloped back to
the seignorial castle with the bastard in my arms, and delivered him in secret
to the child mother, Isabel.

Discretion was my weapon and my desire: the heir, Felipe, loved this girl;
he would wed her; the future Queen would owe me the most outstanding
favors; I would enjoy peace and protection in which to continue my vocation
as friar and painter, and also to extend them to men like you, Chronicler, and
to my brother, the astronomer Toribio. But if someone discovered the truth,
then what confusion there would be, what disorder, what rancor, what uncertainty for my fortunes; Felipe would repudiate Isabel; Felipe's mother, who
had pardoned her husband so many deceptions, would not absolve him of this
particular transgression; my fortune would be unsure; I would be defeated,
like Oedipus, by incest! Through the alleyways of Valladolid I sought out
an ancient blackbird, a renowned procuress expert in renewing maidenheads,
and in secret I led her to Isabel's chamber in the castle, where the old cur-
mudgeon, with great art, mended the girl's ill and stole away as she had come,
a drone in the shadows.

Isabel wept because of her many misfortunes; I asked her about the infant;
that giddy child moaned that, not knowing how to care for him, or nourish
him, or anything concerned with him, she had given him into the hands of
her friend the jester, who was keeping him in some secret part of the castle. I
cursed the girl's imprudence, for she was furnishing more and more weapons
to the intriguing buffoon, who, neither late nor lazy, made known to the
outrageous and whoring Prince, our Señor, what he knew, and asked him
money in exchange for guarding the secret. The Señor called the Fair, you
see, was convinced that the duenna and the marshal—following the King's

direction—had abandoned the newborn child in a basket in the waters of the Ebro. Therefore, the jester's greedy project was short-lived, for that same afternoon, when all the court was gathered in the castle hall, El Señor, our master, offered the jester a cup of wine to animate him in his buffoonery, and the incautious mime, cavorting and capering, died, choked by the poison.

I set about to look for the lost infant and found him in the most obvious of places: on a straw pallet in the cell occupied by the jester. I gave the child to Isabel's duenna, Azucena. The duenna took him to Isabel and explained to her that when he died the jester had left a newborn child in his pallet. She had decided to care for the child, but her breasts were dry. Could she nurse the babe at the teats of the bitch who recently had whelped in Isabel's bedchamber. Isabel, who was still bleeding from her own childbirth, said yes, and to her uncle, El Señor, she said: "Our son can pass as the son of the jester and Azucena. Do not kill anyone else. Your secret is safe. If you do not touch my son I shall tell nothing to anyone. If you kill him, I shall tell everything. And then kill myself."

But that ferocious and handsome Señor did not wish to kill anyone, he wished to make love to Isabel again, he wished to love without limits, he wished to possess every living woman, every bleeding female, nothing could satiate him; that very morning in the chapel he saw Isabel spit out a serpent at the moment she received the Host, he saw the eyes of love with which his own son Felipe gazed at Isabel, and being unable to make love to her again, and thus desiring her more ardently than ever, he drank until he was drunk, rode out on his dun-colored steed, lopping off heads of wheat with his whip, he encountered a trapped she-wolf, he dismounted, violated the beast, howled like her and with her, satiated all his dark needs, his frustration, and burning fires: animal with animal, the act did not horrify him; it would have been a sin against nature to make love again with Isabel, but not beast with beast, no, that was natural: this is what he told me as he confessed another night, the night when Isabel and Felipe had just been wed and after the cadavers burned on the pyre in the courtyard had been carried away in carts; this he confessed to me, in addition to all his earlier crimes, sure of my silence, feeling the need to pour out his tormented soul before someone.

"Have I impregnated a she-wolf?" he asked me through the grating of the confessional, hoping to find solace for his monstrous imaginings.

"Be calm, Señor, please be calm; such a thing is impossible . . ."

"Accursed breed," he murmured, "madness, incest, crime, the only thing lacking was to make love as beast to beast; what do I bequeath my son? Each generation adds scars to the generation that follows; the scars accumulate until they lead to sterility and extinction; degenerate seeks out degenerate; an imperious force impels them to find one another and unite . . ."

"The seed, Señor, exhausts itself from growing upon the same soil."

"What would be born of my coupling with a beast? Did some dark necessity impel me to renovate the blood with a living but nonhuman thing?"

"In spite of classic wisdom, Señor, nature at times makes strange leaps," I said ingenuously, thinking thus to absolve myself of any knowledge concerning the paternity of Isabel's child, and also to promote the current belief about his origin. "For instance, consider a child," I added, "that is not the son of man and she-wolf but the child of jester and scrubbing maid; he bears monstrous signs of degeneration . . ."

"What signs?" cried El Señor, who had never seen the child.

"A cross upon his back, six toes on each foot . . ."

Now El Señor called the Fair howled, he howled, and his animal cry resounded through the domed ceiling of the church; he left, shouting: "Do you not know the prophecy of Tiberius Caesar?, is this the sign of the usurpers, rebellious slaves, have I engendered slaves and rebels who will usurp my kingdom?, parricidal sons?, a throne raised upon the blood of their father?"

I knew he ordered the child killed, but he disappeared, as also disappeared that same night, to his great sadness, Felipe's companions, Ludovico and Celestina; I knew that El Señor ordered that every Saturday be dedicated to hunting wolves until every wolf was exterminated. Only I understood the reason for these orders. I gave thanks when El Señor died, after playing very strenuously at ball; Prince Felipe occupied his place, and my Señora Isabel ascended to the throne reserved for her.

Isabel displayed great austerity and discretion as the wife of the new Señor, Don Felipe, and I never imagined that the maidenhead restored by the magpie of the alleyways of Valladolid remained intact. My respectful friendship with La Señora was constant. I attempted to entertain her, as I always had, with my enamels and miniatures, and by lending her to read the volumes of courtly love of the *De arte honeste amandi* of Andreas Capellanus, for beneath her dignity I noted an increasing melancholy, as if something were lacking; at times she sighed for her dolls and her peach stones, and I told myself that my Señora's transition from young foreigner to solitary Queen and secret mother of a vanished child had been too swift. The people murmured: When will the foreigner give us a Spanish heir? False pregnancies were announced, followed always by unfortunate miscarriages.

Nothing was more disastrous, however, than the accident that then befell my mistress, her husband being in Flanders at war against the Adamite heretics and the dukes that protected them. The humiliation of the thirty-three and one half days she spent lying upon the paving stones of the castle courtyard transformed my Señora's will; it unleashed forces, passions, hatreds, desires, memories, dreams that doubtless had throbbed for a long time in her soul and had awaited only an astonishing event, both terrible and absurd, like this one, to fully manifest themselves. A mouse, then, and not the virile member of our Señor, gnawed away the restored virginity of my Señora. She called me to her chamber, when finally she returned to it: she asked me to complete the work begun by the Mus; I possessed her, finally breaking the network of fine threads the go-between of Valladolid had woven there. I left her in the spell of a delirious dream, cursing myself for having broken my vow of chastity: a renewable vow, yes, but also less sacred than my resolution to pour all my bodily juices into my art. To perfect that art, I have dedicated myself all these years.

I often went out into the countryside searching for faces, landscapes, buildings, and perspectives that I sketched in charcoal and guarded jealously, later incorporating these details of everyday reality into the figures and spaces of the great painting I was secretly creating in a deep dungeon of the new palace El Señor was constructing to commemorate his victory over the dukes and heretics of the vicious province of Flanders. Thus one morning, as I was wandering through the fields of Montiel, I happened to meet a cart being driven by a blond youth by whose side was seated a green-eyed, sun-burned blind man playing a flute. I asked permission of the blind man to sketch his features. He acceded with an ironic smile. The youth was grateful for the rest; he went to a nearby well, drew a bucket of water, disrobed, and bathed himself. I turned from my preoccupation with the blind man, who could not see me, and gazed at the splendid beauty of the youth, so like the perfect figures rendered by Phidias and Praxiteles. Then, with amazement bordering on horror, I noticed the sign upon his back: a blood-red cross between the shoulder blades; and as I looked at his naked feet, I knew I would count six toes upon each foot.

I controlled my trembling hand. I bit my tongue not to tell the blind man what I knew: the youth was the son of my Señora, the brother of our present Señor, the bastard disappeared on the night when wedding and crime were allied; I told him, rather, that I was a friar and painter of the court, in the service of the most exalted Prince Don Felipe, and then it was he who became perturbed, his expression alternately revealing the desire to flee and the need to know. I asked him what he was hauling in his cart beneath the heavy canvas. He reached out a hand, as if to protect his cargo, and said: "Touch nothing, Friar, or the youth will break your bones on the spot."

"Have no fear. Where are you going?"

"To the coast."

"The coast is long, and touches many seas."

"You are good at prying, Friar. Does your master pay you well to go as talebearer throughout his kingdom?"

"I take advantage of his protection and attend secretly to my vocation, which is not that of informer, but artist."

"And what kind of art would yours be?"

I deliberated for a moment. I wished to gain the confidence of the blind man who was accompanying the lost son of my Señora. I did not, however, tell him what I knew. I tried to tie up loose ends: in some manner this man was involved with the child's disappearance; perhaps he had received him from other hands, but perhaps he himself had stolen him that night from the bloody castle; and who had disappeared at the same time as the child? Felipe's companions: Celestina and Ludovico. I knew the rebellious student; I could not recognize him in the blind man. I took the risk, not knowing whether I would be rewarded with the blind man's good faith or a drubbing from his young companion; I took a stab in the dark.

"An art," I answered him, "similar to your ideas, for I conceive of it as a direct approximation of God to man, a revelation of the grace inherent in every man, man who is born without sin and thus obtains grace immediately without the intercession of the agencies of oppression. Your ideas incarnate in my painting, Ludovico."

The blind man almost opened his eyes; I swear, friend Chronicler, that a ray of strange hope flashed across his obstinately closed eyelids; I pressed his coppery hand in my pale one; the youth dropped the bucket back into the well and approached, naked and drying himself with his own clothing.

"My name is Julián. You can rely on me."

When I returned to the palace, I found my Señora upset from a dream she had just experienced. I asked her to tell it to me, and she did so. Feigning stupor, I replied that I had dreamed the same, dreamed of a young castaway tossed on a beach. Where? My dream, I told her, had a site: the coast of the Cabo de los Desastres. Why? The place of my dream, I said, had a history: the chronicles abound in notices of varinels sunk there with their treasures from the Spice Islands, Cipango, and Cathay, of vessels that had disappeared with all the Cádiz crew and all their captives of the war against the Infidel aboard. But also, as if in compensation, they tell of sailing ships broken upon the rocks because lovers were fleeing in them.

She asked me: "What is the name of this youth of whom we both have dreamed?"

I replied: "It depends upon what land he treads."

La Señora reached out to me: "Friar, take me to that beach, take me to that youth . . ."

"Patience, Señora. We must wait two years nine months and two weeks, which are a thousand and one half days; the time it will take your husband to finish his necropolis of Princes."

"Why, Friar?"

"Because this youth is life's answer to the will-for-death of our Señor, the King."

"How do friars know these things?"

"Because we have dreamed them, Señora."

"You lie. You know more than you are telling me."

"But if I told her everything, La Señora would cease to have confidence in me. I do not betray La Señora's secrets. She must not insist that I betray mine."

"It is true, Friar. You would cease to interest me. Do what you have promised. At the end of a thousand and one half days, bring that youth to me. And if you do so, Brother Julián, you will have pleasure."

I lie, my friend. I did not answer her saying, "That is all a contrite and devout soul could ask"; no, I did not wish to be my Señora's lover; I did not want to waste in her bed the vigor and vigilance I must devote to my painting; and I feared this woman, I was beginning to fear her; how could she have dreamed what had happened between Ludovico and me when the blind man told me he was going to the Cabo de los Desastres, the beach where more than sixteen years before he and Celestina, Felipe, Pedro, and the monk Simón had met, and that this time Pedro's ship would sail in search of the new world beyond the great ocean, and that the youth with the cross upon his back would embark upon it and on a precise day, a thousand and one half days later, on the morning of a fourteenth of July, he would return to the same beach, and that then he could go with me, travel to the palace of Don Felipe, El Señor, and there fulfill his second destiny, that of his origins, as in the new world he would have fulfilled his first destiny, that of his future? I was confused by these explanations; the place and the time, on the other hand, were engraved in my mind; I would then see some way my mistress could recover her lost son. But Ludovico added one condition to our pact: that I find a way to advise Celestina that on the same day she should pass by that beach. Celestina? The blind man knew what Simón had told him when, he said, the blind man had returned to Spain: disguised as a page, she was playing a funeral drum in the procession of the Mad Lady, Don Felipe's mother, who bore throughout Spain the embalmed cadaver of her impenitent husband, refusing to bury him. It was not difficult for me to send a message to the page of the lunatic Queen.

But my Señora, I tell you, frightened me: how did she dream that dream?, was it the potions of belladonna I had administered to calm her delirium?, the recollections of some drawing of mine of real or imagined castaways?, was it the presence in her bedchamber of a furtive Mus I saw moving at times among her bedsheets, hiding, watching us?, was it a white and knotted root like a tiny human figure, almost a little man, I occasionally saw move with stealth among the hangings of the bedchamber?, was it a Satanic pact, something of which I was unaware and that caused me to tremble as I entered my mistress's bedchamber, some horrible secret that damaged and hindered the causes of my art as well as the beliefs of my religion?, and was it not my purpose, candid friend who hears me, to conciliate once again reason and faith through art, to return to human intelligence and divine conviction the unity threatened by separation?, for it was, and is, my belief that religion warring against reason becomes the facile prey of the Devil.

In order to rid myself of this increasing fear of the demonic, and also to rid myself of the increasing sexual appetite of La Señora, I searched for gracile youths that I might lead in secret to her bedchamber; I became, I confess, a vile go-between, as much a procurer as that hymen-mending magpie of Valladolid; and in one thing, worse, for these youths led to her bedchamber never left there alive, or if they did, they disappeared forever and no one ever heard of them again; some were found, white and bloodless, in the passageways of the palace and in forgotten dungeons; of others, a very few, I came to know this: one died on the gallows, one on the pillory, another was garroted. I feared more and more for the health of my protectress's mind; I must channel her passions in a manner beneficial to my own desires, and also convincing to hers—whatever they might be. I searched through *aljamas* and Jewries in Toledo and Seville, in Cuenca and Medina. I was searching for someone in particular. I found him. I brought him to the uncompleted palace.

In lands of ancient Castilian Christianity he was called Miguel. In the Jewries he was called Michah. And in the *aljamas* he was known as Mihail-ben-Sama, which in Arabic means Miguel-of-Life. Your husband El Señor, I said, has exhausted his life in the mortal persecution of heretics, Moors, and Jews, and those three bloods and those three religions flow through Miguel's veins; he is a son of Rome, of Israel, and of Araby. Renew the blood, Señora. Enough of this attempt to deceive your subjects; the familiar public announcement of your pregnancy, hoping to attenuate the expectations of an heir, merely forces you to pretense: you must stuff your fathingale with pillows and imitate a condition that is not yours; then follows the equally familiar announcement of a miscarriage. Frustrated hopes are often converted into irritation, if not open rebellion. You must be cautious. Allay their discontent with one theatrical blow: fulfill their hopes by having a son. You may rely on me: the only proof of paternity will be the features of El Señor, your husband, that I introduce upon the seals, miniatures, medallions, and portraits that will be the representation of your son for the multitudes and for posterity. The populace—and history—will know the face of your son only through coins bearing the effigy I have designed that are minted and circulated in these kingdoms. No one will ever have occasion to compare the engraved image with the real face. Combine, Señora, pleasure and duty: provide Spain with an heir.

Conveniently deaf, Chronicler, I did not hear—I swear it, I did not hear—
La Señora's answer to my arguments: "But, Julián, I already have a son . . ."

She said it serenely, but there is no worse madness than serene madness;
I tell you I did not hear her; I continued; I said: Recover the true unity of
Spain: regard this young man, Mihail-ben-Sama, Miguel-of-Life, a Castilian,
Moorish, and Hebrew Miguel; I swear to you, Chronicler, do not look at me
in that way, that is when I said this to La Señora, I did not say it later, when
I took her own son to her, the youth found on the Cabo de los Desastres,
when I told you this, I lied, I accept my lie, yes, because I did not know then
how this story was going to end, I believed I would never reveal my greatest
secret to anyone, I thought today, as I began to speak to you, that the worst
secret would be any secret at all, for example, when El Señor told me what he
saw in his mirror as he ascended the thirty steps, I said to myself, this will
be the secret, the father of El Señor fornicated with a she-wolf, but that she-
wolf was none other than an ancient Queen dead for centuries, the one who
stitched flags the color of her blood and her tears, a restless soul resurrected
in the body of a she-wolf, it was natural that another child should be born of
her belly, blood calls to blood, degenerates seek out one another and copulate
and procreate: three sons of the Señor called the Fair, three bastards, three
usurpers, Felipe's three brothers, is it not enough you know this secret?, is
your curiosity not satiated?, I wished to be honest with you, to win your forgiveness, do not now accuse me of something so frightful, I asked La Señora
to have a child by Mihail-ben-Sama, you, you were the true culprit, you, a
Chronicler made bitter and desperate because your papers are not identical to
life, as you would wish, you interrupted my project with your idiotic poem,
you removed Mihail from life and placed him within literature, you wove
with paper the rope that was to bind you to the galley, indiscreet and candid
friend, you sent Mihail to the stake, do you not remember?, you shared a cell
with him the night before your exile and his death, how could I have been the
iniquitous procurer who delivered a son to the carnal love of his mother?, how
was I to know that was what La Señora desired?, she recognized him, yes, she
recognized him, the cross, the toes, I believed I was compassionately reunit-
ing a mother and a son, she knew who he was, she knew she was fornicating
with her own son, she knew it, and she screamed her pleasure of him, I knew
it, and I lamented it with prayers and breast beating: blood calls to blood, the
son born of incest has closed the perfect circle of his origin: transgression of

moral law; Cain slew Abel, Set, Osiris, Smoking Mirror killed the Plumed Serpent, Romulus, Remus, and Pollux, son of Zeus, rejected immortality at the death of his brother Castor, son of a swan: sons of a witch, sons of a she-wolf, sons of a Queen, these were three, they did not kill one another, their number saved them, but there is no order that is not founded upon crime, if not of blood, then of the flesh: poor Iohannes Agrippa, called Don Juan, it fell to you, in the name of the three brothers, to transgress in order to found anew: not Set, not Cain, not Romulus, not Pollux, your destiny, Don Juan is that of Oedipus: the shadow that walks toward its end by walking toward its origin: the future will respond to the enigmas of the past only because that future is identical to the beginning; tragedy is the restoration of the dawn of being: monarch and prisoner, culprit and innocent, criminal and victim, the shadow of Don Juan is the shadow of Don Felipe: in her son, Don Juan, La Señora knew the flesh of her husband Don Felipe: only thus, Chronicler, only in this way; candid friend of marvels, soul of wax, hear me, I believed I was returning her lost son to her, but instead she recovered her true lover, you are to blame, foolish friend, not I, not I, such was not my intent, I swear it, forgive me, I forgive you, events acquire a life of their own, they escape our hands, I did not propose such a horrible infraction of divine and human laws, you frustrated my project with your literature, now you know the truth, you must now alter all the words and all the intent of this long narration, revise now what I have told you, Chronicler, and try to discover the lie, the deception, the fiction, yes, the fiction, in each phrase, doubt now everything I have told you, what will you do to collate my subjective words with objective truth?, what?, you sent Miguel-of-Life to the stake, and you condemned me to be an accomplice to an incestuous transgression: see the fires of the stake upon every page you fill, Chronicler Don Miguel, see the blood of incest in every word you write: you desired the truth, now save it with the lie . . .

"Señor, this great painting has been sent to you from Orvieto, fatherland of a few somber, austere, and energetic painters. You are the Defender of the Faith. They offer it in homage to you and to the Faith. See its great dimensions. I have measured them. They will fit perfectly within the empty space behind the altar in your chapel."

Translated by Margaret Sayers Peden

WORK

1954, *Los días enmascarados*, Novaro (stories).

1958, *La región más transparente*, Fondo de Cultura Económica (novel).

1959, *Las buenas conciencias*, Fondo de Cultura Económica (novel).

1962, *Aura*, Ediciones Era (novel).

1962, *La muerte de Artemio Cruz*, Fondo de Cultura Económica (novel).

1964, *Cantar de ciegos*, J. Mortiz (stories).

1967, *Zona Sagrada*, Siglo XXI (novel).

1967, *Cambio de piel*, J. Mortiz (novel).

1969, *Cumpleaños*, J. Mortiz (novel).

1969, *El mundo de José Luis Cuevas*, Tudor Publishing Company (essay).

1970, *Casa con dos puertas*, J. Mortiz (essay).

1970, *Todos los gatos son pardos*, Siglo XXI (play).

1970, *El tuerto es rey*, J. Mortiz (play).

1971, *Tiempo mexicano*, J. Mortiz (essay).

1971, *Los reinos originarios*, Seix Barral (play).

1972, *Cuerpos y ofrendas*, Alianza (anthology).

1973, *Chac Mool y otros cuentos*, Salvat (stories).

1975, *Terra Nostra*, J. Mortiz (novel).

1976, *Cervantes o la crítica de la lectura*, J. Mortiz (essay).

1978, *La cabeza de la hidra*, Argos (novel).

1980, *Una familia lejana*, Ediciones Era (novel).

1980, *El Dragón y el Unicorno: La tensión del pensamiento entre las antiguas relaciones de sangre y las nuevas relaciones jurídico-estatales que surgieron con la civilización*, Cal y Arena (essay coauthored by Alejandro Carrillo Castro).

1981, *Agua quemada*, Fondo de Cultura Económica (stories).

1982, *Orquídeas a la luz de la luna. Comedia mexicana*, Seix Barral (play).

1985, *Gringo Viejo*, Fondo de Cultura Económica (novel).

1987, *Cristóbal Nonato*, Fondo de Cultura Económica (novel).

1990, *Constancia y otras novelas para vírgenes*, Fondo de Cultura Económica (novel).

1990, *Valiente mundo Nuevo. Épica, utopía y mito en la novela hispanoamericana*, Mondadori (essay).

1990, *La campaña*, Santillana (novel).

1991, *Dos educaciones*, Mondadori (play).

1991, *Ceremonias del alba*, Mondadori (play).

1992, *El espejo enterrado*, Fondo de Cultura Económica (essay).

1993, *Geografía de la novela*, Fondo de Cultura Económica (essay).

1993, *El naranjo*, Alfaguara (stories).

1994, *Nuevo tiempo mexicano*, Aguilar (essay).

1994, *Diana o la cazadora solitaria*, Alfaguara (essay).

1995, *La frontera de cristal. Una novela en nueve cuentos*, Alfaguara (stories).

1996, *Voluptuario*, Saint Martins (monograph coauthored by Brian Nissen).

1998, *Retratos en el tiempo*, Alfaguara (essay).

1999, *Los años con Laura Díaz*, Alfaguara (novel).

2000, *Los cinco soles de México. Memoria de un milenio*, Seix Barral (essay).

2001, *Instinto de Inez*, Alfaguara (novel).

2002, *En esto creo*, Seix Barral (essay).

2003, *La Silla del Águila*, Alfaguara (essay).

2004, *Inquieta compañía*, Alfaguara (essay).

2004, *Contra Bush*, Aguilar (essay).

2005, *Los 68*, Grijalbo (essay).

2006, *Todas las familias felices*, Alfaguara (stories).

2007, *Cuentos sobrenaturales*, Alfaguara (novel).

2007, *Cuentos naturales*, Alfaguara (stories).

2007, *Santa Anna*, (opera libretto).

2008, *La voluntad y la fortuna*, Alfaguara (novel).

2009, *Adán en Edén*, Alfaguara (novel).

2010, *Vlad*, Alfaguara (novel).

2011, *Carolina Grau*, Alfaguara (stories).

2011, *La gran novela latinoamericana*, Alfaguara (essay).

2013, *Federico en su balcón*, Alfaguara (novel).

ENGLISH TRANSLATIONS

1960, *Where the Air Is Clear*, translated by Sam Hilman, Obolensky (novel).

1968, *The Good Conscience*, translated by Sam Hilman, Farrar, Straus and Giroux (novel).

1972, *Holy Place*, translated by Sam Hilman, E. P. Dutton, Farrar, Straus and Giroux (novel).

1975, *Aura*, translated by Lysander Kemp, Farrar, Straus and Giroux (novel).

1976, *Terra nostra*, translated by Margaret Sayers Peden, Farrar, Straus and Giroux (novel).

1978, *Hydra Head*, translated by Margaret Sayers Peden, Farrar, Straus and Giroux (novel).

1982, *Distant Relations*, translated by Margaret Sayers Peden, Farrar, Straus and Giroux (novel).

1986, *A Change of Skin*, translated by Sam Hilman, Farrar, Straus and Giroux (novel).

1986, *Burnt Water*, translated by Margaret Sayers Peden, Farrar, Straus and Giroux (novel).

1986, *The Old Gringo*, translated by Margaret Sayers Peden, Farrar, Straus and Giroux (novel).

1988, *Birthday*, translated by Sam Hilman, Farrar, Straus and Giroux (novel).

1989, *Christopher Unborn*, translated by Alfred Mac Adam, Farrar, Straus and Giroux (novel).

1991, *The Death of Artemio Cruz*, translated by Alfred Mac Adam, Farrar, Straus and Giroux (novel).

1994, *The Orange Tree*, translated by Alfred Mac Adam, Farrar, Straus and Giroux (novel).

1995, *Diana: The Goddess Who Hunts Alone*, translated by Alfred Mac Adam, Farrar, Straus and Giroux (novel).

1997, *The Crystal Frontier: A Novel in Nine Stories*, translated by Alfred Mac Adam, Farrar, Straus and Giroux (novel).

2000, *The Years with Laura Diaz*, translated by Alfred Mac Adam, Farrar, Straus and Giroux (novel).

2002, *Inez*, translated by Margaret Sayers Peden, Farrar, Straus and Giroux (novel).

2006, *The Eagles Throne*, translated by Kristina Cordero, Random House (novel).

2008, *Happy Families*, translated by Edith Grossman, Random House (novel).

2011, *Destiny and Desire*, Translated by Edith Grossman, Random House (novel).

2012, *Vlad*, translated by Alejandro Branger and Ethan Shaskan Bumas, Dalkey Archive Press (novel).

•

AWARDS AND RECOGNITIONS

1967, Premio Biblioteca Breve for *Cambio de piel*.

1972, Premio Mazatlán de Literatura for *Tiempo mexicano*.

1976, Premio Xavier Villaurrutia for *Terra nostra*.

1977, Premio Rómulo Gallegos for *Terra nostra*.

1979, Premio Internacional Alfonso Reyes.

1984, Premio Nacional de Literatura de México.

1987, Premio Cervantes.

1992, French Legion of Honor medal.

1992, Premio Internacional Menéndez Pelayo.

1993, Orden al Mérito de Chile.

1994, Priz Grizane Cavour.

1994, Premio Príncipe de Asturias.

1994, Medalla Picasso de la UNESCO.

2000, Honorary Doctorate from Universidad Veracruzana.

2000, Honorary Doctorate from Universidad Autónoma de Sinaloa.

2001, Honorary Member of the Academia Mexicana de la Lengua.

2004, Premio Real Academia Español de creación literaria for *En esto creo*.

2008, Premio Internacional don Quijote de la Mancha.

2009, Honorary Doctorate from Universidad de Quitana Roo.

2009, Gran Cruz de la Orden de Isabel la Católica.

2009, Premio González Ruano de Periodismo for the article "El Yucatán de Hernán Lara Zavala."

2009, Honorary Doctorate from Universidad de Veracruz.

2010, Honorary Doctorate from Universidad de Puerto Rico.

2011, Premio Formentor de las Letras.

2011, Honorary Doctorate from Université Michel de Montaigne.

2011, Premio Fundación Cristóbal Gabarrón de las Letras.

JORGE
EDWARDS
(Chile, 1931)

Jorge Edwards is one of Chilean literature's most well-known authors. Born in the capital in 1931, he belongs to one of the oldest families in the country: Brits who arrived to the Pacific coast at the beginning of the nineteenth century, some of whom, over the course of the country's history, would emerge as important figures in the cultural and political spheres.

Edwards inherited his taste for literature from one of his relatives, his great uncle Joaquín Edwards Bello (protagonist of his novel *El inútil de la familia*), a writer disgraced for his sarcastic portrayal of the aristocracy to which he belonged: "An aunt of mine intuited my inclination toward writing. One day on the sly she showed me my uncle Joaquín's books. My father spoke of him with great irritation. He never referred to him simply as tío Joaquín, no, he always added an adjective. He was Useless Joaquín."

Edwards's father didn't want a similar future for their son; they sent him to study at the school Compañía de Jesús, where he had as a teacher Father Hurtado, a priest who was canonized by Benedict XVI in 2005. Later, after finishing his degreee, he continued his education in the Law Faculty at Universidad de Chile and began his long career as a diplomat and writer.

He made his literary debut in 1952 with the book of stories *El Patio*; his diplomatic debut came ten years later, when he was sent to Paris as secretary to the Chilean embassy. In both cases, his name was associated with the two dominant currents in the literary panorama of the time, both in Chile and in the rest of Latin America and Spain: on one hand, there was the generation of 1950, and on the other, the *boom*, which also included Mario Vargas Llosa, Gabriel García Márquez, and Julio Cortázar, young writers who, like Edwards, were also strolling through the streets and the nights of Paris.

In 1962 he was awarded the Premio Municipal de Santiago for his book *Gente de la ciudad* and three years later he published his first novel, *El peso de la noche.* In 1967, the year when his book of stories *Las máscaras* was released, he returned to Santiago and stayed until in 1971, with Salvador Allende already in the Palacio de la Moneda, he was sent as ambassador to Cuba. There he had disagreements with the government of Fidel Castro and the authorities "suggested" that he leave the island. This experience gave birth to his novel *Persona non grata*, "one of the truly vibrant classics of modern Latin American literature," in the words of Octavio Paz. The book, an open criticism of on-the-ground socialism exemplified by the Cuban regime, was censored in Cuba and Chile, and earned its author enmities not only in the political sphere, but also among the circle of Latin American writers.

Upon his return from Havana, the socialist government sent him back to Paris, this time under the tutelage of Pablo Neruda. At the time, the poet was the ambassador to France and they struck up a friendship that would unite them for years. In September 1973, when Augusto Pinochet's military coup took place, unable to return to Chile, Edwards opted for exile in Barcelona, where he dedicated himself to writing and journalism. In 1977 he published *Desde la cola del dragon*, a compilation of essays already sketched out in different articles that appeared in magazines like *La Vanguardia*, *The Times*, *The Washington Post*, or *Le Monde*.

In 1978 he was able to return to his country and he became an active militant against the dictatorship, only resuming the diplomatic life with the return of democracy to Chile. The president, Eduardo Frei, named him ambassador to UNESCO, where he stayed from 1994 to 1996. With the Premio Nacional de Literatura and Premio Cervantes in 1999, the end of the millennium found him receiving the Orden al Mérito Gabriela Mistral from the Ministerio de Educación. The government of Sebastián Piñera named him ambassador to Paris, a post that he currently holds. He continues to write numerous magazine articles that are often published in Latin America and Europe and his most recent novel *La muerte de Montaigne* just came out. Soon the first volume of his memoirs will come out, focused on his childhood, adolescence, and youth, and bearing the title *Los círculos morados*, which "were the stains left behind by the cheap wine in the first literary cafés I knew."

THE ACORN

The Torture of Doctor Johnson

For me, "Family Order" is an emblematic story, a culmination of my work from the sixties, my thirties in Paris. Right now I'm writing away from my library and I don't have the text in front of me, but I write with a renewed, almost painful memory, of the actual process of creating this story and of the place: a more or less dilapidated apartment that reminded me of my childhood home, with garlands hanging from the ceilings and wrought iron balconies opening out in front of the Eiffel Tower, near where I'm now composing these lines. In the selected pages there are images of slow water, where fish leap in the depths, below overhanging willow branches along the banks. They are mental landscapes, where the troubling waters of profound memory meet the verses of Pablo Neruda's *Residence on Earth* (slowly flooded with slow waters), and with the mythical floods of novels like *As I Lay Dying* by William Faulkner. And it's a family order threatened by the most intense disorder: that of incest, of extreme marginality, of personal degradation.

The pages taken from my last book, *La muerte de Montaigne*, are the result of my mature reflection, nurtured over long decades by reading Michel de Montaigne's essays, among other things, which led me to the construction and invention of Montaigne as a novelistic character. It is the most free writing of Europe's past, lucid and ludic, and the most inspiring for a contemporary mind. The result is a text of mine, essay-novel (and not novelized essay), which leaves room for resigned meditation and jest, as evidenced by this morning greeting between an illustrious gentleman who, in his final years, married a prostitute: "Good morning, whore. Good morning, cuckold." In other words, the text emerges from juvenile disorder with a smile; sometimes, with a laugh. Suddenly, with a sneer.

The third is a fragment of dialogue between Fidel Castro and the author: writers confronting power, the reasoning of the State. It's a political and diplomatic experience condensed in writing, in language. The final salvation of literature? Maybe so. In any case, it is an example of serene, detached, ironic nonfiction, in the middle of the baroque proliferation and the revolution.

In Conversation with the Dead

The living dead who speak in our dreams: the Balzac of the short and mysterious novels, from *The Unknown Masterpiece* to *Sarrasine* and *Louis Lambert*; the young Neruda of *Residence on Earth*; the César Vallejo of *Poemas humanas*; Montaigne inside and outside his tower, naturally, and Marcel Proust, and the enigmatic Machado de Assis, who wrote in nineteenth-century Rio de Janeiro "with the pen of jest and the ink of melancholy," among many others. But beyond literature, I spent my childhood and my adolescence in a magical space, the center of Santiago, Chile, of that time, full of stories and storytellers: those of my mother and my maternal grandfather, of father Gana and father Iturrate, of Mariquita Fuentes, who cooked in a heavy wood stove, who moved the plates from the stove with a long hook and who told stories between the underground fire and the smoke coming out of the pans. All of them unknowingly applied Denis Diderot's maxim: tell stories while you can because the story of life is ending soon.

Could you elaborate a little on Neruda's influence on your life and on your writing and your time in Paris?

Neruda was a great storyteller, indeed, an exceptional oral narrator, and I enjoyed that a lot; he taught me something and also helped me kill a lot of time. Now I suppose it was time lost and gained. It didn't influence my writing much: his verse tended toward the solemn and torrential and he started to restrain himself in his final years; from the start, my prose has been economical, brief, miniaturistic, and tended, on the contrary, to swell and grow with maturity. Neruda was a great lover of Paris and I became one too. We met there often and expanded our knowledge together. I remember Pablo when he said: "Jorge is a messenger pigeon."

CODA

Since your exile in Barcelona you've said that literature is created with memory. How did the experience that you recount in Persona non grata *affect you throughout your life?*

With creative memory, memory that invents. In his surrealist manifestos, André Breton spoke about profound memory, a flow that disappears and reappears, that "allows that which floats to float," a phrase I used as an epigraph in my first novel, *El peso de la noche*. My work has been a balanced amalgam of memory and fiction, that sometimes leans more to one side and sometimes more to the other.

I was affected by the experience I tell and the publication of the book that tells it. My worst doubts about true socialism were confirmed with my stay on the island of Cuba between December, 1970 and the end of March 1971. From then on, I've not changed my criticism, but deepened it, and since then, I haven't gone back. The publication caused an immediate, unrelenting ban, in the literary, editorial, and personal. It's a ban that has taught me many things. The red censorship in the West has been one of the greatest and most profound experiences of my life. But I've survived fine, and I notice that the health of my censors from that time, if they are alive, is increasingly precarious.

A THOUSAND FORESTS

On Saturday, just as Verónica had said, the family arrived: the parents, a petite and opinionated aunt, and a boy about ten years old with something monstrous about his face. Verónica had already warned us that her younger brother was a monster. Behind them, in the latest model convertible, came José Raimundo. I found him unpleasant from the start. Short, chubby-cheeked, he gave the impression of a guy who was pampered, soft, and tyrannical at the same time. All of his country clothing looked like it came straight from the store. I watched him get out of the car, shake hands and greet everyone in the same way, with a mechanical nod and smile.

At that time, he showed no preference for you. Not that afternoon either, when we went for a walk with the aunt and the monster. But the following afternoon I noticed that he stayed close to you and tried to make jokes and kid around, and you laughed halfheartedly. Luckily, he announced after lunch that he had to return to Santiago. "Unfortunately," he said, "I have some business in Santiago first thing tomorrow." We waited to hear the car's engine and then, Verónica and I celebrated his departure, Verónica, boisterously, I, with more discretion because I wasn't in my own home. Aunt Charito leaped to José Raimundo's defense; she said he was "talented," always at the top of his class, in high school and university; and his charm was even more significant considering he was an only child, spoiled by a rich family. "Besides," added Aunt Charito, addressing you spitefully, "it seemed to me that he was fawning over you quite a bit." You vigorously denied Aunt Charito's claim, blushing slightly. "Poor Cristina!" Verónica exclaimed. "The admirer she ended up with!" "Why poor?" asked Charito. "A great match! What more could she want?" "Tell me," asked Verónica, exasperated, appealing to your direct testimony: "What did you think of my cousin? Tell me honestly!" "He's not that boring," you responded, conciliatory, and both Verónica and Aunt Charito thought that you admitted they were right. "You see!" exclaimed Aunt Charito, and Verónica protested, absolutely certain that you were speaking that way out of sheer politeness. I had no doubt, for my part, that Verónica was right. With his pudgy plumpness, his clichéd manners, his impeccable clothes, José Raimundo was precisely the type of person we looked down on, who would never have access to the clique that we formed then. We could disagree about many things, you, Verónica, whose affinity had been revealed to us within a few minutes, and I, but a disagreement on this matter seemed inconceivable to us. The discussion about José Raimundo lasted a long time and eventually Aunt Charito retired to her room, upset, emphatically declaring that in that house nobody escaped gossip. "Don't bad-mouth me, please," she said, full of resentment, before leaving the living room, and as soon as she disappeared through the doorway, Verónica burst into laughter that must have burned her ears.

We had a great time with Verónica, there's no denying it. It had been a long time since we'd had such a great time. The monster was a bit annoying, at times; but rather calm. Pallid, with a sickly and hateful expression, he'd rub against his mother's skirts, and she tolerated his most absurd whims. One time he threw a temper tantrum in the dining room and grabbed a steak with his hand and threw it on the ground. It made me want to throttle him. But, in general, he didn't interfere with us; he followed after his mother. On the other hand, Aunt Charito liked meddling and giving her opinion. After that first argument, however, she was more discreet. Of course, she didn't mention the subject of José Raimundo. On the afternoon walks she became philosophical and talked about religion and death. She would look at, for instance, the sunset and say: "How can there be people who do not believe in the existence of God! It's impossible for there to be a sincere atheist. Impossible!" I dared to contradict her, not everyone has received His grace, which allows them to believe; the Catholic doctrine itself supports it . . . "True," she said, and nevertheless, the twilight, the vast horizon, filled with red clouds, which she contemplated with her arms crossed, in rapture . . . We stayed silent. At times, Aunt Charito's passion was contagious.

—What time do you have?, you ask, without lifting your eyes from your sewing.

—It's still early. Five of nine.

We were on the top of a hill and in the background you could see the narrow creek, with deep water, that slowly licked the branches of the willows. One afternoon we got onto a raft of rotting planks, in swimsuits, and Aunt Charito started screaming at us, hysterically, from the shore, to come back, that the raft could break. To upset her, Verónica, who was a very good swimmer, began to rock the raft, and you clung to me shrieking with fright. I swim perfectly, but that afternoon I was afraid, filled with fear and revulsion at the idea of falling into the cold, slow-moving water, teeming with fish that would suddenly leap near us, without our being able to see them (we only saw them circle on the surface; in the depths we imagined slimy creatures, tadpoles, larvae, the mud on the bank would crumble when we tried to get out, eroded by moisture, roots resembling snakes). Verónica anticipated my fear and prolonged the ride, full of sadistic joy. Only your crying was able to reach her, at last, and she brought the raft closer to shore. "Don't joke that way again," pleaded Charito, her nerves shaken. Verónica, without paying her any mind, submerged herself with one leap and swam to the opposite bank. "Get in!" she shouted from there, clinging to some roots, but you said that you swam very badly and I didn't want to get in. The mud in the creek produced an insurmountable revulsion in me.

—How strange!, you say. It got pretty late.

You start to abandon your sewing. You look toward the dining room. Then you decide that you have nothing else to do, that this work is the best for easing impatience. The clock, a few minutes late, chimes nine times.

—You see?, I say, It's not that late.

When we returned to Santiago, my father had become significantly worse. Insomnia kept him from getting any rest. At the dinner table he would drum his fingers and stare into the void. At times, the pace would increase and become troubling. Foods seemed bland to him, after trying two or three bites, he would push the plate away with an expression of disgust. "Don't eat, if you don't want to, but don't leave plates in the middle of the table." His only response, the increasing pace of his fingers. It's not that he didn't want to respond; it's that he hadn't heard a single syllable. He forgot the most fundamental things—putting on a tie, buttoning his pants—and spoke with little coherence. His habit of walking the halls at night and inopportunely entering bedrooms had gotten worse. No one was able to sleep anymore. Once when

I woke up at three in the morning we argued bitterly; I locked my door in his face, trembling with rage. I have the impression that he was on the other side of the door for a long time, stunned, without managing to move, hazily remembering that he'd argued with someone, with whom, about what . . .

We missed Verónica, who stayed in the country. She alone could save us from the infinite, penniless (there was never money in the house) boredom, before the start of classes. We traveled all around the city on foot, often even reaching the nearby hills or the open country. On afternoons that were beginning to grow shorter, wandering through a forest or field where urbanization projects were plotting the courses of future streets or along the slopes of a hill, we discussed every conceivable topic. You said that men were a burden, that you would never get married, that all of my mother's insinuations and anxieties produced in you the opposite effect of what she wanted. Your entrance into the University was settled and you announced that you were going to make a living teaching. However poorly they paid. You didn't need much to live. I mentioned that I hadn't thought about getting married either. Perhaps we could live together; although we might not earn much, two incomes would be combined. We would have to set aside a monthly fund for travel, of course. You found that the travel fund wasn't a bad idea. I wasn't wrong. Although one might earn more than the other, you more than I, the money would be shared and we would use the travel fund equally. "Or differently. If one wants to travel and the other doesn't . . ." Differently. Independence would be fundamental; a firm agreement; no one would try to impose rules, set curfews, rituals of any kind. Questions would be prohibited. We were going to undermine the order my mother sought to establish, otherwise unsuccessfully, despite her futile complaints. We would carry the refusal of that order to its ultimate consequences. "Don't you think?" Were you entirely sure? You would say yes, of course. "Wonderful!" I shouted, raising my arms, elated. The night came too soon, the cold wind of the mountains, and you suggested going back. Hunger was nagging at us. We imagined in advance a disappointing alphabet soup or a plate of spinach; at that time, a fried egg over spinach would have been quite an extravagance.

Translated by Lisa Boscov-Ellen

*

FROM *EL MUERTE DE MONTAIGNE*
(THE DEATH OF MONTAIGNE)
[A NOVEL]

Michel de Montaigne, incidentally, was a marvelous reader. In the Latin American world there are only three or four writers who read, who connect with the history of literature, who converse with the dead (to quote don Francisco de Quevedo), in a comparable manner, akin to his. I think of Jorge Luis Borges, of the Brazilian Joaquim Maria Machado de Assis, of Alfonso Reyes. I think of them and their origin, their relatives, more numerous than one would think, of their progeny. I don't know which Spaniards we might cite: Cervantes, Quevedo, Gracián, Azorín, José Ortega y Gasset? In my adolescence and in my early adulthood, as some people know, I read Azorín with delight, whose short works quoted Montaigne once in a while. Brevity, by the way, was an intention or a weakness to which both writers confessed. Later I abandoned the reading of Azorín in a foolish, probably sectarian way. And now I come to the conclusion that there was an aesthetic itch in his prose, an affectation, a verbal coquetry, which wears thin over time. Even in Borges, suddenly a similar coquetry appears from somewhere. Not, on the contrary, in Alfonso Reyes. One could argue that Alfonso Reyes is the strongest prose writer of all, but this, perhaps, is an abuse on my part. Regarding the writing of the Lord of the Mountain, we might say that it's an astonishingly natural, playful writing, of unparalleled rhythm, predisposed to somewhat disjointed digressions, fragmented almost by definition. Suddenly, without saying "heads up!" he inserts a note that's crude, dissonant, sharp. In this respect, Montaigne is less formal, less cautious, than any of the writers I've referenced above. Furthermore, he frequently introduces dissonance, sets up the effect of surprise, through a quotation. Surreptitiously. As though an indiscreet muse might have whispered something in his ear. For example, he reminds us that Horace, one of his favorite Latin poets, raises the following question: does lack of literacy make one's member less hard? Interesting question, which has a certain and definitive answer. In the opera by Dimitri Shostakovich, Lady Macbeth, the great provincial lady, in love with a worker at her husband's factory, is, without knowing it, proof of what Horace suggests. The worker was less literate, but his manly attributes, as Montaigne would say, were more compelling.

Judging from my own journey through the essays, which often repeat themselves, which tend to relapse, Montaigne's preferred readings are more or less known. Among essayists, ethicists, historians, in a prominent place, in the front row, are Plutarch and Seneca. Austerity and stoicism from Seneca; from Plutarch, the power of his depictions, sentences sculpted with a chisel. A language without fat, without appendages, of stainless steel. Successive and fragmentary writers, who one can start reading from any point. He didn't feel the same identification with or the same affection for Ciceronian discourse. He had the impression that Cicero was bombastic, full of himself, and that his great verbal jabs usually fell a little wide of the mark. He loved, however, Horace's concise, sharp verse, and deep prolonged harmonies, and he felt dazzled by Virgil's lyric tirades. We, ignorant, read the Virgilian strophes cited by Montaigne, those marvelous strophes, and are left flabbergasted. He prefers the *Georgics*, and suggests that in certain passages of the *Aeneid* the author neglected to take it up a notch. He uses an ancient word, *pigne*, which I don't find in my dictionaries, but the *pignon* is a cogwheel that serves to move another wheel. In short, another turn of the cogwheel, of the *pigne* or the *pignon*, valid advice for us all.

I have already said something about the literary succession of Michel de Montaigne and now I'm in a position to add some more detail, some detail that is more than a detail. Montaigne had a sense of nature, of the natural, which touched many things, which influenced his way of being, his style, his way of composing essays and even his manner of writing essays and well-structured, meticulously composed non-literary texts. He maintains somewhere that he is a "naturalist," before that word was invented to apply to men of science dedicated to the study of the natural sciences. That said, what could be defined, essentially, as love for nature, respect for the natural, often leads our figure to express himself bluntly, with minimal affectation. His literary heirs, abundant, diverse, present in the most unexpected areas, did not always understand this aspect of Montaigne's prose, which sometimes stemmed directly from the Latin and Greek classics, but which also related, in another way, by other means, to the rural world around him. We have already seen, for example, that when Montaigne criticizes the know-it-alls, the idolaters of knowledge, among whom, in his completely naïve opinion, figured Pierre

Eyquem, his father, he references Horace without major bias, who pondered whether by being less literate a person would have a more flaccid member. In this respect, Azorín, fussy, skittish, lean in body and soul, wouldn't follow the master in any way. Gustave Flaubert, who kept his essays as bedside reading, probably so. Guy de Maupassant, his spiritual—and perhaps corporeal (as some academic gossips suggest)—son as well. André Gide—elegant, aloof, modern, and classic—less so, but for different reasons than Azorín, given that his relationship with, let's say, the male member, his awareness in that regard, his point of view, were different.

The side that's dirty, mischievous, sensual, provocative, in the Lord of the Mountain's prose appears in many of his anecdotes. The essays consist of interspersed, interwoven reflections and anecdotes, which emerge from the ardor of writing and which come, in many cases, from the personal memory of the author, and in others, from his favorite books, from the library on the third floor of his tower. He tells a story—I don't know now whether regarding inebriation or some other matter—that took place in his region some years ago. A fairly young widow, a peasant, rural, with generous curves, went to a party in the countryside. She tried wines from the new harvest, she became quite animated, and on the way back she fell asleep under some bushes. She didn't remember much the following day, but after a few weeks she realized that she was pregnant. We assume that she was spread out at the edge of the path and that her skirts, rumpled, hiked up, would have revealed the hint of some tempting thighs. The widow, wasting no time, issued a notice, that is, she posted papers on doors, in squares, town halls, in which she claimed she would marry the person who came forward and confessed to being the perpetrator of the crime. A young farmhand from the area around her village came forward, confessed, and together they lived as a happy couple for many years. I imagine that Michel de Montaigne would watch them go by from the vantage point of his tower, beneath beams engraved with phrases of his favorite Latin authors, arm in arm, speaking excitedly and he would smile, content, grateful for life. With a pen in his hand, perhaps.

Jules Michelet, the great nineteenth century historian of the French Revolution, of the History of France, of Joan of Arc, of Henry IV, of Louis XI, of so many things and so many people, passionate, ebullient, romantic, admired Michel de Montaigne's prose, he couldn't help admiring it, but he felt very little affection for the author. He argued that he, Michelet, was the historian of *la foule*, the masses, the multitudes, the people, and that Montaigne, on the other hand, was the historian of himself. In other words, Michelet was an epicist, a rhapsode, a visionary, a creator of worlds, while Montaigne (his Montaigne) was a subjectivist, an intimist, a dandy, completely indifferent to popular voices. I've heard arguments in this vein many times and referring to many writers. Of course, I always fare badly. To put it another way, the subjectivist, the intimist, the limited, is I. Do you think, from here on out, I'm going to maintain that I am Montaigne, as they say Flaubert declared, that *Madame Bovary c'est moi*? Sorry to disappoint you, but I'm not a madman who from remote, dreadful Chile (as the other said), believes himself to be Michel de Montaigne. You're not going to catch me in this unspeakable weakness. No, gentlemen.

But the story about the young widow who got drunk at a party in the countryside, of the notice she issued, of their marital happiness over the years, opens up a whole new world to us. Not in the manner of Jules Michelet, the epicist: in another way. Michelet's narrative prose moves enormous masses, human strength that suddenly seems more than human. When he describes the events of 1588 in France, during the decline of Henry III and the Valois dynasty, at the time of religious wars, on the eve of the arrival of Henry IV of Navarre and the Bourbons to the throne, and relates the steps that Philip II of Spain's Invincible Armada is taking, what happens with his hundred and fifty-odd ships of great importance off the Breton coast, and Elizabeth of England's defensive preparations, and the consequences that the victory of the Invincible might have had for France and for all of Europe, we witness an enormous movement, a grand drama. The Invincible Armada, carrying in its core the Spanish inquisitional darkness, is, in Michelet's narrative, a gigantic bird, spreading its black, ominous wings, over all of northern France and the British Isles. And when Queen Elizabeth descends from a white horse and announces the disaster of the enemy fleet, the English soldiers fall to their knees, weep with emotion, revere their still-beautiful monarch of fifty years of age. It is an opera on a global scale, an astonishing scene. And yet, the thighs of the young widow, who in her misfortune found her happiness, do not move me any less. Montaigne's smile persists, prevails, overcomes all. We have an organ, Montaigne says, that does not always obey us, that leaves us high and dry at the least opportune times, that answers only to itself. Here there are no palaces like El Escorial, no invincible armadas, no white horses of significance. We find ourselves in the realm of the individual soul, and of the body, no less individual. A kidney stone lying across the urethral canal can send us straight to hell in life. During his trip to Italy, and during his 1588 trip to Paris and Chartres on horseback, Montaigne, because of his repeated kidney stones, was subjected to unbearable suffering. The Invincible sailed along the course of its black destiny, and he, on his horse, was sweating from a cold pain. One of the stones that he passed, according to his detailed description, had the exact shape of his phallus in miniature. Can we contrast a phallus in miniature to the massive movements Michelet recounted? No, probably, and, in some sense, yes. Montaigne, from his tower, from his distance, glimpses the fires of Saint Bartholomew's Day, the commotion of battles, the crimes in alleys or in palace verandas. And Michelet, suddenly, precisely, renders a single dignified brushstroke of Montaigne, unforgettable. When he tells, for example, that Louis XVI, already at the gallows, approached a corner, looked at the crowd attending his execution and released a terrible "moo."

They are startling, profound episodes, that cut through us like daggers. For my part, at the end of the readings, opening pages, suddenly closing books, I always return, with delight, with true voluptuousness, to the acerbic, sardonic, incisive, harsh style of the Lord of the Mountain. In one of the essays, a character with an intense, gallant, adventurous life approaches his old age, his retirement, and decides to marry a prostitute who is also on the path to retirement. Once married, Montaigne asserts, they'll be able to greet each other every morning, with good reason, in the following manner:

> *Good morning, whore.*
> *Good morning, cuckold.*

Translated by Lisa Boscov-Ellen

•

FROM *PERSONA NON GRATA*
[A NOVEL]

We got into Meléndez's chocolate-colored Volkswagen, the same car that had taken me off to meet Fidel the night I arrived in Havana. My Alfa, driven by Isidoro, followed.

The Ministry of Foreign Relations was located in a building whose Greek columns and neoclassical sobriety made it resemble every millionaire's mansion in Latin America—and in fact it had once belonged to a sugar magnate. There were three or four lighted windows in the building that night, and two Alfa Romeos parked beside the entrance. In the shadows I made out the darker figures of several soldiers armed with machine guns.

My aide in the Protocol section, who had often attended me before, led me to the diplomats' reception room. After that piece of paper that had been handed me in my hotel room, I could well imagine the nature of this untimely summons. I was exhausted, and depressed, but during the three-minutes' wait for the minister I managed to collect my energies and calm myself. The door opened and the aide showed me into the minister's office.

Standing in the middle of the room, dressed in olive-green fatigue uniforms and with pistols strapped to their waists, Fidel Castro and Raúl Roa were awaiting me.[1] Fidel gestured to a place on the couch and when I was seated took the chair to my left. Roa had always been cordial with me, and we had gotten on well, but now he was extremely tense and serious-looking. According to the notes I made three or four days later, I had entered the Ministry building at exactly 11:25 P.M. I will now try to reproduce that meeting, which though one or another detail may escape me is forever engraved on my memory.

"You recall our conversation that first night that you arrived," began the Prime Minister.

"Of course!" I replied.

---

1 In Geneva, Raúl Roa later told a mutual friend of ours, Vicente Girbau, a publisher and international diplomat from Spain, that he, Roa, had been wearing a dark blue suit and a tie. "Tell Edwards he made a mistake," he told Girbau. I don't know whether he was serious or joking, but I do know that my memory would have to be playing grave tricks on me if he was serious. Unless by calling attention to the one "false" detail Roa had wanted to confirm all the rest.

"That night I took quite a liking to you. I enjoyed that conversation, and I was, as you will recall, quite courteous. But now I must tell you that we were mistaken about you. Because you have shown yourself to be a person hostile to the Cuban Revolution! And hostile to the Chilean Revolution as well! From the first day, you allowed yourself to be surrounded by counterrevolutionary elements, enemies of the Revolution, persons whose interest it was that you be given a negative view of the current Cuban situation, so that you might communicate those views to Chile. We learned all this immediately. As you will fully understand, it would have been stupid of us not to have kept you under a degree of surveillance. We have followed every detail of your meetings, your walks, your conversations—we have followed your every step. By the time of the arrival of the *Esmeralda*, I was already quite well informed about you, and you will have noted that I made my displeasure with you evident when I shook your hand on the deck of the ship. Now, after the warmth I showed you on the day of your arrival, I did not want to let you leave without telling you how deeply displeased and disappointed we have been by your behavior here. We should, no doubt, have declared you *persona non grata*, but we didn't want to do that; it would have damaged our relations with Chile. But you should know that we have communicated our opinion of your mission here to Salvador Allende."

Fidel seemed to want to make his point about his irritation and end the conversation there. He supposed, I imagine, that the news that I had been reported to Salvador Allende would be a mortal blow to me, at least as far as my career was concerned, and that I would be dumbstruck by it. I think that mistaken belief stemmed in the final analysis from his ignorance of Chile and the Chilean way of life. In Chile one can survive even inside the administration in spite of the enmity of the head of state.[2]

I took advantage of the first pause that offered, and I said:

"Prime Minister, I don't think I have allowed myself to be surrounded by a group of counterrevolutionaries, as you call them. I am a writer first and a diplomat second, and I have socialized with the Cuban writers who are friends of mine, and who have been my friends since before my diplomatic

---

2   This sentence was written, according to the dates in my notebooks, in April 1972—a year and a half before the military coup d'état.

posting here, from the time I first came to Cuba as a guest of the Casa de las Américas in January 1968—in some cases, since even before that. I am convinced that I have not met with any counterrevolutionary or enemy of the Revolution. It may be that these friends have critical views of the Revolution's present moment; but there is a very clear difference to me between an intellectual who criticizes a regime and a counterrevolutionary or an agent of the enemy."

Fidel was listening gravely. Suddenly, in fury, he interrupted me and began to openly attack. In spite of this, I insisted that he let me continue, and finally, led perhaps by curiosity to learn my version of things, he did.

"With regard to my alleged hostility to the Cuban Revolution," I went on, "I can tell you, Prime Minister, that the major difficulties I have experienced in my diplomatic career have been due precisely to my support for the Cuban Revolution. In 1965 and 1966, after relations were broken off, at a time when you were violently attacking the Frei government, I was the only South American diplomat in Paris[3] who maintained ties with the Cuban Embassy. The American invasion of the Dominican Republic occurred, and I signed the manifesto published by Cuban intellectuals. My signature appeared in *Le Monde*, and that, as you may imagine, did not sit very well with my boss, the ambassador from the Frei regime. During those years I accepted an invitation from the Casa de las Américas and I came to Cuba in early 1968 even though relations had been broken off between Chile and Cuba and even though I was a career diplomat for the government of Chile. It is true that Gabriel Valdés, who was at that time our minister of foreign relations, approved my trip, but that didn't keep the trip from causing no end of headaches for me at the time and later. My immediate superiors very much disapproved of my coming here, and I suffered a setback in my career because of it. And during all those years I was a contributor to the magazine *Casa de las Américas* and corresponded constantly with its editors. How can you say, given all this, that I have been hostile to the Cuban Revolution?"

I looked at Raúl Roa out of the corner of my eye; he was very serious, watching me, not saying a word. He had always been, as I say, very cordial to me; I felt, therefore, that this scene must be more unpleasant and perhaps

---

3   At the time I was the first secretary of the Chilean Embassy.

more dangerous for him than for anyone else. I never learned, and probably never will learn, what thoughts, what reactions my words provoked in him. Fidel, on the other hand, was following me intently, and his expression hid nothing of what he was thinking and feeling.

"That said, Prime Minister," I continued, "I must explain to you what happens to a Chilean of good faith, a person who has never skimped on his friendship for the Cuban Revolution, who arrives in Cuba today as the representative of the Unidad Popular. A Chilean reads in the situation of Cuba today one of the possibilities of his own country's future. To speak with complete frankness, I think it is only natural that this Chilean not particularly enjoy contemplating that future as it may be seen in the situation of Cuba today. Nor would the people of Cuba have much enjoyed contemplating that future if they had been able to anticipate in 1959 what Cuba would be like in 1971—if, for example, twelve years of a revolution had passed in Ecuador or some other country in Latin America and the Cuban people had been able to look at it and find there the situation that I have found in Cuba today. Because I recall very vividly the predictions that were made in Cuba in 1966 and 1967 about the economy of Cuba in 1970. A huge economic boom was predicted, a boom that would banish forever the specter of foreign economic dependency. There was to be a sensational increase in agricultural production, and it was promised that Cuba would export coffee, that no sugar harvest after 1970 would be less than ten million tons."

Fidel stood up in uncontrollable irritation.

"And you don't know the problems that Cuba has had to face! You don't realize that we have been subjected to a merciless blockade, that the most savage imperialist regime in history lies eighty miles off our coast! You seem not to want to recognize that the sole desire of Yankee imperialism is to destroy us, wipe us off the face of the earth, destroy the Cuban Revolution and all it stands for to the nations of the earth, and that this Yankee imperialist government is the richest and most powerful regime that has ever existed!"

"But I do recognize that," I said. "That is why I wouldn't want to see Chile go through the same experience."

"And do you think the Chilean experiment is going to be so easy?" Fidel broke in. "Do you think that the reactionary forces in Chile will fail to organize themselves, with the direct aid and support of the Yankee imperialists?

Haven't you heard of the Djarkata Plan?[4] So far Allende has only conquered the government—which means he has only breached the first walls of power. When the inner bastion begins to give, the confrontation will be inevitable."

In other words, the Chilean Revolution was still to be won. The electoral process, our historical innovation, was but a prelude, an apparently favorable accident, although it could well turn out to be a two-edged sword. If Allende was not to bog down in the quicksand of constitutionality, his only alternative was to radicalize the process, take it to the point of rupture. It must be granted that when the MIR faction cooled before September 1970, Fidel allowed Allende to play his electoral trump, but this didn't mean that Chile had discovered the formula for a peaceful transition to socialism. Far from it. The Chilean situation had not led Fidel to revise his theories, as some people naïvely thought, but rather to refine them, and to confirm them by another route. I recalled that phrase from our first encounter: "If you Chileans need help, just ask for it. We may not be much good at producing, but we're great at fighting!"

Later, during his visit to Chile, it was at first believed that Fidel really had changed.

But all it took was the "empty pot" demonstration[5] (pots well salted with personal insults against Fidel from the right-wing press), and the Comandante, who theretofore had shown his most conciliatory face in all his public statements, became the Fidel of old. At the end of that day, the protest of the furious housewives, banging their pots and pans in the streets of Santiago, had turned into real street battles between the followers and the enemies of the government. He spent the night of the demonstration beside his machine gun, surrounded by his own armed guards, waiting with exasperated patience, in the internationalist spirit of Latin American revolution, for the Chilean government to ask him for help. But Allende kept his head, and the next

----

4   Rumors of the existence of the so-called "Djarkata Plan" appeared often in the newspapers at this time. This was allegedly a plan by the CIA to organize right-wing death squads to kill Communists in Indonesia (and, by extension, any country) should there by a left-wing coup.

5   During which a large number of middle- and upper-class Chileans, especially housewives, demonstrated against Castro and the Allende government by banging on empty pots, which symbolized the economic chaos of those years. These demonstrations became frequent in the last years of Allende and caused much concern among the Unidad Popular government.

morning Fidel discovered, to his rather noisily expressed surprise, that a reg-
ular-army general was in charge of the state of emergency. Chile was hopeless! In the National Stadium, while some members of his audience got up
and left after the hours of Fidel's speechifying that they were wholly unused
to, Fidel confessed that he was leaving Chile "even more radical" than he'd
come, and "more of a revolutionary" than ever. He attempted to demonstrate
this renewed revolutionary zeal later by inviting Miguel Henríquez, leader of
the MIR party, to Cuba shortly afterward, and going to the airport personally
to greet him.

Fidel, in sum, seemed, in spite of certain indications to the contrary, not
to believe in the real possibility of success via the evolutionary, constitutional
route that Chile had chosen. And the most serious thing about all this was,
as one might see from Fidel's reaction to the "empty pot" episode, that Fidel's
lack of confidence might create further problems for Chile. In a film of a
conversation that Fidel had with Allende, one can see Castro acknowledge
that his trip to Chile was a "voyage from one world to another." Yet there was
little indication that he had reached all the possible conclusions from that
observation. Of course such conclusions would have implied more modesty
than Fidel could probably have mustered.

As a Chilean diplomat, and one accused of hostility toward the Cuban
Revolution, I did not think it my place to enter into theoretical discussions
regarding a country's choice of political strategy. Instead, I returned to the
subject of my relationship with the dissident writers, since that was the most
serious charge leveled against me during that singular conversation with the
Cuban head of state at midnight on Sunday, March 21, 1971.

"I refused to turn my back on my friends," I said. "I knew they were
expressing opinions critical of the government, and that their relations with
the government had become somewhat antagonistic, but they have been my
colleagues and my friends for years. I have probably acted more like a writer
than a diplomat. It is quite possible that after this experience, and this conversation, which I am certain I will always see as very important to me, I will
leave the diplomatic service and devote myself to literature. I'd like nothing
better. I recognize that I've been a bad diplomat in Cuba. But I have one
excuse: The real relations between Chile and Cuba have been carried on in
Santiago. My presence here has been only symbolic. I insist, furthermore,

that my writer friends, however much they have criticized the current situation, are neither *gusanos* nor counterrevolutionaries. And I've met with writers of every stamp, you know, not just with the most critical ones."

"That much is true," Fidel interrupted. "We know that you have been in contact with writers on our side."

I had noted that in one way or another one would often be reminded of the efficiency of secret-police surveillance. The little book about the case of the Mexican diplomat, the TV program on the "CIA operative" Olive, the speech by the Dominican journalist in which he publicly confessed that he was a double agent, were all manifestations of that reminder. With this last statement, Fidel had not only demonstrated his personal knowledge of my "case" (for incredible as it might seem to a peaceful citizen of Chile, my stay in Havana had become a "case" within a socialist country), but also that the agents of State Security were very efficient at their jobs.

"But let's take the case of Heberto Padilla," I then said. "His criticism is always predicated on a standpoint within the Left. He once quoted Enrique Lihn to me, who said that when one leaves Cuba, the Revolution begins to grow larger and more imposing as one looks at it from a greater distance. Heberto talked to me about a period of volunteer labor he had done on a citrus farm, about a year ago. The leader of the project was, according to Heberto, the perfect example of the revolutionary. He wanted the best for his group, he wanted it to thrive and prosper and to live in the best possible material circumstances, and he had even designed the furniture in the project's living rooms and bedrooms. He made sure there was fresh orange juice every morning for breakfast. And at the same time he was a theorist, a great reader. Padilla cited that case in contrast to others who think that discomfort, carelessness of details, can be remedied with high-sounding phrases."

"Excellent!" said Fidel, for whom the mention of Heberto Padilla produced frank displeasure. "Excellent! But I feel I must tell you that Padilla is a liar. And a turncoat! And, *and*," said Fidel, raising his eyebrows and his index finger, and looking me straight in the eye, "he is *ambitious*."

He fell silent after this last phrase, as though giving me time to draw all the appropriate conclusions. It was true that Padilla was given to suggesting the existence of certain mysterious links between himself and secret higher powers. He had given me to understand on more than one occasion that he stayed afloat relatively successfully thanks to the power struggles between factions within the government. Whenever he made these suggestions, he would laugh uproariously and look very self-satisfied.

I always thought, and continue to think, that Heberto's ravings were no more than a game of vanity he played, mostly with himself. Fidel's last phrase, though, intrigued me. It confirmed, of course, that in early 1971 there actually was an underground factional power struggle going on. Had Heberto taken part in this struggle somehow? What fantastic version of things had been reported to Fidel? And how had my own actions, Heberto's contacts with me, been used?—for one had to wonder whether those contacts had intentionally, and with some mysterious plan, been made easier by that hidden hand which had sufficient power to assign people rooms in the Habana Riviera. The list of mysteries in this book, mysteries for which I can only give the most hypothetical sort of explanations, is already long. The fact is that I had learned no more than a few hours ago that Heberto had been arrested, and I was trying, out of conviction and out of simple friendship, but without much real hope, to help him.

"I insist on one thing, Prime Minister," I said. "I am convinced that Heberto Padilla is not an agent for anybody. He is a difficult man, I'll grant you—he is willful, and capricious, and he has a sharp critical bite. But he has never been anything but a man of the Left, and his criticism has come from the Left. And the relationship between the state and the writer has never been anything but troubled, anyway. It can't help but be. The *raison d'être* of the State and the *raison d'être* of poetry contradict one another. Plato said that one should listen to the beautiful words of poets, one should crown poets, anoint them, and then carry them outside the republic's walls the next day. He knew that if they stayed inside they'd cause nothing but trouble! But Plato intended his words ironically, too, since he was not only a philosopher but something of a poet as well. And socialism will just have to learn to live with its writers. That is important for the writers, but it is even more important for socialism."

"And you think that there are real poets in Cuba?" the prime minister asked.

He seemed to have serious doubts about that, but he did not consider himself the best person to decide the issue—not because he did not trust his own critical judgment (I suspect, on the contrary, that his was the only critical judgment he did trust) but because he didn't want to run the risk that an over-generalized and relatively negative pronouncement from him as to the quality of Cuban literature should later be quoted by me.

"We recognize that it has now become quite fashionable in Europe," he said, "among those that call themselves leftist intellectuals, to attack us. We don't care about that! Those attacks mean absolutely nothing to us! Until now we've had no time in Cuba, faced as we've been by the immense amount of revolutionary work to be done—and that needed our *immediate* attention—to worry about the problems of culture. Now we will begin to work at creating a popular culture, a culture for the people and by the people. The little group of bourgeois writers and artists that has been so active, or at least talked so much, up till now, without creating anything that's been of any real worth, will no longer have anything to do in Cuba. Look—every socialist country has come at some point in its development to the stage that we have come to now. The Soviet Union first and China not long ago, with the Cultural Revolution. There's no socialist country that hasn't passed through a stage like this, a stage in which the old bourgeois culture, which managed to hang on after the Revolution, is supplanted by the new culture of socialism. The transition is hard, but as I say, the bourgeois intellectuals are no longer of any interest to us. None! I'd a thousand times rather Allende had sent us a miner than a writer, I'll tell you."

Fidel would not expressly mention Stalin, but his suggestion was clear, perhaps in order to intimidate me, and through me my Cuban friends, and to warn us all that the cultural policy of the Revolution was entering its Stalinist phase. He knew what hackles this would raise in Europe, and among precisely those intellectuals who had previously supported Cuba enthusiastically, and he was declaring from the outset that criticism from that quarter, even an all-out attack, would not change his course one jot. He knew, too, that the criticism had already begun; at this point he opted to take the offensive and precipitate the rupture himself. The pretext, as always, was the need to lay the foundations for a proletarian culture. Why hadn't Allende sent him a miner? It occurred to me that a Chilean copper miner, some worker from the mines at Chuqui or El Teniente, would have been even more disillusioned than I at seeing the absenteeism, the volunteer work turned forced labor, the unpaid hours, the long, grave faces in the lines in Old Havana, the broken and potholed streets, the cracked and peeling walls, the broken windows. But I couldn't be insulting, even if Fidel was; I had to keep the discussion on another plane.

"It's true that there's a certain leftist fashion," I said, "but I, personally, have been pretty reluctant to follow political and literary fashions."

Fidel was disconcerted by the *sangfroid* of my replies, and the tone of the conversation, in spite of his aggressiveness, had begun to change. I took advantage of the moment to bring the talk around to more personal topics. I gave Fidel a history of my education, in order to try to make him understand that I had arrived by a process of natural, organic evolution at my left-wing stance, and that it was not some intellectual fad I had just recently taken up. My early and perhaps emotional rejection of my Jesuit education (the same education Fidel had received) had become more rational, more intellectual. Teenage reading had led me to refutations of those proofs of the existence of God that my professors of apologetics gave us, and from that to losing my religious faith was a short step.

"It's rare to lose one's faith through a purely logical process," Fidel interrupted.

"There was a rejection of Catholicism, at least as it was taught and practiced at the time, that was instinctive, of course, and not at all rational, but the arguments of modern philosophers gave the rejection a rational coherence. I think the strongest motivation after that was my support for Latin American nationalism. I performed my first political act when I joined a demonstration to protest the invasion of Guatemala in 1953 or 1954."

"You must have been pretty young!" Fidel said, his voice surprised and almost friendly.

I smiled.

"Later, as I said, I began, very, very enthusiastically, to follow the Cuban Revolution. After the Twentieth Communist Party Congress in the Soviet Union, when the Soviets were in the full swing of de-Stalinization, Cuba seemed to me to be setting an example for a different sort of socialism. That example thrilled a lot of us. It's true that the period that you are talking about now, the period that you now see as a necessary step in the evolution of the Cuban Revolution, has been taken in every socialist experiment. But that doesn't mean that it's inevitable, much less desirable. On the contrary. We must not abandon the quest for another kind of socialism. That, in fact,

is the significance of the Chilean experiment. Marx tried to find a way to
the integrated liberation of man, liberation at every level and in every aspect
of life; no true socialist, no socialist of good faith, can give up on that ideal
without falling into the blackest kind of pessimism. Remember that the entire
intellectual thrust of Marxism is to dissolve the repressive apparatus of the
state. One of its primary concerns was peace in Europe. Marx lived in an
age of wars between nations, he was intimately familiar with the Prussian
state, and he had come to the conclusion that the main causes of war were
bourgeois states, with their repressive apparatuses that tended to lead them
into conflict with each other, and their struggles for power, and their terri-
torial expansionism. Marx conceived the dictatorship of the proletariat as an
essentially temporary historical stage that would lead to that final stage when
all traces of the bourgeoisie were destroyed or assimilated by the working
class, when the state would be dissolved, and, in consequence, when there
would be peace among the nations. The dictatorship of the proletariat would
of necessity be much less repressive than the dictatorship of the bourgeoisie,
which in Marx's time was totally inhuman, savage; it would be the dictatorship of the vast majority, come to replace the dictatorship of a tiny minority."

"As Marx conceived it," Fidel said, "socialism would triumph first in the
most developed countries—Germany and England. Marx's socialism was
conceived to be applied in the advanced industrial countries of his time. The
factory workers would take over the reins of power and the control of the
means of production. The historical experience of socialism, however, has
been different. And that is why we face the problems that we do in applying
socialism to the challenges of underdevelopment. Believe me, there are very
serious problems, and you Chileans will be facing them very soon yourselves."

At this stage of our conversation, we had both stood and were pacing
the office. The atmosphere had lightened considerably. I insisted that I had
acted in good faith, with no ulterior motives or underhandedness—though I
confessed that I had not always acted with the tact essential to any diplomat.

"Yes," Fidel said at one point, "I believe you. I wish we'd had this conversation before. I think it might have helped. But one is always so very busy.
How can one find time? The problem is that I have already sent a message
about you to Allende."

I said nothing. Fidel seemed to think that the news of his accusation
would crush me. He looked at me out of the corner of his eye as he paced

with long strides back and forth across the room. But what could Allende do
to me? He could order me home to Chile, which would neither frighten nor
displease me. He couldn't throw me out of the diplomatic service without
the required administrative hearings and an order to that effect signed by
the Comptroller-General. The subtleties of our bourgeois institutions! And
if he did manage to have me expelled from the service, he could hardly keep
me from breathing, living, writing, publishing whatever I felt like, at least
at the current stage of our own Revolution—a stage which Fidel, without
the slightest doubt and in fact precisely because of this "softness," scorned,
and considered essentially fragile and temporary. When he realized that I
was basically indifferent to his charges, Fidel reacted very naïvely—unless, of
course, he astutely proposed to explore an area that had so far not been dealt
with in our conversation.

"I see you don't care about Allende," he said. "But you do care about
Neruda. I'll report you to Neruda!"

I smiled again. I refused to tell him that the Cubans had already denounced Neruda himself, and that they had spread the denunciation to the
four corners of the globe, in a campaign they had never used even against
their worst enemies. Fidel knew that perfectly well, and so he knew that the
idea of "accusing me to Neruda" was pure bravado. During this part of our
interview, as we paced in opposite directions—Fidel had the habit of walking
while he talked, especially at crucial moments of the conversation, and so did
I—back and forth across the office of the minister of foreign relations, who
was observing us in absolute silence, something quite funny happened. Fidel
was talking about Cuban agriculture, and he contended that back in the days
of the Sierra Maestra he had been the only person to oppose an agricultural
reform based on the mere subdivision of land, with the aid of a system of
cooperatives. That, he said, would create a privileged, and profoundly conser-
vative, class of campesinos.

"Yet I was in Princeton, Prime Minister," I put in, "studying international
policy, when you went to the United States in early 1959, and I remember your
speech to a group of students and professors there very well. You spoke there,
in English, about an agrarian reform that would create new property owners,
a step which you said showed how original and distinct the Cuban Revolution
was in comparison with the Soviet Union. And you added that that new class
of campesino property owners, as they emerged from the backwardness that

had been their lot up to then, would create an excellent market for Cuban as well as for American industry."

Fidel stopped short and looked at me in amazement.

"It wasn't at Princeton," he said, looking at Raúl Roa. "It was at Yale or someplace. I don't remember too well anymore."

"I heard you speak at Princeton, Prime Minister," I insisted, imperturbably.

"It wasn't Yale?" Fidel asked Roa.

After a moment's silence, Roa, who spoke no other word the entire night, said: "It was Princeton."

Fidel then looked at me wide-eyed, in an expression approaching or pretending to approach childlike wonder, and went from the formal *usted* to *tú*.

"And you were there!" he exclaimed.

At another point in the conversation I spoke to him about Chile's criticism of his government. I told him that on the Chilean Left, sharp criticism was the norm. It was precisely this habit of sharp criticism that had brought the Unidad Popular to power. Criticism of reactionary regimes had led to the electoral triumph of the Left. But this habit of criticism wouldn't just go away, just stop, from one moment to the next, I said, simply because a popular government was in power. Besides, Chilean experts who had worked in Cuba had taken away a very critical view of the Cuban situation.

"But they never aired those views outside!" Fidel exclaimed.

"Nor have I," I replied. "I never invited my writer friends to any of the official receptions I held, in spite of the fact that they were invited to other embassies. Our discussions were strictly private and personal. There is nothing more natural than that a diplomat who is at the same time a writer should get together with his literary brethren in the country he is posted to. That always happens. We writers, especially in Latin America, are almost a family, and people know each other across national borders. How was I supposed to avoid seeing these people in Cuba? Of course we talked, we talked a great deal, and we are by nature a sharp-tongued lot."

"Now I'm even beginning to think," Fidel said, turning to Roa, "that he's a pretty good diplomat!"

Fidel kept returning to the subject of writers, for whom he had what seemed to me a strange distaste.

"Why do you people have to keep appointing writers as diplomats?" he suddenly asked me.

I explained to him about the Chilean tradition of writer-diplomats and politicians: Vicente Pérez Rosales and Alberto Blest Gana.

"Pérez Rosales was active at every step of the building of the Republic," I said. "He was a journalist, a diplomat in Europe charged with handling German emigration, a colonizer of the south, a senator. At the end of his life he wrote his memoirs and produced the best book of his time, better than the work of professional literati. It's as though somebody had taken part in the Revolution and been minister, been put in charge of agriculture in the provinces, been taken into the diplomatic service, and then were to write a book based on his own experience."

"And the book turned out to be better than the writers'," crowed Fidel, who seemed taken with the idea.

"Yes," I said, "but Vicente Pérez Rosales had a real literary calling, frustrated in part by his life as a man of action, and he prepared himself for years for the task of writing."

"You have to send me that book," Fidel said. "Remember that you promised to do that."

I had in fact promised that. It was during the time of the *Esmeralda* visit, and Fidel had just given another demonstration of his prodigious memory.[6]

At another point in the conversation Fidel had asked me, almost sarcastically, if I thought *I* might someday write something worthwhile.

"I've never thought about the subject that way," I said. "I try to be true to my calling as a writer, and to write the best I can. I may never write a book of any real worth, as you put it, but results aren't everything. A writer writes out of certain personal obsessions. When those obsessions coincide with the great issues of a particular historical moment, the result may be a lasting work of art. The artist in that case becomes an interpreter of his or her time. The only thing I can assure you, for my own part, is that for good or ill I will keep writing."

The Prime Minister looked at me in surprise again, as though the imperturbable tone with which I answered him were utterly unheard of. He told me that when I wrote a book I considered worthwhile I should send it to him. He

---

6   Months later, in Paris, I was having lunch with Monsignor Zacchi, who was still papal nuncio in Havana at the time, and I gave him a copy of *Recuerdos del pasado* (*Memories of the Past*) to take for me to the Prime Minister.

promised to read it![7] Later, confirming my impression as to his bewilderment throughout most of our conversation, he said, and these are his exact words: "Do you know what I've been most impressed by in this conversation?"

"What, Prime Minister?"

"Your calmness!"

I raised my eyes and looked straight into his eyes, but I did not say a word.

The last thing he said to me, with great seriousness, before shaking my hand warmly, was that he hoped we'd meet again someday. I understood by those words that he meant that he hoped that in spite of everything I would continue to count myself among the friends of the Revolution.

"I hope so too," I said.

Fidel walked me to the door and closed it slowly after me. The aide from Protocol was still outside in the large reception room waiting for me. I had gone into the minister's office at 11:25. It was now 2:45; the conversation had lasted three hours and twenty minutes.

On the sidewalk outside, near the armed guards, Meléndez was waiting. He'd no doubt assumed that I would emerge from the conversation within minutes of entering, shattered by the Comandante's attacks. I walked up to him calmly, inwardly savoring his perplexity, which he could not altogether mask.

"Well, Meléndez," I said, "Adiós!"

Meléndez looked at me for an instant, his eyes troubled, and then looked quickly to one side. My attitude seemed to indicate that his accusations, his files, his tapes had not been fully successful in landing me among the "bad guys," in some lower circle of the Revolution's Inferno, and that recognition

---

7 The book that followed this conversation was this book. I sent Castro a copy of the first edition, with a respectful dedication that mentioned his request. I sent it by way of a Cuban ambassador in Madrid. I learned later that Carlos Altamirano, the Chilean Socialist politician, had been in the Comandante's office at one point, talking about Chile and other subjects, and the two men's eyes had suddenly, and by pure coincidence, fallen on the book, which had little slips of paper marking some of the pages. "This kind of thing—naturally I don't read this," the Commander-in-Chief said, making a gesture as though to brush it away with his hand and moving quickly on to other subjects. "Naturally"! Other bits and pieces of gossip, however, have made me think that he had read it carefully and even vainly, as he seems to have been irritated by my description of the lined, tired face he showed during our first encounter. As some of my Spanish friends might say, "Read us? We're nobody!"

unnerved him. Something had happened in the world that his philosophy, like Hamlet's friend Horatio's, had not dreamt of.

"Adiós, Edwards," he said, though his eyes were turned away. "Bon voyage!"

I briefed my successor and the consul on the conversation, for the proper functioning of the embassy in the future. My successor stared at me, wide-eyed and pale. I made no comments; they could draw their own conclusions. Fidel had revealed to me, in the course of the conversation, that they had "studied" my replacement and that in their view he was the person "least indicated" for the job who could have come, a person who by temperament and habits would not like Havana.

"He is an old-time diplomat," I had replied, "a man whose career means everything to him. He will try to act professionally. Consequently, he will work to make relations between Cuba and Chile the best that they can possibly be, since his professional success depends on just that."

"You're right," Fidel had finally said.

It was quite likely that my defense would help my colleague; but I said not a word about this part of the interview to him, so as not to make him more nervous than he already was.

There was a note for me on my bed. The young Chilean woman who couldn't take her daughter to Chile was asking for work at the embassy. She hadn't had the courage to ask for work before, but the job would be a lifesaver for her. I suddenly understood the anguish with which she had approached me recently. She, too, naïvely, had believed, as had many others, that I could help her. I called the hotel telephone operator to ask to be waked up at six, and I lay down to try to get a couple of hours' sleep. My bags were packed and sitting at the door. My ticket, my passport, and the keys were on the dresser. I looked out at the ocean, thinking I wouldn't be seeing that ocean again for a long, long time, perhaps a lifetime, and I closed my eyes and tried to sleep.

Translated by Andrew Hurley

WORK

1952, *El patio*, Carmelo Soria Impresor (stories).

1961, *Gente de la ciudad*, Editorial Universitaria (stories).

1965, *El peso de la noche*, Seix Barral (novel).

1967, *Las máscaras*, Seix Barral (stories).

1969, *Temas y variaciones*, Editorial Universitaria (stories).

1973, *Persona non grata*, Barral Editores (novel).

1977, *Desde la cola del dragon*, Dopesa (essays).

1978, *Los convidados de piedra*, Seix Barral (novel).

1981, *El museo de cera*, Bruguera (novel).

1985, *La mujer imaginaria*, Plaza & Janés (novel).

1987, *El anfitrión*, Plaza & Janés (novel).

1990, *Adiós, poeta*, Tusquets (biography).

1992, *Fantasmas de carne y hueso*, Editorial Sudamericana (stories).

1996, *El origen del mundo*, Tusquets (novel).

1997, *El whisky de los poetas*, Alfaguara (journalistic articles).

2000, *El sueño de la historia*, Tusquets (novel).

2002, *Machado de Assis*, Omega (biography).

2003, *Diálogos en un tejado*, Tusquets (journalistic articles).

2004, *El inútil de la familia*, Alfaguara (novel).

2008, *La casa de Dostoievsky*, Planeta (novel).

2011, *La muerte de Montaigne*, Tusquets (novel).

2012, *Los círculos morados*, Lumen (memoirs).

·

ENGLISH TRANSLATIONS

1993, *Persona Non Grata*, translated by Andrew Hurley, Paragon House (novel).

•

AWARDS AND RECOGNITIONS

1962, Premio Municipal de Cuento de Santiago for *Gente de la ciudad*.

1965, Premio Atenea de la Universidad de Concepción for *El peso de la noche*.

1969, Premio Pedro de Oña for *El peso de la noche*.

1970, Premio Municipal de Santiago for *Temas y variaciones*.

1979, Guggenheim Fellowship.

1985, Knight of the French Order of Arts and Letters.

1990, Premio Comillas for *Adiós, poeta*.

1991, Premio Municipal de Ensayo de Santiago for *Adiós, poeta*.

1994, Premio Atenea de la Universidad de Concepción for *Fantasmas de carne y hueso*.

1994, Premio Nacional de Literatura de Chile.

1997, Premio de Ensayo Mundo for *Desde la cola del dragón*.

1999, Premio Cervantes.

1999, Knight of the French Legion of Honor.

2000, Orden al Mérito Gabriela Mistral.

2005, finalist for Premio Altazor for *El inútil de la familia*.

2005, Premio José Nuez Martín for *El inútil de la familia*.

2008, Premio Iberoamericano Planeta, Casa de América de Narrativa for *La casa de Dostoievsky*.

2009, Premio Fundación Cristóbal Gabarrón de las Letras.

2010, Premio ABC Cultural & Ámbito Cultural.

2011, Premio González Ruano de Periodismo.

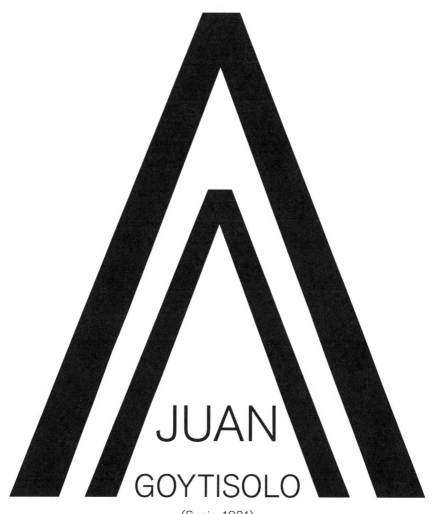

JUAN
GOYTISOLO
(Spain 1931)

Juan Goytisolo, born in Barcelona in January of 1931, was the second of three brothers who were all writers: the poet, José Agustín, passed away in 1999, while Luis is also a fiction writer. Reserved and nomadic, the author of *Juan sin Tierra* is an intellectual who has found his place thanks to his condition as a perpetual foreigner. As he himself has indicated, he was a Castilian in Catalonia, a Catalan in Spain, and now he's a Spaniard in Morroco, a country where he's lived for more than fifteen years.

In 1938, when he was seven, his mother was killed in one of the many nationalist bombings of Barcelona. That Goytisolo's adolescence unfolded replete with the conflict and unease of that period is reflected, naturally, in his first books: *Juegos de manos*, in 1954, and *Duelo en el Paraíso*, in 1955, novels that portray the lives of the young people of those years, saturated in Francoism and seeking to approach reality in a different way.

In 1956 he went to Paris. He worked as a consultant for Gallimard, he married Monique Lange (a close friend of William Faulkner and very well known in the Parisian intellectual and artistic sphere), and struck up friendships with writers like Jean Genet. As the years passed, his time spent in France would be like a door opening onto a new world and closing on another, an experience that inspired Goytisolo and would accompany him forever: it was there that he accepted his homosexual desire and left behind existential subjectivism in order to observe reality from a critical point of view.

That's how the trilogy *El mañana efímero* (composed of the novels *El circo*, 1957; *Fiestas*, 1958; and *La Resaca*, in the same year) was born. In it he sought to offer himself up as a voice of the silenced Spanish people. He also engaged with other genres like the essay (*Problemas de la novela*, 1959) or political reportage (*Pueblo en marcha*, about the Cuban Revolution), in which he always exalts the hyperrealist perspective.

Censored by the Francoists beginning in 1963, in 1966 he started the Álvaro Mendiola trilogy (*Señas de identidad*, 1966; *Reivindicación del conde don Julián*, 1970; and *Juan sin Tierra*, 1975) with which he sought to break away from traditional narrative forms and, at the same time, depict Catholic Spain and the Catalan bourgeoisie, of which, as a dissident writer, he was no longer a member, even though that was his culture and heritage. During that time, he was a professor of literature at universities in California, Boston, and New York, and he was becoming more and more interested in Maghreb.

Beginning in 1980, Goytisolo carried out a study of his origins in autobiographical texts like *Coto vedado* (1985) or *En los reinos de taifa* (1986) in which he offers a personal version of his trajectory as a writer and an alternate vision of Spanish literature itself, conceived more as an encounter of cultures than a lineage. During the '90s he covered the crisis in the Balkans for the newspaper *El País* and those reports are collected in *Cuaderno de Sarajevo* (1993) and *Paisajes de guerra* (2001). In 2003 he said goodbye to fiction with a crepuscular book: *Telón de boca*; but he withdrew his farewell and a few years later he revived an old character, el Monstruo of the Parisian neighborhood Sentier, in *El exiliado de aquí y allá*. A heterodox and chameleonic author, he has received, among others, the Premio Octavio Paz de Poesía y Ensayo (2000), el Formentor (2012), and more recently he was the finalist for the Man Booker Prize for fiction.

THE ACORN

The demiurge of *The Blind Rider* is a compression of my experience. I am about to turn eighty years old and I believe it is the only text in Spanish literature that connects with Calisto's soliloquy in *Tragicomedy of Calisto and Melibea and the old prostitute Celestina*. No character exists that looks right at God and rebukes him for having made the world as it is. This idea was very present in my mind when I wrote this. It is a way of confronting human life absent the protective dome of the divine.

A lament for the loss of your wife, Monique Lange, and the recognition of impermanence?

We had a very intense relationship, despite all the sorrows. It was a brutal loss and then you have to ask yourself: why are we born or, why are we still here? A lot of the time when I see so many dead friends, I say: what am I doing here? Why them and not me? Ever since I reached a certain age I've had the feeling that I'm here and not here. I'm still here but I'm already not here. The end. We are looking for a stairway and we don't know how many stairs we have left in us. I had a very Catholic education and life was always presented to us under the protective dome of the divine, but in *Tragicomedy of Calisto and Melibea and the old prostitute Celestina* it demonstrably does not exist. And this is what has always attracted me to Fernando de Rojas work. It is the most radically negative work of Spanish and Western literature of that time period—there is no equivalent. Shakespeare came much later, at that time it was unique. And you can only really understand this by taking into account the circumstances of Fernando de Rojas life. The Inquisition persecuted his entire family and several of them were burned at the stake while others were subject to public ridicule. How do you explain a twenty-three-year-old man having such a negative vision of the world? Clearly it was this—his experience.

In Conversation with the Dead

My dead are the writers who have survived the test of time. Within Spanish literature those who have indirectly influenced my books, Góngora in *Don Julián*, always Cervantes, San Juan de la Cruz in *The Virtues of the Solitary Bird*. [Joseph] Blanco White was fundamental for me. When I started to read his English work, as I was translating, I had the impression that what I was writing was not a translation, that I was writing it myself. The criticisms he made of the Spain of his time were the same as those I could make of the Spain of my own time. It was almost an exercise of creation. His voice was my voice. And from outside I would say that the authors I have most recently reread have always been very close, Diderot, Tolstoy, Flaubert; I have completely reread the work of all of them. In addition a long catalogue of twentieth century novelists and poets. But I also continue reading the works of young people and I am very open to them. My life is reading and writing and then traveling or walking.

Coda

Jean Genet was someone who believed very much in marginality and he was some-one you admired greatly for his unflagging honesty with respect to literature.

The precise word would be radicality, his radicalism had a great influence on my life. Before I participated in what you might call "the literary life" and after I met him I separated myself completely from that. He would say very clearly that literature is one thing and the literary life another and you have to know how to choose. And I chose. I have always thought that looking in at the center from the periphery is much more interesting than looking out from the center at the periphery. I have always managed to avoid situating myself within the literary scene and studied it in reverse, from an assumed marginalization. Without fitting myself into the canons of religious, nationalist, and ideological orthodoxy. Literature is the area of life as shown to us by Cervantes in the *Quixote* and by Scheherazade in *A Thousand and One Nights*; I believe the writer should never give the readers answers, rather plant in them new doubts.

"History is the realm of the lie. The greatest enemy of the lie is not the truth; it is another lie."

All of our national histories are lies, since Spanish history always begins with the invasion of the Arabs. Then the battle of Guadalete, no one knows if this battle took place or not, or if Saint James who made us win all the battles. Well obviously he was not transported from Lake Tiberias in Palestine to Galicia by angels. It is all legend. This was verified in the Balkans, with Serbian nationalism, that it's all lies on top of lies.

A THOUSAND FORESTS

FROM *The Blind Rider*

[A NOVEL]

Although he avoided a face-to-face encounter in the shadows of nightfall, did he visit him once he'd crossed over?

"I shall tell you in cruel Castilian: you were born to perpetuate oblivion. Grief at loss abates, memory wanes, feelings and affections lose their strength and intensity. It is the law of the world, which I supposedly created and to which you are subject. There is no such thing as an inconsolable child or wife. Those around you will shed some tears over you but your image will dissolve like snow in a glass of water.

You no longer think of her daily and need to look at her photo to bring her to mind. Everything blurs, darkens, and is extinguished. It is my only manifestation of goodness. For if those who belong to your incorrigible species enjoyed the power of telling the future, do you think they'd procreate alien children, grandchildren or great-grandchildren whose behaviour and ideas they wouldn't understand and would be appalled by? If the father of the father who begat you could have imagined what you'd turn into and how you'd write about him, there's no doubt he wouldn't have done his duty, he'd have got off the moving train. All you are today would horrify him. That's why I regularly send you off to push up daisies: to spare you the spectacle of a descendency contrary to your dreams . . ."

The stars weren't still twinkling or were covered in cloud; darkness enveloped him, the patio remained silent and the only sound was a child crying next door, or perhaps on a corner of his side-street. He curled up in the patchwork quilt and let him monologue on.

"You who imagine me blissfully surrounded by my angels and devotees, don't realize it's only the deeds of ill-doers which amuse me. No perversity is alien to me. You are now entertained by televised images of wars, mutilated bodies and the savagery of the soldiery, unaware that I've been enjoying them from the day you conceived me. You are so easily deluded by what your minds concoct!

I know you don't believe in me, but you are powerless before those who do. I exist through them and so it will always be as the centuries clock up.

What I'm saying goes for you and your admired Tolstoy, although he didn't altogether lose his peasant faith: he diluted me into a kind of generic, rather bland entity. Such was his greatness: the intuition or doubt which drew him to the railway station of Astapovo in a third-class train. He wanted to go south, beyond the White Mountains and, in his quest for a coherent end, died before reaching them.

As for you . . ."

"There are no big differences between you and me. Though you were engendered by a droplet of sperm and I was manufactured by dint of speculation and Councils we both hold something primordial in common: non-existence. We are chimera or spectres dreamed up by something other, call it chance, contingency, or caprice. You were still-born and already belong to the kingdom of shadows. I was invented over millennia of Byzantine quarrels and will cease to exist the day the last of your fellows stops believing in me. Each of my imaginary attributes or properties has been the cause of disputes, amendments, clarifications, battles to the death. Am I One, am I a Trinity, am I Merciful? Or a cruel, bloodthirsty monster, an impassive spectator before your evil-doing and outrages? Those who transform me into Supreme Goodness immediately face the problem of the world's merciless brutality. What the devil am I doing up here if I don't stir a finger to halt it? Have I granted myself an interminable holiday or am I blind, insensitive, and useless? It is impossible to resolve that contradiction, however much my invention has been perfected over the passage of time. If I am not that furious Being ravaging all he has created in blood and fire, imposing himself through terror on the consciences of his children, what am I? A bland, anaemic phantom, an idea so tenuous it fades into nothingness. In the beginning, when you started to forge my fantastic existence, I was amused by your theories and hypotheses.

The nouns defining me, the adjectives fleshing them out, strengthened my substance and its specific weight. I'll be frank with you. The additions and finishing touches to my person fanned my greed, kept me in a state of stressful anxiety. The equilateral triangle with the watchful eye at its centre or the imitation triangular sun adorned with clouds didn't meet my expectations. Why Triple and not Quadruple? Didn't my Son's mother perhaps harbour the requisites of a real Deity? And, if we're into dreams, why couldn't I, the Dreamèd, be a Hexagon or, better still, a Decahedron with as many faces and corners as the commandments sculpted on the Tablets of Law that I handed to Moses? I could see myself as a prismatic, crystalline block, like the eyes of flies able to examine things and beings from different angles. I will confess to you my envy of pagan gods: they had limited competencies, but lived their passions and hatreds to the full, did not take themselves too seriously, lied to you, but were ready to be bribed and placated. On the contrary, you deny me humour and laughter. I am as solemn as your autocrats or Napoleon on the day of his Coronation. If hell is a psychic state, as the old man grotesquely encapsulated in a mobile plastic bubble argues, whatever happened to the beautiful, awesome, Dantean vision of fire, cauldrons and flames where the condemned were eternally consumed? If you erase all that with one stroke of the pen you strip me of a fundamental part of myself, reduce my powers as an absolute monarch to a species of constitutional president! If my competitors in other creeds hold on to theirs, they will finish me off irrevocably, for what sustains my authority is the secret weapon of intimidation. I know all about turning the other cheek, sacrificing the Son and other pious legends destined to alleviate the harshness of the first part of the story, like the sweet arbor the tyrant cultivates next to the barbed wire fences and watch-towers of his extermination camps. But none of that can compensate the removal of my best arguments and attributes. Your species behaves according to the alternate currents of abject submission and the longing to transgress. Would you, for example, have surrendered to an angel's insipid beauty, without the stunning power of those tough skulls, rough chins, voracious lips, sinewy bodies to which you have yielded throughout your life?"

"When you lived as hirsute animals in caves, two-footed and tottering, perhaps yearning after your plantigrade support, in what ways did you differ from other primates?

Your rustic lights were only exercised satisfying elemental needs, searching for roots, hunting and devouring whatever inferior or weaker species fell into the grip of once hairy extremities it would be an insult to call hands.

Guided by female oestrus, you bolted into grottos where they sheltered and, in order to shaft them, stuck crude stone weapons into the thoraxes or skulls of their males, cut them up and swallowed down their testicles and cocks to bolster your potency, just as a few rickety aficionados still down the piping hot nuts of fighting bulls (such atavism survives, however civilised and wise you may think you are).

I don't know if you'd discovered the secret of fire and celebrated your victories and captives by leaping and grunting around bonfires, or I may have seen such like in one of your Tarzan or dinosaur films; I hadn't yet been born into your minds. Millions of years went into my invention.

But ever since you created me omnipotent and eternal, I have contemplated you retrospectively over time and can measure your advances and regressions, the struggle between lucidity and your animal heritage. Frankly, I don't see a big difference between your predatory appetites and those you displayed when fresh out of the cave.

You haven't been modified by the hundred thousand light-years passed since then (forgive the scant rigor of my calculations); you still dance your ritual dances around bonfires, grind down the bones of your adversaries and copulate with their deities on heat: centuries and centuries of culture and enlightenment vanished in the smoke of the conflagration and collapse of skyscrapers.

Like young Tolstoy, you saw the massacres and devastation in Chechnya.

Tell me: what has changed on the Earth which, according to legend, I created in a week?

Close your eyes for a moment: only the wild fastnesses of the Caucasus mountains, like the one you anticipate behind the peaks you admire from your terrace, retain their luminosity for you. The bodies sacrificed accumulate dust and rancour in the deep valleys and my laughter resounds around the Roof of the World."

Occasionally, the voice condescended to converse with him.

"You're a fictional being. Your destiny was written in advance."

"In the Uncreated Text?"

"I discovered it in the work a calligrapher composed centuries ago. The incidents and episodes in your life, even the most sordid, are there, and not a detail missed. I won't elaborate or you'll get bored."

"Won't you let me take a peek?"

"Curiosity was always your downfall! Don't you remember the first chapter of the Book?"

"Where the devil did you find the manuscript?"

"Don't look in libraries destined to burn. The manuscript is your own life."

"Did my double have my name?"

"Name, surname, date and place of birth coincide. But you're the one written, not him. Everything figures in its pages."

"Even this dialogue between you and me?"

"I have it before my eyes as if on a computer screen. All that occurs was foretold."

"What happens then if I keep quiet?"

"There are blank spaces. But you don't want to keep quiet. When you talk, you prolong your life. You have come onstage and aren't in a rush to leave."

"And how about yourself?"

"Let's just say that in order to exist I need an audience. The day when the theater empties I'll be gone as well. But that won't happen tomorrow or the day after, do you think?"

"A long story!"

"Very, very long. Unless your world becomes uninhabitable and you put an end to it."

"I won't live to see that."

"Will you be sorry?"

"Who doesn't have the odd dream of dying and taking the world with him?"

"Perhaps you haven't the wherewithal, but soon that won't be the case. The desire to reach me and my promises of happiness contain the threat of my disappearance. By longing for me thus, those who love me can reduce me to ashes!"

"Tell me what is written there."

"Don't be impatient. The inevitability of happenstance is the world's best kept secret. What would become of me if I were to bring my offspring in on the act?"

"History is the kingdom of the lie. As soon as you invented the alphabet and skilled yourselves in the mechanics of writing, you discovered the deceptions of palimpsests, the preparation of codices to justify myths and foundational legends, of commandments dictated by divinities which you both create and are victims of. You forged my miracles and attacks of rage, the searing fires of Sodom, the sayings attributed to prophets and messengers. Would the titles granting earthly power, the Vicariate of Christ in Peter's Seat at Rome, the crowns and sceptres of kings and sultans have been possible without the fraudulent labours of venal scribes and copyists? Biblical texts, conciliar resolutions and books of revelation don't merit the slightest credit: they've been rehashed, rewritten, corrected and erased again.

If you allow yourself to be duped by this cybernetic era of instant communication, think what might have happened a thousand years earlier with relics, apparitions and miraculously identified cadavers, savage struggles over thrones and crosiers, centuries-old genealogical trees, if no caliph, pontificate, or tyrant had had the good wit to base the undeniable source of his nobility on Adam's coupling with Eve.

Be convinced once and for all: there is no person, family, lineage, nation, doctrine or State that doesn't base its pretensions to legitimacy on a flagrant falsehood. Those who burn libraries to erase awkward traces ignore the fact that the burnt manuscripts are themselves spurious. The greatest enemy of the lie is not truth but another lie. The calligrapher who penned you did so in the full knowledge that you didn't exist."

"When I shat your physical world and from My Heights contemplated the Finished Job, I shook in horror: it was worse than a turd, than foul dung, than a fetid pile of dough threaded like a beaten meringue. Its spheric form gyrated in the stratosphere obscenely complacent, not noticing it was shown up by the sun and was clearly a zero minus in the myriad asteroids, meteorites, stars, and planets you stupidly call the Creation. An ass sprinkled it with some of its own and it almost drowned in its piss, but that hapless drunken prophet of ill-omen constructed his ark and saved your bacon. Saved you from what? From envy, evil, oppression, crime, war, corrosive lust after power and wealth? From pain, sickness, decrepitude and death? Mentally you placed yourselves at the center of the universe and imagined that the nightly spectacle of the moon and constellations had been created to pleasure your eyes and never for a moment did you understand that you are but a microscopic grain of sand on a huge, constantly expanding beach. And if I existed, would I have taken so much trouble to ensure your delight and entertainment? Or do you really believe I hang on your every word and deed however puerile and malign they are, in order to note them in a record book so I don't forget them? Such a presumption would make me die of laughter if I weren't by definition mortal. Yesterday, when you were on your café terrace in the square, I noticed you absent-mindedly watching the little fellow who daily pushes the chair of someone disabled and who stops in front of you to soften your heart and extract a coin or two. His twisted head, tortured eyes, foaming, gaping mouth didn't extract a single tear of pity from you. The repetition of things numbs their effect and enters the category of the over-familiar. I don't escape that rule either: your cruelty and pettiness rehearsed over the centuries make me yawn. That's why I invented eternity, not because I want to give out prizes and punishments like an arrogant deity subject to rages and caprice, but so, like any idler, I could sustain the immensity of my boredom."

"The cordillera you contemplate is a theater safety curtain: lift it up, enter there. The world stretching out on the other side answers to your emotional longings: precipitous, wild, scorched by the sun and sculpted by the four elements. You anticipated it first in Gaudí's volcanic space, then in the lunar wastes of the Great Erg and endless dunes of Tarfaya. There is no vegetation, there is no green, no human trace softens its nakedness and sumptuous austerity. The sorties and occultations of the tiny star warming you repeat their cycles for millions of years before an empty amphitheatre. All colours and shades of the spectre combine in an apotheosis staged for you. You will be its only spectator if you rid yourself of the goods and chattels keeping you on this ephemeral islet.

What are you waiting for? Do you think you'll always see the bulls from the barrier, never from the sand itself?

The worst that could happen to you already has. You live without her, far from her and hardly see her diminished by distance. Make the necessary arrangements for those who look after you and for the children who will forget you, only to grow and multiply, in their cruel innocence. Don't cling to what you will soon abandon. The greater your detachment, the easier will be your passage.

Tweak your ear, don't use your deafness as a shield: you catch me on a good roll and I speak without malice aforethought. Nothing you cast off, the routine and comforts of old age are worth a jot in comparison with what awaits you. You will receive a whole tunnel of light to yourself. You will accompany me across the White Mountains and peaks of Black Dust, along ravines and gullies where scurries the rascal I lovingly instructed and armed. The most lethal, polished artefacts won't prevail against him for I will clone others and yet others possessed by his same appetite for destruction. Such has been the law of your stupid world from long before you invented me. But beyond the horrors you glimpse on television, veiled from you by zealous manipulators, lies the beauty hidden behind the safety curtain. Enter there and lose yourself in the spectacle. I will be there to close the parenthesis between nothing and nothingness. My voice will boom round the heights as in that far-fetched bible story. As I said, or so they say I said, to the dead man you will be: Arise and walk!"

Translated by Peter Bush

WORK

1954, *Juegos de manos*, Destino (novel).

1955, *Duelo en el Paraíso*, Planeta (novel).

1957, *El circo*, Destino (novel). First volume in the El mañana efímero trilogy.

1958, *Fiestas*, Emecé (novel). Second volume in the El mañana efímero trilogy.

1958, *La Resaca*, Club del Libro Español (novel). Third volume in the El mañana efímero trilogy.

1959, *Campos de Níjar*, Seix Barral (novel).

1959, *Problemas de la novela*, Seix Barral (essay).

1960, *Para vivir aquí*, Bruguera (stories).

1961, "La isla," Seix Barral (travel story.)

1962, "La Chanca," Seix Barral (story).

1962, *Fin de Fiesta. Tentativas de interpretación de una historia amorosa*, Seix Barral (stories).

1963, *Pueblo en Marcha. Instantáneas de un viaje a Cuba*, Librería Española (essay).

1966, *Señas de identidad*, J. Mortiz (novel). First volume in the Álvaro Mendiola trilogy.

1967, *Furgón de cola*, Ruedo Ibérico (essay).

1970, *Reivindicación del conde don Julián*, J. Mortiz (novel). Second volume in Álvaro Mendiola trilogy.

1975, *Juan sin Tierra*, Seix Barral (novel). Third volume in the Álvaro Mendiola trilogy.

1977, *Disidencias*, Seix Barral (journalistic articles).

1977, *Obras Completas. Tomo I*, Aguilar (novels).

1978, *Obras Completas. Tomo II*, Aguilar (stories and essays).

1978, *Libertad, libertad, libertad*, Anagrama (essay).

1979, *El problema del Sáhara*, Anagrama (essay).

1979, *España y los españoles*, Lumen (essay).

1980, *Makbara*, Seix Barral (narrative poem).

1982, *Paisajes después de la batalla*, Montesinos (novel).

1982, *Crónicas Sarracinas*, Ibérica de Ediciones y Publicaciones (essay).

1985, *Contracorrientes*, Montesinos (essay).

1985, *Coto vedado*, Seix Barral (memoir).

1986, *En los reinos de taifa*, Seix Barral (memoir).

1988, *Las virtudes del pájaro solitario*, Seix Barral (novel).

1989, *Estambul otomano*, Planeta (essay).

1990, *Aproximaciones a Gaudí en Capadocia*, Mondadori (essay).

1991, *La cuarentena*, Mondadori (novel).

1993, *Cuaderno de Sarajevo*, Aguilar (magazine articles).

1994, *Argelia en el vendaval*, Aguilar (miscellaneous).

1995, *El sitio de los sitios*, Alfaguara (novel).

1995, *El árbol de la literatura*, Círculo de Lectores (essay).

1996, *Paisajes de guerra con Chechenia al fondo*, Aguilar (miscellaneous).

1997, *Las semanas del jardín*, Alfaguara (novel).

1997, *Lectura del espacio en Xemaá-El-Fná*, Galaxia Gutenberg (monograph, with photographs by Isabel Muñoz).

1999, *Cogitus interruptus*, Seix Barral (essay).

2000, *Carajicomedia*, Seix Barral (novel).

2000, *El peaje de la vida*, Aguilar (essay coauthored with Sami Naïr).

2000, *Diálogo sobre la desmemoria, los tabúes y el olvido: diálogo con Günter Grass*, Galaxia Gutenberg (essay).

2001, *Pájaro de guerra: Sarajevo, Argelia, Palestina, Chechenia*, Aguilar (magazine articles).

2002, *Memorias*, Península (new edition of the two volumes of his memoirs *Coto vedado* and *En los reinos de tiafa*).

2003, *Telón de boca*, El Aleph (novel).

2003, *España y sus Ejidos*, Hijos de Muley-Rubio (essay).

2003, *Tradición y disidencia*, Fondo de Cultura Económica (articles and essays).

2004, *El Lucernario. La pasíon crítica de Manuel Azaña*, Península (essay).

2005, *Obras completas vol. I. Novelas y ensayo (1954-1959)*, Galaxia Gutenberg.

2006, *Obras completas vol. II. Narrativa y relatos de viaje (1959-1965)*, Galaxia Gutenberg.

2006, *Obras completas vol. III. Novelas (1966-1982)*, Galaxia Gutenberg.

2007, *Contra las sagradas formas*, Galaxia Gutenberg (essay).

2008, *El exiliado de aquí y de allá*, Galaxia Gutenberg (novel).

2008, *Obras completas vol. IV. Novelas (1988-2003)*, Galaxia Gutenberg.

2008, *Obras completas vol. V. Autobiografía. Viajes al mundo islámico*, Galaxia Gutenberg.

2009, *Genet en el Raval*, Galaxia Gutenberg (essay).

2009, *Obras completas vol. VI. Ensayos literarios (1967-1999)*, Galaxia Gutenberg.

2010, *Blanco White. "El Español" y la independencia de Hispanoamérica*, Taurus (essay).

2010, *Ella, Elle, Heyya*, Sirpus (memoir).

2011, *Muros caídos, muros erigidos; Berlín a salto de mata*, Katz Barpal / CCB (conference published in conjunction with the essay *Muros caídos, muros erigidos* by Tzvetan Todorov).

2011, *Obras completas vol. VIII. Guerra, periodismo y literatura*, Galaxia Gutenberg.

·

ENGLISH TRANSLATIONS

1969, *Marks of Identity*, translated by Gregory Rabassa, Grove Press (novel).

1974, *Count Julian*, translated by Helen Lane, Seaver Books (novel).

1977, *Juan the Landless (Masks)*, translated by Helen Lane, Viking Penguin (novel).

1991, *Landscapes After the Battle*, translated by Helen Lane, Serpent's Tail (novel).

1992, *The Virtues of the Solitary Bird*, translated by Helen Lane, Serpent's Tail (novel).

1992, *Space in Motion*, translated by Helen Lane, Lumen Books (novel).

1994, *Quarantine: A Novel*, translated by Peter Bush, Dalkey Archive Press (novel).

2000, *The Garden of Secrets*, translated by Peter Bush, Serpants Tail (novel).

2001, *Landscapes of War: From Sarajevo to Chechnya*, translated by Peter Bush,

City Lights Publishers (reportage).

2001, *The Marx Family Saga*, translated by Peter Bush, City Lights Publishers (novel).

2002, *State of Siege*, translated by Helen Lane, City Lights Publishers (novel).

2003, *Forbidden Territory and Realms of Strife: The Memoirs of Juan Goytisolo*, translated by Peter Bush, Verso (memoir).

2005, *A Cock-Eyed Comedy*, translated by Peter Bush, City Lights Publishers (novel).

2005, *The Blind Rider*, translated by Peter Bush, Serpent's Tail (novel).

2011, *Exiled from Almost Everywhere*, translated by Peter Bush, Dalkey Archive Press (novel).

•

AWARDS AND RECOGNITIONS

1985, Premio Europalia.

1993, Premio Nelly Sachs.

1994, Prix Méditerranée Étranger for the best foreign novel translated into French for *Barzkh* and *Cuaderno de Sarajevo*.

1995, Premio Rachid Mimumi.

1996, Premio de la Paz awarded by the Fundación León Felipe.

1997, Premio Jorge Isaacs de Narrativa Iberoamericana.

2001, Honorary member of the Union of Moroccan Writers.

2002, Premio Octavio Paz de Poesía y Ensayo.

2004, Premio de Literatura Latinoamericana y del Caribe Juan Rulfo.

2005, Premio Extremadura a la Creación.

2008, Premio Nacional de las Letras Españolas.

2009, Premio de las Artes y las Culturas de la Fundación Tres Culturas.

2010, Premio Don Quijote de la Mancha.

2011, Finalist for the Man Booker.

2011, Premio Mahmoud Darwish.

2012, Premio Formentor.

JUAN
MARSÉ
(Spain, 1933)

Juan Marsé was born in Barcelona in 1933 and given the name Juan Faneca Roca. His mother died in childbirth, which led his father, a taxi driver who, besides being a widower, also had a daughter, to give him up for adoption to a couple who got in his taxi and were bemoaning the fact that they didn't have any children. From them, he took his surnames: Marsé Carbó.

Marsé's education was autodidactic and he found his literary voice walking the streets of the neighborhoods of Gràcia, Guinardó, or Monte Carmelo, places where a good portion of his novels take place. Those walks, along with adventure novels and American films, allowed him to escape from an atmosphere full of misery: the memory of the war was still intact in his family, who was aligned with the side of the vanquished, mulling over the defeat in silence, under the Francoist regime.

In 1946, just thirteen years old, he started working as an apprentice in a jewelry shop. When he got home at night, he frequently sketched out his first literary exercises in a notebook, texts full of risks and errors that were shaping a very personal style that in Ceuta, while doing his military service, led him, in 1960, to write his first novel, *Encerrados con un solo juguete.* As his literary career was beginning, his encounter with Paulina Crusat was fundamental—she was a great friend of Carles Riba and J. V. Foix who worked as a literary critic for the magazine *Insula.* He maintained an intense correspondence and exchange of essential readings with Crusat throughout his first years as a writer.

Thanks to a friend, the poet Jaime Gil de Biedma, who convinced him to get out of Spain for a while, Marsé left for Paris. He stayed there until 1962, working whatever jobs he could: as a Spanish teacher, as a translator, even as a laboratory assistant at Institut Pasteur.

When he came back from Paris, in the early '60s, he tried to make a living as a translator (the first edition of *The Temple of the Golden Pavilion* by Yukio

Mishima, for example, was a result of his work). But it wasn't until 1965, on his return to Barcelona, that the name Juan Marsé began to circulate forcefully in the Spanish literary world. In 1965 he won the Premio Biblioteca Breve for *Últimas tardes con Teresa*, a beautiful novel that is also an oblique parody of the Barcelona Bourgeoisie at the end of the 1950s. His central character, the Pijoaparte—a young murciano who seduces a girl from the upper class—immediately became one of the most emblematic characters in Spanish literature.

Carlos Barral, overjoyed with the discovery of "that proletariat writer, who I was watching with perplexed curiosity," had a lot to do with the place Marsé occupied in the post-war literary sphere, turning him into one of the banner writers of the publishing house. His work has been translated into German, French, Hungarian, English, Polish, Romanian, Swedish, Portuguese, Chinese, Korean, Greek, Hebrew, Czech, and Slovak.

With *La oscura historia de la prima Montse* (1970), his next novel, Marsé aimed to investigate traditional Catalan families and, at the same time, offer an ironic and bruising perspective on Francoist and Catholic Spain. Three years later, when the convictions of his new novel, *Si te dicen que caí*, were unable to evade the censor, Marsé decided to send it to the Premio Internacional de Novela "Mexico," which it then won. In 1976, one year after the death of the dictatorship, it was finally able to be published in Spain.

Following the path he'd sketched (to show the moral and social degradation that the civil war produced and keep alive the memory of the defeated, his childhood years in neighborhoods of post-war misery), in 1982 he published *Un día volveré*. The story of an old soldier who, when he's released from prison, realizes that, no matter how hard he tries to correct past errors, many people are not ready to forgive him. Two years later, Marsé gave us *Ronda del Guinardó*, a brief but perfect novel whose action takes place on May 8, 1945, the day of the German surrender.

In the '90s, with *El amante bilingüe*, the writer weighed in on questions of identity, fidelity, and heartbreak, to then, in 1993, return to neighborhood landscapes with *El embrujo de Shanghai*. In the year 2000, he won the Premio Nacional de Narrativa with *Rabos de lagartija* and in 2008, the Premio Cervantes. Several of his books have been turned into films by directors such as Vicente Aranda and Fernando Trueba, among others. *Caligrafía de los sueños* (2011) was his last published novel.

Throughout his oeuvre, Juan Marsé's realist style has been characterized by the integration of the most avant-garde literary techniques, and the way he modulates his testimonial voice with the use of parody and humor has served as a template for new generations of writers.

THE ACORN

The Torture of Doctor Johnson

I chose this fragment because it develops a theme that is central in my writing—the conflict between appearance and reality—and, at the same time, it foreshadows that conflict's denouement. Here we see the lie that Teresa, a progressive university student, is living. She's trapped in the illusion of an idyllic future, and this makes her believe that she is in love with the promise that future holds. But the illusion dissolves and dies in these pages when she suddenly realizes that she is not really in love with an ideal, but with a man, who for her, and her alone, embodies that ideal. *Últimas tardes con Teresa* is a novel I conceived of in Paris, but wrote in Barcelona. I came back to write it because I needed to see Monte Carmelo again, the setting for the novel. Around that same time, I read two novels that were very influential. There are three actually, but two important ones. One was *The Red and the Black* by Stendhal, about Julien Sorel, a provincial youth, poor but attractive in a way, who is searching for his place in the world. It's the story of any immigrant—first it was the Andalusians, *charnegos* we called them, and now people from Maghreb, and from Eastern Europe—trying to find a place in Catalan society. So there are these allusions to provincial youths from nineteenth century novels by Balzac and Stendhal. Another important novel was *An American Tragedy* by Theodore Dreiser. The other novel I didn't actually read at the time. But I read *The Liberal Imagination*, an essay by Lionel Trilling, in which he described Henry James's novel, *The Princess Casamassima*, so well that it made me feel like I had read it. The story really resonated: it's about a secret society and a young man who tries to join it. These influences came together in the protagonist of *Últimas tardes con Teresa*, the Pijoaparte. Behind every novel there are always other novels, sometimes the author admits it and sometimes not.

The tension between appearance and reality is exacerbated in an environment like the one lived in under Franco.

It overwhelms and impacts every aspect of life, as much intellectually as physically. Life was appearances. The regime's official story about the country and what was happening to people was pure appearance, it was false—it was a lie. In this sense, all dictatorships present a reality that is constantly contradicted by daily life. This is a theme intrinsic to fiction since *Don Quixote*. The great theme of *Don Quixote* is appearance and reality. The appearance is the giants and the reality is the windmills. In my opinion, it's the mother of the modern novel and so it contains everything.

In Conversation with the Dead

The Quevado poem brings to mind the following dead friends: Jaime Gil de Biedma, Carlos Barral, Manuel Vázquez Montalbán, Ángel González, Juan García Hortelano, José Agustín Goytisolo, Gabriel Ferrater, Joan Petit, Jaume Perich, Terenci Moix, Gabriel Celaya, Víctor Seix, Toni López, Mario Lacruz, Luis Palomares, Paulina Crusat, Ramón Bartra, Charles Dickens, R. L. Stevenson, Gustave Flaubert, F. Scott Fitzgerald, Hemingway, Stendhal, and Pío Baroja. But I have created my own fictional space and the obvious referent is Faulkner, although there are others like the Santa María of Onetti, a writer I admire a lot. You have to write about what you know. I never lived in Monte Carmelo, but I lived very nearby. When I was a kid we would go play in Monte Carmelo because we were attracted to the danger, the risk. Kids with shaved heads lived there, and the uneducated children of immigrants. They lived freely and we were jealous because we had to go to school and they were always playing soccer. Those excursions to Monte Carmelo involved a certain amount of risk because those kids were scary. The same was true for Guinardó, Parque Güell. But I lived farther down, near Plaça de Rovira in the Barrio de la Salud. So I worked with that setting, because it's one I lived in, one I know.

Coda

Like the character of the Pijoaparte, you came from outside the powerful and influential bourgeoisie and literary groups and you made it on your own. Was that hard?

It was sudden and almost improvised in the sense that, though I liked reading a lot, I never studied at a university and barely even in secondary school. When I was thirteen years old my mother told me that I had to drop out of school and start working. This wasn't a problem and didn't upset me at all—I wanted to get out of that school. They made us recite the rosary every day; it was a terrifying thing. It was an awful, old-fashioned school, and I was excited to do something that would get me out of there. So, when I decided to submit my first draft to an editor, I knew no one in the literary world, I had no idea what a literary life could be like. And then I met this group of people who were very refined, but who, on the other hand, with respect to social and political ideas of the nation, were openly leftist. I realized right away that these people were "señoritos" from the country's upper class—Goytisolo, Carlos Barral, Castellet—and for them, I was probably the first working-class person they knew. They advised me right away to get out of the country, and I'd been wanting to travel, so I published my first novel and I went to Paris. I lived with abandon. They thought while I was in Paris I would write, but I wrote absolutely nothing. I bought books—or sometimes stole them because I had no money at first—and went to the cinema to see movies that weren't shown here, and listened to music and went to the theatre . . . in other words, I devoted myself to living. A love affair now and then . . . in the end—freedom. And I joined the Party and became close friends with Jorge Semprún, who taught us classes on international politics. And it was there I conceived of *Últimas tardes con Teresa*. I gave a few talks in Spanish to some young French students, they were upper class, very refined, and one of them was named Teresa. Nothing at all to do with the character, but that's where the name came from. Then I quit my job at the Pasteur Institute with Jacques Monod, a famous researcher who won the Nobel Prize. My first novel was translated and published by Gallimard, the famous publisher who translated Faulkner and Dos Pasos, Maurice-Edgar Coindreau. I worked in film;

I started translating screenplays from French into Spanish for co-productions in France and Spain. But *Últimas tardes* was already in my head and I needed to come back. And taking advantage of a film that was being shot here and in Paris, I came with the crew and I stayed.

To finish the story, when I got back to Barcelona everyone asked: "So, how was your experience in Paris?" I told Carlos Barral, "I didn't bring anything." That is to say, yes, I brought an idea that I'm going to start working on right away, but it doesn't take place in Paris, it takes place here. More than anything I remember a conversation with old man Lara, who said to me in his Andalusian accent: "How is it possible that you came back from Paris without a novel? Those French women will do anything. Not one story about a French woman? Those things sell like pastries." Everyone was a little frustrated with me about that. And I started to work on *Últimas tardes con Teresa*.

The Pijoaparte has become one of the most beloved characters in Spanish literature.

The only thing I wanted to do was recount a few dreams. Some of this character's dreams could be attributed to me as a kid. Like having a fling with a blond-haired blue-eyed girl who drives a sports car and belongs to the Catalan bourgeoisie. That might have been an erotic or romantic dream from my youth, maybe. But that's not where it came from; it came from conversations I had with that group of girls and Teresa Casadesus in Paris. Her father was a well-known pianist, Robert Casadesus, he was from Catalonia and he came here to perform. She was an unlucky girl really, she was blond and very beautiful, but she'd been in a car accident and was in a wheelchair. She was eighteen. Those girls just wanted to hear me speak Spanish, so I'd improvise and make up stories. I made up things about where I was from, the neighborhood I lived in, things that happened to me there, visits to Parque Güell and to Monte Carmelo. In those conversations I found they were particularly attentive when I talked about visiting the Chinese neighborhood in Barcelona. I saw something in them that might be called call slum nostalgia. They were French high school girls and of course they'd never been in a Chinese neighborhood; they weren't familiar with that type of life. But that was where I came up with the character of that young university student—a progressive, a romantic who mistakes appearance for reality.

The doomed romantic?

Exactly. Everything gets confused and Teresa mistakes the maid's boyfriend, Manolo, for a member of the Communist Party, thinking he's a militant labor activist, but he's not. Just like how those girls were projecting their romantic ideas onto the marginal neighborhoods where life is a little bit difficult. The seed of the novel came from there. And this character joined a literary tradition that comes from the nineteenth-century novel—the tradition of the poor provincial youth. I've been criticized many times for describing him as a handsome or attractive boy. Okay, he's poor, almost illiterate, and he doesn't know Catalan, so if I didn't make him a little bit attractive, he'd get absolutely nowhere, you know. He wouldn't go anywhere.

A THOUSAND FORESTS

FROM *Últimas tardes con Teresa*
(Last Evenings with Teresa)
[a novel]

The flash of some terrible reality leaping, as its way is,
out of the heart of spring. Because youth . . .
—*Virginia Woolf*

Years later, looking back on that passionate summer, both of them would recall not only the suggestive light that fell on every event, its variety of golden reflections and false promises, its illusions of a free future, but also the fact that, in the middle of their mutual attraction, even in the heat of their summer kisses, there were shadows where the cold of winter was already nesting, the fog that would eclipse the mirage.

—Are you honest with me, Manolo? Sometimes I'm scared . . .

—Scared of what?

—I don't know. Is this real, what's happening to us?

The internal erosion of the myth took place without weakening Teresa's growing love for the boy from the south. His true character was revealed to her precisely (and it took only three nights) when she realized she hadn't been seduced by an idea, but by a man. First came a feeling of disorientation, a need to reevaluate certain notions about the strange world in which we live, when she made some unexpected connections, the scandalous way illusion wrapped itself around reality.

On a Sunday afternoon of sun and sudden showers, it was the end of August, Teresa insisted they go into a popular dance club in Guinardó. They had taken refuge from the rain in a bar across the street from Salón Ritmo, where a crowd of boys and girls, who arrived running through the rain, were waiting to go in. Manolo mentioned that years ago that place had been his favorite dance club. "Why don't we go in?" she said, her eyes lighting up. "You won't like it, that place is full of degenerates," Manolo said. But she insisted ("Rain and no car, what else can we do?") and he had no choice but to indulge her whim. Right then the rain was coming down in torrents. Manolo took off his jacket and used it to protect the girl as they crossed the street. Teresa leaned against him and smiled. At the ticket window a fat, pink man was smoking Ideales and Teresa tried to bum one. "Don't be rude," joked Manolo. "Oh be quiet, *hombre*. This will be fun, you'll see." Boys: 25 pesatas, Girls: 15. "Discrimination," said the happy university girl. One drink included in the cover. Performing: Orquesta Satélites Verdes, their singer Cabot Kim (Joaquín Cabot), Maymó Brothers (Afro-Cuban rhythms), Lucieta Kañá (young Catalan *cuplé* performer) and some other big names from that era. "This is going to be great," said Teresa. From the beginning she showed an odd excitement. Exclusive, special appearance by Trio Moreneta Boys (the lovely sounds of *sardana* fused with modern rock). "Spectacular," said Teresa as they went in, "I can't wait." The place was packed and loud, no room to move on the dance floor. Men dressed to the nines, with sardonic eyes and impertinent expressions roved around in tight packs, harassing girls, leaning over them, scrutinizing their necklines and whispering come-ons. Almost all of them were Andalusians. The fiery looks Teresa received were more than suggestive. Manolo's constant presence at her side saved her from an advance that, if she were alone, would have moved beyond simple admiration. Fortunately, on that day she was dressed plain enough for church (white pleated skirt, blue blouse with a high neck, and a wide black belt), which, in that milieu, might have made her the subject of mockery if it hadn't been for her long, blonde hair and lustrous, sun-flattered skin, two charms that betrayed her, that is of course if she wanted to pass unnoticed. There were stationary groups of girls in the galleries and in chairs lined up around the dance floor, whispering among themselves every now and then. At the far end, on a small stage were the Satélites Verdes dressed in sequin shirts, their singer (unusually melodic, according to popular opinion) with a thin, black mustache and a nasal, Gregorian voice. Previously, the place had belonged to an old cultural and recreational workers society (Home of the Weavers Guild), which, along with their Choir, their Library, and their Theater—now converted into Salón

Ritmo—had disappeared along with the Republic. Outdated and solemn decoration: four walls with plaster crown molding embossed with bouquets of flowers, bunches of grapes, and coats of arms—a face within, an illustrious name below (Prat de la Riba, Pompeu Fabra, Clavé). Glorious Catalans, leaders of *orfeó i caramelles*, the long lost labor movement, whose severe profiles seemed to express scorn for the Sunday invasion of illiterate Andalusians. In the first floor gallery, through the rancid odor of the wooden box seats, wandered the ghost of a familiar, artisan spirit that reigned in the past and that today occupied one remaining refuge: the stockroom for beverages and artifacts. It had been a library and billiard room, now it housed the mutilated and still quivering remains of Catalan translations of Dostoevsky and Proust alongside Salgari, Dickens, *the Patufet*, and Maragall, and rusted trophies and old Home of the Weavers standards sleeping alongside the dream of oblivion.

The dance hall was infernally hot and the generous aroma of body odor prevailed. Teresa was suppressing indulgent exaltations. Dancing on a Sunday, the world is yours! Wild, overpopulated islands, violent skies, primal impulses, abashed tenderness, fragrance free gardens where love flowers anyway—*carpe diem!* She hung on Manolo's arm or sat with him in the galleries, her body relaxed but her head held up at the same angle, vigilant and awake, as at the movies (breathing in air full of phantasms), revealing her beautiful, naked throat. She didn't miss a detail of the spectacle, and made pleasant comments about the couples clinging to one another, revolving around the dance floor, tireless, like an anthill. Manolo recognized a few notorious members of the community, he knew them well: the same ones who went dancing with maids on Thursdays at Salón Price, and at Las Cañas, and Metro, and Apolo, and at the Iberia, Máximo, Rovira, Texas, and Selecto theaters, small, sweaty *Murcianos* with striped, starched shirts and suffocating double-breasted blazers, soft *bailarines* that never got a girl, who spun and spun around on the dance floor with their faces lifted to the gallery, devouring with their eyes the girls, sitting in the box seats like sphinxes, whose contemptuous silence or cutting responses to the boys' entreaties ("Want to dance, baby?" "No." "Why not?" "Because I don't." "Go fuck yourself, *tuberculosa*." "Shameless dwarf.") were of course, Teresa told Manolo, unjust and infinitely crueler than the insults they received. Perhaps for this reason, and aware that Manolo didn't seem to share her desire for excitement (she had only convinced him to take

her to the dance floor twice, and even then he had resisted), Teresa was reluctant to turn down a request to dance from a short man who approached them
unexpectedly and tried to get Manolo to remember a night they spent drinking together a long time ago. Teresa told Manolo to introduce her and she
asked the man where he was from and what he did for a living. He turned out
to be from Torre Baró, a distant suburb, and he claimed to be an electrician.
"Would you like to dance?" he asked very politely. Teresa wasn't sure (she saw
that Manolo was smiling ironically, disinterested), but something was about
to happen that would prompt her to accept. They were standing in one corner
of the room; everyone was waiting for the band to start the next song (Domin
Marc had just finished and the Trio Moreneta Boys were being introduced).
Just then, there was a commotion that rippled through the middle of the
dance floor; some girls shrieked, some couples became agitated, and everyone
looked in their direction. Apparently a prankster had come through and
pinched a few of the girls. Teresa laughed as if it were the most natural thing
in the world. "What fun!" she said. She was looking at Manolo's friend,
whose head only came up to her chin; still, the small man seemed oddly
graceful, very compact, a slim body enveloped in the furious aroma of cologne,
a narrow, checkered blazer, small, doleful Japanese eyes, and a grease sculpted
toupee. Teresa looked at him kindly but remained indecisive, and it was then
she felt on her ass the pinch of a master, very slow and precise, opportunistic.
She said nothing, but turned around surreptitiously, red as a tomato, in time
to see a stooped silhouette, the hunched and skeptical shoulders of a man who
slipped, laughing, between the couples. At the same time, she heard the voice
of a girl next to her telling her friend: "I know him, his name is Marsé, a
short guy with brown, curly hair. He's always putting his hands in inappropriate places. Last Sunday he pinched me and then gave me his phone number,
just in case I wanted something from him, shameless." "Did you call him?"
asked the friend. Teresa didn't hear the answer because the brave little pygmy
in front of her was still staring dumbly and insisting: "Let's dance, Teresina?"
Delightful, charming, the electrician, she thought. The band started playing,
and Teresa, still feeling the warm sting on her buttocks, perhaps impelled by
the stealthy and distinguished work of the groper, or perhaps fascinated by
the atmosphere, abandoned herself to the arms of the little *Murciano* from
Torre Baró and fearlessly threw herself into the jostling sea of elbows and
perspiration. The Trio Moreneta Boys started playing their most popular

song, a bolero ideal for dancing in low light. Contrary to what Teresa expected, in that confused ocean of heads revolving slowly in the half-light, there
was no wholesome exuberance, free from bourgeois complexities: everyone
danced pressed together in silence, a strange seriousness on their faces. There
was an unbearable air of respectability, grotesquely romantic and circumspect,
more so even than a society ball organized by rich housewives. For a while,
Teresa followed Manolo with her eyes, watching his back move disinterest-
edly away. She watched him from a distance at the peaks of the waves, until
she realized that she was sinking beyond saving. It was awful—in spite of the
fact that at first it allowed her a certain freedom of movement—she had forgotten about the sheerness of her skirt, that she was not wearing a bra under
her blouse, and of the hemorrhage of golden dreams this unexpected discovery was going to provoke in her partner. The result: all of a sudden the electrician revealed himself to be an insatiable scumbag, a desperate octopus with
fifty hands, his mouth panting on her left breast in the darkness. He stopped
speaking and pushed himself against her, sweating and exerting himself. She
endured it out of pure courtesy until, pushed by the mass of couples to the
middle of the floor, unable to take a step, they were rendered immobile,
trapped, him pushing against her (Teresa felt his small hand running over her
back and her ass like a spider), his back arched like a skilled and vigorous
tango dancer. The electrician achieved the desired erection and she felt it
rubbing against her thigh. Where was the wholesome joy of popular dances?
Body odor and furtive, depressing urges, that's all it was. Around them, the
couples had stopped dancing and were standing still, faces turned toward the
stage, listening to the song the Trio Moreneta Boys were playing. Hands
desperately groped waists and breasts, strange and shameful flirtations in the
shadows. Still Teresa tried to laugh, but it was the last time she would that
day. Soon she stood rigid: the little electrician held her so tightly that her feet
were lifted off the floor. She had lost sight of Manolo a while ago (Has he left
me in the hands of these savages?) and, suddenly frightened, believing that
she was alone and that she'd be unable to get out of there, she looked angrily
at her partner, who she found was already in a pathetic state of dissolution.
When she looked into his small eyes (for a long time she would remember
those congested and sad eyes, looking up at her like a little beaten dog: it was
his first reality check) she saw that he was about to have a panic attack. He
dropped her right away and she began to clear a path with her elbows, feeling

like she was drowning. It was all a lie: the melodic Trio, Manolo's worker friends, popular dances . . . The couples glanced at her and smiled, but nobody seemed willing to let her leave the dance floor. "What a tease! She ditched him," she heard some girl say. "Poor boy. That's not right." Finally she got back to where she'd left Manolo. No sign of him. She stood, flustered in the darkness. "Manolo," she murmured weakly. He might have been any of the shadows she saw. Unknown faces, weirdly illuminated and sweaty, like a nightmare, leaned in over hers, oscillating to the beat of the horrendous babbling music. A daring hand ran through her fine, blonde hair, and a pair of lips pushed rudely against her soft ear whispering obscene words. "Looking for me, blondie?" "Fresh *señorita*, so nice to see you." "Don't run away, *princesa*, you'll lose your panties." A heavy-set girl with red lips protected her, insulting the gawkers. Her legs shaking, embarrassed and furious at the same time, her eyes desperate, Teresa searched for Manolo everywhere, even in the first floor gallery, where a few dancing couples were clinging tightly to each other in the shadows. In the hallway, she thought she saw Manolo going into a room and she hurried after him. Inside, a yellow light bulb, wrapped in iron mesh, old friend of the flies, cast a weak, dirty light on the boxes of beer bottles stacked next to a few damp bookshelves, and on broken glassware, covered in cobwebs. On the floor, in the middle of the room, some dusty books and old magazines were piled as if for a bonfire. "Manolo, is that you?" she whispered. The room smelled damp. A stifled cough behind the boxes of beer. Teresa's feet bumped into the pile of books (she thought she heard an amused feminine laugh) or more accurately, with one volume that was separated from the pile, a volume with a red jacket and a photograph, yellowed by time, featuring some venerable older men with white beards, stuck to the cover: Madame Bovary and Karl Marx rolling together across the floor clinging tightly to each other, aroused, escaping from that mountain of science and knowledge ready for the fire or the trashcan. She heard whispers coming from one corner, and a licentious giggle, mocking her—her shock, her fear in the face of reality. Then something moved behind the boxes: a dark-haired girl with braids and big, dreamy black eyes backed into the corner straightening her skirt. She looked at Teresa, smiling, a little startled, but unblinking and uncomplaining, hiding instinctively behind the stack of boxes. Next to her appeared a strapping redheaded boy in a waiter's jacket with a bottle of cognac in each hand. "Looking for something?" A full, sonorous laugh burst out of the girl with the braids, her eyes fixed on her friend. Teresa looked down; glancing for the last time at the unusual literary couple, stuck together at her feet, surrounded by the smell of damp velvet. She muttered an apology, turned around, and ran out. She went back to the gallery overlooking the dance floor. The lights were on now. Leaning over the rail, she could see the whole dance floor and the gallery. Manolo had disappeared. "Maybe he got mad. I'm so stupid . . ." When she turned around she was given another start: the small, greasy electrician was behind her, staring, his hands deep in his pants pockets, smiling with an inscrutable expression. He was waiting, respectful, humble, ready to pounce. Teresa escaped again and went down the stairs, from one room to the next. Finally she got out to the foyer, to the coat check and the bar.

Manolo was standing at the bar drinking a beer. Teresa's first impulse was to run to him and throw herself into his arms. But she made an effort to calm herself and went up to him from behind, her eyes lowered. When she got to him she stood on tiptoes and kissed him on the cheek. Manolo turned and looked at her, smiling affectionately: "Tired of dancing already?" Teresa nodded, looking at him with a kind of learned humility. And then she stopped pretending and laid her head on his shoulder. "Don't do that again, please, don't leave me alone again!" She asked him to get her out of there right away.

"What world do you live in, little girl?" he said affectionately, when she had told him everything. "I told you, this place isn't for you."

And, embracing her, he stroked her hair tenderly until she calmed down.

They finished the night in the Cristal City Bar, in the company of respectable, discreet couples who would be home by nine o'clock. They ended up kissing in peace on a balcony inaccessible to overzealous *Murcianos* and sly gropers, in front of two gin-and-tonics with twin, aseptic slices of lime.

Then, on consecutive nights, Teresa's emotional state was slowly and subtly fractured. Other cracks: warm and happy nights in Monte Carmelo, noisy neighbors, good-looking boys dressed in T-shirts, romantic walks in the moonlight, slogans for workers' rights in the famous Delicias bar . . . For a long time, the young university student had craved to experience that seething vitality. But she discovered and came to know Monte Carmelo, a mythic realm (like Florida was for conquistadors in their day), too late. Up until then, the neighborhood had only been circle of blurry shadows, admired from a distance, because Manolo had always refused to take her to Carmelo and introduce her to his friends. But one name was very familiar to her: Bernardo.

Manolo—freeing himself from having to talk about certain activities (that's how he referred to them, although Teresa used a snarky, biological term: cell meetings) that she amusingly attributed to him, but that he'd actually never experienced—decided some time before that when he talked about Bernardo he would always imitate the mysterious style he had learned listening to the students talk about Federico. The result was that Bernardo became a renowned, clandestine leader, inaccessible and impenetrable keeper of the greatest secrets: "Do you know Bernardo? Have you heard of him? Bernardo could explain how this works better than I, I know nothing," the Pijoaparte would often tell Teresa, when her curiosity put him in a tight spot. "Will you introduce me to him someday, Manolo?" "It wouldn't be wise," he said. And so Teresa admired Bernardo even though she'd never met him. In part it was a reflex of her attraction to Manolo and in part it was due to her own rash moral sensibility. But her moral sensibility was as generous as it was reckless: Teresa's moral realism didn't come from analytical effort, as she believed, but from love; in any event, more disappointments were still in store for her.

On one of the nights she went with Manolo to upper Carmelo, as they were about to say goodnight, she suggested they take a walk through the neighborhood. He started to say no, but the desire to embrace the girl behind some bush on the other side of the hill, and talk to her in earnest about something that'd been bouncing around in his head for a while (the possibility of obtaining a job through Mr. Serrat) made him change his mind. "Okay, we'll take a walk on the other side, I'll show you Valle de Hebrón." They left the car on the highway. Putting his arm around Teresa, protecting her from the eyes of some neighbors out in their doorways getting fresh air, he guided her toward Calle Gran Vista. Past Delicias bar, some children were playing in the middle of the gutter, and, in the light spilling from a doorway, two little girls were holding hands, singing:

> *The patio at my house*
> *is special,*
> *when it rains it gets wet*
> *just like all the rest . . .*

Teresa approached the girls and, squatting down, sang with them for a while. Her mood began to improve again, dangerously. The night was warm and full of stars, the moon rolled lazily over the terraces, surrounded by green silks, and there was a red glow at the edges of the sky. All that was missing was a radio, a radio playing loudly from some terrace, sending a simple, corny melody out into the night. In a vacant lot at the end of Calle Gran Vista was a cart path leading down to Parque del Guinardó. They sat down on a wall of crumbling semicircular stones. After a while, they went down the hill through the small fir trees, holding hands. They heard the metallic chirp of crickets. Teresa lay down in the grass. Her lips were vivid that night, her eyes overwhelmed, full of generosity and tenderness. Maybe it's the right moment to level with the girl, he thought, the moment to tell her that I'm out of a job, that the future looks bleak, and that maybe her father could, if she asks him, get me a job with real responsibilities and prospects . . .

—Baby, hey, your father . . . your father, maybe your father might . . . ?

It was her inviting mouth and her small, perky strawberry breasts that made him stutter, not indecision; it was that parallel universe that he held in the space between his hands, burning him, anticipating all the sweet, warm spasms of future dignity and prosperity . . . He sat up to collect his thoughts. Teresa looked up at him from the ground with sleepy eyes. And he turned back to her, hesitating: he could make her his and be her lover for a time, it was true; maybe even for months and months; but what would be gained by that? What does it mean, that enormous word: lover? What modern girl— student or not, but rich and with new ideas—doesn't take a lover these days? No big deal. Then later on, do I know you? It was lovely, but goodbye. Fleeting passion and ephemeral unions of the sexes, you know, that's life. No, kid, your idea of Teresa in bed: you haven't thought it through. Sure you can possess this adorable creature, so educated and respectable (although in truth, her moral foundations are not as solid as her social standing might proclaim), but you'll never possess the world that comes with her: distinction, cultural values, grace, and decorum. Look, caress her lovely golden hair, her pretty silken knees just once; hold that parallel universe of strawberries and pearls in the palm of your hand just once, and you'll understand that those are the opulent offspring of social struggle, and you only earn them through equivalent struggle, it's not enough to reach out your trembling claws and take them . . .

Teresa stood up, went over to her friend, and hugged him from behind. "Everything is so beautiful from up here, isn't it?" she said. The smell of fir and pine trees rose around them. The lights of Montbau and Valle de Hebrón shone in the distance, down on the highway cars rolled by, headlights aglow, entering the city one after another, like a procession. Teresa let go of him, laughing, and took a few spins around him. "I like your neighborhood," she said. "Let me take you out for a *carajillo* at the Delicias bar." "It's called a *perfumado*," he corrected, smiling. "Right, a *perfumado*," she said. "I want a *perfumado* from Delicias." Manolo approached her slowly, mumbling words, smiling, floating, as in a dream, and kissed her again and again, bit her neck, nestled his face in her blonde hair (your father, your-fa-fa-fa-ther-could . . .) until she pulled away again, laughing, making him chase her. Manolo followed her, stumbling, he caught her, he lost her. Little girl, you're driving me crazy. "I want a *carajillo*, I want a *perfumado!*" she repeated stubbornly. "Take me to Delicias and then we'll come back here," she said with an irresistible smile. And all of a sudden she ran off up the hill to the path, where she stopped for an instant and looked back at him, then continued to Calle Gran Vista. Manolo followed her slowly, head down, hands in his pockets. The crickets' song annoyed him. When he got to the first houses on the street he picked up his pace. He didn't see Teresa. And that's when it happened: he heard her scream. The girl must have been about fifty meters away; it was dark, he couldn't see anything, but he knew what had happened the moment he started running toward Teresa. He found her leaning against a wall, covering her face with her hands, her back turned to the other side of the street. Her shoulders were trembling.

—What happened?

Teresa made an effort to compose herself, she sighed, her hands on her hips. She seemed more angry than frightened.

—Over there . . . There's a man . . .

She pointed to a shadowy corner, one of the archways built into the retaining wall abutting the hillside around Casa Bech. The light from the only streetlamp illuminating the street did not reach the archway, but it revealed something of the stranger: a pair of old shoes and the muddy folds of pants that were too long. "He scared me to death, the lunatic," said Teresa. "He must be crazy, because all of a sudden he jumped out of the dark in front of me with his arms wide open and with . . . everything unbuttoned, laughing, staring at me, I can barely believe it!" A panting came from the shadows, the stranger's feet moved. Manolo flew in that direction like an arrow and buried his hands in the dark, grabbing the greasy collar of a shirt (his fingers touched a three- or four-day-old-beard and a huge nose that felt familiar) that gave off an unbearable stench of wine. "Come on, pervert, let's go! I see you," he shouted, and pulled: what came out of the shadows, shaking like a ragdoll, in the feeble light of the streetlamp, was none other than El Sans, or what was left of him after almost two years of serving as a target for Rosa's lethal conjugal machinations. "Aren't you ashamed, you piece of shit, you've got a family!" Manolo said, shaking him, and overcome by a sudden rage, he started hitting him. El Sans's prank was nothing new in remote, poorly lit neighborhoods like that one, it happened all the time and Manolo knew it. Still he punished El Sans so harshly (really he was moved by a desire for vengeance that went beyond what the offense against Teresa could have inspired in him) that Teresa was shocked. "Don't hit him anymore, let him go." But Manolo kept on. "He's got no right to live!" he shouted. "I told him a long time ago, I warned him! Piece of shit! Look at what you've become!" El Sans, completely drunk, smiling sadly, covered his face with his arms, pinned against the wall. "I didn't know!" he moaned, and stuttered, inverting his vowels: "I didn't see you, I swear I never saw you!" Finally, stumbling, almost dragging himself, he broke away and started to run. Manolo shouted after him: "*Trinxa*, animal! You were bound to end up like this, you piece of shit, scaring defenseless women! Disappear, go die already, you've got no right to live." He turned back to Teresa, who was looking at him with astonished eyes. He put his arm around her and explained: "These neighborhoods . . . Like I said. Dark streets, decent girls can't go out alone at night. It happened to my sister-in-law too, one night she came home crying . . . Did he do anything to you?" "No, no . . . he's from this neighborhood? It seemed like you knew him." "I could've killed him, look. He wasn't bad . . ." he muttered thoughtfully. "He didn't used to be bad, believe me. His life got complicated, things went bad for him, but it was all his fault. I always told him, I warned him. Now he's finished, he drinks all the time and goes around acting like an idiot. Someday he's going to turn up with a cracked skull." "But," said Teresa, "if he's your friend, why'd you hit him like that? He didn't even touch me."

"Didn't I tell you already? Because he deserved it . . . He was asking for it," said Manolo angrily.

Of course, he didn't tell her that this horny reprobate was the famous Bernardo, the other nameless hero of Carmelo. But there was no saving him now. When they got back to the car, the girl still wanted to get a drink at Delicias bar (although not with the same enthusiasm as before, saying she needed it to get over the fright). By the time Manolo realized it was a bad idea, Teresa was already inside. And there was Bernardo, alone, at a table in the corner, still panting, bleeding from his nose, frozen like a frightened rat. It's possible that Teresa might never have suspected the truth if they hadn't run into Manolo's brother. Everyone turned around to watch her come in: two bus drivers leaning on the bar, talking to the brother of the Pijoaparte, four boys playing dominos, and an old man sitting by the doorway. Manolo's brother came over to them, smiling warily and shaking his head. He was in his thirties, tall and stooped, with a tired, brown expressionless face and yellow teeth. He was easy-going and slow, rural, given to effusive greeting. He wore only a grease-stained jumpsuit. In the neighborhood he was considered half-crazy and no one paid attention to him. He liked simple jokes (there was this, then this happened, then the trees chased the dogs, ha, ha, ha), but, paradoxically, he was very talkative and attentive to detail when telling stories, with many opinionated and generally ignored digressions. In the bar, people tried to get away from him. For this reason, because he was often left alone, his words hanging in the air, he had an odd, broken way of telling stories: he always seemed to have begun to tell them somewhere else, to someone who had left without waiting for him to finish, and there he was, all of a sudden, searching for company with his eyes, ready to continue the story. As this recurred quite frequently, it resulted in installments that never ended, spread out equitably between various acquaintances, none of whom seemed to care about the beginning or the end. But Teresa would care about the end of his story that night. It referred directly to Bernardo. Manolo had no choice but to introduce Teresa. "A friend," he said. "We aren't going to stay long." His brother insisted that the girl drink a shot of Calisay ("It's really good for women" he explained, without revealing what was good about it) that Teresa accepted politely. She thought Manolo's brother was very nice, with a docile face that, in a way, recalled that of a horse. But she only had eyes for her damaged assailant, curled up in his corner, ashamed. It pained her to see him rub his bloody nose with the back of his hand. Manolo's brother had gone back to the bus drivers who were drinking beer at the bar; he started to tell

them something, but when they continued to ignore him, he turned back to
Teresa, continuing:

". . . and you know they really thrashed him this time, look at him, come
on take a look at him. He's got a pretty good cut, but I don't think he's dangerous; it's his wife who's terrifying. This worthless (he pointed at Manolo)
brother of mine can tell you, he and Bernardo (he pointed at Bernardo, and
Teresa was left in suspense hearing his name) used to go out together all the
time, when things were going well for everyone, when there was good work
and a shred of dignity. Bernardo has had bad luck with Rosa. She's a tyrant.
Rosa's his wife," he said, adding a touch of precision.

That was the end of his story for the evening. Teresa imagined that the
beginning probably contained more, no less surprising, revelations, impossible
to recover now, already dissolving in the memories of the two bus drivers. In
any event, the terrible suspicion had returned: could the great Bernardo, of
whom Manolo had spoken so much, and whom she had compared with Federico (rebellious, arousing, Parisian *sombra*), be that same worthless specimen
bleeding in the corner? Her suspicion increased when at her side she caught a
furtive glance from Manolo, a glance that spied on her thoughts, and suddenly
she experienced the same nausea and the same feeling of disappointment that
had overcome her at the Sunday dance. Right then she saw Bernardo get up
to leave: this poor staggering man, hunched over, leaning forward, pushing
his face out like he's blind or a depraved madman, this moral and physical
disaster is Bernardo, the militant worker and comrade who worked in *la sombra* with Manolo? . . . If that back, those dragging feet, that worn-out specter
of Carmelo hadn't seemed so sad, she would've started laughing. That same
delinquent, that future sex-offender worked printing pamphlets for students?
She knew it, she'd always suspected it: Monte Carmelo was not Monte Carmelo, Manolo's brother wasn't a car salesman, he was a mechanic, there was
no working class consciousness here, Bernardo was the product of her own
revolutionary fantasy, and Manolo was the same . . .

Without realizing what she was doing, she ordered a *perfumado* (which
provoked a loud burst of laughter from Manolo's brother) while at the same
she interrogated the boy with her eyes, bewildered, depressed by what she had
just realized. But she saw nothing but adoration in her friend's black eyes, no
secret power, no heroism in the face of danger, nothing but adoration for her.
She hurried out of Delicias and went to her car. She heard a neighbor's radio

playing loudly: a delightful but ill-timed tune, nothing missing now, no more good-looking slum boys in T-shirts strolling in the moonlight. Manolo was at her side, watching her, watching her movements with a kind of paternal concern, as if she were a little girl taking her first steps and might fall. He feared Teresa's reaction, the avalanche of questions that was going to crush him at any moment. But Teresa was silent. Walking fast with an air of offended dignity. All he could do was accompany her down the street in the middle of the night. When they got to the car she sat in the driver's seat and didn't move, lost in thought, staring straight ahead. Manolo slipped into the car with feline smoothness, not wanting to disturb her thoughts. He studied her profile in silence for a while, then he brushed her temple with his lips.

—Stop it, Manolo, please, said Teresa. Do you think I'm just a stupid girl?

—I tried to tell you many times how things are in this neighborhood, that you shouldn't have too many illusions . . .

—Stop talking. You're an imposter.

Teresa turned and stared at him coldly. The chirping of crickets came into the car from both sides of the street. Manolo held the girl's blue gaze. He adored her in that moment more than ever; it seemed to him that in a matter of minutes Teresa had become a woman, a woman who was just as likely to bury a knife in his chest as to let him into her bed and into her life forever. He thought: and if I were to be honest with her right here, right now, if I were to confess that I'm nothing, a nobody, poor and unemployed, a fucking petty thief from the slum, shameless and in love? . . . Wait, relax.

—I just want to know, she said, her voice breaking, what happened to the pamphlets you promised us.

Manolo ran a hand through his hair: he'd completely forgotten that random, impulsive promise, and now he had no way to explain it.

—Get out, Teresa said.

—What?

—Get out of the car . . .

Now her voice broke completely.

—Why weren't you honest with me? I think . . . I think that's the least I deserve.

He was going to say something, but Teresa had already opened the door and gotten out. She slammed the door, leaving him inside, and stood in the street, her arms crossed. Behind her the crickets sang, the city lights twinkled.

—This is ridiculous! she shouted. I wish Maruja would just get better already and I could be done with this once and for all, and get out of here, to hell with summer, with vacation, with these walks, with everything. I'm sick of it, so sick of it!

—Forgive me, he said, I'll explain everything. Come on, get in.

She didn't move. Manolo opened the door.

—Come on, get in.

—As soon as you get out, if you don't mind.

She looked into the distance, chin on her chest, with a forlorn air more accusatory than the scornful twist of her upper lip. He studied her for a moment: this new Teresa excited him, she seemed ready to stab him, her anger turned him on. He told her so. "Go to hell," she muttered. Her eyes were full of tears. When he saw this, Manolo jumped out of the car and went toward her. But then she dodged him and slipped into the driver's seat. "Teresa, listen to me . . ." he begged. She started the car, but didn't drive off right away. She struggled with the transmission (she couldn't get it into first) or pretended to; maybe she was waiting for him to say something. Manolo realized that he shouldn't let her leave without offering some explanation, whatever it was. It was clear, he thought darkly, for this creature, love and conspiracy were still one and the same. Then a revelation:

—It's okay, he said, venturing a hand toward her hair. She dodged him suspiciously. Tomorrow I'll get the pamphlets for your friends. Will you come? I'll wait for you at the clinic at ten in the morning. Okay? At ten.

Teresa fixed him with one last, sad look. The car pulled rapidly away, with that maddening, childish whine that always made the *Murciano*'s skin crawl.

The boy went slowly up the street. When he got home, he took his white pants out of the closet and asked his sister-in-law to iron them for the next day. Then he lay down on his bed (his brother called to him from the dining room, insulting him, but Manolo ignored him) and devised a plan in full detail.

Teresa called the clinic as soon as she got home: Maruja was the same. Then she showered, and, barefoot, in her underwear, pajama top unbuttoned, her hair down, she sat alone at the dining room table. Her father had gone to Blanes that afternoon at the last minute. Vicenta served her dinner, but she barely ate anything. She put on an Atahualpa Yupanqui record, drank two shots of gin with ice, and went to bed with a third, her head exploding with doubts and wandering thoughts. She formulated a hundred serious questions about Manolo and then realized, astounded, that she wasn't being honest with herself. She was haunted by the delightful shadow of self-criticism: the change in her mind frightened her. She was angry with herself, the way she behaved with Manolo seemed ridiculous, foolish—admit that the boy's political persona stopped mattering to you some time ago, acknowledge it, she thought, lying in bed in her blue painted room, unable to sleep (her abdomen pulsing, registering the rhythm of a guitar), sweating a musical gin surrounded by dolls and records and books, rubbing her cheek softly against her naked shoulder. When will I learn to control my emotions? Liberty, resistance, militancy in the party . . . In the end, what is resistance? What does being a militant in a cause even mean? The same for communism, what is it?

Teresa's thighs are sweating honey, a motorcycle tears through the tranquil San Gervasio night. Deep down, I'm alone, she thinks; I've been living, until yesterday, surrounded by ghosts. Solitude, generosity, sentimentality, curiosity, interest, confusion, enjoyment—she could enumerate all of these emotions because she believed she already had an explanation for the boy's behavior and for her own: both of them, each in their own way, were at war with fate. But she was still curious. What was the idea of freedom for a poor boy like Manolo? To be with me in Floride, driving over ninety miles an hour? Kissing my mother's hand properly? Making love on the beach with a rich tourist? Or maybe those were just ways to gain time, to steal time from poverty, from misfortune, from obscurity. Yes: a man trying to gain time, at war with fate, that's Manolo, that's all of us. But his idea of freedom? A sports car. A fast, flashing convertible. A single white Renault Floride for everyone in the world (don't step out of the line, step *with* the line) instead of a world where there would be a Floride for all of us. An error of perspective—it's not your fault— it's normal. He's intelligent, attractive, generous, but manipulative, insolent, and probably a liar: he protects himself however he can. And what do I know about the strange effects of poverty on the mind! What do I know about cold and hunger, about the true horrors of the oppression a boy like him must suffer? I haven't even asked him how much he earns. If we always try so hard not to talk about what a man earns, only about his behavior (well, my friends, I assert that a man's behavior depends on what he earns). If even today, acting like a stupid rich girl throwing a tantrum in front of her chauffer, I made him get out of the car, if I want to interrogate him instead of helping him, if he's so attentive, so handsome, so kind and patient with me! . . . Has he ever asked about my ideological affiliation? No. And still, he promises to give me the pamphlets tomorrow; it's very possible that all of it is just a bunch of non-sense. I couldn't care less. A hundred useless questions and a hundred useless answers about my Manolo: true or false, whatever his class consciousness, his vision of the future, the real question is . . . (*ay mamá*, and still I can't sleep!)

The real question is this: How far will I let him take me?

Translated by Will Vanderhyden

WORK

1961, *Encerrados con un solo juguete*, Seix Barral (novel).

1962, *Esta cara de la Luna*, Seix Barral (novel).

1966, *Últimas tardes con Teresa*, Seix Barral (novel).

1970, *La oscura historia de la prima Montse*, Seix Barral (novel).

1970, *1939-1950, Años de penitencia*, Difusora Internacional (monograph).

1971, *1929-1940, La gran desilusión*, Difusora Internacional (monograph).

1973, *Si te dicen que caí*, Novaro (novel).

1975, *Señoras y señores*, Punch (magazine articles).

1976, *Libertad provisional*, Sedmay (guión).

1977, *Confidencias de un chorizo*, Planeta (magazine articles).

1978, *La muchacha de las bragas de oro*, Planeta (novel).

1981, *El Pijoaparte y otras historias*, Bruguera (stories).

1982, *Un día volveré*, Plaza & Janés (novel).

1984, *Ronda del Guinardó*, Seix Barral (novel).

1985, "La fuga del río Lobo," Debate (children's story).

1985, *El fantasma del cine Roxy*, Almarabú (short story).

1986, *Teniente Bravo*, Seix Barral (includes the stories "Historia de detectives," "Teniente Bravo," and "El fantasma de cine Roxy").

1990, *El amante bilingüe*, Planeta (novel).

1993, *El embrujo de Shanghai*, Plaza & Janés (novel).

1996, *Las mujeres de Juanito Marés*, Espasa-Calpe (anthology).

2000, *Rabos de lagartija*, Lumen (novel).

2001, *Un paseo por las estrellas*, RBA (articles).

2002, *Cuentos Completos*, Espasa-Calpe (stories).

2005, *Canciones de amor en Lolita's Club*, Lumen (novel).

2011, *Caligrafía de los sueños*, Lumen (novel).

ENGLISH TRANSLATIONS

1981, *Golden Girl*, translated by Helen Lane, Farrar, Straus and Giroux (novel).

2005, *Lizard Tails*, translated by Nick Caistor, Harvill (novel).

2006, *Shanghai Nights*, translated by Nick Caistor, Harvill (novel).

·

AWARDS AND RECOGNITIONS

1959, Premio Sésamo for the story "Nada para morir."

1960, Finalist for the Premio Biblioteca Breve for *Encerrados con un solo juguete*.

1965, Premio Biblioteca Breve for *Últimas tardes con Teresa*.

1973, Premio Internacional de Novela México for *Si te dicen que caí*.

1978, Premio Planeta for *La muchacha de las bragas de oro*.

1985, Premio Ciudad de Barcelona de Literatura en Lengua Castellana for *Ronda del Guinardó*.

1990, Premio Ateneo de Sevilla de Novela for *El amante bilingüe*.

1993, Premio de la Crítica de Narrativa Castellana for *El embrujo de Shanghai*.

1994, Premio Europeo de Literatura Aristeion for *El embrujo de Shanghai*.

1997, Premio Juan Rulfo.

1998, Premio Internacional Unión Latina.

2000, Premio de la Crítica de Narrativa Castellana for *Rabos de lagartija*.

2001, Premio Nacional de Narrativa for *Rabos de lagartija*.

2002, Medalla de Oro de Barcelona al Mérito Cultural.

2003, Premio de la Associació d'Amics from UAB.

2004, Premio Extremadura a la Creación.

2008, Premio Cervantes.

2008, Premio Carlemany.

2010, Premio Fundación Cristóbal Gabarrón de Letras.
2010, Premio de Cultura de la Comunidad de Madrid.
2011, Insignia de Oro from UAL.

SERGIO

PITOL

(Mexico, 1933)

Writer and diplomat, Sergio Pitol's life has taken place between literary creation and comings and goings from his country of origin. Born on March 18, 1933, his childhood was tremendously difficult. He lost his mother and father, and his sister shortly thereafter, and in the middle of all those tragedies, he contracted malaria, which left him bedridden from ages six to twelve.

At that time, he and his brother were living under the care of their grandmother. In her long and detailed monologues, she told her grandsons, time and again, about that journey of scholastic formation that in her childhood had taken her to Italy, along with her father and sisters; but, above all, the hardships she lived through upon her return to Mexico, where the Revolution stole her young husband, along with several properties, and she was beset by difficulties of every sort. Since that time, his grandmother had tried to mitigate her suffering by incessantly rereading the books that she had filled the house with. His illness and those books made him a premature and voracious reader. In this way he became "a full-time traveler, a treasure hunter." While his brother went to school, played tennis, and rode horses, he spent his time traversing his grandmother's library, his first world map. So, hand in hand with Kipling and Conrad he came to know India and discovered the heart of Africa, and with Jack London, he began the difficult climb up the Chilkroot Trail, in search of destiny. "Literature saved my life," he has been recalled as saying on multiple occasions.

With the illness overcome, the longing to continue those travels would mark his future as a writer. He earned degrees in Law and Philosophy from Universidad de México, to then began his diplomatic career. In the years that followed he lived in a state of perpetual travel: he was an attaché and cultural advisor in Belgrade, Warsaw, Rome, Beijing, Paris, Budapest, Moscow, and

Barcelona. His knowledge of Polish, Italian, Russian, and English led him to excel in the field of translation. He has translated more than a hundred books. Among them were many standout writers, such as Henry James, Jane Austen, Vladimir Nabokov, Lewis Carroll, Virginia Woolf, and Joseph Conrad. The cities where he traveled became the settings for many of his stories.

Sergio Pitol says that he first started writing in a country house, where he had taken refuge to recover from a failure in love. The readings of those days, especially of Faulkner, would impel him to write his first story, "Victorio Ferri cuenta un cuento." For fifteen years he kept writing stories, making them his training, until in 1959 he published his first book *Tiempo cercado*. It would be followed by a body of work characterized by great narrative agility and a marked transgression of literary genres. This style is a response to Pitol's visceral relationship with literature, and it turns his writing into a kind of autobiography where the lived and the read intermingle.

After having already published dozens of books (among the most important ones *El tañido de una flauta*, *Nocturno de Bujara* and *El desfile del amor*), he returned to Mexico in 1988, and settled in Xalapa, where he currently resides. He continues to write and publish, and has received numerous awards and recognitions, noteworthy among them the Premio Nacional de Lingüística y Literatura, the prestigious Juan Rulfo, and in 2005, the Premio Cervantes. He's never participated in literary groups and has looked with suspicion at those closed nuclei that seem to exert a kind of power that has nothing to do with his concept of the life of a writer.

THE ACORN

The Torture of Doctor Johnson

It was thanks to this story that I was able to write again after a long period of creative paralysis.

In the early eighties I took a short trip to Bukhara. A Mexican friend living in Berlin came to see me in Moscow, where I was staying at the time. She'd gotten pregnant and she asked us, myself and another friend, a Russian, to accompany her to the Uzbek city in search of the father's family.

We made the trip by plane, first, and then by train. I had a notebook with me and during the trip I began to compulsively take notes about everything I was seeing: the landscape, the people, the fantastical cities in the Asian Russia, delirious places that easily combine dreams and the best of the Arab, Asian, and Slavic worlds.

I took detailed notes on these imaginary-seeming places, piecing together the form and tone of a story that, without knowing it, I'd already begun to write, and which would attempt to recreate the atmosphere of those spaces built between dream and wakefulness, between enchantment, history, and something resembling madness.

I returned to Moscow and immediately began working on the story. Everything I'd seen and noted down began to take shape, to organize itself into thick language, full of dark corners and demented stories. I wrote the story with vertiginous speed, with the vivid sensation of passage, not only because I was returning to writing after a period of absence, but also from the intuition that something in me had transformed, had advanced precipitously, after a period of incubation, to a place in which I felt myself fully employed as a writer.

In Conversation with the Dead

I have to acknowledge the influence of many writers, including William Shakespeare, Miguel de Cervantes, Tirso de Molina, Jorge Luis Borges, Pérez Galdós, Leo Tolstoy, Choderlos de Laclos, Anton Chekhov, Virginia Woolf, Luis Cernuda, William Faulkner, Christopher Isherwood, E. M. Forster, Thomas Mann, Hermann Broch, Henry James, Charles Dickens, Ford Madox Ford, Nikolai Gogol, Witold Gombrowicz, Franz Kafka, Alfonso Reyes, Bertolt Brecht, Carlo Goldoni, Arthur Schnitzler, Juan Rulfo, Marcel Schwob, Carlo Emilio Gadda, and Samuel Beckett.

I've been fortunate enough to translate some of these authors, and what I've learned from them is beyond repayment. I've said it elsewhere: few activities are as fruitful for a writer as translation. Translating allows access to the most hidden corners of a work, opening it up and then seeing how it takes shape before our eyes.

Few experiences have been more useful to me than translating that stylistic marvel that is Ford Madox Ford's *The Good Soldier*. Translating it meant untangling that confusing network of secrets, gossip, lies, and truths woven together to make the story. I was transformed by that experience, and found a previously unknown desire and energy to begin writing novels.

Those that I haven't translated I've read fervently. One of my great literary idols is Benito Pérez Galdós, so abused for so long by Spanish critics. The acceptance speech that Octavio Paz gave when he received the Cervantes Prize is practically a love letter to the author of *Episodios nacionales*. Anyone who ventures into the complex universe of his language can't help but come out dazzled at the narrative monument that he created, admired by authors like Luis Cernuda, María Zambrano, Luis Buñuel, Ramón Gaya, Jaime Torres Bodet, and Christopher Domínguez Michael.

Another of my great passions is the theater. I've read and reread the plays of Tirso and Chekhov. I've taken elements from them without which several of my novels would never have taken shape. Dialogue, for example, is difficult to take on successfully without referring to this genre; the same goes for the use of space, the movement of characters. The theater teaches, better than any other genre, how a story is woven together, how it unravels, changes, and ends.

We know, for example, that when Mann was writing his masterpiece, *Doctor Faustus*, and he reached a dead end, he would automatically resort to the theater. Especially Shakespeare's comedies, which he read to expand and enliven his writing—looking for plots, analyzing the English playwright's fantastical parade of characters—or simply in order to enjoy, with the pleasure and admiration of a student, the musicality of his language.

Coda

You started writing at twenty-three, in the shadow of Faulkner. Then you began taking trips all over the world. At fifty, the act of writing became a pleasure for you. Can you add to this statement?

I can tell you from personal experience that returning to one's first texts demands an activation of all of your defenses in order not to succumb to the negative vibrations that time builds up in them. It would be better to take a vow never to look backward! One risks that return becoming an act of penitence or atonement, or what's a thousand times worse, that you feel tenderness for the ineptitudes that really should embarrass you.

My first stories inevitably concluded in an agony that led to the death of the protagonist or, in the most benign cases, to madness. This was in 1957, and I was twenty-four. I moved with relish through a world of intense eccentricity where friends and teachers of various ages, nationalities, and professions coexisted with perfect ease, although, as is to be expected, the young people were dominant. Alfonso Reyes, Carlos Pellicer, Juan José Arreola, Juan Rulfo, María Zambrano, Rosario Castellanos, Augusto Monterroso, Margo Glantz, Elena Poniatowska, Juan García Ponce, Carlos Monsiváis, José Emilio Pacheco, and Luis Prieto made up part of that group, to which were added, over the years, after my return to Mexico, the young Juan Villoro, Mario Bellatin, Fabio Morábito, Jorge Volpi, and Álvaro Enrigue. Apart from the orthodox eccentrics, the rest of the group was characterized by a passion for lively and intelligent conversation, a penchant for irony, a lack of respect for preconceived values, for false glory, for petulance, and, especially, for complacence.

One fine day I realized that my time and space had been saturated and contaminated by the external world and that the noise was reducing, in an unfortunate way, two of my greatest pleasures: reading and dreaming. I had to leave, to change scenes, emerge from the magma. I rented a house in Tepoztlán, which at the time was a small town, apart from the world, lacking electricity even, and I fixed it up in order to spend holidays there. I remember that during my first stay I plunged fervently into the prose of Quevedo and the novels of Henry James. At times it seemed like my spiritual health was returning.

In a few weeks I'd written my first three stories: "Victorio Ferri cuenta un cuento," "Amelia Otero," and "Los Ferri," which take place in San Rafael, a version of Huatusco, the small city in Veracruz where my grandmother lived for many years, where my parents were born and grew up and were married, where my brother was born as well. The plots, the characters, and a slew of details with which I tried to create the right atmosphere came from the stories that I heard my grandmother tell over and over during my childhood and adolescence, stories based on a forever longed-for Eden, the world that the Revolution had turned to ashes. That was my first active incursion into literature, my leap into writing.

To *Infierno de todos* I owe the ability to let go of that expired world that wasn't my own, only tangentially related to me, and this allowed me to take on a literature with greater fidelity to the real. When *Infierno de todos* was published I was living in Warsaw. Three years before I'd begun a trip through Europe that at first I thought would be very short. I visited all the essential places and eventually stayed in Rome for a while. For various reasons, I stayed away from Mexico from that point on, changing location often, almost always through the intervention of chance, until late in 1988, when I returned to the country.

The last story to appear in *Infierno de todos*, "Cuerpo presente," finished in Rome, 1961, signified the closing and farewell to that vicarious world about which I'd been writing up till then. At that point I began a new narrative period in which I used these travels as backdrops for dramas suffered by various characters—the majority of them Mexican—who unexpectedly confronted the different beings who inhabited them, and whose existence they hardly suspected. They concerned interior voyages whose stops included

Mexico City, a few towns in Veracruz, Cuernavaca, and Tepoztlán, but also Rome, Venice, Berlin, Samarkand, Warsaw, Belgrade, Beijing, and Barcelona.

Years later, in the latter of these, I was able to finish *El tañido de una flauta*, my first novel. I was thirty-eight at the time with very few skills to my name. When I wrote it I established a tacit promise with literature. I decided, without knowing what I'd decided, that instinct should impose itself over every other mediation. Instinct would be what determined form.

El tañido de una flauta was, among other things, an homage to German literature, to Thomas Mann in particular, whose novels I'd often revisited since my adolescence, and in whose journals and essays I've submerged myself with a pleasure that is beyond words: his *The Story of a Novel*, that amazing workshop of narrative creation, has been of vital importance to my work.

Afterward, as a tacit or explicit homage to some of my tutelary gods— Nikolai Gogol, H. Bustos Domecq, and Witold Gombrowicz, among others—I wrote *El desfile del amor, Domar a la divina garza,* and *La vida conyugal*, a trilogy of novels closer to the Carnival than to any other ritual. I've written elsewhere about that experience:

> As the official language that was spoken and heard every day became more and more rarified, in my novels, to compensate, it became more animated, more sarcastic and lowbrow. Every scene was a caricature of the world, which is to say, a caricature of a caricature. I found refuge in vacillation, in the grotesque . . . I quickly became aware of the function of the communicating vessels in the three novels that make up the *Tríptico del Carnaval*: they were working to reinforce a grotesque vision that gave rise to them. Everything that aspired to solemnity, to sanctification, to self-complacence, would suddenly decline into mockery, vulgarity, and ridicule. A world of disguises took hold. The situations, both together and separately, exemplify the three fundamental phases that Bakhtin located in the carnivalesque farce: the coronation, the dethronement, and the final sacrifice.

In Xalapa, where I moved in 1993, three later books came together, *El arte de la fuga, El viaje,* and *El mago de Viena,* a compendium of passions and profanations that as it moves along becomes a subtraction. With the end of the worldly environment that for decades surrounded me, the disappearance from my vision of the scenes and characters that for years suggested the cast that populated my novels, I was forced to transform myself into an almost unique character, which was in a sense pleasurable, but also disturbing. Leo Tolstoy wrote in his journal that he could only write about what he knew and had lived through personally. His masterful work feeds from the experiences that he accumulated over his life.

Writing, it seems to me, is ultimately a process of weaving and unweaving various narrative threads that are tightly wound and where nothing is ever closed and everything is always conjecture; it's up to the reader to sort them out, to solve the mystery at hand, to choose among a number of suggested possibilities: dream, delirium, wakefulness. Everything else, as always, is words.

A THOUSAND FORESTS

"By Night in Bukhara"

FROM *Nocturno de Bujara* (By Night in Bukhara)

for Margo Glantz

I

We'd tell her, for instance, that the flutter and cawing of the crows would drive travelers insane. To say that the birds invaded the city by the millions was to say nothing. You had to see the branches on the tall eucalyptus, on the leafy chestnuts, at the point of splintering, where that intense mass of feathers, beaks, and scaly legs congealed, to realize the absurdity of reducing certain phenomena to a number. What did it mean to say that a flock of a thousand crows, or better yet of hundreds of thousands of crows, swarmed deafeningly under the Samarkand sky before gathering in its tree-lined parks and avenues? Not a thing! You had to see those pitch-black swarms in order to stop trying to count them and yield to a vague but discernible notion of the infinite.

"At the hour when the crows begin to fall," Juan Manuel would say, "it's not unheard of for some Portuguese tourist to throw himself from an eighth-floor balcony of the Hotel Tamerlane, or for a Scandinavian diplomat exploring the city to start cawing, flapping his arms and hopping around, trying to take flight, until a medic shows up to take him someplace where they can give him the necessary sedative injection."

"It's the ferocity of the crow's screech just as it's torn to pieces," I would interject. "At that hour, at nightfall, you see them falling from the trees like rotten fruit, gutted, their wings broken, pieces of brains, legs, a cloud of feathers—a fucking spectacle, I swear to God—while in the thick foliage above, the survivors hop fearfully from branch to branch or crouch down attempting to camouflage themselves because they wouldn't dare try to flee."

"There are these desert cranes with long, narrow beaks and powerful teeth," he'd cut in, "the *Ciconida dentiforme*; it swoops down and tears them to pieces. You probably know all about this; from what I've read they fly in from the coasts of Libya, and they've taken over huge sections of Calabria. It's the terror that makes the birds give out that dreadful sound. Have you ever seen them attack? Feri, the Hungarian, almost lost his mind during his convalescence because of those musical slaughters."

She'd give us this annoyed sort of look and then, deciding to take part in the conversation, would declare insolently: "I believe that actually the Lapland gulls are the ones who feed off the flesh of other birds."

"Lapland gulls? The *Larus argentatus laponensis*?" Juan Manuel would ask with an absolutely straight face. "The truth is I don't know the first thing about that species. Well, as you know, when it comes to ornithology I'm a complete ignoramus . . . Are you sure it's called a *Lapland* gull? My reference books are terribly rudimentary, but they don't mention it. I should probably consult something more technical."

Then the birds would be forgotten and without the slightest transition we'd start giving her a tour of the holy, mysterious, and opulent city of Samarkand. Of its history, its architecture, its culture. What mattered most was that she not talk, that she be kept quiet as long as possible.

"It doesn't have the charm or the cultural prestige of Bukhara," we admitted a few days before she left on her trip. "Bukhara is the city of Avicenna, and Samarkand of Tamerlane and Genghis Khan. That's the difference, and it's enormous, can't you see that?"

II

I'm certain that when I was first in Warsaw my ignorance about Bukhara was absolute. It's possible that I'd glimpsed its name in a novel. Is it possible there's a "Wizard of Bukhara" in the *Thousand and One Nights*? I may have seen the name by chance in a carpet seller's window. But from the day that Issa showed up with her travel brochures, Juan Manuel and I devoted ourselves, each in his own way, to reading everything we could about the Uzbek cities of central Asia to add a layer of verisimilitude to our stories.

Only a few weeks ago, just before traveling to that region, I heard a Mexican theosophist who was passing through Moscow say that Bukhara was one of the navels of the Universe, one of the points (I believe he spoke of seven) where the earth is able to form a connection with the heavens. I don't know how factual that is, but when I arrived to that city at dusk and saw for myself the pale color of the celestial dome above I started to feel like I was at the very center of the planet. It's possible that this idea burrowed into me, and when I crossed the walls that encircled the old city it intensified the sensation of magnetism and magic I felt: I approached the bazaar, the Kasbah, and the inextricable Jewish quarter with the same utter astonishment that the encounter with certain books and films had produced in me as a child.

The heart of Bukhara doesn't seem to have seen a single change in the last eight centuries. I walked with Dolores and Kyrim through the labyrinth of alleys barely wide enough for two people. Extremely narrow paths that opened amazingly onto wide plazas from which rose the mosques of the Po-i-Kalan, of the Lab-i-Hauz, the Samani and Chashma-Ayub mausoleums, the slender, herculean Kalan minaret, the ruins of the ancient bazaar. At a certain hour, late into the evening, the traveler wandering through empty alleys (flanked by one-story, and occasional two-story, windowless houses with wooden doors whose every centimeter is carved over, each different from the one before, narrating in some way the history and signaling the position of the family that inhabits it, reinscribed every hundred-and-fifty or two-hundred years with the same designs, legends, and symbols they bore in the eighteenth, fifteenth, and twelfth centuries) can hear the echo of his own steps coming back to him from another time.

I look over the postcards I bought in Bukhara. I'm sure I don't completely recognize those places, maybe I was there, maybe I wasn't. I'm overwhelmed by the thought that I saw for myself the marvels that I shuffle before my eyes; I can barely reproduce the city; what I remember in particular is the sound of my steps, my conversations with Dolores and Kyrim, the sense of intoxication, of delight, that came over me every time one of those alleys opened onto the smooth angles of a mausoleum; I remember the Islamic music filtering through windows, music that possibly had changed very little since the current inhabitants' ancestors built the religious center that quickly became a commercial emporium where caravans from every corner of Turkistan and even farther off—from China, from Byzantium, from the nascent Russia—converged; they communicated with signs, speaking words that were understood by few, displayed their merchandise between the arcades and in the nearby bazaar, exchanged money, knotted cords, bartered; small tubes of gold dust and pieces of silver, coins from Toledo, from Crete, from Constantinople, from across the whole Orient, changed hands in an intricate network of marketplaces. After walking one night through Bukhara, the grandeur of Samarkand, experienced the following day—so much gold, so much splendor, such long walls, such tall cupolas!—seemed like vulgar riches in comparison, a strange vision of wealth that prefigured a kind of Hollywood. As if Tamerlane had intuited the future work of Griffith or De Mille and amused himself by showing them the way!

But not all was still and silent by night in Bukhara!

It was the beginning of November. The cotton harvest was ending in Uzbekistan and in its rich cities weddings were being celebrated. A moment came when Bukhara was submerged in sound and madness. It must have been then, while witnessing one of these wedding processions, that I felt the first brush, the first flutter, without ever quite managing to locate it, of a story that had taken place twenty years before, when Juan Manuel and I would talk with an Italian painter, a perfectly detestable woman actually, and we suggested that she travel to Samarkand. I realize now that Bukhara is the city we should have recommended: everything that we eventually invented to urge her along seemed plausible in Bukhara. When we described Samarkand to her what was somehow being sketched out in our imaginations was this other city.

While we walked the alleys trying to find the center of the city, the true navel of the universe to which the theosophist must have been referring, Kyrim recounted with delight horrifying stories he'd heard in the homes of his friends' parents, stories no doubt passed down from one generation to another, to be passed on in this way for centuries to come; stories describing spine-chilling crimes, cadavers carved up in extremely complex manners. Their narrator's delight revealed the cruelty that possesses the tribes of the desert in the most unexpected moments; but, like in the *Thousand and One Nights*, those stories lacked any true gore, they were a kind of metaphor for fatality, for the grace and misfortune that comprise all human destiny (because Allah is always most wise!) and rather than terrifying us they inspired a kind of relief, a kind of calm.

It's not unthinkable that Issa, the Italian painter, visited Bukhara when she made the trip to central Asia. It's possible that it was there she contracted the illness that shattered her reason and whose details we never managed to fully understand.

III

The extravagance of our stories exasperated her more often than not, though some did amuse her. They made her forget her idiotic sentimental problems with Roberto, the Venezuelan student she'd inexplicably taken as a lover. It was one thing for her to sleep with him and quite another that she took him everywhere and encouraged him to talk all the nonsense that she gushed over later. But if that wasn't absurd enough, Roberto's reciprocation of her passion was even more so: that neurotic, bitter, and rapacious woman bore absolutely zero resemblance to the young, moon-faced blondes that he was always with, those fun-loving waitresses from the bar near the Plac Konstytucji.

When Juan Manuel was in Warsaw we'd get together at a small café in the Hotel Bristol. There came a moment, after we'd met the painter, when we almost stopped going there; Issa drank too much, she talked too much; the only thing that interested her was the story of her life, reliving her past triumphs (which we assumed were lies!), and eventually forcing us to listen to the endless litany of grievances she held against Roberto, who would promise to come by for her and almost always stood her up.

Before I met her, I'd seen her several times in the Bristol's restaurant. Always alone. At once desolate and charged with disdain for everything around her. By chance, I came to know some of her circumstances. She was a very rich woman, related to large industrialists from the north of Italy. She painted. Or rather she had painted at one time; she'd exhibited in several important galleries in Europe (at great personal cost). It wasn't clear exactly what she was doing in Poland. Apparently she'd come in pursuit of a Varsovian lover and had stayed in the country out of inertia. She may have been afraid to return to the bosom of her family and to a city saturated with failures, hoping that by some miracle her work would be recognized. One day I found her sitting with Roberto, who I knew vaguely. The Venezuelan stood to greet me with an affability that must have struck me as suspicious. He took me to the table and introduced me to his friend, then he announced that he had to step away for a few minutes and he left us alone. We waited until the restaurant closed, but he never came back for her. From then on I never managed to shake her off. She transformed me against my will into her confidant, her audience. The exhaustion that she produced in me was totally oppressive.

Jealousy began to take an alarming toll on her. She wept in public, she'd make scenes. One day her manner was less dismal than usual and she announced that she'd decided to cure herself of such an unsatisfying love. The best way, she thought, was to put some distance between them. No, she didn't think it was the right time to go back to Italy; what she needed was to travel, to see new places, and earlier that day she'd passed by the Wagons-Lits office and hadn't been able to contain herself. She'd booked a ticket for an excursion that included Moscow, Kiev, and Leningrad. She had a handful of travel brochures with her. In about three weeks, she'd be leaving for Moscow. She couldn't work; she'd started a large oil canvas that could be her master work, she explained, but she'd been suddenly overcome with apathy, and the smallness of her studio was suffocating; besides, Roberto's vulgarity had drained her more than she could ever have imagined it would, and now he'd gone to the mountains without even bothering to tell her except at the very last moment and only by telephone. When he came back he wouldn't find her in Warsaw; she'd be on the steppe. This trip would help her to recover the necessary strength to break it off with that lout and return to her work with the rigor to which she was accustomed.

Juan Manuel started leafing through one of the tourist pamphlets: it listed the itinerary that Issa had chosen, along with another that featured several other cities, including Samarkand. There was a full-page color photograph of the Registan.

"How is it possible you didn't choose this trip?" he exclaimed after reading a few paragraphs of the leaflet. "Is it because you lack the money or the curiosity? Do you realize you might never have a chance to see these places again? Think about it! Did you know that Samarkand was built at the same time as Babylonia? It's the only city from that period that's still inhabited today! The strangest things happen in Samarkand. Do you remember Feri, the Hungarian pianist who lived in Dziekanka last year? He went there to spend the holidays with some friends who were from there. When he came back he told us the most incredible things."

We set about using every tool we keep in storage for times when we attempt a description of places like this, an assortment of clichés, of facile images, of non-specifics that confuse the Caucuses with Byzantium, Baghdad with Damascus, the Near with the Far East, mentioning Yakut and Samoyedic princes, barbarian rituals, and refined cruelties whose setting was Samarkand and whose informant and protagonist were the young Feri, who'd survived extraordinary experiences that began the moment he got off the train and discovered that the friends who should have been there to meet him, his old friends from the conservatory in Budapest, were not on the platform; instead, he found two men with thick beards, one old and the other young, wearing cloaks with astrakhan collars, hats of the same material, and knee-high black leather boots, who studied him carefully as if they were trying to recognize or identify him. Feri thought they might have been his friends' relatives and that for some unforeseen reason they'd come instead to welcome him; he approached and asked in an extremely rudimentary Russian if they were there for him; he clarified that he was Feri Nagy, and gave the names of his classmates in Budapest. They replied affirmatively in Russian; then they spoke briefly in their own language, a conversation that seemed unnaturally formal to him. The young one took his suitcase and with a ceremonial gesture invited him to follow them.

They entered the Asian city, a true bazaar of narrow alleys, Feri said, of low walls, ornately carved doors that opened onto courtyards filled with pomegranate trees, rose bushes, and swarms of children producing a sound almost as deafening as the crows he would later observe every evening in the city's parks. The children peered through the doorways, chubby and fat-headed, muttering strange sounds in their language that sounded like warnings for him to leave, telling him he still had time to turn back to the station and catch the first train that would take him away from Samarkand. As he put it, the sounds resembled a phrase in Hungarian that meant, "Return to thine own house, Satan!"

One of us described the house they came to, which was just like every other. In one corner, a blind wall and a door; on a second floor, a tiny window covered in iron bars. Once inside, they crossed a courtyard that was also planted with roses and pomegranates; the only difference was the absence of children. Both the old and the young man in astrakhan-collared coats walked very upright, their movements identically martial; they led him up a narrow staircase that ended at a terrace. Across this terrace there was a very simple, almost monastic room whose furniture consisted only of a narrow bed and a small table with a washbasin. The older one clapped a few times and launched a volley of barking shouts that contrasted harshly with the sobriety of his manner. A young woman appeared with a pitcher of water and filled the basin. Feri had always been bothered by having to bathe with other people around, but he felt compelled to take off his shirt and wash his face, neck, and arms in front of the two men who, standing in the doorway, now seemed more like guards than hosts. He took a shirt from his suitcase and was about to put it on when the young woman returned with an Arabic djellaba, and through the older one's gestures, which were practically orders, he was made to understand that he had no option but to put it on.

"He felt completely ridiculous. You met Feri, didn't you?" Juan Manuel asked again. "No? He was an extremely timid young man, incapable of offering even the slightest resistance. It's easy to picture him in that situation, obeying every order they gave him, not arguing back. Because, when it came to it, with what language would he have responded? Every time he tried to say anything in Russian they responded yes, of course, certainly, and went right back to talking to each other in that language he didn't understand a single word of."

Then they went to the living room. A young man around his age, dressed in European style, to the point that that anyone might have mistaken him as Mediterranean, someone from Palermo or Athens, perhaps, welcomed him in and sat him down next to the princess.

"What princess?" the Italian finally asked with a hint of interest.

We had to explain that Feri had been taken to the house of Circassian aristocrats.

"In Samarkand you can still find the descendants of some of the oldest families in the world."

They were sitting on rugs, between heaps of cushions and pillows. The room was elegant and at the same time extremely filthy. The elegance wasn't obvious, it took work to detect it, knowing where and in what it resided. Only someone with a trained eye could see it. The average mortal would have seen only confusion, filth, and disorder. The aging princess was draped in rich brocades, but she was barefoot, and the stench emanating from her body was unspeakable—a mixture of sweat, grimy feet, unwashed clothes, rancid oil, and vulgar perfumes. The men, on the other hand, seemed very clean. The grandson was the only one dressed in European clothes; everyone else, men and women, were dressed up in the most extravagant manner imaginable; almost all of them had on knee-high black boots, some wore gilded tunics, and others leather and chamois jackets and pants with astrakhan hoods and collars; the women's brightly colored tunics barely concealed their underwear. The ensemble, according to Feri, who wasn't terribly observant—looked like an enlargement of a Persian miniature.

"Does that mean anything to you?" I interrupted, turning to Issa. "To me, nothing. A Persian miniature? What does that mean? A Persian miniature could be anything, a harem or a hunt. And Hungarians, as you know, are Asians, and because of this our beloved Feri Nagy was starting to feel like a fish in water. He didn't need words to make himself understood. And he never managed a good description of the party because at bottom there was nothing strange about it to him. It was as natural as attending a birthday dinner at the Gellert in Budapest—the only thing was that the aging princess didn't seem to like him at all."

"But where was he? In the bazaar?"

"You haven't understood a thing, because deep down you're just like Feri. You take everything naturally, no matter where you are. How could he have been in the bazaar when we've been trying to explain to you for hours that he was at a party in the home of Circassian princes!"

"For starters, I know there aren't any houses like that or princes there. To me it seems like the only thing this Feri did was sell you a pack of lies, which you bought completely."

"Possibly. But I can guarantee that he didn't invent the scars; we saw them ourselves."

"That's right, we saw them, and I promise you they weren't anything to laugh at. Alright, let's start at the beginning. First came a lamb stew, bunches of aromatic herbs, and at the same time, without the least sense of order, sweets made from honey, from pine nuts, from pistachio, spicy seeds, bowls of soup, and according to him an exquisite peach brandy to accompany the food. At first the old lady kept herself aloof even though she was right next to him, and treated him with arrogance, disdain, like some interloper trespassing in her home by who knows what trickery, but by the second or the third glass

she started smiling at him, offering him incomprehensible words, feeding
him sweets between her swollen fingers and her perpetually black fingernails.
The young man in Western clothes didn't eat: he sat in a corner monoto-
nously playing a drum and intoning a very languid, very soft Oriental song;
at moments his face took on an almost feminine expression. That food, that
mixture of fats and honey, would have made me sick; Feri, on the other hand,
was enchanted. Everyone approached him, crowded around, smiling, serving
him glass after glass of brandy, feeding him lamb chops or sweets with their
fingers, putting dates in his mouth. Feri was a real specimen! By now he was
perfectly at home with the stench that at first had bothered him so much,
and in fact he inhaled it with delight, as though it complemented perfectly
the honey sweets and the aroma of the brandy. Yes, at a given moment, he
had the sensation of having reached the promised land; he wanted to stand up
to give a toast but he discovered that his legs barely worked. Feri's ineptitude
is legendary, and with alcohol, he's a disaster. By this point the group was
crowded close around him, smiling, expectant, anticipating his words, his
gestures. Their faces and open collars poured sweat. Only one girl, the same
one who'd brought the water and the djellaba to the small bedroom, moved
away at that moment to the other corner of the room and began to whisper
a contrapuntal melody to her companion, the boy dressed as a European.
The features of the musical duo were severe, absent, as if they were both in
a trance, in contrast to the rest of the family, who would explode into laughter and then hush suddenly; there was no doubt that they were waiting for
something to happen; their eyes glowed, their teeth glowed. Feri had never
in his life seen such glowing white teeth. Now completely unable to stand, he
thrust out his chest, extended an arm, lifted his glass, and toasted to love, to
the song of the nightingale, to friendship, to the color of the pomegranate, to
their encounter that afternoon. Did you ever hear his voice? What a shame! I
can't believe you never heard it! Feri was the prince of Dziekanka, a boy with
a truly harmonious voice, grave and baritone and very well cultivated. When
he spoke in Hungarian it was like he was singing. These apparently were the
words that the aristocrats had been waiting for. The moment he stopped,
the drums crashed in a frenzy and the whole gathering let out a savage cry,
although the right adjective isn't savage but *ancient*, an archaic howl, in fact.
Someone, no doubt the old woman, refilled his glass and took advantage of
the movement to erupt into coarse laughter and to stroke his cheek with her

filthy, calloused hand. That was the last thing he remembered. When he woke up he was naked in the narrow cot in the room they'd first taken him to. He thought he was dying. His body ached miserably, but not everywhere, because there were some parts, his legs, for instance, that he couldn't feel at all. For a terrifying instant he thought that they'd been amputated. An agonizing movement brought his hand to his thighs—they were still there. He lifted his head slightly and could see his whole body, stained as if a bucket of pomegranate dye had been poured on him. It didn't take much effort to realize that the stains were in fact streaks of black crusted blood, that his body had been horribly injured, that some of the wounds, inflicted several days before from what he could tell, had an unsettling look, that surely several days had passed since they'd been dealt and that they would soon be infected. He sat up as much as he could and covered his body with a sheet. He didn't have the strength to dress. He went down the stairs, through the courtyard, deserted at that hour, and reached the street. It was dawn. He walked for several blocks. Lights were coming on in some windows. He heard steps close by. With the last of his strength, he screamed, and then he fainted. He woke up in a hospital, and was never able to gather whether hours or days had passed since he'd fainted. While his wounds healed (despite their grim appearance, they were not so severe, although the ones on his groin were very painful) his only diversion—if you could even call it that!—consisted in spending his afternoons watching the sun set from the balcony and awaiting the frightening arrival of the desert cranes on the hunt for crows. When they released him, he looked desperately for the house where the dinner had been, but he never managed to find it. Several times he went to the station just as the trains were arriving; he hoped that chance would offer him another encounter with his hosts, but they never appeared. That's the way Feri is, utterly Oriental: he'd found his slice of heaven and he didn't want to lose it. Finally they forced him to leave the city and he came back to Warsaw. He was in another world. He wanted to drop out and talked about elixirs and the kind of pleasure that we could never comprehend, and because no one paid any attention to him he ended up returning to his country. They say he lost interest in the piano, and it's a shame because he really did have a gift for it."

"I have no doubt whatsoever that the only thing this Feri ever did was amuse himself with you. He wouldn't have dared try to slip me all that nonsense."

"Possibly. You Europeans are shrewder when it comes to this sort of thing. In any case, no matter what the people are like, just seeing the monuments would be worth it. Think of the bazaars, the fabrics! The point, ultimately, is to see another continent!"

"It might be worth it."

And one day she announced that she'd changed her ticket, that she'd be leaving in three or four days, and that when she got back she'd tell us all about her time in Samarkand. We were never able to hear the story.

IV

Juan Manuel once gave me a text by Jan Kott, "A Short Treatise on Eroticism." I found it among my Polish books, with the quote I was thinking of the day after our nocturnal walk through Bukhara, as we were preparing for our return to Samarkand, and Kyrim and Dolores were recalling the wedding ceremonies. I'll attempt a translation: "In darkness the body is split into fragments, into separate objects. They have an independent existence. It is my touch that makes them exist *for me*. Touch is a limited sense. Unlike sight, it does not embrace the entire person. Touch is inevitably fragmentary; it decomposes. A body experienced through touch is never an entity; it is just a sum of fragments that exist side by side."

I had tried to remember that quote as we were leaving Bukhara, and rereading it I was glad to learn that I hadn't missed the sense of it. We were at the airport, in an ivy-covered waiting area in the open air, with small tables and wood benches around a wide garden. It was filled with German tourists. They were all old. The childish rose color on the men's cheeks faded on their noses, revealing networks of tiny veins and purple blotches; the women's robust legs (like the Jack in a Spanish deck) repeated the same veiny pattern, but their violet knots looked less innocent. They were stretched out on benches in the early November morning, absorbing the last solar rays of the year. That scene, the ivy, the roses, the tourists asleep in the sun, created an atmosphere as distant as possible from anything that could be associated with an airport. Everything there refused the idea that, within thirty minutes, Dolores, Kyrim, and I would be aboard a machine that in less than an hour would deliver us, along with that blonde horde, to Samarkand.

I was suddenly bothered by the presence of those men and women, most likely from the Bundesrepublik. Everything about them, their emphatic laughter, their explosive voices, the clumsiness of their movements, seemed vulgar to me, and as a result, quite repellent. Fifteen hundred years before, when Bukhara was already a city, the ancestors of these invaders were still catching deer from the forests surrounding them and tearing them apart with their bare hands. Notwithstanding the quality of their clothing, the price of their cameras, and the evident desire to demonstrate their superiority, their gestures and their manners, in contrast to the locals, signaled a historical novelty, something extravagant and profoundly garish.

A dark mood washed over me. It wasn't just that the presence of those foreigners was a blight on the city—ultimately, I was one of them, despite my efforts to convince myself that at the root Mexicans were Asian. What most irritated me, recalling the events of the previous night with my traveling companions, Kyrim and Dolores, the marriage ceremonies that we'd witnessed, was my erasure of certain key details that I could only reconstruct, and vaguely at that, when I heard their recollections of them. I tried again to hear the screams, the drums, tried to picture the young people, jumping and skipping, the sharp red color of a jacket, the maddened, almost parodic steps of their dance, their eyes shining from a drunkenness produced not only by the alcohol but also by the communal excitement of the multitude; I saw a golden brocade tunic that contrasted with the jeans and the modern jackets of the majority of the guests. But what escaped me was the fire, the large bonfire that (I thought after hearing the story from my friends) no doubt represented a test of purification and virility. Kyrim, who had spent a good part of his life in Tashkent and of the three of us was the only one familiar with the region, explained that those ceremonies had nothing to do with Islam, but dated back to previous historical periods; recalling a time when this region witnessed the height of the cult of Zoroaster.

We had left the old city behind us. We were walking back to the hotel along a wide avenue and decided to sit and rest on a bench. I said that I'd like nothing more that night than to attend a theater performance; by watching the audience and observing their reactions I'd be able to catch a glimpse of the social fabric of Bukhara. To see how the public came in, where they sat, how they dressed, which sections were filled with older people, which with younger, when and how they laughed, the intensity of their applause. I'd done it elsewhere: I'd seen a Turkmen opera, a puerile and stirring piece called *Aína*, in Ashgabat, and a play very much like Faulkner's *As I Lay Dying*, written by a contemporary Siberian author, in a theater in Irkutsk. I wasn't interested in seeing anything Uzbek or Tajik or Russian in Bukhara. But how I would have loved to see the public's response to something more distant, more foreign, *Die lustige Witwe*, for instance—the degraded and marvelously banal foam of the ritual! Coinciding with a touring operetta from Tashkent, or Dushamne, or Moscow would have been a sublime experience!

Suddenly we heard a distant thunder, an abrupt howl, a drum roll followed by an impressive silence. The conversation stopped. A group of people appeared in the distance, illuminated by torches and emerging from one of the barbicans that gave passage to the interior city. Suddenly the multitude was on top of us. Two boys and an old man led the procession, followed by a cluster of drums and a handful of uncommonly large trumpets, and behind them a disordered mass of some two-hundred to two-hundred-fifty people; they jumped in place as if bouncing off the pavement. The dancers' faces and gestures were extremely sober, almost inexpressive; then they started running and went for a good distance. We stood up and started following the parade. The three dancers (always two young men and an old one) that lead the procession went in turns: they danced frantically, sprung into the air, twisted their bodies as though they were falling, and righted themselves just before touching the ground, reestablishing a perfect balance; after a hundred meters they were absorbed into the mass and a new trio emerged to take the soloist roles. At moments the procession moved very quickly, at others it dragged along at a slow crawl, following the rhythm of the trumpets. Then the drums would roll and the human swarm seemed to freeze momentarily, then jumped in place, silently, their faces almost transfigured in ecstasy. When the immense trumpets took up again, the multitude issued a kind of strange moan, something bestial and primitive, an echo of the first sounds of man, and then everyone would start to run, never losing the rhythm of the dance, stopping once again for the drums and then repeating the entire ritual over again. Only the soloists, the dancers and acrobats who led the procession, danced constantly, in the moments of rest as well as the advance.

We followed them a ways, walking alongside, down the sidewalk, stunned, amazed, dazzled.

As a final walk that night, Kyrim proposed a visit to a park that housed the ancient tombs of the Samanids. We crossed a small birch grove. In the distance we could hear the thunder of the parade mixing with Uzbek or Turkmen music from nearby radios. There was no one around. We were the only people in that forest. The darkness made the tombs invisible. The tales of throat-slittings and mutilations that Kyrim had recently been telling us in the alleys of the old city started to weigh ominously on us. When we emerged from the park we heard the thunder again, and saw the mob in the distance. The parade didn't seem to be moving now. A glow illuminated a low building, wider than the others but likewise closed off to the outside. A much larger crowd than the one we'd seen before swarmed in front of its door.

We approached. The multitude was in fact no longer moving: it jumped and screamed with an unusual frenzy around what the next day Dolores and Kyrim told me was a bonfire. I can't understand how in only a few hours I could have forgotten everything about that fire, which was the central feature of the scene. Instead, I could remember, as if I was still seeing them, the intensity of some of the drunken gazes, the acrobatics, the fragment of a gold brocade tunic, a scarlet jacket, the monotonous rhythm of the drum, the screams, the expression of the young bridegroom who they took by the arms and shook to the rhythm of the dance, the calm faces of several women who looked out from the courtyard where they were, no doubt, guarding the purity of the bride. We had returned to the beginning of time. A mysterious intensity brought me to the earth. I wanted to dance with the natives, to shout like they did. When Dolores and Kyrim later described the huge bonfire that the howling multitude forced the bridegroom to jump over several times, I was shocked by the bias of my vision. How could I have forgotten the fire, not noticed it, when it was the fundamental element of the party?

A fragmentation of vision, just as in Jan Kott's treatise on eroticism, could be extended to every intense sensory experience. When touched, the world disintegrates, its elements separate, they become disconnected and are only perceptible in one or two powerful details that annihilate the rest. Why, for instance, a piece of red brocade under a distorted face, or a certain filthy turban, and not the bonfire that even now I cannot manage to reconstruct with any precision? Afterward, and this I did remember well, the young bridegroom passed through the doorway under two rows of torches that formed the roof of the universe, and he was handed to the women who would lead him to the bride. As soon as the bridal party was inside the house, the shouts and the sounds of the drums and the trumpets stopped, replaced by languid, undulating music; this was man's passage from the wilderness to the refinements of Islam. For reasons that aren't worth recalling, we didn't accept the invitation made by several young people to join in the celebration; for me, the crucial moment had already passed.

And it was in the airport in Bukhara (while we waited for the plane that would take us to Samarkand, and the fire that I was tormented at having forgotten was described) when the memories that had been trying to gather themselves together since the night before began to emerge: my years as a student in Warsaw, the unforgettable conversations with Juan Manuel in the Bristol café, the way we encouraged that tiresome painter, from whose overbearing stupidity the world fled like a plague, to extend her trip through the Soviet nation into Central Asia, the fabricated adventures of Feri, and, especially, an intense nostalgia for my lost youth. My hatred for the mob of sunbathing tourists flared up again, along with a momentary twinge of uneasiness about our role in the outcome of that Italian's trip to this same region twenty years before.

"It wasn't our fault—I have no reason to feel responsible," I said, and felt my companions staring at me without the slightest idea what I was talking about.

V

What could we have to feel guilty about? That Issa slowly became infected with our enthusiasm for the exoticism of the places she would be visiting, for the artistic relics that she'd soon come to know for herself, for the picturesque customs and the unfamiliar landscape that she'd soon witness? Because it was impossible that she really believed the story about Feri, the young Hungarian pianist we'd invented to misdirect her, to stupefy her, to free ourselves, if only temporarily, from her complaints, from the catalog of offenses that she held against Roberto, the unfaithful lover who at those hours, the ones we spent talking in the café, would be dancing with one of the waitresses whose aura of beer and sweat seemed to attract him so much. Blame? The thought was absurd. Not even at the time did it pass through my mind.

The painter's trip lasted three weeks. It was a relief knowing that we were free of her. When the holidays ended, Juan Manuel returned to Lodz to continue his studies, and I accepted an invitation to spend the season in Drohycin, a small ecclesiastical city in southeastern Poland, where the solitude allowed me to revise a book of stories that I wanted to publish when I returned to Mexico. I had suddenly begun to take literature seriously. Naïvely, I thought that from then on I'd be able to dedicate myself to it almost exclusively. One of the stories, vaguely gothic in color, was inspired in part by the image of the Italian painter. I began by imagining her living in that city. The theme was very simple, and developing it I attempted to explain something that typically leaves me stunned when I encounter it in reality: the passion of certain women for repugnant men. The protagonist of that short story is an Italian artist spending a season in Warsaw; she meets an individual of Polish extraction (he could have been Australian or an American), someone morally and intellectually primitive, with zero sensibility, without family in Poland but determined to live in Drohycin, the city of his ancestors.

The narrator, who had known the protagonist in a previous time, runs into her at a restaurant in the old marketplace, accompanied by an older man whose enormous bald head is completely out of proportion with his tiny body. He sits down with them at the table. The guy doesn't let anyone else speak. His stories are chillingly vulgar, he strings together nonsense about every possible subject and in the same breath mocks what he considers to be his companion's intellectual pretensions. The few words that she manages to slip into the conversation are met with disgusting jeers and comments on the part of that demon, whose abnormal head reddens at those moments and pours forth thick sweat.

The narrator gets up a few minutes later, nauseated by the couple. Almost more repugnant than his manners is the woman's submission, the beatific smile with which she listens to his platitudes. He is amazed by the couple's moral and intellectual disparity, and the perfect equilibrium that they've apparently managed to establish.

Years later, when he returns to Drohycin, he remembers that this was the city his friend mentioned as her future residence. Driven by inertia, indifferently, and then with more open curiosity, he begins to make inquiries after the couple. A crime has taken place whose causes he will never be able to determine. An extremely macabre and inexplicable conclusion remains a mere play of conjectures.

When I returned to Drohycin I called Juan Manuel and we agreed to meet in Warsaw. He arrived crestfallen and ill-tempered. He'd spent the previous weeks living through a love story with a film student who had been given an important role in a new movie by a famous director, instantly transforming her into a celebrity. He had been spending his time in cafés and restaurants engaged in intensely literary arguments about the difference between the reactions of the body and the mind at the moments when love ends. Everything we accept rationally meets its refutation in the senses, he said, aware that he wasn't discovering the Mediterranean, yet speaking with absolute conviction. A few times it surprised us that Issa never came around to abuse us with her travelogues. It never occurred to us to seek her out.

It wasn't until Juan Manuel visited later that we ran into Roberto with one of his happy barmaids. He was a bit drunk. At first we didn't understand much of what he was saying; after making him repeat the story several times, we started piecing things together. Issa had returned. She was in the hospital. The story that the doctors had told him was extremely strange. It seems that she'd been found one morning in one of those Asian cities she'd visited, wrapped up in a sheet, her body completely destroyed, as if she'd been attacked by a pack of animals that apparently had turned her body into a sieve. They had kept her in a clinic to cure her wounds and bruises, then they'd put her on a plane and when she landed in Warsaw she was hospitalized again. No one understood what she was talking about. Her conversation was peppered with incomprehensible words in an unknown language. He'd gone to see her twice, but Issa wouldn't let him or anyone else approach her bed. They had her on sedatives almost constantly. Her mother and a nephew had arrived from Italy to care for her and take her back as soon as she'd recovered. What annoyed him the most was that the painter owed him almost four hundred dollars for a leather jacket that he'd bought her in Bulgaria, and the family wouldn't even let him mention the subject. It was a lesson for him, he added, not to be such a jackass next time and just settle for the local flavors.

That was it. The thought of looking for her worried us. What was the point of visiting her if she couldn't or wouldn't see anyone? We never found out what happened or where she'd been. I wonder if she visited Bukhara, if the accident that so affected her had happened there. Soon afterward they took her to Italy and we never heard from her again.

A voice over the loudspeaker announced the next flight. The Aryan beasts, and us along with them, began to shake ourselves awake, to check our flight numbers, and to walk listlessly toward the gate that separated the garden from the landing strip.

Moscow, November 1980

Translated by Steve Dolph

WORK

1959, *Tiempo cercado*, Estaciones (stories).

1959, *Victorio Ferri cuenta un cuento*. Estaciones, La Aventura y el Orden (story).

1965, *Infierno de todos*, Universidad Veracruzana (stories).

1966, *Los climas*, J. Mortiz (stories).

1966, *Sergio Pitol*, Empresas Editoriales (autobiography).

1967, *No hay tal lugar*, Alacena/Era (stories).

1967, *Antología del cuento polaco contemporáneo*, Era (stories collection).

1970, *Del encuentro nupcial*, Tusquets (stories).

1972, *El tañido de una flauta*, Era (novel).

1975, *De Jane Austen a Virginia Woolf*, SEP-Setentas (essay).

1980, *Asimetría*, Difusión Cultural-Universidad Nacional Autónoma de México (stories).

1981, *Nocturno de Bujara*, Siglo XXI (stories).

1982, *Cementerio de tordos*, Océano (stories).

1982, *Juegos florales*, Siglo XXI (novel).

1983, *Olga Costa*, Gobierno de Estado de Guanajuato (essay).

1984, *Vals de Mefisto*, Anagrama (stories, new edition of *Nocturno de Bujara*).

1984, *El desfile del amor*, Anagrama (novel).

1988, *Domar a la divina garza*, Anagrama (novel).

1989, *La casa de la tribu*, Fondo de Cultura Económica (essay).

1990, *Cuerpo presente*, Era (anthology of stories).

1991, *La vida conyugal*, Era (novel).

1991, *El relato veneciano de Billie Upward*, Monte Ávila (anthology, new edition of *Cuerpo presente*).

1993, *Luis García Guerrero*, Gobierno del Estado de Guanajuato (essay).

1994, *Juan Soriano. El perpetuo rebelde.* Conaculta/Era (essay).

1996, *El arte de la fuga,* Era (essay).

1998, *Pasión por la trama,* Era (essay).

1998, *Todos los cuentos,* Alfaguara (stories).

1998, *Soñar la realidad. Una antología personal,* Plaza & Janés (essays and stories).

1998, *Olga Costa,* La Rana (monograph).

1999, *Un largo viaje,* Universidad Nacional Autónoma de México (anthology of stories).

1999, *Tríptico del Carnaval,* Anagrama (edition collecting the novels *El desfile del amor, Domar a la divina garza,* and *La vida conyugal*).

1999, *Una adicción a la novela inglesa,* ISSTE (essays).

2000, *El viaje,* Era (reportage).

2000, *Todo está en todas las cosas,* Lom Ediciones (stories).

2001, *Hasta mañana y buenos días,* Gobierno del Estado de Aguascalientes (essay).

2001, *El oscuro hermano gemelo,* Editora de Gobierno de Veracruz (stories).

2001, *La relación con India,* Instituto di Cultura-Biblioteca Gaspara Stampa (story).

2002, *Los cuentos de una vida,* Debate (complete collection of stories).

2002, *Adicción a los ingleses. Vida y obra de diez novelistas,* Lectorum (essays).

2003, *De la realidad a la literatura,* Fondo de Cultura Económica (essay).

2003, *Obras reunidas I,* Fondo de Cultura Económica (anthology).

2003, *Obras reunidas II,* Fondo de Cultura Económica (anthology).

2004, *Obras reunidas III,* Fondo de Cultura Económica (anthology).

2005, *El oscuro hermano gemelo y otros relatos,* Norma (stories).

2005, *El mago de Viena,* Pre-Textos (essay).

2005, *Los mejores cuentos,* Anagrama (story collection).

2006, *Obras reunidas IV,* Fondo de Cultura Económica (anthology).

2007, *Trilogía de la Memoria,* Anagrama (edition collecting *El arte de la fuga, El viaje,* and *El mago de Viena*).

2007, *Ícaro,* Almadía (stories).

2008, *Obras reunidas V,* Fondo de Cultura Económica (anthology).

2011, *Una autobiografía soterrada,* Anagrama (essay-story).

2011, *Memoria. 1933-1966,* Era (relato).

AWARDS AND RECOGNITIONS

1973, Premio Rodolfo Goes for *El tañido de una flauta.*

1980, Premio La Palabra y el Hombre for *Asimetría.*

1981, Premio Xavier Villaurrutia for *Nocturno de Bujara.*

1984, Premio Herralde for *El desfile del amor.*

1993, Premio Nacional de Lungüistica y Literatura.

1997, Premio Mazatlán de Literatura for *El arte de la fuga.*

1998, Guggenheim fellowship.

1998, Gran Premio de la Asociación de Cultura Europea.

1999, Premio Juan Rulfo.

2003, Honorary Doctorate from Universidad de Veracruz.

2005, Premio Roger Caillois.

2005, Premio Cervantes.

2007, Premio Italio nel Mondo, XII Edizione.

2011, Orden de Isabel la Católica del Reino de España.

JOSÉ
DE LA
COLINA
(Mexico, 1934)

José de la Colina is considered one of the most singular writers of Mexican prose. Although he was born in Santander on the 29th of March 1934, very soon thereafter, while his father, a printer and captain in the republican infantry, was fighting at the front, he left Spain with his mother and brothers to reside for a few years in France and Belgium. When the war ended, the whole family began a definitive exile that took them to Santo Domingo, Cuba and, finally, to Mexico, where the author has lived since 1941. Those formative years, as he himself has recounted, built in him many affinities that, different from other writers of his generation, had been born elsewhere and had taken root in him in an entirely natural way. The ambivalence of his unstable situation made his worldview, and his writing for that matter, "something slightly apart, something troubled by feelings of insecurity, of fragility, of the transience of all things." Since those years, exile has shown itself to be something exceedingly important to his literary creation.

He spent his childhood years between one job and another, escaping whenever he could to movie theaters, where he spent hours fantasizing about one calling or another: now a painter, now an actor (he even went to audition for Buñel's *Los olvidados*, for which he wasn't a great fit because he didn't have enough of a Mexican appearance), and he even dreamed of being a soldier in some other part of the world. When he was thirteen, however, his interest in literature imposed itself over all the rest, and he started working as a scriptwriter for the radio program *La legión de los madrugadores*. A few years later, he took his first steps into journalism as a film critic.

In 1955, at the age of twenty-one, he published his first book, *Cuentos para vencer a la muerte*. From that time onward, a path began to open up for him in the world of literature as a writer, editor, and critic. Those were years of discovery and voracious reading of all kinds of books, years during which he struck up friendships with a few writers and artists, and he began to frequent gatherings in cafés, to walk through the streets, fervently debating with Eugenio Olmedo, Arturo Souto, Juan Espinosa, Inocencio Burgos, Isidro Covisa, Guillermo Rousset, Antonio Montaña, and others. His second book, *Ven, caballo gris*, represented for the author a definitive transition to narrative art. He became interested (to the point of obsession) in the power of the word and the manipulation of literary language and narrative structure. Out of that, his next book was born, *La lucha con la pantera*, in which space is carved out for two recurrent themes in the author's oeuvre: film and the struggle to find love.

His work as a writer has always been coupled with his activity as a journalist; he has been a member of the editorial committee for the magazines *Nuevo Cine, Plural, Revista Mexicana de Literatura y Vuelta*. Along with Eduardo Lizalde he launched the venture of "El Semanario Cultural" in *Novedades*, and the publication remained in his hands for more than twenty years. For his work on that supplement he was awarded the Premio Nacional de Periodismo Cultural in 1984. Currently his blog *Correo fantasma* is a throng of cultural criticisms of every variety. His collaborations with a plethora of magazines— *El Nacional, Letras Libres, La Gaceta* (Cuba), *Le Chanteau du verre* (Belgium), *Contrechamp y Positif* (France), among many others—are interspersed with the publication of books of stories like *Tren de historias* (1998), *Álbum de Lilith* (2000), and *Muertes ejemplares* (2004).

The master of experimentation and nonconformity, the poet Octavio Paz said of him: "The figure of this solitary man is exemplary for more than one reason: as director and promoter of magazines and cultural supplements, as a critic and journalist of literature and film, as a writer and storyteller, as a translator. I said solitary, but I must add: cordial. I could also have said, without toying with opposites, impassioned and ironic, strict and generous, furious and tender. An incorruptible conscience, an open and loyal friend, a unique writer: his prose style is one of the best in Mexico. More than a solitary man, a libertarian: more than a libertarian, a free spirit." A free spirit, a proud anti-patriot yet to be recognized by his home country as the author of some of the best pages written in Spanish in recent times.

THE ACORN

The Torture of Doctor Johnson

In "La última música del *Titanic*," I was trying to show how among the most heroic characters of that historic shipwreck were these humble chamber musicians who were charged with playing songs to calm the passengers, which they did until the very end when every one of them was lost with the ship. This aspect of the *Titanic* story has always had a particular effect on me, and, at the same time, I was trying an approach to "continuous" prose—not detained or delayed by semicolons or periods—as a means to create a kind of fluid and "musical" narrative. Beyond that, and outside the merely literary reasons, I'm from the Spanish port city of Santander, where the news of the great shipwreck naturally had a great impact. (When I was a child, my father, who was sixteen at the time, would recount his memories of the event to me.) So the *Titanic* has always been part of my family mythology, and so in the seventies, when Mario Lavista, a composer and the editor of the magazine *Pauta*, asked me for something on the subject of music, and because I'm the kind of music lover who doesn't know much beyond the location of *do* on the piano, I wrote and sent him this piece, which you might call a fetish-text.

In Conversation with the Dead

I think before everything else a writer is in conversation with himself or with his other self. On the other hand, the writers who I reread the most in order to learn something about the texture and rhythm of prose, in my language, range from Cervantes to Luis de Granada, from Azorín to Corpus Barga, to Ramón Gómez de la Serna, to Octavio Paz, and, in other languages, from

Conrad to William Faulkner, to Marcel Proust, to Blaise Cendrars, to Michel Leiris, to Italo Calvino . . . and others.

CODA

Alejandro Rossi has described your prose as "open and at the same time pitch-perfect, free of dead phrases, tightly woven and rich in lateral gazes." Your style has also been praised by Octavio Paz. You've described your style as "madreporic."

I found the idea of madreporic writing in Blaise Cendrars. I often write with a "technique" that consists of putting down a first phrase or sentence and then expanding it, enriching it, with asides that are informative, narrative, descriptive, and sometimes even imagined or metaphoric, where the text itself "invites" me to add to it without disrupting the flow of the paragraph with periods and commas. This story is trying to be a complete and continuously fluid ("madreporic") narrative paragraph almost 1,350 words long.

It seems impossible to separate the experiences of a life of exile, a childhood in France, Belgium, Santo Domingo, Cuba, and finally Mexico, from literary work like yours. Can you speak about how this experience influenced your writing, the gaze of "the other" in your prose?

You're asking me to explain something that to me is still a mystery, but it's true that my writing has a certain geographical variety. With the risk of overly schematizing and falling into "the sublime," I'll say that I often define myself as an atheistic, stateless anarchist, and that from History and from "my" history I'm attracted to solitary, marginal characters, at odds with others. Besides that, I think that we're all exiled (starting from our mother's womb), although some, consciously or not, deceive themselves with a national or social or political identity or some creed.

A THOUSAND FORESTS

"The Final Music of the Titanic"
from Muertes ejemplares (Exemplary Deaths)

for Gerardo Deniz

Je sens vibrer en moi toutes les passions d'un vaisseau qui souffre
—*Baudelaire*

Just before midnight, between the 14th and the 15th of April, 1912, on its maiden voyage and during its fifth day crossing the Atlantic from Southampton, England, to New York, United States of America, the RMS *Titanic*, of the British company White Star, the largest and most luxurious passenger liner of all time, a Babylonian grand hotel on the water, in expert opinion unsinkable, with two thousand two hundred people aboard (aristocrats, multi-millionaires, people from the middle class, emigrant workers, sailors, machinists, service personnel, stokers), received a glancing lateral blow from an iceberg that suddenly appeared and before passing by scraped across the metal plates on the starboard side with a sound that the crewmen and passengers would describe as a soft grinding or the rolling of a thousand marbles or the brush of a piece of silk or the grazing of a giant finger on the metal hull of the ship, but which the machinists and stokers felt as the explosion of an enormous firearm, as a thunderclap, or the gush of a powerful surge of icy water, and following a shudder that awoke several passengers, the boat stopped in what would be the final point of its horizontal and surface trajectory, at 41° 46' N, 50° 14' W, and Captain Edward J. Smith, who that same night had been celebrating a party given in his honor by some of the most distinguished passengers, who may have danced a waltz with the beautiful

255

and talkative Countess of Rothes, the white-bearded and dignified Captain
Smith whose imposing demeanor didn't correspond to the commonness of his
surname and who at sixty-two had decided to crown his long and efficient
career with the White Star maritime company by retiring after that famous
voyage on the sumptuous boat that he considered invulnerable enough to have
ignored over the course of the day no less than seven radio messages from
other ships regarding the abundance of icebergs in the area, immediately
understood that the *Titanic* would go under in at most two hours and that
he had to keep it afloat as long as possible, carry out an orderly evacuation
of the passengers into lifeboats which, all together, could hold just over half
of the people aboard, send into the vast sea and the vast night surrounding
them the radio distress call, establishing the use of a signal composed of three
letters in Morse code: three dots, three dashes, three dots, S.O.S. (which can
mean both *Save Our Sailors* and *Save Our Souls*), order the broadside launch
of rocket flares, and accept that he would go down with the ship in the tradition of the navy, the navy mistress of the seas, the navy of "Rule Britannia,
Britannia Rule The Waves," can't you hear that song in the head of Captain Smith, if that head still exists somewhere, can't you hear him order his
radio operators and pyrotechnists to send their distress signals, advising his
crewmen to *behave like subjects of His Royal Majesty*, and among other hasty
measures to forestall the panic of the passengers just starting to come on
deck, most of them pulled from sleep, unable to understand or believe what
was happening, several still with a glass in hand because the toasts in the
Parisian ballroom had been prolonged, others playfully throwing pieces of ice
left behind by the cunning iceberg before it continued its anonymous destiny
into the night, some trembling now at the whistling and shuddering from
the boiler rooms and at the gradual inclination of the prow, Captain Smith
called for the members of the *Titanic*'s orchestra, who that same night had
been playing waltzes, polkas, romances, tangos, cakewalks, and ragtime at
the party in his honor, and who, now aware of the situation, began playing
again, fifteen minutes after midnight, in the same first class ballroom, and
then on the deck near the main staircase, and while the other passengers were
running, crowding together, colliding, embracing, putting on life jackets, and
trying to find a place among the insufficient lifeboats, there stood those seven
musicians among whom I can regretfully only name their leader, Wallace
Hartley, because the only image of them I've seen is from a book, a group

of oval photographs reproduced so poorly that, while I can see their faces clearly, two have mustaches, two wear hats (one of these a top hat), none of them are old, and one may as well be a boy, their names and the specific instruments they played are tiny and illegible, though in one of the images the subject's hand rests on the neck and strings of a cello, so that, without further information, I have to assume that the orchestra was composed like many others of the period for this purpose, which is to say a small portable piano, a saxophone, a flute or clarinet, a violin or cello, and possibly a banjo or ukulele for the ragtime, and maybe a drum kit, I don't know, the only thing that wouldn't have dissolved and corroded at the bottom of the sea would be a metal instrument, but when the scattered remains of the *Titanic* and the body of the ship were discovered by Robert D. Ballard and his team in 1985, seventy-three years later, nothing resembling a musical instrument was found, though they did find a number of miraculously intact bottles of wine and champagne, along with a doll's head and even shoes and boots, nor does anyone know, because the survivors' testimonies are inconsistent, what genre of music they were playing, they only describe "lively tunes," "happy medleys," "upbeat and highly syncopated rhythms," "ragtime," and ultimately I can only suppose that toward the end, two hours and fifteen minutes into the morning of Monday, April 15th, when the prow had already submerged and the bridge had been swept under the water and the majority of the fifteen hundred passengers who had not found a place in the lifeboats were huddled together at the stern (by now Captain Smith would have said it was every man for himself), as Thomas Byles, the chaplain, was hastily taking confessions and offering absolution, the seven brave musicians may have played a religious piece, or "God Save the King," or one of the four solemn military marches written between 1901 and 1907 by Edward Elgar under the title "Pomp and Circumstance," I can almost hear the music, almost see the seven men in black ties, standing very close together in a tight circle, trying to dilute their fear and exerting themselves with concentration, love, and professionalism, to play their music, virtually isolated from the chaos around them, the turmoil, the people shouting as they run past, struggling, colliding, weeping, screaming, moaning, praying, those seven apparently impassive Anglo-Saxons who, knowing it was useless to try to save the ship or to save themselves, applied their technique, their artistic pride, regardless of their musical background, to creating the perfect sound, to keeping the tempo, to not missing a note, to ultimately achieve what surely, though none of them would have realized it, was the best performance of their lives, each of them perhaps taking one solo during the *tutti* sections, as the water reaches their feet and it becomes difficult to stay upright because the deck is now inclined almost forty-five degrees, and suddenly they're interrupted and silenced by the tremendous explosion of the furnaces, and the flickering and sudden extinguishing of all the lights, and the shuddering of the stern as it splits after the explosion of the furnaces and detaches from the rest of the ship, and finally they drop their instruments or cling to them, everything tips vertically, everything goes down into the grasping, cold, black, savage waters, and our seven (im)mortal musicians drown and are dragged to the bottom of the ocean, down there, four kilometers deep, into silence, without music, where they have since lain, becoming *something rich and strange*, as Shakespeare would say, until the silent depths of the sea corrupts and dissolves their bones.

Translated by Steve Dolph

WORK

1955, *Cuentos para vencer a la muerte*, Los Presentes (stories).

1959, *Ven, caballo gris y otras narraciones*, Universidad Veracruzana (stories).

1962, *La lucha con la pantera*, Universidad Veracruzana (stories).

1962, *El cine italiano*, Universidad Nacional Autonoma de México (essay).

1971, "Los viejos," in *Papeles de Son Armadans* (story).

1972, *Miradas al cine*, SEP (film criticism).

1982, *El mayor nacimiento del mundo y sus alrededores*, Penélope/FONAPAS (stories).

1984, *La tumba india*, Universidad Veracruzana (stories).

1984, *El cine del Indio Fernández*, Ministerio de Cultursa de España (essay).

1986, *Luis Buñuel. Prohibido asomarse al interior*, J. Mortiz/Planeta (film essay coauthored by Tomás Pérez Turrent).

1987, *La tumba india y otros cuentos*, SEP (stories).

1992, *Aunque es de noche*, Vuelta (novel).

1993, *Viajes narrados*, Universidad Autónoma Metropolitana (stories).

1993, *Buñuel por Buñuel*, Plot (film essay coauthored by Tomás Pérez Turrant).

1998, *Tren de historias*, Aldus (stories).

2000, *Álbum de Lilith*, Daga (stories).

2001, *Libertades imaginarias*, Aldus (essay).

2004, *Traer a cuento. Narrativa (1959-2003)*, Fondo de Cultura Económica (anthology).

2004, *Muertes ejemplares*, Colibrí (stories).

2005, "Las medias fantasmas de Leda R." Ermitaño (erotic story).

2005, *Personerío (del siglo XX mexicano)*, Universidad Veracruzana (stories).

2005, *Zigzag*, Aldus (miscellaneous).

2007, *Portarrelatos*, Ficticia/UNAM/Difusión Cultural (micro stories).

2009, *Cuentos*, Universidad Nacional Autónoma de México (stories).

AWARDS AND RECOGNITIONS

1983, Premio Nacional de Periodismo de México.

1984, Premio Nacional de Periodismo de México.

2002, Premio Mazatlán de Literatura for *Libertades imaginarias*.

2005, Homenaje Nacional de Periodismo Cultural Fernando Benítez.

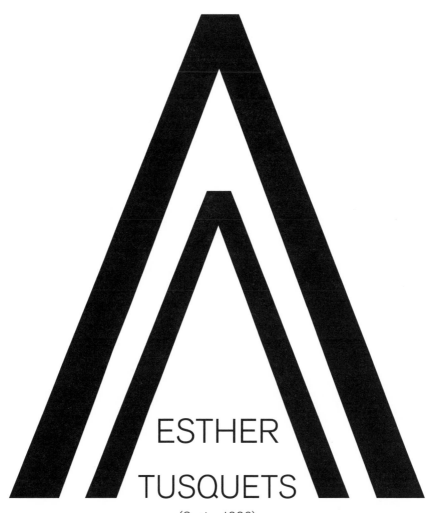

ESTHER
TUSQUETS
(Spain, 1936)

Since she was a girl, it was clear to Esther Tusquets that neither laziness nor caution would force her to give up anything in her life. Born in Barcelona in 1936, her childhood unfolded in the bosom of one of the most traditional families of the Catalan upper class that, immune to the clashes of the Spanish Civil War (which began that same year), enjoyed a social prestige gained, among other ways, thanks to belonging to the side of the victors.

So, in a tower in Pedralbes, Esther Tusquets grew up with her brother Óscar, today a well-known architect, who, in 1969, with his then wife Beatriz de Moura, founded Tusquets Editores. Along with their friends and colleagues, the siblings would form part of the *Gauche Divine*, that group of "good kids" who wanted to spend those Barcelona nights of the 1960s less prudishly.

During that time, her father bought her the publishing house Lumen, which her uncle had founded. As the head of the house, she kept its original name, but completely changed the religious and Francoist line that her uncle had followed, and began to publish authors like Umberto Eco and Virginia Woolf, and also took charge of introducing Spain to the celebrated Mafalda comic strips and the rest of Quino's body of work. But despite the great success she achieved at the head of Lumen (which she frequently describes as a miracle), Esther Tusquets has never thought of herself as a publisher by vocation: "I didn't choose to be a publisher; I was, I enjoyed it, but it was never my vocation." With the death of her father, the rock and administrator of the business, and with Lumen consolidated as one of the most important publishers in the Spanish book market, she decided to sell it in order to dedicate herself entirely to writing: "When I sold Lumen, I'd been the head of the business for 35 years. I wanted to write, and the business part of the company didn't interest me. Not only do I not remember my years as a publisher with nostalgia, but now there is nothing that could make me go back."

Her career path as a writer had begun in 1978 with *El mismo mar de todos los veranos*, which she had written in complete secrecy and which she decided to publish herself in order not to compromise any of her publishing friends. In that book, she was already hinting at some of her most recurrent literary motifs: the struggle between pain and pleasure, memories of childhood, her ambivalent relationship with her mother, etc. With flexible and sinuous syntax, her work, pioneering both in its structure and thematics, made Esther Tusquets one of the great revelations of Spanish literature at the time. Success encouraged her to continue and so, after that first novel, she published *El amor es un juego solitario*, which won the Premio Ciutat de Barcelona the following year, and *Varada tras el último naufragio*, with which she concluded a trilogy that, at its time, was surprising for its capacity to delve into the feminine conscience without subterfuge and, at the same time, do so with a style and language that slides between memory and evocation. Her oeuvre, since then, has diversified in books that possess a strong biographical imprint and in works that approach the feminine universe and the world of her childhood, not relying on plot development, but more attentive, in every case, to the internal resonances of the particular story.

Her short but fruitful incursion into the world of children's literature has left behind characters as celebrated as *La conejita Marcela*, paragon of tolerance and rebellion, revisiting, in a tone for children, one of the literary themes often found behind her novels—social denunciation and the rejection of injustice.

In recent years, before her death in 2012, her books focused on recalling the post-war period without nostalgia and affirming a sensibility of playfulness in her writing. Faithful to her famous honesty, she has published her most confessional works: *Correspondencia privada* (2001), *Confesiones de una editora poco mentirosa* (2005), *Habíamos ganado la guerra* (2007), *Confesiones de una vieja dama indigna* (2009), and *Tiempos que fueron* (2012), this last written by four hands along with her brother Óscar. In its pages appear portrayals of travel companions who over the years have walked beside Esther Tusquets, that most dignified of ladies who was able to open a window onto the world of Spanish letters through which arrived the pages of Hemingway, Proust, Alice Munro, Walt Whitman, Emily Dickinson, and so many others, and able to close it in time to passionately live her love for the craft of writing.

THE ACORN

The Torture of Doctor Johnson

Since I was a girl I have always enjoyed being told stories. Out loud, on the radio, at the theater, at the cinema, on television. I enjoyed them so much that there came a day when I wanted to write them. And it's frustrating for a genuine consumer and producer of stories when they get all hacked up. I will always remember with particular disappointment a recital by Maria Callas at Liceo. Maybe the series of arias made for a better show, but I would have preferred a whole opera. So, when invited to select a text of mine for an anthology, I prefer that it be a story that is, if not entirely whole, as complete as possible, in other words, a short story.

"Summer Orchestra" is one of the few texts I've written in which I would change nothing. One of the few that, after fifty years, is still the same. My same subjects as always already make an appearance: love and the sea, my rejection of bourgeoisie society, my conviction that we are not living in the best of worlds, my difficulty connecting with my family (who is my family and what is my place?), the love-hate conflict with my mother, it's all there, for good or ill, in one of my oldest pieces of writing.

In Conversation with the Dead

The word *dead* is not adequate if we are going to talk about the great creators of the past whom I am only able to imagine living. Who are my favorite authors? I'm changeable, I feel great passions (I've felt them since I was a girl) for an author and I read them—I used to read, I barely read at all now—from their first work through their last. Except, of course, "the untouchables." Who can replace Shakespeare?

Coda

What do you think about Virginia Woolf, the majority of whose work you published, and about other female writers?

My enthusiasm for Woolf's work is always taken as a given, but, although I recognize her extraordinary talent, she's never been one of my passions. There are many women writers I admire. In my publishing house's catalogue there is a greater percentage of women than what is typical. I feel, for example, a special predilection for Carson MacCullers and for Flannery O'Connor. I don't think there have been as many female thinkers in Spain but there haven't been as many male thinkers either.

Social criticism lies behind many of the plot lines in your stories and novels. But you also often shift between registers and styles, and your texts range from the most experimental to autobiographical stories that display a great sense of humor. What comes first the style or the plot?

I think social criticism does lie behind my novels. It is the fundamental theme in "Summer Orchestra." I have never considered myself a leftwing radical, but I remember always feeling uncomfortable living in such an obviously unjust system.

As far as changes in style and theme with my writing, I don't think they are very obvious. I feel, on the contrary, like I am always writing the same novel.

I don't think I change much between register, style, thematic. For good or ill, I consider myself a monothematic and reiterative writer. Someone once said that, yes there are writers that always write the same novel, Esther Tusquets was always writing the same page. The only notable change is the tendency to greater simplicity.

The ludic element—an important element that has nothing to do with jest or making jokes—is a personal choice in life and in literature. To me it seems indispensable.

A THOUSAND FORESTS

"Summer Orchestra"

from *La niña lunatica y otros cuentos*

(The Lunatic Girl and Other Stories)

Summer was already well advanced—more than halfway through August—when it was decided to begin renovating the smaller dining room of the hotel and move the children, together with their governesses and their nursemaids and their mademoiselles, into the grown-ups' dining room. Throughout the whole of July and the first two weeks of August the children had formed a wild, unruly and increasingly uncontrollable gang that invaded the beaches, raced through the village on bikes with their bells ringing madly, prowled with restless curiosity around the stalls at the fair, or slipped—suddenly surreptitious, silent, almost invisible—into secret places amongst the reeds. Year after year they built the huts that housed their rarest treasures and where they initiated each other into marvelous, secret, and endlessly renewed transgressions (smoking their first cigarettes, often communal, crumpled and slightly damp; getting enmeshed in poker games played with a ruthlessness that would have astonished the grown-ups—games so intense and hard-fought that the participants often preferred to play on rather than go down to the beach—and venturing into other stranger and more ambiguous games, which Sara associated obscurely with the world of grown-ups and the forbidden, and to which, during that summer, she had reacted with both fascination and shame, eager to be a spectator but very reluctant to take part. She—possibly alone amongst all the girls—had been astute or cautious enough when playing forfeits and lucky enough at cards to get through those days without once having to let anyone kiss her on the mouth or touch her breasts or take her knickers down), transgressions which were doubly intoxicating because they were the culmination of that parenthesis of temporary freedom provided by the summer and would be unthinkable once they were all back in the winter environment of schools and city apartments.

But within a matter of two or three days the summer community had broken up and with it the band of children, some being transported inland to spend what was left of their holidays in the mountains or in the country, most of them going home to prepare for the September resits. And Sara had stayed on as the one female straggler amongst the decimated gang of boys (Mama and Mademoiselle had promised consolingly that, at the end of August, her four or five best friends would be allowed to come up for her birthday) but the atmosphere had changed, it had grown suddenly tense and unpleasant, the general mood of irritability and discontent aggravated perhaps by the frequent rain and the shared feeling that all that remained now of summer were a few unseasonable, grubby remnants. One thing was certain, the boys' pastimes has grown rougher and Sara had simply had enough of them, of their fights, their games, their practical jokes, their rude words and their crude humour, had had enough of them spying on her through the window when she was changing her clothes, of them upending her boat, of having three or four of them corner her amongst the reeds. That was why she was so pleased about the change of dining room: there, at least during mealtimes, the boys would be forced to behave like civilized beings. And they must have had the same idea, for they protested and grumbled long and loud, complaining that, now there were so few of them and the rain deprived them not only of many morning at the beach but also of almost every afternoon previously spent among the reeds, it really was the end to be expected now to sit up straight at table without fidgeting, barely saying a word, eating everything that was put in front of them, being required to peel oranges with a knife and fork and, to crown it all, wear a jacket and tie to go into supper.

But Sara was radiant and so excited on the first night that she changed her dress three times before going down—opting in the end for a high-necked, full-skirted organdie dress that left her arms bare and which her mother did not much approve of, saying that it made her look older than her years and was inappropriate for a girl who had not yet turned twelve—and then caught up her long, straight, fair hair with a silk ribbon. What most excited Sara that first night was the prospect of getting a good look at the adult world, until then only glimpsed or guessed at, since during the long winters the children's lives were confined to school, walks with Mademoiselle, and the playroom. There was hardly any contact between children and parents during the summer either—not this year nor in any previous year. (Sara had overheard Mademoiselle making a comment to one of the chambermaids about the delights and charms of the family holiday, at which they had both laughed, only to fall silent the moment they realized she was listening, and the whole episode had filled Sara with a terrible rage.) For the fact was that while the grown-ups slept on, the children would get up, have breakfast, do their homework or play table tennis and be coming back from the beach just as their parents would be finishing breakfast and lazily preparing themselves for a swim; and when the grow-ups were going into the big dining room for lunch, the children would already be off somewhere, pedaling down the road on their bikes or queuing at the rifle range at the fair. It was only occasionally, when Sara—quite deliberately—walked past the door of one of the lounges or the library, that she would catch sight of her mother sitting, blonde and evanescent, amongst the curling cigarette smoke. She would feel touched and proud to see her here, so delicate and fragile, so elegant and beautiful, like a fairy or a princess hovering ethereally above the real world (the most magical of fairies, the most regal of princesses, Sara had thought as a child, and in a way still thought), and for a moment her mother would stop playing cards or chatting to her friends to wave a greeting, call her over to give her a kiss, or pick out a liqueur chocolate from the box someone had just given her. At other times her father would come over to the children's table and ask Mademoiselle if they were behaving themselves, if they did their homework every day, if they were enjoying the summer. And, of course, they did coincide at church on Sundays because there was only one mass held in the village and the grown-ups had to get up early—relatively speaking—but even then they would arrive late and sit in the pews at the back, near the door. Although they did wait for the children on the way out to give them a kiss and some money to spend on an ice-cream or at the rifle range.

So Sara dressed with great care the first night the children moved into the big dining room—where they occupied only four tables—and she entered the room flanked by her brother and Mademoiselle, both of whom looked bad-tempered and morose. Her own face was flushed and her heart beat fast, and she was so excited and nervous that it was an effort to finish the food they put on her plate, and she felt she could see almost nothing, that she was unable to fix her gaze on anything, such was her eagerness to see and record every detail: the women in their long dresses, with their shoulders bare and their hair up and the earrings that sparkled on either side of their neck; the men, elegant and smiling, so different from the way they looked in the morning on the beach or on the terrace, and talking animatedly—what about?—amid the laughter and the tinkling of crystal glasses. The unobtrusive waiters slipped furtively between the tables, treading lightly and barely uttering a word, so stiff and formal and impersonal that it was hard to recognize in them the rowdy, jokey, even coarse individuals who, up until yesterday, had served them in the children's dining room. And no one, neither the waiters nor the other diners, took the slightest notice of the children, so that any attempts by governesses and mademoiselles to stop the children fidgeting, make sure they left nothing on their plates and used their knives and forks properly were futile. As was the music played by the orchestra (hearing it as she crossed the foyer or from far off on the terrace, Sara had imagined it to be larger, but now she saw that it consisted only of a pianist, a cellist and a violinist, and the pianist it seemed to her, had terribly sad eyes) for no one appeared to be listening to it, or even to hear it. People would merely frown or raise their voices when the music increased in volume, as if they were obliged to superimpose their words over some extraneous noise. There wasn't a gesture, a smile, even a pretense at applause. That surprised Sara, because in the city her parents and their friends attended concerts and went to the opera (on those nights her mother would come into their room to say goodnight, when the children were already in bed, because she knew how Sara loved to see her—the way she was dressed now in the dining room—in her beautiful, long, low-cut dresses, fur coats, feathered hats, jingling bracelets, with the little gold mesh bag where she kept an embroidered handkerchief and her opera glasses, and all about her the sweet heavy perfume that impregnated everything her mother touched and that Sara would never ever forget.) And in the library there were several shelves full of records which on some nights, when her parents were not at home, Mademoiselle would play so that Sara could hear them from her bedroom and drift off to sleep to the music. But here no one paid the least attention and the musicians played for no one and for no reason, so that when Sara went over to her parents' table to kiss them goodnight she couldn't help asking them why that was, at which they and their friends all burst out laughing, remarking that "that" had little to do with real music, however hard the "poor chaps" were trying. And that remark about "poor chaps" wounded Sara and without knowing why, she associated it with the jokes the boys told, with the stupid acts of cruelty they perpetrated amongst the reeds. But she immediately discounted the thought, since there was no possible connection. It was as irrelevant—and she had no idea why this came back to her now either—as Mademoiselle's tart sarcastic comment about the delights of family holidays.

Nevertheless, the following night, because she still thought the music very pretty and because it infuriated her that the grown-ups, who did not even bother to listen, should then condescendingly pass judgment on something to which they had paid not the slightest attention, she said to Mademoiselle— "The music's lovely, isn't it? Don't you think they play well?"—and Mademoiselle said yes, they played surprisingly well, especially the pianist, but in the dining room of a luxury holiday hotel in summer it made no difference if you played well or badly. It really was a waste of good musicians. Then, screwing up all her courage, with her cheeks flushed and her heart pounding but without the least hesitation, Sara stood up and crossed the empty space separating her from the orchestra and told the pianist how much she enjoyed the music, that they played very well. She asked why they didn't play something by Chopin, and the man looked at her, surprised, and smiled at her from beneath his moustache (although she still thought he looked terribly sad) and replied that people there didn't normally expect them to play Chopin, and Sara was on the verge of saying that it didn't matter anyway since they wouldn't be listening and wouldn't notice and then she felt—perhaps for the first time in her life—embarrassed by her parents, ashamed of them, and now that flittering grown-up world seemed suddenly rather less marvelous to her. And before returning to her table, without quite knowing why, she apologized to the pianist.

From then on Sara put on a pretty dress every night (alternating the three smart dresses she had brought with her but had not worn all summer, because up till then she had gone around in either jeans or a swimsuit) and she did her hair carefully, brushing it until it shone, tying it back with a silk ribbon. But she still felt awkward and self-conscious when she entered the dining room (the boys made angry, spiteful, possibly jealous comments but Sara no longer heard them, they had simply ceased to exist) and she would mechanically eat whatever was set before her because it was easier to eat than to argue. She still observed the women's lovely dresses, their new jewels and hairstyles, their easy laughter and chatter amongst the clink of glasses; she still noticed how elegant the men looked and how gracefully they leaned toward their wives, smiled at them, lit their cigarettes and handed them their shawls, whilst a few waiters as insubstantial as ghosts bustled about them. The music played and outside the full moon shimmered on the dark sea, almost the way it did in technicolour films or advertisements. But her eyes were drawn more and more toward the orchestra and the pianist, who seemed to her to grow ever sadder, ever more detached but who, when he looked up from the keyboard and met Sara's gaze, would sometimes smile and make a vague gesture of complicity.

Suddenly Sara felt interested in everything to do with the pianist and discovered that the pale, thin woman (though she was perhaps faded rather than pale, like the blurred copy of a more attractive original) whom she must have often seen sitting on the sands at the beach or strolling along the farthest-flung and least frequented paths of the garden, always accompanied by a little girl who would hold her hand or be running about nearby, this woman was the pianist's wife and the little girl was their daughter. Sara had never seen a lovelier child, and she wondered if at some time in the past the mother had also been like that and wondered what could have happened since then to bring her so low. And, having definitely broken off relations with the gang of boys, and Mademoiselle having raised no objections, Sara began to spend increasing amounts of time in the company of the woman and the little girl, both of whom inspired in her a kind of transferred or displaced affection, for Sara loved the pianist—she had discovered this on one of those nights when he had looked up from the piano at her and their eyes had met; it was a discovery that brought with it no surprise, no confusion or fear, it merely confirmed an obvious reality that filled her whole being—and because the little girl and the woman were part of him, Sara bought the child ice-creams, candied almonds, bright balloons and colored prints and took her on the gondolas, the big wheel, the merry-go-round, to the circus. The little girl seemed quite mad with joy, and when Sara glanced at the child's mother, perplexed, the mother would always say the same thing: "it's just that she's never seen, never had, never tried that before," and here her look would harden, "we've never been able to give her such things"; and then Sara felt deeply troubled, as if she were somehow in danger—she would have liked to ask her forgiveness, as she had of the pianist one night, long ago now it seemed, though she did not know for whom or for what—perhaps because she could not understand

it or perhaps because something within her was doggedly coming to frui-
tion—and because when it did finally emerge and spill out of her she would
be forced to understand everything and then her innocence would be lost for
ever. The world would be turned upside down and she would be shipwrecked
in the midst of the ensuing chaos with no idea how best to adapt in order to
survive.

At nightfall—by the end of August it was already getting darker earlier—
while the woman was giving the little girl her supper and putting her to bed
in the servants' quarters, Sara almost always met the pianist in the garden
and they would walk up and down the road together, holding hands, and
the man would speak of everything he could have been, of all that he had
dreamed in his youth—his lost youth, even though he couldn't have been
much more than thirty—of what music had meant to him, of how much he
and his wife had loved each other and of how circumstances had gradually
caused everything to wither and crumble, forcing him to abandon everything
along the way. It was a bleak, terrifying speech and it seemed to Sara that
the man was not talking to her—how could he unburden such stories on a
child of eleven?—but perhaps to himself, to fate, to no one, and on the road,
in the darkness of night, they couldn't see each other's faces, but at certain
points the man would hesitate, a shiver would run through him, his voice
would tremble and then Sara would squeeze his hand and feel in her chest a
weight like a stone, whether pity or love she no longer knew, and she would
have liked to find the courage to tell him that there had doubtless been some
misunderstanding, that fate had conspired against them, that at any moment
everything would change, life and the world could not possibly go on being
the way he described them. And on a couple of occasions the man stopped
and held her tightly, tightly to him and, although she had no way of knowing
for sure, it seemed to Sara that his cheeks were wet with tears.

Perhaps the woman felt subtly jealous of their walks alone together in
the dark or perhaps she simply needed someone to whom she could pour out
her own anguish, someone she could justify herself to (although no one had
accused her of anything) because she sometimes alluded bitterly to "the things
my husband has probably told you" and, however hard Sara tried to stop her
or tried not to listen, she would go on. "Did he tell you that now there are
fewer guests in the hotel, the management won't even pay us the pittance they
originally promised us, something he simply doesn't want to know about?"

"Did you hear what the manager did to me the other day, right in front of him and did he tell you that he didn't say a word in my defense?" "Did you know that I've borrowed money from everyone, that we don't even own the clothes on our backs, that we have nowhere to go when the summer seasons ends in a few days' time and that he just stands on the sidelines as if none of this had anything to do with him at all?" And one day she grabbed her by the shoulders and looked at her with those hard eyes that left Sara defenseless and paralyzed: "Yesterday I felt so awful I couldn't eat, but do you think he cared or bothered to ask me what was wrong? No, he just picked up my plate and, without a word, finished off both our suppers. I bet he didn't tell you that." And Sara tried to explain to her that the man never talked to her about real events, about the sordid problems of everyday life, about what was going on just then between him and his wife; he talked only, in melancholy, desolate tones, of the death of love, of the death of art, of the death of hope.

The day of Sara's birthday came round, the last day of the holidays, just before the hotel was to close and they were all due to go back to the city and, just as Mama and Mademoiselle had promised, her best friends traveled up specially and even the boys behaved better, wearing their newly pressed suits and their Sunday smiles, and she got lots of presents that she placed on a table for everyone to see, including a new dress and, from Papa, a gold bracelet with little green stones that had been her grandmother's and which signaled that Sara was on the threshold of becoming a woman. There were sack races, lucky dips, fireworks, mountains of sandwiches, a vast cake, and a fruit punch with lots of champagne in it which, because it was the first time they'd ever been allowed to drink it, got them all a little merry and was just one more sign that they were leaving childhood behind them. And the whole afternoon Sara was so excited, so happy, so busy opening her present and organizing games and attending to her friends that it was only when night fell, when the party was over and some of the guests were already leaving to go back to the city, that she realized that the musician's little daughter had not been among them, and, however much she tried to deny what to her seemed at once both obvious and inconceivable, she knew instantly what had happened. She knew even before she grabbed Mademoiselle by the arm and asked, shaking her furiously: "Why didn't the little girl come to my party? Tell me!" and there was no need to specify which little girl she was talking about, and Mademoiselle blushed, she did her best to act naturally but instead blushed to the roots of her hair and, not daring to look at Sara, said: "I don't know, Sara, really I don't, I think it must have been the porter who wouldn't let her in," adding, in an attempt to placate her, "but she is an awful lot younger than all your other friends . . ." She knew before she confronted the porter and spat out her rage at him, and man simply shrugged and explained that he'd simply done as he was told, that her mother had issued instructions about who should be allowed into the party; and she knew before she went over to her mother, swallowing back her sobs, her heart clenched, and her mother looked up from her book with surprised, unflinching eyes and said in a slow voice that she had had no idea they were such good friends and that anyway it was high time Sara learned the kind of people she ought to be associating with, and then, seeing Sara's eyes fill with tears, seeing that she was shaking, said: "Don't cry, now, don't be silly. Maybe I was wrong, but it's not so very important. Go and see her now, take her a slice of cake and some sweets and it'll all be forgotten." But in the musician's room, where she had never set foot before, the woman gave her a hard look, a look, thought Sara, that was now fixed, a look that woman had been rehearsing and learning throughout the summer, but her voice quavered when she said: "The worst thing, you see, was that she didn't understand, she saw you all having tea and playing games and she didn't understand why she couldn't go in; she cried a lot, you know, before she finally went to sleep." But the woman didn't cry. And Sara dried her own tears and did not ask forgiveness—now that she knew for whom and for what, she also knew that there are some things for which one does not ask forgiveness—and she took them no cakes or sweets, made no attempt to give them presents or to make anything better.

She went up to her room, tore off the ribbon, the dress, grandmother's little bracelet and threw it all down in a heap on the bed, then she pulled on her jeans and left her tousled hair hanging loose over her shoulders. And when she went into the dining room, no one, not Mademoiselle or the boys, her parents or the head waiter, dared say one word to her. And Sara sat down in silence, without even touching the food they put on her plate, sitting very erect and very pale, staring at the orchestra and repeating to herself that she would never ever forget what had happened, that she would never wear a long, low-cut dress and a fur coat and jewels or allow men in dinner jackets to fill her glass and talk to her of love, that she would never—she thought with surprise—be like the rest of them, that she would never learn what kind of people she ought to be associating with, because her place would always be at the side of men with sad eyes who had had too many dreams and had lost all hope, at the side of hard-eyed, faded women, old before their time, who could barely provide for their own children, not after this terrible, complicated summer in which Sara had discovered first love and then hate (so similar, so intimately linked), not after this summer in which, as the grown-ups kept telling her in their very different ways, she had become a woman. She repeated all this to herself again and again while she looked and looked at him and he looked at no one but her, not even needing to look down at the piano on which, all through supper, he played nothing but Chopin.

Translated by Margaret Jull Costa

WORK

1978, *El mismo mar de todos los veranos*, Lumen (novel).

1979, "Juego o el homre que pintaba mariposas," Lumen (story).

1979, "La conejita Marcela," Lumen (children's story).

1979, *El amor des un juego solitario*, Lumen (novel).

1980, *Varada tras el último naufragio*, Lumen (novel).

1981, *Siete miradas en un mismo paisaje*, Lumen (stories).

1982, "Las sutiles leyes de la simetría," Alianza (story included in *Doce relatos de mujeres*).

1985, *Para no volver*, Lumen (novel).

1986, "Olivia," Visor (story in *Revista Litoral*).

1987, *Libro de Moisés: Biblia I, Pentateuco*, Lumen (novel).

1989, *Después de Moisés*, Lumen (novel).

1990, *Relatos eróticos*, Castalia (stories).

1993, "La reina de los gatos," Lumen (children's story).

1994, *Libros "de lujo" para niños*, Torre de Papel (article in *Cuadernos de literatura infantil y juvenil*).

1995, "Recuerdo de Safo," Lumen (story included in *Cuentos de este siglo: 30 narradoras españolas contemporáneas*).

1996, *La niña lunática y otros cuentos*, Lumen (stories).

1996, *Carta a la madre*, Anagrama (story included in *Madres e hijas*).

1997, *Con la miel en los labios*, Anagrama (stories).

2001, *Correspondencia privada*, Anagrama (collected letters).

2002, *Orquesta de verano y otros cuentos*, Debolsillo (stories)

2005, *Confesiones de una editora poco mentirosa*, RqueR (memoir).

2005, *Entrevistas: Maitena por Esther Tusquets*, RqueR (interview).

2006, *Prefiero ser mujer*, RqueR (articles).

2007, *¡Bingo!*, Anagrama (novel).

2007, *Habíamos ganado la guerra*, Bruguera (memoir).

2008, *Pasqual Maragall: El hombre y el político*, Ediciones B (biography co-authored by Mercedes Vilanova).

2009, *Confesiones de una vieja dama indigna*, Bruguera (memoir).

2009, *Carta a la madre y cuentos completos*, Menoscuarto (stories).

2010, *Pequeños delitos abominables*, Ediciones B (essays).

2011, *Trilogía del mar*, Ediciones B (includes the novels *El mismo mar de todos los veranos*, *El amor es un juego solitario*, and *Varada tras el último naufragio*).

2012, *Tiempos que fueron*, Bruguera (memoir).

·

ENGLISH TRANSLATIONS

1986, *Love is a Solitary Game*, translated by Bruce Penman, Riverrrun Press (novel).

1990, *The Same Sea as Every Summer*, translated by Margaret E. W. Jones, University of Nebraska Press (novel).

1991, *Stranded*, translated by Susan E. Clark, Dalkey Archive Press (novel).

1994, "Summer Orchestra," translated by Margaret Jull Costa, Serpent's Tail (story included in *The Origins of Desire: Modern Spanish Short Stories*).

1999, *Never to Return*, translated by Barbara F. Ichiishi, Bison Books (novel).

2011, *Seven Views of the Same Landscape*, Barbara F. Ichiishi, Host Publications (novel).

2013, *We Had Won the War*, translated by Barbara F. Ichiishi, Peter Lang International Academic Publishers (memoirs).

·

AWARDS AND RECOGNITIONS

1979, Premio Ciutat de Barcelona for *El amor es un juego solitario.*

1997, Premio Ciutat de Barcelona for *La niña lunática y otros cuentos.*

2005, Received the "Cross of Sant Jordi"

2008, Finalist for Premio Salambó for *Habíamos ganado la guerra.*

2011, Medalla de Oro al Mérito en el Trabajo.

HEBE
UHART
(Argentina, 1936)

ebe Uhart was born in 1936 in Moreno, twenty kilometers from Buenos Aires. Her paternal grandparents were French Basques; her maternal grandparents had come from Italy to Argentina, which is where she grew up, in a family environment, with neighbors who besides being neighbors were relatives: the doctor uncle, the crazy aunt, an older brother who would become a priest, and her parents: a bank employee and a severe school mistress.

Although her mother often told her colorful stories, in her home there was no curiosity for reading and Uhart only had access to the few books her brother owned, theological and of a highly moralistic content. It was her cousin who introduced her to the works of Neruda, Guillén, and Vallejo, and, already studying in the Philosophy Faculty, literary gatherings were frequent in her circle of friends. She wasn't encouraged to write either, but already in her childhood a peculiar attention to language came awake inside her, attention to the way people spoke, how they expressed themselves, the things they said. Working as a teacher in public schools, she listened attentively to her students, children of Italians, speak in *cocoliche*, a jargon used by Italian immigrants to make themselves understood in Spanish.

When she was twenty-three she went to live in Rosario, taking with her the texts she had written over the past four years. In 1962, in that city, she published her first book, *Dios, San Pedro y las almas*, a series of stories that hadn't been shown to anyone, except one friend who knew how to tell her when her writing was alive and when it wasn't. When she got back to Buenos Aires, she stopped working as a teacher, finished her studies, and continued writing and publishing. Still, she never lost her calling to teach: for years, she organized literary workshops in her home, out of which many writers have emerged.

A tireless traveler, Hebe Uhart has visited rural towns in Argentina and Uruguay, Latin American capitals, and Italian cities like Naples and Taormina, where the colloquial dialects fascinated her, the street-level stories: the stuff small towns are made of. She was integrating all of it into her work, made up of a great variety of stories, three novels, a pair of novellas, and various articles. Greater public recognition came to her beginning in 2003, when *Del cielo a casa* appeared, a book of stories published by the prestigious publishing house Adriana Hidalgo.

"A writer has the obligation to keep an ear attentive to speech," Hebe Uhart has said. Her passion for speech has led her to delve into a strangely familiar world, equidistant from dream and memory, perceived, basically, through the ways people express themselves. Although until relatively recently she was considered "a secret writer," this image is beginning to crack, even against the will of the writer herself who has always carried out her work with the humility of someone distrustful of fame. In Buenos Aires, the theater director Laura Yusem, premiered an acclaimed play *Querida mamá o guiando la hiedra* in 2010, based entirely on the work of Uhart. Recently, apart from the publication of a new selection of her work by Alfaguara, from going off on several research trips and giving a lecture on Simone Weil at the Cátedra Bolaño in Santiago, Chile, her book *Viajera crónica* has been published, in which she describes her travels to southern Italy, Rio, Asunción, Ecuador, Peru, and Uruguay, among others, and which includes studies and information about the history and literature of each place.

THE ACORN

The Torture of Doctor Johnson

Overall, I'm guided by the taste of readers. It's like tangos, many are nice but there are a dozen that everyone likes. I picked the excerpt from the novel *Mudanzas* because of a very subjective feeling I recall that this combined "The feeling of the importance of the thing at hand" the Romans spoke of and a very special spirit of humility. I still remember the gray skirt I wore while writing *Mudanzas* and the café where I went very early every day. I had a lot of drive to do it because it was like contract work, as though my ancestors charged me with providing testimony of their lives, and so, because of that contract, it's easier, because the weight of the potential meaninglessness of writing is lifted off the writer, there's a kind of obligation.

In the case of the story "Him," it was hanging over me for many years. When a subject resurges time and again it's because it's for you and must be attended to. I wasn't finding the form and tone necessary to write it; it was only when I was more mature—that is, at another stage, separated from the experience of the events involving the idealized male character—that I was able to write it. When I stopped idealizing my partners, I was able to resolve it.

"Training the Ivy" is different from what I normally do, because it has a type of philosophy behind it and is full of reflections and, well, sometimes you want to reveal yourself.

In Conversation with the Dead

I don't recognize the Quevedo poem and if I ever knew it I don't remember it, and all this about solitude, books, and such doesn't provoke any reflection in me. As for non-literary influences, one of them was my aunt María, dead for a long time now, who was completely insane. I studied her relentlessly between the ages of ten and sixteen because I couldn't believe the things she would say. She drew a little doll and called her "The lady of sport and steering wheel." Another was "The lady of the bidet and toilet." I'd play ball with her and when it got lost, she would say: "It went to the locker room." And I'd think: "Where does she get all of this, and why have I never heard anything like it from anybody else?" I was trying to find some order in those words, some explanation, and in everything I thought, I found no meaning. And by the time I was sixteen what she said didn't shock me anymore but instead elicited annoyance and pity, realizing that her insanity was not a source of discovery, it was something chronic, incurable.

As far as this conversation with the dead. When I write I don't converse with anybody, or don't believe I'm connected to anyone, I'm aware of what I'm going to write so that what I want to say comes out.

But on occasion you've mentioned Clarice Lispector and Simone Weil, and there are also some who consider you to be a devoted student of Felisberto Hernández.

Simone Weil interested me since I was young, I've read her in different stages of my life and she's given me the same impression, that of speaking at a soul level which you can either accept or reject, you can't be indifferent. When I know that she's right but don't want to lend her credence it's because I find her very demanding and I want diversion, I look at her photo in the book and I call her "Spinster" and "Ugly." But then I return to her. Regarding Clarice Lispector, I like her but not all of her. There's a story in which she ponders the subject of an egg and I find it absurd and tiresome. But she has beautiful articles. Then there's Chekhov. What's there to say? He has an extraordinary ability to identify with the most dissimilar characters, he's able to put himself in the shoes of a two-year-old boy, in the mind of a princess on a spiritual retreat, in the reasoning of a corrupt official, etc.

CODA

Above all an oral register predominates in your work. Is there a deliberate process to attaining this style or does it have a more intuitive character?

It's related in part to the register people use when they say things, their gestures, intonations, and not so much what they say. While people tend to have a similar register relative to their education, social class, and habits, I discover them more starting from certain fissures where I can enter, from the language, and this applies when I take travel notes on an individual level as well as a regional one. The most genuine manifestations are onomatopoeias; in Río de la Plata, for example, they are exclamations and in Bolivia they're inward sighs. All of these details interest me.

A THOUSAND FORESTS

FROM *MUDANZAS* (MOVING)
[A NOVEL]

The house in Moreno had two entrances, a vestibule, an entrance hall with yellow flagstone floors, a dining room, and not one, but two courtyards.

To get to the bathroom from the other rooms you had to pass through the courtyard, through the first courtyard with red and white tiles. Beyond the bathroom, the house became increasingly informal: the second courtyard was brick and behind the bathroom there was a small room and a chicken coop. "Animals shouldn't live with people," said Domingo, who paid for the house and brought the family to live in the center of town. They came from a house that didn't have a dining room or garage, where the chickens regularly escaped from the coop until someone thought to put them back. After moving to the new house, the chickens were kept apart and strictly confined to the coop, they belonged on the brick courtyard and would have soiled the beautiful tiles of the front courtyard. After the chickens were restricted to the coop once and for all, they acquired a cautious and pensive stride, appropriate to a smaller space. As for the bathroom, the inconvenience wasn't so bad, here you only crossed the courtyard; in the previous house the bathroom was outside. Domingo said he was going to do his best to enable them to live like people, that's why he had a good job, worked twelve or fourteen hours a day and when he got back he wanted to see everything clean and his mother and sister smartly dressed and happy. They were well-dressed but odd, especially María. His sister María was not altogether adjusted to the new house and when she cleaned she would put on a headscarf, tied in a knot at ear level, and you couldn't tell whether it was a bonnet or a scarf. When she cleaned she would put on a tattered dress that she refused to part with;

she would clean with her lips sucked inward, in an expression that distorted her mouth, as if this, instead of being a means of outward communication, would send internal messages to her brain. His mother was almost always in the kitchen—as though it were the only place she could understand and take charge—or with the chickens. When she would go to the dining room—only to attend to visitors—she handled the situation well, but they had to remind her to take off her apron when she went in, which was like going to China. She would grow irritated because she wanted to return to the kitchen; taking off her apron, putting on her apron, greeting, have a glass of port, yes, no, she looks fatter, no, thank you very much, tute, muse, muse, musaie. When María would very politely offer the visitor another glass of port, yes, no, the mother would say "pardon me" because she already knew what was happening: the chickens had been clucking for half an hour, and sticking their necks out through the chicken wire; the coop was so far away that when it rained you had to bring an umbrella to stay dry: in the other house you had to bring an umbrella to the bathroom: now the chicken coop, always the same. Atilio was the one who was always happy, but according to Domingo his happiness was unwarranted: he spent everything he earned, and if he didn't spend it, he gave it away. He didn't put money in the Bank, he saved it in a box, without distinguishing between coins, pesos, large bills. Domingo thought that even though Atilio worked and wasn't inclined to complain, something was bound to go wrong for someone who keeps money in an unlocked box, someone who never knows how much he has. He often told him to put the money in the bank, but Atilio would say that his feet hurt. These excuses struck him as even worse. Domingo didn't think that anyone's feet could hurt. How is someone going to walk if their feet, their foundation, so to speak, are unstable? If something is unstable at the base you have to fix it, change it, or destroy it.

So the mother had to reconcile the children, the chickens, and worst of all, when there was no alternative, to tolerate a visitor.

The father had remained at the old house to look after the horses. He was a coachman and Domingo said that the carriage wouldn't fit in the new house, because he was going to buy a car. A car, when there were only three cars in all of Moreno! The father strongly objected to such ambition because he thought the higher you fly, the farther you fall. Domingo thought otherwise:

with horses comes manure, they can break free if they're poorly tethered and he wasn't about to let them run all over this tiled courtyard as if it were a racetrack, which had actually happened with a colt they gave Atilio: he didn't tie him up properly, at night he got loose and went galloping around the yard in such a way that it sounded like an entire cavalry squadron. And he'd even predicted that, but in the realm of carelessness . . . Their mother had another idea: there was so much grass growing in the garden—they had a garden with palm trees and everything—so much grass needlessly squandered, enough to feed two or three horses. But she had learned to keep such ideas from Domingo: eventually she didn't have any more ideas like that because they were useless in the new house. She didn't have any idea about the garden either, she couldn't care less: the only thing that she enjoyed was gathering peaches when she felt like it: she put them in her apron, which had to be done out of Domingo's sight, because he would tell her:

—Baskets were invented for a reason.

And so gathering peaches in her apron or soaking her feet with water and salt in a washbasin were things that had to be done out of Domingo's sight. When all the ideas that seemed perfectly possible to her, but couldn't be applied at the new house, had left her, she started to hide things: empty candy jars for the future, old shoes in case a worldwide war arrived, cloth of good quality or design. Domingo ignored all of this; and he also ignored that when their father came to visit—and now it was just that, a visit—she would kill a chicken, personally twisting its neck, she would skin it, and give it to their father to take with him: because he did not like to kill chickens or any living creature and Domingo didn't know how many chickens there were: he was in charge of important things, he was the chief traffic officer for the English railroad, he directed the movement of the trains. He had learned scheduling, discipline, and how to dress well from the British. Ramondi, a great-uncle who became a doctor through personal sacrifice, had also trained him extensively. Ramondi had two grown daughters and did not let them leave his house or go out in short sleeves, lest they provoke some miscreant. Ramondi stayed up late into the night and personally hunted cockroaches. As soon as Domingo hired a woman to do the laundry at home, Ramondi asked for María to come to his house occasionally to keep his daughters company, to darn socks, very random tasks in the end. Domingo thought that being near Ramondi's daughters would be good for María because that way she could copy the coveralls, so hygienic, that they wore to clean and the caps that cover all your hair and especially those mannerisms, so sure and resolute. He thought that what María lacked was resolve. But although she lacked resolve, there was something María was absolutely certain about: she didn't want to go and darn Ramondi's socks. She would have liked to be a high fashion dressmaker, but had some reservations. She told her mother:

—Horizontal stripes make you look wider, vertical ones imprison the body. Florals, if they're large, are very noticeable, and if they are small they get lost on the body, they do nothing. Diagonal stripes would be best, but she didn't see them in the store.

When the mother grew tired of hearing about dresses of dubious design, she said:

—Stripes are stripes and flowers, flowers. They're going to make it to your measurements, tute, muse, muse, musaie.

It seemed convenient to the mother for María to go to Ramondi's occasionally, so she got a break from these conversations about sewing that went nowhere. On the rare occasion that María produced a dress—which was like the birth of the mountains—the resulting product was complicated, with designs that avoided flowers, stripes, the fabric wasn't smooth either, she didn't know what it was. She would try it on and show it to her mother. Last time, her mother told her:

—So much time just for that? Mother of God!

And María went to cry in her room.

No, she would not go to Ramondi's, she didn't want to wear the coveralls or the dustcap his girls wore, she didn't want to darn socks, she wasn't going to be anyone's maid.

One morning Domingo found a pamphlet on Atilio's bedside table. At the top was written "Radical Civic Union" and beneath "Forward, radicals, united we overcome." When he saw him, he asked scornfully:

—And that?

Atilio defended the radical party: he talked about the dignity of the people and the deceit of the conservatives, which infuriated him. Atilio would eat anything—give him a boiled shoe and he'd manage to say that it was delicious—he was the only one who approved of the dresses that María made and he never fought or got worked up over anything, but he couldn't tolerate the

deceit of the conservatives. He told Domingo that he'd gone to a demonstration: that's where he got the pamphlet. Domingo said to him:

—*That* doesn't hurt your feet.

Then he jumped up and answered back that he was in full agreement with
the radical party, because a radical is born just as he'd been born, who knows
how, he would be radical until he died, he could be nothing else.

—Worker's Party? More like Worthless Worker's Party . . . Domingo said.

Atilio said that he wouldn't talk politics with him anymore, it would only
make things worse and it was precisely that manner of speaking, "worthless"
that failed to respect human dignity.

The leader of the radical party was Doctor Yrigoyen. He was called don
Hipólito, the doctor, and "the Armadillo" by his opponents, because he sel-
dom left his house to be seen in public. He moved between different houses,
as if to hide, and when he spoke he used complicated language, he'd say, "the
conducive effects," or "the submission of the motherland to foreign interests."
The remarkable thing was that people loved what he said: everyone seemed
to understand him.

Teresa met Domingo at Ramondi's; she was his second cousin but on the
other side of the family. She knew how to sew well, from time to time she
made a dress for Ramondi's girls, but as an exception, a favor. Because Teresa
worked in the store Gath and Chaves, she brought dresses home from the
shop for Ramondi's girls to try on; their father did not want them to go out to
try on dresses. At first they raised objections in the store about taking dresses
home to try on—it was a large shop, with strict rules—but since the dresses
Ramondi's girls chose rarely left the racks, they had very long sleeves, high
collars, and a monastic cut, they eventually agreed to let Teresa take them
home. Teresa had her job, dressed well, knew how to wrap things beautifully.
Yet how many humiliations she had to endure in life! To begin with she was an
orphan and lived with her aunt and her cousin Adolfo. Her aunt kept Adolfo
around as an adult and let him drive her up the wall all day. She couldn't
bring her co-workers to her house, bah, to her aunt's house, where Adolfo
was always flying off the handle and moreover that woman, fortunately for
her but not for Teresa, never noticed anything. Her aunt wore a high bun
that ended in a point like a meringue, she would say silly things to people.
She'd say: "You were uglier before and now you're better, what did you do?"

Or if the person wasn't an adult: "I see you're taller now than before." The aunt didn't recognize people easily, but when she did, a sort of exaggerated happiness overcame her as though she had been thinking about that person constantly, but at the same time as if that person had become someone else. Her aunt's house was a total mess and when Teresa would return exhausted from so much work, she nevertheless lovingly served a soup that seemed to be made with grape leaves and a meat that seemed to be guinea pig caught by Adolfo. For this reason she wanted to get married as soon as possible not just to be a wife and not endure any more humiliations, rather to apply some ideas she had acquired about life, some learned from old Ramondi. These were: 1) The feeding of children must be healthy, simple, and hygienic. 2) In the summer you should wear light-colored clothing, to refract the sun's rays. 3) People who make fun of others are unrefined, ignorant, and have no composure. It was because of her composure that Domingo was interested in her: she was always well-dressed, reserved, and prudent. Since she didn't want to bring a man who was so well-dressed, so important, to her house, they agreed to have lunch at a tearoom in Barrio Once, in María's presence.

Convincing María to go out to lunch at the Once tearoom in the role of the fiancé's sister was a difficult task for Domingo. When he'd persuaded her—and it was already a lot of work for María, who'd never had lunch outside of her house—then came advice on how to behave in front of the woman who, God willing, would be his fiancée: she should be unassuming, without seeming simple, pleasant with good judgment, and shouldn't order an apple for dessert, because you have to know how to cut it properly. She enjoyed the conversation with Domingo a lot because he knew how to handle everything. What an instructive conversation! But when Domingo left, she realized she had to go more or less to Mars and she didn't consider herself ready for that. She took out the four dresses that she had and put them on the bed: she looked at them at length, sucking her lips inward, and thought that the natural-toned one would be nice if it had brown stripes and on the other hand, the sky blue top part went perfectly with the blue skirt. And if she were inclined to cut up all of the dresses and combine them differently, making others that were splendid, perfect? As she was quietly saying "no, no" her mother appeared and said:

—Where were you?

She said:

—I don't have a dress to go out.

—You're not lacking a dress, you're lacking a head—her mother said.

When Domingo arrived, their mother said:

—Why yes, buy her a golden jackfruit. The robe of Saint Margaret.

The dress that Domingo bought for her fit her well: but the fabric made her itch, it caused a strange itching all over her body and in addition it had a superimposed design and you couldn't tell if it was drawn or printed, but it made her a little dizzy. When Domingo saw that María was not convinced, he said to their mother:

—You aren't coming, mamá?

—No, no, María will go.

And María had to go.

The Once tearoom was so magnificent, so enormous, that it couldn't be taken in with a single glance. This is how María saw it when she entered, carried by the current of people coming and going—you could be carried anywhere by that current of people and be lost forever, because the tearoom, rather than being a refuge, was another way of getting lost. There were festooned chandeliers; there was one in María's house, but here there were five hundred. And they were larger, with more festoons, and all alike. At home they had different lamps in each room, but here they had to make them all alike so that people wouldn't complain about being seated under an inferior chandelier. They weren't on but were dazzling all the same, reflecting the light of the sun. The waiters were dressed in uniforms, and there were so many that María wondered how they knew which table to go to and also which waiter was responsible for their table. The tables were also set in an identical manner, with the knife and fork equidistant from the plate so that they seemed about to move on their own and begin cutting the food automatically. Domingo's fiancée arrived right away: of course, she was easy to pick out because of her height. She was dressed in blue and looked a bit sour. Domingo said to her:

—This is my sister.

And María, in her best polite tone, said:

—I am the little sister.

Teresa's mood did not seem to improve with the introduction and after that, María essentially said nothing: she was far away from them at the table, their conversation didn't reach her. Both of them were of an imposing height and spoke very seriously, without looking at the chandeliers or the waiters or the table. In any case, María had so many things she was busy thinking about, that once the initial temptation to go flying out of there passed, this place held many lessons to be learned. To begin with, the waiters who were all dressed alike were similar to Ramondi's maid, who wore a raw silk smock and a bonnet for hair hygiene, which at the same time was similar to the one Ramondi's girls used. Consequently, both the waiters and Ramondi's maid wore something like household symbols while Vicenta, who did the laundry at their house, didn't wear a uniform; it would have been like putting a uniform on a horse. Furthermore Vicenta acted of her own accord, she addressed others informally and that wasn't in good taste. The number of waiters in the tearoom was so great that it took half an hour to find one with the calluses of a farmer and that perplexed her greatly: an imperfection in the midst of perfection. A threatening imperfection, because at any moment someone might come to punish the waiter with the calluses and also her because her hands were too small and fat: that's why she didn't rest them on the table, but hid them in her skirt. The couple ate hardly anything and María thought that she should also eat hardly anything: this is how it should be: all alike. The couple seemed to discuss a difficult issue, from time to time there was a silence. During one of them, María said to Teresa:

—Would you like a little of mine?

—No, Teresa said.

—Have a little of mine, this is sufficient for me.

She liked to use the word *sufficient*, it seemed delicate to her.

Teresa told her:

—Frankly, no.

It was an emphatic "frankly," it left no room for María to deploy courtesy. At home, she'd repeat the question two or three times to the visitor, often the visitor would refuse and the third or fourth time would say: "If you insist . . ." The tone of voice in which she said "frankly" made such an impression on her that even much later, when she would think about her, she didn't call her "Teresa" but rather "frankly." At another point she wanted to take part in the conversation, she wanted to say: "What lovely festooned chandeliers." She realized, from both of their faces, that she shouldn't say that. She wanted to say the word *festooned* and for them to know something: she was no fool; she knew her words.

When Domingo moved to get up, María said:

—I must get back to my chores.

Yes, the Once tearoom had many lessons for her, but she would never go back again.

Translated by Lisa Boscov-Ellen

•

"HIM"
FROM *RELATOS REUNIDOS* (COLLECTED STORIES)

That summer, I was about to start university. The year before, I had protruding shoulder blades like an angel, obtained through a diet of steak and halved tomatoes (I once passed out in the bathtub). Now I was slightly overweight and every night, in a small notebook, I counted calories: carrot, eighty calories; lettuce, forty-five. Turnip greens, I read in a magazine, eighty-four. I didn't want to add turnip greens to my diet, which, like almost everything that added up to eighty calories, had to be crap. My thinking had also changed: from delving into books debating whether Jesus was the son of God or an ordinary man, I moved on to an essay on the verities of faith and of reason. The author attempted to reconcile them like this: "In refuting the biblical account because it attributes nine hundred years to Noah, we must consider that this involves God's measurement of time . . . which is quite different from our own." It seemed to me that there was not any possible conversion table of God's time to ours, and that space between the verities of faith and of reason felt to me like a temporary fix. Anyway, at the time I was not willing to follow those theses to their ultimate conclusions: I was just browsing. After that year when I had pondered in a serious way whether Jesus was the son of God or an ordinary man, which coincided with my diet of steak with halved tomatoes, I had returned to the frame of mind I had been in when I was eleven. At eleven years old, a friend had told me: "Hell is in this life." I had found that statement very interesting; I had never heard it. It seemed possible but unverifiable; the statement meant less to me in itself than in relation to how my friend seemed to me after having come up with it: she was suddenly a mysterious person—who knows what strange paths she had taken to arrive at saying, "Hell is in this life."

But at seventeen I danced both alone and with a partner. With sweeping steps and spins I danced alone until I got dizzy: "On a Monkey Honeymoon." A monkey honeymoon seemed much more fascinating to me than human honeymoons. I also listened to a singer named Frankie Lane: I felt that life was a sweet depravity and I was only able to share it with Frankie Lane: he was singing for me. When I listened to Frankie Lane, which ended up being every day, in my mind I acquired a great allure—that of a girl disillusioned with life. That disillusionment was temporary; if it was Saturday and there was dancing at the club or in a house, I would bathe much later; I would put my dress on a chair in the bathroom and I didn't have to suffer through dinner; I would eat whatever, in passing. Instead of eating dinner I would dance to "Skokian"; it was a very dynamic type of music, it was the appetizer to the dance and everything was permeated by Skokian, even the cripple I saw go down the street every day at eight in the evening. Why not? Being crippled could be an alluring thing. At the dance, a cute, blue-collar young man asked me to dance and leaned against me. I really liked dancing with him, but I forgot him as soon as he left me. I danced once with Guillermo Echecopar, his hair like a scrub-brush, narrow shoulders, and a frail body; it was there that, for the first time, I heard that history should be revised. His frailty was disconcerting and made me want to run my hand through his scrub-brush hair, but I couldn't reconcile the topic of revised history with the aforementioned feelings; they were separate like the verities of faith and of reason. I danced with him all night and never saw him again because he was from Mendoza.

Yes, I was going into Philosophy; when I was asked why, I would say: "By discarding." They would ask me again: "Descartes?" "Oh, no, by discarding other majors," I'd say with apparent weariness and with a certain sense of superiority over such repetitious humanity. I had said as much to a visitor, Ernesto, who sought my brother's friendship; whenever he came by, my brother would reject him. Since my brother wouldn't spend time with Ernesto, I would listen to him. He was fat and boring; he wanted to study Philosophy although he had already started Medicine. I followed my brother's lead and didn't want to see him either, so then my mom would listen; she thought highly of him because he told her that he waxed the floors at his house. It seemed she would have been happy if my brother or I had kept him company, either one of us, and in the end I chatted with him a little because my mom had said to me: "How unfriendly and rude! A boy who's worth his weight in gold . . ." One day he told me he had bought all of the materials for the upcoming year; he invited me to study at his house, which was in a nearby town. His house was twice the size of mine, but I couldn't bring myself to admire it. His parents weren't around and one afternoon I put on "Skokian" and accompanied the album with some dreadful onomatopoeic English, some foolish and obnoxious onomatopoeia; at that time, I began to develop the conviction that you could get to know people much more intimately through onomatopoeia or by the way they sneezed than through the most varied ideas they could possibly sustain. When the album ended he told me that there was an isolated room upstairs; in the room there was a bed and in the bed he had slept with a girlfriend he'd had. He said that the bed creaked. I thought that the bed must creak with sounds similar to the onomatopoeia with which I accompanied "Skokian" and changed the topic of conversation; a while later I left and refused to go back to that house to study Philosophy. Ernesto kept coming to my house every week, my mom let him in and they made progress in their conversations about the quality and application of floor wax.

The year before my entrance into Philosophy I had examined my body from the front, side, and rear, with a mirror. I was utterly dissatisfied, I didn't like my feet or my thorax, which seemed big to me, or my wavy hair; although I was relatively tall, I wanted to be taller, with straight, blonde hair. But I also beat myself up for being tepid, both externally and internally. Perhaps I would have preferred to be the kind of ugly that's startling. And as the Holy Spirit spews out the tepid, I dressed in black, to cover my terrible internal ugliness and my nothing exterior. I covered myself so I wouldn't offend my fellow man; but when I danced with the young blue-collar worker and with Guillermo Echecopar, I wore prettier dresses, I put on lipstick and came to consider myself acceptable; and yet something was missing. That year I went to a huge party; in the center, a blonde with a perfect body danced nonstop, surrounded by the four most intriguing men at the party. It had to be acknowledged that she was older, she was twenty-three; but she wasn't chosen just because she was blonde and beautiful; she was funny, intelligent, flirtatious, self-absorbed, and smiling. Her triumphs didn't provoke any outburst from her, like galloping across the dance floor, something that I would have done if I'd been so successful. First I felt pain, "I'll never be like her," but then when everyone sat down to watch her dance, I was part of everyone and it was as if I were dancing with those boys. The other girl who danced a lot wasn't pretty and yet she had almost as much success as the blonde: but she'd had a *savoir faire* since the age of nine. When we were nine all the girls wanted to fit in with Mirta and being her friend was a sort of consecration; she was friends with everyone and with no one; she was friends with the group. Once she invited me to her house to play; there were a lot of us girls. The cohesion of the group seemed so pronounced, so compact and perfect, with such sophisticated codes that were over my head, that I couldn't understand what they were saying; they were arguing. It made me very upset to intervene or argue; I took a bat and went off to play by myself. I hit the ball, spilled a little bit of soil from a pot, and she said to me, harshly:

—Sweep that up.

I swept the floor in silence and went home crying, without saying good-bye, so no one would see my tears; I was never going back to her house. Back at her house was the group, triumphant and glorious and I had been left alone and ordered to sweep; I would never forgive them.

But now, at seventeen, a kind of status quo existed between the two of us; we were grown up and I had learned the art of saying one thing and thinking another and of speaking without saying anything that was important to me. Every time I saw her, as we exchanged a few words, I was thinking: "Do you remember when you ordered me to sweep?"

I ran into her one day in September; we were on our bicycles and she suggested that we ride through the outskirts of town where the houses were small, spread out, and there were occasional logs that looked like natural seats, flowering acacias, and nearby, the river. When we had gone a short distance, I was feeling happy that she had taken notice of me and that I had maintained this new adult frame of mind and she was happy because she believed that she deserved everything she had, and she said to me:

—Let's say hi to a friend of mine who lives out here.

We stopped at a house, older than the others, with tall weeds in the

front yard. It looked deserted; if the owners inhabited it, they didn't seem
to care whether they lived there, outdoors, or in the city. She rang the bell
like someone accustomed to visiting that house and the handsomest man I'd
ever seen in my life emerged sleepily. He was a man, not a boy like the ones
I danced with; he had to be twenty-seven years old. He had the beginnings
of a beard, about two days' growth; he must've been someone who didn't care
about trifles like shaving. His body and his face were perfect, with very large
and sensual lips and a mocking expression. She said to him:

—How's it going? Mirta behaved casually, as if she were this grown man's
equal.

I was struck dumb by his presence and he could tell: he became more
casual, yawning, speaking like someone who had just rolled out of bed. My
fascination grew. He said:

—Want to come in?

—No, no, another time, Mirta said as though she was used to entering his
house and wouldn't now because she had more important things to do. I was
as stunned by his presence as by the fact that he didn't have any effect on her.
When we were leaving (I almost fell off my bike but by the grace of God, I
didn't) I asked Mirta:

—Have you known him long?

—Yeah, about two years. I met him at a party.

She'd had the privilege of interacting with this creature for about two
years; she said this as if it were perfectly natural. She added:

—He doesn't live there all year, he's passing through. He lives in Buenos
Aires.

Of course, I thought, it couldn't be any other way; he would inhabit a
shabby house when he wanted to wear a shabby beard; he would go there to
hide out, but he would have another splendid house in Buenos Aires in which
he would do splendid things.

Mirta said:

—He eats tangerines in bed and tosses the peels on the sheets.

That was the best of what I would get to hear. Obviously he was an
entirely free being, he could be civilized or savage according to his wishes . . .

—He's game for anything, she said. Last time I saw him in the river with
a tall, skinny blonde.

How could a prince be game for anything? It was a mystery that I wasn't prepared to ask her about, so I didn't say anything. I hid the effect that he had on me and translated it into something superficial.

—He's really cute, I said.

She changed the subject and we headed downtown.

After that, I couldn't stop thinking about him: "He was with a tall, skinny blonde." Of course, who was he going to go out with, he wasn't going to go out with a little wavy-haired lamb like me. He would rotate women constantly but he would prefer the tall, skinny blonde because they formed a couple totally distinct from others. She probably had very long nails; she was beautiful, slightly older than him, and with those witch nails she would pick up the tangerine peels from the bed, without comment; never a reproach. Sometimes at night, before going to sleep, I imagined him alone. I saw his face as if I were seeing it in reality, imagined that he lived with me under the following conditions: he would put me in a kind of kennel that he had at the back of his house and keep me tied up there all day. He would go out and when he'd return, he would untie me; he would treat me with respect. I would prepare dinner and he would call me indispensable. Then I began to imagine him during the day as well, and in the evening my feet carried me to his neighborhood of their own accord; I didn't make it to his house.

When I got close and turned back it was as if I had been saved from some danger; I looked carefully at the fallen logs, the small houses, the stone benches near the doors, as though the only thing that I had intended was a pleasant stroll. One time, on one of my many walks around that neighborhood, I turned down a street parallel to his. I was carrying a bag to buy fruit from a produce market out there, so I'd have an excuse in case I ran into him, although I loathed crossing those lawns with a shopping bag. Upon reaching his house, I had the feeling that he was hiding inside. I was certain that he wasn't a man who walked around the neighborhood; he wasn't someone easily found on the street, and as befitting an important person, he wouldn't walk around without rhyme or reason.

One day I said to myself: "I'm going to make it through the door of his house." I forged ahead, saying, "hopefully he's not there," but I sensed that he was.

He was, he was repairing his fence, but it's possible that was a figment of my imagination. He smiled at me as though he had seen me the day before and said to me:

—What are you doing out here?

—Nothing, I was in the neighborhood . . .

I didn't know what to say. Then he said to me:

—Want to come in?

—No, thanks, I said. I have to go.

I waved to him and left. How could it occur to him so naturally that I would go inside? Perhaps I would go inside and he would tie me to the bed, or who knows what, it had to be dark in that house. When I got home, I thought: "Good thing I escaped, if I'd gone in there, chances are I would not have come out again."

When I got back to my house Ernesto was there talking with my mom; he was explaining the ideas of Thales in comparison to Anaximander. My mom wasn't interested in Philosophy; she was interested in World War II. She said to us:

—How interesting! I'll leave you two alone.

Then he continued expounding, and I considered all of his thoughts flawed and invalid and I wasn't willing to listen to him nor to read any history of Philosophy he wrote in this way, that refuted everything before it. Meanwhile, Ernesto was still talking to me, and I listened to him, embarrassed: if "he" were to find out that I had a friend like this, he would never look at me again; he would look down on me. I used to think that Ernesto bored me, but in that moment I started to think that Ernesto contaminated me; if I listened to him too much, tediousness and fatness would contaminate me.

—Very interesting, I said to him. I have to go.

—I'll go with you, he said.

—No, no, another time.

From then on he started to come every other day; he was finally resigned to the fact that my brother wouldn't come out, because he never came out anymore and you could see that my mom, however much she appreciated Ernesto, didn't know what to say to him. She kept on saying that he was a lovely boy, but after the conversation about Thales and Anaximander, every time he rang the bell, she would say to me: "Ernesto's here."

I dealt with him at the door; I consistently told him that I had to go out, his face would fall, like a kicked dog, and he would leave. I had no pity.

I entered the department of Philosophy and started to meet a number of fascinating people. Cristina, for example, was twenty and already had a six-year-old, a little girl with thick glasses. She introduced her like this: "My daughter. She's a little less cross-eyed than Sartre." Also Esther: when I asked to stop at a place to get coffee, she told me: "I don't go in here; I have ghosts here." At first I was childishly frightened and then I understood that it was a subtle image; of course, they were private ghosts. And also Mario, who struck up long discussions with his friends, debates that I didn't understand because they were older and spoke in French and English. When someone defeated him in an argument, Mario would gesture like someone who had been disarmed and would say, "Touché."

Because of all these new developments I had forgotten about "him." One winter day I went to the station to take the train; he was on the platform and I recognized him from half a block away. He was clean-shaven; he was wearing a beautiful coat. The thrill of seeing him was so strong that I had to concentrate all my effort to not show it, I wanted to appear indifferent. On the stairway to the platform I rehearsed how I was going to handle this; I decided that it was best to pretend I hadn't seen him and then let my gaze wander, as if by chance. But when I emerged from the stairwell, he saw me, he smiled at me and I immediately walked over to him.

—Hi, he said to me.

—Hi, I said.

The train arrived and he asked:

—Should we sit here?

—Yeah, I said. I didn't care whether I was sitting on the floor or on the roof of the train.

He asked where we should sit with some hesitancy, I didn't understand how a god could ask where to sit; everything was so surreal that I told myself: "I'm going to act completely natural."

I had said "yeah," my voice squawking like a crow. I had to fix that, I had to show that I was relaxed and selective. He saw me with my thick books and asked me:

—What are you reading?

—Baudelaire, I said.

Baudelaire seemed like appropriate reading to mention to him.

—Have you read Hermann Hesse?

—Yes, I told him. I had to make up for that crow voice.

I said:

—I also read Neruda and Guillén. But I dislike everything by Guillén.

—Why?, he asked, mildly irritated, like a strict teacher.

I'd read the literary supplements in the newspapers: "The Picasso of the early years," "The early Vallejo." I couldn't distinguish "The early Guillén" from any other, but I said:

—Because he uses a lot of onomatopoeia.

He remained silent and I had an attack of desperation. May God help me from here on out not to do anything outside my plan! He still didn't speak, I looked out the window, we passed about five gypsies.

—Gypsies . . . I said with exaggerated enthusiasm, as though the spectacle excited me.

He smiled and remained silent. Then I asked him:

—Have you ever dreamed in technicolor?

—Oh, I've never had the privilege, he said.

He said it as if it were a dubious or uninteresting privilege. I noticed the refinement of his expression: he might have wanted to say: "I don't care," but he said it graciously. I thought: "No, he's not a god, he's an English gentleman." Although I was struck by his response, I said:

—I dream in color.

I recounted a dream with large tropical flowers, I described them for him.

I had dreamed about him, but I didn't tell him that; he might become irritated with me for such an imposition. When I finished telling him about the dream, he said to me:

—We're here.

He was smiling, he was stretching in his seat and looking at me, a little amused and also a little weary.

—Yes, I said.

He was an English gentleman.

Three days after that episode, my mom told me:

—Someone sent you flowers.

They were red roses, very beautiful, recently delivered and wrapped in paper. I couldn't figure out who had sent them. I thought and thought. My mom said to me:

—Aren't you going to put them in water?

I wasn't going to until I knew who had sent them, I didn't like flowers very much, I would have preferred fruit or chocolates . . . unless he had sent them. Yes, I thought with increasing conviction; he must have sent them to me, because if I, who did not like flowers, liked these so much, they were so gorgeous, so present . . . Yes, he had been the one who sent them. The entire day I thought of nothing else, I looked at them every time I went in or out of the house. I put them in water, I gave them water five times that day so they would last forever. The next day, when the buds opened and were in their glory, my mom told me:

—Ernesto came by.

— . . .

—He sent you the roses. It was to be expected.

She said that and left with the newspaper to take a nap.

—That can't be, I said.

—Yes, she said to me from the room.

What was to be expected? I hated her, as though her prediction was part of the scam.

It is possible that my mom changed the water of those roses, because she did not tolerate wastefulness or unfinished tasks; I didn't look at them again myself, may all the gardens catch fire and may those roses burn in hell forever.

Translated by Lisa Boscov-Ellen

•

"Training the Ivy"
from *Relatos Reunidos* (Collected Stories)

Here I am arranging the plants so they don't crowd each other, or have dead parts, or ants. It gives me pleasure to see how they grow with so little; they are sensible, adapting to their containers; if the containers are small, they stay small, if they have space, they grow more. They are different from people: some people, with a petty constitution, acquire some luxuriance that obscures

their true size; others, of great heart and ability, remain crushed and overwhelmed by the weight of life. This is what I think about when I water and
transplant and also about the various modes of existence of plants: I have
one that is resistant to sunlight, tough, as though from the desert, that takes
for itself only the green necessary to survive; and then a large ivy, beautiful, insignificant, which doesn't have the slightest pretension of originality
because, with its iridescent green, it resembles any ivy that can be bought
anywhere. But I have another ivy, uniformly green in color, which turned out
small; it seems to say: "Iridescence is not for me"; it responds by growing very
slowly, shaded and secure in its cautiousness. It's the plant I love most; from
time to time I train it, I know where I want it to go and it understands where
I want to lead it. I sometimes call the iridescent ivy "stupid" because it does
a few pointless arabesques; I respect the desert plant for its resilience, but
sometimes it seems ugly to me. But it seems ugly to me when I see it through
the eyes of other people, when a visitor comes: generally I like them all. For
example, there's a variety of small daisy, called mayweed; I don't know by
what criteria it is distinguished from the daisy. Sometimes I look at my garden as if it belonged to another and discover two flaws: one, that few plants
fall gracefully, with a certain lushness and sinuous movement; my plants are
very still, short, contained within their pots. The second flaw is that I have a
lot of small flowerpots, of different sizes, rather than large, structured, well-
planned flowerbeds; because I was really putting off the task of culling, as we
say, that same expression, culling, or cleaning up, referring to my plants, has
a sort of maliciousness about it. I was putting off, as much as possible, the
use of the maliciousness necessary for survival, ignoring it in myself and in
others. I associate malice with the mundane, with the ability to immediately
discern whether a plant is a mayweed or a daisy, whether a stone is precious or
worthless. I associate or used to associate malice with selective scorn based on
objectives that are no longer foreign to me: dealing with people, with a lot of
people, the resentments, the repetitiveness of people and situations; ultimately,
the replacement of wonder with the detective spirit also corrupted me with
wickedness. But some things continue to amaze me. Four or five years ago I
had prayed to God or the gods not to make me severe, scornful. I used to say,
"Dear god, don't make me like the mother in *Las de Barranco*." That mother's
life was a perpetual uproar, a witches' Sabbath; she invaded the affairs of
those around her, lived her life through them, so that her true desires were

not known; she had no pleasure other than shrewdness. I, before becoming a little like the Barranco woman, viewed that model as something appalling, but once incorporated, I felt more comfortable: the comfort of culling and forgetting, when there is so much to remember that you prefer not to look back. Now, in the morning I think one thing, in the afternoon, another. My decisions don't last more than an hour and are free of the feeling of inebriation that often accompanied them before; now I decide out of necessity, when I have no other alternative. This is why I assign limited value to my thoughts and decisions; I loved my thoughts before; I liked what I thought; now I think what I like. But what I like is confused with what I should do and I lost the ability to cry; I should distract myself a lot from what I like and should do, or I'm just in a kind of limbo where I suffer a little: some setbacks (the effect of which can be anticipated), small frustrations (able to be examined and offset). I discovered the part that needs and duties have in invention: but I respect them suddenly, without a lot of attachment, because they organize life. If I cry, it's somewhat without my consent, I should distract myself from what I want and what I should do; I only allow a little water to emerge. Feelings toward people have also changed; what was once hate, sometimes for very elaborate ideological reasons, now is just a stomachache, boredom becomes a headache. I lost the immediacy that facilitates dealing with children and although I know it's regained with three short races and a couple funny faces, I have no desire to do that, because I envy everything they do: run, swim, play, want a lot, and demand ad infinitum. Lately I've spent a lot of time criticizing—with whomever, particularly taxi drivers—the upbringing of young *porteños*. In general we agree; young *porteños* are indeed quite rude. But it's such a sad agreement that no conversation blossoms from this topic.

Now I think that the reason they burned witches was not because they traveled through the air on broomsticks, or the meetings they had; rather it was the mincing of bones, mincing of brains until they were left finely ground. They also saved pig ears and used the stock to polish the floors; it's possible that someone, in passing, might slip and fall, a very remote benefit; they didn't assign it much importance. In this way the witches killed three birds with one stone and that was their power. Mulling things over, they reconstructed their ideas, they cooked them up and also cooked up the condition to obtain the same product in different forms. For example, the cat:

the witch has no ancestors, no husband, no children: the cat represents all of that for her, with the cat she negates death. The witch works like the Jivaro, to reconstruct an order of the semi-alive; this is why she steeps, boils, and mixes fragrances with revolting substances: it is to rescue the revolting substances from oblivion; she reminds those that want to forget them in the name of enchantment, aesthetics, and vivid life. No, they were not punished for freely traversing distances; it was for the secret scheme of experimentation that could alter the immediacy of feelings, of decisions, of beings, which life sustains with rules of its own. And she does not recoil from the cross, as they say, because it is an inanimate object; she recoils from the Paschal Lamb.

Now that I'm a bit of a witch, I observe a coarse streak in myself. I eat straight from the pan, very quickly, or I do the opposite, I go to a restaurant where everyone chews each bite six times according to regulation, for health and because chewing gives me pleasure—like if we were horses—I become infatuated with old slippers, I dump too much water on the plants after washing the balcony so that mud falls and gets the clean part dirty (wasting time, since I have to clean it again), I cook a lot, because I find pleasure in the raw becoming cooked and I completely reject ecological arguments; if the planet is destroyed within two hundred years, I'd like to come back to life to witness the spectacle. I exchange impressions with some witch friends and our conversation comes down to fleeting statements, stories of different obstinacies, mutual tests of witchcraft, perfecting it, for example, learning to kill three birds with one stone, not necessarily to do evil deeds, but perhaps to save time, never wasting powder on a dead duck, not giving something more importance than it deserves, when in reality that thing is very difficult to evaluate.

But it wasn't always this way, it wasn't this way. Before I thought about culling the plants and about killing two birds with one stone, I suffered for two years as I'd never suffered in my life; one morning I cried with equal intensity for two different reasons.

I understood what happens to those who die and those who leave; they return in dreams and say: "I am, but I'm not; I am, but I'm going" and I say to them: "Stay a little longer" and they offer no explanation. If they stay they do so as outsiders, as something else, and they watch me as distant visitors. In that realm of oblivion where they've gone they have other callings and have acquired another way of being. And everything that we have eaten, quarreled over, talked and laughed about passes into oblivion and I don't want to meet new people or see my friends; as soon as I start to talk to someone, I've personally already sent them to the realm of oblivion, before their turn to leave or to die arrives.

I wake up and I sense that I'm alive; day breaks. Not a single idea enters my mind; nothing to do, nothing to think. I don't intend to continue smoking in bed without any idea in my mind. I'm suddenly seized by very good intentions but with no relation to anything concrete: I bathe, comb my hair, heat up water; I liven up and the good intentions increase. It's a March day and the light is growing even, the little birds are working, they go here and there. I am also going to work. I know what I'll do: I'm going to train the ivy, but not with a coarse string, I'll tie it up with garden twine. There it is, securely against the wall: I remove the dead leaves from the ivy and from everything that I see. You could say that I have an attack of removing dead leaves but the expression isn't adequate because it is a calm attack, but I don't intend to finish until I've removed the last ant and the last leaf that serves no purpose. I stack all of those small flowerpots, they will go to other homes, perhaps with other plants. An airplane passes very high overhead and suddenly I'm overcome by a happiness and a peace so great upon doing this work that I do it more slowly so it won't end. I'd like someone to come and find me like this, in the morning. But everyone is doing other diverse tasks, perhaps they're suffering or grumbling or catching the flu; it doesn't matter, that will pass and at some point they will have some happiness like mine now. I feel so humble and so gracious at the same time that I'd thank someone, but I don't know whom. I look over my garden and I'm hungry, I deserve a peach. I switch on the radio and I hear them talking about the troy ounce: I don't know what that is, nor do I care: get a move on, beautiful life.

Translated by Lisa Boscov-Ellen

WORK

1962, *Dios, San Pedro y las almas*, Menhir (stories).

1963, *Eli, Epi, Pamma sabhactani*, Goyanarte (stories).

1970, *La gente de la casa rosa*, Fabril (stories).

1974, *La elevación de Maruja*, Cuarto Mundo (stories).

1976, *El budín esponjoso*, Cuarto Mundo (stories).

1983, *La luz de un nuevo día*, Centro Editor de América Latina (stories).

1986, *Leonor*, Per Abbat (stories).

1987, *Camilo asciende*, Torres Agüero Editor (novel).

1992, *Memorias de un pigmeo*, Pluma Alta (stories).

1995, *Mudanzas*, Bajo la Luna Nueva (novel).

1997, *Guiando la hiedra*, Simurg (stories).

1999, *Señorita*, Simurg (novel).

2003, *Del cielo a casa*, Adriana Hidalgo (stories).

2004, *Camilo asciende y otros relatos*, Interzona (stories).

2008, *Turistas*, Adriana Hidalgo (stories).

2010, *Relatos reunidos*, Alfaguara (stories and novellas).

2011, *Viajera crónica*, Adriana Hidalgo (articles).

2013, *Un día cualquiera*, Alfaguara (stories)

·

AWARDS AND RECOGNITIONS

2004, Premio Konex in the story category (quinquenio 1999-2003).

2011, Premio Fundación El Libro al Mejor Libro Argentino de Creación Literaria, for *Relatos reunidos*.

2011, Several of her texts were combined in the play *Querida mamá o guiando la hiedra*, which was a popular success.

MARIO

VARGAS

LLOSA

(Peru, 1936)

Mario Vargas Llosa was born in 1936 in Arequipa, Peru. During his early years he was in the care of his maternal grandparents and his mother, as his parents had separated a few months before his birth. Years later the marriage was reignited and the whole family moved to Lima, where he was sent to a military prep school, which ended up being, after some time, the setting for his first texts.

From a very young age he demonstrated a natural capacity to connect to speech and the written word. Before turning fifteen he had already published articles in a local magazine and had premiered his first play: *La huida del Inca*. He studied Literature at Universidad Nacional de San Marcos in Lima and, though convinced of his literary calling, he also took classes in Law. His passion for writing was soon combined with activist fervor and, then, desire and love: he met Julia, his political cousin, whom he married in 1955; he was ten years younger than her and his family did not look favorably on the marriage.

In 1957, with two books published (*Los jefes* and *El abuelo*), he moved to Madrid and three years later, to Paris. In 1963, *La ciudad y los perros*, a novel whose argument revolves in turn around several students in a military prep school, raised him to prominence with the Premio Biblioteca Breve and, shortly thereafter, it won the Premio de la Crítica Española. The next year, divorced from Julia, Vargas Llosa married Patricia, with whom he had three children: Álvaro, Gonzalo, and Morgana.

La casa verde (Premio Rómulo Gallegos, 1965) and *Conversación en la Catedral*, published in 1969, situated him in the front line of the *Boom* of Latin American literature: his virtuousic technique, the richness of his language, and his capacity to compose complicated and imaginary worlds were the virtues many readers recognized immediately as a stamp of his personal style. Previously, his distancing himself from the Cuban Revolution made him an uncomfortable figure, both in Spain and Latin America, for progressive sectors.

In the '70s, Vargas Llosa dedicated himself equally to the essay and to satire (*Pantaleón y las visitadoras*) and to the novel (*La tía Julia y el escribidor*). In the '80s, on the other hand, he delved into the history of the Americas (*La guerra del fin del mundo*, 1981; and *Historia de Mayta*), with a pair of novels examining messianism and the revolutionary ideal on the continent. Premio Cervantes in 1984, Premio Príncipe de Austurias de las Letras de Perú in 1986, the decade ended with his candidacy for president of Peru in the elections of 1990, where he was beaten by Alberto Fujimori.

In 1993 he published his memoirs, *El pez en el agua*, and the novel *Los cuadernos de don Rigoberto*. In 2000 he recreated the figure of the Latin American dictator in *La Fiesta del Chivo* and in 2003, in *El paraíso en la otra esquina*, he sketched the lives of Flora Tristán (one of the pioneers of feminism) and her grandson Paul Gauguin. Celebrated with various honorary doctorates from the most prestigious universities in the world (Yale, 1994; Ben Gurión Ber-Sheeva in Isreal, 1998; Harvard, 1999; San Marcos de Lima, 2001; Oxford, 2003; Europea de Madrid, 2005; the Sorbonne, 2005) and awarded various prizes, the French government gave him the Legión of Honor in 1985. Since 1994 he's been a member of the Spanish Real Academy and in 2010 he received the Nobel Prize.

His most recent work is made up of various essays (*La tentación de lo imposible* about Victor Hugo's *Les Misérables*, 2004; *El viaje a la ficción*, about Juan Carlos Onetti, 2008), various collections of articles (*El lenguaje de la pasión*, 2001; *Diario de Irak*, 2003; and *Sables y utopías*, 2009), and two novels: *Travesuras de la niña mala* (2006) and *El sueño del celta* (2011).

THE ACORN

The Torture of Doctor Johnson

I selected these fragments according to two criteria. First, that each one of them had dramatic significance within the story, and that each alludes to crucial elements of the plot. And second, that these fragments might be read and understood on their own, by someone unfamiliar with the context within which they appear in my books. Two criteria that are difficult to reconcile but that I think I've managed to sustain with some success.

In Conversation with the Dead

The list of unforgettable dead to whom I return time and again, in my memory or by rereading, is long and would fill several pages. Picking a small number of names from among them I have to cite the great novelists of the nineteenth century like Tolstoy, Dostoevsky, Victor Hugo, Dickens, Flaubert, Balzac; from the classics like Cervantes, Quevado, and Góngora, to Martorell's *Tirant lo Blanch*, to the Homeric poems I discovered in my old age, to many writers who revealed to me miracles of technique and prose in the telling of a story: Proust, Kafka, Joyce, and Faulkner. The writer I have probably reread most is Faulkner. I discovered him in my first year of university, in 1953, in Lima, and since then I have never ceased to be amazed by the complexity and subtlety that his stories attain thanks to the way he organizes the points of view, the movement of the narrator, the creation of his own literary time, and also, of course, thanks to that enveloping style of extraordinary sensoriality that makes the changes in atmosphere and landscape in which the stories illuminate, or blur, or vanish, creating expectation, uncertainty, and always keeping readers in a kind of trance. Faulkner is perhaps the writer who taught me most about the type of novelist I wanted to be and the type of novels I wanted to write.

CODA

From your position with respect to Cuba and Hugo Chávez, and later as a candidate for president of Peru, you have always defended individual freedoms. What's your perspective on the political and social panorama since 1993, when you wrote El pez en la agua? *Has there been an erosion of freedoms or have they been lost?*

I think all the opinions I expressed in *El pez en la agua* I still maintain. I might clarify some details and add others regarding phenomena like Chávez in Venezuela and Evo Morales in Bolivia that did not exist when I wrote down those memories. When I began writing, the idea was widespread that a writer had, in addition to an artistic and intellectual responsibility, a civic responsibility and should participate in the political debate regarding the problems of the time. I learned this reading Sartre, about whom my opinion has greatly changed, but I have always shared his idea that writers should engage in expressing their opinions about politics and social problems. I don't believe writers should exempt themselves from such participation, just like I don't believe any other citizen should either. If we want things to improve in our society, we must be involved in political life and writers can contribute to this activity without renouncing their own vocation. In the dominion of the word, for example, political language tends to be clichéd, full of the commonplace, a disseminator of slogans and mottos more than ideas. A writer can give back to politics language that is clean, fresh, that expresses concepts, ideas and not just sensations and clichés. On the other hand, a writer can add imagination and inventiveness to a world that, owing to the advance of specialization, is becoming increasingly routine and predictable, deprived of idealism and creativity. If we want democracy to survive and not to drown in dictators or in total mediocrity, it's indispensable for us to inject imagination and novelty into democratic life. In this way writers can provide a service to the political life of nations.

A THOUSAND FORESTS

from *The Way to Paradise*
[a novel]

Many times he would recall those first months of conjugal life with Teha'amana in the hut in Mataiea in the middle of 1892 as the best he had known in Tahiti, and maybe the world. His little wife was an endless source of pleasure. Willingly, without reservations, she gave herself to him when he asked, and loved him freely, with gratifying delight. She was a hard worker, too—so different from Titi Little-Tits!—and she washed clothes, cleaned the hut, and cooked with as much enthusiasm as she made love. When she swam in the sea or the lagoon, her inky skin was dappled with reflections that moved him. On her left foot she had seven toes instead of five; two were fleshy growths that embarrassed the girl. But they amused Koké, and he liked to stroke them.

Only when he asked her to pose did they quarrel. It bored Teha'amana to stay still in a single position for a long time, and sometimes she would simply walk away with a scowl of annoyance. If it hadn't been for his chronic problems with money, which never arrived in time and slipped through his fingers when it did arrive—the remittances sent by his friend Daniel de Monfreid from the sale of paintings in Europe—Koké would have said that in those months happiness was at last catching up with him. But when would you paint your masterpiece, Koké?

Later, with his habit of turning minor incidents into myths, he would tell himself that the *tupapaus* destroyed the sense he had in the early days with Teha'amana of nearly being able to touch Eden. But it was to those demons of the Maori pantheon that you owed your first Tahitian masterpiece, too: you

319

couldn't complain, Koké. He had been on the island for almost a year, and still he knew nothing about the evil spirits that rise from corpses to poison the lives of the living. He learned of them from a book he was loaned by Auguste Goupil, the richest colonist on the island, and this—what a coincidence—at almost the same time that he had proof of their existence.

He had gone to Papeete, as he often did, to see if there was any money from Paris. These were journeys that he tried to avoid, because a round trip on the public coach cost nine francs, and there was the bone-jarring torment on the wretched road, too, especially if it was muddy. He had left at dawn in order to return by afternoon, but a downpour had washed out the road and the coach let him off in Mataiea after midnight. The hut was dark. That was odd. Teha'amana never slept without leaving a small lamp burning. His heart skipped a beat: might she have left him? Here, women changed husbands as easily as they changed clothes. In that respect at least, the efforts of missionaries and ministers to get the Maori to adopt the strict Christian model of the family were quite futile. In domestic matters the natives had not entirely lost the spirit of their ancestors. One day, a husband or wife would simply decide to move out, and no one would be surprised. Families were made and unmade with an ease unthinkable in Europe. If she had gone, you would miss her very much. Yes, Teha'amana you would miss.

He entered the hut and, crossing the threshold, felt in his pockets for a box of matches. He lit one, and in the small bluish-yellow flame that flared between his fingers, he saw a sight he would never forget, and would try to rescue over the next days and weeks, painting in the feverish, trancelike state in which he had always done his best work. As time passed, the sight would persist in his memory as one of those privileged, visionary moments of his life in Tahiti, when he seemed to touch and live, though only for a few instants, what he had come in search of in the South Seas, the thing he would never find in Europe, where it had been extinguished by civilization. On the mattress on the ground, naked, facedown, with her round buttocks lifted and her back slightly arched, half turned toward him, Teha'amana stared at him with an expression of infinite horror, her eyes, mouth, and nose frozen in a mask of animal terror. He was frightened himself, and his palms grew wet, his heart beating wildly. He had to drop the match, which was burning the tips of his fingers. When he lit another, the girl was in the same position, with the same expression on her face, petrified with fear.

"It's me, it's me—Koké," he said soothingly, going to her. "Don't be afraid, Teha'amana."

She broke into tears, sobbing hysterically, and in her incoherent murmuring he caught several times the word *tupapau, tupapau*. It was the first time he had heard it, though he had read it before. As he held Teha'amana on his knees, cradled against his chest while she recovered, he was immediately reminded of the book he had borrowed from Goupil, *Travels to the Islands of the Pacific Ocean*, written in 1837 by a French consul to the islands, Jacques-Antoine Moerenhout, in which there appeared the strange word that Teha'amana was now repeating in a choked voice, scolding him for leaving her there with no oil in the lamp, knowing how afraid she was of the dark, because it was in the dark that the *tupapaus* came out. That was it, Koké: when you entered the dark room and lit the match, Teha'amana mistook you for a ghost.

So those spirits of the dead did exist, evil creatures with hooked claws and fangs, things that lived in holes, caves, hidden places in the brush, and hollow trunks, and came out at night to frighten the living and torment them. Moerenhout's book was meticulous in its descriptions of the disappeared gods and demons that existed before the Europeans came and eradicated the Maori beliefs and customs. And perhaps they even made an appearance in that novel by Loti, the novel Vincent liked so much and which first put the idea of Tahiti in your head. Not all was lost, after all. Something of that lovely past still beat beneath the Christian trappings the missionaries and pastors had forced on the islanders. It was never discussed, and every time Koké tried to get something out of the natives about their old beliefs, about the days when they were free as only savages can be free, they looked at him blankly and laughed—what was he talking about?—as if what their ancestors used to do and love and fear had disappeared from their lives. It wasn't true; at least one myth was still alive, proved by the fretting of the girl you held in your arms: *tupapau, tupapau*.

He felt his cock stiffen. He was trembling with excitement. Noticing, the girl stretched out on the mattress with that cadenced, slightly feline slowness of the native women that so seduced and intrigued him, waiting for him to undress. He lay down beside her, his body on fire, but instead of climbing on top of her, he made her turn over and lie facedown in the position in which he had surprised her. He was still seeing the indelible spectacle of those buttocks tightened and raised by fear. It was a struggle to penetrate her—she purred, protested, shrank, and finally screamed—and as soon as he felt his cock inside her, squeezed and painful, he ejaculated with a howl. For an instant, while sodomizing Teha'amana, he felt like a savage.

The next morning he began to work at first light. The day was dry and there were sparse clouds in the sky; soon a riot of colors would erupt around him. He went for a brief plunge under the waterfall, naked, remembering that shortly after he had arrived, an unpleasant gendarme called Claverie had seen him splashing in the river with no clothes on and fined him for "offending public morality." Your first encounter with a reality that contradicted your dreams, Koké. He went back to the hut and made a cup of tea, tripping over himself. He was seething with impatience. When Teha'amana woke up half an hour later, he was so absorbed in his sketches and notes, preparing for his painting, that he didn't even hear her say good morning.

For a week he was shut away, working constantly. He only left his studio at midday to eat some fruit in the shade of the leafy mango tree that grew beside the hut, or to open a can of food, and he persisted until the light faded. The second day, he called Teha'amana, undressed her, and made her lie on the mattress in the position in which he had discovered her when she mistook him for a *tupapau*. He realized immediately that it was absurd. The girl could never reproduce what he wanted to capture in the painting: that religious terror from the remotest past that made her see the demon, that fear so powerful it materialized a *tupapau*. Now she was laughing, or fighting to hold back laughter, trying to make herself look frightened again as he begged her to do. Her body lacked the right tension, too, the arch of the spine that had lifted her buttocks in the most arousing way Koké had ever seen. It was stupid to ask her to pose. The raw material was in his memory, the image he saw every time he closed his eyes, and the desire that drove him those days while he was painting and reworking *Manao tupapau* to possess his *vahine* every night, and sometimes during the day, too, in the studio. Painting her he felt, as he had only a few times before, how right he had been in Brittany at the Pension Gloanec when he assured the young men who listened ardently to him and called themselves his disciples, "To truly paint we must shake off our civilized selves and call forth the savage inside."

Yes, this was truly the painting of a savage. He regarded it with satisfaction when it seemed to him that it was finished. In him, as in the savage mind, the everyday and the fantastic were united in a single reality, somber, forbidding, infused with religiosity and desire, life and death. The lower half of the painting was objective, realist; the upper half subjective and unreal but no less authentic. The naked girl would be obscene without the fear in her eyes and the incipient downturn of her mouth. But fear didn't diminish her beauty. It augmented it, tightening her buttocks in such an insinuating way, making them an altar of human flesh on which to celebrate a barbaric ceremony, in homage to a cruel and pagan god. And in the upper part of the canvas was the ghost, which was really more yours than Tahitian, Koké. It bore no resemblance to those demons with claws and dragon teeth that Moerenhout described. It was an old woman in a hooded cloak, like the crones of Brittany forever fixed in your memory, timeless women who, when you lived in Pont-Aven or Le Pouldu, you would meet on the streets of Finistère. They seemed half dead already, ghosts in life. If a statistical analysis were deemed necessary, the items belonging to the objective world were these: the mattress, jet-black like the girl's hair; the yellow flowers; the greenish sheets of pounded bark; the pale green cushion; and the pink cushion, whose tint seemed to have been transferred to the girl's upper lip. This order of reality was counterbalanced by the painting's upper half: there the floating flowers were sparks, gleams, featherlight phosphorescent meteors aloft in a bluish mauve sky in which the colored brushstrokes suggested a cascade of pointed leaves.

The ghost, in profile and very quiet, leaned against a cylindrical post, a totem of delicately colored abstract forms, reddish and glassy blue in tone. This upper half was a mutable, shifting, elusive substance, seeming as if it might evaporate at any minute. From up close, the ghost had a straight nose, swollen lips, and the large fixed eye of a parrot. You had managed to give the whole a flawless harmony, Koké. Funereal music emanated from it, and light shone from the greenish-yellow of the sheet and the orange-tinted yellow of the flowers.

"What should I call it?" he asked Teha'amana, after considering many names and rejecting them all.

The girl thought, her expression serious. Then she nodded, pleased. *"Manao tupapau."* It was hard for him to tell from Teha'amana's explanation whether the correct translation was "She is thinking of the spirit of the dead" or "The spirit of the dead is remembering her." He liked that ambiguity.

A week after he had finished his masterpiece he was still giving it the final touches, and he spent whole hours standing in front of the canvas, contemplating it. You had succeeded, hadn't you, Koké? The painting didn't look like the work of a civilized man, a Christian, a European. Rather, it seemed that of an ex-European, a formerly civilized man, an ex-Christian who, by force of will, adventure, and suffering, had expelled from himself the frivolous affectations of decadent Paris and returned to his roots, that splendid past in which religion and art and this life and the next were a single reality. In the weeks after finishing *Manao tupapau* Paul enjoyed a peace of mind he hadn't known for a long time. In the mysterious way they seemed to come and go, the sores that had appeared on his legs shortly after he left Europe a few years ago had disappeared. But as a precaution, he kept applying the mustard plasters and bandaging his shins, as Dr. Fernouil had prescribed in Paris, and as he had been advised by the doctors at the Vaiami Hospital. It had been a while since he'd hemorrhaged from the mouth as he had when he first came to Tahiti. He kept whittling small pieces of wood, inventing Polynesian gods based on the pagan gods in his collection of photographs, and sitting in the shade of the big mango tree, he sketched and started new paintings only to abandon them almost as soon as they were begun. How to paint anything after *Manao tupapau*? You were right, Koké, when you lectured in Le Pouldu, in Pont-Aven, at the Café Voltaire in Paris, or when you argued with the mad Dutchman in Arles, that painting wasn't a question of craft but of circumstance, not of skill but of fantasy and utter devotion: "Like becoming a Trappist monk, my friends, and living for God alone." The night of Teha'amana's fright, you told yourself, the veil of the everyday was torn and a deeper reality emerged, in which you were able to transport yourself to the dawn of humanity and mingle with ancestors who were taking their first steps in history, in a world that was still magical, where gods and demons walked alongside human beings.

Translated by Natasha Wimmer

.

FROM *The Feast of the Goat*
[A NOVEL]

"Manuel Alfonso came for me right on time," says Urania, staring at nothing. "The cuckoo clock in the living room was sounding eight o'clock when he rang." Her Aunt Adelina, her cousins Lucinda and Manolita, her niece Marianita, avoid one another's eyes so as not to increase the tension; breathless and frightened, they look only at her. Samson is dozing, his curved beak buried in his green feathers.

"Papa hurried to his room, on the pretext of going to the bathroom," Urania continues coldly, almost legalistically. "'Bye-bye, sweetheart, have a good time.' He didn't have the courage to say goodbye while he was looking me in the eye."

"You remember all those details?" Aunt Adelina moves her small, wrinkled fist, without energy or authority now.

"I forget a good number of things," Urania replies briskly. "But I remember everything about that night. You'll see."

She remembers, for example, that Manuel Alfonso was dressed in sports clothes—sports clothes for a party given by the Generalissimo?—a blue shirt with an open collar, a light cream-colored jacket, loafers, and a silk scarf hiding his scar. In his peculiar voice he said that her pink organdy dress was beautiful, that her high-heeled shoes made her look older. He kissed her on the cheek: "Let's hurry, it's getting late, beautiful." He opened the car door for her, had her go in first, sat down beside her, and the chauffeur in uniform and cap—she remembered his name: Luis Rodríguez—pulled away.

"Instead of going down Avenida George Washington, the car took an absurd route. It went up Independencia and drove across the old city, taking its time. Not true that it was getting late; it was still too early to go to San Cristóbal."

Manolita extends her hands, leans her plump body forward.

"But if you thought it was strange, didn't you say anything to Manuel Alfonso about it? Nothing at all?"

Not at first: nothing at all. It was very strange, of course, that they were driving through the old city, just as it was strange that Manuel Alfonso had dressed for the Generalissimo's party as if he were going to the Hipódromo or the Country Club, but Urania didn't ask the ambassador anything. Was she beginning to suspect that he and Agustín Cabral had told her a lie? She remained silent, half listening to the awful, ruined speech of Manuel Alfonso, who was telling her about parties long ago for the coronation of Queen Elizabeth II, in London, where he and Angelita Trujillo ("She was a young girl at the time, as beautiful as you are") represented the Benefactor of the Nation. She was concentrating instead on the ancient houses that stood wide open, displaying their interiors, their families out on the streets—old men and women, young people, children, dogs, cats, even parrots and canaries—to enjoy the cool evening after the burning heat of the day, chatting from rockers, chairs, or stools, or sitting in the doorways or on the curbs of the high sidewalks, turning the old streets of the capital into an immense popular get-together, club, or festival, to which the groups of two or four domino players—always men, always mature—sitting around tables lit by candles or lanterns, remained totally indifferent. It was a show, like the scenes of small, cheerful grocery stores with counters and shelves of white-painted wood, overflowing with cans, bottles of Carta Dorada, Jacas, and Bermúdez cider, and brightly colored boxes, where people were always buying things; Urania preserved a very vivid memory of this spectacle that had perhaps disappeared or was dying out in modern Santo Domingo, or perhaps existed only in the rectangle of streets where centuries earlier a group of adventurers came from Europe, established the first Christian city in the New World, and gave it the melodious name of Santo Domingo de Guzmán. The last night you would see that show, Urania.

"As soon as we were on the highway, perhaps when the car was passing by the place where they killed Trujillo two weeks later, Manuel Alfonso began . . ." A sound of disgust interrupts Urania's story.

"What do you mean?" asks Lucindita after a silence. "Began to what?"

"To prepare me." Urania's voice is firm again. "To soften me up, frighten me, charm me. Like the brides of Moloch, pampered and dressed up like princesses before they were thrown in the fire, into the mouth of the monster."

"So you've never met Trujillo, you've never talked to him," Manuel Alfonso exclaims with delight. "It will be the experience of a lifetime, my girl!"

Yes, it would. The car moved toward San Cristóbal under a star-filled sky, surrounded by coconut palms and silver palms, along the shores of the Caribbean Sea crashing noisily against the reefs.

"But what did he say to you?" urges Manolita, because Urania has stopped speaking.

He described what a perfect gentleman the Generalissimo was in his treatment of ladies. He, who was so severe in military and governmental matters, had made the old proverb his philosophy: "With a woman, use a rose petal." That's how he always treated beautiful girls.

"How lucky you are, dear girl." He was trying to infect her with his enthusiasm, an emotional excitement that distorted his speech even further. "To have Trujillo invite you personally to his Mahogany House. What a privilege! You can count on your fingers the girls who have deserved something like this. I'm telling you, girl, believe me."

And then Urania asked him the first and last question of the night:

"Who else has been invited to this party?" She looks at her Aunt Adelina, at Lucindita and Manolita: "Just to see what he would say. By now I knew we weren't going to any party."

The self-assured male figure turned toward her, and Urania could see the gleam in the ambassador's eyes.

"No one else. It's a party for you. Just for you! Can you imagine? Do you realize what it means? Didn't I tell you it was something unique? Trujillo is giving you a party. That's like winning the lottery, Uranita."

"And you? What about you?" her niece Marianita exclaims in her barely audible voice. "What were you thinking, Aunt Urania?"

"I was thinking about the chauffeur, about Luis Rodríguez. Just about him."

How embarrassed you were for that chauffeur in his cap, a witness to the ambassador's hypocritical talk. He had turned on the car radio, and two popular Italian songs—"Volare" and "Ciao, Ciao, Bambina"—were playing, but she was sure he didn't miss a word of the ploys Manuel Alfonso was using to cajole her into feeling happy and fortunate. A party that Trujillo was giving just for her!

"Did you think about your papa?" Manolita blurts out. "Did you think my Uncle Agustín had, that he . . . ?"

She stops, not knowing how to finish. Aunt Adelina's eyes reproach her. The old woman's face has collapsed, and her expression reveals profound despair.

"Manuel Alfonso was the one who thought about Papa," says Urania. "Was I a good daughter? Did I want to help Senator Agustín Cabral?"

He did it with the subtlety acquired in his years as a diplomat responsible for difficult missions. And wasn't this an extraordinary opportunity for Urania to help his friend Egghead climb out of the trap set for him by perpetually envious men? The Generalissimo might be hard and implacable when it came to the country's interests. But at heart he was a romantic; with a charming girl his hardness melted like an ice cube in the sun. If she, being the intelligent girl she was, wanted the Generalissimo to extend a hand to Agustín, to return his position, his prestige, his power, his posts, she could achieve it. All she had to do was touch Trujillo's heart, a heart that could not deny the appeals of beauty.

"He also gave me some advice," says Urania. "What things I shouldn't do because they annoyed the Chief. It made him happy when girls were tender, but not when they exaggerated their admiration, their love. I asked myself: 'Is he really saying these things to me?'"

They had entered San Cristóbal, a city made famous because the Chief had been born there, in a modest little house next to the great church that Trujillo had constructed, and to which Senator Cabral had taken Uranita on a visit, explaining the biblical frescoes painted on the walls by Vela Zaneti, an exiled Spanish artist to whom the magnanimous Chief had opened the doors of the Dominican Republic. On that trip to San Cristóbal, Senator Cabral also showed her the bottle factory and the weapons factory and the entire valley watered by the Nigua. And now her father was sending her to San Cristóbal to beg the Chief to forgive him, to unfreeze his accounts, to make him President of the Senate again.

"From Mahogany House there is a marvelous view of the valley, the Nigua River, the horses and cattle on the Fundación Ranch," Manuel Alfonso explained in detail.

The car, after passing the first guard post, began to ascend the hill; at the top, using the precious wood of the mahogany trees that were beginning to disappear from the island, the house had been erected to which the Generalissimo withdrew two or three days a week to have his secret assignations, do his dirty work, and negotiate risky business deals with complete discretion.

"For a long time the only thing I remembered about Mahogany House was the rug. It covered the entire room and had a gigantic national seal, in full color, embroidered on it. Later, I remembered other things. In the bedroom, a glass-doored closet filled with uniforms of every style, and above them, a row of military hats and caps. Even a Napoleonic two-cornered hat."

She does not laugh. She looks somber, with something cavernous in her eyes and voice. Her Aunt Adelina does not laugh, and neither does Manolita, or Lucinda, or Marianita, who has just come back from the bathroom, where she went to vomit. (She heard her retching.) The parrot is still sleeping. Silence has fallen on Santo Domingo: no car horns or engines, no radios, no drunken laughter, no barking of stray dogs.

"My name is Benita Sepúlveda, come in," the woman said to her at the foot of the wooden staircase. Advanced in years, indifferent, and yet with something maternal in her gestures and expression, she wore a uniform, and a scarf around her head. "Come this way."

"She was the housekeeper," Urania says, "the one responsible for placing fresh flowers in all the rooms, every day. Manuel Alfonso stayed behind, talking to the officer at the door. I never saw him again."

Benita Sepúlveda, pointing with a plump little hand at the darkness beyond the windows protected by metal grillwork, said "that" was a grove of oaks, and in the orchard there were plenty of mangoes and cedars; but the most beautiful things on the place were the almond and mahogany trees that grew around the house and whose perfumed branches were in every corner. Did she smell them? Did she? She'd have a chance to see the countryside— the river, the valley, the sugar mill, the stables on the Fundación Ranch— early in the morning, when the sun came up. Would she have a Dominican breakfast, with mashed plantains, fried eggs, sausage or smoked meat, and fruit juice? Or just coffee, like the Generalissimo?

"It was from Benita Sepúlveda that I learned I was going to spend the night there, that I would sleep with His Excellency. What a great honor!"

The housekeeper, with the assurance that comes from long practice, had her stop on the first landing and go into a spacious, dimly lit room. It was a bar. It had wooden seating all around it, the backrests against the wall, leaving ample room for dancing in the center; an enormous jukebox; and shelves behind the bar crowded with bottles and different kinds of glasses. But Urania had eyes only for the immense gray rug, with the Dominican seal, that stretched from one end of the huge space to the other. She barely noticed the portraits and pictures of the Generalissimo—on foot and on horseback, in military uniform or dressed as a farmer, sitting at a desk or standing behind a lectern and wearing the presidential sash—that hung on the walls, or the silver trophies and framed certificates won by the dairy cows and thoroughbred horses of the Fundación Ranch, intermingled with plastic ashtrays and cheap decorations, still bearing the label of Macy's in New York, that adorned the tables, sideboards, and shelves of the monument to kitsch where Benita Sepúlveda left her after asking if she really didn't want a nice glass of liqueur.

"I don't think the word 'kitsch' existed yet," she explains, as if her aunt or cousins had made some observation. "Years later, whenever I heard it or read it, and knew what extremes of bad taste and pretension it expressed, Mahogany House always came to mind. A kitsch monument."

And she herself was part of the kitsch, on that hot May night, with her debutante's pink organdy party dress, the silver chain with the emerald and the gold-washed earrings that had belonged to her mama and that Papa allowed her to wear on the special occasion of Trujillo's party. Her disbelief made what was happening unreal. It seemed to her she wasn't really that girl standing on a branch of the national seal, in that extravagant room. Senator Agustín Cabral had sent her, a living offering, to the Benefactor and Father of the New Nation? Yes, she had no doubt at all, her father had arranged this with Manuel Alfonso. And yet, she still wanted to doubt.

"Somewhere, not in the bar, somebody put on a Lucho Gatica record. *'Bésame, bésame mucho, como si fuera esta noche la última vez.'*"

"I remember." Manolita, embarrassed at interrupting, apologizes with a grimace: "They played 'Bésame Mucho' all day, on the radio, at parties."

Standing next to a window that let in a warm breeze and a dense aroma of fields, grass, trees, she heard voices. The damaged one of Manuel Alfonso. The other, high-pitched, rising and falling, could only be Trujillo's. She felt a prickle at the back of her neck and on her wrists, where the doctor took her pulse, an itch that always came when she had exams, and even now, in New York, before she made important decisions.

"I thought about throwing myself out the window. I thought about getting down on my knees, begging, crying. I thought I had to clench my teeth and let him do whatever he wanted, so I could go on living and take my revenge on Papa one day. I thought a thousand things while they were talking down below."

In her rocking chair, Aunt Adelina gives a start, opens her mouth. But says nothing. She is as white as a sheet, her deep-set eyes filled with tears.

The voices stopped. There was a parenthesis of silence; then, footsteps climbing the stairs. Had her heart stopped beating? In the dim light of the bar, the silhouette of Trujillo appeared, in an olive-green uniform, without a jacket or tie. He held a glass of cognac in his hand. He walked toward her, smiling.

"Good evening, beautiful," he whispered, bowing. And he extended his free hand, but when Urania, in an automatic movement, put forward her own, instead of shaking it Trujillo raised it to his lips and kissed it: "Welcome to Mahogany House, beautiful."

"The story about his eyes, about Trujillo's gaze, I had heard it often. From Papa, from Papa's friends. At that moment, I knew it was true. A gaze that dug deep, all the way down to the bottom. He smiled, he was very gallant, but that gaze emptied me, left me a hollow skin. I was no longer myself."

"Benita hasn't offered you anything?" Not letting go of her hand, Trujillo led her to the best-lit part of the bar, where a fluorescent tube cast a bluish light. He offered her a seat on a two-person sofa. He examined her, moving his eyes slowly up and down, from her head to her feet, openly, as he would examine new bovine and equine acquisitions for the Fundación Ranch. In his gray, fixed, inquisitive eyes she perceived no desire, no excitement, but only an inventory, a gauging of her body.

"He was disappointed. Now I know why, but that night I didn't. I was slender, very thin, and he liked full-bodied women with prominent breasts and hips. Voluptuous women. A typically tropical taste. He even must have thought about sending this skeleton back to Ciudad Trujillo. Do you know why he didn't? Because the idea of breaking a virgin's cherry excites men."

Aunt Adelina moans. Her wrinkled fist raised, her mouth half opened in an expression of horror and censure, she implores her, grimacing, but does not manage to say a word.

"Forgive my frankness, Aunt Adelina. It's something he said, later. I'm quoting him exactly, I swear: 'Breaking a virgin's cherry excites men. Petán, that animal Petán, gets more excited breaking them with his finger.'"

He would say it afterward, when he had lost control and his mouth was vomiting disjointed phrases, sighs, curses, discharges of excrement to ease his bitterness. Now, he still behaved with studied correctness. He did not offer her what he was drinking, Carlos I might burn the insides of a girl so young. He would give her a glass of sweet sherry. He served her himself and made a toast, clinking glasses. Though she barely wet her lips, Urania felt something flame in her throat. Did she try to smile? Did she remain serious, showing her panic?

"I don't know," she says, shrugging. "We were close together on that sofa. The glass of sherry was trembling in my hand."

"I don't eat little girls," Trujillo said with a smile, taking her glass and placing it on a table. "Are you always so quiet or is it only now, beautiful?"

"He called me beautiful, something that Manuel Alfonso had called me too. Not Urania, Uranita, girl. Beautiful. It was a game the two of them were playing."

"Do you like to dance? Sure you do, like all the girls your age," said Trujillo. "I like to, a lot. I'm a good dancer, though I don't have time to go to dances. Come on, let's dance."

He stood up and Urania did too. She felt his strong body, his somewhat protruding belly rubbing against her stomach, his cognac breath, the warm hand holding her waist. She thought she was going to faint. Lucho Gatica wasn't singing "Bésame Mucho" now, but "Alma Mía."

"He really did dance very well. He had a good ear, and he moved like a young man. I was the one who lost the beat. We danced two boleros, and a guaracha by Toña la Negra. Merengues too. He said they danced the merengue in clubs and decent homes now thanks to him. Before, there had been prejudices, and respectable people said it was music for blacks and Indians. I don't know who was changing the records. When the last merengue ended, he kissed me on the neck. A light kiss that gave me gooseflesh."

Holding her by the hand, their fingers intertwined, he walked her back to the sofa and sat down very close to her. He examined her, amused, as he breathed in and drank his cognac. He seemed serene and content.

"Are you always a sphinx? No, no. It must be that you have too much respect for me." Trujillo smiled. "I like beautiful girls who are discreet, who let themselves be admired. Indifferent goddesses. I'm going to recite a poem, it was written for you."

"He recited a poem by Pablo Neruda. Into my ear, brushing my ear, my hair, with his lips and his little mustache: 'I like it when you're quiet, it's as if you weren't here; as if your eyes had flown away, as if a kiss had closed your mouth.' When he came to 'mouth,' his hand moved to my face and he kissed me on the lips. That night I did so many things for the first time: I drank sherry, wore Mama's jewelry, danced with an old man of seventy, and received my first kiss on the mouth."

She had gone to parties with boys and danced, but a boy had kissed her only once, on the cheek, at a birthday party in the mansion of the Vicini family, at the intersection of Máximo Gómez and Avenida George Washington. His name was Casimiro Sáenz, the son of a diplomat. He asked her to dance, and when they had finished she felt his lips on her face. She blushed to the roots of her hair, and at Friday confession with the school chaplain, when she mentioned the sin, her voice broke with embarrassment. But that kiss was nothing like this one: the little brush mustache of His Excellency scratched her nose, and now, his tongue, its tip hot and sticky, was trying to force open her mouth. She resisted and then parted her lips and teeth: a wet, fiery viper pushed into her mouth in a frenzy, moving greedily. She felt herself choking.

"You don't know how to kiss, beautiful." Trujillo smiled at her, kissing her again on the hand, agreeably surprised. "You're a little virgin, aren't you?"

"He had become aroused," says Urania, staring at nothing. "He had an erection."

Manolita gives a short, hysterical laugh, but her mother, her sister, her niece don't follow suit. Her cousin lowers her eyes in confusion.

"I'm sorry, I have to talk about erections," says Urania. "If the male becomes aroused, his sex stiffens and grows larger. When he put his tongue in my mouth, His Excellency became aroused."

"Let's go up, beautiful," he said, his voice somewhat thickened. "We'll be more comfortable. You're going to discover something wonderful. Love. Pleasure. You'll like it. I'll teach you. Don't be afraid of me. I'm not an animal like Petán, I don't enjoy being brutal to girls. I like them to enjoy it too. I'll make you happy, beautiful."

"He was seventy and I was fourteen," Urania specifies for the fifth or tenth time. "We were a mismatched couple, climbing that staircase with the metal railing and heavy wooden bars. Holding hands, like sweethearts. The grandfather and his granddaughter on their way to the bridal chamber."

The lamp on the night table was lit, and Urania saw the square wrought-iron bed, the mosquito netting raised, and she heard the blades of the fan turning slowly on the ceiling. A white embroidered spread covered the bed, and a number of pillows and cushions were piled against the headboard. It smelled of fresh flowers and grass.

"Don't undress yet, beautiful," Trujillo murmured. "I'll help you. Wait, I'll be right back."

"Do you remember how nervous we were when we talked about losing our virginity, Manolita?" Urania turns toward her cousin. "I never imagined I'd lose it in Mahogany House with the Generalissimo. I thought: 'If I jump off the balcony, Papa will really be sorry.'"

He soon returned, naked under a blue silk robe with white flecks and wearing garnet-colored slippers. He took a drink of cognac, left his glass on a dresser among photographs of himself surrounded by his grandchildren, and, grasping Urania by the waist, sat her down on the edge of the bed, on the space left open by the mosquito netting, two great butterfly wings crossed over their heads. He began to undress her, slowly. He unbuttoned the back of her dress, one button after another, and removed her belt. Before taking off her dress, he kneeled, and with some difficulty leaned forward and bared her feet. Carefully, as if a sudden movement of his fingers could shatter the girl, he pulled off her nylon stockings, caressing her legs as he did so.

"Your feet are cold, beautiful," he murmured tenderly. "Are you cold? Come here, let me warm them for you."

Still kneeling, he rubbed her feet with both hands. From time to time he lifted them to his mouth and kissed them, beginning at the instep, going down to her toes and around to her heels, asking with a sly little laugh if he was tickling her, as if he were the one feeling a joyful itch.

"He spent a long time like that, holding my feet. In case you're interested, I didn't feel the least excitement, not for a second."

"You must have been so scared," Lucindita says encouragingly.

"Not then, not yet. Later on, I was terrified."

With difficulty His Excellency stood, and sat down again on the edge of the bed. He took off her dress, the pink bra that held her budding little breasts, the triangle of her panties. She allowed him to do it, not offering any resistance, her body limp. When Trujillo slid the pink panties down her legs, she noticed that His Excellency's fingers were hurrying; they were sweaty, burning the skin where they touched her. He made her lie down. He stood, took off his robe, and lay down beside her, naked. Carefully, he moved his fingers through the girl's sparse pubic hair.

"He was still very excited, I think. When he began to touch and caress me. And kiss me, his mouth always forcing my mouth open. Kissing my breasts, my neck, my back, my legs."

She did not resist; she allowed herself to be touched, caressed, kissed, and her body obeyed with the movements and postures that His Excellency's hands indicated for her. But she did not return the caresses, and when her eyes were not closed, she kept them glued on the slow blades of the fan. Then she heard him say to himself: "Breaking a virgin's cherry always excites men."

"The first dirty word, the first vulgarity of the night," Urania declares. "Later, he would say much worse. That was when I realized that something was happening to him. He began to get angry. Because I was still, limp, because I didn't kiss him back?"

That wasn't it: she understood that now. Whether or not she participated in her own deflowering wasn't anything His Excellency cared about. To feel satisfied, it was enough for her to have an intact cherry that he could break, making her moan—howl, scream—in pain, with his battering ram of a prick inside her, squeezed tight by the walls of that newly violated intimate place. It wasn't love, not even pleasure, that he expected of Urania. He had agreed to the young daughter of Senator Agustín Cabral coming to Mahogany House only to prove that Rafael Leonidas Trujillo Molina, despite his seventy years, despite his prostate problems, despite his headaches with priests, Yankees, Venezuelans, conspirators, was still a real man, a stud with a prick that could still get hard and break all the virgin cherries that came his way.

"I had no experience, but I knew." Her aunt, cousins, and niece lean their heads forward to hear her whisper. "Something was happening to him, I mean down below. He couldn't. He was about to go wild and forget all his good manners."

"That's enough playing dead, beautiful," she heard him order, a changed man. "On your knees. Between my legs. That's it. Take it in your hands and mouth. And suck it, the way I sucked your cunt. Until it wakes up. Too bad for you if it doesn't, beautiful."

"I tried, I tried. In spite of my terror, my disgust. I did everything. I squatted on my haunches, I put it in my mouth, I kissed it, I sucked it until my gorge rose. Soft, soft. I prayed to God it would stop."

"That's enough, Urania, that's enough!" Aunt Adelina isn't crying. She looks at her in horror, without compassion. Her eyes roll back in her head, the whites bulging, sclerotic; she is shocked, violently agitated. "What are you telling us for, Urania? My God, that's enough!"

"But I failed," Urania insists. "He covered his eyes with his arm. He didn't say anything. When he moved his arm away, he hated me."

His eyes were red and his pupils burned with a yellowish, feverish light of rage and shame. He looked at her without a hint of courtesy, with belligerent hostility, as if she had done him irreparable harm.

"You're wrong if you think you're leaving here a virgin so you can laugh at me with your father," he spelled out, with mute fury, spitting as he spoke.

He seized her by the arm and threw her down beside him. Assisted by movements of his legs and waist, he mounted her. That mass of flesh crushed her, pushed her down into the mattress; the smell of cognac and rage on his breath made her dizzy. She felt her muscles and bones crumbling, ground to dust. She was suffocating, but that did not prevent her from feeling the roughness of that hand, those fingers, exploring, digging, forcing their way into her. She felt herself pierced, stabbed with a knife; a lightning bolt ran from her head down to her feet. She cried out, feeling as if she were dying.

"Go on and screech, you little bitch, see if you learn your lesson," the wounding, offended voice of His Excellency spat at her. "Now open up. Let me see if it's really broken or if you're faking it."

"It really was. I had blood on my legs; it stained him, and the spread, and the bed."

"That's enough, that's enough! Why tell us more, Urania?" her aunt shouts. "Come, let's make the sign of the cross and pray. For the sake of what you hold most dear, Urania. Do you believe in God? In Our Lady of Altagracia, patron saint of Dominicans? Your mother was so devoted to her, Uranita. I remember her getting ready every January 21 for the pilgrimage to the Basilica of Higüey. You're full of rancor and hate. That's not good. No matter what happened to you. Let's pray, Urania."

"And then," says Urania, ignoring her, "His Excellency lay on his back again and covered his eyes. He was still, very still. He wasn't sleeping. He let out a sob. He began to cry."

"To cry?" Lucindita exclaims.

Her reply is a sudden jabbering. The five women turn their heads: Samson is awake and announces it by chattering.

"Not for me," declares Urania. "For his enlarged prostate, his dead prick, for having to fuck virgins with his fingers, the way Petán liked to do."

"My God, Urania, for the sake of what you hold most dear," her Aunt Adelina implores, crossing herself. "No more."

Urania caresses the old woman's wrinkled, spotted hand.

"They're horrible words, I know, things that shouldn't be said, Aunt Adelina." Her voice sweetens. "I never use them, I swear. Didn't you want to know why I said those things about Papa? Why, when I went to Adrian, I didn't want anything to do with the family? Now you know why."

From time to time he sobs, and his sighs make his chest rise and fall. A few white hairs grow between his nipples and around his dark navel. He keeps his eyes hidden under his arm. Has he forgotten about her? Has she been erased by his overpowering bitterness and suffering? She is more frightened than before, when he was caressing her or violating her. She forgets about the burning, the wound between her legs, her fear of the bloodstains on her thighs and the bedspread. She does not move. Be invisible, cease to exist. If the weeping man with hairless legs sees her, he won't forgive her, he'll turn the rage of his impotence, the shame of his weeping, on her and annihilate her.

"He said there was no justice in this world. Why was this happening to him after he had fought so hard for this ungrateful country, these people without honor? He was talking to God. The saints. Our Lady. Or maybe the devil. He shouted and begged. Why was he given so many trials? The cross of his sons that he had to bear, the plots to kill him, to destroy the work of a lifetime. But he wasn't complaining about that. He knew how to beat flesh-and-blood enemies. He had done that since he was young. What he couldn't tolerate was the low blow, not having a chance to defend himself. He seemed half crazed with despair. Now I know why. Because the prick that had broken so many cherries wouldn't stand up anymore. That's what made the titan cry. Laughable, isn't it?"

But Urania wasn't laughing. She listened, not moving, scarcely daring to breathe, hoping he wouldn't remember she was there. His soliloquy was discontinuous, fragmented, incoherent, interrupted by long silences; he raised his voice and shouted, or lowered it until it was almost inaudible. A pitiful noise. Urania was fascinated by that chest rising and falling. She tried not to look at his body, but sometimes her eyes moved along his soft belly, white pubis, small, dead sex, hairless legs. This was the Generalissimo, the Benefactor of the Nation, the Father of the New Nation, the Restorer of Financial Independence. The Chief whom Papa had served for thirty years with devotion and loyalty, and presented with a most delicate gift: his fourteen-year-old daughter. But things didn't happen as the senator hoped. And that meant—Urania's heart filled with joy—he wouldn't rehabilitate Papa; maybe he'd put him in prison, maybe he'd have him killed.

"Suddenly, he lifted his arm and looked at me with red, swollen eyes. I'm forty-nine years old, and I'm trembling again. I've been trembling for thirty-five years, ever since that moment."

She holds out her hands and her aunt, cousins, and niece see it is true: she is trembling.

He looked at her with surprise and hatred, as if she were a malevolent apparition. Red, fiery, fixed, his eyes froze her. She couldn't move. Trujillo's eyes ran over her, moved down to her thighs, darted to the bloodstained spread, and glared at her again. Choking with revulsion, he ordered:

"Go on, get washed, see what you've done to the bed? Get out of here!"

"A miracle that he let me go," Urania reflects. "After I saw him desperate, crying, moaning, feeling sorry for himself. A miracle from our patron saint, Aunt Adelina."

She sat up, jumped out of bed, picked up the clothes scattered on the floor, and, stumbling against a chest of drawers, took refuge in the bathroom. There was a white porcelain tub stocked with sponges and soaps, and a penetrating perfume that made her dizzy. With hands that barely responded she cleaned her legs, used a washcloth to stanch the bleeding, got dressed. It was difficult to button her dress, buckle her belt. She didn't put on her stockings, only her shoes, and when she looked at herself in one of the mirrors, she saw her face smeared with lipstick and mascara. She didn't take the time to wash it off; he might change his mind. Run, get out of Mahogany House, escape. When she returned to the bedroom, Trujillo was no longer naked. He had covered himself with his blue silk robe and held the glass of cognac in his hand. He pointed to the stairs:

"Get out, get out," he said in a strangled voice. "Tell Benita to bring fresh sheets and a spread and clean up this mess."

"On the first step I tripped and broke the heel of my shoe and almost fell down three flights of stairs. My ankle swelled up afterward. Benita Sepúlveda was on the ground floor. Very calm, smiling at me. I tried to say what he had told me to. Not a word came out. I could only point upstairs. She took my arm and walked me to the guards at the entrance. She showed me a recess with a seat: 'Here's where they polish the Chief's boots.' Manuel Alfonso and his car weren't there. Benita Sepúlveda had me sit on the shoeshine stand, surrounded by guards. She left, and when she came back, she led me by the arm to a jeep. The driver was a soldier. He brought me to Ciudad Trujillo. When he asked: 'Where's your house?' I said: 'I'm going to Santo Domingo Academy. I live there.' It was still dark. Three o'clock. Four, maybe. It took them a long time to open the gate. I still couldn't talk when the caretaker finally appeared. I could only talk to Sister Mary, the nun who loved me so much. She took me to the refectory, she gave me water, she put wet cloths on my forehead."

Samson, who has been quiet for a while, displays his pleasure or displeasure again by puffing out his feathers and shrieking. No one says anything. Urania picks up her glass, but it is empty. Marianita fills it; she is nervous and knocks over the pitcher. Urania takes a few sips of cool water.

"I hope it's done me good, telling you this cruel story. Now forget it. It's over. It happened and there's nothing anyone can do about it. Maybe another woman might have gotten over it. I wouldn't and couldn't."

"Uranita, my dear cousin, what are you saying?" Manolita protests. "What do you mean? Look what you've done. What you have. A life every Dominican woman would envy."

She stands and walks over to Urania. She embraces her, kisses her cheeks.

"You've really battered me, Uranita," Lucinda scolds her affectionately. "But how can you complain? You have no right. In your case it's really true that some good always comes out of the bad. You studied at the best university, you've had a successful career. You have a man who makes you happy and doesn't interfere with your work . . ."

Urania pats her arm and shakes her head. The parrot is quiet and listens.

"I lied to you, Lucinda, I don't have a lover." She smiles vaguely, her voice still breaking. "I've never had one, I never will. Do you want to know everything, Lucindita? No man has ever laid a hand on me again since that time.

My only man was Trujillo. It's true. Whenever one gets close and looks at me as a woman, I feel sick. Horrified. I want him to die, I want to kill him. It's hard to explain. I've studied, I work, I earn a good living. But I'm empty and still full of fear. Like those old people in New York who spend the whole day in the park, staring at nothing. It's work, work, work until I'm exhausted. You have no reason to envy me, I assure you. I envy all of you. Yes, yes, I know, you have problems, hard times, disappointments. But you also have families, husbands, children, relatives, a country. Those things fill your life. But Papa and His Excellency turned me into a desert."

Translated by Edith Grossman

WORK

1959, *Los jefes*, Roca (stories).

1963, *La ciudad y los perros*, Seix Barral (novel).

1966, *La casa verde*, Seix Barral (novel).

1967, *Los cachorros*, Seix Barral (novel).

1969, *Conversación en la Catedral*, Seix Barral (novel).

1971, *García Márquez: Historia de un deicidio*, Barral (essay).

1971, *Historia secreta de una novela*, Tusquets (essay).

1971, *Día domingo*, Amadís (stories).

1973, *Pantaleón y las visitadoras*, Seix Barral (novel).

1975, *La orgía perpetua: Flaubert y "Madame Bovary,"* Seix Barral (essay).

1977, *La tía Julia y el escribidor*, Seix Barral (novel).

1981, *La guerra del fin del mundo*, Seix Barral (novel).

1981, *Entre Sartre y Camus*, Huracán (essay).

1981, *La señorita de Tacna*, Seix Barral (drama).

1983, *Contra viento y marea (1962-1982)*, Seix Barral (essays and articles).

1983, *Kathie y el hipopótamo*, Seix Barrel (drama).

1984, *Historia de Mayta*, Seix Barral (novel).

1986, *¿Quién mató a Palomino Molero?*, Seix Barral (novel).

1986, *La Chunga*, Seix Barral (drama).

1986, *Contra viento y marea (1972-1983)*, Seix Barral (essays and articles).

1987, *El hablador*, Seix Barral (novel).

1988, *Elogio de la madrastra*, Tuquets Editores (erotic novel).

1990, *Contra viento y marea (1964-1988)*, Seix Barral (essays and articles).

1990, *La verdad de las mentiras: Ensayos sobre la novela moderna*, Seix Barral (essay).

1991, *Carta de batalla por "Tirant lo Blanc,"* Seix Barral (first comprehensive collection of essays).

1993, *Lituma en los Andes*, Planeta (novel).

1993, *El pez en el agua*, Seix Barral (memoirs).

1994, *Desafíos a la libertad*, El País-Aguilar (essay).

1996, *La utopía arcaica: José María Arguedas y las ficciones del indigenismo*, Fondo de Cultura Económica (essay).

1996, *Ojos bonitos, cuadros feos*, PEISA (drama).

1997, *Los cuadernos de don Rigoberto*, Alfaguara (novel).

1997, *Cartas a un joven novelista*, Ariel (essay).

2000, *La Fiesta del Chivo*, Alfaguara (novel).

2001, *El lenguaje de la pasión*, El País (articles).

2001, *Bases para una interpretación de Rubén Darío*, Instituto de Investigaciones Humanísticas, Facultad de Letras y Ciencias Humanas, UNMSM (essay).

2003, *El paraíso en la otra esquina*, Alfaguara (novel).

2004, *La tentación de lo imposible*, Alfaguara (essay about Victor Hugo's *Les Misérables*).

2006, *Israel/Palestina Paz o guerra santa*, Aguilar (articles).

2006, *Travesuras de la niña mala*, Alfaguara (novel).

2007, *Odiseo y Penélope*, Galaxia Gutenberg (drama).

2008, *El viaje a la ficción: El mundo de Juan Carlos Onetti*, Alfaguara (essay).

2008, *Al pie del Támesis*, Alfaguara (drama).

2009, *Las mil noches y una noche*, Alfaguara (drama).

2009, *Sables y utopías*, Aguilar (articles).

2010, "Fonchito y la luna," Alfaguara (children's story).

2011, *El sueño del celta*, Alfaguara (novel).

2012, *La civilización del espectáculo*, Alfaguara (essay).

2013, *El héroe discreto*, Alfaguara (novel)

·

ENGLISH TRANSLATIONS

1966, *The Time of the Hero*, translated by Lysander Kemp, Grove Press (novel).

1968, *The Green House*, translated by Gregory Rabassa, Harper Perennial (novel).

1975, *Conversation in the Cathedral*, translated by Gregory Rabassa, Harper Perennial (novel).

1978, *Captain Pantoja and the Special Service*, translated by Gregory Kolovakas and Ronald Christ, Harper Perennial (novel).

1979, *The Cubs and Other Stories*, translated by Gregory Kolovakas and Ronald Christ, Harper Perennial (stories).

1982, *Aunt Julia and the Scriptwriter*, translated by Helen R. Lane, Farrar, Straus and Giroux (novel).

1984, *The War of the End of the World*, translated by Helen R. Lane, Farrar, Straus and Giroux (novel).

1985, *The Real Life of Alejandro Mayta*, translated by Alfred Mac Adam, Farrar, Straus and Giroux (novel).

1986, *The Perpetual Orgy: Flaubert and Madam Bovary*, translated by Helen Lane, Farrar, Straus and Giroux (essay).

1987, *Who Killed Palomino Molero?*, translated by Alfred Mac Adam, Farrar, Straus and Giroux (novel).

1989, *The Storyteller*, translated by Helen Lane, Farrar, Straus and Giroux (novel).

1990, *In Praise of the Stepmother*, translated by Helen Lane, Farrar, Straus and Giroux (novel).

1994, *A Fish in the Water*, translated by Helen Lane, Faber & Faber (autobiography).

1996, *Death in the Andes*, translated by Edith Grossman, Farrar, Straus and Giroux (novel).

1998, *Notebooks of Don Rigoberto*, translated by Edith Grossman, Farrar, Straus and Giroux (novel).

2001, *The Feast of the Goat*, translated by Edith Grossman, Farrar, Straus and Giroux (novel).

2003, *The Language of Passion*, translated by Natasha Wimmer, Farrar, Straus and Giroux (essays).

2003, *The Way to Paradise*, translated by Natasha Wimmer, Farrar, Straus and Giroux (novel).

2007, *The Bad Girl*, translated by Edith Grossman, Farrar, Straus and Giroux (novel).

2007, *The Temptation of the Impossible: Victor Hugo and* Les Misérables, translated by John King, Princeton University Press (essay).

2010, *The Dream of the Celt*, translated by Edith Grossman, Farrar, Straus and Giroux (novel).

•

AWARDS AND RECOGNITIONS

1959, Premio Leopoldo Alas for *Los jefes*.

1963, Premio Biblioteca Breve for *La ciudad y los perros*.

1964, Premio de la Crítica de Narrativa Castellana for *La ciudad y los perros*.

1966, Premio de la Crítica Española for *La casa verde*.

1967, Premio de la Crítica de Narrativa Castellana for *La casa verde*.

1967, Premio Internacional de Literatura Rómulo Gallegos for *La casa verde*.

1967, Premio Nacional de Novela de Perú for *La casa verde*.

1981, Premio de la Crítica (Argentina).

1981, Medalla de Honor del Congreso (Peru).

1985, French Legion of Honor.

1985, Premio Ritz París Hemingway for *La guerra del fin del mundo*.

1986, Premio Príncipe de Asturias de las Letras.

1987, Official decoration from the French Order of Arts and Letters.

1990, Honorary Doctorate from Florida International University.

1992, Honorary Doctorate from University of Boston.

1992, Honorary Doctorate from University of Genoa.

1993, Premio Planeta for *Lituma en los Andes*.

1993, French Order of Arts and Letters at the order of Comander.

1994, Premio Cervantes.

1994, Member of Real Academia Española.

1994, Honorary Doctorate from Yale University.

1994, Honorary Doctorate from Georgetown.

1997, Peace Prize from the German Booksellers.

1998, Honorary Doctorate from Ben Gurión of Isreal.

1998, Honorary Doctorate from University College of London

1999, Honorary Doctorate from Harvard University.

1999, Premio Ortega y Gasset de Periodismo for his article "Nuevas inquisiciones."

1999, Premio Internacional Menéndez Pelayo for revitalizing fantasy and for the ethical breadth of his work.

2001, Orden El Sol de Perú on the order of Gran Cruz con Brillantes.

2001, Honorary Doctorate from Universidad Nacional Mayor de San Marcos.

2002, Nabokov Prize, from the PEN American Center.

2002, Honorary Doctorate from Trobe University of Melbourne.

2003, Honorary Doctorate from Oxford University.

2005, Honorary Doctorate from the Sorbonne University.

2005, Honorary Doctorate from Humboldt University of Berlin.

2008, Honorary Doctorate from Universidad Católica del Perú.

2010, Honorary Doctorate from Universidad Nacional Autónoma de México.

2010, Nobel Prize for Literature.

2011, Orden del Águila Azteca.

2011, Medalla de Honor "Sanmarquina" on the order of Gran Cruz from Universidad de San Marcos.

2011, Honorary Doctorate from Universidad Peruana Cayetano Heredia.

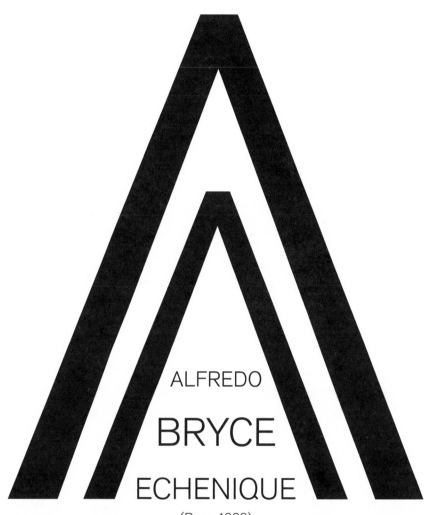

ALFREDO

BRYCE

ECHENIQUE

(Peru, 1939)

When you talk about Bryce Echenique it's difficult to discern between the man himself and his fame. The "artistic lie" (which he learned from Wilde) and an irrepressibly ironic view of life go hand-in-hand with this inexhaustable writer and his mischievous memory.

Born in Lima in 1939, Alfredo Bryce Echenique had to turn away from a destiny that had not exactly driven him to become a writer. His parents were members of the Peruvian upper class: his father, Francisco Bryce, was a prestigious banker; his mother, Elena Echenique, was a descendent of José Rufino Echenique, president of Peru between 1851 and 1855. The family wanted Bryce Echenique to have a fulfilling career as a lawyer, one day to even see him become president of Peru. But he wanted nothing but to travel, read, get away from a country where, he was sure, he'd never be able write.

So after he was educated in elite schools and graduated with degrees in Law (to please his father) and Literature (to please himself), in 1964 the French government awarded him a scholarship and he went to Paris to study at the Sorbonne. The next year he tried to get his scholarship renewed for another year and, when he didn't get it, he sold his return ticket and traveled around France, Italy, Greece, and Germany. In Perugia he wrote his first manuscript, which he ended up losing on one of the many trains he took during his trip around Europe. In 1965, while making a living as a Spanish teacher in a high school in Paris, he resolved to write it again, but this time writing was a whole new experience: he was finding his voice, his style, so oral and so full of digressions. Those stories would comprise his first book, *Huerto cerrado*, published in 1968.

By then, he was already a professor at the Sorbonne. In May of that year, he randomly found himself in Nanterre and witnessed firsthand and with certain skepticism, the youth and student movement that was in its gestation.

Even though, like Cortázar, Bryce's heart was always on the left, he found disillusion there as well: "Now everyone shows up wearing ties, like business executives, like my first wife. Today the woman who left me for a Marxist is an executive and if you remind her of it, she blushes." In his relationships with women, through the years, he also suffered disappointments, "but I have the pleasure to be waiting for my third divorce, so I can get married for the fourth time, as soon as possible."

So, after publishing his first book, Alfredo Bryce kept writing stories, short texts, until one of them surpassed six hundred pages and ended up turning into the novel *Un mundo para Julius*. Published in 1970, it portrays, through the eyes of a boy and in a shamelessly ironic and enormously vital tone, what childhood was like in the heart of the Lima oligarchy. *Un mundo para Julius* gained prominence in 1972 with the Premio Nacional de Literatura del Perú and was selected as the best foreign novel published in France in 1974. The success overwhelmed Bryce, sinking him in a profound depression that led to his being checked in to a psychiatric hospital. The diagnosis: a lack of vanity. Throughout the years, the writer has suffered several relapses, but he insists he's made the most of his depression: "I've recouped my investment with a profit." In those years, he also gave us *La felicidad ja ja*, where he continues his reflection on the world of Lima's high society, only now his characters have grown up and are on the brink of adolescence and melancholy.

Paul Valéry University in Montpellier contracted him in 1980 and there he wrote the novels *La vida exagerada de Martín Romaña* (1981) and *El hombre que hablaba de Octavia de Cádiz* (1985). Together they made up the dyptich *Cuadernos de navegación en un sillón Voltaire* and centered on the life of Latin American intellectuals in Europe, tied together by the figure of Martín Romaña, a young professor who, after breaking with his familial past in Peru, responds only to his desire to write.

In 1985, he abandoned France and settled in Spain, where he lived both in Barcelona and Madrid. In 1986, he published *Magdalena peruana y otros cuentos* and in 1995 the novel *No me esperen en abril*, a sort of colophon for *Un mundo para Julius*. In 1998, *Reo de nocturnidad* won the Premio Nacional de Narrativa in Spain. The following year, down on himself and the country, the writer decided to go back to Peru, a decision that, with time, he came to consider rushed, and presently he splits his time between the two countries. In 2007, Alfredo Bryce was embroiled in a bizarre accusation of multiple plagarisms. The episode, itself with the coloring of a spy novel, carried with it a certain enmity, but also the unconditional support of those who, like Enrique Vila-Matas and Mario Vargas Llosa, have been uncompromising in defending their faith in the writer, who continues to steer his literary course between suffering and laughter.

THE ACORN

The Torture of Doctor Johnson

Above all I like the pages I picked from *Un mundo para Julius* for their efficiency. Let's not forget that they're the first pages in the book and, in a condensed way, although not lacking in subtleties, they contain a lot of information about the novel's central characters, with the exception of Juan Lucas—Julius's stepfather and the novel's antagonist—whose presence is implied in the nocturnal outings of Susan, Julius's frivolous, widowed mother. But in addition to introducing the book's main characters, these pages also introduce the book's principal settings. The boy's house is a microcosm of Peru, with borders that he crosses for the first time when he goes from the elegant part of the large mansion where he lives into the so-called "servants' quarters," an accurate reflection of a whole country that is profoundly and cruelly divided between the very rich and the very poor, and into distinct regions such as the coast, the world of the Andes, and the Amazon. From these immense and varied regions of Peru come the so-called servants of this wealthy family who, instead of taking interest in their own country, live with their eyes fixed principally on Europe and secondarily on the United States. And so Julius and his siblings attend British and American schools, where the few Peruvian teachers working there come off as deeply pretentious in the eyes of their students.

"Manzanas" is the long monologue of a young and beautiful nympho-maniac who competes with any good-looking girl who crosses her path, and who, at the same time, maintains a romantic relationship with an important musician who is much older, and is able to see her in a good light, even to overlook her infidelities. The tension comes from her admiration for the refined, cultured, and respectable man combined with her desire to surpass him in some way, petty as it may be. She doesn't say any of this. She just suggests it. A murder, although only symbolic, might be the only way for the guilt-ridden girl to escape from her constant and spiteful obsessions and contradictions.

In Conversation with the Dead

I'm convinced that this depends on the book I'm working on. For example, in the case of *Un mundo para Julius*, in which all the characters were invented and the style was spoken and "spontaneous" (the fruit of a lot of work and many corrections), I was only "in conversation" with myself. When this novel was published, they talked about the influence of Salinger. But it was only at that point that I read Salinger—I only discovered him afterward, which shows how oftentimes you invent even the authors who influence you. No, in my case, the Quevado idea doesn't apply at all, but it's true that on a day when I'm writing and I feel "blocked" or I need help to keep going, I always revisit the poetry of César Vallejo, which has nothing to do with my work. Vallejo, even though I open his book entirely at random, to any old page, always moves me and "puts me back in working order," helping me to keep writing.

On the other hand, right now I'm writing about the origin, apogee, and decadence of a traditional Peruvian family from the nineteenth and twentieth century (it ends between 1970 and 1980), and in preparation, I read some Peruvian history books relevant to the topic and novels like *Bearn, El Gatopardo,* and *Buddenbrooks* by Lorenzo Villalonga, Lampedusa, and Thomas Mann; the novels that accompany me as I write now are far removed from what I'm interested in talking about. For example, Virginia Woolf, Edith Wharton, Tom Sharpe, Nathaniel West, Chester Himes, or Henry Miller. If I'm away from home, yes, but not in the peace of the deserts, not on a crowded beach. Sterne fascinates me, I'll never deny it, and I've reread him several times. But humor steers me away from the sentimental novels of the eighteenth century—there's too much crying, they never laugh.

Once you said that it was Cortázar who had a "liberating influence," teaching you that, in the space of a single sentence, you can diverge, make digressions, work with spoken language, that he "opened up your style."

Yes, Cortázar could be one, of course. And others no doubt, such as Rabelais and Cervantes, Sterne, and Stendhal—the author I reread the most, especially *The Charterhouse of Parma*.

Coda

You were teaching university classes during May of '68 on some writers of the boom and you've said that it was in Paris that the image of the Latin American writer (guevarism) was established. Can the myth of the professional Latin American be given up for dead or do you think it still survives?

Actually, I think that myth's own sickness killed it many years ago. No one believes in Castro anymore, nor do they dream of "El Condor Pasa" (the best rendition of which is by Simon and Garfunkel, and it is also the aria of an unfinished opera that a rich Peruvian gentleman wrote in Paris thinking more about La Scala in Milan than about the Andean man of his own country . . .). And as for Guevara, today it's well known that he was just a fanatic individualist combined with a lousy man of action (he failed everywhere he went) who was only looking for death, I think.

Many of your readers consider you a humorist. But behind every humorist there's a moralist. And behind this moralist a pessimist. Right? You are quoted as saying: "I think that sometimes people have been mistaken reading my books because they only perceive humor."

I don't pretend to be a moralist nor do I even think of starting a book with a predetermined goal. No, I don't think there is a purpose or even a design behind my ironic—never cruel or sarcastic—humor. It just gives, like an apple tree gives an apple, without caring by whom or how it gets eaten. As far as pessimism goes, I've always considered myself "a pessimist who wants everything to turn out okay."

A THOUSAND FORESTS

FROM *A WORLD FOR JULIUS*
[A NOVEL]

Remember how during those trips that our mother would take us on
when we were children, and we used to escape from the sleeper cars
to run through the third-class cars. We were fascinated by the men we
used to see sleeping against strangers' shoulders, or simply stretched
out on the floor, in the packed cars. They seemed more real than our
families' friends. At the Toulon station one night, during our return
to Paris from Cannes, we saw the third-class travelers drinking from
the water fountain on the platform; a worker offered you some water
from a soldier's canteen and you gulped it down, looking quickly at
me like the little girl who had just had her first adventure in life . . .
We were born to travel in first class but, in contrast to the rules of the
great ocean liners, it seemed to prohibit us from third class.
　　　　　　　　　　　　　　　—*Roger Vailland*, Beau Masque

Julius was born in a mansion on Salaverry Avenue, directly across from the
old San Felipe Hippodrome. The mansion had carriage houses, gardens, a
swimming pool, and a small orchard into which two-year-old Julius would
wander and then be found later, his back turned, perhaps bending over a
flower. The mansion had servants' quarters that were like a blemish on the
most beautiful face. There was even a carriage that your great-grandfather
used, Julius, when he was President of the Republic, be careful, don't touch!
it's covered with cobwebs, and turning away from his mother, who was lovely,
Julius tried to reach the door handle. The carriage and the servants' quarters

always held a strange fascination for Julius, that fascination of "don't touch, honey, don't go around there, darling." By then his father had already died.

Julius was a year and a half old at the time. For some months he just walked about the mansion, wandering off by himself whenever possible.

Secretly he would head for the servants' quarters of the mansion that, as we've said, were like a blemish on a most beautiful face, a pity, really, but he still did not dare to go there. What is certain is that when his father was dying of cancer, everything in Versailles revolved around the dying man's bedroom: only his children were not supposed to see him. Julius was an exception because he was too young to comprehend fear but young enough to appear just when least expected, wearing silk pajamas, turning his back to the drowsy nurse and watching his father die, that is, he watched how an elegant, rich, handsome man dies. And Julius has never forgotten that night—three o'clock in the morning, a lit candle in offering to Santa Rosa, the nurse knitting to ward off sleep—when his father opened an eye and said to him poor thing, and by the time the nurse ran out to call for his mother, who was lovely and cried every night in an adjoining bedroom—if anything, to get a bit of rest—it was all over.

Daddy died when the last of Julius' siblings, who were always asking when he would return from his trip, stopped asking; when Mommy stopped crying and went out one night; when the visitors, who had entered quietly and walked straight to the darkest room of the mansion (the architect had thought of everything), stopped coming; when the servants recovered their normal tone of voice; and when someone turned on the radio one day, Daddy had died.

No one could keep Julius from practically living in the carriage that had belonged to his great-grandfather/president. He would spend the entire day in it, sitting on the worn blue velvet, once gold-trimmed seats, shooting at the butlers and maids who always tumbled down dead by the carriage, soiling their smocks that the Señora had ordered them to buy in pairs so that they would not appear worn when they fell dead each time Julius took to riddling them with bullets from the carriage. No one prevented him from spending all day long in the carriage, but when it would get dark at about six o'clock, a young maid would come looking for him, one that his mother, who was lovely, called the beautiful Chola, probably a descendant of some noble Indian, an Inca for all we know.

The Chola, who could well have been a descendant of an Inca, would lift Julius from the carriage, press him firmly against her probably marvelous breasts beneath her uniform, and not let go until they reached the bathroom in the mansion, the one that was reserved for the younger children and now belonged exclusively to Julius. Often the Chola stumbled over the butlers or the gardener who lay dead around the carriage so that Julius, Jesse James, or Gary Cooper, depending on the occasion, could depart happily for his bath.

And there in the bathroom, two years after his father's death, his mother had begun to say good-bye. She always found him with his back to her, standing naked in front of the tub, pee pee exposed, but she never saw it, as he contemplated the rising tide in that enormous, porcelainlike, baby-blue tub, which was full of swans, geese, and ducks. His mother would call him darling, but he never turned around, so she would kiss him on the nape of his neck and leave very lovely, while the beautiful Chola assumed the most uncomfortable postures in order to stick her elbow in the water and test the temperature without falling in what could have been a swimming pool in Beverly Hills.

And about six-thirty every afternoon, the beautiful Chola took hold of Julius by his underarms, raised him up and eased him little by little into the water. Seeming to genuflect, the swans, geese, and ducks bobbed up and down happily in the warm, clean water. He took them by the neck and gently pushed them along and away from his body, while the beautiful Chola, armed with soapy washcloths and perfumed baby soap, began to scrub gently—ever so gently and lovingly—his chest, shoulders, back, arms, and legs. Julius looked up smiling at her, always asking the same questions, such as: "And where are you from?" and he listened attentively as she would tell him about Puquio, a village of mud houses near Nasca, on the way up to the mountains. She would tell him stories about the mayor or sometimes about medicine men, but she always laughed as if she no longer believed in those things; besides, it had been a long time since she had been up there. Julius looked at her attentively and waited for her to finish talking so he could ask another question, and another, and another. And it was like that every afternoon while his two brothers and one sister finished their homework downstairs and got ready for dinner.

Those days, his brothers and sister already ate in the formal dining room of the mansion, which was an immense room replete with mirrors where the beautiful Chola would carry Julius, first, to give his father a sleepy kiss and then, after a long walk to the other end of the table, the last little kiss of the day to his mother, who always smelled heavenly. But that was when he was just a few months old, not now when he would go to the main dining room by himself and spend time contemplating a huge silver tea service, looking like a cathedral dome on an immense china cabinet that his great-grandfather/president had acquired in Brussels. Without luck, Julius tried over and over to reach that enticing polished teapot. One day, though, he did seize it; but he couldn't manage to stay on his tippy-toes nor let go of it in time, whereupon the teapot came crashing down with a big noise, denting its lovely shape and crushing his foot; it was, simply put, a complete catastrophe. From that point forward Julius never again wanted to have anything to do with silver tea sets in formal dining rooms in mansions. Along with the tea service and mirrors, the dining room had glass-paneled cabinets, Persian rugs, porcelain china, and the tea set that President Sánchez Cerro gave us the week before he was assassinated. That's where his brothers and sister ate now.

Only Julius ate in the children's dining room, which was now referred to as Julius' dining room. It was like Disneyland: the four walls were covered with Donald Duck, Little Red Riding Hood, Mickey Mouse, Tarzan, Cheetah, Jane, properly dressed, naturally, Superman, probably beating up Dracula, Popeye, and a very, very skinny Olive Oil. The backs of the chairs were rabbits laughing raucously, the legs were carrots, and the tabletop where Julius ate was shouldered by four little Indians who were not related to the Indians that the beautiful Chola from Puquio would tell him about while she bathed him in Beverly Hills. Oh! and besides, there was a swing with a tiny seat when it was time for the bit about eat your soup little Julius (at times, even more endearingly, cutie pie Julie), a little spoonful for your Mommy, another for little Cindy, another for your brother Bobby and so on, but never one for your Daddy because he had died of cancer. Sometimes his mother would pass by the room while they swung Julius and fed his soup to him, and she would hear those horrendous nicknames the servants used that were ruining her children's real names. "Really, I don't know why we ever gave them such attractive names," she said. "To hear them say Cindy instead of Cinthia, Julito instead of Julius, what a crime!" she said to someone on the telephone, though Julius hardly ever heard her because, what with finishing his soup and that swinging motion embracing him like a somniferous plant, he would get drowsy, ready for the beautiful Chola to pick him up and carry him off to bed.

But now, unlike when his brothers and sister ate in Disneyland, all the servants hovered over Julius while he ate, even Nilda, alias Jungle Woman, who was also the cook, smelled of garlic, and terrorized everyone with a meat cleaver in her domain, that is, the pantry and the kitchen. She was always in their company too, but she never dared touch him. It was he who would have liked to have touched her, but then his mother's words were stronger than the smell of garlic. For Julius everything that smelled bad smelled like garlic, the way Nilda smelled. Since he didn't understand very well what garlic was, he asked Nilda about it one evening, and she began to cry. Julius remembers that day: it was the first saddest day of his life.

Julius was fascinated with Nilda's stories about the jungle and especially about the word Tambopata; the fact that it was located somewhere in Madre de Dios province made it special, something that really excited him, and he wanted to hear more and more stories about naked tribesmen, stories which led to intrigues and secret hatreds that Julius discovered when he was about four years old. Vilma, the name of the beautiful Chola from Puquio, attracted his attention while she bathed him, but then, when she took him down to the dining room, it was Nilda and her stories teeming with pumas and painted jungle savages that captivated his attention. Poor Nilda only tried to keep Julius entertained so that Vilma could feed him. But that's not true, no, because Vilma was consumed with jealousy and looked at Nilda with hatred. Amazingly, Julius quickly became aware of what was going on around him and figured out how to solve the problem astutely: he began to pump the butlers for information, then the laundress and her daughter who also washed clothes, then the gardener Anatolio, and even Carlos, the chauffeur, whenever he didn't have to take the Señora somewhere and happened to be around.

Celso and Daniel were the butlers. Celso would tell the story that he was the nephew of the mayor of the district of Huarocondo, province of Anta, in the department of Cuzco. Besides, he was the treasurer of the Friends of Huarocondo Club, located in the Lince neighborhood of Lima, where butlers, waiters, servants, cooks, and even a bus driver on the Descalzos-San Isidro line would meet. And if that wasn't all, Celso also said he was treasurer of the club, he was in charge of the cashbox and, moreover, since the lock on the club door was old, he kept the money upstairs in his room. Julius' imagination left him dumbfounded. He had forgotten all about Vilma and Nilda. "Show me the cashbox! Show me the cashbox!" he begged. And there, in Disneyland, the servants would delight in wondering why Julius, the owner of a big, plump piggy bank, which he found uninteresting, would insist on seeing, touching, and opening the cashbox belonging to the Friends of Huarocondo Club. That evening, Julius decided he would sneak out and enter, once and for all, the distant and mysterious servants' quarters that now also concealed a treasure. He would go there tomorrow, not tonight, no, because having polished off his soup, he felt the sway of the swing becoming more and more comfortable, the tiny flying seat would soon reach the moon, but it was the same as always: Vilma would surprise him with her chapped hands, frankly, they were like broomsticks, and carry him off to Fort Apache.

Fort Apache (that's what it said on the door) was Julius' bedroom. There all the known cowboys were affixed life-size to the walls; others, made of cardboard holding plastic pistols that shone like metal, stood in the middle of the room. All the Indians had been wiped out and now Julius could easily go to sleep without causing a ruckus; in fact, the battle was already over in Fort Apache and only Geronimo, for whom Julius showed a liking, perhaps he would become a friend of Burt Lancaster some day, for only Geronimo had survived and continued to stand pensive and proud at the back of the room.

Vilma adored Julius. His unlikely appearance, it must have been those huge floppy ears, had awakened in her an enormous affection and a sense of humor, which was almost as delicate as that of Señora Susan, Julius' mother, whom the servants had been reproaching a little recently because she was going out every evening and would stay out all hours of the night.

She always woke him up, even though Julius would fall asleep long after Vilma thought she had left him fast asleep. In reality, he faked it and as soon as she would leave he would open his eyes wide and usually spend a couple of hours thinking about a thousand and one things. For instance, he would think about how much love Vilma had for him; after a while everything became utterly confusing because Vilma, though she was light-skinned, was also half-Indian and, besides, she never seemed to mind walking among the dead Indians in Fort Apache. In addition, she had never shown any liking for Geronimo, she always looked at Gary Cooper instead; of course, all that occurred in the United States, but Indians, and my bedroom, and Celso, for sure, he's an Indian . . . That's the way it would go until he fell asleep, perhaps waiting for Mommy's footsteps on the stairs to awaken him, there she is, she's coming up. He would listen for her footsteps and adored her, here she comes, now she's by my door, and then continues down the hallway toward her room at the end, where Daddy died, where tomorrow I'll go and wake her, lovely . . . He would fall asleep immediately so that the moment to wake her might come even sooner. He would always wake her up.

For Vilma, it was a temple; for Julius, a paradise; and for Susan, it was her bedroom, that's where she slept, a widow, thirty-three years old, and lovely. Vilma would take him there every day around eleven o'clock in the morning. It was always the same: Susan would be sleeping deeply and they would be reluctant to enter the room. They would just stand there spying on her from the half-open door until suddenly Vilma got up the courage to nudge him forward toward the dream bed replete with canopy, veils, carved bedposts, and tiny sculpted baroque angels high up on the four corners. Julius would turn to look toward the door where Vilma stood motioning for him to touch Susan, then he would extend his hand, pull back the veil and see his mother as she really was, without a trace of makeup, sleeping soundly, stunning, and lovely. Finally he would get up the courage to touch her, his hand barely grazing her arm, and she, who always woke up reliving the last moments of the previous night's outing, would respond with the same smile she gave the man who caressed her hand across the table at some nightclub. Julius would touch her again and Susan would turn over, facing away from him, burying her face in the pillow and trying to go back to sleep. For a second it was as if she had just returned tired from dancing and couldn't wait to fall into bed. "Mommy," he would say, daring to speak forcefully yet in a soft way, scolding her teasingly while being prodded all the while by Vilma who motioned from the door. When Julius touched her for a second time, Susan would start becoming aware of the new day but, having yet to open her eyes, would smile again across the table at the nightclub and turn over once more, sinking deeper into the bed on the other side to where she had turned when she finally went to bed feeling so tired; then, in a fraction of a second, she would sleep through the whole night all over again and then let the echo of

"Mommy" coming from Julius initiate the arrival of another day and finally produce a sweet and lazy smile that this time was for Julius.

"Darling," she would yawn, lovely. "Who's getting my breakfast?"

"Me, Señora; I'll tell Celso to bring up the tray."

Susan was fully awake when she saw Vilma standing in the distant doorway. That was the moment when she truly thought that Vilma, even though she was fair-skinned, could be a descendant of a noble Indian: why not from some Inca king? After all, there were fourteen of them.

Julius and Vilma were always present for Susan's breakfast. It began with the arrival of the butler-treasurer who, without the slightest clinking, brought the demitasse of hot black coffee, the crystal glass of orange juice, the little sugar bowl and the dainty silver spoon, the silver coffeepot, just in case the Señora wished to make her coffee stronger, toast, Holland butter, and English marmalade. With the first little sounds of breakfast—knife spreading marmalade, spoon stirring sugar in the coffee, chinking cup returned to little saucer, crunching toast—as soon as these sounds were heard, the bedroom took on a warm and caring atmosphere, as if those first sounds of the morning had awakened infinite possibilities for affection in those who were present. It was hard for Julius to remain still, and Vilma and Celso would smile while Susan ate under their watchful eyes, admired and adored; she seemed to know what feelings her breakfast noises could bring forth. From time to time she raised her head and smiled at them as if to ask: "More little sounds? Do you want to play the game of the little sounds?"

When breakfast was over, Susan would begin making numerous phone calls and Vilma would leave with Julius for the orchard, the swimming pool, or the carriage. On this occasion, Julius didn't wait for Vilma to take him by the hand, for he ran after Celso who was taking out the tray. "Show me the cashbox! Show me the cashbox!" he blurted out while the butler was going down the stairs. At last Julius caught up with him in the kitchen and the butler-treasurer agreed to show it to him as soon as he had finished setting the table; Julius' brothers and sister would soon be arriving hungry from school. "Come back in fifteen minutes," he said.

"Cinthia!" Julius shouted, appearing in the big hall at the foot of the stairs.

As usual, Carlos, the family Negro-in-uniform-with-chauffeur-cap, had just brought them home from school and they were on their way upstairs to greet their mother.

"Dumbo!" Santiago shouted without stopping.

Bobby didn't turn around to look; Cinthia, however, had stopped at the landing.

"Cinthia, Celso is going to show me the cashbox that belongs to the Friends of Gua . . ."

"Huarocondo," she smiled, correcting him. "I'll be down for lunch in a minute."

Whereupon for the first time Julius ventured into the servants' quarters of the mansion. He looked all around: everything was smaller in comparison to the rest of the mansion, more common, plain, and ugly, too; in fact, everything there was smaller. All of a sudden he heard Celso's voice telling him to enter and just then he remembered that he had gone looking for him; but upon seeing the cold, dark-brown metal bed he realized that he was in a bedroom that really smelled bad.

The butler said: "There's the cashbox," pointing toward the little round table.

"Which one?" Julius asked, looking straight at the table.

"That one, of course."

Julius couldn't believe his eyes. "Which one?" he asked again, like when you look at something that's right in front of your nose waiting for someone to point it out to you. Don't you see it? That one! There! Right in front of your nose!

"Are you blind, Julius? Here, take it."

Celso reached over to pick up the cookie tin from the table and handed it to him. Julius grasped it the wrong way, by the lid, which came off spilling a wad of filthy paper money and coins onto his pants and all over the floor.

"What a child! Look what you've done . . . Help me."

"Hurry up, I got to serve lunch to your brothers and sister . . ."

"I have to go eat with my sister."

Translated by Dick Gerdes

•

"Manzanas"

from *Cuentos completos* (Collected Stories)

*For María Eugenia
and Francois Mujica*

There are some excursions, not even excursions, but just walks through the city, through one neighborhood, which somehow turn into endless, painfully condensed adventures, adventures of discovery. Some discoveries are nothing but the enumeration of all our problems, Juan. Flowers for you, I say to myself, I repeat to myself, anxious to get to your apartment, struggling through streets, all these streets where I could turn right or turn left, and never bring you anything. And that one definitive street I've sometimes wanted to turn down forever. I've tried, but I already know, I already know that your love wins, like all the times I ran away leaving behind traces so you'd be able to come and find me. I've never loved like this, and that's what scares me.

There is no past with you, there is only the present, there is no future because I don't want a future with you. There is only the interminable present. I already left the flowers; you'll find them in front of your door. But I keep on walking. Flowers for you, I repeat to myself. It hurts me horribly. Today I wanted to kill you. I put some half-rotten apples next to the flowers, and realized that with those I might kill you. Just then I realized it. Until then they'd just been a gift. You like them that way, half-rotten, for your compotes. Then the idea struck me: he'll find those beautiful flowers, so fresh; beautiful, fresh, and young like me. And since he's such a sensitive man, since he's a man who next to me looks old, much older than me, he'll see the bouquet of flowers that are me, when he gets to his door he'll see the apples that are him, and he'll realize that I wanted to kill him. And this will kill him. It will kill him. Little by little. When he understands what I've thought, what I've imagined, that knowing all of this, I still left the apples, the apples that will kill him.

And none of this is your fault, Juan. Along the long road of the present I want to give your flowers to so many people. Juan, there is one type of girl that frightens me more than any other. On the way, carrying your flowers, I see some of them. Today's your birthday and I woke with a smile, loving you. I imagined you waking up in your apartment crammed with objects, with paintings, your old Parisian apartment where, if there were a future, I'd want to lose myself, where fear would never find me.

Your piano, your passion for music, your passion for something, the hours you study, the integrity with which you quietly work while I run away and want to escape and flee, leaving behind traces so you'll come find me. Forgive me, Juan. Forgive you for what? you always ask me. And then you always find the perfect Spanish word so that you never have to acknowledge that I've tried to hurt you. Your piano, your hours of study, your apartment crammed with music books, with so many paintings, and so many objects. I can't paint. I didn't give you those objects. Forgive me, Juan. Forgive you for what? And so many times, Spanish words, which instead of revealing my faults obscures them, evades them forever, with so much love, with so much tenderness, with all the kindness in the world. I surrender myself to your arms when you find the words in Spanish that make you forget what I am, and you turn my attempts to run away into the mischief of a wayward child who still has a future.

But there is only the present and today is your birthday and I woke up already dreaming about your apartment and about these flowers I'm bringing you. I'll go buy Juan the most beautiful bouquet of flowers I can find. I'll go and buy the rottenest apples they sell in the market and, tonight, when he gets back from his trip, after a successful concert in Brussels, he'll find the flowers and will make himself a compote. Juan, this was my whole plan for the day. Juan, this is the only thing I have to do all day. Nothing else. Well, maybe I'll go meet up with one of the boys I hate, one of the boys with whom I betray you, and I'll arrogantly tell him that Juan is coming back tonight after another performance in Brussels, hiding the fact that today is your birthday and that you're much older than I am.

I had tears in my eyes when I woke up dreaming about this lovely day, about your return, about the surprise I was going to give you. The flowers. Your compote. It was as if you had just said a word in Spanish that described my plan, the idea that was already forming inside me to meet up with one of those boys with whom I betray you, to brag about myself. But you weren't there. You weren't there and there were no Spanish words to turn me into a wayward child. And I recalled your long hours of work, your strength of will, the way you can practice piano for hours and hours, and love me, and know everything. Yes, you know everything. I wanted to kill you.

Juan, there is one type of girl that terrifies me more than any other. Flowers for you, I repeat and repeat. Two of these girls have already crossed my path, and I've wanted to give them your flowers. The girls are taller and younger than I, and they're so terribly chic. They cross streets with ease, Juan. They have things to do, Juan. They wouldn't care about your piano, Juan, or your lack of style, or your age. Don't ever look at them, Juan, please. But, of course, you wouldn't even see them. I adore your kindness. Those girls, Juan, they're the death of me. I don't know what it is, I can't stand them and yet I want to bow before them. I don't know if I want them to hit me or make love to me. In any case, I want to steal the boy that's with them. Even if they're alone, I want to steal their boy forever. Juan, you and I know, there're no Spanish words that can turn me into a wayward child when I see those beautiful girls. You told me I was *una reina*. Another day you found me *la más encantadora*, another day you cited the most beautiful verse by Yeats. I smiled at you. And you knew your failure, you didn't find a word, and I hate your piano. My smile lied and you knew that too. Juan, you must suffer so much because of me.

Flowers for you, I repeat and repeat, but I stare insolently at those girls. They walk with such ease. Their clothes fit so nicely. How calmly they live and how calmly they walk. Their eyes, their hair, their legs, their thighs, their asses. I've already seen two of these girls on my way to bring you flowers. It takes so much effort to get to your apartment. And there is still the anxiety attack in the elevator. It's the only thing I've mastered in this life, silent anxiety attacks that no one notices. I almost enjoy them because my eyes open wide and I look without seeing and people lower their eyes and I feel strong, almost strong enough to frighten people, the best would be to frighten those terribly chic girls. Why, my God, why, if I'm so pretty, so young, if I love you so much, if you love me so much, if I need nothing from these terribly chic girls, who look like adolescents, walking calmly, serene in the bustle of the metro cars. I already know that life isn't like that; you explained it to me lovingly, patiently, but maybe if instead of the tears that filled your eyes, maybe if you had said a few words in Spanish. But you didn't. And so I want to kill you.

I've returned to the disaster of my life. On my way here I ruined this day, your birthday. I woke up dreaming of flowers and apples for you. I searched for them with such tenderness; I bought them with such tenderness, picking them out one at a time, for you, my love, for your birthday. Searching, buying, picking—that was my day, it was for you, Juan, it was for you. Tonight you return from Brussels. And now, walking to your apartment has brought me to this bed where I lie. The present continues, Juan. I'm desperate, so alone, so sad, so uselessly beautiful. I've stolen a boy from one of those girls. We made love and I told him I just killed a pianist named Juan. He didn't understand me at first, or actually I told him that it started as a birthday present, a surprise for your return, and then, later, all of a sudden, it became a premeditated crime, a perfect telepathic crime. At last he understood: leaving you my gift, I was the flowers and you were the apples. I'm the flowers, you're the apples—old, rotten, dead.

I go on alone, Juan, I keep running away, how frightening to have fled without leaving a trace. I'm sitting in a train station and I don't know what train to take. Go back to Paris . . . I don't dare, I don't dare, not without calling you first. And the telephone's right there, but I don't dare, this time I don't dare call you. And you, how could you call me since this time I've left no trace? Poor Juan, you'll play your piano for hours and hours every day until I come back. I don't deserve to be taken back, Juan. Don't forget that I've killed you.

Juan, there's a one in a million chance that I'll be saved. And it all depends on you. I'm crazy, I'm totally crazy, but all of a sudden I'm happy and optimistic because it all depends on you. Juan, you must call me here, it's not possible, it's not possible, I'm in the train station in Marseilles, you must intuit this. This is where we met, remember? And when we talk, thank me for the flowers, Juan, and don't mention the apples. Call them *manzanas*, thank me for *las manzanas*, please, Juan. There is always a future for a wayward child. Don't forget: *manzanas*, Juan, please, thank you, from Marseilles . . .

Paris, 1979

Translated by Will Vanderhyden

WORK

1968, *Huerto cerrado*, Casa de las Américas (stories).

1970, *Un mundo para Julius*, Barral (novel).

1972, "Muerte de Sevilla en Madrid"; "Antes de la cita con los Linares," Mosca Azul (stories).

1974, *La felicidad ja ja*, Barral (stories).

1977, *Tantas veces Pedro*, Plaza & Janés (novel).

1977, *A vuelo de buen cubero*, Anagrama (articles).

1979, *Todos los cuentos*, Mosca Azul (stories).

1981, *La vida exagerada de Martín Romaña*, Argos Vergara (novel).

1985, *El hombre que hablaba de Octavia de Cádiz*, Anagrama (novel).

1986, *Magdalena peruana y otros cuentos*, Plaza & Janés (stories).

1987, *Crónicas personales*, Anagrama (articles).

1987, "Goig," PEISA (children's story written in collaboration with Ana María Dueñas).

1988, *La última mudanza de Felipe Carrillo*, Plaza & Janés (novel).

1990, *Dos señoras conversan*, Plaza & Janés (novel).

1993, *Permiso para vivir: Antimemorias I*, Anagrama (memoirs).

1995, *No me esperen en abril*, Anagrama (novel).

1995, *Cuentos completos*, Alfaguara (stories).

1996, *A trancas y barrancas*, Anagrama (essay).

1997, *Reo de nocturnidad*, Anagrama (novel).

1997, *Guía triste de París*, Suma de Letras (stories).

1999, *La amigdalitis de Tarzán*, Suma de Letras (novel).

2000, *La historia personal de mis libros*, Fondo Editorial Cultura Peruana (articles).

2002, *El huerto de mi amada*, Planeta (novel).

2002, *Crónicas perdidas*, Anagrama (articles and lectures).

2003, *Doce cartas a dos amigos*, PEISA (collected letters).

2003, *Cuentos completos 1964-1974*, Anagrama (stories).

2004, *Entrevistas escogidas*, Fondo Editorial Cultura Peruana (articles and interviews).

2005, *Permiso para sentir: Antimemorias II*, Anagrama (memoirs).

2005, *Entre la soledad y el amor*, Debate (essays).

2007, *Las obras infames de Pancho Marambio*, Planeta (novel).

2009, *La esposa del Rey de las Curvas*, Anagrama (stories).

2009, *Penúltimos escritos*, PEISA (articles).

2012, *Dándole pena a la tristeza*, Anagrama (novel).

•

ENGLISH TRANSLATIONS

2001, *Tarzan's Tonsillitis*, translated by Alfred Mac Adam, Knopf (novel).

2004, *A World for Julius*, translated by Dick Gerdes and J.A. Marzan, University of Wisconsin Press (novel).

•

AWARDS AND RECOGNITIONS

1964, Scholarship from the French Government (1964-1965).

1966, Scholarship from the Geothe Institute.

1968, Longlist for Premio Casa de las Américas for *Huerto cerrado*.

1972, Premio Nacional de Literatura Ricardo Palma for *Un mundo para Julius*.

1974, Premio a la Mejor Novela Extranjera for *Un mundo para Julius*.

Orden El Sol del Perú, from the government of Fujimori, rejected by Bryce Echenique because of his democratic convictions.

1975, Guggenheim Fellowship.

1983, Prix Passion for the best novel of the year in France for *La Vie exagérée de Martin Romaña.*

1986, Title of Knight of French Arts and Letters.

1990, Recognition of his international trajectory at the hands of the president of the Unión de Ciudades Capitales Iberoamericanas.

1990, Medalla cívica de la ciudad de Lima.

1993, Title of Comander of the Orden de Isabel la Católica.

1995, Title of Official of French Arts and Letters.

1997, Premio Internacional de la Paz Dag Hammarskjöld.

1998, Premio Nacional de Narrativa de España for *Reo de nocturnidad.*

2002, Premio Planeta 2002 for *El huerto de mi amada.*

2002, Prix Grinzane Cavour (Italia) for *La amigdalitis de Tarzán.*

2012, Gudalajara Book Fair Prize for Romance Language Literature.

EDGARDO
COZARINSKY
(Argentina, 1939)

Edgardo Cozarinsky was born in Buenos Aires in 1939. His grandparents were Ukranian immigrants who, at the end of the nineteenth century, pursued by the specter of the incipient anti-Semitism that was already beginning to move through Europe, fled the old continent and moved to Argentina. His paternal grandparents, from Kiev, settled in the province of Entre Ríos, to the north of the capital. They were part of the so-called "Jew gauchos," a name given to those men and women who had come from far away to work land that promised them a fertile future. His maternal grandparents, from Odessa, opted to make their home in Buenos Aires and dedicate themselves to peddling, touring around the twenty streets that comprised the neighborhoods Once, Abasto, Almagro, and Villa Crespo.

Edgardo Cozarinsky passed his adolescence in those *porteño* streets. A young taciturn man who frequented the neighborhood cinemas of the capital to see double features of old Hollywood films, he spent days devouring the pages of Stevenson, Conrad, and James, among others, while studying literature at the university. When he was twenty, he met Silvina and Victoria Ocampo, Adolfo Bioy Casares, and Borges, writers with whom he maintained close friendships. Around that time, he was working as a columnist for film magazines and also published a few articules in the legendary journal *Sur*.

In the middle '60s, Cozarinsky traveled to Europe for the first time and in 1967, after a few months in New York, he returned to Buenos Aires. He contributed to the magazines *Primera Plana* and *Panorama* and, at the same time, he stole away on the weekends to work on ". . ." (*Puntos suspensivos*), his first film, which agilely eluded the censor then reigning in Argentina and was very well received at festivals in Europe and the United States. In 1973, he shared with José Bianco the Premio de ensayo del diario *La Nación* for his "El relato indefendible," a text he would expand on later in *Museo del chisme*

(2005). The next year he published his "long-seller" *Borges y el cine*, which he added to in later editions and which has been translated numerous times.

That same year, faced with the atmosphere of anarchy, violence, and repression that was being lived in Buenos Aires, he packed his bags and exiled himself to Paris. There he dedicated himself to films of a very personal nature: *Fantasmas de Tánger*, *Scarlatti en Sevilla*, *Citizen Langlois*, and *Boulevares del crepúsculo* are a few of the many films in which, like a true documentarian, he retained images and sounds of the present but in the disguise of a story that, in the end, expressed his own passions and his own desires. Of an essentially nomadic spirit, his work in cinema took Cozarinsky to cities like Budapest, Tallinn, Rotterdam, Tangier, Vienna, Granada, Saint Petersburg, and Seville. During those years he wrote only one book, which became a cult classic: *Vudú urbano* (new edition published by Emecé in Spain and Argentina in 2002 with prologues by both Susan Sontag and Guillermo Cabrera Infante), in which, like in his films, he disregards genre to circulate freely between memory, history, and reflection. The publication of the book in 1985 coincided with his return to Argentina, two years before the end of the military dictatorship.

At the turn of the new century, writing was slowly replacing film for Cozarinsky, but he never did stop filming: at sixty he began a new stage in his cinematographic voyage, characterized by formal and lively exploration; films of a lyrical style *Apuntes para una biografía imaginaria* (2010) and *Nocturnos* (2011) earned him honors and invitations to festivals in Venice, Vienna, and Istanbul, as well as a retrospective in April of 2012 at the boldest laboratory of independent film: The Jeonju International Film Festival (South Korea). In 2013, he debuted *Carta a un padre* to a great amount of critical acclaim.

Nevertheless, it has been in recent years that Edgardo Cozarinsky has fully developed his literary career. His celebrated collection of stories *La novia de Odessa* and the essays and articles in *El pase del testigo*, were published by Emecé in 2001. In short order he has become one of the most interesting Argentine writers of the moment, unraveling a fiction in which biography is fair game, serving to delve into memory, into identity. Novels like *El rufián moldavo*, *Lejos de dónde*, or *La tercera mañana* are good examples of this.

THE ACORN

THE TORTURE OF DOCTOR JOHNSON

I looked through my most recent work, and although I am not the best judge of what I write (I don't think anyone is) I chose "December 2008," the fifth section of *Lejos de dónde*. Excerpted in this way it doesn't have the impact that it acquires as the conclusion of the novel, but I think that it can be read almost like a short story and that the mystery of the bond that unites the characters, although unspoken, is vaguely perceptible and impregnates the situation with mystery. It contains a tone, a hidden *pathos*, a crushing sense of the disaster of History and of individual lives, recurrent motifs in my fiction.

IN CONVERSATION WITH THE DEAD

When you get to a certain age, inevitably you have more dead friends than living ones. My list is long yet that doesn't make me sad. My dead live with me and share my new feelings and my work. First of all, I want to mention Alberto Tabbia, who was my best friend and who left me his exquisite collection of books in English. He was an example of the "writer who doesn't write" and I planned, and I still plan, to edit his notebooks. In them I found the couplet that I used as an epigraph for my novel *El rufián moldavo*: "To speak with the living I need / words that the dead taught me." Also José Bianco, Silvina Ocampo, Héctor Murena, among the writers. And thinking about the crossroads that Paris was for me: Raúl Ruiz and Severo Sarduy among those of my own language, and the great Danilo Kiš among those from Eastern Europe. With my parents, the paying of debts never ends, but I am nourished by what I write.

Coda

You spent a lot of time with Bioy Casares, Borges, and the Ocampo sisters, Victoria
and Silvina. Is it true that there existed a "Grupo Sur?"

I was never part of the "Grupo Sur," if such a thing existed outside of a few
assiduous collaborators. (Borges, Bioy Casares, and Silvina Ocampo, although
they all published in the journal, annoyed Victoria Ocampo). In my case, it
was José Bianco, when he was editor-in-chief, who approached me in a bookstore on Calle Viamonte and invited me to write a review. I was nineteen or
twenty years old. Later on I occasionally published in the journal. I met Bioy
because of that same review, which was of his book *Guirnalda con amores.* He
liked the review and invited me to his house and there I sat at the same table
as Silvina and Borges for the first time. I saw Borges frequently when he was
teaching English literature at the University, we talked, mostly I listened to
him before and after his classes, and I went to his house a few times. My
relationship with Silvina was more personal, kind of private.

What was life like for a young Argentine in Paris during the seventies?

I got by, like any imigrant. The hardship was tempered by the city's literary
and artistic mythos, which has been worn down over the years. Paris is not
France and foreigners who in one way or another belong to the world of high
culture are always welcome there, not because of generosity but because of the
superego ("it's only natural that they want to come here") held over from the
years when it was the capital of arts and letters, something like the glow of
a dead star that distance leaves visible. For me Paris was and is a crossroads
where I can connect with other Latin Americans and people from Eastern
Europe who I happened to meet in that horrible Buenos Aires of the nineteen
seventies.

A THOUSAND FORESTS

from *Lejos de donde*
(Far from Somewhere)
[a novel]

Chapter 5
December 2008

*Mother, whose
hand did I clasp
when with your
words I went to
Germany?*
—Paul Celan, *"Wolfsbohne."*

As soon as she saw the man—around fifty years old, a grizzled three-day-old beard unstylish and untrimmed, a wrinkled raincoat that seemed to weigh on his shoulders, an air of fatigue or maybe carelessness—she knew he'd come in and force her to stay open even later. Bistro Samowar was the only bar open at that hour in the gallery of Dresden's central station. If he spends more than ten euros I'll wait on him, she decided as she responded to his greeting without a smile.

The man ordered vodka. She didn't recognize his accent, maybe Italian, or Romanian; in any event, it wasn't Slavic, she was sure of that. She put a small glass on the bar, hesitated a moment after filling it, and left the bottle beside it. The man downed the glass in one swallow and poured another without asking. He wasn't Russian, but he drank like he was; looks like I'll be able to charge him for the whole bottle. She had selected the most expensive, a Finnish vodka. Now, for the first time, she smiled.

Two Africans moved through the gallery with mops, an indication that the station expected no more visitors.

"I don't think I can keep the bar open much longer," she said, not knowing if she intended to close or simply get the guy to pay for the bottle.

"What's the problem?"

"If the manager finds out, we could get fined."

"Don't worry. I can cover it."

She studied him: was he drunk or just full of himself? He was still speaking German, slowly, without faltering.

"I got on a train in Krakow, there was a problem at the Görlitz station, I don't know what, we had to wait for another train, now I've missed the connection to Frankfurt, and I'm going to have to spend the night here."

"When you leave the station, across the Pragerstrasse, there are a few hotels, French. New and cheap."

He didn't seem to take the hint. He served himself another glass and gestured for her to join him. She hesitated a moment before accepting. The man looked around, his eyes lingering on the fresco that covered the wall facing the bar: silhouetted against an intense blue sky, a cathedral with domes shaped like onions crowned a hill whose flowery slopes dropped to the banks of a turquoise river.

"That looks like Kiev. Is it the Petchersk monastery?"

"I don't know. When we opened, the owner had a painter decorate the place. He brought in all these *mamushkas* and painted wooden spoons. He also contacted an importer of Russian vodka and beer and hired a cook who makes *solyanka* and homemade *kvas*. I never saw the painter again and I never asked him about this painting. The owner wanted to give the place some character. He said that such a small bar, surrounded by so much fast food, needs atmosphere, if it wants to attract patrons of a different sort . . ."

"Do many Russians come through here?" The man's German was overly proper, obviously studied. "Although today one should probably distinguish between Russians, Ukrainians, and Belarusians . . ."

She laughed.

"Doesn't bother me. I'm Polish and at one time all of it was part of Poland."

His smile seemed to her like the memory of a smile.

"Do they still teach that in the schools? Do they have maps from different periods that show how the country has shrunk?"

"Now? I don't know. When I was in school we had to climb over rubble to get there and in the winter, in the classroom, we had to wrap ourselves in blankets."

He refilled the glasses, downing his again in a single swallow.

They were silent for a moment that seemed to stretch out, not because they were searching for words, but as if the evocation of the past, fleeting as it was, had awoken ghosts that demanded respect, imposed silence, maybe the ghosts of the hundreds of thousands of refugees from the East who had camped in Dresden in 1945, running from the Soviet advance, only to die, burnt to ashes by twenty-four hours of British-American bombing that served no strategic purpose, corpses carbonized among the ruins, destined for putrefaction and stench, remains that some loved-one, facing the impossibility of burial, placed inside a suitcase and carried with them on their flight to the south, in search of some corner untouched by bombs, where they could find a place in the ground; but the graves had not been consecrated, and now the specters had arisen amid the concrete and glass architecture of the twenty-first century, evading the ubiquitous neon of advertising, and had begun to slip through the shadows toward the ancient center of the city, perhaps to see how fidelity to the past, or the irrational force of patriotism, had rebuilt palaces, theaters, and churches according to their original design, rescuing from among the ruins a few stones that might have come from the Frauenkirche in order to place them among the new ones, until the baroque cathedral was returned to the city meticulously reproduced: in the same way the ancient Egyptians, when building a new temple, inserted rubble from their ruined temples into the foundations, to ensure the continuity of the divine presence, in the same way that a leftover crumb of yesterday's bread is added to the starter for today's loaf.

Because the dead always come back, and ghosts of victims are the most tenacious.

In that moment of silence, those ghosts were more real than the Polish woman—sixty-five-years old, poorly dyed hair, broken fingernails—and the tired Argentine at the end of a long journey: foreigners, displaced people, survivors of forgotten wars. When they spoke again, it was as if that silence had been a long night of shared secrets. They had been moved by something imperceptible they would not know how to name anyway—an invisible presence, a gust of wind, a breath. Now they struck up a conversation that minutes before they would not have imagined.

"I wanted to visit Krakow," the man said, "for family reasons. Simple curiosity. I think my mother was from there. She went to Argentina after the war. I was born in Buenos Aires."

"I never knew my mother. I'm a 'child of war,' one of many. She couldn't take care of me, and I think for her a baby might have embodied the memory of violation, nothing more. I don't blame her. She gave me to a family of Polish peasants, but I guess she was Austrian. What she was doing in Poland in the middle of the war, who knows. They told me when I turned fifteen. They didn't remember my mother's name, or maybe they didn't want to say it. She never came back. She might have died during the war. Or with a little luck she started a new life."

When he went to refill the glasses, he found that the bottle was empty. She grabbed another one.

"On the house."

He shook his head and put a one-hundred-euro bill on the counter.

"No woman pays for my drinks," he said, laughing, but his tone was firm. "The liquor calls for something solid. My treat."

She took a plate with two *pelmeni* on it from under a glass cover and put it in the microwave. Minutes later, a beeping signaled the food had come back to life.

They were eating in silence when he, obeying a sudden, inexplicable impulse that left him startled by his own words, said:

"My mother was a Jew." After a silence, he added: "She never wanted to talk about what she lived through before arriving in Argentina. I said she grew up in Krakow, but the truth is that I don't know where exactly. All I know is that at one time she was eighty kilometers from Krakow, in Oświęcim . . ."

He paused—guided once again by an impulse that he was unable to explain—and translated the name, which in German was charged with resonances that had not contaminated the Polish equivalent.

"In Auschwitz . . ." he said. And as if to mitigate the possible impact of that word he hurried to add, "that's all I know about her life before Argentina. And that she survived with one goal: to get as far from Poland as possible."

He emptied the glass of vodka again and remained silent. She studied him before speaking.

"You don't need to tell me about it. I don't have anything against the Jews. I just don't like them. And I don't like to talk about the past either, it makes no sense. Others were killed afterward in other countries. And today the killing continues. The killers are different, those who die are different. Don't ask me where, I don't watch television anymore." As if to excuse her frankness, she lifted her glass and tapped it against his. "To the future," she said.

He smiled.

"I see you're an optimist. We're not young anymore."

"Believe me, I'm not an optimist. There is a Polish song that goes: 'I am worse today than yesterday, but better than tomorrow.'"

They laughed and together finished the second bottle.

The station's sliding doors let in a frozen gust of wind swirling with needles of snow: the man, making a farewell gesture as he walked away, had gone out into the elements. He had left the change from the hundred euros on the bar; she put it in her apron pocket with a smile for the silhouette disappearing into the night, smaller all the time under the neon circles out in the street. She stood there watching until she could no longer make him out through the fog on the windows.

In the station, only the little lights on the towering Christmas tree in the central hall remained lit. She removed some clogs and a heavy hooded jacket from the closet, turned off the light, lowered the metallic curtain. Now it was time to go to sleep.

Translated by Will Vanderhyden

WORK

1964, *El laberinto de la apariencia: Estudios sobre Henry James*, Losada (essay).

1974, "Borges y el cine," *Sur* (essay, new edition published in 1991 by Editorial Fundamentos as *Borges en/y/sobre cine*).

1985, *Vudú urbano*, Anagrama (stories and essays).

2001, *La novia de Odessa*, Emecé (stories).

2001, *El pase del testigo*, Sudamericana (essays and articles).

2002, *Borges y el cinematógrafo*, Emecé (new edition of "Borges y el cine").

2004, *El rufían moldavo*, Emecé (novel).

2005, *Museo del chisme*, Emecé (essay and stories).

2006, *Tres fronteras*, Emecé (stories).

2006, *Palacios plebeyos*, Sudamericana (articles and one story).

2007, *Maniobras nocturnas*, Emecé (novel).

2007, *Milongas, crónicas y cuentos*, Edhasa (articles and stories).

2009, *¡Burundanga!*, Mansalva (stories).

2009, *Lejos de dónde*, Tusquets (novel).

2010, *Blues*, Adriana Hidalgo (article and essays).

2010, *La tercera mañana*, Tusquets (novel).

2013, *Dinero para fantastmas*, Tusquets (novel).

2013, *Nuevo museo del chisme*, La Bestia Equilatera (essays).

•

ENGLISH TRANSLATIONS

1992, *Urban Voodoo*, translated by Edgardo Cozarinsky, "The Sentimental Journey" translated by Edgardo Cozarinsky and Ronald Christ, Lumen (stories).

1992, *Borges in/and/on Film*, translated by Edgardo Cozarinsky, Lumen (film reviews and critical analyses).

2004, *The Bride from Odessa*, translated by Nick Caistor, Farrar, Straus and Giroux (stories).

2007, *The Moldovian Pimp*, translated by Nick Caistor, Vintage Books (novel).

•

AWARDS AND RECOGNITIONS

1973, Premio "La Nación" de Ensayo for "Sobre algo indefendible."

2004, Premio Konex de Platino y Diploma al Mérito.

2004, Premio Cóndor a la trayectoria, from Asociación Argentina de Críticos de Cine.

2008, Premio de Narrativa (bienio 2001-2003) del Ministerio de Cultura de Buenos Aires for *La novia de Odessa*.

2011, Premio de la Academia Argentina de Letras for the best novel 2008-2010 for *Lejos de dónde*.

JOSÉ
MARÍA
MERINO

(Spain, 1941)

José María Merino, writer, academic, and master of the short story, was born in 1941 in A Coruña, but he's always considered León to be the place of his greatest sentimental attachment. That's where his father was born, who, when the Spanish Civil War began, was a member of the Federación Universitaria Escolar. Given this republican affiliation he thought it necessary to go into hiding in Galicia.

When the war was over, he did just that. José María Merino's father married a girl from A Curuña. Once José María was born, the family went back to León, where Merino's father opened a law firm. He was a voracious reader and he consequently instilled this love for reading in his children, which was good because at the time interest in reading was as scarce as food itself. "*Novelas, no verlas*," Merino said, remembering one of the many phrases used by his teachers, whose greatest preoccupation was to get their students to recite in succession the dates and periods of Literary History.

On his own, Merino read the great adventure novelists and the most important writers of the Spanish Golden Age, the universal classics, ancient legends and American myths, which immediately got him interested in the mysteries that words concealed, in the search for significations through the constant consultation of dictionaries. As he recalls in his book *Intramuros*, imagination and words were his living refuge: he couldn't understand the world without reading. "For me, reading a book was an interior adventure, a secret voyage that I took," he has remarked about the years of his adolescence.

When he finished high school, he left León and went to Madrid to study Law. Shortly thereafter, in 1972, he published his first book. It was a book of poetry, but poetry, as he has said, ended up abandoning him in order to reveal that his true destiny lay elsewhere: writing fiction. His zealous curiosity and his desire to always explore new forms of expression have, over the course of his career, given him an astonishing capacity to change genre and register. So, the imprecise borders between sleep and wakefulness, between reality and dream, the vast legion of myths, the double, these have been the main themes Merino has engaged with across his extensive oeuvre, from the first book of fiction (*Novela de Andrés Choz*, a text that evades general classification and that critics read as a literary novel, a science fiction novel, and even as metafiction) to his most recent microfictions.

In essential novels like *El caldero de oro*, *La orilla oscura*, and *El centro del aire* (grouped by the author under the title *Novelas del mito*), in stories that explore the uncertainty of living in a strange world, free from chance, and in the microfictions that he started to write randomly and upon request, José Mária Merino has learned how to explore the labyrinths of identity and memory and he has glimpsed, for a fleeting second, the encounter of the real with the sinister, the fantastic. As he has indicated on various occasions: "Literature is the instrument that allows you not only to travel through the reality of the waking world, but also through the reality of dreams. And you cannot travel through both places simultaneously without making use of the fantastic, fantasy, imagination."

Along with other writers from León, like Juan Pedro Aparicio, Luis Mateo Díez, and Antonio Pereira, he has revived the lost tradition of the *filandón*, nocturnal meetings where, while spinning, tales and stories are told that have been passed down from generation to generation.

Father of two daughters (one of them, Ana, is a poet and creative writing professor in Spanish at the University of Iowa), awarded the Premio Nacional de la Crítica in 1986 for *La orilla oscura*, since March 27th 2008, José María Merino sits every Thursday in the seat "M" of the Real Academia Española as an honorary member, an appropriate fate for a writer whose love of words has led him to spin fascinating stories, concocted in the incessant stillness of unanimous nights.

THE ACORN

The Torture of Doctor Johnson

I chose the opening of my novel *La orilla oscura* because it is the work in which I think my literary obsessions really start to take shape: the tension between sleep and waking, the question of the double—in this case, with Spanish America mixed in—metamorphosis, the tricks that memory plays, my taste for metafiction and for texts that are nested like Russian dolls . . . Then I include three microfictions, a form I discovered after writing several novels and about a hundred short stories, because they represent not only the flexibility of the genre, but also show different aspects of my bewilderment at reality, which is the main inspiration for my writing. Finally, I chose the first story from my latest work, *El libro de las horas contadas*, in which I play with the idea of composing a novel as a short story writer would, and a collection of short stories and microfictions as a novelist.

In Conversation with the Dead

The dead whose voices I hear with my eyes? My favorite books come to mind in schools, in flocks, and I find it hard to choose just a few. I will settle for a painfully incomplete historical overview of the books that have shaped me. After my first, Johanna Spyri's *Heidi*, which I read when I was seven, there were the ones I read in my childhood and adolescence, over which hung the shadow of *Don Quixote*—*Tom Sawyer, Kim, Around the World in 80 Days, William Brown* . . . and a few dictionaries and encyclopedias, among which Salvat's *Universitas*, where I discovered Hoffman and things like the solar system and mythology, stands out. After that, various eighteenth to twentieth century novelists: Voltaire, Fleming, Jane Austen, Dickens, Balzac, Stendhal, Galdós, Baroja, Mann, Faulkner and other Americans . . . to say nothing of the Russians, from Pushkin to Shalamov, whom I still adore, or those authors of fantasy and science fiction—from Stoker to Borges and Cunqueiro, via Asimov, Fredric Brown, and Arthur Clarke, for example. After the *Thousand and One Nights*—I forgot to mention *Life is a Dream*!—my original trinity of short story writers—Poe, Maupassant, Chekov—has since expanded to include innumerable others, of which I'll only mention Isak Dinesen, Aldecoa, and Ribeyro. As for poetry, I still enjoy reading Lucretius, Omar Khayyám, Garcilaso [de la Vega], Bécquer, Prévert, Whitman, Neruda . . . And what can I say about those who published accounts of their travels to the Indies, especially Bernal Díaz de Castillo? And so, just that; my eyes listen to many of the dead. Not as many of the living, but between the two there is enough to keep me from getting bored . . .

CODA

Do you see intuition as an indispensable quality in writing fiction?

For years I've argued that all living beings have language, some form of communication, and that the real significance of human language lies not in its expression, but rather in our ability to organize it through narratives, and that these have provided our universe with symbolic structures that allow us to understand it. Intuition, which does not depend on logical reasoning, is an indispensable part of this process, which long predates philosophy and science. *Homo sapiens* are what we are thanks to this intuition for creating narratives, even though this has also been used to conjure up the hereafter and a world presided over by the gods. Without the intuition for coming up with fictions and, along with that, for trying to understand who we are and what makes up the world around us, we would still be living in caves and barely surviving on berries and animals we struggled to kill. In my case, I can't write a story I have not arrived at by intuition, even if I organize it logically later.

A THOUSAND FORESTS

FROM *LA ORILLA OSCURA* (THE DARK SHORE)
[A NOVEL]

I. IN THE MUSEUM

Faint flashes in the half-light, his visions all faded away: the doorway, off to one side of the vestibule, that opened onto a clearing in the forest; the hall that extended past the dresser, under two dark paintings, and intermittently became a path lined by thick brush and enormous tree trunks; a brilliant light at the far end that spilled out from between the folds of a brownish curtain the same way it filtered into spaces where no vegetation grew but where the dense foliage's shade was still strong. The ticking of a clock reverberated in the air, its symmetrical rhythm splintered by its echo, a flutter of wings, the clamor of a prolonged hailstorm, the sound of some distant brook.

"You think you're awake, but maybe you're dreaming," he thought. He opened his eyes and revealed the day. A moment earlier, when they were still closed, the night in which those images had dissolved stretched across from the other side, but it seemed that the simple act of opening them had opened the floodgates that held back the light, causing its sudden arrival; a deluge of brightness splashed all surfaces, broke on the moldings, and swirled around the nightstand, turning it into a compact little island. And so, nearly every object was defined by a presence so striking that it seemed impossible to imagine a past in which the darkness had concealed them, or a future in which the light was once more extinguished, and they disappeared again.

It was morning, and the day, like all others at that latitude, had arrived suddenly, without a dawn; it would be easy to imagine someone turning on a light with the simple flip of a switch. The milky quality of that first light—the grayish veil that muffled its gleam, the subtle dirtiness that clouded it—reinforced this idea and convinced him that maybe it wasn't that the sun's rays were gliding through planetary space until they filled the streets, reached his window and spilled into his room, but rather that the bright beam of a distant spotlight was focused on the units of some new building. Artificial light illuminating a habitat. Then he thought that, if the plaza outside his window was just one part of a covered area, this area must be of enormous proportions, contain great distances: perhaps far, far away, on the other side of distant walls—also enormous—it was still night; perhaps there the night was much longer, and much deeper, than the ones he was used to. A night to match the measure of such a vast territory.

He imagined that the light that had so suddenly been turned on was a sign that preceded the hustle and bustle of some daily activity, and was seized by the suspicion that the immense place in which he found himself was actually some kind of mysterious depository, a strange museum in which beings and objects of different origins were kept. And he thought that maybe he was one of those goods, that his room was just the container in which he was stored.

The image of an immense depository sitting placid in the night, lit suddenly by a milky white bulb, eventually brought his own measurements to mind and he was overcome by the frightful certainty that, compared to the dimensions of those outer spaces, he was fairly miniscule. He understood then that the hotel was just a medium-sized box forgotten on some shelf; that similar, tiny, weak beings fated to circulate in ways they could not foresee and closed in little boxes like his own room, were being kept on the same shelf of those colossal units.

Stacked up in some immeasurable depository. Or classified according to an unknown order in some mysterious museum. The idea of the museum, which on the one hand seemed to confirm, however subtly, several of his intuitions, brought him back, nonetheless, to his incipient wakefulness: he pushed the sheets back with a stretch of his legs and forced himself to believe that his suspicions were imagined, that they were nothing but fictions rooted in the rough surfaces of sleep, ultimately innocuous, taking comfort in the knowledge that the threat they posed was impossible. He had let himself get carried away by the faltering logic of half-sleep, but he was not a miniscule being: he was, without a doubt, exactly the right size relative to the height and appearance of the other residents and to the space that surrounded them.

It occurred to him that his obsessive trips to the Museum of the City had, through the mysterious workings of a still-drowsy mind, been behind some of the horrifying transformation. "I'll never go back to that museum," he decided. "I'll never go back, never," he whispered, moving his lips furiously to emphasize the determination behind the thought.

He lay there motionless, his eyes fixed on the world outside. But, still shaken by this unique confusion, he speculated that perhaps the light wasn't light, but rather the color of some solid material, because the illumination that accumulated on the other side of the window presented an unusual density that seemed composed, more than of light and space and clusters of clouds, of something compact and nearby that had been stuffed inside a grayish cloth, an enormous parcel that had fallen from the sky and gotten caught among the dark green leaves and red flowers of the Royal Poinciana growing in the middle of the plaza, which, seen from his bed, their crowns barely visible at the bottom of the window looked, without the benefit of perspective, like a thick crop of shrubs; as though, instead of adorning the towering height of the trunks, they emerged directly from the ground just a few inches below.

And so his suspicions that the light was artificial, that the plaza was a vast enclosed space, and that he himself was a miniscule being, were interrupted by the peaceful contemplation of that fallen package that had come to rest against his window, which spilled over into the fantasy of being in some subterranean space: the crowns of the Poinciana were just shrubs growing out of the ground at the height of the windowsill, and the second floor became the most elevated part of some basement. But he had already left his dream state, and these illusions were no more than the product of a fanciful laziness: the light continued to accumulate, flowing in from the outside like a fine solid, and the noises he heard attested definitively to reality, triumphant in the end over any chimera, far removed from the trappings of his nightmare; the faint ticking that in the final images of his dream had become the sound of a pendulum that was also the echo of clucks and growls and currents in a forest clearing, now came to rest on the nightstand, surrounded by the noises of the morning: the elevator humming along its route after starting up with a faint grunt; the murmur that announced the approaching wheeze of a vacuum; the sound of retreating footsteps that followed the click of a door latch. There was no question that another day was beginning in the hotel while he stayed

in bed, waiting for the phone call that would come at any minute to tell him
it was time to get up.

Translated by Heather Cleary

•

"FLY"

FROM *LA GLORIETA DE LOS FUGITIVOS*
(THE FUGITIVE'S ROUNDABOUT)

The fly circles listlessly around the bathroom. I look at it with disgust. What's
a bug doing in my luxury hotel room—in February, no less? I hit it with a
towel and it falls, lifeless, onto to the marble sink. It's a strange, reddish fly,
not very big. It occurs to me that it is the last of a species that will disappear with its death. It occurs to me that the bathroom is its refuge from the
winter. That in the garden under my window there is a plant, also very rare,
which can only be pollinated by this fly. And that, within a few millennia,
the presence of enough oxygen to ensure the survival of our own species will
depend on the pollination and proliferation of that plant. What have I done?
By killing this fly I have sealed your fate, humans of the future. But a slight
twitch moves its legs. Maybe it isn't dead! Now it is moving them with more
force, now it has managed to stand, now it's rubbing them together, stretching out its wings, getting ready to take flight; now it's circling around the
bathroom. Live! Breathe, humans of the future! But its clumsy movements
bring that first, repellant image back to mind. I am snapped out of my trance.
What is this disgusting bug doing here? I grab the towel, follow it, hit it, kill
it. I finish it off.

Translated by Heather Cleary

•

"The Toaster"
from *Cuentos del libro de la noche*
(Stories from the Book of the Night)

It's a beautiful spring morning and we are going to have breakfast on the terrace. While my wife makes coffee, I bring the fruit, the marmalade, the honey, and the coffee cups outside. On the table I find a new toaster, already plugged in. It must be a surprise from my wife, since the one we had was old and hard to use; it always burned the bread. This one is oblong and shiny, its design aerodynamic—modern and without any sharp angles. Right away, I wonder where the bread goes, since there is no opening on top. Finally I see, on the side opposite the power cord, a long, horizontal, transparent panel. It seems to be a tray, but I can't pull it out; while I am trying I discover something amazing, but horrible: there are little bugs with pale heads and strange prehensile appendages inside. I shout and my wife comes running. *I didn't put that there*, she says, looking at the bugs with the same disgust. Suddenly, the cord that connects the supposed toaster to the outlet breaks loose and retracts inside the object, which scoots across the table, rises into the air, hovers for a few seconds, and then flies quickly off until it is lost in the bright sky. We are terribly upset by the incident: my wife's antennae tremble with fear, and I can feel the hairs on my abdomen standing on end, all my legs shaking beneath me.

Translated by Heather Cleary

•

"The Coffee Cup"
from *El libro de las horas contadas*
(The Book of Numbered Hours)

I've poured the coffee in its little cup, added the sweetener, and stirred it with a small spoon, which, as I take it out, creates a little eddy on the surface of the hot liquid that catches the foam of the dissolving sweetener and spreads

it in an ellipse. It reminds me of a galaxy that I imagine, in the four or five
seconds before it disappears, is actually real, with stars and planets. Who
knows? When I lift the cup to my lips I will imagine that I am about to drink
a black hole. The duration of our seconds is certainly on a different scale, but
maybe our universe is made up of drops of some substance in the process of
dissolving in a liquid just before sliding down some enormous gullet.

Translated by Heather Cleary

•

"The House with Two Doors"
from *El libro de las horas contadas*
(The Book of Numbered Hours)

When I was there during Holy Week this year, I saw that they had torn down
the house with two doors. A multi-storey building is going up in its place.
Perhaps because so many years had passed, the change didn't affect me the
way it should have. Still, deep down in some distant part of me, I was relieved
to know that the house and its back door no longer existed. When by one of
those twists of fate I ran into Publio, whom I hadn't seen in twenty-five years,
the first thing he said to me after we exchanged a few words of recognition
and greeting, was:

"Did you hear that they tore down the house with two doors?"

Publio, the twins, and I went to school together. We would meet up in the
Plaza Circular and, once we were all there, start our walk along Julio de
Campo, crossing Padre Isla to take de la Torre on the other side.

The house with two doors was right at the intersection of Padre Isla and
de la Torre. It was a huge, stately structure made of bricks and capped with
slate, with a second floor and a tall mansard roof. It had two doors, but
neither of them opened onto the street: one of the side walls, with two big
picture windows covered in ivy, faced that way. The doors opened onto opposite sides of the lot that surrounded the house: a little estate surrounded by a

high brick wall with shards of glass embedded at the top. Toward the back on one side, a sliver of an overgrown garden and the door of a shed could be seen. The wall separated the estate from the neighboring buildings. In the part of it that faced Padre Isla, there was a large, rusted iron gate.

We stared at it every day as we passed. It had been abandoned for years, and a mysterious force emanated from it, a place no human being had set foot for so long, with foliage that grew wild and unchecked in the garden and impenetrable blinds that never changed position, drawing us in.

Publio's father, a lawyer, also handled the administration of real estate and was charged with selling the house. Publio told us a garbled story about deaths and escapes to America that we listened to with a mix of disbelief and fascination.

We must have stared at that house hundreds of times, in all seasons—in the dark days of winter, when the branches of the trees were covered with frost, and in the spring, when the new leaves started coming out on the ivy in a brilliant, pale green and the birds filled the garden with their din; when, sometime around June, all sorts of flowers would bloom in disarray in the abandoned planters, and in autumn, when the ground turned yellow with the dry leaves that had been blown down by the first winds of fall—the place always stirred in us the same thoughts of unexplored forests, of the ruins of fantastic temples or forts, of some hidden kingdom.

That year we sought out remote places. We were a group of explorers charting a meandering course into the heart of an unknown continent. When the days got cooler, we would go to where the rivers met and, surrounded by willows and blackberry bushes that grew in a tangle under the poplars while the gulls, so exotic inland, flew over the water, we would imagine perilous routes through lands filled with piranhas and shrunken heads.

One sunny morning, after we had stood staring at the house with two doors for a long time, someone expressed our shared desire out loud: it would be an amazing expedition to explore that house, the wild garden, the garage, the rooms where solitude had stagnated for so long.

Publio ran through a list of obstacles. His father was strict, and if he found out that we had lifted the keys from him, he would be punished. We responded that it would only be once, one afternoon, and that we would be discreet, making the most of the quiet after the midday meal, so that no one would see us.

The matter was not decided for some time. Finally, during the anguished lapse after our exams but before our grades were announced, it was. We met at the big clock at four sharp. The June sun beat down on the empty streets and a soft hum streamed from the houses.

Publio brought the big key to the gate and two smaller, old-fashioned ones for the doors. It seemed that the garage wasn't locked.

Inside, the garden turned out to be much bigger than it seemed from the street. There was a fountain with a cherub holding a goat by the horns and two benches in the middle of the dense vegetation. In the garage, the door to which it took us a while to open—the wood had expanded and it scraped the ground—there was a big, dark Hispano-Suiza covered in dust; in the eaves—the ceiling was unfinished—sparrows and swallows had nested.

We stayed in the garage for a while; first in the car, moving the seats, changing gears and turning the huge wheel; later, rummaging around in the old junk piled up along the back wall. We finally made our way to the front door and, while the twins stood by the gate and kept an eye out for passersby, Publio and I—after a struggle—unlocked and opened the door. A few pieces of plaster fell on our heads from the cracked and mildewed lintel, giving us a scare.

The stairs heading up to the second floor and the attic were just ahead of us. The house had many rooms, though there was no furniture in any of them. Cautiously, we opened the blinds and the afternoon light fell on the dusty parquet floors and the walls marked by the traces of missing paintings, armoires, and headboards.

A peculiar stain on the wood floor in one room lent credibility to whatever stories of secret murders that Publio might have told us. And so that isolated, stately old house gradually took on the dimensions of our dreams of adventure.

When there was no corner left unexplored, we realized that at no point in our meticulous survey had we come across the door to the back entry seen from outside.

We carefully inspected the far wall of the vestibule, which sounded hollow, but weren't able to find an opening. Eventually the twins found, hidden among the wood panels that covered the bottom third of the wall under the staircase, a tiny door that couldn't have been more than two and a half feet tall by maybe one and a half feet wide.

The discovery of that niche fueled our curiosity further still, and not even Publio—who had acted like our chaperone throughout the adventure, as though he were protecting the interests of the property's owner—put up much resistance to the idea of breaking the lock on the tiny door. The twins, who had come prepared with a few tools, set about the task with a screwdriver, and before long the lock popped and the door opened with a creak of its hinges.

There was, in fact, a door like the one on the façade at the bottom of a few steps, which no doubt opened onto the back of the house. For some reason the owners had decided to reduce that exit to a tiny concealed door.

We crossed through the little doorway on all fours and went down the stairs. The lock opened smoothly. We stepped outside, into a space that was no more than an alleyway surrounded by the high wall. It was not connected to the garden in the back; the wall met the side of the building abruptly.

The darkness caught us by surprise. While we had been distracted by our explorations, time had passed and we needed to be getting home. It was then that we noticed a change in the wall bordering the street we had not seen before: a gaping hole behind the ivy, and several bricks that had come loose. In the dim light of the evening, the whole wall had an air of ruin to it.

When we stepped out into the street, we immediately noticed that the panorama was not the one we were used to. Despite the hour, the streetlights were still unlit. But it wasn't just the urban gloom of the half-light that suggested something had changed; more than anything, it was the emptiness of the place: there wasn't a soul in the street, and not a single car passed by. The silence was profound.

We closed the gate and started walking. Little by little we noticed, bewildered, that the city had changed drastically. An unbelievable amount of dried rinds, scraps, crumpled paper, and all sorts of waste were scattered across the sidewalks. When we got to Santo Domingo Plaza, the sudden accumulation of dirt took on immense proportions: in the middle of the plaza, as though left there by countless trucks dumping their loads in the exact same place, rose a veritable mountain of trash. Ordoño Street was also silent and abandoned, the neon signs that normally announced the names of its businesses unlit.

We didn't say a word, but all could feel our confusion turn to fear. And so, instead of saying goodbye, we just stood there together, frozen.

"Walk me home," Publio begged.

We did. Publio lived right next to Pícara Justina Plaza, above a newsstand that also sold used books and comics. But the newsstand had vanished, and in its place was a dark little shop that sold coal, in which an old woman knit by the light of an oil lamp amid the shards and dust and cobwebs. Publio took in the scene, catatonic.

"Bye," he said finally, quietly, and disappeared through the front door.

We couldn't move, either. The plaza seemed unusually desolate: the trees, which had been so green with the first days of summer heat, were completely without leaves, stretching out their bare branches in a wintery gesture; the bars, which at that hour would always be packed with a lively crowd, were almost completely dark, serving only a few old men who stood motionless at the bar under the dying light, also unusual. That was when we saw that first passerby, a skinny kid who walked haltingly, a pack slung over his shoulder.

The city seemed to have been taken over by a sudden shabbiness. The light of dusk, which should have been rosy, shone a dark violet on the rooftops. Growing more and more frightened by the transformation, we slowly left Publio's house behind us. The twins lived nearby and I followed them without hesitation, unable to part ways and meet my own fate.

We had barely stepped onto the plaza when we heard a cry behind us. Publio came running toward us with his arms spread in an outrageous gesture. Distraught, we watched him approach, almost ready to raise our arms and start screaming in terror, ourselves.

"That's not my house," he murmured.

His hair was standing on end and his ears were as red as tomatoes.

"My mother isn't there, neither is my sister. Just strangers. Even the porter is different."

We continued in silence toward the twins' house. The whistle of a train echoed through the silence in an unfamiliar way, sounding more like a groan or a howl.

This time we all went upstairs. The twins rang the bell, but no one answered. Finally, the door opened and a face appeared, pale with broad features like those of the twins' disabled brother, set into a head that bobbed on a thick, twisted neck. He looked around as though he didn't see us, and then thumped his way back down the hall. The twins went in, too, and we stayed in the vestibule, on the other side of the curtain that separated it from the hallway.

The house always smelled of the stews Mrs. Balbina, the twins' mother, used to make for her big family; stews that were never short on onion, bay leaf, and hot pepper. But that afternoon that delicious aroma had been replaced by the smell of mold, of air gone stale or rancid for being shut in too long. An unintelligible hum, like that of a long monologue, could be heard through the half-open doors that led to the central courtyard.

Publio and I were about to leave when the twins returned. They had the same expression of dejected powerlessness on their faces. They, too, spoke in a murmur. Of the whole family, only that faded likeness of poor Fermín preserved the memory of their home.

"There's no beds or dressers in our room," they said. "Only cages. Stacks of empty cages, like ones for rabbits or chickens."

We went out into the street. The night had taken over the city and there was a faint light coming from the streetlamps, the kind of glow that belonged to times of great scarcity. Over by the bullring, three enormous trailers, like the ones used by the circus but with their paint chipped and faded, were pulled up the street by a pack of skinny mules.

We were all shaking.

"Let's go to my house," I said.

The statue of Guzmán was surrounded by thick vegetation, a tangle of creepers that enveloped its base and climbed aggressively toward the figure. In the distance the cathedral glowed dimly, and we were horrified to see that its spires were blunted, their points eaten away as though some terrible ruin had taken it over. The branches of the chestnut trees in La Condesa and the poplars along the river were also as bare as they would have been in winter. Dark spots mixed with the glint coming off the windows: many of the panes were missing and everything around us had the appearance of neglect and decay.

As I stepped through the front door of my house, the first thing I noticed was that the elevator no longer performed its old function. The outer grate was gone, along with the cables from which it had hung, and in its place was a wooden panel with a little window; it now served as a porter's dorm. Paco, the porter, nodded off inside with his hands resting on the newspaper and a strange pair of dark glasses on his face that looked like the ones worn by the blind.

The stairwell looked like it always had, but with more scratches, writing, stains, and drawings on the walls, so dense around the doorbells that the plaster took on the look that afternoon of a collection of bas-reliefs.

I unlocked the door and turned on the light. It was my house, but it had changed, had become almost unrecognizable. In some instances, it was only that the placement of the furniture or objects had changed; in others, the objects themselves were different, completely unknown to me. It was my house, but mixed together with something else by a mysterious process of transmutation.

At first, I thought there was no one else there, but when I got closer to my bedroom I heard heavy, strained breathing. It was my room, there was no doubt about it: the same portraits were still hanging on the walls—the one of me in some field, very young, wearing Tyrolean suspenders and a striped shirt, standing between my father and my mother, and the one from my first communion, with the whole school there in the cloisters, flanked by children dressed as angels and little shepherds—and there, above the headboard, was the old metal crucifix. But there was a stranger in my bed, a man with gray hair. His eyes were closed. It was his breathing that was so loud, that sounded like snoring or a death rattle. There was something vaguely familiar in his features that only added to my terrified confusion.

I left my room and walked toward the balcony, but didn't make it all the way out there: through a crack in the door I was able to see, seated in a rocking chair and rocking gently back and forth, with a rosary in one hand and a fan in the other, my grandmother. I held back a scream; my grandmother had been dead for two years. The sight of her corpse, lying still in the coffin the morning after she passed away, had left a terrible mark on me.

It was my grandmother, there was no question. She slowly whispered her prayers as she opened and closed her fan.

We went back out into the street. Some phenomenon had transformed our city and our homes, and there we were: orphaned, alone, and with no idea what to do.

The twins decided we should spend the night in the house with two doors, where at least we would have the protection of a roof. We were so frightened that we weren't even hungry.

Our fear turned to even greater distress as we got closer to the estate. As though it were coming from above, an incessant wailing could be heard beyond the dark eaves of the houses. Someone was crying and their cries echoed through the emptiness, in the silence of that inanimate city, replacing the everyday bustle to become the new sound of the streets and buildings.

We opened the gate and went toward the back door, which was the only one that was illuminated in all that darkness, even if only faintly, by the dim glow of the streetlamps. Once inside, we climbed the stairs, crossed through the little door in the wall and found ourselves once again in the enormous vestibule, our flashlights carving into the darkness as though it were something solid.

The smaller twin had taken charge of the group. He had us go into a room that faced the street and found a pile of old sacks somewhere that he set about laying across the floor.

"We can sleep here," he said.

Immersed in our suffering, it seemed to us that, precisely because of his calmness, which seemed so out of place, he too belonged to the immense confusion of the city. Then he went over to one of the windows and pulled on the cord to the blinds, which slowly gave way.

"We should save our batteries," he said.

All of a sudden, he shouted to us. We went over to him, and he pointed at the street. The streetlamps were glowing with their usual light, and the sound of a car horn could be heard.

We managed to unlatch the window and it opened with the creak of old wood. Outside, the night had changed completely. The familiar sounds of a living city reached us. It smelled like summer, like new buds, like pollen.

We followed the smaller twin, who left the room, walked down the stairs to the front door, slid back the deadbolt and, after cautiously peeking outside, called out in relief. We all went out then and started running for the gate: the vision we had glimpsed from the window had been real. People strolled along the sidewalks or stopped in front of well-lit shop windows; cars drove down the street with their white, yellow, and red lights. We had gotten our city back.

"Yes," I said. "I saw that they'd torn it down. I saw."

I'm sure that somewhere deep in my own gaze the embers of that old flame still burn the same way they did in his. The memory has colored all the events of my life, and when I step out into the street through the only door to my house, I'm often overcome by the fear of finding myself in that inert, corroded, infinitely sad city, bound to the other like an invisible shadow.

Translated by Heather Cleary

WORK

1972, *Sitio de Tarifa*, Helios (poetry).

2973, *Cumpleaños lejos de casa*, Seix Barral (poetry).

1976, *Novela de Andrés Choz*, Magisterio Español (novel).

1981, *El caldero de oro*, Alfaguara (novel).

1982, *Cuentos del reino secreto*, Alfaguara (stories).

1984, *Mírame Medusa y otros poemas*, Ayuso (poetry).

1985, *La orilla oscura*, Alfaguara (novel, Cátedra edition, 2012).

1986, *El oro de los sueños*, Alfaguara (novel).

1987, *La tierra del tiempo perdido*, Alfaguara (novel).

1987, "Artrópodos y hadanes," Almarabú (story).

1989, *Las lágrimas del sol*, Alfaguara (novel).

1990, *El viajero perdido*, Alfaguara (stories).

1991, *El centro del aire*, Alfaguara (novel).

1992, *Las crónicas mestizas*, Alfaguara (triology comprised of *El oro de los sueños*, *La tierra del tiempo perdido*, and *Las lágrimas del sol*).

1994, *Cuentos del Barrio del Refugio*, Alfaguara (stories).

1995, *Los trenes del verano*, Siruela (children's novel).

1996, *La edad de la aventura*, Altea (essay/children's literature).

1996, *Las visions de Lucrecia*, Alfaguara (novel).

1997, *Cincuenta cuentos y una fábula. Obra breve 1982-1997*, Alfaguara (stories).

1998, *Intramuros*, Edilesa (memoirs).

1998, *Adiós al cuaderno de hojas blancas*, Anaya (children's novel).

1999, *Cuatro Nocturnos*, Alfaguara (novellas).

1999, *La casa de los dos portales y otros cuentos*, Octaedro (anthology).

1999, "La memoria tramposa," Edilesa (story).

2000, *Los invisibles*, Espasa (novel).

2000, *Novelas del mito*, Alfaguara (triology comprised of *El caldero de oro*, *La orilla oscura*, *El centro del aire*).

2000, *Cuentos*, Castalia (anthology).

2002, *Días imaginarios*, Seix Barral (micro stories).

2002, *Leyendas españolas de todos los tiempos: Una memoria soñada*, Temas de hoy (stories).

2003, *El heredero*, Alfaguara (novel, Castalia edition, 2012).

2004, *Ficción continua*, Seix Barral (essay).

2004, *Cuentos de los días raros*, Alfaguara (stories).

2005, *El anillo judío y otros cuentos*, Castilla (anthology).

2005, *Cuentos del libro de la noche*, Alfaguara (micro stories).

2006, *Cumpleaños lejos de casa: Obra poética completa*, Seix Barral (poetry).

2007, *El lugar sin culpa*, Alfaguara (novel).

2007, *La glorieta de los fugitivos*, *Minificción completa*, Páginas de Espuma (stories).

2009, *La sima*, Seix Barral (novel).

2010, *Las antiparras del poeta burlón*, Siruela (novel).

2010, *Historias del otro lugar*, Alfaguara (stories).

2011, *El libro de las horas contadas*, Alfaguara (stories and micro stories).

2012, *El río del Edén*, Alfaguara (novel).

•

ENGLISH TRANSLATIONS

1987, *Beyond the Ancient Cities*, translated by Helen Lane, Farrar, Straus and Giroux (novel).

1994, *The Gold of Dreams*, translated by Helen Lane, Sunburst (novel).

•

AWARDS AND RECOGNITIONS

1976, Premio Novelas y Cuentos for *Novela de Andrés Choz*.

1986, Premio Nacional de la Crítica for *La orilla oscura*.

1993, Premio Nacional de literature infantile y juvenil for *Los trenes del verano*.

1996, Premio Miguel Delibes for *Las visiones de Lucrecia*.

2002, VII Premio NH de relatos for *Días imaginarios*.

2003, Premio de Narrativa Ramón Gómez de la Serna for *El heredero*.

2006, Premio Torrente Ballester for *El lugar sin culpa*.

2007, Premio Salambó for *La glorieta de los fugitivos*.

2008, Premio Castilla y León de las Letras.

2009, Premio Fundación Germán Sánchez Ruipérez.

2013, Premio de la Crítica de Castilla y León for *El río del Edén*.

2013, Premio Nacional de Narrativa for *El río del Edén*.

RICARDO
PIGLIA
(Argentina, 1941)

I t's been said that Ricardo Piglia (Adroqué, Buenos Aires, 1941) is one of the most challenging novelists in Latin American literature. It was his father who inculcated in him a passion for reading; he gave him collections of *Robin Hood* and *Thor* and it was not unusual to hear him recite from memory a few verses from *Martín Fierro*.

In 1955, after the fall of Perón, the family decided to move to Mar del Plata, a port and beach city reclining against the Atlantic, and there, between the ocean mist and his nighttime strolls, Piglia discovered North American literature and film, and was convinced he would become a writer: in a notebook with a black cover he began to write a diary, a habit he would maintain, and as the years passed and his readings continued, would serve as a laboratory of reflections and experiences.

When he finished high school he didn't study Literature, as might be expected; he enrolled in the History program at Universidad de La Plata because he was sure that this would teach him to read from a less bureaucratic and academic position. Later he moved to Buenos Aires and, fascinated by detective fiction, he put together the famous collection of the genre "Serie Negra," which introduced authors such as Horace McCoy, Raymond Chandler, Dashiell Hammett, and David Goodis.

His first book, *La invasión*, appeared in 1967 in Cuba, where he had been honored by Casa de las Américas. In 1975 *Nombre falso*, another book of stories, appeared, but it wasn't until 1980 that his name became an undisputed reference point in Argentine literature. That year, in the middle of the military dictatorship, he published *Respiración artificial*, a key novel in the literature of that country, for the way that it breaks down historical events in a way that encapsulated the situation being lived at the time. Populated by intellectuals who reflect on history and literature, reproducing the tensions of

411

the literary discourse of that time period, he manages to fracture the complex relationships between the genres of criticism and fiction.

Following *Respiración artificial*, Piglia gave us *La ciudad ausente*, at which point the pianist Gerardo Gandini composed the eponymous opera, which premiered in 1995 at Teatro Colón in Buenos Aires.

In addition to fiction, he is also the author of numerous essays, especially in the field of literary criticism, in which he reflects on Argentine literature and developes ideas mingling psychoanalysis, Kafka's diaries, and Brecht's poetry. There is high regard for texts he has written on the story, on Joyce, on the two antagonistic lines in Argentine literature, represented, on the one hand, by the work of Arlt, and on the other, in that of Borges.

A distinguished academic, between 1977 and 1990 he was a visiting professor at various universities in the United States like Princeton and Harvard, in addition to giving seminars in the Literature program at Universidad de Buenos Aires. He gained more public recognition with his novel *Plata quemada* (1997), whose film adaptation by Marcelo Piñeyro won the Premio Goya in the year 2000 for the best foreign feature film in Spain, awarded by Academia de las Artes y Ciencias Cinematográficas de España.

In 2010 he published *Blanco nocturno*, a short detective novel that won him the Premio Rómulo Gallegos. The book's plot revolves around the life and experiences of a solitary inventor and is faithful to Piglia's intriguing and intense style. His work has been translated into English, French, Italian, German, and Portuguese, among other languages, and has been read as "the necessary bridge between the Buenos Aires Argentine literature of Borges and Cortázar, and the more recent writing of Pablo de Santis and Rodrigo Fresán."

THE ACORN

The Torture of Doctor Johnson

"The Girl" was the first story created by the storytelling machine in *La ciudad ausente*. That's why I picked it. I wrote the novel and the stories that compose it between 1990 and 1992 attempting (unsuccessfully) to alter the rigid boundaries between short forms and longer pieces of writing. After publishing the book I found many other situations and plots that seemed to form part of the rotation of stories of that novel. For example, the first Chinese translation of *Don Quixote* was the work of the prestigious writer Lin Shu and his assistant Chen Jialin. Since Lin Shu did not know any foreign languages, his assistant came every afternoon and recounted episodes from Cervantes's novel. Lin Shu translated the book based on those accounts. Published in 1922, with the title *The Story of a Crazy Knight*, the book was received as a great event in the history of literary translation in China. It would be interesting to translate this version of the *Quixote* into Spanish. Personally, I would like to write a story about the conversations between Lin Shu and his assistant Chen Jialin as they worked on the transcription of the Cervantes novel and add it to some future—and uncertain—reissue of *La ciudad ausente*. Sometimes I think that what I've written since (*Plata quemada*, *Blanco nocturno*, or the screenplay for *La sonámbula*) are really stories from the machine.

In Conversation with the Dead

At a certain point I realized that in Joyce's *Ulysses* and Proust's *In Search of Lost Time* the word metempsychosis seemed linked to the act of reading. Dead souls rest on the page. My favorite reincarnations have been Hemingway and

Roberto Arlt; I read them when I was very young and I tried—futilely—to write like them. At my age, one is very attentive to posthumous mutations and the written voice of ancestors. Literary tradition as the spiritualism of writing. There is something of this in the poems of Yeats and also—more carnal—in the poem *Metempsychosis* by Rubén Darío: ("I was a soldier, and Cleopatra the Queen / took me to her bed for sex . . .").

CODA

Your literary upbringing is also inscribed with the writing of the Río de la Plata. What kind of fiction does this area generate?

Starting in the '40s, I think the Río de la Plata—let's say Borges, Cortázar, Onetti, Felisberto Hernández—established a kind of fiction focused on a narrator who does not understand very well what he is narrating, a weak narrator who vacillates throughout the plot and investigates. This is in opposition, it seems to me, to the despotic narrator who instills his world with total certainty and without vacillations like in the novels of Rómulo Gallegos, García Márquez, or Isabel Allende.

A THOUSAND FORESTS

FROM *THE ABSENT CITY*
[A NOVEL]

THE GIRL

The matrimony's first two children were able to lead a normal life, especially considering the difficulties associated with having a sister like her in a small town. The girl (Laura) was born healthy. It was only with time that they began to notice certain strange signs. Her system of hallucinations was the topic of a complicated report that appeared in a scientific journal, but her father had deciphered it long before that. Yves Fonagy called it "extravagant references." In these highly unusual cases the patient imagines that everything that occurs around him is a projection of his personality. The patient excludes real people from his experience, because he considers himself much more intelligent than anyone else. The world was an extension of herself; her body spread outward and reproduced itself. She was constantly preoccupied by mechanical objects, especially electric lightbulbs. She saw them as words, every time one was turned on it was like someone had begun to speak. Thus she considered darkness to be a form of silent thinking. One summer afternoon (when she was five years old) she looked at an electric fan spinning on a dresser. She thought it was a living being, a female living being. The girl of the air, her soul trapped in a cage. Laura said that she lived "there," and raised her hand to indicate the ceiling. There, she said, moving her head from left to right. Her mother turned off the fan. That is when she began having difficulties with language. She lost the capacity to use personal pronouns. With time she stopped using them altogether, then hid all the words she knew in her memory. She would only utter a little clucking sound as she opened

415

and closed her eyes. The mother separated the boys from their sister because
she was afraid that it was contagious. One of those small town beliefs. But
madness is not contagious and the girl was not crazy. In any case, they sent
the two brothers to a Catholic boarding school in Del Valle, and the family
went into seclusion in their large house in Bolívar. The father was a frustrated
musician who taught mathematics in the public high school. The mother was
a teacher and had become principal, but she decided to retire in order to take
care of her daughter. They did not want to have her committed. So they took
her twice a week to an institute in La Plata and followed the orders given
by Doctor Arana, who treated her with electric shock therapy. He explained
that the girl lived in an extreme emotional void. That is why Laura's language
was slowly becoming more and more abstract and unpersonalized. At first
she still used the correct names for food. She would say "butter," "sugar,"
"water," but later began to refer to different food items in groups that were
disconnected from their nutritive nature. Sugar became "white sand," butter, "soft mud," water, "wet air." It was clear that by disarranging the names
and abandoning personal pronouns she was creating a language that better
corresponded to her personal emotional experiences. Far from not knowing
how to use words correctly, what could be seen was a spontaneous decision
to create a language that matched her experience of the world. Doctor Arana
did not agree, but this was the father's hypothesis, and he decided to enter
his daughter's verbal world. She was a logic machine connected to the incor-
rect interface. The girl functioned according to the model of a fan—a fixed
rotational axis served as her syntactic schema, and she moved her head as
she spoke to feel the wind of her unarticulated thoughts. The decision to
teach her how to use language implied also having to explain to her how to
compartmentalize words. But she would lose them like molecules in warm
air. Her memory was a breeze blowing in the white curtains of a room in an
empty house. It was necessary to try to take that sailboat out in still air. The
father stopped going to Doctor Arana's clinic and began treating the girl with
a singing teacher. He had to give her a temporal sequence, and he believed
that music was an abstract model of the order of things in the world. She
sang Mozart arias in German with Madame Silenzky, a Polish pianist who
directed the chorus in the Lutheran Church in Carhué. The girl, sitting on
the bench, howled to the rhythm. Madame Silenzky was frightened to death
because she thought the child was a monster. She was twelve years old, fat

and beautiful like a madonna, but her eyes looked as if they were made out of glass and she clucked before singing. Madame Silenzky thought the girl was a hybrid, a doll made out of foam, a human machine, without feelings, without hope. She screamed more than she sang, always out of tune, but eventually she was able to follow the line of a melody. Her father was trying to get her to incorporate a temporal memory, an empty form, composed of rhythmic sequences and modulations. The girl did not have any syntax (she lacked the very notion of syntax). She lived in a wet universe, time for her was a hand-washed sheet that you wring out in the middle to get the water out. She has staked out her own territory, her father would say, from which she wishes to exclude all experiences. Anything new, any event that she has not yet experienced and which is still to be lived, seems like something painful, like something threatening and terrifying to her. The petrified present, the monstrous and viscous and solid stoppage of time, the chronological void, can only be altered with music. Music is not an experience, it is the pure form of life, it has no content, it cannot frighten her, her father would say, and Madame Silenzky (terrified) would shake her gray head and relax her hands on the piano keys by playing a Haydn cantata before they began. When he finally got the girl to enter a temporal sequence, the mother fell ill and had to be hospitalized. The girl associated her mother's disappearance (she died two months later) with a Schubert lied. She sang the melody as if she were crying over someone's death and remembering a lost past. Then, using his daughter's musical syntax as a base, the father began working on her lexicon. The girl did not have any form from which to construct references, it was like teaching a foreign language to a dead person. (Like teaching a dead language to a foreigner.) He decided to begin by telling her short stories. The girl stood still, near the light, in the hall facing the patio. The father would sit in an armchair and narrate a story to her as if he were singing. He hoped the sentences would enter his daughter's memory like blocks of meaning. That is why he chose to tell her the same story, only varying the version each time. The plot would become the sole model of the world and the sentences modulations of possible experiences. The story was a simple one. In his *Chronicle of the Kings of England* (twelfth century), William of Malmesbury tells the story of a young, sovereign Roman noble who has just gotten married. After the feasts and the celebrations, the young man and his friends go out to play bocci balls in the garden. In the course of the game, the young man puts his

wedding ring, to avoid losing it, on the barely extended finger of the hand of
a bronze statue. When he goes to retrieve it, he finds that the statue's hand is
now a tight fist, and he cannot get his ring back. Without telling anyone, he
comes back at night with torches and servants and discovers that the statue
has disappeared. He keeps the truth from his bride, but when he gets into bed
that night, he feels that there is something between them, something dense
and hazy that prevents them from embracing. Terrified, he hears a voice that
murmurs in his ear:

"Kiss me, today you and I were united in matrimony. I am Venus, and you
have given me the ring of love."

The first time he told the story, the girl seemed to fall asleep. There was a
breeze from the garden at the end of the patio. There were no visible changes,
at night she dragged herself into her room and curled up in the darkness
with her normal clucking. The next day, at the same time, her father sat
her in the same place and told her another version of the story. The first
important variation had appeared about twenty years later, in a German compilation from the mid-twelfth century titled *Kaiserchronik*. In this version,
the statue on whose finger the young man places the ring is not Venus, but
the Virgin Mary. When he tries to unite with his bride, the Mother of God
comes between the couple to chastise him, which incites a mystical passion
in the young man. After leaving his wife, the young man becomes a priest
and devotes the rest of his life to the service of Our Lady. An anonymous
twelfth-century painting depicts the Virgin Mary with a ring on her left ring
finger and an enigmatic smile on her lips.

Every day, in the early evening, the father would tell her the same story in
its multiple variations. The clucking girl was an anti-Scheherazade, she heard
the story of the ring told a thousand and one times at night by her father.
Within a year the girl is already smiling, because she knows how the story
ends. Sometimes she looks down at her hands and moves her fingers, as if she
were the statue. She looks up at the garden and, for the first time, gives her
version of the events in a soft whisper. "Mouvo looked at the night. Where
his face had been another appeared, Kenya's. Again the strange laugh. All of
a sudden Mouvo was in a corner of the house and Kenya in the garden and
the sensorial circles of the ring were very sad," she said. From that point on,
with the repertory of words she had learned and with the circular structure
of the story, she began to build a language, an uninterrupted series of phrases

that allowed her to communicate with her father. In the following months she was the one who told the story, every evening, in the hall facing the patio in the back of the house. She reached a point where she was able to tell, word for word, the version by Henry James—perhaps because his story, "The Last of the Valerii," was the last in the series. (The action has shifted to Rome in the time of the Risorgimento, where a young woman, who has inherited a fortune, in one of those typically Jamesian moves, marries an Italian noble from a distinguished, but impoverished, lineage. One afternoon, a group of laborers working at a dig in the gardens of the villa discover a statue of Juno. *Signor Conte* begins to feel a strange fascination with that masterpiece from the best period of Greek sculpture. He moves the statue to an abandoned greenhouse and hides it mistrustfully from anyone's view. In the days that follow, he transfers a large part of the passion he feels for his beautiful wife to the marble statue, and spends more and more of his time in the glass structure. At the end, the *Contessa*, in order to free her husband from the spell, tears the ring off of the goddess's ring finger and buries it at the far end of the gardens. Her life becomes happy once again.) A gentle drizzle was falling in the patio and the father was rocking in his chair. That afternoon the girl left the story for the first time, she left the closed circle of the story like someone walking through a door, and asked her father to buy her a gold ring (*anello*). There she was, singing softly, clucking, a sad music machine. She was sixteen years old, a pale dreamer, like a Greek statue. As steadfast as an angel.

Translated by Sergio Waisman

WORK

1967, *Jaulario*, Casa de las Américas (stories).

1967, *La invasión*, Anagrama (stories).

1968, *América Latina: De la traición, a la conquesta*, Jorge Álvarez (essay).

1975, *Nombre falso*, Anagrama (stories).

1980, *Respiración artificial*, Anagrama (novel).

1986, *Crítica y ficción*, Anagrama (essays).

1988, *Prisión perpetua*, Anagrama (novel).

1992, *La ciudad ausente*, Anagrama (novel).

1993, *La Argentina en pedazos*, La Urraca (essays).

1995, *Cuentos morales*, Espasa-Calpe (stories).

1997, *Plata quemada*, Anagrama (essays).

1999, *Formas breves*, Anagrama (essays).

2000, *Diccionario de la novela de Macedonio Fernández*, Fondo de Cultura Económica (essays).

2001, *Tres propuestas para el próximo milenio (y cinco dificultades)*, Fondo de Cultura Económica (essays).

2005, *El último lector*, Anagrama (essays).

2010, *Blanco nocturno*, Anagrama (novel).

2013, *El camino de Ida*, Anagrama (novel).

•

ENGLISH TRANSLATIONS

1994, *Artificial Respiration*, translated by Daniel Balderston, Duke University Press (novel).

1995, *Assumed Name*, translated by Sergio Gabriel Waisman, Latin American Literary Review Press (stories).

2000, *The Absent City*, translated by Sergio Waisman, Duke University Press (novel).

•

AWARDS AND RECOGNITIONS

1962, Premio de la revista *El Escarabajo de Oro* for "Mi amigo."

1963, Premio de la revista *Bibliograma* for "Una luz que se iba."

1967, Special recognition Premio Casa de las Américas for *Jaulario*.

1997, Premio Planeta Argentina for *Plata quemada*.

2005, Premio Iberoamericano de Letras José Donoso.

2011, Premio de la Crítica España for *Blanco nocturno*.

2011, Premio Rómulo Gallegos for *Blanco nocturno*.

2011, Premio Hammet for *Blanco nocturno*.

2012, Premio Casa de las Américas de Narrativa for *Blanco Nocturno*.

2013, Premio Iberoamericano de Narrativa Manuel Rojas.

EDUARDO
MENDOZA
(Spain, 1943)

E duardo Mendoza is considered one of the best storytellers of his home city, Barcelona, where he was born in 1943. After being educated in a school belonging to La Congregación de los Hermanos Maristas, he opted to pursue a law degree. But then he left and went traveling around Europe, spending time in London thanks to a fellowship. In 1967, two years after he left, he came back to his home city and dedicated himself to studying law, until in 1973, stifled by the political and cultural climate in Spain, he decided to abandon his incipient profession and he went to live in New York to work as a translator for the United Nations.

Mendoza has acknowledged that the cult of literature within his family influenced him in his vocation as a writer. He was going to call his first novel *Los soldados de Cataluña*, a title that would have had trouble eluding the Francoist censor, so he decided to call it *La verdad sobre el caso Savolta*, a title that was more in keeping with the central storyline, the mysterious atmosphere where the plot unfolds, and better, in any case, at concealing the novel's political undertone.

Published in 1975, a short time before Franco's death, *La verdad sobre el caso de Savolta*, was a breath of fresh air in the dubious Spanish fiction of the time; in it, Mendoza presents an innovative structure, open to various narrative discourses, functioning like parts of a puzzle that, all together, end up resembling Barcelona at the beginning of the twentieth century, a city that found itself in the middle of tension and the struggles of unions and revolutionaries.

In his next novel, *El misterio de la cripta embrujada* (1979), he started down another literary path, the detective saga, through which he sought, via an exceedingly peculiar character (a nameless detective locked in an insane asylum), to parody the noir novel and the gothic genre and, at the same time, to offer his vision of Barcelona at that moment. In 1982, this first title was followed by *El laberinto de las aceitunas*; and the trilogy culminated in 2001, with *La aventura del tocador de señoras*.

Back in New York in 1983, Mendoza became an author who was preferred by readers and celebrated by Spanish critics. In 1986, with *La ciudad de los prodigios* (considered by many to be his best novel) he managed to unite the admiration of both with a story set between the World Expos of 1888 and 1929, whose protagonist, Onofre Bouvila, functions as an archetype and a reflection of a period marked by anarchism and corrupt power. Settled now in Barcelona, for years he has maintained a close relationship with the poet and academic Pere Gimferrer, who has been the editor of almost all of his works in Spain, and also with Félix de Azúa.

Humor, one of the secret weapons of Mendoza's oeuvre, almost a genre all its own, also characterized other essential titles of his like *La isla inaudita* (1989), which tells of a Catalan executive's trip to Venice in search of love; *Sin noticias de Gurb* (1990), which presents the delirious and personal diary of an extraterrestrial who arrives in a city that is preparing to receive the Olympic torch; or *El año del diluvio*, in 1992. In 2006 he published *Mauricio o las elecciones primarias*, a novel whose plot unfolds in the years leading up to the Transition, also set in Barcelona, and in 2008 *El asombroso viaje de Pomponio Flato*, a satire that explores the confines of the Roman Empire. The writer's most recent novel, *El enredo de la bolsa y la vida* (2012), where he revives his famous nameless detective, has already garnered enormous popular success.

THE ACORN

The Torture of Doctor Johnson

My selection corresponds less to criteria of quality—difficult to apply to fragments that should be viewed all together—than to a criterion of representation. Successful or not, the chosen text is a model of my preoccupations and
my methodology, if you can call it that: the predominance of action, sacrifice
of craft in service of economy, prominence of dialogue over other narrative
techniques. And constant reference to traditional narrative or, to be more
precise, to the nineteenth-century novel.

In Conversation with the Dead

Since you are citing Quevado, I will cite Gracián: the young dialogue with
the dead, with those who have gone before; the adult, with the living; the old,
with themselves. I think I'm at the third stage. But I've spoken with many
dead. Since I started writing at quite a young age, I had children's writers as
models (Verne, Rider, Haggard, Conan Doyle) and I've never renounced their
legacy. Baroja opened the door for me to find my own style. I've always kept
my eyes on the great classics of the nineteenth century (Stendhal, Dickens,
Tolstoy) and of the eighteenth century (Voltaire, Swift, Diderot). But I think
the great classics are like great mountains. From a distance they oxygenate
and strengthen; scaling them is dangerous.

Coda

*Your first novel, today considered one of the first novels of the Transition, was pub-
lished during the Franco era, although its recognition by readers and critics came
after his death. You wrote the novel in New York. How did that city and the fact of
living far from Spain influence you?*

I wrote *La verdad sobre el caso Savolta* before leaving for New York, during
the long and dark years of the late Franco regime. It was published after I
already left, but the distance in no way intervened its conception, although it's
true that before New York I had lived in London and elsewhere. I've always
enjoyed getting outside, I don't know whether to enrich my experience or to
see the bulls from behind the barricade. I spent a prolonged period in New
York. Of course the city and the work I did there as an interpreter had an
important influence on me. I wrote some other novels there that I consider
characteristic of my work: *El misterio de la cripta embrujada,* a moralistic novel
à la Voltaire's *Candide* and openly humoristic, and *La ciudad de los prodigios.*
As for Franco, to whose demise I am invariably linked in literary treatises that
talk about me, I don't think it should be considered a factor in my personal
evolution or in evaluations made of my work.

A THOUSAND FORESTS

FROM *The Truth About the Savolta Case*
[A NOVEL]

We were married on a spring morning at the beginning of April. Why? Why did I make such a reckless decision? I have no idea. Even now, after having so many years to think them over, my own acts are still an enigma to me. Did I love María Coral? I think not. I think I confused (my life consists of a continual confusion of feelings) the passion that young, sensual, mysterious, and unfortunate young woman inspired in me with love. Probably my solitude, my boredom, my being aware that I'd wasted almost all of my youth so pitifully also influenced me. Desperate acts and the various forms and degrees of suicide are the patrimony of sad young men. Lepprince was the one who ultimately tipped the balance with his solid reasons and his persuasive promises.

Lepprince wasn't stupid: he was aware of the unhappiness around him and wanted to remedy it to the degree his capabilities, which were many, allowed. But we musn't exaggerate: he wasn't a dreamer who aspired to change the world, and he certainly didn't feel guilty about the problems of others. I said he admitted, to himself, a certain responsibility, not a certain guilt. It was out of responsibility that he decided to help María Coral and me. And he judged this to be the best solution: María Coral and I would marry (if and when we would give our mutual consent); that way the gypsy's problems would be resolved in the most absolute way, and the Lepprince name would not be involved. I, for my part, would stop working for Cortabanyes and start working for Lepprince, with a salary commensurate with my future needs. That way, Lepprince did not have to resort to charity: I would earn my living and that of María Coral. The favor came from Lepprince, but not the money.

It was better for all of us and more dignified. The advantages María Coral derived from this arrangement are too obvious to list. As for me, what can I say? It's certain that without Lepprince's intervention, I would never have decided to take such a step, but, rethinking things, what did I have to lose? To what could I aspire? At best, a brutalizing, ill-paid job, a woman like Teresa (to make miserable, just as Pajarito, poor man, had done to his wife), or a stupid soubrette like the ones Perico Serramadriles and I chased in the streets or at dances (and with whom I would dehumanize myself to the point of putting up with their vegetable, chattering company without resorting to violence). My salary was miserable: it barely allowed me to subsist; it costs a lot to maintain a family; a future of permanent loneliness horrified me—even today, as I write these words, it still horrifies me . . .

"To tell the truth, man, I don't know what to say. The way you put it, so matter-of-factly . . ."

"You don't have to reveal great truths to me, Perico; all I want is your opinion."

Perico Serramadriles swallowed some beer and wiped off the foam that clung to his incipient mustache.

"It's hard to give an opinion about such an unusual case. I've always held the opinion that marriage is a very serious thing and shouldn't be decided on the spur of the moment. And now you yourself say you're not really sure you love this girl."

"What is love, Perico? Have you ever known true love? The longer I live the more I think love is pure theory. A thing that only exists in novels and movies."

"That we haven't found it doesn't mean it doesn't exist."

"I'm not saying that. I'm saying that love in the abstract is the product of idle minds. Love doesn't exist unless it materializes in something corporeal. A woman, I mean."

"Obviously," admitted Perico.

"Love doesn't exist; all that exists is a woman with whom we fall in love under certain circumstances for a limited time."

"Well, if you put it that way . . ."

"Tell me: how many women have crossed our paths that we might have fallen in love with? Not a one. What were they? Clothes pressers, seamstresses, daughters of minor employees like us, future Doloretases *in potentia*."

"I don't see why it has to be that way. There are other women."

"Sure, I know all about it: princesses, beauty queens, movie stars, refined, cultured, sophisticated women. . . . But those women, Perico, are not for you and me."

"In that case, follow my example: don't get married," said my highly rhetorical friend.

"Now you're just showing off, Perico. You say that today and feel like a hero. But the sterile years will pass, and one day you'll feel alone and tired, and the first one to cross your path will eat you alive. You'll have a dozen kids, she'll get fat and old in the twinkling of any eye, and you'll work until you drop just to feed your kids, pay the doctor bills, dress them, get them a bad education, and make them into honest, poor office workers like us, all so that the species of the miserable will be perpetuated."

"I just don't know . . . you paint everything so black. You think all women are the same?"

I kept my mouth shut because the long-buried memory of Teresa passed before my eyes. But her image did not change my arguments. I evoked Teresa and for the first time I asked myself what Teresa had meant in my life. Nothing. A frightened, unprotected little animal who aroused a naïve tenderness in me like an anemic, hothouse flower. Teresa was miserable with Pajarito de Soto and miserable with me. All she got from life was suffering and disillusion; she wanted to inspire love but garnered only betrayal. It wasn't her fault, or Pajarito de Soto's, or mine. What did they do to us, Teresa? What witches presided over our destiny?

When the appetizers, the entrée, the fish, the fowl, the fruit, and the dessert were finished, the guests left the table. The men gasped for air and patted their bellies with happy resignation. The ladies mentally bade farewell to the dishes they'd refused with great effort, dissimulating their eagerness under a rictus of disgust. The orchestra went back to the bandstand and played the first notes of a mazurka, which no one danced. Conversation, suspended for a long while, became general again.

Lepprince looked for Pere Parells among his guests. During dinner he'd watched him: the old financier, taciturn and sulky, barely ate anything and answered the questions asked by his dinner companions with dry monosyllables. Lepprince became nervous and gave Cortabanyes a questioning look.

From the other end of the table, the lawyer answered him with a gesture of indifference, as if it were a matter of little importance. After dinner, he and Lepprince met.

"Go to him, go now," said the lawyer.

"Wouldn't it be better to wait until later? In private perhaps?" insinuated Lepprince.

"No, right now. He's in your house and won't dare to make a scene in front of everyone. Besides he's eaten little and drunk more than usual. You can get whatever he knows out of him, and that's important for us. Go on."

Lepprince found Pere Parells alone, near the orchestra, immersed in his own thoughts. He was pale, and his bloodless lips trembled slightly. Lepprince did not know whether to attribute those symptoms to irritation or to the digestive disorders of old age.

"Pere, would you mind talking with me for a few minutes?"

Parells made not the slightest effort to conceal his annoyance; his only answer was silence.

"Pere, I'm sorry I was a bit brusque with you. I was nervous. You know how things have been going lately."

Without turning to face Lepprince, Parells responded.

"Do I really know? Tell me, how are things going?"

"Don't dig in your heels that way, Pere. You know better than I how things are."

"Do I indeed?" said the old man with unrelenting sarcasm.

"Since the war ended, business has been flat, I agree. I don't know how we're going to resolve all our problems, but I'm convinced we will resolve them. There are always wars. I don't think we have any reason to be nervous as long as we're united and work together to restructure the business."

"When you say *work together* you mean work with you, of course."

"Pere," Lepprince insisted patiently, "you know that I need your help, your experience now more than ever . . . It isn't fair for you to blame me alone for what might happen; why is it my fault the Americans won the war? You yourself favored the allies . . ."

"Look, Lepprince," Parells stopped him without changing position or looking into his young partner's face, "I made this business out of nothing. Savolta, Claudedeu, and I, through our work, without stopping to take a breath, stealing time from sleep, forgetting we were tired, we made the business what it was until a short time ago. The business matters to me. It's my whole life. I've seen it grow, bear its first fruits. I don't know if you understand what something like that means because when you walked in it was all there. But no matter. I know conditions are unfavorable, I know all our work is on the point of going under. Savolta and Claudedeu are dead, I feel old and tired, but I'm not so stupid," here the tone of his voice changed, "I'm not so stupid that I don't know things like that can happen. I've seen lots of failures in my life, so I'm not shocked about my own. Moreover, even if it were certain we were going to fail, and even if I do feel as worn-out as I do, I wouldn't hesitate to start all over again, to dedicate all my hours and energies to the company."

He paused. Lepprince waited for him to continue. "But, and take careful note of what I'm saying to you," the old financier went on calmly, "I would destroy what means so much to me before I'd allow certain things to happen."

Lepprince lowered his voice until it was a whisper.

"What do you mean?"

"You know better than I."

Lepprince looked around. Some of the guests had noticed them and were watching with unabashed curiosity. Ignoring Cortabanyes's advice—to speak to Parells in public—he suggested they retire to the library to speak alone. Unwillingly at first, then with sudden firmness, Parells accepted. That tactical error would precipitate the tragedy.

"Explain just what you mean," said Lepprince once they were safe from public view.

"You explain!" screamed Pere Parells, forgetting the decorum he'd maintained until then. "Explain to me what's going on and what's been going on these past years. Explain to me what you've been hiding from me until today, and then perhaps we can begin to talk things over."

Lepprince turned red with rage. His eyes shone, and his jaw was tight.

"Pere, if you think I've been juggling the books we can go over to the office right now and look them over."

Pere Parells looked Lepprince directly in the eye for the first time that night. The defiant eyes of the two partners met.

"I'm not just talking about the accounts, Lepprince."

Parells knew he'd said too much, but he couldn't control himself. Too much to drink, all the rage he'd held in for so long made him say what he thought, and he listened to his own words as if a third person were saying them. But what he heard did not seem badly put to him.

"I'm not just talking about the accounts," he repeated. "For a long time now, I've been noticing serious anomalies inside and outside the business. I had certain investigations carried out on my own."

"And what did you find out?"

"I'd rather not divulge that information. You'll know what it is at the proper time."

Lepprince exploded.

"Listen here, Pere. I came here to clear up what I thought was a simple misunderstanding, but now I see that things are taking a direction I simply will not allow. Your allusions are an insult, and I demand an immediate explanation. And as for your fears about the future of the business, well, you can get out whenever you please. I'm willing to buy your stock at whatever price you'd care to name. But I don't want to see you anymore at the office, understand? I don't want to see you anymore. You're old, you're senile, you can't think straight. You're a useless wreck, and if I've put up with your absurd interference until now it's been out of respect for what you were and to honor the memory of my father-in-law. But now I'm fed up, once and for all, fed up."

Parells turned white, then gray. He seemed to choke and brought his hand to his heart. A savage glitter flooded Lepprince's eyes. The old man recovered slowly.

"I'll bury you, Lepprince," he muttered with a strangled voice. "I swear I'll bury you. I've got more than enough proof."

Rosita the Idealist, the generous prostitute, was coming back from the market, grumbling and cursing out loud about the high price of everything. Cabbage leaves and a loaf of bread protruded from her basket. She stopped to buy goat milk and cheese. Then she went on her way, stepping around puddles. *The streets of the poor are always wet*, she was thinking. Along the gutters ran a blackish, shining, and putrefied water that poured into the drains with a lugubrious gurgle. She spat and blasphemed. Sitting on a tiny stool, with a little metal plate at his feet, a blind man strummed out a sad chant on his guitar.

"Congratulations on your little outings, Rosita," said the blind man with a crowlike cackle.

"How did you recognize me?" she asked, coming closer.

"By your voice."

"And what do you know about my outings?" she said, resting her empty hand on her hip.

"Just what people are saying," answered the blind man, stretching forward a hand and feeling around. "Would you let me?"

Rosita shook her head no, as if the blind man could see her.

"Not today, Uncle Basilio, I'm not in the mood."

"Come on, just a little, Rosa. God will reward you."

"I said no, and no is no."

"You're worried about this business with Julián, eh, Rosa?" asked the blind man with his idiotic grin.

"What does it matter to you?" she growled.

"Tell him to watch his step. Inspector Vázquez is looking for him."

"Because of the Savolta thing? He didn't do it."

"Sure, but he'll have to convince Vázquez," declared the blind man.

"Well, he won't find Julián. He's well hidden."

The blind man strummed the guitar again. Rosita the Idealist went on her way, stopped, went back, and gave Uncle Basilio a piece of cheese.

"Here, take it. It's fresh cheese, I just bought it."

The blind man took the cheese from Rosita's hands, kissed it, and put it in his jacket pocket.

"Thanks, Rosa."

The two of them remained silent for an instant. The blind man, in an indifferent tone, said. "You've got a visitor, Rosa."

"Cops?" asked the prostitute in fear.

"No. That squealer . . . you know. Your lover boy."

"Nemesio?"

"I don't know any names, Rosa. I don't know any names."

"You wouldn't have told me if I hadn't given you the cheese, right, Uncle Basilio?"

The blind man put on a miserable face.

"I just didn't remember, Rosa. Don't be that way."

Rosita the Idealist walked through the dark doorway of the building in which she lived, took a careful look into the corners, and, seeing no one, made her difficult way up the steep stairs. She was puffing when she reached the fourth floor. On the landing she saw a huddled shadow.

"Nemesio, get up out of there. You don't have to hide."

"Are you alone, Rosita?"

"Can't you see?"

"Here, let me help you."

"Get your hands off the basket, you pig!"

She put it down on the floor, dug through the pleats of her skirt, took out a key, and opened the door. Nemesio walked in behind her and closed the door again. The apartment consisted of two rooms separated by a curtain which concealed an iron bed. In the first room there was a table with a heater attached to it underneath, four chairs, a chest, and a camp stove. Rosita turned on the light.

"What do you want, Nemesio?"

"I have to speak to Julián, Rosita. Tell me where I can find him."

Rosita made a disdainful gesture.

"I haven't seen Julián for months. He's got another girl."

Nemesio shook his head sadly without raising his eyes from the floor.

"Don't lie. I saw both of you walk into this very building last Sunday."

"Oh, so you're spying on us, eh? And who's paying you, if you don't mind telling?" asked Rosita as she emptied the basket, her voice a blend of indifference and scorn.

"No one's paying me, Rosita, I swear. You know that for me, you . . ."

"That's enough. Get out."

"Tell me where Julián is. It's important."

"I don't know."

"Tell me. It's for his own good. Someone killed a man named Savolta, Rosita. I don't know who he is, but he's a big shot. I suspect Julián is mixed up in the affair. I'm not saying he did it, but I know he's got something to do with Savolta. Vázquez is in charge of the case. I've got to warn Julián, don't you see? It's for his own good. It doesn't matter one way or the other to me."

"It must matter, otherwise you wouldn't be making such a fuss. But I don't know anything. Get out and leave me in peace. I'm tired, and I've still got a lot to do."

Nemesio studied Rosita's face with a mixture of pity and respect.

"You're right. You don't look so hot. You're tired and it's still morning. That's no good. This life's no good for you, Rosita."

"So what do you want me to do, fool? Sell stories to the cops?"

When Nemesio left, he had the feeling something bad was going to happen.

Lepprince took care of speaking with María Coral. I didn't have the nerve to do it, and I was happy for his mediation. It took him three days to give me the answer, but the tone of his voice was festive when he told me that the gypsy would be happy to marry me. Almost at the same time we began the preparations for the wedding, my work with Lepprince began. I was finally leaving Cortabanyes's office. Doloretas shed a few tears when I left, and Perico Serramadriles patted me on the back with affected camaraderie. Everyone wished me good luck. Cortabanyes was a bit cold, perhaps jealous that I would leave him for someone else (a feeling many bosses allow themselves with regard to their employees, over whom they think they have certain proprietary rights).

At the beginning, the work Lepprince assigned me made me dizzy. Then with time, as happens with all jobs, I ended by sinking into a soft, grayish routine in which the number and format of a document counted for more than its content. (Besides, until Lepprince's political projects became clearer, my work consisted merely in the selection and classification of newspaper articles, letters, pamphlets, reports, and texts of various kinds.) No sooner had María Coral agreed to the marriage than we proceeded to transform her into the worthy bride of a young and promising secretary to the mayor. We visited the best shops in Barcelona and fitted her out with the latest-style clothes and shoes from Paris, Vienna, and New York. I began, following Lepprince's advice, the project of refining María Coral, since the gypsy's style left a lot to be desired. Her vocabulary was obscene, her manners rough. I taught her to carry herself elegantly, to eat properly, and to converse discreetly. I gave her a superficial but sufficient culture. The gypsy responded to this program with an interest that moved me. She was astonished, as well she should have been. She was, after all, living a fairy tale. She made notable progress, because she possessed a lively intelligence and an iron will, befitting someone who lived in such turbulent places with the lowest levels of human scum. The underworld is a good school.

The months that preceded our wedding were a whirlwind of activity. Aside from María Coral's education, arranging our home cost me hours of pleasing labor. I decorated our house according to the most modern style; there was nothing missing, neither the necessary nor the superfluous: we even had a telephone. I bought or chose everything myself. The frenzy of the preparations kept me from thinking, and I felt almost fortunate. I bought new clothes, carried my books and other possessions from my old apartment to my future home, fought with bricklayers, painters, carpenters, decorators, and tailors. The time flew by, and I was taken by surprise on the eve of the wedding.

To tell the truth, my dealings with María Coral during those febrile days had been frequent, but for some unconscious though foreseeable reason, we'd kept our contacts at a formal, almost bureaucratic level, that of student and teacher. Even though the imminence of our marriage must have been floating in the air of our relations, we both pretended to know nothing about it, and we behaved as if, once my educational labors were finished, we would have to separate and never see each other again. I showed I was efficient and courteous; she, submissive and respectful. There was never an engagement with such an air of fastidious decorum. Far away from our respective families, tutors, and moral or social obstacles (I was rootless; María Coral a common cabaret performer), we behaved paradoxically with greater circumspection than if we'd been surrounded by a wall of modest mothers, fainthearted chaperones, and strict guards.

One morning in April we were married. No one attended the ceremony except Serramadriles and a few of Lepprince's employees (ones I didn't know), who signed as witnesses. Lepprince did not attend the church ceremony, but he was waiting for us at the door. He shook hands with me and did the same with María Coral. He took me aside and asked if everything had gone well. I said it had. He admitted he was afraid the gypsy would change her mind at the last minute. It's true that María Coral did hesitate before saying, "I will," and her voice was almost imperceptible and tremulous. The priest's blessing closed like a door over her assent.

Then we went on our honeymoon. It was Lepprince's project, and he'd organized it in secret. I didn't want to go along with such a foolish idea, but he gave me the train tickets and the hotel reservation, insisting with such firmness that I simply could not say no. After a tiring journey, we reached our destination. On the train, we didn't speak. The other passengers saw we were newlyweds, gave ironic looks, and, at the first opportunity, left the compartment alone to us.

The place Lepprince selected was a spa in the province of Gerona, which we reached in a broken-down coach pulled by four half-dead nags. It consisted of a seignorial hotel surrounded by a few houses. The hotel had an extensive, well-tended garden in the French style, filled with cypresses and statues. At the end of the garden was a small woods with a path that led to the thermal baths. The view was splendid and rural, the air of the greatest purity.

We were received with disproportionate cordiality. It was teatime, and in the garden, sitting at cast-iron and marble tables protected by colored parasols were families and small groups. There was a tranquility in the air that warmed my heart.

Our rooms were on the second floor of the hotel, and, to judge by those I saw later, they were the most sumptuous and expensive. We had a suite—bedroom, bath, and sitting room. The bedroom and sitting room had windows that opened onto a terrace with rosebushes in blue ceramic vases. The furniture was superb and the bed, wider than it was long, was covered by a canopy that held up the mosquito net. In each one of the rooms there was an electric fan that kept the air fresh and fluttered strips of paper that frightened away the insects that came in from the garden.

María Coral stayed in the suite to unpack, and I took a walk outdoors. As I passed by the tables, the gentlemen stood up to say hello, the ladies nodded their heads, and the young girls stared timidly into their steaming cups of tea—as if they were reading a romantic future in the leaves. It amused me to respond to these ceremonious greetings with a tip of my Panama hat.

Pere Parells's wife and other ladies signaled to all the guests whose eye they could catch and whispered back and forth, accompanying their chatter with malicious giggles or severe gestures of repulsion according to whatever was being said. The arrival of the old financier silenced them.

"We're leaving," said Pere Parells to his wife.

"What!" exclaimed the ladies. "You're not leaving now, are you?"

"We are," said Mrs. Parells, as she got to her feet. The years had taught her not to ask questions and certainly not to contradict. Theirs was a happy relationship. In the vestibule, she asked her husband if something was wrong.

"I'll tell you everything right away. Now, let's go. Where's your coat?"

A young maid brought various overcoats until the old couple identified their own. She begged their pardon for her awkwardness, alleging she was new to the house. Pere Parells accepted this incongruous excuse and asked her to get him a cab. The maid didn't know what to do. Pere Parells suggested she consult the butler. The butler was equally perplexed. There were no taxis in that neighborhood. Perhaps down in the plaza they would find a taxi stand or a carriage stop.

"And couldn't you send someone?"

"Sorry, sir, but the entire staff is busy with the party. I'd be happy to go myself, but I have express orders not to leave the house for any reason. I'm sorry, sir."

Pere opened the door and walked out into the garden. The stars were shining, and the breeze had died down.

"We'll take a little stroll. Good night."

They crossed the garden. A man was standing guard next to the entrance gate. Pere and his wife waited for him to open the gate, but he didn't move. So Pere tried to open it himself but couldn't do it.

"It's locked," said the man. He didn't look like a guard, to judge by his manners, although, at the same time, he was dressed like one.

"So I see. Open up."

"I can't. Orders."

"Orders? Whose orders? Has everyone gone crazy?"

The man, wearing a striped waiter's vest, showed Pere his identification. "Police."

"So what does this mean? Are we under arrest or something?"

"No, sir, but the house is under guard. No one can enter or leave without authorization."

"Whose authorization?"

"The chief inspector's."

"And where is the chief inspector?" howled Pere Parells.

"Inside, at the party. But I can't go get him, because he's incognito. You'll have to wait. Orders are orders. Got a cigarette?"

"No. And will you please open this gate right now? Do you know with whom you're dealing? I'm Pere Parells! This is ridiculous, understand? Ridiculous! What are all these precautions about? Are you afraid we're going to steal the silverware?"

"Pere," said his wife calmly, "let's go back to the house."

"I don't want to! I'm fed up with that house! We'll wait here until they open the gate!"

"As long as you're thinking of staying awhile, I'll just slip off to the bathroom," said the policeman. "I'm just about wetting my pants."

The old financier and his wife went back to the vestibule and spoke with the butler, who spoke with Lepprince. Finally, a guest who was wandering through the rooms with a solitary, circumspect air joined them.

"My wife is feeling ill, and we'd like to go home. I suppose that's still not a crime. I'm Pere Parells," he said in a cutting tone. "Please do me the favor of having the gate opened."

"Instantly," said the inspector. "Allow me to accompany you, and please excuse the annoyance. We're expecting the arrival of some people whose presence obliges us to take these uncomfortable precautions. Believe me, it's as big a bother for us as it is for you."

The policeman at the gate was urinating behind a bush when the three of them arrived.

"Cuadrado, open the gate!" ordered the inspector. Cuadrado buttoned his trousers and ran to carry out the order. In the street, Pere Parells felt a shiver of indignation.

"Shameful!"

There were police stationed on the sidewalks, and at every corner there were mounted *Guardia Civiles* wearing swords and three-cornered hats. Whenever the police spied the old couple, they scrutinized them from head to toe. On the hill just above the plaza, they heard muffled noises, and the ground began to shake. They stepped back against a garden wall. Up on the hill came horses and coaches. The police posted on the sidewalks brought their hands to their holsters, alert for the slightest irregularity. The mounted men guarding the corners unsheathed their sabers and presented arms. The coaches came closer, the horses' hooves echoed against the cobbles. Trumpets blared. Some neighbors, astounded by the unexpected commotion, poked their heads out of windows, only to be violently called back inside by the police stationed inside the house. There were armed men even in the treetops. The fog gave a ghostly aspect to the procession.

Pere Parells and his wife, paralyzed with astonishment and huddled against the wall, saw pass before their eyes a regiment of cuirassiers and several carriages flanked by hussars whose lances tore leaves off the lower branches off the trees. Some coaches had their curtains lowered, others did not. In one of the last coaches, Pere glimpsed a face he recognized. The galloping procession left the still-frozen couple covered by a cloud of dust. Pere recovered from his stupefaction and said in a low voice, "This is too much."

"Who was it?" asked his wife, with a slight tremor in her voice.

"The king. Let's go."

"Inspector Vázquez, you must hear me out. Just listen to what I have to tell you and you won't be sorry. A crime is always a crime."

Inspector Vázquez threw the papers he was reading down on the desk and focused a fulminating stare on his ragged confidant, who was rubbing his hands together and balancing first on one foot, then on the other in a desperate attempt to be noticed.

"Who the hell let this bird into my office?" bellowed the inspector, addressing the peeling paint on his ceiling.

"There was no one here, so I took the liberty . . . ," explained his confidant, advancing toward the desk covered with newspapers and photographs.

"I swear by Christ's blood, by the eternal salvation of my . . . !" Vázquez started to say, but he stopped when he realized he was using the same religious terminology as his annoying visitor. "Why can't you leave me in peace? Get out!"

"Inspector, I've been trying to speak with you for five days now."

There were only two days left of the seven the conspirators allotted Nemesio, and he hadn't found a single clue related to Pajarito de Soto's death. The Savolta murder had cut him off, and the police were concentrating on solving that crime to the exclusion of all others. Also, his efforts to find the conspirators and warn them of the fact that Inspector Vázquez was looking for them in connection with the Savolta affair had been met by an absolute rejection from every one of the sources he'd approached during those five unlucky days.

"Five days?" said the inspector. "They've seemed like five years to me! Let me give you some advice, buddy. Get out and stay out. The next time I see you snooping around here, I'll have you locked up. You've been warned. Now get out of my sight!"

Nemesio walked out of the office and down to the ground floor filled with dire foreboding. But he was soon distracted by an unexpected incident. As he reached the bottom stair, Nemesio detected unusual movement: there were shouts, and policemen were running in every direction. *Something's going on. I'd better get out of here now.* He was trying to do just that, when a uniformed policeman grabbed him by the arm and dragged him to the far corner of the room.

"Out of the way."

"What's going on?"

"They're bringing in some dangerous prisoners."

Nemesio waited, holding his breath. From his corner, he could see the entrance, and, parked in front of it, a paddy wagon. A double file of armed police formed a path from the wagon to the building. They brought the prisoners out of the wagon. Nemesio tried to run, but the policeman still held him by the arm. The silence was only broken by the clinking of chains. The four prisoners entered. The youngest was weeping; Julián had lost his beret, had a black eye and bloodstains on his sheepskin jacket, held a manacled hand against his ribs, and his legs gave way as he walked; the man with the scar looked serene, although he had deep circles under his eyes. Nemesio thought he'd die.

"What did they do?" he whispered in the ear of the policeman guarding him.

"It looks like they're the ones who killed Savolta."

"But Savolta died at midnight on New Year's Eve."

"Shut up!"

He didn't dare say that he'd been with the prisoners at that precise moment in the photographer's studio, that Julián had brought him there by force. He was afraid of being implicated in the matter, so he obeyed and kept silent. Uselessly, however, because the man with the scar had seen him. He nudged Julián with his elbow, and when Julián caught sight of Nemesio, he shrieked, in a voice that seemed to boil out of his guts, "You finally sold us out, you son of a bitch!"

One of the guards hit him with the butt of his rifle, and Julián fell to the floor.

"Take them away!" ordered an individual dressed like a poor man.

The sad procession passed by Nemesio. Two agents were dragging Julián by his armpits, blood pouring out of him. The man with the scar stopped opposite Nemesio and gave him a freezing scornful smile.

"We should have killed you, Nemesio. But I never thought you'd do this."

He was pushed forward. It took Nemesio a few seconds to regain his composure. He tore himself violently away from the policeman holding his arm and ran back up the stairs. In the hall, he ran into Inspector Vázquez.

"Inspector, it wasn't those men! I swear. They didn't kill Savolta."

The inspector looked at him as if he were seeing a cockroach walking over his bed.

"But . . . you're still here?" he said, turning bright red.

"Inspector, this time you'll have to listen to me whether you want to or not. Those men didn't do it, those men . . ."

"Get him out of here!" shouted the inspector, pushing Nemesio aside and striding forward.

"Inspector!" implored Nemesio, while two powerful agents dragged him bodily toward the door. "Inspector! I was with them, I was with them when Savolta was killed. Inspector!!"

Cortabanyes met with Lepprince in the library. Lepprince was pacing nervously, his face serious, and his gestures brusque. Cortabanyes, nursing his laborious digestion, heard explanations sprawled in an armchair, attentive to Lepprince's words, his eyes half-open, his lip hanging. When Lepprince finished, the lawyer rubbed his eyes with his fists, taking his time before speaking.

"Does he know more than he says, or is he saying more than he knows?"

Lepprince stood stock-still in the center of the room and looked Cortabanyes up and down.

"I don't know. But this is no time for word games, Cortabanyes. Whatever he knows, he's dangerous."

"Unless he's got nothing concrete in his hands he isn't. He's old and alone, as I've already said. I really doubt that at this time in his life he's going to embark on an adventure that will do him no good. If he only suspects, he'll keep quiet. Today he was excited, but tomorrow he'll see things in a different way. It's to his benefit not to make trouble. We'll convince him to retire and resign himself to the pleasant labor of clipping coupons."

"And if he's got more than the mere suspicion going through his head?"

Cortabanyes scratched the few hairs he had on his bumpy cranium.

"What can he know?"

Lepprince began pacing again. The lawyer's calm restored his confidence but maddened him at the same time.

"Why the hell ask me!? Do you think he'll just tell us?" He stood still, his mouth open, his eyes fixed, and one hand in the air. "Wait! Remember . . . ? Remember Pajarito de Soto's famous letter?"

"Yes, do you think Pere Parells has it?"

"It's a possibility. Someone had to receive it."

"No, it isn't probable. All that happened a long time ago. Why would Parells have kept quiet for three years and only now . . . ? Because business is bad," he answered himself, as he usually did. "It's a hypothesis. But I doubt it. Especially, and we've argued this point a thousand times, it isn't certain the letter ever existed. The only proof was what that lunatic said who told Vázquez."

"Vázquez believed him."

"Sure, but Vázquez is a long way from here."

Lepprince added nothing more, and both men were silent until Cortabanyes said, "What do you think you'll do?"

"I still haven't decided."

"I'd advise you to be . . ."

"I know, calm."

"And above all, no . . ."

A huge commotion came from the salon next door. The orchestra stopped playing, trumpets sounded, and horses stamped their hooves in the garden.

"They're here," said Lepprince. "Let's be with everyone else, we'll go on talking later."

"Listen," said the lawyer before Lepprince reached the library door.

"What do you want?" answered Lepprince impatiently.

"Is it absolutely necessary for you to keep Max with you at all times?"

Lepprince smiled, opened the door, and joined his guests. The voice of the butler asking for attention imposed an expectant silence in which the high-sounding announcement echoed.

"His Majesty the King!"

We had dinner in the hotel dining room, and afterward took a walk through the various salons. In one, people were dancing to an orchestra playing waltzes, but since the guests at the spa had come to cure illnesses rather than to amuse themselves, there were only a few clumsy dancers. In another salon, where a fire was blazing, some matrons with complicated hairdos and huge stomachs were chattering. The third room was reserved for gambling. When we got back to our rooms, the unnaturalness of the situation became obvious to us, our movements became awkward, and we dragged ourselves aimlessly around. Finally María Coral broke the silence with some simple and logical words, which in those circumstances sounded like a declaration of principles. "I'm sleepy. I'm going to bed."

It was a motion, and I seconded it without comment. I took my pajamas and robe out of the wardrobe and went into the bathroom. There I calmly changed, giving María Coral time to do the same. When I'd finished, I lit a cigarette and smoked it, thinking it would help me meditate. But it wasn't the case: it burned, leaving my head as empty as it had been during the past weeks. In the bathroom it was cold; I noted that my extremities were stiff, and my back had a tremor. It was foolish to stay there, sitting on the edge of the tub, fleeing from nothing in no direction. I decided to face facts and improvise appropriate behavior as I went along. I opened the door and walked out. The bedroom was in darkness. The light from the bathroom allowed me to see the silhouette of the bed. I put out the light and felt my way. I had to go around the bed, tracing the edge because María Coral was on the side closest to the bathroom door—I wasn't going to climb over her. Her breathing seemed regular and deep, and I concluded she was asleep. I told myself it was better that way and took off my robe and slippers and slipped between the sheets. I closed my eyes and tried to go to sleep. It wasn't easy; before I drifted off, I had time to think over a long list of banalities: that I hadn't wound my watch, that I didn't know if Lepprince had paid the hotel in advance, that I didn't know how to tip the staff, that I hadn't sent my clothes out to be washed. I don't know how long I slept, but no doubt it was a short, light sleep because I woke up suddenly with my head clear and my nerves tense. Next to me, I felt the presence of a warm body, and my fingers held the pleats of a silky nightgown. The situation called for one kind of action or another, but both God and the devil seemed to have abandoned the battle-ground. There are moments in life when we know that everything depends on quick intuitions and abilities; I was in one of those moments, but in my head there was a blur instead of ideas. I heard the bells of a distant clock: two o'clock. I experienced the same sense of helplessness as an exhausted camper lost in a thick woods who sees the sun setting and realizes he's been in that same place before. Finally I fell back to sleep.

Against all expectations, I woke up in a good mood. It was a radiant morning: the sunlight came in through the spaces in the curtains and formed circles on the floor, turning it into a Lilliputian stage. I jumped out of bed, went into the bathroom, shaved, brushed my hair, and dressed, carefully choosing the most appropriate clothes for that solemn spring day. When I finished, I went back to the bedroom. María Coral was still asleep. She had an unusual way of sleeping: stretched out on her back, with the covers pulled up to her chin, and her hands on top of the covers. I remember the way dogs roll over on their backs and raise their legs to have their bellies scratched by their masters. Was this the right moment? I hesitated, and, in these cases, as everyone knows, hesitation means giving up. Or a defeat. I opened the curtains, and the sun poured in, not leaving even a corner in darkness. María Coral half opened her eyes and emitted some complaining noises, half grunt, half deep breath.

"Get up; look what a beautiful day it is," I exclaimed.

"Who told you to wake me up?" was her reply.

"I thought you'd want to enjoy the sun."

"Well, you thought wrong. Have breakfast sent up and close the curtains."

"I'll close the curtains, but I won't order breakfast. Right now I'm going down to have breakfast in the garden. If you want, you can join me; if not, fend for yourself."

I closed the curtains, took my stick and hat, and went down to the dining room. The French doors were wide open, and a few people were sitting at the tables on the terrace. Only some old people chose to take the sun inside, protected from the air, which was cool and even painful because of its incredible purity. An intermittent breeze swayed the bushes in the park.

"Would you like to order breakfast, sir?"

"Yes, please."

"Hot chocolate, coffee, or tea?"

"I'd like café au lait, if the coffee's good."

"It's excellent, sir. Would you like croissants, toast, or some rolls?"

"A bit of everything."

"Will you be breakfasting alone, or shall I also serve madam's breakfast?"

"I'll be alone . . . No, just a moment, bring the same thing for my wife."

As I was ordering, I saw María Coral walk in, still sleepy and ill-humored. But her appearance didn't fool me: she'd come down to have breakfast with me. I stood up, helped her be seated, told her what I'd ordered, and buried myself in the newspaper. The ordeal of the night was over, and yet an electric charge floated in the air and presaged new anguish. I decided to speed things up. After breakfast, I suggested to María Coral that we go up to our suite "to take a little rest." She stared at me.

"I know what you want. Come for a walk, and we'll talk."

We strolled silently through the garden, and when we came to the end, we sat down on a stone bench. The stone was cold, the leaves on the trees were rustling, a bird was singing; I'll never forget that scene. María Coral told me she'd thought things over and that the situation demanded absolute clarity. She declared she'd married me out of self-interest, that no feeling of any kind had entered into her decision. Her conscience was clear because she supposed I wasn't the victim of any hoax and that I myself had married her as a way of getting ahead; therefore, what was blameworthy in such a marriage was compensated for by the fact that in entering into it she'd avoided having its anguishing circumstances lead her to situations a thousand times worse.

"We've begun in reverse," she added. "Most people get to know each other first and then get married. We're married, and we barely know each other."

Starting from that basis, and above and beyond the formality of our union, we should proceed like sensible people. A premature intimacy could only lead us to tensions and misgivings. It would only nurture hatred and rancor. Besides, she considered herself a decent woman (she said it humbly, lowering her eyes, while a slight blush passed over her smooth cheeks). To give herself to me would seem like a kind of prostitution.

"I know that my life does not authorize me to demand respect. It's true I worked as an acrobat in the most sickening shows, but away from my work, I was always proper."

The need to be believed burned in her eyes. A tear formed in her eye like an unexpected visitor, like the first breeze of spring, like the first snow, like the first flower to bloom.

"If I went with Lepprince, it was for love. I was a girl, and his personality and his wealth dazzled me. I didn't know how to be his equal. I killed myself trying to please him, but I could see the irritation in his gestures, his words, and his eyes. When he threw me out, I accepted it as fair. He was the first man in my life . . . and the last, until now. I will always respect you, if you respect me. If you want my body, I will not refuse you, but you may be sure that you will be vilifying me if you take me. And it's quite possible I will run away from you. If that happens, you will be responsible for the rest. You decide: you're the man, and it's only logical you should give the orders. But just realize that whatever you decide, you'll have to live with it."

"I accept your conditions," I exclaimed.

She bent over and kissed my hand. That's how our days passed at the spa. At the time I thought they were pleasant; now I consider them happy. Better that way. There are events that are happy when they take place and become bitter in memory, and others, insipid in themselves, which with time take on a nostalgic hue of happiness. The happy days last only briefly; the second kind fill our whole life and provide solace when disaster strikes. I, personally, prefer them. María Coral and I carried out our pact to the letter. Our relationship was of a geometric correctness; on my side at least there was no violence or effort in observing all the clauses. María Coral turned out to be a silent, discreet partner, one with whom I barely exchanged half a dozen insignificant comments over the course of a day. We would take separate walks; if by chance we ran into each other in the labyrinthine garden, we would stop briefly and exchange a few words before going back to our independent strolls. The words we exchanged were cordial.

We ate lunch and dinner together merely out of social propriety and because it was more comfortable for María Coral if I chose the dishes: the menu, with its French names, upset her.

"I wonder if you ever ate anything but sausage sandwiches," I said to her one day.

"Maybe, but at least I don't try to give the impression that I've only eaten caviar and lobster," she retorted.

I would laugh at her rough-and-ready comebacks, because it was in those instants when María Coral showed her best side, her true personality of a poor, frightened girl. At the time, she was nineteen. She didn't realize it, but until then no one understood her as I did. And for my part, even though I wouldn't confess it even to myself, I held the hope that the opaque tenderness I felt for her would one day, not in the distant future, have its reward. The spa setting, so calm, favored those kinds of daydreams. Tranquility reigned with undisputed ubiquity. María Coral and I were the only young members of that ailing community. Many guests, as I found out from a waiter, never left their rooms; some never left their beds, expecting to end their days in that spot. And except for the two of us, no one ever reached the end of the garden, unless it was in a wheelchair or hanging onto the solicitous arm of a staff member.

Among those wrecks, I made friends with an old mathematician, who claimed to have invented several revolutionary engines, which, incomprehensibly, the government ignored. He went on about perpetual motion and its application to pumping water out of the lower strata by the movement of those very strata. The incoherence of his arguments and a certain stutter in his voice gave his terminology a distant, poetic dimension, like a fairy tale. I also discovered a dusty politician from the Radical Party who was hell-bent on making me admire his scandalous amatory adventures, which without a doubt were the fruit of his imagination over the course of his long stay at the spa, the fruit of solitude, like the sprouting of a vine in the cracked walls of an abandoned cloister. One afternoon, just before sunset, we happened to be on the terrace, he and I, half asleep. The garden seemed to be deserted.

Suddenly, María Coral emerged from a cypress grove cut to form an arch. She was walking by herself with a decisive air. The politico put on his glasses, scratched his goatee, and nudged me with his elbow.

"Young man, did you see that beauty?"

"That lady, sir, is my wife."

Translated by Alfred Mac Adam

WORK

1975, *La verdad sobre el caso Savolta*, Seix Barral (novel).

1979, *El misterio de la cripta embrujada*, Seix Barral (novel).

1982, *El laberinto de las aceitunas*, Seix Barral (novel).

1986, *La ciudad de los prodigios*, Seix Barral (novel).

1986, *Nueva York*, Destino (essay).

1989, *La isla inaudita*, Seix Barral (novel).

1989, *Barcelona modernista*, Planeta (essay).

1990, *Restauración*, Seix Barral (novel).

1990, *Sin noticias de Gurb*, Seix Barral (play).

1992, *El año del diluvio*, Seix Barral (novel).

1996, *Una comedia ligera*, Seix Barral (novel).

2001, *La aventura del tocador de señoras*, Seix Barral (novel).

2001, *Pío Baroja*, Omega (essay).

2002, *El ultimo trayecto de Horacio Dos*, Seix Barral (novel).

2006, *Mauricio o las elecciones primarias*, Seix Barral (novel).

2007, *¿Quién se acuerda de Armando Palacio Valdés?* Galaxia Gutenberg (essay).

2008, *El asombroso viaje de Pomponio Flato*, Seix Barral (novel).

2008, *Gloria*, Seix Barral (play).

2009, *Tres vidas de santos*, Seix Barral (includes the stories "La Ballena," "El final de Dubslav," "El malentendido").

2010, *Riña de gatos. Madrid 1936*, Planeta (novel).

2011, "El camino del cole," Alfaguara (children's story).

2012, *El enredo de la bolsa y la vida*, Seix Barral (novel).

·

ENGLISH TRANSLATIONS

1990, *City of Marvels*, translated by Bernard Molloy, Pocket Books (novel).

1992, *The Truth About the Savolta Case*, translated by Alfred Mac Adam, Pantheon (novel).

1996, *The Year of the Flood*, translated by Nick Caistor, Harvill Press (novel).

2000, *A Light Comedy*, translated by Nick Caistor, Random House, (novel).

2007, *No Word From Gurb*, translated by Nick Caistor, Telegram Books (novel).

2009, *The Mystery of the Enchanted Crypt*, Nick Caistor, Telegram Books (novel).

2011, *The Olive Labyrinth*, translated by Nick Caistor, Telegram Books (novel).

2013, *An Englishman in Madrid*, translated by Nick Caistor, Maclehose Press (novel).

•

AWARDS AND RECOGNITIONS

1976, Premio de la Crítica for *La verdad sobre el caso Savolta*.

1987, Premio Ciutat de Barcelona for *La ciudad de los prodigios*.

1988, Best Book of the Year Award, *Lire* magazine (France) for *La ciudad de los prodigios*.

1988, Finalist for Premio Grinzane Cavour in the category of Foreign Fiction (Italy) for *La ciudad de los prodigios*.

1988, Finalist for prix Médicis y Femina (France) for *La ciudad de los prodigios*.

1992, *Elle* magazine Readers Award for *El año del diluvio*.

1998, Best Foreign Book Award (France) for *Una comedia ligera*.

2002, Premio al major libro del año, awarded by Gremio de Libreros de Madrid, for *La aventura del tocador de señoras*.

2007, Premio Fundación José Manuel Lara for *Mauricio o las elecciones primarias*.

2009, Premio Pluma de Plata for *El asombroso viaje de Pomponio Flato*.

2010, Premio Planeta for *Riña de gatos*.

2013, Premio del Libro Europeo for *Riña de gatos*.

CRISTINA

FERNÁNDEZ

CUBAS

(Spain, 1945)

C ristina Fernández Cubas is part of the lineage of female writers with a special gift for the short story. She was born in 1945 in Arenys de Mar, a Catalan coastal town where she lived until she was fifteen, when she moved to Barcelona. She finished high school there, studied Law, participated in university and independent theater groups (she met Mario Gas, Carlos Canut, Carlos Velat, Santi Sans, Emma Cohen, Enrique Vila-Matas, and Carlos Trías, among others) and in December of 1973, along with her then husband Carlos Trías, she embarked on an adventure to Latin America, a trip without a return ticket that ended up lasting two years. In 1978, and after spending a long period in Barcelona, she settled in Cairo for ten months. It was while she was there that she received a letter from Tusquets Editores expressing their interest in publishing her first book: *Mi hermana Elba*.

The book appeared in 1980 and it was well received by both critics and readers. Far from more popular forms, Fernández Cubas stuck, from the beginning, to the genre of the short story to show her vision of the world: an estranged look in the face of the thing that reality, so alien and changeable, presents on a daily basis. With *Los altillos de Brumal*, in 1983—previously adapted for film by Cristina Andreu with the title *Brumal—El ángulo del horror*, in 1990, and with *Con Agatha en Estambul*, in 1994, the author went back to some of the settings of her first stories—points on the map where her biography and literature coexist—and insisted on her best-loved subjects: the double, dreams, the disturbing nature of the quotidian, and the threshold of the unknown.

In 1985 she published her first novel, *El año de Gracia*, an unsettling adventure set within the framework of a mysterious island inhabited by bloodthirsty sheep and murderers; a genre she would return to ten years later in *El columpio*, a story that moves between a mother's evocative dream and a reality comprised of disconnected memories. She is also the author of a play, *Hermanas de sangre* (1998), adapted for Catalan television in 2001 by Jesús Garay. That same year she published a book of recollections, *Cosas que ya no existen*, five years later, *Parientes pobres del diablo*, three disturbing stories, not without humor, in which appearances, ghosts, and dreams pull us into the hidden interiors of the individual.

Todos los cuentos, a volume that collected the entirety of her short oeuvre, published in 2008, won, among others, the Premio Ciudad de Barcelona and the Premio Salambó de Narrativa, deserved recognition for an essential career in Spanish fiction.

THE ACORN

I figured I couldn't leave out "The Journey." Rarely have I been able to express so many things with such a small number of words. And ever since then, since the moment I wrote it, this short story that's barely a page long has stuck with me wherever I've gone. Like a letter of introduction. Like a business card.

I've been similarly affected by "The Angle of Horror." Of all my work it's probably one of the "coldest'" stories. But it's also the best reflection of my poetics, of the importance I give to something so inseparable from the genre as perspective. In "The Angle of Horror" everything is perspective.

With respect to the novel *El año de Gracia*, I'd like to recall its origin. The starting point was a story in the newspaper *El País*. It was about an environmental group, "Operation Dark Harvest," and their failed expedition to the island of Gruinard, one of the Hebrides off the northwest coast of Scotland. The island had been contaminated with anthrax in 1941, as a precaution against a possible biological war with Germany, and the goal of the environmentalists was to make off with soil samples and denounce the dangers posed by its mere existence. But what I really found interesting was the geographical location, its characteristics, the setting. An island closed to public curiosity, less than two kilometers from civilization, with the only people granted access being a team of scientists who, with the necessary precautions, visited the island every two years. And above all, this fact: the former inhabitants of the island, mostly shepherds, had been forced to evacuate. On the island, then, there only remained a number of sheep, abandoned to chance . . . And from there my imagination took over. I wondered about the effects of the anthrax on those flocks of sheep; I wondered if it were possible the sheep had become feral and developed murderous tendencies; I thought that perhaps, one shepherd—just one—hiding among the fog and craggy rocks, had refused to follow the order and stayed on the island . . . And so *El año de Gracia* was born. The story of a young man, well versed in theology and dead languages—though completely unaware of the ways of the world—whose sister Grace gives him "the gift of a year" and fate ends up taking him to the island . . . I still remember the writing process with a mixture of nostalgia and fondness. Gruinard gave me the opportunity to go on an anachronistic adventure in the middle of the twentieth century. And I took it as far as it would go.

In Conversation with the Dead

With all my respect for Quevedo (and his beautiful sonnet) I have to express my resistance to using the word "dead" to refer to authors I've enjoyed—and still enjoy—reading, without respect to dates, centuries, or other trivialities. Literature is immortality. In many cases, at least. And it has been in my readings of Homer, Cervantes, Coleridge, Potocki, Bécquer, Poe, Kafka, James, Hoffmann, Rulfo, stories by Pardo Bazán or the anonymous authors of the Spanish narrative tradition, just to name a few by way of example. Their works have lives of their own, and therefore, they persist among us.

Coda

You've been one of the pioneers of the short story in Spain. Has it been difficult to find a place among the reading public?

For a long time, the short story wasn't highly respected in Spain. Or, wrongly, it was considered an apprenticeship, a stepping-stone to the novel. If I were to reread the interviews I did in 1980, when I published my first book, I imagine I would be surprised by two things: the insistence on asking me when I was going to write a novel, and my stubbornness (of which I'm more than proud) in defending the short story and making it clear that it is a genre in and of itself. But to answer your question, the truth is that, in my case at least, I found a place among the reading public right away. And I'll mention something that lots of people overlook and that might clarify the reason the short story still isn't as popular and as widespread as the novel. The reader. The marvelous reader of stories. An accomplice. Because it's a very special reader who appreciates intensity more than length, who isn't lazy, and above all—contrary to what people believe—who isn't hurried. A reader who doesn't mind going back to the beginning if something isn't entirely clear, who doesn't mind meditating a while upon reaching the end. In sum, an active reader. And I think there are more and more readers like that. Just like there are more and more writers cultivating the genre. Now there are lots of us. And that suggests that the short story is in excellent health.

In your writing there's often a transition from childhood to loss of innocence, portrayed as a sort of rite of passage. In narrating this you use some elements of horror or of the fantastic in order to create an effect of disruption of everyday norms. Can you elaborate on this?

I like to move in everyday scenarios where, suddenly, a disruptive element barges in. I don't know if it can be considered a "fantastic" technique, or if, on the contrary, it constitutes something just as real as life itself. I have my doubts. I rely on Blaise Pascal, whom I cite frequently: "The ultimate function of reason consists of recognizing that there is an infinite number of things that surpass it . . ." But anyway, regarding the passage from childhood to adolescence, I think that, very often, that brutal and painful transition doesn't even need external elements. It's sufficient, even excessive, in and of itself. Or going back to what I said earlier: "life itself."

To what extent do you think you've been influenced by living near the Mediterranean?

Naturally. It's influenced me quite a lot. I was born in Arenys de Mar and I lived there until I was fifteen. I used to fall asleep to the sound of the waves, and the first thing I saw when I got up was the sea. The Mediterranean was like an extension of the house. The beach, the sunshades, the striped beach huts of summer . . . these things appear in some of my stories. And maybe because I always thought of the Mediterranean as domestic, familiar, and quotidian, any time I wanted to stage a tempest, a shipwreck, or an extraordinary adventure, I passed over my friend and invariably turned to the Atlantic. The *Mare Tenebrosum* of the Old World!

In an interview with El País *you mentioned the stories that don't let you go until you've finished them, that leave you exhausted, and you cite Cortázar, who calls them "stories against the clock."*

You could also call them "hijacking stories." You can't break free from them until you finish them. And then yes, then you can breathe easy, as if you'd just taken off an enormous backpack, a burden . . . They're usually not very long (it would be hard to stand so much tension) and very frequently they turn rather mysterious even for the author. For a time, at least. Afterward, you start tying up loose ends, understanding where they came from and why they grabbed you like that . . . But all of this belongs to the secret life of stories.

A THOUSAND FORESTS

One day a friend's mother told me a strange story. We were at her house, in the historic district of Palma de Mallorca, and from the interior balcony, which overlooked a small garden, you could see the façade of the enclosed convent next door. My friend's mother used to visit the abbess; she'd bring ice cream for the community, and they'd chat for hours through a lattice window. By then the rules of enclosure were less strict than in years past. Nothing was stopping the abbess from interrupting her seclusion once in a while to go out into the world, if she'd wanted to. But she flat-out refused. She had lived within those four walls for nearly thirty years, and the lure of the outside world didn't interest her in the least. That's why my friend's mother thought she must be dreaming when one morning the doorbell rang and a dark figure appeared, silhouetted against the light in the doorway. "If it's alright with you," the abbess said after the obligatory greetings, "I'd like to see the convent from the outside." And then, on the same balcony where I was told this story, she sat for some minutes in silence. "It's very pretty," she said finally. And, just as cheerfully as she'd come to the door, she said goodbye and returned to the convent. I don't think she ever left again, but at this point it doesn't matter. I still think of the abbess's journey, as I did then, as one of the longest journeys of all the long journeys I've ever heard of.

Translated by Emily Davis

•

FROM *EL AÑO DE GRACIA* (THE YEAR OF GRACE)
[A NOVEL]

The first word the ancient shepherd mumbled over my sickbed—or the first one I seem to remember—was *Grock*. At the time, confused by what appeared to be a strange being that was half sheep and half man, it didn't occur to me that my timely visitor was capable of naming himself, and I assumed it was bleating. But the long recovery, and that strange lucidity that sometimes comes with fever, led me to babble different phrases in various languages until I understood that Grock was speaking a rudimentary English peppered with an abundance of expressions in Gaelic—a language that, unfortunately, I knew nothing about other than its mere existence—and that if I dispensed with any sort of flourish and instead resorted to the purest simplification, my rescuer's eyes lit up, he nodded or shook his head, and he tried, in turn, to reduce his language as much as possible and limit himself to naming things.

Learning Grock's language wasn't terribly burdensome. What helped wasn't so much my knowledge of English as the evidence that the old man's peculiar syntax was extremely similar to that of primitive languages, and even to that of many of our children when, provided with a certain vocabulary, they start to express their needs. Grock's sentences frequently began directly with the material object of interest, then moved on to the accessory information, to the how and why, to the circumstances, and only later, much later, to the real answers to my questions. I asked him repeatedly about the name of the island we were on, and his answer was: "Grock." I tried to be much more explicit, and adding gestures and faces, I said: "Island . . . This island . . . What is it called?" The answer was invariable: "Grock." It was obvious that he didn't distinguish between his name and what was an object of his property. Grock had spent too many years among sheep.

But I couldn't curse my luck. Thanks to the shepherd's care and the bits of information I managed to drag out of him with a great deal of patience, I was able to form an approximate idea of where we were located. In an earlier time the Island of Grock had been inhabited by several families of shepherds. Later, "many, many years ago . . . ," for reasons the old man wasn't aware of or didn't know how to explain, the families gathered their belongings, left their flocks behind, and abandoned the land. Only Grock remained on the island, in charge of hundreds of sheep, the mothers of the mothers of the mothers of those quadrupeds that had made such an impression on me and that, as I seemed to understand, either because they were too many to be controlled by one man, or because the shepherd avoided them, didn't take long to go from tame flocks to feral, bloodthirsty packs. "They did very bad things to Grock," he said. "Very bad things." I soon discovered that the shepherd utterly despised them. When he talked about sheep, his face took on a terrifying appearance, his eyes shone with wild fury, and he reveled in reciting the long list of punishments he'd made them suffer to show them that he was Grock, the master of the island, and that they had done "very bad things." When I finally asked him what constituted the wicked actions of those beasts (secretly afraid he'd tell me), the ferocious gleam again dilated his pupils for a moment, then was replaced, almost immediately, by an unexpected expression of tenderness. "They killed Grock," he said.

For the first few days, I often had to resort to imagination, sometimes pure invention, to interpret the shepherd's perplexing statements. He insisted that I was from Glasgow—though, maybe, he was using that name to mean anywhere off the island—and he seemed very surprised by the story of the shipwreck, of my rescue, and of the subsequent disappearance of the remains of the *Providence*. I don't think Grock knew how to pretend, but the absurd possibility that the old man—almost like a child—might be unaware of the ship's mysterious destination left me baffled. Again I faced the large number of enigmas yet to be solved, and I had a feeling that the limited narrative faculties of my rescuer weren't going to be of much help to me for the time being.

I had surrendered myself to dark conjectures when Grock, who had just polished off my last bottle of gin, broke into wild laughter. I didn't have time to be startled. As if he'd suddenly remembered the reason for his boundless joy, the old man grabbed a case that was hanging from his neck, pulled out a wrinkled card and, still laughing, handed it to me. Here I had to rub my eyes to be sure I wasn't dreaming. What I had in my hands was a color photograph, a portrait of the shepherd himself, taken by an instant camera. So the island wasn't as deserted as I'd been led to believe. I didn't stop to think about what sort of disturbed mind would come up with the macabre idea of photographing Grock, nor did it seem appropriate to submit the shepherd to a new interrogation. All I knew how to do was join in his laughter as a simple proof of my good intentions. Between bursts of laughter, he told me about a little box with a button you could push, and little by little, shadows would appear, then colors, and finally, the image of a man. "A man," he said. The apparent magic of the camera was what truly amused the shepherd. I looked back at the snapshot with a shudder. I held in my hands the cold, raw embodiment of horror. In front of me, convulsing with laughter, was little more than an old, mad child who had absolutely no idea he was laughing at himself.

Translated by Emily Davis

•

"The Angle of Horror"
from *Todos los cuentos* (Collected Stories)

As she was knocking on the door for the third time, Julia realized that she should have done something days ago. She looked through the keyhole, couldn't see anything, and angrily paced up and down the roof terrace. She should have done something the moment she discovered her brother was hiding a secret, before the family had taken matters into their own hands and built up a wall of interrogations and reprimands. Because Carlos was still there. Locked inside a dark room, pretending to be mildly indisposed, he abandoned the solitude of the loft only to eat, and he was constantly annoyed, hidden behind opaque sunglasses, taking refuge in a strange, exasperating silence. "He's in love," his mother said. But Julia knew his odd behavior had nothing to do with the ups and downs of love or disillusionment. That's why she decided to keep watch on the top floor, at the door to his bedroom, peering through the keyhole, searching for the smallest sign of movement, waiting for the heat of summer to compel him to open the window overlooking the roof terrace. A long, narrow window she would jump in through, like a cat being chased, like the shadow of one of the sheets drying in the sun, appearing so quickly and unexpectedly that Carlos, overcome with surprise, would have no choice but to speak. At the very least, he would ask: "Who said you could burst in like that?" Or maybe: "Go away! Can't you see I'm busy?" And she would see. She would finally see what mysterious things were keeping her brother busy, she would understand his extreme paleness, and she would rush to offer help. But she had been keeping strict vigilance for more than two hours, and she was starting to feel ridiculous and humiliated. She abandoned her lookout post by the door, went out onto the roof terrace, and, as she had already done so many times that afternoon, again started counting the broken and cracked tiles, the plastic clothespins and the wooden ones, the exact number of steps separating her from the long, narrow window. She knocked on the glass and said to herself with a tired voice: "It's me, Julia." Really she should have said: "It's still me, Julia." But what did it matter now! This time, however, her ears pricked up. She thought she heard a faraway moan, the creak of rusted bedsprings, a few dragging steps, a metallic sound, another creak, and a clear, unexpected: "Come in. It's open." And at that moment, Julia felt a shudder very similar to the strange trembling that had gone through her body days earlier, when she'd suddenly understood that *something* was happening to her brother.

It had already been a couple of weeks since Carlos had come back from his first study abroad. September 2nd, the date she'd colored red on the calendar in her room and that now seemed to be getting further away and more impossible. She remembered seeing him at the foot of the stairs to the British Airways jumbo jet, waving one of his arms, and she could see herself, amazed that at eighteen he could still be growing, jumping excitedly on the airport terrace, blowing kisses and waving, pushing her way through to welcome him in the lobby. Carlos had returned. A little skinnier, quite a bit taller, and much paler. But Julia thought he was even more handsome than when he'd left, and she ignored her mother's comments about the deficient diet of the English or the incomparable excellence of the Mediterranean climate. They got in the car, her brother delighted by the prospect of spending a few weeks at the beach house, and when his father shot him a few innocent questions about the blonde girls in Brighton, Julia didn't laugh at her family's wisecracks. She was too excited and her head was buzzing with plans and projects. The next day, when their parents stopped asking questions and pestering him, she and Carlos would talk in secret about the summer's events. On the roof, like always, with their legs dangling off the edge, just like when they were little, when Carlos taught her to draw and she showed him her collection of trading cards. When they got to the front yard, Marta came bounding out to meet them and Julia marveled again at how much her brother had grown. "At eighteen," she thought. "How absurd!" But she didn't say anything.

Carlos had become entranced, staring at the front of the house as if he were seeing it for the first time. He had his head tilted to the right, his brow furrowed, and his lips stuck in a weird grimace that Julia couldn't interpret. He remained motionless for a few minutes, staring straight ahead with hypnotized eyes, unaware that the others were moving, hauling in luggage, and that Julia was right next to him. Then, hardly changing his posture, he rested his head on his left shoulder. There was a look of shock in his eyes, and the weird grimace was gone, replaced by an unambiguous expression of weariness and depression. He wiped his forehead with his hand, and focusing his eyes on the ground, he kept his head down as he followed the cobblestone path across the garden.

At dinner, his father kept bugging him about his conquests, and his mother was still worried about his lack of color. Marta made a couple of witty remarks that Carlos met with a smile. He seemed tired and drowsy. From traveling, maybe. He kissed the family goodnight and went to bed.

The next day Julia got up very early, reviewed the list of readings that Carlos had recommended to her when he left, gathered up the sheets of paper she'd taken notes on, and climbed up onto the roof. After a while, tired of waiting, she jumped onto the terrace. Her brother's window was ajar, but there didn't seem to be anyone in the room. She went to the balustrade and looked down into the garden.

Carlos was there, in the same position he'd been in the night before, staring at the house with a mixture of astonishment and consternation, tilting his head, first to the right, then to the left, gluing his eyes to the ground and dejectedly following the cobblestone path that separated him from the house. It was then that Julia suddenly understood that *something* was happening to her brother.

The impossible love hypothesis was gaining strength during the family's tense lunchtime conversations. An English girl, a young, pale, blonde girl from Brighton. The melancholy of first love, the sadness of distance, the apathy that boys his age tended to direct toward everything that was unrelated to the object of their passion. But that was at the beginning. When Carlos was only acting shy and unsociable, startled by questions, averting his eyes, rejecting little Marta's attempts to comfort him. Maybe at that point she should have acted with conviction. But now Carlos had said: "Come in. It's open," and gathering her courage, she had no choice but to push the door open.

At first she failed to notice anything besides the suffocating heat and a halting, plaintive breathing. After a while, she learned to distinguish among the shadows: Carlos was sitting at the foot of the bed, and his eyes seemed to reflect the only glints of light that had managed to enter his fortress. Were those his eyes? Julia opened one of the window shutters just slightly and sighed with relief. Yes, that dispirited boy, hidden behind those impenetrable sunglasses, his forehead dotted with little gleaming drops of sweat, was her brother. The only thing was that his pallor now seemed too alarming, his behavior too inexplicable, for her to be able to explain it to the rest of the family.

—They're going to call a doctor, she said.

Carlos didn't react. He sat there for a few minutes with his head hanging down toward the floor, knocking his knees together, twiddling his fingers as if he were playing a children's tune on the keys of a nonexistent piano.

—They want to make you eat something . . . They want you to leave this filthy room.

Julia thought she saw her brother shiver. "The room," she thought. "What could he possibly find in this room to keep him here for so much time?" She looked around and was surprised to find that not everything was as messy as she'd expected. From the bed, Carlos was breathing heavily. "He's going to speak," she thought, and smothered by the stifling atmosphere, she timidly pushed one of the shutters and opened the window a crack.

—Julia, she heard. I know you won't understand a word of what I'm going to tell you. But I need to talk to someone.

A glimmer of pride lit up her eyes. Carlos, just as in other times, was going to let her in on his secrets, make her his most faithful ally, ask her for help, which she would rush to offer. Now she knew that she'd done the right thing in keeping watch by that shadowy room, acting like a ridiculous amateur spy, bearing the silence, measuring the dimensions of the bleak, scorching roof terrace ad nauseam. Because Carlos had said: "I need to talk to someone . . ." And she was there, next to the half-open window, ready to listen attentively to everything he chose to confide, without daring to intervene. It didn't matter that he was speaking to her in a low voice, hard to understand, as if he were afraid of hearing from his own lips the secret motive behind his unease. "It all comes down to a matter of . . ." Julia couldn't make out the last word uttered under his breath, nearly a whisper, but she didn't want to interrupt.

She took a wrinkled cigarette from her pocket and held it out to her brother. Carlos refused without looking up.

—It all started in Brighton, on a day like so many others, he said. I went to bed, closed the window so I wouldn't hear the rain, and fell asleep. That was in Brighton . . . did I say that already?

Julia nodded and cleared her throat.

—I dreamed that I'd aced my exams, that they were showering me with diplomas and medals, that suddenly I wanted to be here with all of you and, without thinking twice about it, I decided to come home as a surprise. So I got on a train, an incredibly long and skinny train, and before I knew it, I'd arrived here. "This is a dream," I told myself and, extremely pleased, I did all I could to keep from waking up. I got off the train and headed toward the house, singing. It was early morning and the streets were deserted. Suddenly I realized I'd left my suitcase in the train compartment, the gifts I'd bought for you, the diplomas and medals, and that I should go back to the station before the train headed back to Brighton. "This is a dream," I told myself again. "Let's say I sent my luggage here by mail. We can't waste time. The story will just get complicated." And I stopped in front of the house.

Julia had to make a conscious effort not to interrupt. These things happened to her too, but she'd never attributed much importance to them. Ever since she was little she'd known she could control some of her dreams: she knew she could suddenly realize, in the middle of the worst nightmare, that she, and only she, was absolutely in control of that magical succession of images and that she could, just by making a decision, eliminate certain characters, invoke others, or increase the speed of what was happening. She didn't always succeed—to do that it was necessary to gain conscious ownership of the dream—and besides, she didn't find it especially fun. She preferred to let herself travel through strange stories, as if they were really happening and she were just the protagonist, but not the author, of those unpredictable adventures. One time her sister Marta, despite how young she was, told her something similar. "Today I was in control of my dream," she'd said. And now she suddenly remembered certain conversations about the topic with her classmates from school, and she even thought she remembered reading something similar in the memoirs of a baroness or countess that she'd borrowed from a friend. She lit the wrinkled cigarette that she was still holding in her hand, inhaled a mouthful of smoke, and felt a harsh burning that scorched her throat. When she heard herself cough she noticed that the room was absolutely silent and that it had probably been a long time since Carlos had stopped talking and she had lost herself in stupid reflections.

—Please go on, she said finally.

After a moment of hesitation, Carlos continued:

—It was this house, the house you and I are in now, the house where we've spent all our summers ever since we were born. And yet, there was something very strange about it. Something tremendously unpleasant and distressing that at first I couldn't put my finger on. Because it was exactly *this house*, except that, because of some strange gift or curse, I was looking at it from an unusual angle. I woke up sweating and anxious, and I tried to calm down by reminding myself it was only a dream.

Carlos covered his face with his hands and stifled a cry. His sister thought she heard him mutter an unnecessary "until I got here . . ." and she recalled, with a bit of disappointment, the transformation she'd observed days earlier at the garden gate. "So that's what it was," she was going to say, "just that." But she didn't say anything this time either. Carlos had stood up.

—It's an angle, he said. A strange angle that horrifies me but doesn't stop being real . . . And the worst part is that there's no remedy. I know I won't be able to break free from it ever in my life . . .

The last sobs forced her to redirect her eyes toward the terrace. She suddenly felt uncomfortable being there, not being able to understand most of what she was hearing, feeling decidedly alarmed by the breakdown of that person she'd always thought was enviably strong and healthy. Maybe her parents were right and whatever was wrong with Carlos couldn't be solved with kindness and confidence. He needed a doctor. And her task would consist of something as simple as abandoning that suffocating room as soon as possible and joining in the concern of the rest of the family. "Well," she said with determination, "I promised Marta I'd take her to the movies . . ." But she quickly noticed that her face betrayed her fake sense of calm. Carlos's sunglasses confronted her with a double image of her own face. Two heads of messy hair and very wide, frightened eyes. That must have been how he saw her: a child trapped in an ogre's den, making up excuses to quietly leave the room, waiting for a chance to slip through the doorway, take a deep breath, and run down the stairs. And what's more, now Carlos seemed to have fallen into a daze, scrutinizing her from the other side of the dark glasses, and she noticed, below those two heads of messy hair and frightened eyes, two pairs of legs that were starting to shake, too much to keep talking about Marta or the movies, as if that afternoon were just any afternoon when Marta or the vague promise of going to the movies even mattered. The shadow of a sheet waving in the wind blocked her view of her brother for a few seconds. When the light came back, Julia noticed that Carlos had come closer. He was holding his glasses in one hand, revealing his swollen eyelids and a stunned expression. "It's amazing," he said in a tiny voice. "You, Julia, I can still look at you." And again that preference, that uniqueness that he granted her for the second time that afternoon, achieved its purpose with incredible velocity. "He's in love," she said at dinner, and she forced down a plate of bland vegetables she'd forgotten to put salt and pepper on.

It didn't take long for her to realize she'd acted stupidly, that night and the ones that followed the first visit to the loft. When she set herself up as mediator between her brother and the world; when she took on the task of making the untouched dishes disappear from his room; when she told Carlos, like the faithful ally she'd always been, about the doctor's diagnosis—severe depression—and the family's decision to put him in an institution. But it was already too late to turn back. Carlos accepted the news of his immediate committal with surprising apathy. He lowered his dark glasses—those impenetrable glasses that he dared remove only in her presence—expressed his desire to leave the loft, walked through various rooms of the house on Julia's arm, greeted the family, responded to their questions with reassuring answers. Yes, he was feeling well, much better, the worst was over, they had nothing to worry about. He went into his parents' bathroom for a few minutes. Through the door, Julia heard the metallic click-clack of the medicine cabinet, a crinkling of paper, a squirt of cologne. He came out washed and groomed, and he looked much more calm and tranquil. She took him to his room, helped him get into bed, and went downstairs to the dining room.

It was some time later when Julia suddenly felt scared. She remembered her father taking the lock off the loft door a few days earlier, her mother's worry, the meaningful look on the doctor's face when he declared him powerless

against the pains of his soul, the metallic click-clack of the medicine cabinet
. . . A white, organized cabinet that she'd never thought to nose around in,
the medicine cabinet, her mother's pride, nobody else could have placed so
many remedies for so many situations in such a small space. She ran up the
stairs two at a time, panting like a greyhound, terrified at the prospect of
having to say what couldn't be said. When she got to the bedroom she pushed
the door open, opened the shutters, and dropped onto the bed. Carlos was
sleeping peacefully, without his inseparable dark glasses, oblivious to torment
and anguish. Neither all the sunlight from the terrace that was streaming in
through the window, nor Julia's efforts to wake him, managed to make him
move a muscle. She heard herself crying, shouting, going to the top of the
stairs and calling out her family's names. Then everything happened unbe-
lievably quickly. Carlos's breathing was getting weaker, nearly imperceptible.
For a few moments his face regained the relaxed, tranquil beauty of earlier
times; his mouth was drawn into a calm, blissful half-smile. The evidence
could no longer be denied: Carlos was sleeping for the first time since he'd
returned from Brighton, that September 2nd, the date she'd colored red on her
calendar.

She didn't have time to regret her stupid actions or to wish with all her
might that time could turn back on itself, that it were still August and that
she, sitting on the edge of the roof next to a pile of papers, were anxiously
awaiting her brother's arrival. But she closed her eyes and tried to convince
herself she was still little, a child who played with dolls and collected trading
cards during the day and sometimes, at night, had terrible nightmares. "I'm
in control of my dream," she told herself. "It's just a dream." But when she
opened her eyes she knew she couldn't keep fooling herself. That awful nightmare wasn't a dream and she didn't have any power to rewind the images,
alter situations, or even make that beautiful, peaceful face regain the anguish
of illness. Once more the shadow of a sheet waving in the wind took over the
room for a few seconds. Julia looked back toward her brother. For the first
time in her life she understood what death was. Inexplicable, impossible to
grasp, hidden behind the false appearance of rest. She looked at Death, at
all the horror and destruction it holds, decomposition and the abyss. Because
that person lying on the bed wasn't Carlos anymore, it was Death, the great
thief, clumsily disguised with another's features, laughing hysterically behind
those red, swollen eyelids, revealing the deception of life, proclaiming its dark

kingdom, its capricious will, its unyielding, cruel designs. She rubbed her eyes and looked at her father. He was her father. That man sitting at the head of the bed was her father. But there was something enormously unpleasant about his features. As if a skull had been made up with melted wax, powdered, and painted with theater makeup. A clown, she thought, a clown of the worst kind . . . She clung to her mother's arm, but a sudden repugnance made her let go. Why was her skin suddenly so pale, her touch so slimy? She ran out to the terrace and leaned on the balustrade.

—The angle, she cried. My God . . . I've discovered the angle!

And that's when she noticed that Marta was next to her, with one of her dolls in her arms and a half-chewed candy between her fingers. Marta was still a beautiful little child. "You, Marta," she thought. "I can still look at you." And although the words struck her brain in a different voice, with different intonation, with the memory of a loved one she would never see alive again, that wasn't what startled her or what made her throw herself to the floor and pound the tiles with her fists. She had seen Marta, the eager look on Marta's face, and deep in her dark eyes, the sudden realization that *something* was happening to Julia.

Translated by Emily Davis

WORK

1980, *Mi hermana Elba*, Tusquets (stories).

1982, *El vendedor de sombras*, Argos Vergara (stories).

1983, *Los altillos de Brumal*, Tusquets (stories).

1985, *El año de Gracia*, Tusquets (novel).

1988, *Cris y Cros; seguido de El vendedor de sombras*, Alfaguara (stories).

1990, *El ángulo del horror*, Tusquets (stories).

1994, *Con Agatha en Estambul*, Tusquets (stories).

1995, *El columpio*, Tusquets (novel).

1997, *Drácula de Bram Stoker, un centenario: vampiros*-banpiroak, Diputación Foral de Guipúzcoa (essay).

1998, *Hermanas de sangre*, Tusquets (play).

2001, *Emilia Pardo Bazán*, Omega (biography).

2001, *Cosas que ya no existen*, Lumen (memoirs).

2006, *Parientes pobres del diablo*, Tusquets (stories).

2006, *La ventana del jardín*, Kliczkowski (stories).

2008, *Todos los cuentos*, Tusquets (stories).

2009, *El vendedor de sombras. El viaje*, Alfabia (stories).

2011, *Cosas que ya no existen*, Tusquets (memoirs).

2013, *La puerta entreabierta*, Tusquets (novel). Published under the pseudonym Fernanda Kubbs.

·

AWARDS AND RECOGNITIONS

2001, Premio Mario Vargas Llosa NH de relatos for *Cosas que ya no existen.*

2006, Premio Setenil for the best book of short stories published in Spain for *Parientes pobres del diablo.*

2006, Finalist for Premio Salambó for *Parientes pobres del diablo.*

2007, Premio Xatafi-Cyberdark de literature fantástica for *Parientes pobres del diablo.*

2008, Premio Tormenta for the best book published in Spanish for *Todos los cuentos.*

2008, Premio Salambó for *Todos los cuentos.*

2009, Premio Cálamo "libro del año 2008" for *Todos los cuentos.*

2009, Premio Ciudad de Barcelona for *Todos los cuentos.*

ELVIO
GANDOLFO
(Argentina, 1947)

E lvio Gandolfo was born in San Rafael on August 26, 1947. A year later, his family moved to Rosario, the city he considers his real home. He didn't receive his literary education in the family library, but through a discovery of modern literature that he made along with his father. His father had two powerful vices: cigarettes and reading. His son didn't inherit the former; the latter captured him forever. Don Francisco Gandolfo had an additional devotion: his job at a printer. In the business's workshops, father and son printed *El Lagrimal trifurca*, a literary magazine they ran between 1968 and 1976. The magazine became a megaphone for a new generation of poets and ignored authors—both from in the country and from the world map of international literature—and a forum for lively discussion.

In 1969 Elvio Gandolfo moved for the first time to Montevideo, where he got married and lived for two years. Then he went back to Rosario, where his daughter Laura was born and where he stayed until 1976. Around that time, he started what would become a prolific career as a journalist. He contributed frequently to the newspapers *Clarín* and *La Opinión*, among other publications. Over the years, he has stood out as prominant columnist and, above all, as a literary critic. Especially well known are the reviews he wrote for the magazines *Minotauro* and *El Péndulo*, where he wrote a popular column "Polvo de estrellas," dedicated to his great passion: fantastic literature.

In 1978 he went back to Uruguay, where he stayed until 1994. Since that time, he has traveled regularly between Montevideo, Buenos Aires, and Rosario. His work and geographical displacements inevitably translate into the literary sphere; his two novels *Boomerang* and *Ómnibus*, are stories of discovery and belonging, voyages "into the unknown," where dialogues mingle with reflections and film references, where one picks up all kinds of details. Parallel to the work he's done as cultural journalist, poet, and novelist, Elvio Gandolfo has developed an important career as a writer of short stories. Many of them are characterized by having everyday individuals as protagonists, whose routine lives are interrupted by something that disturbs them, transforming the common and banal into something unsettling and extraordinary. Gandolfo himself tells how this technique serves to wake up the reader, who often lives in that same state of banal numbness. *La reina de las nieves* (1982), *Sin creer en nada* (1987), and *Cuando Lidia vivía se quería morir* (2000) include stories like "El manuscrito de Juan Abal," "La oscuridad bajo la mesa," and "El momento del impacto," which have been considered indispensable in understanding the glory of the science fiction of Río de la Plata. As an anthologist, critic, editor, fiction writer, journalist, poet, typeographer, and translator, whether in his critical articles, in his fiction, or in his poetry, Gandolfo has fought to break up the fixed structures of "cultured" and predetermined literature, in favor of another literature, the fantastic, intense, and subtly revelatory.

THE ACORN

The Torture of Doctor Johnson

My activities as a reader and writer are ludic, they follow strict laws that I don't fully understand, they take place on a different level from all the rest—journalism, translation, prologues. One of these laws is an unrelenting attempt to avoid repetition. For "other people" there is nothing more reassuring than a style, a theme, regular breathing, but me, I choose to put off writing something for months and sometimes years, until I "find a way" to avoid repeating what I and other authors have done. Even so, I often discover later that writers in other languages and different countries tried something similar around the same time. But what's important to me is the choice to find something new, something different. That's why I picked "The Moment of Impact." I tried to make something impossible, at least in terms of the physical laws and limits we are bound by at this moment in science and history, plausible. In that sense, the story satisfies me fully. Besides, it seems to be written for nobody.

But there is second dimension: along the arc traced by my stories, only I know what reflects a moment of serendipity, a surge of energy. At another time I might have come up with a single short sentence ("a whale falls on a city") and I wouldn't even have written it down. When I did, however, I filled in all of the details composing that precise moment and "the space of the impact." The businesses, the streets, names of the residents of 1043 on Peatonal Cordoba (taken from the name plates on the building's intercom) are (or were) real. When you use actual landmarks you discover the limits of what is really real for the people living in that place. I remember that Patricio Pron (who I often saw on those streets around that time) looked at me out of the corner of his eye with an expression of sarcasm, distance, a certain dose of disdain, and said: "So, there's a bar called Cordoba y Sarmiento on, say, Cordoba and Sarmiento?" he paused briefly to accentuate his disdain for my invention: "I don't believe it," he concluded. I took him by the arm and we walked to that corner (it was only two blocks away). I told him to look up. The bar's sign read exactly that. He accepted it with a smile: something that more than once during that time saved him from coming off as a pedant.

I wanted to write a strange story, something charged with energy, unique (like "The Heat Death of the Universe" by Pamela Zoline, like "Los buques suicidantes" by Horacio Quiroga). And besides it enabled me to silence the zealotry of a young friend, and, years later, to know with clarity, without the stains of sentimentality or conventional narrative tricks, exactly what existed, sometime in January of 1996, a couple blocks from the center of Rosario.

In Conversation with the Dead

One of them, as far as I know, is still alive and well. Years after the first time I read it, I reread *I Am Legend* by Richard Matheson, and I discovered with horror that I'd taken too many jewels from the grandfather's coffer: the manipulation of tension, the harshness of the streets, the lines of dialogue, the way women function in a story. Around that time the same thing happened with Alfred Bester, whose effect has lessened a bit with the passing of time, leaving intact *The Demolished Man*. On a global level, the list would be endless, entire cemeteries. All of Witold Gombrowicz, Borges, Macedonio Fernández, Marosa di Giorgio, Roberto Arlt (from the beginning I couldn't unpack the wisdom in his statement that he wrote "bad"), Ballard, Mario Levrero, Carlos Mastronardi, my father Francisco, Hebe Uhart, Felisberto Hernández, Jose Idem (the one of *Martín Fierro*), the flood of Fogwill, all of Nicanor Parra, over and over (he teaches incessantly like a streetcorner guru, like a cool high school teacher). Closer: David Foster Wallace, Felipe Polleri, Pablo De Santis's eight best books, Ted Chiang, Cesar Aira's fifteen best books, Scott Fitzgerald's best book. And the caravan continues, guided by the masterful hand of George Romero.

Coda

You play with the idea of synchronicity. Do you consider your writing to be part of the tradition of fantastic literature rooted in Argentina since the work of Borges or Cortázar, or do you consider your work to be more experimental than fantastical?

On one hand, synchronicities and rhythms are themes I've often focused on. On the other, I've been amazed to discover the same themes in sociology texts (Erving Goffman), etiology texts (Konrad Lorenz and others), or in the movement of multitudes. In a long piece that I'm working on now something similar occurs in the context of a Sunday market (Tristán Narvaja) in Montevideo: if you catch the rhythm, you can move with the crowd—if you don't end up getting trapped. And it's best to catch it intuitively. The first *Matrix* movie has the same theme, and so does an old novel by Fritz Leiber, which a number of years ago I included in a collection for Coluhue: *Los que pecan*, which is based on the idea that everyday life depends on this rhythm.

I think being a part of the fantastic tradition in Argentina is inevitable, even Leopoldo Lugones, Roberto Arlt, or Macedonio Fernández have wonderful texts of that kind. More than a genre, I think it's a way of looking at the real. This is accentuated in the eastern or Uruguayan branch, authors like Felisberto Hernández, Mario Levrero, and even the overly-scrutinized territory of Onetti (*La vida breve*, *Dejemos hablar al viento*, or even *El pozo*).

A THOUSAND FORESTS

"The Moment of Impact"
From *Cuando Lidia vivía se quería morir*
(While Lidia Was Alive She Wanted to Die)

For P.S.

THE APPEARANCE

A blue whale, also known as a blue rorqual, materializes over the city of Rosario, at an altitude of 452 meters, in the cool blue sky of spring day.

The sudden monumental presence is preceded tenths of seconds before by a soft hissing sound (as if the body, 28 meters in length, had filtered in through a crack in the firmament), then an explosive *bang!* caused by the displacement of the empty air suddenly occupied by the enormous body. No one hears it, because no one is paying attention on that day at that hour in the center of Rosario, which stretches out below.

In that immobile hundredth of a second between its appearance and the beginning of its fall, the prodigious, wide tail of the blue whale jerks as if it were still underwater (in the ocean, almost simultaneously, it produces a sudden silent implosion as the salt water rushes to fill the photogravure of its gigantic disappeared body), scattering the water still clinging to it, in the exact moment that its 172-ton body begins its descent.

Seen like this, in the empty sky, the blue whale completes the roundness of that sky, serving as a reference point, similar to a thin line of white cloud at an altitude of 1,550 meters barely visible through squinted eyes. But there is nothing surreal in the stark appearance of the whale. To be more precise:

in no way does it recall a painting by Magritte, a painter who might well have put a huge blue whale hanging in a blue sky.

But in that case the whale would be unblemished, smooth, pure. Here we're dealing with a gigantic blue rorqual, numerous pleats traversing the length of its underbelly indicating how far it can open its jaw in order to swallow, for example, 60 tons of water, which it filters through the densely barbed grill of its mouth, trapping all the edible material it needs to keep its 172-ton body moving, living. There are of course patches of skin that are smooth, like a black eggshell, others are rough, with colonies of barnacles clinging to them like a thick plaster. But the most important thing, in that hundredth of a second of stillness, is the sense of physical weight, of muscularity and blubber.

If you were to compare the size of the blue whale—suspended briefly in midair, before beginning its fall—to something, it would have to be a passenger jet airplane, but a whale is much denser; a jet, of course, is hollow.

There is an additional difference. A jet airplane falling on the center of a city, however tragic—given the victims, the flattened buildings, the explosion of the fuel tank—would at least be thinkable. The appearance, and above all the plummeting fall of a blue whale is, on the other hand, *un*thinkable, *un*acceptable, *un*possible. So the enormous cetacean, suddenly submerged in air when it was just underwater, stunned, will fight to grasp what the hell is going on, why the sonic profile provided in the depths by echolocation has been amplified and complicated to the point of saturation, why all of a sudden, in the hundredth of a second when it rotates to the vertical and begins to fall, it feels a terrible heat on its skin. In addition, without knowing it, in its cetacean slowness accustomed to feeding cycles, songs of courtship and commentary, and the pure joy of floating, it will fight to impose the impossible reality of a blue rorqual falling suddenly on a city, the mere idea of such an occurrence is refuted, at least prior to today, not only by science, common sense, and custom, but by the very fabric of reality.

THE FALL

Vertical, immense, the whale, or blue rorqual, begins to fall. After a hundredth of a second of immobility, its velocity increases astonishingly, second to second. Parts of its body begin to change shape. The long sack of pleats under the mouth starts to contract upward, something that never happened underwater. Even beached on land, without the total violence of a fall from an altitude of 452 meters, the dense volume of the rorqual would have been enough to crush its internal organs. Now it is not motionless, stretched out on land. It is falling at a velocity impossible to calculate, because there are no measuring instruments and no onlookers to witness this phenomenon that by its mere existence puts to test the very fabric of reality, which refuses to account for blue rorquals falling on a river city one spring day.

As the tapered form of the blue whale falls toward the city of Rosario, which stretches out serene and gray, inside the whale there takes place a slow and bulging displacement of its internal organs—without detaching or being crushed—in the direction of its tail. The light of the sun, which other species, namely the inhabitants of the city, would consciously or unconsciously experience as pleasant and warm, is for the whale, on the other hand, experienced as insufferable. First and foremost because the friction from the first 80 or 100 meters dries the whale out entirely, not just the surface water but also the moisture in its skin. The enormous four-ton tongue, on top of which an elephant could comfortably sit, is stuck by its own inertia to the cathedral ceiling of the falling blue whale's palate.

After the first hundred meters, if someone were paying attention, he would begin to hear the increasing hum of the more than 170-ton body plummeting like an unimaginable missile of meat, blubber, bones, and minuscule barnacles toward the center of the city. The hum is strange, opaque, curiously similar to an airplane falling toward the earth, but lacking the aggression of engines going crazy, out of control. It's a sort of dreadful note, low and intensifying, that in the whale's delicate ears, accustomed only to a multitude of flat ocean echoes, adds to the massive general disorientation that the cetacean's senses are suffering, falling irrevocably through the blue sky toward the city.

After the first two hundred meters of the fall the body undergoes further modifications, now intolerable. Many of the baleens or whalebones—four to five meters in length—protected by the enormous lower lip, break with small cracks on the inside of the mouth, detach and, combined with the tongue sticking to the palate, contribute to the suffocation of the whale. At that altitude the whale is clearly suffering, defenseless, turned into a pitiless mass of geometric acceleration, pierced by a stab of nostalgia for salt water, for slow liquid days.

THE VIEW

The eye of the whale is much less impressive than other parts of its body, especially like this, in the air. It's no bigger than the eye of a cow. But it sees. First it sees an assaulting flood of blue, blue extending out in every direction where transparent air collects to form color. In that first hundredth of a second in which the whale is immobile, the eye closes defensively.

But when the body rotates 45 degrees to the vertical and begins to fall, the eye opens. And what it sees, approaching at an incredible velocity, and confirming the signals the great blue rorqual receives from echoes off the solid surface, is the city, stretching out below as infinite as the sky, although there is a clear limit along one border: the river. In its slow absorption of everything, the whale identifies the brown and silver surface as water, and an ancient reflex allows it to recognize water as its only chance of salvation, unaware in that fleeting moment of the certainty with which physics dictates (keeping in mind figures of weight and velocity of impact) that crashing into the liquid surface would be just as fatal as colliding with the dirt or concrete.

But as certain zones of the whale's senses are overcome by the effects of gravity—the growing heat on its skin, the soft internal tearing, the fleeting sensation of the burnt barnacles ripped off by friction with the air—others inform it in tenths of seconds that it will not fall into the water, but onto the uneven contours of concrete—buildings, streets, and plazas of the city center.

There is one profile that stands out, a sort of vertical spike standing upright alongside the river. If it's possible that there exists something like feelings in blue rorquals, the one that is falling over the city on September 24th, 1995, feels that it would prefer to fall there, vertical, rectilinear onto that blunt but long and tall shape, to be impaled, to at the very least become a spectacle with some modicum of dignity, and not just a simple, albeit colossal, pulverized cetacean.

Now the shapes down below become even clearer, now the eye takes in everything in a thousandth of a second before the socket is closed forever by the overwhelming weight of acceleration, by lack of moisture, by friction, in the same way the whale's sex organs—tucked up in the genital slit near the tail so it can swim unencumbered—bury themselves inside even farther, with a kind of primordial terror all their own, protecting themselves against the cauterizing heat on the skin. In that flash of fleeting and final perception, the eye sees that the body—accelerating, barely 150 meters above the surface—will crash, that it will be entombed between the buildings at the intersection of the streets the inhabitants of the city know as Bulevar San Martín and Avenida Córdoba.

THE TARGET

Eight seconds before the blue rorqual hits the corner of Córdoba and San Martín, there are six stationary people standing on that corner and another four approaching the intersection. On the corner there are two couples, one middle-aged (over forty, under fifty) and one young (between twenty and thirty) standing around a small green table covered with pamphlets. There are, in addition, two venerable senior citizens, who don't seem to have any kind of relationship with one another. A pair of posters fixed by thumbtacks to the table hang down in front of it, clearly indicating that these people are members of a group advocating the protection of animals, including whales of every kind.

The people in motion, who will arrive at the intersection at the precise moment of impact, are:

A young thirty-four-year-old officer worker coming down San Martín toward the river, a briefcase hanging from one hand and a gray suit jacket draped over one shoulder—to relieve himself from the insufferable heat he is imagining that same intersection in the winter;

A forty-eight-year-old woman, whose thinning hair is an indistinct color between orange and brown, the result of the accumulation of countless dye jobs carried out over the years, walking down Córdoba, also toward the river;

A young man of twenty-six years, who looks younger, long, fine hair falling down his back. An hour earlier he swallowed a substance whose consumption is punishable by law and it has added a luminous halo to the lines that he sees (doors, windows, signs, storefronts). He is walking parallel to the woman, and due to a phenomenon of synchronicity that no one (least of all the two of them) is aware of, their legs are moving in unison, like a ballet performance or a parade;

A thirty-two-year-old man, a professional soccer player, famous in his day but realizing now that it is time for him to retire, an idea that sinks his mind into a wash of shimmering melancholy, intermingling the memory of past goals with the bleakness of the coming future.

If the eye of the whale—the blue rorqual—could open now, in the ferocious rush of air and the viscous secretion with which it tries to protect itself from the unfamiliar aggression enveloping it, it would see, eight seconds prior to impact, the ten people down below align to receive it directly, in a seemingly predetermined formation, ten points increasing in size, still mobile.

Counting down, eight seconds prior to impact, the ten people, as well as others in the vicinity, become aware of the falling blue whale. First and foremost, the shadow of the plummeting mass falls across the intersection. They might mistake this for a dense cloud suddenly blocking out the sun. But, additionally, there is the monumental hum of the tons of flesh, bones, and blubber, produced by the blistering and implacable descent of the condemned marine beast.

The ten people, and others at a distance, outside the intersection, all look up at the same time. Catching sight of the jaw or the enormous bottom lip misshapen by its velocity, the great curving tail coming behind, and they freeze, caught as if in the flash of a photograph.

The jaw of the office worker drops, his jacket and briefcase too, his arms go limp. "My God, my God," the woman murmurs through her teeth, flooded with a dark guilt, the color drains from her face, accentuating the contrast of her white skin and dyed hair. The animal rights activists react as if according to a plan, taking a small step backward, separating themselves slightly from the small table. The soccer player is jerked out of his melancholy humor and without knowing why, he smiles, as if the terrific humming of the next eight seconds were his old fans cheering one of his moves. The only one who comprehends what he sees is the boy with long hair, whose face is overwhelmed by a beatific expression, as he thinks, euphorically: "A whale—outstanding!" right before impact.

THE IMPACT

It's sad. The whale, the blue rorqual, grew in the belly of another blue whale, emerged from the water, nursed like a cow, stared into the marine depths with a bovine eye, filtered infinite liters of water through its baleens, sang and commented with its underwater voice, grew to its current size, and now it's going to crash into an endless mass of concrete: the city of Rosario.

In a way, that same body, already injured by the friction of the rectilinear fall, burnt by the air, comprehends its dark fate when the hard, sharp wall of the Sedería Eiffel, which occupies one of the four corners, slices open its side like a huge knife. Then everything gets confused. Many of the employees of Banco Nación, across from the Sedería, will wonder to the end of their days whether they did or did not see the massive wall of plummeting-blue-whale-body, covered suddenly with a wave, like red paint, of its own blood. Those not directly in the intersection will wonder the same thing, especially because of the faithful reflection provided by Banco Nación's smooth and reflective glass walls, of the biological mass, larger than a locomotive, bellowing desperately as it is torn open and crashes.

Nobody will ever ask anyone else what they witnessed. But the employees and customers of Casa Chemea—which, as it has done since time immemorial, has shirts, jeans and jackets on display in a glass storefront occupying one of the other four corners—will never have to wonder what they did or did not see. Protected as they are by the small windows, by signs showing the discounted prices, if asked they would say they felt nothing, saw nothing, and had no doubts about what they saw or felt. On the other hand, the two or three people on the opposite corner, sitting at McDonald's white plastic tables, will experience, just like the ten people in the intersection, the impact of the whale's terrible mass without even being able to move.

Given the velocity of the fall and impact, it's impossible to know if the whale, blue rorqual, hits the hard surface of the intersection with its mouth open or closed. In any event, its powerful bellow, a sound that's impossible to distinguish from the awful tearing of the flesh against the corner of the Sedería Eiffel, will make people both indoors and outdoors for fifteen or twenty blocks of the surrounding area, in the middle of taking a step or motionless in bed, clutch a hand or both hands to their chest or, in the most sensible cases, stop what they are doing and cover their ears.

Because now, in the precise instant that the two lines—the vertical fall of the dense cetacean, and the horizontal plane of the concrete—meet, the challenge or attack on the fabric of reality is carried out and resolved in something less than a second, something immeasurable.

Although it materialized, rotated vertical, fell and ended up stuck like a massive cork into the intersection of Bulevar San Martín and Avenida Córdoba, the blue whale could not have materialized, fallen, and crashed, because that does not happen within the fabric of reality. While the whale was in action, in motion, it was able to follow its trajectory, its unfathomable fate. But now, when at last it crashes, it pulverizes the ten bodies standing in the intersection, flattens the little green table like a piece of paper, shakes and even cracks the marble and concrete of the ancient doorway of Banco Nación, which stands alone on the corner, without a building, like a relic. While the whale is falling, it is flesh and bones and muscles that are falling.

But every part of the whale that touches the hard floor of the city, of reality, self-destructs. First becoming a soft pulp, between gray and green, a wave that washes down the streets from the intersection like a surging tide, the salty and semi-putrefied odor of the sea invading the nasal passages of anyone struck and carried by the wave, created by the enormous body as it is entombed, erased, sucked up by the horizontal plane.

As it disappears, the wave of dissolving whale slips into the wide lobby of the Victoria Mall, although it doesn't reach the central indoor fountain. At this point, only the tail has yet to disintegrate, though the whole thing is erased at the same rate that it falls and embeds itself in the concrete of San Martín and Córdoba, and in the end, hundredths of a second later what actually inundates the streets from the intersection is no longer even pulp but liquid.

The liquid waves of destroyed whale splash the businesses at the entrance to Galería Córdoba, one of which displays an Enciclopedia Espasa, for an instant it almost pushes the joystick controlling the arm that grabs stuffed animals out from inside the transparent glass box at the entrance to Juguetería Gulliver, and in the end it is lost, like a low tide absorbed by the sand, before even making it to the corner of Sarmiento. None of the patrons of the bar tautologically baptized "Sarmiento y Córdoba" notices a thing, and in the end, with the whale totally erased, liquefied, absorbed a block away, the liquid flows back, drops, dissolves.

THE EBB

The reality into which the blue rorqual crashes has no trouble withstanding it. As massive as the whale is, it's nothing, not even a molecule, compared to that fabric. Well not exactly nothing: at least it's a loose end, unraveling. Unaware and disoriented, it was ripped from the depths of the ocean and hurled down on the city. Flesh and animal suffered the change of environment terribly during the fall. Its weight pulverized at least ten people, but it found the peace of dissolution when it hit the concrete.

In the moment that its last molecule disappeared, those who suffered the impact were standing again in the intersection, knowing that something had happened but not knowing what, feeling a strange sensation in their legs, like wet clothes, like the smell of the sea, like fingers cooled by water. Even more: in the surrounding blocks, those who heard, in one way or another, the bellow of intolerable agony, and especially those who saw or received the impact, experienced a feeling that is also provoked by causes other than a falling whale: a death in the family, the unconfessed desire to crash and be eclipsed, to disappear, to escape the limits of mind and body.

A slight anguish, not psychological but physical: a bubble bursting under that vulnerable spot of white skin right at the base of the throat, that point of infinite surrender and risk that lovers know. Something that, if they were able to concentrate and put it in words, which they don't even think of doing, the inhabitants of the city might describe as a dark internal bubble of death. In reality they experienced it as a closing of the throat, not from emotion (because they saw and felt nothing) but from weariness, from heat. The next day, Rosario's only newspaper would include a small section about the dangers of heat stroke, and the appropriate measures to avoid it.

The whale dissolved, disappeared violently and sweetly, gone. That night, those in charge of cleaning the pavement on Peatonal Córdoba would smell, from out of the grates and the sewer systems, an odor that would fill them with nostalgia for maritime coasts, so different from the rivers surrounding the city, but they would register it as the leftovers of seafood dishes from some restaurant that probably fell through the grate at some point, and they would increase the pressure of the water from their hoses.

Reality, undaunted, continues on its path, free of whales falling on centrally located corners. The suitcases and belts in Cepero Cueros seem to be waiting, satisfied, resting in windows under the glow of electric lights. In 1043 of Peatonal Córdoba, the doorman, as well as Mr. F. Cristiá, Dr. Molveznick and Dr. Gruegg and Mr. Héctor F. Pastore, sleep the serene sleep of the righteous. Whales in the city are limited to illustrations that languish in the Biblioteca Argentina or Biblioteca Vigil, to the moving images of videos recorded for programs like *National Geographic*, to any number of flat, motionless posters in kiosks or old bookstores.

Although the sacrificed blue whale did not alter the fabric of reality, it did have effects: unique thoughts, lumps in throats, sudden feelings of chaos and catastrophe, imprecise but real, especially for those close to the point of impact. And although the architectural surface of the city is wholly monolithic and hard, although there are few things in the world with more common sense than one of its residents, in the long nights the empty streets still communicate something soft and sorrowful, but at the same time almost nourishing, to those passing through them alone or in the company of others. And old friends stop seeing each other one day to the next or keep seeing each other with a sudden and inexplicable mutual irritation. So, in a way, what the impact of the whale unleashed can be explained by the sometimes violent gusts of senselessness that permeate the supposedly serene and comfortable lives of the city's inhabitants, gusts which those inhabitants try, just as senselessly, to attribute to the heat, to the humidity, or to the mosquitoes.

In fact, for a few seconds, the fabric of reality, although destroying it afterward, allowed the body of the whale to plummet through the spring air of Rosario at an increasing velocity. It allowed the uneven ground to receive the body, the flank to be torn open by the Sedería Eiffel, but in the end it dissolved it, evaporated it in the exact instant that its existence was about to have effects, cause damage.

But the fabric of reality is not just calm, it's also struggle, resistance; it's not just precise, enduring details, it's also displacements. Exactly three and a half months after the fall and definitive obliteration of the blue rorqual, on a date more significant, more disposed to unusual occurrences, the 24th of December of 1995, a black and gray sperm whale materializes in the burning sky of a summer day above the nearby city of Santa Fe. The process follows, like almost everything that ends up imposing itself on the fabric of the real, the same pattern. One hundredth of a second of immobility, in which the characteristics of the sperm whale, in the event that someone is watching, can be captured, more masculine and headstrong, with a square, destructive forehead, ready to withstand any impact, the skin covered with scars, the eye opening on a reflection of absolute surprise, before, in the next hundredth of a second, the sperm whale rotates and begins to fall toward the city.

Translated by Will Vanderhyden

WORK

1972, *De lagrimales y cachimbas*, El Lagrimal Trifurca/La cachimba (poetry anthology of various authors).

1976, *Poesía viva de Rosario*, La Ventana (poetry anthology of various authors).

1978, *La Huella de los Pájaros*, El Lagrimal Trifurca/La cachimba (poetry anthology of various authors).

1982, *La reina de las nieves*, Centro Editor de América Latina (stories).

1986, *Caminando alrededor*, Ediciones de la Banda Oriental (stories).

1987, *Sin creer en nada (trilogía)*, Punto Sur (stories).

1990, *Rete Carótida*, Ediciones de la Banda Oriental (stories).

1992, *Dos mujeres*, Alfaguara (stories).

1993, *Parece mentira*, Fin de Siglo (stories and articles).

1993, *Boomerang*, Planeta (novel).

1994, *Ferrocarriles argentinos*, Alfaguara (stories).

2000, *Cuando Lidia vivía se quería morir*, Perfil (stories).

2006, *Ómnibus*, Interzona (novel-report).

2007, *El libro de los géneros*, Editorial Norma (essays).

2010, *The Book of Writers*, Caballo Negro (stories).

2011, *Dos mujeres* (new edition), Periferica (stories).

•

AWARDS AND RECOGNITIONS

1992, finalist for Premio Planeta for *Boomerang*.

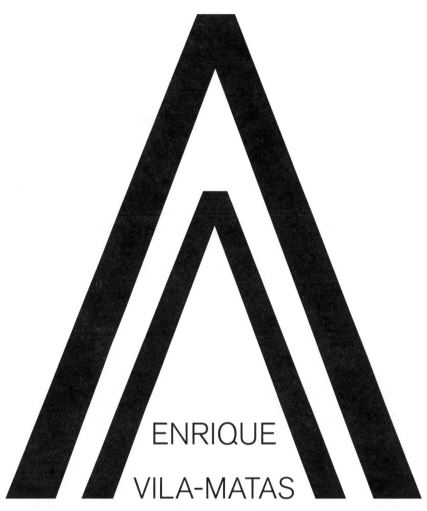

ENRIQUE
VILA-MATAS
(Spain, 1948)

Very early in his imaginative and ironic oeuvre, Enrique Vila-Matas achieved a precise *tone* and a particular contemporary sensibility that allows for a natural continuity between the real and the fictional. To put it another way: he is a master of "fictionalizing" the I and the real in very convincing literary ways.

He was born in Barcelona in 1948. His childhood transpired right across from the Cinema Metropol, awaking in him an early passion for film. In fact, he worked as a writer for *Fotogramas* magazine (where he invented a ton of interviews that he managed to pass off as genuine) and in 1970 he even directed two short films: *Todos los jóvenes tristes* and *Fin de verano*. The following year, deprived of cinematographic activities because of obligatory military service (in Africa), he wrote his first novel, *Mujer en el espejo contemplando el paisaje*, published by Tusquets in 1973.

In 1974 he went to Paris. Marguerite Duras rented him a loft and during the two years he lived in the French capital, he dedicated himself to writing his second novel, *La asesina ilustrada* (1977). When he published *Historia abreviada de la literatura portátil* in 1985, a important text in Spanish fiction, his work was not only beginning to be appreciated by the readers of his country, but also by readers in Latin America, who viewed him as an original writer, able to combine the essay with fiction in an attempt to understand the world, to make some sense of a reality beyond definition. *Una casa para siempre* (a novel divided into stories, or stories that can be read as a novel whose protagonist is a ventriloquist, who witnesses the birth of his own voice) did nothing less than confirm him as an essential author of the Spanish language.

Between 1990 and 1995, Vila-Matas gave us his first books of essays (*El viajero más lento* and *El traje de los domingos*) and two collections of stories: *Suicidios ejemplares* and *Hijos sin hijos*. From then on, and until the end of the '90s, he focused on themes like family (*Lejos de Veracruz*), the vocation of writing (*Extraña forma de vida*) and Catalan nationalism (*El viaje vertical*) to then, after the turn of the century, continue creating an oeuvre that understands literature as a game, always new and dangerous.

So, in the year 2000, he published *Bartleby y compañía*, an unclassifiable novel that won the Premio Ciudad de Barcelona (2001), the Prix du Meilleur Livre Étranger (France 2002), and the Prix Fernando Aguirre-Libralire (France 2002). In it, through a fascinating blend of essay and biography, Vila-Matas traces the paths of those authors who, faithful to the phrase that Melville put in his character Bartleby's mouth ("I prefer not to"), stopped writing and opted for silence.

Stunned and overwhelmed by the response of readers and critics, Vila-Matas suffered a creative paralysis from which he recovered by writing his next novel, *El mal de Montano* (2002) where the *malady* suffered by his protagonist, Montano, is nothing other than literature itself. It won the Prix Médicis in 2002, for the best foreign novel published in France, and he became a regular contributor to *Le Magazine Littéraire*.

With *París no se acaba nunca*, published in 2003, Vila-Matas returned to his years in Paris with an ironic version of the time he spent in that city. The book preceded *Doctor Pasavento* (2005), a novel about the disappearance of the subject in the West and more concretely about "the difficulty of being no one."

A health problem during the Feria del Libro de Buenos Aires led to his being taken directly to a hospital in Barcelona, and from those days arose the stories of *Exploradores del abismo* (2007). The next year, in *Dietario voluble*, again he erased the lines between fiction, essay, and biography with a book where, as the author himself said, "the genres succeed one another like moods."

In 2010, Vila-Matas returned to the novel with *Dublinesca*, in which, at the same time as narrating the lived experience of an elderly publisher from Barcelona, he interrogates himself about the future of the novel as a genre, about the fate awaiting the literature of the future. His most recent novel, *Aire de Dylan*, is garnering the enthusiasm of the critics and public alike, and it has reaffirmed him as one of the most singular and prestigious voices of contemporary European literature.

THE ACORN

The Torture of Doctor Johnson

I chose this text because, four years after writing it, I still like this story that I began when Sophie Calle and I made a pact that resembled, in a way, the pact made by the two travelers in *Strangers On a Train*, the two men who agree to murder their mutual enemies simultaneously. In our case, the pact consisted of agreeing that, over the course of a year, I would write a life for Sophie and she would live it. I wrote the first chapter for her right away, but months went by and she—just like with the second murderer in *Strangers On a Train*—did not decide to act. If Sophie didn't do anything, I couldn't keep writing and I ran the risk, in addition, of ending up blocked forever, waiting for her to make her move . . .

Seeing that she would never act and after a desperate period of writer's block, I decided to go back and write the story of what had happened with Sophie Calle. And I went back, I told the story, but something strange happened. Normally, we writers tend to try to pass off a fictional story as real. In "Because She Did Not Ask" it was just the opposite: to make sense of my real story I had to present it as fiction.

In Conversation with the Dead

A long time ago someone said to me: "See the things your pain creates." It's a beautiful sentence—enigmatic, unique, I'd say feminine—and it is also a sentence that, in the most moving way, makes me feel closer to my dead.

Coda

Your work combines literature, life, and a sense of playfulness. How are these three elements related?

Literature and life are like a game. Something that we sometimes forget or sometimes think of as frivolous. We forget that in the tracks of the earliest discovered humans we see an adult couple walking through the snow, and coming behind, the more irregular tracks of a child who is understood to be walking crookedly, but no, it's the image of a child at play. That playfulness is as ancient as the human condition. And literature is viewed as a game and as life itself. A game in which one appropriates and changes the work of other writers. It's a game that horrifies some translators, those who don't know that I sometimes use this approach in my work.

The strange thing about writing is that one separates oneself from life, to write about life and about the world. When it comes to writing about what is separate, the combination of literature and life must be found completely outside of both things. There are people who think that I am some kind of library rat but really it's just the opposite. Still, in appearance it might be so because of the metafiction in all my stories; it would appear that I never get outside of books, but that isn't true. There are also people who believe that when you write you are not living; that is another error. Because clearly when one is writing one is also living. And when you are living, frequently, as in my case, you can be writing. There are times when I am aware that I'm living something that I will later write. Normally, if there is this incentive, I am more interested in the habitual sequence in which I find myself. For example: I give public lectures and speeches that, for a writer who prefers to be writing, can be a bit tedious. Still, I give them as if they were part of my own work; they are experiences that I try to use to later turn into something that is reflected in my writing. That way I do not feel like I've lost time in activities that are separate from writing. In other words, I steer everything toward the literary, in reality toward my work. When I'm at the bus stop I forget that I'm working. I simply forget myself. But I also observe many things in the streets, like a boy with an ice cream who slips and falls; this becomes a story: everything, everything is there. The mind also works in a literary way. That's why in *Dublinesque*, anticipating that it might pull more readers into the book, on the third page I alert the reader that the main character sees life in a literary way. Those who don't know me will not stumble over this oddity. It's like alerting the reader that a butcher is obsessed with seeing shapes in the clouds, so that, when the butcher looks at the clouds, the reader knows that this is normal and doesn't find it strange. So, readers discover that there is a character who sees everything through a kind of literary lens. Often times, when I'm alone I don't think about anything literary; I don't really even care at all about literature. I guess it's like the rule that alongside love, hate must also exist. Even when I'm not there.

A THOUSAND FORESTS

FROM "Because She Didn't Ask"

FROM *EXPLORADORES DEL ABISMO* (Explorers of the Abyss)

II. DON'T MESS WITH ME

1.

I wrote the story *The Journey of Rita Malú* for Sophie Calle. You could say I did it because she asked me to. It all began one afternoon when she called me at my home in Barcelona. I was flabbergasted. I revered her, considered her out of my reach. I'd never met her in person and didn't think I ever would. She called to say that a mutual friend (Isabel Coixet) had given her my phone number, and that she wanted to propose something, but couldn't do it over the phone.

Her words carried an odd, mysterious charge to them, however involuntary. I suggested an encounter in Paris at the end of the month since I planned on spending New Year's Eve there; the year 2005 was drawing to a close. We arranged to meet at the Café de Flore in Paris at noon on the 27th of December.

On the appointed day, I arrived in the neighborhood a half hour early, a little apprehensive about the encounter. Sophie Calle had something of a reputation for being capable of practically anything and I was well aware of her eccentricities and audacity, partly thanks to Paul Auster's novel, *Leviathan*, in which Sophie was a character called María Turner. The novel's dedication reads: "The author extends special thanks to Sophie Calle for permission to mingle fact with fiction."

I was aware of all this, but I knew a lot of other things, too. For example, I recalled having read that once, when she was young, she had felt lost in her home city of Paris after a long trip through Lebanon. She wasn't familiar with anyone anymore and felt compelled to follow behind people she had never met, leaving them to decide where she was supposed to go. I recalled this and some of her most famous "happenings": how she invited strangers to sleep in her bed as long as they let her watch them and take photographs of them, and if they would answer her questions (*The Sleepers*); or how she had pursued a man one time, after finding out purely by chance, that he was traveling to Venice that evening (*Venetian Suite*); or how she got her mother to hire a private detective to take photographs of her and follow her, knowing the whole time that she was being trailed, to get him to profile her in his reports with the fake bare truth of an objective observer.

As I headed for our appointment at the Café de Flore, I was reminded of what Vicente Molina Foix had said about Sophie Calle, how she belonged to the kingdom of verbal imagination. If we take into account the models that inspired her and the fact that words were always at the origin of her visual projects, and given the earnest personal accounts and strong prose of her stories, along with the fact that she establishes herself as the protagonist, victim, plot and subject of an omniscient narrative, she stands as one of the greatest novelists of the moment.

I came to the appointment feeling uneasy, and asked myself what she could possibly have in store for me, if it might be something eccentric or dangerous. To buck up my self-confidence before our meeting at Café de Flore, I ducked into the nearby Café Bonaparte and threw back two shots of whisky in less than five minutes, standing at the bar *Far West* style. I left Café Bonaparte walking slowly (it was ten minutes to twelve) and stopped to have a look in the window at La Hune bookstore, which is only 10 meters away from the Flore. The French translation of one of my novels was on display, but I didn't pay much attention to it, I was too busy drilling myself about what Sophie Calle was going to say.

Suddenly, a short man with North African features asked very politely if he could talk to me for a minute. I thought he was going to ask for money and was irritated that he had broken my concentration on Sophie Calle.

"Excuse me, I've been observing you and I would like to offer my help," the man said. And he handed me the address for Alcoholics Anonymous, written out in longhand on a piece of paper torn from a small notebook. He had been following me since the Bonaparte. I didn't know how to respond.

I considered telling him that I wasn't an alcoholic, nor was I anonymous. I thought of explaining to him that I didn't drink as much as it might appear and also of telling him that I was not exactly an anonymous person, and draw his attention to my book on display in the window. But I didn't say a word. I pocketed the address for Alcoholics and tried to walk into the Flore without slouching or seeming full of complexes.

I recognized Sophie Calle immediately among the others. She had arrived early and got a table in a good spot. I asked her permission to sit down, in a show of respect. She smiled and extended it. She said that we would speak in Spanish, she had lived in Mexico for a year and knew my language well. I sat down, and to curb my shyness, started talking immediately. I told her the story about how I had been spied on and pursued just a moment earlier by a recovering alcoholic, which is something that could have come straight out of the *wall novels* she was so addicted to—the man and the chase, that is. Might she have been the person who had put him up to it?

Sophie smiled slightly and almost without further ado, pointed to an excerpt from my most popular novel. The excerpt, she said, related directly to what she wanted to propose. I could hardly recall that particular episode in my book. It recounts a story that Marcel Schwob tells in *Parallel Lives*: a story about the life of Petronius, who, when he turned 30, it's said, decided to narrate his sorties into the seamy side of the city. He wrote sixteen books of his own invention and when he had finished, read them aloud to Sirius, his accomplice and slave, who laughed like a lunatic, and applauded nonstop. So together, Sirius and Petronius came up with the plan of living out the adventures he had written, taking them from parchment to reality. Petronius and Sirius dressed up in costumes and fled the city, took to the road and lived out the adventures Petronius had composed, who abandoned writing from that moment on, once he began living the life he had imagined. "In other words" (I ended by saying in the excerpt), "if the theme of *Don Quixote* is about the dreamer who dares to become what he dreams, the story of Petronius is that of the writer who dares to experience what he has written, and for that reason stops writing."

What Sophie suggested was that I write a story, any story. That I create a character she could bring to life: a character whose behavior—for one year, maximum—would be contingent upon what I wrote. She wanted to change her life and what's more, she was tired of having to determine her own *deeds*,

now she preferred to have someone else do it for her, let somebody else decide
how she was supposed to live. She would obey the *author* in everything . . .
There was a brief silence. Everything except killing.

—In short, she said, you write a story and I'll bring it to life.

2.

We remained silent for a few slow seconds till she regained her voice and
explained to me that she had made the same proposition to Paul Auster some
years earlier, who found the responsibility too risky and so declined. She also
told me that she had recently suggested the same thing to Jean Echenoz, who
also ended up declining the invitation.

It seemed to me that the intention behind Sophie's proposition was to
make the author disappear, precisely what I had written about in my latest
texts, claiming that's what I desired. Yet I had never dared to follow through
with it, only to blurring my personality into what I wrote. I told myself that
Sophie seemed aware of my concerns and that must be why she had now
chosen me, to finally bring my literature to life.

She explained that her mother had only two or three months left to live
and it was important for me to keep this in mind, since it's the only thing that
could condition or temporarily delay our project, as long as I was willing to
accept the proposition, that is.

—I haven't said so yet, but I'm happy to accept, I said.

Sophie smiled—I've always considered a smile to be the perfect form of
laughter—and she seemed happy to see that I hadn't doubted a second before
accepting. But I shouldn't forget—she reminded me again—that everything
depended on the state of her mother's health.

3.

Half an hour later, I was back in the Hotel Littré, on rue Littré, where my
wife was waiting for me, and I excitedly explained the strange assignment to
her. I was both excited and satisfied with the prospect that had just opened in
my life, although better to say in my work, since the life bit was Sophie's job.
The problem now was figuring out what kind of a story to write. At first, all I
came up with were stupidities: make Sophie travel to Barcelona, for example,

and sign up for Catalan classes. Things like that, truly asinine. My wife suggested that I make more of an effort. "You'll come up with something. You always find a way out when you get stuck," she told me.

I returned to Barcelona with my wife the next day. I figured the sooner I wrote the story, the better it would be for me. I had a burning curiosity to clarify things as soon as possible; in other words, to see how things would play out as quickly as I could, and calculate whether I was truly interested or not in being involved in this attractive, though strange and ambiguous project. I worried that if I let too much time go by, Sophie Calle might back out or maybe even forget her proposition. So I went straight to work as soon as I got back to Barcelona and wrote *The Journey of Rita Malú* within a short time.

I sent *The Journey of Rita Malú* to Sophie by email as an attached document, precisely on the 12th of January, confident she'd try to live the story out (and eager to see how she would go about it: would she find the ghost, for example, who was my own self, only fifty years older?). But her answer by return email was slow to arrive. Days went by without a word, not a single message. I was obliged to write something every day in my diary (I had been keeping a sort of diary in a red notebook since September), so I jotted down that she hadn't yet given any sign of having received my story.

Had my story not appealed to her? Could she have figured out that it was really about the exploration of mental geographies in search of a ghostly writer who was me, myself, although visibly older?

Her failure to respond certainly provoked uncertainty. I didn't think my work was poorly written. My story was in keeping with what she had requested. What's more, it was an elastic narrative that could either be a closed story, or else the first chapter of a novel. So it offered the freedom to climb aboard the story and live it out as a complete novel, or to dig into the first chapter and live it like a short story, hopping off early in the journey.

The days rolled by with no news from Sophie, until one afternoon I realized that her strange silence was crippling me as a writer, since for the first time in my life I depended on someone else to be able to write. I needed the other person to move into action, I mean she had to start living what I wrote and if the occasion called for it, ask me to continue the story. Obviously, what I couldn't do now (which is what I was accustomed to doing when I wrote novels), was continue writing about the ghost of the Azores alone, I couldn't write anything else until she acted on the story, discovered the ghost, and questioned me about what happened next, if in fact she wanted to carry on.

Sophie's silence made me anxious. In fact, her failure to answer left me vulnerable, literally paralyzed and incapable of writing until I heard from her. I was poised for a new book that couldn't go anywhere because it wasn't in my hands to make it happen. I began to wonder whether what Sophie Calle's project really intended was to do me in as a writer.

4.

I had warned Sophie when we met in the Flore that I would be traveling on January 23rd to a literary conference in Cartagena de Indias, Colombia. She seemed to make a mental note of the information. Because when her long overdue answer finally arrived by email, it came on exactly the 23rd of January (eleven days after I had sent my story to her), precisely and peculiarly on the selfsame day I left Barcelona for Colombia. My wife, worried over how uneasy the whole affair was making me, called my hotel in Cartagena to let me know that Sophie Calle had finally responded and that the email went like this: "I haven't received anything from you yet. No rush. I've had problems with the Internet. It broke down last week. I'm afraid you might think (in case you sent me something) that I've been keeping silent."

I realized we'd practically have to start all over again. So when I got back from Cartagena de Indias, I resent *The Journey of Rita Malú* to Sophie. And that's when it got worse. Because the days went by once again in a strange, newfound silence. My angst expressed itself in troubled notes, written in my diary or red notebook.

Finally, a message from Sophie arrived on February 3rd: "My mother wanted to see the sea one last time before she dies and we've traveled to Cabourg. As to what concerns us, I finally found out why I never received your emails or your story: it all went into my spam box, including poor Rita Malú. Anyway. I'm going to read your story soon."

I remember that day's night, when I dreamt that Cabourg was the capital of one of the Azore Islands. But the dream was much calmer than those of the previous ones. As if Sophie's promise that she would read my story had worked a soothing effect.

5.

Remember to distrust.
—Stendhal

The next day I went to Girona to give a conference and had dinner later with some friends. I outlined a few details of the project I had gotten myself into with Sophie Calle, feeling edgy the whole time due to alcohol; I felt compelled to explain everything, as if writing by proxy, since I couldn't do it for real. I had to cross my arms and wait for Sophie to decide to do something. Naturally, I could begin a story or a novel that had nothing to do with Sophie's project, but I felt incapable of setting off on a parallel venture.

—I'm paralyzed, I told them, because I can't hope for the death of Sophie's mother in order to resume work on the novel. I can't do anything, not even write her a measly email. Neither can I politely ask after her mother's health, since it might seem as though I was eager for something critical to happen that would allow me to get back to work on the project.

I ended by invoking the pathetic case of Truman Capote from *In Cold Blood*: the writer who suffered unspeakably because he couldn't deliver the book he had completed without the execution scene.

When I got back from Girona, I couldn't stand the inactivity any longer and was overcome by a suicidal urge to press the send key, shooting over to Sophie a beautiful image of the volcanic Island of Pico looking vaguely reminiscent of Roberto Rosellini's movie *Stromboli*. Something new had to happen, anything, if only a slight breeze, I remember telling myself.

She answered that same day, surprisingly quickly. The picture she sent frightened me, because it was her elderly mother's face: there was an intense look in her eyes, as if reproaching my obscene impatience to see her dead.

Sophie had written at the bottom of the photo: "I'm sending a picture of my mother. It's the one she picked for her grave and the epitaph will read: *I was getting bored.* I'm sending it because in a way, she's standing in the way of Pico Island and me. I've heard that you'll be in Paris on the 16th of March. Perhaps we could see each other then."

In fact, I did have to be at the Salon du livre in Paris on the 16th of March. But it was so far away. It seemed way too long to have to wait for another encounter. It's as though—I thought—we were doomed to being in touch in little trickles of communication. But what else could I do? Even though this lack of action had me on edge, I couldn't very well murder her mother so that Sophie could move into gear and complete her journey.

I jotted down in my red notebook: "Someone in Paris wants me to realize that I no longer want to write. And they're going about it in infinitely perverse ways. I must write about it in order to continue writing."

A few days later, I dared myself to send Sophie a new email that might break the deadlock I found myself in—though I didn't get my hopes up. I wrote:

"All life is a process of breaking down (Francis Scott Fitzgerald)."

I pressed the send key. No way to go back. It was irreversible. The sentence about breaking down had already travelled to Sophie's address. Minutes later, again with surprising speed, Sophie answered with the photo of a grave that read *"Don't expect anything."*

I took it very hard. As if the *"don't expect"* was meant for me. I responded immediately, desperate and to defend my own sense of self-respect. I sent her a quote by Julien Gracq that went: "The writer has nothing to expect from others. Believe me, he writes only for himself!"

Silence fell over our correspondence once again. A silence that reigned for days. One afternoon at the end of February, I ran into my friend Sergi Pàmies and vented my frustration by conveying the entire story of Sophie Calle and the strange labyrinth of emails into which I had gotten lost. To keep him interested, I tried to get him to identify with the story reminding him, absurdly, that like Sophie, he had also been born in Paris. Obviously, it wasn't necessary. Sergi listened with his customary kindness and curiosity, and after thinking it over a while, insinuated something rather dreadful, though it had already occurred to me, too. He said that perhaps Sophie's mother wasn't dying after all, and the center of the game was the exchange of emails, which Sophie Calle would turn into a *wall novel* and a study on my ethical behavior during the silent wait for the supposed death of her mother.

—You might just find all the emails you've been writing to Sophie, Pàmies told me, reproduced someday in large format on the walls of some museum. Be careful what you write from now on, because you might read it through a magnifying glass in the near future.

When I described how the relationship with Sophie had taken on the mental structure of a love story (the jealousy of one person not knowing what the other was thinking, which is really what lover's jealousy has always been about: not knowing what the other is thinking; read Proust to understand it better), Sergi preferred to avoid the transcendental and instead mentioned a French song titled *Les histoires d'amour*, sung by the Rita Mitsouko Duo. She sang: "*Love stories generally end badly.*"

6.

When I got home later that same day, I was surprised to find Sophie's response to my Julien Gracq quote. This time there was no text, only the tiny photograph of a funerary cross. Irritated by the mute and solitary cross, I decided to banish the image by re-sending it to Sergi, who had just emailed me the full text of the song by the Rita Mitsouko Duo.

"Sergi, look at what that Sophie sent me," I wrote to Pàmies. But horror of horrors. I hadn't been paying enough attention and in my haste, I had actually resent the message to Sophie herself. It wouldn't be long before she found out that I had referred to her somewhat disrespectfully as "that Sophie," and what's worse, that I was resending her emails to someone else named Sergi.

I was mortified when I realized my mistake.

The days went by in ominous, strict, horrendous silence on her part. Surely, it was all over.

One afternoon when I least expected it, an email suddenly arrived: "I hope you didn't think my *plurien* meant anything."

Did this *plurien* refer to her: *Don't expect anything*? Her sentence came accompanied by the picture of a road leading into a town called FAUX. I understood this as a clear message: she was calling me a "fake." And what became clear, or was finally confirmed: it was over between us; I had proved that I was a pig.

7.

I spent several days totally bewildered, writing small, ridiculous notes in my red notebook. Crushed. Until one morning, carried away by the previous evening's alcoholic exultation, I began telling myself that I had nothing to lose by trying to reconcile with Sophie, so I dared send her an email: "I will be in Paris from the 16ᵗʰ to the 21ˢᵗ of March, in the Hotel de Suède, on Rue Vaneau. Since they don't always inform their guests of missed telephone calls, I wanted to advise that if you would like to reach me, it would be best to communicate by fax."

The real motive—should Sophie decide to answer—was to see whether an intrusive fax would be admitted into the collection of emails that were probably on route to becoming one of her hypothetical *wall novels*. I sent the message and—as my mother said when my father went off to do the lengthy military service required in their day, when she had to brace herself against the fact she had no idea when he would be coming home—I sat down to wait. That's what I did over the following days: I sat down to wait, at all hours, nestled at my desk, not writing a thing, steadfastly waiting and thinking, thinking about a variety of subjects. I ruminated. I calculated, for example, how long it would take for spring to arrive and remember saying things to my self like: When spring comes, I must be sarcastic. Only by so being, will I survive the next season. Things like that, sometimes without making much sense. Until the 16ᵗʰ of March came around and off I went to the Hotel de Suède on Rue Vaneau, in Paris.

I was only there for a few hours before a fax from Sophie arrived, encouraging me to call her at home. My first reaction was a combination of happiness and annoyance. On the one hand, there was nothing I wanted more than her forgiveness, but on the other, I thought of how aggravating the rebirth of that complicated relationship might be.

After much hesitancy, I finally made up my mind to call her. The telephone rang three times. Someone picked up.

—It's me, I'm . . . I babbled.

A brief silence. Followed by Sophie's voice:

—Oh! You got my fax?

—Yes. I'm here in Paris. Is everything well, Sophie?

Another brief silence. And then these words, nearly a whisper:

—My mother died yesterday afternoon.

It's the last thing I expected to hear.

I didn't know whether to believe her or not. It seemed too much of a coincidence that her mother would have waited until I got to Paris to die. I was at a loss. Finally, I mumbled a few words of condolence.

—Oh, come on . . . , she interrupted.

Another phone rang in Sophie's house, probably her cell phone. She asked me to "excuse her for a second." I heard part of the conversation with the other person who had called. She pronounced the word "funeral" several times and it made me think that for however unlikely it seemed to me, it actually confirmed the truth—it would have been a beastly farce—regarding her mother's death.

She hung up her cell phone and came back to our conversation. She told me the funeral would take place two days later, in the cemetery of Montparnasse, and that it would be nice if I could come. The obituary would appear in *Liberation* on the day of the funeral. In any case, she added, now she had the time to see me. If I wanted, we could meet someplace in Paris within the hour. In the Hotel de Suède, for example.

One hour and five minutes later, Sophie walked into the hall of the Hotel de Suède with a video camera and a broad smile. I was there waiting for her. She ordered two coffees from reception and though I didn't want to see them, showed me recent images of her dead mother and a copy of the peculiar obituary that would appear in *Liberation* two days later.

It didn't take long for her to explain that following the experience with her mother, there was still one more obstacle between her and Pico Island. She had been invited to the Venice Biennale and needed time to prepare her show for this significant exhibition. She was so sorry, but our project would have to be postponed. She had studied maps of the Azores and was also drawn to the idea of going back to Lisbon, a city she wasn't very familiar with after all. It wasn't a lack of interest in Rita Malú's journey, on the contrary, she was very intent on it, but the Venice Biennale was—as I must perfectly understand—of paramount importance to her.

Of course I could understand her perfectly, but there was a pending question that I didn't hesitate to ask:

—When will you have time to live out *The Journey of Rita Malú*?

—May of next year, she said, without blinking.

My God! May 2007 seemed so far away. What could I possibly do in the meantime?

—I've been waiting a long time, over eight years, to tackle this experience of *living* a story and I don't mind waiting another year, she added by way of an explanation.

—Eight years?

—Yes, eight years have gone by since I first proposed the idea to Paul Auster. I can wait a little while longer, don't you think?

It seemed the perfect occasion to stage a break-up, to convey to her that by no means would I wait 14 months longer; so be it, our imaginary contract had come to an end. No way would I wait such a ridiculous amount of time!

But instead I was all smiles and resignedly docile.

We said our goodbyes at the door of the hotel an hour later and arranged to see each other again the following day, in the Salon du livre, Porte de Versailles, where I would be signing copies of my latest novel. She would come to see me, she said, since it was close to her home. I took my leave and we both headed to our respective appointments, walking in opposite directions. I went to a friend's party near Bastille Square, where I described a few details of my recent encounter with Sophie. A journalist from a magazine dedicated to rock music and literature heard my story and blurted: "Oh my God! She proposed it to you, too?"

I didn't really want to know what was behind the "you, too." But I ended up saying, "Yes, she approached me, too." And then I asked if she had approached anyone other than Paul Auster or Jean Echenoz. And yes, she had suggested the idea to two other writers. She had also approached Olivier Rolin, for example.

The next day, I found out that there weren't only three more writers, but at least four. Just before I left Littré for the Salon du livre, I received a call from a good friend who was in Segovia, the writer and filmmaker Ray Loriga, who invited me to Madrid to participate in *Carta libre*, an hour-long program on Spanish public television where he interviewed artists from his imaginary tribe. He wanted to invite Sophie and me, he said, to be among his guests, to talk about our project. I asked him how he had found out about it, and he told me that Sophie had told him herself, they're longtime friends. She made the same attractive proposition to him three years ago. He'd almost gone mad, he said, working relentlessly to move the seductive plan forward, but he'd come up against all sorts of peculiar glitches, including Sophie herself. Luckily for him, he hadn't gone so far as to write the story. My case was definitely much worse, since the story was already written and yet nothing had come of it.

It seriously aggravated me to find out that there had been more people invited previously than what I'd been told. But I didn't say a word and kept

my anger to myself. I accepted Loriga's invitation to his program because
I figured at least it would give me another opportunity to see Sophie, and
more material to put into writing about my relationship with her, always
awaiting—which was threatening to become eternal—her decision to embark
on the adventure, the journey of Rita Malú, toward the encounter with my
ghost.

8.

Two hours later, I was signing copies of my novel in the Salon du livre when
Sophie showed up with a friend whom she introduced as Florence Aubenas,
that is, as the famous journalist of *Liberation* who had been kidnapped and
then freed in Iraq. Though I had signed the manifesto for her freedom in
Barcelona, I hadn't seen photographs of her. So inevitably, I doubted that she
was the real Aubenas. Inertia lead me to suspect that everything Sophie did
was a bluff, that she had lied to me about her mother and now she wanted to
poke fun at my expense by introducing me to the fake Aubenas.

—Stop pulling my leg, I said to Sophie.

It was a gut reaction. I uttered it spontaneously; it just burst out as a result
of all the ambiguities. Now I'd even begun to get familiar with her.

—What does it mean, stop pulling my leg? Do you mean that you don't
want me to play with you? Sophie said in more than correct Spanish.

—Exactly, I smiled. Don't mess with me.

(It seemed to me like a good title for a novel.)

But Florence Aubenas was in fact Florence Aubenas. Everyone around me
confirmed it. Even Aubenas, who, to confirm that she was herself, invited
me to her stand where she signed a copy of her recently published book, *La
méprise*. So I went back to mine, to my stand, and continued signing books.
Every once in a while Sophie would show up, going back and forth between
Florence's and my publisher's stands.

Sophie would show up and stare at me, then laugh in an infectious way.
I would end up laughing too, my expression distorted by uselessly trying to
keep a straight face, or try to express anger.

—Don't mess with me, I told her again.

I let out a giggle. And that was it. The next day I returned to Barcelona
and she attended her mother's funeral. It seemed silly to reproach her for

having propositioned so many men to bring a written adventure to life, so many broken friends. It seemed grotesque to criticize her and what's more, I had no right.

The idea was hers, after all, and she could undertake it with whomever she pleased, whenever she pleased. I convinced myself, on the other hand (so as not to lose my wits), that it was all beyond reproach. I had no reason for being so apprehensive. Why not wait until May? But . . . it was May of the following year! I was now peeved, annoyed over having been so submissive the whole time, when we had agreed that I would be in control of what had to be done and what had to be lived. I myself didn't understand why I was being so docile. In any case, I thought, I'll have another opportunity to rebel against the situation on my friend Ray Loriga's television show, at least to pound my fist on the table a little. I felt hostage to the strange impression of holding a heavy hammer in my hand that I couldn't use because the handle was in flames.

9.

Back in Barcelona, I received an email from Sophie letting me know that as long as Ray Loriga confirmed that I would be on the show, she would arrive in Madrid on the 6th of April to tape it, although she had to say that she didn't see much sense in a televised encounter when the question remained: what are we going to talk about on camera when the project hadn't begun?

On the 6th of April I went to Madrid and taped the show with Ray Loriga, during which I explained what had happened so far with Sophie. It's not that many things occurred to me to talk about, but I knew how to find water where there was no fountain. Sophie never showed up at the studio. She completely missed the appointment in Madrid, alleging a mix-up over the date and time, and Loriga decided to turn her into the program's invited ghost. When I got back to Barcelona, trying to control my frustration, I sent Sophie the picture of a clock with a Portuguese caption: CONTAGEM DECRESENTE.

The message was a modestly furious protest and possibly the seedling of a rupture, meaning to express that the clock of my patience was now in countdown mode. Sophie answered immediately. She explained that she was preparing a *wall novel* on the subject of "the missing" for the Venice Biennale, and would be traveling the next day to the south of France where she would spend some time with Florence Aubenas, the renowned missing person who had disappeared in another era in Iraq. She bid adieu for a few weeks and asked me to remember that in May 2007, we could take up our project again.

I observed that although I had begun playing the part of the ghost, things had taken an unforeseen turn of events and now she was the specter, like in the story of Rita Malú. Surely the ghost of the red house on the hill on Pico Island had done well by closing the door on her softly.

10.

I traveled to Buenos Aires at the beginning of May, ostensibly to promote my novels, but more than anything else to disappear for a few days. I ended up hospitalized in Barcelona's Vall d'Hebron clinic. I'll never again feel the urge to go missing in an Argentine hotel room. The peculiar thing is that when I was in Buenos Aires, I even boasted about gaining strength in the hotel room in Recoleta, of not setting foot in the streets of the city, except for the two hours I spent in a public appearance at the Book Fair. The audience smiled when I said that I had become a shadow and how, like the character in one of my books, I hadn't stirred from the hotel since arriving in the city. But this was merely literature in the style of *Journey Around My Room*, the desire to cover up a private secret: I got tired just walking down the hall. It's the only reason for not going to see Recoleta Square, for example, which I remembered from previous visits, and that was only 200 meters from my hotel.

I didn't yet know the worst of it: I was experiencing severe kidney failure and headed for an irreversible coma. But, how could I possibly imagine something like that? How could I imagine I was dying? Days passed before I would come to full knowledge, when I returned to Barcelona and walked through El Prat airport like a somnambulist (a poisonous current of uric acid was reaching my brain and I didn't even notice it). I responded bizarrely when asked why I had arrived without a suitcase, my eyes rolled to the whites:

—Life has no idea of the life it leads.

I had spent four full days squatting in that Argentine hotel room playing hide and seek, observing a single, funereal landscape (almost as if it were a premonition) outside my window: the tombs of the neighboring Recoleta Cemetery, the pantheons of some of the national heroes of the Argentine homeland. Flowers for Evita Peron's mausoleum. An obsessive, sickly, mortal view. What a trip!

II.

I remember W.G. Sebald's obsessive view from the hospital, which he tells about in the beginning of *The Rings of Saturn*: "I can remember precisely how, upon being admitted to that room on the eighth floor, I became overwhelmed by the feeling that the Suffolk expanses I had walked the previous summer had now shrunk once and for all to a single, blind, insensate spot. Indeed, all that could be seen of the world from my bed was the colorless patch of sky framed in the window."

Sebald recounts how he was overwhelmed throughout the day by the desire (by looking out the hospital window draped strangely in black netting) to make certain that reality, as he had so dreaded, had vanished forever. The desire, by dusk, had grown so strong for Sebald that he contrived a way to slip over the edge of the bed onto the floor, half on his belly and half sideways, and crawl over to the wall on all fours. He raised himself up despite the pain, holding himself upright for the first time against the windowsill. Like Gregor Samsa, or any other garden-variety beetle.

Anyway. In my case it took three days to reach the blind, insensate spot of my window on the 10th floor for the first time and contemplate, incredulous, the view—surprisingly full of life—that extended from Vall d'Hebron to the sea. So, the world is still there, I told myself. It seemed amazing to me, that anthill of people I observed from way up there, feverishly crossing avenues and streets: the same mad human stream that never even shifted when the young man from Kafka's "The Judgement" threw himself out the window of his paternal home.

How far away and yet how near they were, I thought, my hotel in Recoleta, Sophie Calle, the tombs and mausoleums with their funerary flowers, Rita Malú and Eva Perón, my dangerous days as a missing person overseas.

12.

I remember how when I would finally feel optimistic for a moment, I'd end up suspecting that optimism was just another form of sickness.

13.

The fourth day I was able to begin reading a little. I asked for a book by Sergio Pitol, recalling a sentence that had always called my attention: "I adore hospitals." I couldn't remember what came after that shocking sentence. I found that what Pitol wrote couldn't have been closer to my own experience: "I adore hospitals. They bring back the security of childhood: all nourishment is brought to my bedside punctually. All I have to do is push a button and a nurse appears, sometimes even a doctor! They give me a pill and the pain disappears, they give me an injection and I fall asleep on the spot . . ."

The most difficult time came with nightfall. Pain became more of a blind, insensate spot than my window did a spot of life and the sea. I remember spending time the last night exploring the word *hospitality* to scare away the anxiety—just another way to forget I was in hospital. Luckily, the Guinean nurse on the night shift caught my pensive mood and came to my aid asking what I had on my mind, hoping to calm my disquiet. I told him I was meditating on the word *hospitality*. First he fell quiet for a while, but broke his silence telling me abruptly never to forget that everything was relative. For example, the French had a great reputation for being hospitable and yet nobody dared go into their homes. It made me laugh and I felt at ease the rest of that night. But the anxiety came back with remarkable drive at sunrise, with the first rosy light entering the blind and insensate spot of my window at Vall d'Hebron, and once again I wished for a breath of air, if only one slight breeze, a single movement: proof that I was still alive and waiting.

14.

While I await the operation that will alleviate my problems, scheduled in a few weeks, I have to wear an uncomfortable orthopedic device—a catheter in my penis—that hampers my movement. I can go outside if I want. The catheter empties into a little bag where the urine gathers, tied discreetly around my right leg, under my trousers. It's well hidden, but for now the only time I go out is to take a cab to a medical center on Calle Aribau for tests, or to the hospital to see the nephrologist or the urologist who are caring for me, or to sit in the patio of the bar on the corner. Even though the doctor said I could lead a normal life, I only go out when it's strictly necessary, and never very far.

15.

I read in a note on the Internet that said "the third section of *Double Game* arose from the invitation Sophie Calle extended to Paul Auster: to become the *author* of her acts, to invent a fictional character that she would try to resemble, do what he wanted her to do, for a period of one year maximum." Apparently, Paul Auster didn't want to be made responsible for what could happen to Sophie, and in exchange, he sent her a few *Personal Instructions for S.C. on How to Improve Life in New York City (Because she asked . . .).* Sophie followed his instructions and the result was a project titled *Gotham Handbook.* The rules of the game were: smile at all times, talk to strangers, distribute sandwiches and cigarettes to the homeless and cultivate a spot of her choice. It lasted for one week in the month of September 1994, whose epicenter was a phone booth located on the corner of Greenwich and Harrison. According to Sophie Calle, the result of the operation was the following: 125 smiles given for 72 received, 22 sandwiches accepted for 10 rejected, 8 packs of cigarettes accepted for 0 rejected, 154 minutes of conversation.

I read it all as if years had gone by since I had been excited about Sophie's proposition. My physical collapse had put my health ahead of everything else and the concerns of our project had been relegated to sixth or seventh place in my life. So much so, that her name and surname, Sophie Calle, had become dissociated from the notes I took daily (making things up a lot since December) in my red notebook.

Every once in a while, of course, the memory of that note I had read on the Internet returned and brought to mind the title that Paul Auster had given his work, especially the part in parentheses, *because she asked.* I didn't know why, but at the most idiotic moments I would return to reminiscing about Sophie Calle, and obsessively ponder the phrase "*because she asked.*"

Whenever this occurred, I couldn't help but go over the things that had happened with Sophie, and over them again, and agree that the ghost of the house on Pico Island had done very well to close the door on Rita Malú *softly.*

My catheter stubbornly insists on characterizing—as is happening now— one of those Harlequin sneers that interrupts the drama developing on stage and unravel the plot.

In fact, the only thing the catheter, the illness, the collapse—whatever you

want to call it—did, is doing, is to unravel the plot of my story with Sophie
and distance me the whole while, softly, from her.

III. THE TANGLE

1.

I thought about a friend yesterday, who said that at some point we all ask
ourselves what would have happened had we approached that woman in a
different way, if we'd given some sign that we hadn't . . . I recalled something
else he said, too: "We consider our past life as if it were a sort of rough draft,
something that can be transformed."

Maybe it's a good technique for escaping my life in this prison cell of my
catheter. Yesterday, I went through my diary entries of the past few months,
all the notes I've been jotting down in my red notebook since last September.
They serve as inspiration for reenacting my relationship with Sophie Calle
in the computer. Since she hasn't made up her mind whether or not to live
out *The Journey of Rita Malú*, I thought, I might as well make the jump from
literature to life on my own, particularly since the only thing tying me to
her, to life, is a catheter. To do it, I suggested to myself that I choose a few
fragments from my red notebook and in the style of Petronius (who dared to
live out what he had written), carry the episodes over into real life, or better
said, live them over again and correct them, if necessary. Until now, my diary
notes are mere rough drafts of my own life.

2.

I go over the first lines in my red notebook. I wrote them down last year, on
the 1st of September: "The sun is rising in my study with high windows as
I inaugurate my red notebook or diary, where I'll write about Barcelona and
other nervous cities, asking myself my name, who is it that's writing these
words, and it occurs to me that my study is like a cranium from which I
spring anew, like an imaginary citizen . . ."

How the devil could I bring such intensely literary sentences to life? I'm
in the same room where I wrote them the first time around, but it's hard to

feel as though my study were a cranium from which I spring anew, like an imaginary citizen.

I realize the sentences that inaugurate my diary can't possibly be brought to real life, they're pure literature. How could I saunter around my desk leisurely, thinking I'm walking around the inside of a skull? As a result I yawn, I mope, I feel more paralyzed than ever. Then suddenly it dawns on me that by yawning, by opening up my mouth, I've found the best way of feeling these literary sentences of mine as something *experienced*. Yawning worked a small miracle and I stretched and began splintering like an abyss and went so far as to merge with the void.

In my memory only the cranium remains, which my imagination is depositing at this exact moment on top of my table, like someone lowering their head to rest on their desk at work.

3.

At home that evening, I read through the remaining entries in my red notebook, confirming my suspicion that until that December day when I registered Sophie Calle's call to my home in Barcelona, there's nothing of relevance to the trivial events of my life. There's nothing significant there, the minutes are rightly rough drafts. Nothing is worth correcting. In fact, it would be best to leave them alone, as what they are: the grey outlines of my own life.

It's often said that literature carries a considerable advantage over life: one can go back and correct things. But in my case, I'm not interested in going back or correcting anything; I think it's better to leave things be, at least until the day in question, when Sophie Calle called me at home. The game changed after that. It marked a before and after in my diary, because it's when I started to pretend. Until then, my notes communicate things that really happened to me. But something changed that day, and I came up with the idea of pretending that Sophie Calle had called me at home, to propose a mysterious project she couldn't mention over the phone. After a while, I elaborated on this quick, pretend note, transferred it to the computer and created a parallel fiction that I continued constructing in my energetic red notebook.

Why did I pretend that Sophie Calle telephoned me? And why did I make believe that she had asked me to write something for her to bring to life? Perhaps I made it all up precisely because she didn't ask.

Sophie Calle never telephoned me at home, that part belongs to my imagination. The same goes for the story of our agreements and disagreements—all
make believe. I guess I concocted the phone call and everything else because
I was fed up with my own lethargic existence and needed to describe a more
interesting life in my diary.

I think about it carefully now, and realize that I have an imaginary story
with Sophie and it's written down. Now I could dare myself to bring it to life
instead of only imagining it. But how? First of all, I don't know Sophie Calle
so it would be complicated to get her to call me at home. Even more difficult
would be getting her to meet me at Café de Flore to do all these things, like
suggesting I do what she had already tried with Paul Auster, eight years ago.
It's a tricky story to bring successfully to life, but nothing's impossible and I
don't want to feel defeated before I get started. I'll take the necessary steps
toward bringing the story with Sophie Calle to life, which I've been composing and writing. In other words, if Don Quixote is about a dreamer who dares
to become his own dream, my story will be that of the writer who dares to
bring what he has written to life, specifically in this case, what he's invented
about his relationship with Sophie Calle, his favorite "narrative artist."

4.

It isn't so difficult to get Sophie to call me at home, anyway. All I need to do
is talk to Ray Loriga, the person who explained what Sophie had been going
through over the past few months. He's who told me about the slow agony of
her mother and the funeral in Montparnasse, and the details of the Biennale
of Venice and her friendship with Florence Aubenas. Ray explained so many
details about Sophie, that I was able to invent the story of my understandings
and misunderstandings with her. He also said that three years ago, Sophie
had asked Ray himself to write a story that would allow her to bring literature to life. She had proposed the same thing to Paul Auster, Jean Echenoz,
Olivier Rolin, and very likely to other writers, as Ray soon found out.

In fact, my pretend relationship with Sophie exactly began on the day
when Ray, who's been a friend of hers for many years, recounted the story of
Sophie's invitation for him to write her a story that she would try to bring
to life. Ray said that things had ended in nothing, the same as with Auster, Echenoz and Rolin. I remember feeling immediately envious when I

learned about it, since I would have loved for Sophie Calle to have proposed or asked me for something like that, especially considering all the years I've spent speculating on the relationship between life and literature, rummaging around for a technique to go beyond them, especially beyond literature.

Finding a way to get close to Sophie Calle was the only way to bring a little joy into my life. Why shouldn't I have a stab at getting my favorite "narrative artist" to suggest bringing something that I had written to life? It seemed to me that I had as much a right as anyone else to hear the proposal. Didn't I? Not only was Sophie's proposition as dangerous as it was attractive, it opened the door to a fascinating, outlandish test to push further; to go, once and for all, beyond writing itself. In fact, from a certain point of view, it turned writing into a mere rag, reduced it to a scrap, a measly bureaucratic procedure to gain access to life: life, it's so important. Isn't it? Isn't that what we always say? I was suddenly overcome with doubt. Life, so primordial. I repeated it to myself again: Life, so primordial. So essential, I added. Blood and the liver, so fundamental. The doubts increased. Should life be given such a place of preference? Since the very beginning, since Cervantes, I told myself, this tension between literature and life is the conversation that the novel has advanced all along. Really, what we call the "novel" is nothing more than this ongoing discussion.

Some days later, I recall, I reflected on similar subjects in *Carta libre*, Ray Loriga's program for Spanish television where I talked about my Sophie Calle story as if it were true, the supposedly professional relationship I had spent time developing with her, never once letting on that it was all make believe. Ray, who loves making up false stories, played along and turned Sophie into a sort of ghostly guest presence which, if you think about it, was the only way she could be on the show at all, and where we talked about a project that couldn't really be talked about since, just as I had rightly explained to Sophie in the fictional account, "What are we going to talk about on camera when the project hasn't begun?"

5.

When I woke up, I exchanged the briefcase-bag I'm hooked up to while I sleep (a torment) where the nocturnal urine gathers, for the smaller plastic sack that's tied around my right leg by day. I showered and wrote down the simple dream I had just had about a woman who never turned the faucets off completely, and who always closed doors very softly. I hobbled around behind her with my catheter and a whip, or the shadow of that catheter, and my dream inside the dream bore an unprecedented image of myself: I was smacking her ass with my shadow.

Afterward, I called Ray Loriga and got straight to the point. I told him I wanted Sophie Calle to call me at home as soon as possible, for her to suggest a project, and tell me that she can't explain it over the phone, and that we should find a city and a place to meet. He giggled. I'm serious, I told him. And I would appreciate that he do it sooner rather than later, I said, Sophie has to set a date to meet in Paris, in the Café de Flore, to talk about this secret project, because I want to bring the make believe story that I've been writing in my computer about our relationship to life myself, and the story demands that there be a scene in this particular café in Paris, where I would like Sophie, even if she's faking it, to ask if I would like to write a story that she can later try to live.

Ray seemed a little skeptical. He had called a few days earlier to inquire after my acute renal condition that required surgery. "You can't be serious," he said. "Oh, completely," I responded. "You honestly want to go to Paris wearing a catheter and half screwed up to meet Sophie and play this game with her?" he said, and laughed. There was a brief silence. "What for?" he asked. It seemed a bit zealous to talk about Petronius (that's why I kept quiet) and how I wanted to see what would happen when one lived out the adventure they had previously written, or in other words, when one takes the leap from their own literature to their own life. "Answer me," he insisted. "Why?" Another brief silence. I answered as best I could. "To be in Paris, and more than anything else, to spend time living what I've written, instead of writing," I finally said. Ray wanted to know why I didn't do something else. "Such as?" I asked, more curious than a very curious boy. He didn't think twice: "There are plenty of ways for you to have fun and none of them include going to Paris wearing a catheter, to live out what you've written." I felt bad, even suspicious of acting against my own interests. I had the troubling impression that since I wanted to reach way beyond everything, I was actually putting obstacles in my own path. I told this to Ray. "The world's a tangle," was all he said. I can't explain it, but his words relaxed me, as if for the first time in my life I shared one of the stillest, most evident truths with someone else.

6.

Two days later, I was lying on the hard shell of my back (it's just an expression, what I mean is that I was half asleep, lying naked in bed, on my back, which felt very hard due to the amount of time I had spent in that position with the catheter showing, since I hadn't bothered to keep up decorum and cover myself with the sheets, knowing that I was home alone) when the telephone rang. It was Sophie Calle.

"At last, we speak again. It's about time, don't you think?" she said in Spanish with a thick French accent. The phone number, I saw, was from Paris but it hadn't yet occurred to me that it could be Sophie Calle calling and I asked, half alarmed, who it was on the other end of the line. "It's Sophie, I just wanted to talk to you again, so you don't think I've abandoned our project. It's still on but I have been very busy lately . . ." My legs trembled slightly as I abandoned my beetle-on-its-back position and sat up in bed. She acted as though we were a couple making up romantically. It wasn't what I had asked Ray for. Regarding whether it was really her on the phone, the real Sophie Calle, there was no room for doubt. I had heard (even studied) her voice in different recordings. It was her.

I felt as though I should play along. "Believe me, I don't expect anything from you, I've also been very busy, it'll work out," I said. But she seemed bent on clarifying things: "Venice took up a lot of my time, but the worst was the bureaucratic paperwork after my mother passed away, which was and still is utterly exhausting. I just wanted to let you know that nothing has been dismissed, I still want to bring your story to life . . ." I let her know that everything was fine, that she shouldn't worry, and for a few minutes had the impression that I was speaking with a sense of familiarity, as if we had known each other for a long time. I might have ended up giving details of the problems with my liver and urethra, letting her know I was in a clinical period just before surgery, if it hadn't been for a sudden change in her tone of voice, which turned serious, even slightly aggressive.

"Are you sure everything is alright? I hear a slight hint of disappointment in your voice," she said suddenly. I kept silent and unmoving, sitting upright in bed, naked, confused, with sudden heart palpitations. "Huh?" I asked. "I want to make a proposition, but I can't do it over the phone. Can we meet? I would like to know if you will be coming to Paris anytime in the next few weeks," she said. We wasted no time in arranging an encounter in four days in the Café de Flore, on Friday the 16th of June, to set the scene for the farce. But what if it wasn't a farce and she seriously wants to propose that I write a story for her? That was my great expectation. If she asks me for the same thing as with Auster and Loriga, I could surprise her by tendering a copy of *The Journey of Rita Malú*. I called Ray to thank him for his help but couldn't reach him. Later, through mutual friends, I found that he had left— something to do with the movie he had just filmed about Santa Teresa—and wouldn't be back for a few weeks.

I decided to ask my wife to accompany me to Paris, but she flat out refused to have anything to do with such a cockamamie scheme. First surgery—she said—and then, when the catheter was removed, I could spend time talking to Sophie Calle and whatever other hogwash. "Anyway," she said, "what's got into you with Sophie Calle? Its one thing to admire what she does or even get jealous of her proposals to your friend Ray, but to put your own life at risk just to see her is something very different."

I knew that what she said made sense, but I also knew that art isn't a sensible thing, it never has been; in fact quite the contrary, it's always been an assault on common sense and an effort to reach beyond the beaten trail. Anyway, my wife was clearly exaggerating since I had all the necessary medical authorizations for air travel and I wasn't risking my life by going to Paris. And besides, the adventure of living out what I had written seemed entertaining and nothing impeded me from returning to Barcelona in time for my appointment with the anesthesiologist in Vall d'Hebron hospital on Thursday, June 22nd.

"What if the hospital moves the anesthesiologist's appointment forward? They told us it could happen. What then? Huh? What? You'd postpone an emergency operation because you feel like having coffee at the Flore?" my wife said, beyond exasperation. I don't remember how I answered her; all I know is that I couldn't convince her to accompany me.

So I boarded a plane early on the 16th of June, lonely as a rat, with a pang of self-reproach and my wife's resultant righteous indignation, and showed up in Paris like a poor, crippled bachelor, with a return ticket to Barcelona that same evening. I showed up a half hour early in the neighborhood of Saint-Germain where the Flore is located, a little flustered over the encounter, more than I had expected, to be honest. Ideally, I should have gone to the

Café Bonaparte first and thrown back a few shots of whisky, to keep wholly faithful to the story I had written in my computer and wanted to recreate. But drinking like that would be nearly suicidal, since my kidneys would have a hard time processing the alcohol. They would have been forced to work overtime and given my physical condition, put them in a high-risk situation. So I strolled into the Bonaparte and asked for sparkling water at the bar. I drank it back in a single shot and immediately asked for another. I drank that one back, too. I looked around to see if my eager attitude toward the water had attracted attention, but, obviously, the world remained unmoved, continuing on its course without a care, without anyone asking why I did or didn't drink water. I went to the restroom and emptied the urine from the little plastic bag that was tied to my right leg. I returned to the bar, paid and left the Bonaparte at a leisurely stride since there were still twenty minutes to go before the clock struck twelve o'clock noon. I stopped at the window of La Hune bookstore, ten meters away from the Flore, and looked around to see if anyone had followed me, but nobody had. I didn't want to seem paranoid so I stopped looking around. But, how silly. Who would think I was paranoid if there wasn't anyone, not a single person, watching me?

I turned to look in La Hune's window and saw that the books of the writer I most despised in the whole world were on display. Luckily, the books shared space with a magnificent, large reproduction of *The Bride Stripped Bare by Her Bachelors, Even*, the enigmatic double glass piece by Marcel Duchamp that's painted in oil and divided horizontally into two equal parts with iron wire. At the top of the upper rectangle, the Bride's Domain, was the perfectly reproduced grey cloud (I've always heard that it's the Milky Way) painted by Duchamp. The cloud surrounded three unpainted squares of glass whose function (I've always heard) was to transmit to "the bachelors" located at the bottom half of the glass, the Bride's concerns, possibly her orders, her commands. I paid particular attention to what has always intrigued and interested me the most about this Duchampian glass: the spots located in the far right section of the upper half. This area, these dots, have always been known as the Bachelors' shots.

I had almost reached a point of ecstasy contemplating those dots, but my eyes betrayed me, and once again I caught sight of the books by the writer I hated. I considered sending him a bachelor's bullet. Should I entertain the likelihood that Sophie Calle put those books there just to irritate me? It was highly unlikely. Then I thought of the surgery that was waiting for me back in Barcelona, and of death, and I also thought—I don't know why—that I could lose everything.

Death led me to reflect on life. But, what life? It was high time, I told myself, that in the chaos of our present time, we started asking ourselves what we mean by *life*, exactly what are we talking about when we talk about it and whether what we're talking about all the time isn't actually death. Surely we should start to qualify the definition of experience . . . I have a somewhat distant, kind of fuzzy memory of it. Who lived in complete self-realization? Does anyone truly live? And, while we're at it, what kind of a life did life live?

I decided to pull myself out of the twilight zone I'd gotten myself into and began speculating on what Sophie might say when we finally saw each other. That's what really mattered. Will she ask me to write a story for her to bring to life, and should I understand the request as a farce, as if it were a theatrical representation? Or might she be taking it all seriously and so when she suggests that I bring my writing beyond writing itself, I ought to hand her *The Journey of Rita Malú*, whose twelve pages were folded ever so carefully in my suit pocket?

As I played it all over in my mind, I realized that I was no longer looking at the books in the window, or paying attention to what was going on around me, but almost felt wrapped in a floating cloud. So I was slightly startled when someone stepped between the window and me, greeted me in French with a heavy Spanish accent and an outstretched hand, and politely asked what I was doing there. I'd never seen this young person in my life, with his dark glasses, black suit and tie, and carefully groomed four-day beard. My offbeat sense of humor reared its head and I asked if he was the window decorator. "Because if you are, I have some serious complaints," I said, letting a slight giggle erupt, which made me realize I wasn't all there. I had been trying to concentrate on my meeting with Sophie Calle but all these obstacles were getting in my way, from negative thoughts to characters wearing dark glasses.

"You've been following me since the Bonaparte," I asked, mostly just to say something since all he did was stand there, completely still, with a strange expression on his face as he stared at the slight bulge toward the bottom of my right leg, where the small bag of urine was. "Don't you recognize me?" he

asked looking again at the tiny bulge. I swallowed hard. Could it be a drunk
instead of that "anonymous alcoholic" I'd made-up in my story based on the
red notebook? "Honestly, you don't remember who I am?" he asked again. But
suddenly it came to me, I did recognize him. The dark glasses had thrown me
off a little. He's a Spaniard who's been there for a while—more or less since I
started coming back to this area of Paris—and who walks around the streets
of the district, saying hello to people and politely asking if they remember
him. If you say yes, of course I remember you, then he'll leave you alone. But
since I had a few minutes left to kill before going to the Flore, I decided to
respond that of course I remembered him perfectly, but I forgot what it was
he did for a living. He got very serious. He pretended to be embarrassed by
the question, but it was obvious that in fact the contrary was true, he was
delighted to have the chance to answer. He took a deep breath, pleased, and
said: "I'm a retired artist and now I wander the world." That's perfect. A
retired artist. No one had ever defined themselves that way to me before. I
smiled at him. He said: "Nobody cared about the things I used to paint, so
one day I got fed up and asked myself why I painted and why it mattered
to me if anybody cared. So, you know what I did? I retired. And I went on
painting, as if nothing had happened. But I only paint in my imagination.
Look at this window, for example, to me it's a still life. There's a dead crow in
it. You may not see it. There are days when nothing else exists but the world
in my mind. You have my word as a retired artist."

His words had far surpassed everything I had expected to hear from him.
But now it was time to figure out how to get rid of the guy. Sophie Calle took
precedent. The retired artist had to retire from my sight. "Fine, I'll be seeing
you, I'll always remember you," I said. And slipped away with a lively step,
body leaning slightly forward, head inclined a bit as I walked, as if a blustery
wind were whooshing me from one side to the other of the Boulevard Saint-
Germain, the catheter bouncing wildly from one side to the other, hands
crossed behind my back, stride lengthy.

7.

I arrived at the Flore five minutes early, but Sophie Calle was already there
and she had gotten a good table. I approached her, trying to control my slight
panic.

It's me, I said with a degree of coyness unknown to this world. As a gesture of respect, I asked permission to be seated. She assented and then smiled at me. I tried to conceal my difficulty in sitting down with the catheter. But hiding it only made it worse, since the clumsy movement jerked hard at my penis and the pain lasted almost a minute. Unaware of my private drama, she said that we would speak in Spanish, as we had done by telephone, since she had spent a year in Mexico and could speak the language well. I curbed my shyness and anxiety by speaking up immediately. I started off by telling her the story about how I had been spied on and pursued just a moment earlier by a recovering alcoholic, which is something that could have come straight out of the *wall novels* she was so addicted to—the man and the chase, that is. Might she have been the one who had put him up to it?

Sophie smiled slightly. She caressed the video camera that sat atop the table and got straight to the point, no further ado. I tried to change my position to accommodate my genital equipment and the catheter a little more comfortably. But I wasn't able to improve anything. What she wanted to propose, she said, was that I write a story. That I create a character she could bring to life: a character whose behavior—for one year, maximum—would be contingent on what I wrote. She wanted to change her life and what's more, she was tired of having to determine her own *deeds*, she preferred to have someone else do it for her now, let somebody else decide how she was supposed to live.

—In short, she said, you write a story and I'll bring it to life.

We remained silent for a few slow seconds until she went on to explain that she had made the same proposition to Paul Auster some years earlier, who found the responsibility too extreme and so declined. She had also suggested the same thing, without any luck, to Jean Echenoz, Olivier Rolin, to my friend Ray Loriga, and to Maurice Forest-Meyer.

Who's that last person? I asked suspiciously and almost incoherently, my question like a humble bullet of water in a lake—like a ridiculous bachelor's shot. But Sophie answered saying that now was not the time for this and simply refused to tell me who this Maurice Forest-Meyer individual was, whose name she uttered with a hint of connotation. I realized, moreover, that what I wanted to know was something else, something completely different. What I truly wanted to get out of her was whether this was a simple mise-en-scene, or if she was being serious. But why question her about it, if her response, whatever it may be, wouldn't serve to clarify the situation or orient me in any way? It was useless. So I fired another shot, this time with a little more passion. I asked if what she really wanted was for me to become a retired artist, and at first she regarded me with stupor, which grew into an ice-cold glare.

I broke a long silence by saying that someone had once said that our species' commanding intelligence, the rich and yet vulnerable result of evolution, finds itself at times before doors that are better left unopened, or that should be closed very softly. Another ice-cold glare, but at this specific moment, it turned into a look of utter bafflement. I could no longer contain myself, so I just said it, straight from the gut, every word vocalized carefully:

I am not particularly interested in reaching beyond literature.

Did she hear me correctly?

Just in case—I added—let me express it another way. I don't want to jump any further into the abyss, I mean, what lies beyond literature. There's no life there, only the risk of death. It's like these biochemical breakthroughs we're starting to see that are really a human trap. That's why some doors are better left unopened.

I can't deny, I continued, that I'm not tempted to go beyond my writing. But on second thought, I would prefer to stay put. No, not another step further into the void, or passage from literature to life. I don't want to abandon my writing in the arms of the sinister hole we call life anymore. I've been researching, exploring the shady abyss I intuited in the ambiguous beyond of my writing and figure it's about time we ask ourselves—especially because of the times we're living—what are we really talking about when we talk about "life."

Sophie said that she had to think it all over, and concealed what seemed like a smirk. But I decided to bring it to an end, to finish off what I had rationalized and let her know that literature would always be more interesting than this famous thing called life. First, it's more elegant, and secondly, I've always found it a much more intense experience.

I wasn't sure of what I was saying. The elegant part was what I had said, but life will always be life, that much I knew . . . No, I wasn't at all sure of what I had just said with such confidence. Literature is intense, but life doesn't lag behind, either.

No, I wasn't the least bit sure of what I'd just said, but I had already said it. Deep down, I was annoyed that she hadn't asked me for a story to live out on her own initiative and that's why I was behaving this way. But why should she have done it? Who did I think I was? Wasn't I merely a ghost?

That song came to mind in the face of Sophie's new and awkward silence, that went "love stories usually end badly." I looked her in the eye and it dawned on me that without her knowing it yet, Sophie had the ghost of Pico Island sitting in front of her. There was no way she could know it, but all she had to do was film me for a few seconds with her video, and *The Journey of Rita Malú*, the story I held so carefully in my pocket, would have come to its end right then and there.

Anyway, I'm already out of here, I said.

And I left. Out on the street, I ran into that famous thing called life and a traffic jam that went on forever. And I crossed the street to the other side, to the other side of the boulevard.

Translated by Valerie Miles

WORK

1973, *Mujer en el espejo contemplando el paisaje*, Tusquets (novel).

1977, *La asesina ilustrada*, Tusquets (novel).

1980, *Al sur de los párpados*, Fundamentos (novel).

1982, *Nunca voy al cine*, Laertes (stories).

1984, *Impostura*, Anagrama (novel).

1985, *Historia abreviada de la literatura portátil*, Anagrama (novel).

1988, *Una casa para siempre*, Anagrama (novel).

1991, *Suicidios ejemplares*, Anagrama (novel).

1992, *El viajero más lento*, Anagrama (essays).

1993, *Hijos sin hijos*, Anagrama (stories).

1994, *Recuerdos inventados*, Anagrama (stories).

1995, *Lejos de Veracruz*, Anagrama (stories).

1995, *El traje de los domingos*, Huerga y Fierro (essays).

1997, *Extraña forma de vida*, Anagrama (novel).

1997, *Para acabar con los números redondos*, Pre-Textos (essays).

1999, *El viaje vertical*, Anagrama (novel).

2000, *Desde la ciudad nerviosa*, Alfaguara (essays).

2000, *Bartleby y compañia*, Anagrama (novel).

2002, *El mal de Montano*, Anagrama (novel).

2003, *París no se acaba nunca*, Pre-Textos (essays).

2003, *Aunque no entendamos nada*, JC Sáez (essays).

2003, *Extrañas notas de laboratorio*, El otro, el mismo (articles).

2004, *El viento ligero en Parma*, Sexto Piso (essays).

2005, *Doctor Pasavento*, Anagrama (novel).

2007, *Exploradores del abismo*, Anagrama (stories).

2008, *Dietario voluble*, Anagrama (diaries).

2008, *Y Pasavento ya no estaba*, Mansalva (essays).

2008, *Ella era Hemingway, No soy Auster,* Alfabia (stories).

2010, *Dublinesca,* Seix Barral (novel).

2010, *Perder teorías,* Seix Barral (novella).

2011, *En un lugar solitario,* Debolsillo (novel and stories).

2011, *Chet Baker piensa en su arte,* Debolsillo (stories of fiction criticism).

2011, *Una vida absolutamente maravillosa. Ensayos selectos,* Debolsillo (essays).

2012, *Aire de Dylan,* Seix Barral (novel).

2013, *Fuera de aquí,* Galaxia Gutenberg (conversations with his French translator, André Gabastou).

2014, *Kassel no invita a la lógica,* Seix Barral (novel).

•

ENGLISH TRANSLATIONS

2004, *Bartleby & Co.,* translated by Jonathan Dunne, New Directions (novel).

2007, *Montano's Malady,* translated by Jonathan Dunne, New Directions (novel).

2011, *Never Any End to Paris,* translated by Ann McLean, New Directions (novel).

2012, *Dublinesque,* translated by Ann McLean and Rosalind Harvey, New Directions (novel).

•

AWARDS AND RECOGNITIONS

2001, Premio Rómulo Gallegos for *El viaje vertical.*

2001, Premio Ciutat de Barcelona for *Bartleby y compañía.*

2001, Premio de Narración Breve UNED for "Monólogo del Café Sport."

2002, Award for Best Foreign Book (France) for *Bartleby y compañía*.

2002, Premio Fernando Aguirre-Libraire for *Bartleby y compañía*.

2003, Premio del Círculo de Críticos de Chile for *El mal de Montano*.

2003, Premio Herralde de Novela for *El mal de Montano*.

2003, Premio Nacional de la Crítica for *El mal de Montano*.

2003, Prix Médicis – Roman Étranger for *El mal de Montano*.

2006, Premio Internactional Ennio Flaiano for *El mal de Montano*.

2006, Premion Fundación José Manuel Lara for *Doctor Pasavento*.

2006, Premio de la Real Academia Española for *Doctor Pasavento*.

2007, Premio Letteraria Elsa Morante for *El viajero más lento*.

2009, Premio Letterario Internazionale Mondello for *Doctor Pasavento*.

2009, Premio ABC Cultural & Ámbito Cultural.

2009, Honorary Doctorate from Universidad de los Andes (ULA).

2010, Premio Leteo for his body of work.

2010, Premio Jean Carriére for *Dublinesca*.

2010, Premio Observatorio D'Achtall in the category of Literature.

2011, Premio Bottari Lattes Grinzane for *Dublinesca* and his body of work.

2012, Premio Argital Ciudad de Bilbao for *Aire de Dylan*.

2012, Premio Gregor von Rezzori for *Exploradores del abismo*.

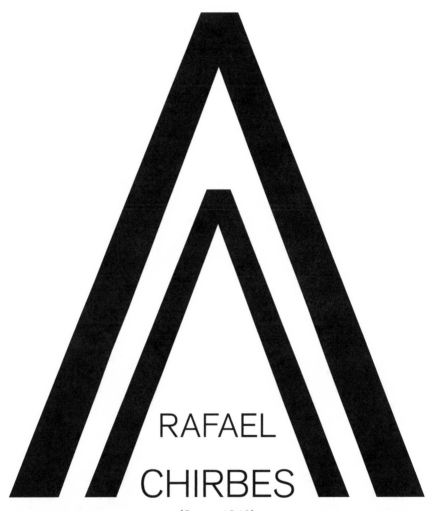

RAFAEL
CHIRBES
(Spain, 1949)

Rafael Chirbes is an author who has been creating his work—indispensable to understanding Spain's recent history—in the shadows. Born the 27th of June, 1949, in Tabernes de Valldigna, in the province of Valencia. He is the son of a republican family, but above all a child of the post-war—social and historical conscience have marked both his life and his writing. From the age of eight, he studied in schools for the orphans of railway workers, and he spent parts of his childhood and adolescence in Ávila, León, and Salamanca. When he was sixteen, he left for Madrid, where he got a degree in Modern and Contemporary History, perhaps to better understand that particular time in history (the second half of the twentieth century) of which he considered himself a product, that moment when a generation—his—succumbed to "chronic amnesia" right when they took power.

An insatiable reader, he worked for several years in bookstores and spent others writing literary criticism. Then he lived in Morocco (where he was a Spanish teacher), Paris, Barcelona, La Coruña, and Extremadura, and finally he went back to his city of birth, Valencia. For years he did various journalistic activities; writing restaurant reviews for the magazine *Sobremesa* and travel reports. It wasn't until he was thirty-nine, in 1988, that he became known as a writer. His first novel, *Mimoun*, was a finalist for the Premio Herralde. Since then, Chirbes has published eight novels that have composed a bitter portrayal of modern-day Spain, blending realism and introspection, history and story, in what the author defines as "a boomerang effect": you have to look behind you to get back to the present. Rafael Chirbes's novels are populated with individuals who long to change history and who, nevertheless, end up succumbing, confronting the impossibility of intervening in anything, torn away toward the end of the world; revolutionaries who shield themselves behind a historical past in order to justify their uslessness in the present.

After publishing *En la lucha final* (1991), *La buena letra* (1992), and *Los disparos del cazador* (1994), in 1996 appeared *La larga marcha*, a novel that along with *La caída de Madrid* (2000) and *Los viejos amigos* (2003) that formed a trilogy about Spanish society from post-war times, through the Transition. The ethical sensibility in Chirbes's writing consists precisely in situating the reader in front of a moral conflict, forcing the reader to take part. Through his minutely detailed stories, the minature world of his characters, Rafael Chirbes manages to shed light on the mechanisms that make the real world run. In his most recently published novel, *Crematorio* (for which he received the Premio Nacional de la Crítica and the Premio Dulce Chacón), he depicts a world adrift, eaten away by corruption and speculation, where that game of masking the real within the fictional becomes rawer and savager. Skeptical and happy, he has accepted the recognition with his characteristic discretion, which serves him so well in Beniarbieg, a small Valencian town, where he currently lives, far away from literary cliques.

Rafael Chirbes states that up until this moment he has the impression of having written only one book. In that book "they don't talk about the war, though the war is present; they don't talk about hope, though they carry the aspirations of the twentieth century." The book he's referring to is a place where you go to try to understand the past in order to attend to the present; it's a place where you find yourself forced, simply, to find out who you are.

THE ACORN

This is the end of my most recent novel, and although the protagonist who's speaking in the text isn't very much like me, I do share a certain texture of his dark outlook.

IN CONVERSATION WITH THE DEAD

There are a lot of deceased authors I love crowding my bookshelves at home. I talk to them; I listen to them. From Aub and Galdós, to Tolstoy, Montaigne, Yourcenar, Lucretius and Virgil, Faulkner, Döblin, Proust, Balzac, Eça de Queiroz, and on and on. I don't leave the house much, so I reread them either at random or impelled by some intuition that tells me that this one and no other is the dead author I should hear at a particular time. For the most part, I'm not mistaken. I also dream about the dead people I knew when they were alive; I've touched them, even, and now they're nowhere, and knowing that they're not here and that I can't talk to them or hear their voices distresses me when I go to bed. Some nights they take control of the room: their absence leaves me breathless and I have to turn on the light so I don't suffocate. With the light on, it's easier to send them back to the peaceful nothingness they're struggling to escape from.

CODA

You said once that literature is like a lover. Either you go all the way or they leave you. You have to know the value of hitting bottom.

I think texts betray any sort of imposture on the part of their authors; they're an extremely sensitive detector. They contain what the author wants to say, but also—and almost more importantly—what's up his sleeve. And yes, I have the impression that writing saves me—I know, I know it's sort of a romantic idea—don't ask me from what, even if it's from myself, it helps me stay afloat. It puts my doubts, my anxieties, at a certain distance and, more importantly, in the service of something.

Do you think there's an ethical place for literature or is it merely an aesthetic exercise?

I don't believe in an aesthetic without ethics, there's no such thing: all aesthetics suggest a particular outlook on the world, and no outlook is innocent.

A point of view situates you somewhere, in a location where potentialities—ways of being—battle one another. When you write, or paint, as when you read or look at something, you have to be conscious of the fact that the author wants to invite you to look from where he's looking. Your mission is to protect yourself. Know that they want to seduce you.

A THOUSAND FORESTS

from *Crematorio* (Crematorium)

[A NOVEL]

At the time, I told her: let it rain now, as much as God wants, let it thunder, let the hail pummel the orange and grapefruit trees; I'm protected, a roof over my head. I'd needed them once, when they were in their prime—those virginal fields gleaming in the aerial photos surrounded by all those old building sites, the perfect lines of orange trees ringing the house, the grove of evergreens, the palm trees, the Chilean pines, like an oasis in the concrete desert in the aerial photos they put in the city and regional tourism brochures, in the windows at real estate agencies—but when Mom and Matías made me an offer, I didn't want them anymore. I told them I had more interesting things to get involved with; they didn't even offer to make me a co-owner; instead they wanted to get something out of it, they wanted me to pay the same amount anyone else would have paid. Now that everything had been reassessed and prices were approaching insane levels, it was not the time to buy. I said it just like that, it's time to sell, but not time to buy, and I told them to do business with somebody else, swallow their pride, and haggle with Bataller, or Guillén, or Dondavi, or Maestre, or Rofersa, with all the builders in the area. I don't want it, I told them. I can't get involved with that now. It's not time, I said. Anything I'd ever had to do, I'd done on my own. I'd rolled up my sleeves, looked for something to start with, something with lift: hydrogen, helium, the gas that makes hot air balloons float, because in that first moment, before charting a course, the important thing is to take off; if you don't ascend, if you don't touch the sky and look at the land below, like a checkered kerchief, there's no voyage. You have to go up, even if it's no more than a few feet, a few yards; after all the sky starts a few feet above your head, but you must experience height, look at things from above, even if it's only a few yards, and then you will be able to chart a course; but the high and mighty Gothic tower refused to help me take that flight. Hermetic, closed, completely sealed off. Deaf, mute, blind stone. Unfeeling stone hewn from God knows what quarry. Showing off the fact that, in its dense structure, there wasn't a single weakness, not a single hole to let the water of feeling seep through. Unmentionable was the god who said let there be, *fiat*, and there was light, who said, open, and the earth broke in two, and a hole opened up to be filled with the blue waters of the swimming pools, the multi-story abyss rose straight up and the air-conditioning units started humming on its walls; everything in the cells of the rising honeycomb switched on, the ovens in the kitchens, and the ceramic stovetops, and every cell was filled with life, those cavities were filled with the shouts of children running down the stairs of their houses with inner tubes and plastic flippers and scuba goggles: the joy of a seaside vacation. All the blue of the Mediterranean, all the calm of the Mediterranean. My God, what would the bus drivers in the big European cities do if there were no Mediterranean, the clerks, the secretaries, the welders, the butchers, what would all those poor people do if on the horizon of their sad working lives there were no Mediterranean. And what about the millionaires who like to float around on rafts, and swim without getting their clothes wet. At this point I know all of this so well it bores me. Now everything can turn stupidly transparent (despite what Guillén thinks). Through the aquarium glass the children watch how whales mate and how sharks sharpen their teeth before going for their morning swim, the world squeezed into a fish tank where everything is visible, like in the houses on those TV shows, *Big Brother*, *The Island* of who knows what, you can see everything, the enormous fish tank of the world, the sharks swimming over the heads of the aquarium visitors, showing their teeth to the kids who aren't afraid of anything anymore. There's something childish about that zeal for transparency, as if societies, like homes—public life is, after all, a simulacrum of private life—didn't need to have their dark zones, the places where potential energy accumulates. We, ourselves, our own bodies, have glass walls. All it takes is the push of a button to show our insides functioning on a screen. My daughter is delighted because she gets to wrinkle her nose every time I light a cigar after a meal; and because she gets to ask Mónica: Has Dad had his triglyceride levels tested this year? And his sugar levels? Urea? Cholesterol? I just see him gobbling up pig's feet, rabbit paté, that gelatinous, greasy, spicy tripe, and how bad they are for him. How's your uric acid, your glucose, your cholesterol? Are you watching them, Dad? Looking at Mónica: Is he watching them? His face looks so red. The last thing I need is for her to say that to Mónica, who has blind faith in nutrition facts and spends the whole day badgering me about probiotics and the antioxidant properties of kiwis and loquats (it seems Silvia reminds her just so she'll annoy me even more). It's getting more difficult every day to drink a glass of whiskey at home. I'm fine, I can drive perfectly with a glass of whiskey in me, no matter what the Department of Health says, I can drive my Mercedes 600 with excellent reflexes at 140 miles per hour in a straight line farther than you can see, feeling the excitement of zero gravity. I can do it, but they won't let me. It's become difficult to smoke a good cigar after a meal in a restaurant without getting piercing glares from somebody at a table in the opposite corner, or without the waiter coming over to tell you that the house has set aside a small room for that activity that everyone used to find exciting. Or, to put it more directly, if you'd please put out your cigar, smoking is not allowed. The women used to go crazy when they put their lips close to your mouth, which smelled of a recently-smoked cigar, the men envied that faint, expensive aroma that wafted from your suit when you sat down at the boardroom table to close your business deals. And now that very thing seems to make them uneasy, even embarrassed. As if you were the *Bounty*, and you'd run aground on a beach, and your hull had started rotting, while the ocean liner of the world continues its journey toward a more tranquil, bluer sea. I ask my son-in-law: Juan, has my daughter managed to get rid of all your tobacco? And Juan, laughing: I smoke in the bathroom with the window open, so the boss doesn't catch me. Silvia shoots him an icy look. Then I start ranting: These days, people call the hotline the government set up for smokers who want to quit, and ask: Can a bus driver smoke in his booth while he's driving? Can parents smoke at home if they have young children? Chewing gum, danger of choking; short-sleeved shirts, danger of skin cancer, fatal melanoma. The radio says they're going to make fat children eat diet food in school (in the U.S. they already issue demerits for obesity every month), and they're banning the burger joint ads for high-calorie fast food—the State pretends to be a parent, but really it's a spy. Things future newspaper readers and radio listeners will analyze, virgin eyes and ears, for whom the beginning of history is what you think of as the end. For all the people for whom history starts today, just when it ends for you, Matías. Night falls in Paris, while a delicate piece of orange-colored china appears on the horizon announcing that the sun will soon rise over Peking. Reconstructions never contain a glimmer of truth. *Memoirs of Hadrian*—which my wife read to me and Silvia in front of the Caravaggios in San Luigi dei Francesi—speaks of that exciting moment when the old gods have died and the new god has not yet arrived. Fruitful moments, when humanity rises on its strength alone, but also terrible, because they suffer inconsolably. The old gods of the region are still kicking, in their last death rattles: Gimeno is still laundering rubles into dollars for Traian, and the politicians and their friend Bolroy, the city councilman, are getting more greedy every day, because they're doing business with Guillén, another dollar-ruble laundering operation. They're still doing business with him, they cover for Guillén, and you already know those business opportunities are options, either for you or for me, no two bodies can occupy the same space. Guillén deals with politicians, who have to act as if they've fallen from another planet and divided the earth with a sword, blindfolded like the statues that represent justice, but everyone knows it's not like that, that justice doesn't have a blindfold covering its eyes. And nevertheless, he decides: here's a space that's suitable for building, here a garden, here facilities for social events, sports, tertiary uses, it depends on who the owner is; and every one of those transactions benefits Guillén, and Bolroy, and they do it because Guillén and his partners are still receiving outside investments, what Traian and the Russians contribute under the table, and the Colombians (even though Guillén told me he split with them, it's not so easy to hide that he has more than enough, his intoxicating cologne among the scaffolds is too obvious)—all that is what I tried so many times to explain to Matías at the beginning, to my brother, who understood the mechanisms so well when he read them in a sociology book, but refused to see them when they materialized before his eyes, look, look carefully: can't you see in action the model that Marx and his followers described for you, the practical application of your theoretical model? Isn't it fascinating? Mercury the thief is king of the world. Don't you see, Matías? This time Matías comes to find me with his head down: he's a child, the child who—when he got angry because they'd scolded him for something and he thought it was unfair—would hide and read books in the laundry room, behind a rocking chair. The vengeful Edmond Dantès. Matías, an egotistical dandy who pretends he doesn't understand that, outside the model, there's nothing left. What the hell was he doing in that bar in Benalda, that man with all the makings of a leader, with four retired men, a gin and tonic in his hands, his eyes lost in the direction of the broad with silicone tits on the calendar . . . Matías, looking in the mirror that reflected his despair, the stamped and embroidered crests of soccer teams hanging on the wall behind the bar, the little triangular flags with the crests of Valencia and Barça. At the end of the world (today we'll live the epilogue of his world, the cold ashes of the anticlimax), even that grimy bar ended up on the good side, it was a sort of door for the future of humanity to pass through. What can you do? Life slips between our fingers, it goes by so fast. I should turn my phone back on, even though I'm sure it'll be full of messages and then people at the company will immediately start pestering me, some about work, others with condolences. Turn it on even if it's just for a minute, to call my daughter, or, even better, Ángela, to find out if they've transferred Matías to the funeral home. I refused to watch the last part. I couldn't handle it. I left. Surely, Matías, if you had a thread of consciousness remaining, you wouldn't have wanted to see me at the last second either. They were whispering, speaking in quiet voices on this side of the glass, the widows and my daughter, while I was thinking: I hope he doesn't hear me, I don't want him to remember me in these moments. I said goodbye quickly, my brother slipping through the shadows and into my room, his cadaverous body becoming a cold hollow between Mónica's body and mine. At that moment I decided I needed to put my arms around her, take a couple of sleeping pills, not the Soñodor I took last time, that does nothing, take a couple of Orfidals, Tranxiliums, something stronger, and fall asleep with my arms around Mónica, my legs between hers, flesh against flesh, flesh against death, warmth against death and its ghosts. I hear the doctor's words in my head again: He's clinically dead. And suddenly, I get emotional. My vision gets all blurry, and my face contorts in a pout. I'm in the car trying to hold back tears, but I can barely see the traffic passing me on the left. Where the hell did this sorrow come from, where is this pain coming from. I shut and open my eyes several times, not with the normal rhythm of blinking, and not that softly; it's more like I'm trying to close something, the way you close and open a box, keeping my eyelids down for a moment and then lifting them; sinking into the coolness of shadows and coming out into light, the way you come up from a dip in the sea: drops of water vanish from your eyes, you can see again, first a flickering image, double because of the water, and little by little, it gains definition, you can see clearly, and you breathe, filling your lungs completely, thinking you could have drowned down there. Filling your lungs with the iodized air that floats on top of the water, bathing in sunlight. Matías. You're there, stretched out on a bed sheet, on a sheet of metal, on a slab of marble. As if there were still time for something. I say: brother; I say: mother, while I think: I was in the womb for months but I don't remember her breasts, her hands, I never had a mother who took me by the hand. Do you see, Matías? I took her by the hand, I'm leading her by the hand in her dementia, in her bitter nonpresence. My eyes closed, my head leaning on the headrest. Later, my arms resting on the steering wheel, my head between them. If anyone looks over from the highway, they'll think I'm sleeping, a weary driver who stopped to take a nap. She's managed to get between us, asking us for her part, just like she demanded it from our father, joint properties, she, the guardian. Mom. Genetics, biography. Who controls a person's movements, desires. Darwin or Marx. Always that insoluble dilemma, useless. But it comes up every time. My brother is dead: I think it, I recite it aloud, I sob it, I repeat it, and I don't know why I'm sobbing, or why I'm saying it, or why I'm declaring it, but hearing myself say it I become once more the child who, running a piece of chalk over the surface of the chalkboard, learned his first letters. An old man dies and the still living child wakes: I watch myself writing my first letters. What did we not become. I return to the chalkboard, to the chalk, to the inkwell set in the recess of the writing desk, and I'm suffering like I'm trying to memorize an exam that I have to recite to the letter in front of the teacher, and I feel like a can't say a single word of it. When I was little, I used to recite poems that I'd copied from my literature book. I recited them on the beach. I did this as a teenager, too, on stormy days. Matías was afraid of lightning and used to shut himself in the closet, in the laundry room, he'd hide there and read (I'm sure he also prayed); I on the other hand preferred to hop on my bicycle, go down to the seashore, and recite poems. Alone, or sometimes with Brouard: if we both went, we'd shout poems that you couldn't hear over the noise of the surging waves, just as we'd see Marlon Brando do years later, letting off steam under cover of the din of the Paris metro. On blue summer days I liked to take Matías with me, holding his hand—he'd be outfitted with scuba goggles and flippers—holding his hand on the road, and holding his hand underwater: showing him the caves, the fish, the seagrass meadows, the underwater flowers, the sponges, the sea

urchins. The most dazzling part of Misent, the part that lay hidden: he discovered it with me, holding my hand, his little hand enveloped in mine. The
angel of life was flying high and passed quickly, there was hardly time to
notice it crossing the country, east to west like a comet, we only saw a few
sparks from its tail when it was already past us, starting to cross the ocean on
who knows what trajectory (*Yesterday, When I Was Young*). Oblivion. Forget
about life. Return to oblivion. Bertomeu Demolition. Leave behind no monuments to commemorate all this. Matías, you, who will be but ash passing
through a furnace, now that you have time in that boredom we call nothingness, grab the Blue Guide to Rome, and re-read what it says about those
graves along the Via Appia, unscathed though mistreated by the passage of
time (who isn't mistreated by the passage of time?), elevated sepulchers among
the cypresses, arrows to the sky, symbols of eternity, of something lasting, a
concept hated by contemporary society, mother of ephemeral architecture,
ephemeral ideas and lives. In Rome, near Porta Maggiore, the baker Eurisace
had an oven built for him and his wife, an oven that would also be a tomb:
the tourists and archaeologists still visit it to study the funereal architecture
as an homage to their labor: a baker, too, can aspire to eternity. Gaius Cestius
had a pyramid built that we still stop to contemplate on the Via Ostiensis, so
he'd be remembered for his works in the East: he suffered there and identified with that land. Read what the guides say about those tombs of soldiers,
kings, even wealthy middle-class wheat traders who are still remembered
centuries later. Now that seems incredible. Life escapes us with the last
breath. They'll scatter your ashes, Matías, and no symbols will remain, neither the sickle, nor the hammer, nor the star that showed its five points as it
appeared in the East, that you thought was going to be hard as diamonds but
it was just a mirage, a mistaken interpretation of sunlight melting in the air,
a mirror that reflects nothing. The face of a vampire is not reflected in a
mirror, remember the movie? We saw it together. You would have been eight
or ten. You were really scared. You clung to me. No marble or basalt or por-
phyry or lapis lazuli. We won't have anything like that: ashy remains in the
funeral home whose façade has a stained glass image of a crowd walking
toward sunset, tiny painted pieces of red glass, a sunset on the façade that
actually faces the East, what does all that matter now, representations, theme
parks, meaningless architecture, mere decorations. You become one more, a
little yearling sheep who wants to graze in the green meadows and doesn't

know the way, who's bleating because he got into the thistles and doesn't know how to get out, and sees that night is falling fast, night is coming. He's bleating, afraid, and the shepherd doesn't hear it, but the wolf is lying in wait and the bleating excites his taste buds . . . Lonely ashes that will dissolve beneath the trunk of a carob tree, in the middle of the country—with its waning purity—that didn't come in time to cure your infection, or tossed into the sea, contaminated by the contemporary sin of tourism (was Montaigne not a tourist? Was Goethe? And Byron. And earlier, Ibn Khaldun, Ibn Battuta, Ptolemy, Herodotus: tourists), ashes mixed up with the abandoned earth on the mountain, the scrub fields that nobody cultivates, the olive trees that nobody prunes, because, despite what you wanted, they're waiting for topographers, surveyors, architects to come take measurements, to start digging with backhoes, removing those thousand-year-old stones. *I want to be Providence, for the greatest, the most beautiful, and the most sublime thing I know of in this world is to reward and punish.* Do you remember? It's Edmond Dantès. My father is crying. He has his back to me, he's sitting on the bed, and then I see his face, his fists are pressed to his eyes. He doesn't see me. How long has it been, where are his tears now, and what do you think, did that make them useless? They served their purpose in their moment, fleeting like everything, and they were only his, and mine. Our rightful part, to be inherited by both of us. They evaporated, but am I going to stop listening to Bach because of that? Because my ears are going to turn to dust and soon the Bach I've listened to will lie there with me, as he has also turned to dust? Because these *Klaviersonaten* by Brahms, performed by Anatol Ugorski, that I started listening to just now in the middle of this traffic jam, not knowing if I should continue toward the freeway or head back home, will be dust along with my ears? Should I renounce them because of that insignificant detail? Because they will be dust? I know. The philosophers said. When I'm gone, the world no longer exists, all this hustle and bustle no longer exists, this cruelty is redeemed. But beyond such relativism rises the very beginning of life. Beyond the evidence that you're here and then gone, that you are and then you are not. Take the fruit and bite into it; let the juice soak into your lips. It is that bite that matters. That's life, a waste, daughter of mine. An explosion of wastefulness that the universe allows. Pure arbitrary consumption of energy. Trophism (and tropism). Silvia: You don't need to get all intellectual about it, Dad. I can't tell you anything. Sometimes I do it to provoke you a little bit, but it's like you have less of a sense of humor every day, she says. And I say: Don't tell me you're trying to provoke me, trying to get a reaction out of me. That you tell me things just to encourage me, to cheer me up, revitalize me, jumpstart me. At my age, a certain apathy is a natural—dare I say medicinal—state. Don't worry about me. The trick is to keep doing things, stones are made for walls, logs to feed the fire, I know that, I tell myself so every day, it's my job, that's what I do, and when every last centimeter of soil has been compacted, the beaches, the plains, the mountains, when everything is built up, and you can't squeeze anything else into this armpit of the world that you care about so much, I'll say goodbye, if I start to care about it too, and if I have one last breath left. But for now, it's exciting enough. What do you want me to do. That's my fate. This pact of apprenticeship to Mephistopheles has allowed me to enjoy good health at seventy-three years (pacemakers, triglycerides, cholesterol, and all: maybe I have one day left, but I'm alive)—should I ask to be forgiven for that? By whom? If I were poor, and if I got sick, would I deserve different treatment, different respect, different admiration? Is that what you mean to tell me? The region is full of scoundrels who ruined their lives and now they ask for justice, idiots who were conned when they wanted to con other people but didn't know how—are they better? Worry about yourself. Don't worry about me. I've had seventy long years. And I'm doing just fine. I sleep like a baby, I wake up in a good mood, just as with almost everything else, though, ever since they put in the pacemaker, I'm a little more careful; I smoke a cigar or two, I have a drink, what more can I ask for? The years I still have left could be great. And your best years are ahead of you. You'll see, maturity, common sense. The paradise of your forties. You know I don't pity myself, I don't tend to think I'm better than I am, but I'm too old to talk about all that again. I talked about it with Matías, with Brouard, with Montoliu the painter, with your mother; I've been arguing with you about it for almost thirty years; I argued with myself about it back then and I settled on a pact of tolerance with my other self—only money can make us sparkle, briefly reflecting the brilliance of the gods. I've already earned my keep, and if I feel like it, my little chickadee, pumpkin, sweet pea, I can pick up and go live somewhere else, near some kind of nature preserve, one of those protected areas you say you like more than I do, though, if I were to go anywhere, I think I'd move closer to one of those hives that should drive you nuts, but that you still visit when you get the chance, places where you can find the whole pack of contemporary civilization, the most you can get out of life: New York or London or Paris, that city that smells like withered lilacs, where you can get yourself a hotel room and have everything you need just a few steps away. Yes, I'll shut myself up in one of those little hotels in the center of Paris where you don't have to walk more than two hundred yards to get everything that the most civilized person in this world could want: delicatessens, wine shops, cheese shops, all the great restaurants, the movies, the theater, painting, music, clothing. Or, to be more ascetic—why not?—a contemporary hermit, a monk in this era, you know, I could do it: I could go to Rome. Spend the rest of my life lying on the bed and reading in a hotel room in Rome; drinking Campari oranges on the terrace at Rosati, eyes half-closed in the sweet autumn sunlight, or contemplating the symmetry of the cupolas around the Piazza del Popolo; eating some really good fettuccine, spaghetti alla matricciana, tasty entrails (trippe alla romana), and greasy animal parts in tomato sauce (coda a la vaccinara) at Checchino; deboning a nice squab at Il Convivio, washing it down with one of those strong Sicilian wines, fifteen-percent-alcohol wines that coat your mouth with velvet and warm your blood, one of those stylish Super Tuscans (a Sassicaia, an Ornellaia). Eating, drinking, reading, and looking at architecture and paintings: spending the days running around to see Raphaels, Michelangelos, Caravaggios, like we used to do on those trips with your mother; spending entire days at the Pantheon, that place where you breathe space instead of air, every architect's dream, spending hours looking through the oculus and contemplating the rain falling on the most beautiful flag in the world; or avoiding the major tourist routes and looking at the paintings and mosaics that are a little out of the way. Visiting San Lorenzo, San Clemente, I Quatri Coronati, mysterious churches that tourists consider second-rate and don't bother to visit. Imagine it. Rome, the old wasp's nest that Augustus filled with bricks and marble: don't forget that the marble was just an overlay, the thin Wonder Bread of the sandwich; underneath, the ham of the sandwich was almost always—as it is now—brick or cement. You don't appreciate it, I get that impression, and yet there's so much beauty in finely crafted brickwork: it lasts longer than stone, it's more flexible, it can be molded, it breathes, and, what's even more beautiful, it carries the imprint of the hands that laid it in place, it embodies ability, wisdom, and soul—it has a soul. Brick, like the human body, is animated by a spirit that lives inside it, and it, too, is dust that slowly returns to dust, architecture that becomes geology. It's a shame that the times don't allow us to treat it with the respect it deserves. Even though, at my age, I know the only place I can go is where, unfortunately, I won't even be able to see the clay wall they put in front of me, where somebody will leave their imprint, their knowledge, a piece of their soul that will accompany me, pulsating in my nothingness. Have you ever noticed that artisanal moment at a funeral, when the twenty or so relatives and friends of the deceased contemplate how the bricklayer prepares the mortar and smears the rows of clay bricks in the wall that closes the niche? Nobody moves until he and his trowel have finished the work, everyone hanging on his movements. Every time I've had to watch that scene, I haven't been able to feel anything: that labor seems the best antidote for pain, for the sharp-pointed nihilism that threatens you every time somebody you love, or somebody you've lived with, dies. Those twenty suffering friends and relatives watch the work of the bricklayer as it evolves before them, an elegant and restrained ballet dancer, an athlete of precise movements, who displays authentic art—or is art not precisely the mixture of work and representation? He prepares the mortar, measures, sets equal rows of bricks, plasters, smoothes. Through his work, he announces that life goes on. These days, if you take care of yourself, if you watch your cholesterol, your glucose, your blood pressure, your prostate, your colon; if you take care of yourself and you're lucky, you can live up to a hundred years, but I've clocked a lot of extra miles on top of my seventy years. When you rent a car, you pay for the number of days you use it, and for the number of miles you drive. Well, my body, the rental vehicle they gave me, it's a machine in good condition, but what can I say, it's traveled around a lot, I've taken it for a lot of drives. Don't doubt for a second that I'm paying for a high overage on my mileage, I've been dragging around my extra weight for a long time already, but also, and most importantly, it's a lot, an enormous amount, an infinite number of miles, an infinity of Havana cigars, of alcohol, tons of sirloin steaks, T-bones, and cutlets, oily, spicy tripe, grouper fresh from the sea, tasty prawns, lobsters on the grill, lobster with rice, lobster Thermidor. They say that all those things, which I call beauty, sink like lead inside the body—beautiful food, or gastronomic weight. The counterweight of earthly beauty: sugar, cholesterol, uric acid, saturated fats, unsaturated and polyunsaturated fats, triglycerides, aminotransferases, who knows what else. All that verbal diarrhea they use to chastise us in the news and on TV. I know it

weighs on me. Too much. But my heart, well-oiled by the mechanics, keeps
on ticking. You can see that I keep in pretty good shape—miraculously, with
my extra weight and my pacemaker—maybe not like an angel, but certainly
like an exemplary, early twenty-first century, septuagenarian human being. If
Silvia'd had her way, when my wife died I would have had to end the life
cycle; I would have been left to go around as a widower, circling a perpetual
grief. I would have gone about closing off spaces, shutting doors. That was
the project my daughter had for me, the place where, most likely, she thought
we would see each other again. She hasn't forgiven me for not accepting that
the only thing deserving of pity has already happened; for believing instead
that the only thing deserving of pity is precisely what hasn't happened yet,
what's happening now. The day the old woman, almost a hundred years old,
went to see her dying son. A cadaver ready to be cooked, well-spiced, seasoned, sprinkled with salt and pepper, she looks with indifference at another
cadaver that's already cooking. She didn't even cry. As if, for her, the passageway is closed, the one that still reduces me to a sentimental sludge, connected to my childhood. We pushed her chair onto the hospital's service
elevator, wheeled her down the hall, and set her facing the bed, on the opposite side of the glass. Where is he? she asked. Is it that one? with displeasure,
as if she were facing a field laborer asking for an advance on his daily wages.
It was hard to recognize him with the facemask, the tubes coming out of him
everywhere. She stared at him for ten minutes and then asked to be taken
away, in that voice of hers, that commanding squawk. That was it. Silvia had
gotten what she wanted. I was in favor of letting her believe that Matías was
still on the mountain, like John on Patmos; Simeon Stylites atop his pillar
like Napoleon in the Place Vendôme, looking down at the world from above,
looking down at the jewelers' windows, the multimillionaires going in and
out of the Ritz with their fancy suitcases, the porters in their gold-braided
livery from another era. Everything from another era and, at the same time,
from this one. Silvia had insisted. Nature has fitted human beings with security systems that allow them to cope with the death of their father, their
mother. But not this, Silvia. There is no genome that can anticipate the death
of a child. That's chaos, Silvia. A sign that the gods, for whatever reason,
have abandoned you. Priam slips in the blood of his child before stepping in
his own. The death of a child is the climax of any tragedy. The death of a
father leaves a halo of peace, a sense of a completed cycle, of nature imposing

its norms, its rites; the death of a child makes the gods tremble. But she was obstinate: the old woman had to see the dying man. Another right exercised. I wish the family could have been a ceasefire zone. That I didn't have to keep fighting for what should have been mine, against the people who were supposed to be on my side. Business is an especially nerve-wracking activity, and even more so if it's construction, possibly the best metaphor for capitalism. Growth means destruction, and that's not my fault: growing means don't stop growing, and building means don't stop destroying. You have to destroy something in order to build something else. Was nothing destroyed when they made terraced fields? They pulverized the mountains. Now you people call it dry stone architecture, you venerate it, sacred, millennial, dry stone architecture, and you try to get UNESCO to name it a World Heritage site, but that was the great destruction of the primitive Mediterranean forest, of the native scrubland. This land has been destroyed for thousands of years. There isn't a patch that hasn't been desecrated. Look right here, in Misent. All you have to do is read the newspapers. In one project, they destroy a Roman villa, an Almohad minaret, a caliphal wall, and half a dozen *fonduks* (it seems, the newspapers say, this was a commercial city in the twelfth century: contacts with Alexandria, Tunis, Sicily). That's what the journalists say we builders do. As if the minaret or the caliphal wall hadn't destroyed the wall or the temple that preceded them. Which stratum is the one where truth resides? At what point should humanity have stopped in order to be authentic? The Russian, hyperactive insomniac that he is: this morning his eyes were pasty, he smelled of alcohol and that distilled sourness that cocaine leaves in your sweat, and it was obvious he hadn't gone to sleep yet. I'm sure he's still dealing with Guillén, I thought. And also that capitalism and cocaine have some things in common. Construction and cocaine have a lot in common, besides the rapidly inflating checking accounts. Hyperactivity, the determination to fight against time. Capitalism and cocaine, this frenetic not-stopping. Shovels have been digging for three days in the place where we had the stable, and they've started uncovering the skeletons of the horses. When I saw the skulls that the workers had arranged on a corner of the property, I thought they looked like sculptures, the ivory bones flecked with spots of clay and iron oxides from the soil, dense as coagulated blood. The company that owned the riding school disappeared without a trace. That was so long ago. Guillén, Bolroy, and I, there were half a dozen owners. I think even Collado ended up having some shares in it. I sold them to him myself. It's at this moment that I get to thinking about how I wanted to be an artist when I was young, and now I've become the creator of this sculpture park where the trunks of orange trees mingle with the bones of horses: tormented forms, animal and vegetable in the process of becoming mineral—when you put it like that it sounds sort of epic—the reddish earth rising like a muddy veil over the machinery, a scene very much in harmony with the new artistic tendencies, the most avant-garde installations: artists request cadavers from the morgues for their installations, human organs in formaldehyde, pig's heads, entrails, mummified bodies, taxidermied corpses. Those unearthed bones, the shreds of leather tanned by the passage of time, those are my secret architecture. I'd like to go up to Brouard's house, which I can see from here, from this freeway entrance that I've decided not to take, the house at the foot of the mountain, behind the dust cloud kicked up by the diggers. I'd like to sit down with Brouard, light a cigar with him (I wonder if he still smokes?), talk as if time hadn't passed, as if my father were still telling him, you're a good writer; I'd bring up some moral question, ask him who's better, talk about moral drift, the swerve of atoms, the difference between rigid Democritus and flexible Epicurus, topics that occupied us in our youth; I'd talk about how Matías burned his money and his health at the same time; I'd describe in minute detail the papers that Matías and my mother signed behind my back. I'd like to see Brouard: the protagonist of his greatest novel, the unscrupulous speculator of *Wandering Volition*, he visits the author, in a scene that's very Pirandello, very Unamuno, to talk, reason, argue, quarrel; let the character defend himself and explain to the author that he hasn't exactly been wandering (I'd talk to him about that emptiness the protagonist seems to be guarding, the unfurnished space where you can hear footsteps echo). Brouard, what happened to our twenty-year-old selves. What did they become. The memories come rushing back and I feel like crying, not even because I'm mad, I just feel like crying, here, surrounded by this white light that stains everything and shamelessly illuminates it, a sun that seems less like a source of life than a bitter punishment. But it's late, it's already late. On the bar, the glass left a ring of alcohol and tonic, on the wood, on the zinc, is it true, Matías? The pact of the righteous. Even though I was the older brother, I felt like the younger one. Is it true, mother? I used to cry at night. Any time of day, I would close my office door and burst into tears. Over and over the distressing phrase comes to mind: I was in the womb for months but I didn't have a mother who took me by the hand, I never had a mother who took me by the hand. I've read that somewhere, too, in some novel; or maybe not, maybe it's just an idea of mine, something that haunts me, an absence that turns into words. I guess I can see why Matías did it, but I've never understood why my mother had to do it, was it just to hear the music? So that he, Matías, would touch her hair on winter afternoons, let it fall onto her shoulders, arrange the bunch of jasmine on her collar, tell her how pretty she is? Now the tears come back, I'm parked on the shoulder, surrounded by this white light, the haze, the cars passing me on the left, the landscape that's been a cage, I've been moving around inside it for so many years; in front of me, all around me, everything covered in this dazzling white dust, blinding and sticky. I'm crying with a sorrow that seems bottomless. At this moment, nothing can soothe it, I'm crying through this hollow inside me, I'm weeping soundlessly, an inaccessible cry, my arms on the steering wheel, my head on my arms, my tears wetting the skin of my arms, macerated skin, full of dark spots, wrinkly Galápagos tortoise skin whose smoothness can't be restored by any sort of moisturizing cream. *Yesterday, When I Was Young.* Everything goes back in time sixty years, everything inside me goes back, but it's immature, undercooked. Inside, beneath the covering of skin, among the bones, in the circulatory torrents and in the pipes where the vegetables and meat are turned to paste, the passage of time hasn't changed anything, or it's changed everything without changing anything—let's say it's left everything intact, but cold, like a broth that you drink at the wrong time and it's lost its qualities, its charm: everything is the same, the same stew, but in that gooey, rubbery state that foods take on when you eat them several hours after they've been cooked. In the distance, the sea, a sheet of boiling metal. And the two words (*Matías, mother*), together, connected, entwined; and along with them, other words from back then, a wave of domestic warmth that crests and breaks and crests again. There's ice cream in the freezer, there's hot chocolate in the mug, there's scented soap in the soap dish in the bathroom, there's black shoe polish in the box where we keep the shoe creams. I smell the shoe polish, the ink, the chalk. The words contain everything, the smell, the color, the taste. They contain nothing, but they do contain something, a representation of something in a particular place. They contain the lie that you can recover something; and yet you can't, they're just deceitful words that make you see without

seeing, smell without smelling. That smell on my hands, the cold in the
morning, the scarf, the gloves. Don't go outside without covering your mouth
with your scarf, wrap yourself up warm—not my mother, the maid, pulling
on my jacket and saying: Cover your mouth with your scarf. Back then,
Matías was still in his cradle, in a bundle of white cloth. To be Providence.
To impart justice. Separate the good from the bad. I look at Brouard's house
and, down below, those properties of mine where the machines are working,
felling the trees we used to play under, and a hundred yards from there, what
remains of the riding school buildings, the red earth that envelops the skeletons of the horses they buried there. Brouard. The injustice of time. Matías,
I don't know whether you finally realized that time always puts things where
they belong. Your Providence. Mother. Women are seduced by what's unpro-
ductive, by words that run over the surface of actions, without touching them,
or words that have little to do with actions, the humming that floats above
the reality of the world like a sticky, green slime, the grand ideas they plan,
like ectoplasm hovering over life. Most likely, she did it only to keep hearing
the music of Matías's words: What did you do today? Let me look at you,
you're beautiful, that lotion is working well for you, it makes your skin so
smooth. Did she do it just for that? Here in my car, if I close my eyes I can
smell shoe polish, I can hear voices: there's scented soap in the soap dish, the
maid says, there's hot chocolate in the mug, ice cream in the freezer. Somewhere near Brouard's house are the horse skeletons that the workers have
started piling up, the materials of my secret architecture that the backhoe is
unearthing, scraps of dry leather, bones covered in wet clay. They shine in the
sunlight, enveloped in the reddish earth laden with oxides, intermediate colors, earth tones, like a Tàpies canvas, dense, complex materials, somewhere
between painting, pottery, and sculpture. They could be part of one of those
installations assembled by contemporary artists. And you too, Matías, now
you are an installation in a contemporary art museum, stretched out on a bed
sheet, on a sheet of metal, or on a slab of marble.

Translated by Emily Davis

WORK

1988, *Mimoun*, Anagrama (novel).
1991, *En la lucha final*, Anagrama (novel).
1992, *La buena letra*, Anagrama (novel).
1994, *Los disparos del cazador*, Anagrama (novel).
1996, *La larga marcha*, Anagrama (novel).
1997, *Mediterráneos*, Debate (essay).
2000, *La caída de Madrid*, Anagrama (novel).
2002, *El novelista perplejo*, Anagrama (essay).
2003, *Los viejos amigos*, Anagrama (novel).
2004, *El viajero sedentario. Ciudades*, Anagrama (novel).
2007, *Crematorio*, Anagrama (novel).
2010, *Por cuenta propia*, Anagrama (essay).
2013, *En la orilla*, Anagrama (novel).

•

AWARDS AND RECOGNITIONS

1988, Finalist for the Premio Herralde for *Mimoun*.
1999, German SWR-Bestenliste prize for *La larga marcha*.
2003, Premio Cálamo "Libro del Año 2003" for *Los viejos amigos*.
2007, Premio Cálamo "Libro del Año 2007" for *Crematorio*.
2007, Premio Nacional de la Crítica Narrativa Castellana for *Crematorio*.

2008, Premio Dulce Chacón for *Crematorio*.

2013, *El País*'s "Best Spanish Language Book of the Year" for *En la orilla*.

2014, V Premio Francisco Umbral for *En la orilla*.

ALBERTO

RUY

SÁNCHEZ

(Mexico, 1951)

Alberto Ruy Sánchez was born in Mexico City in 1951, but his childhood was divided between the Mexican capital, the state of Sonora, and a tiny town in Baja California. Those landscapes were absorbed in such a way that they ended up building the atmosphere of his writing. In an almost Proustian way and after more than twenty years, those places would be evoked again when he visited the Sahara for the first time, around 1975. So he established a particular relationship with the Moroccan desert and even more with the port of Mogador, an ancient point of departure for the trans-Saharan caravans, which would become the setting for many of his stories.

Long before, when he was young, he studied in a school of the Compañía de Jesús where he learned to look at the world "as a complicated reality that can only be fully understood and lived in using intelligence and the senses in equal measure." This baroque conception of existence, combined with the pleasure with which he listened to his relatives tell stories of distant times, shaped his nature as a writer.

In 1975 he got a doctorate from the University of Paris, where he attended seminars taught by philosophers like Michel Foucault and Gilles Deleuze, and worked with Roland Barthes as his thesis adviser, from whom he learned to accept the challenge of finding his own voice to express himself artistically.

Back in Mexico in 1984, he was an editorial secretary and later the books editor at *Vuelta* magazine, which was then run by Octavio Paz, who years later would say of Ruy Sánchez: "His writing is nervous and agile, his intelligence sharp without being cruel, his spirit compassionate without condesencion or complicity." That was an intellectually fertile time, during which, after having published a book of essays, he wrote his first novel, *Los nombres del aire* (1987), a story in which the author delves into feminine desire, in the territory of dreams and longings, with the city of Mogador as backdrop. Ruy Sánchez was honored with the Premio Xavier Villaurrutia, the most prestigious award given in Mexico. With this book, Ruy Sánchez began a path of aesthetic and existential exploration—captured in his next novels—conceived of as the creation of a quality, artistic object.

The next year, along with his wife, the historian Margarita de Orellana, he relaunched the magazine *Artes de Mexico*, which since that time has received more than one-hundred-fifty national and international awards for the art of publishing. With Margarita, he had two children: Andrea, born in 1984, and Santiago, born in 1987.

His career as a writer keeps moving forward, in 1996 he published his second novel, *En los labios del agua*, in which he explores masculine desire through a Mexican of Arab origin (in whom the sands of the Sahara and Sonora deserts converge). With *Los jardines secretos de Mogador* (2001) he finished the trilogy he began with *Los nombres del aire*, but four years later he went back to Mogador with *Nueve veces el asombro*, and by 2007 he finished the pentology about desire with *La mano del fuego*.

In February 2000, the French government decorated him as a member of the Order of Arts and Letters, in recognition of his literary and publishing oeuvre. In 2008, the publishing industry in Mexico awarded him the greatest honor a publisher can receive for his professional trajectory, the Premio Juan Pablos al Mérito Editorial. Although he presently lives in Mexico City, he travels frequently, both because he is in demand at conferences, and also because of his work conducting research and spreading the cultures of his home country, work he carries out with his wife.

THE ACORN

THE TORTURE OF DOCTOR JOHNSON

The pain of choosing. After being grateful for the attention as an author and also for my books, the request to choose a fragment from them that I consider my definitive "favorite pages" has been uncomfortable and even painful. I'm trying to figure out why that is.

After a bad experience with my first published story, which I ended up regretting, after having received frankly undeserved praise from admired writers when that story already seemed detestable to me, I decided not to publish again until I could consider every fragment and every book "the best" I could do for every project and every challenge. Thinking in terms of craft, in other words comparing myself with the Mexican craftspeople whom I admire and who work obsessively until they produce an object that they can feel proud of. I realize that every one of my books has only been published after having been rewritten at least fifteen times. Some fragments within those several times more than that.

So throughout all these years, writing and rewriting obsessively, I've only published what I've considered "the best." Although this is always a relative concept. In terms of craft, every single one of my books is the best I have been able to achieve. And over the test of time up till now I've neither regretted nor believed I could improve any one of them. In terms of their position and function within each book, each project.

Although from a reader's perspective it might be possible, logical, and necessary to choose one above the others, from my perspective it's painful and the term "the best" makes no stable and definitive sense. For the baroque craftsman that I am, focused on my process of invention, nothing and everything is best at the same time.

I try picking out diverse fragments and defending them. I see a thousand reasons to choose any one of them. I question, question again, and revise my selections. In the end I am inclined toward one scene from *Los nombres del aire* in which the protagonist Fatma enters and moves the eyes of us readers around a public bathroom in Mogador, the Hammam, where she will find or has already found her lover, Kadiya.

When I wrote that book I was possessed by the desire to construct a story that was atmosphere above all else, in the way that architecture is an atmosphere. When you go into an interesting building you let yourself be guided by the lights, the smells, the moistures, and everything you feel, and not by the classic idea of suspense.

Why does literature have to be a slave to one traditional idea of what moves us as human beings? I thought about boycotting suspense as much as possible and meticulously intensifying the spaces that the reader passes through, interested more in following a light or a taste than an idea. The opposite of a traditional narrative thread: get to know the pleasure of the labyrinth. I wanted to create a literature of atmosphere that would build across all the senses of the reader a collection of powerful, enveloping sensations.

I was interested as much as possible that readers abandon their interest in the contents of the story, in the anecdote, so as to incite the harmonious explosion of all their senses: beginning with sight, listening and smelling, touching and tasting. And that they would want to continue the story only because a mysterious luminosity called to them. The Hammam in Mogador was ideal to put in practice this project of sensorial storytelling. With its successive rooms, it was the space of spaces most resembling a narrative that I knew of.

The old idea of baroque art from the seventeenth and eighteenth centuries—that you can reach God via sensation, contrary to the classic Protestant idea that only in the contents of the words revealed in the Bible resides the key—led to the creation of baroque cathedrals that were immense mechanisms of enveloping sensation. In a distinct way, even more corporeal and more pleasurable, sensorial atmospheres, like I wanted my books to be. So, this fragment describes and offers up an edifice converted into an experience of sensorial initiation of the lover moving toward the luminous body of her love.

There is a sort sexual animism throughout the whole book, things have soul and sex and in the Hammam more than anywhere else. That's how the protagonist feels and she transmits it to us. It is there that everything is sparked.

And as such Fatma finds her love everywhere, in the air, in the water, in everything she touches. The edifice of the Hammam is also, at the same time, a concentration of her, of the absent love turned into a sensorial presence and it is simultaneously the path toward her.

Along this route of hyper-sensorial-signification, where everything is a metaphor for something else, the infinite, the Hammam is an implicit sensorial metaphor for the city of Mogador, converted in turn into love and longing. In the city of longing.

Another reason for choosing this fragment: the narrative mechanism that was the key challenge in terms of temporal subtlety within the book is actualized in the Hammam: it is a story in which everything has yet to happen but everything is significant because in the Hammam everything has already happened. The protagonist passes through this atmosphere before and after simultaneously.

Another reason for this choice: everything I describe is documented, even the most implausible things. I conducted a detailed investigation to arrive at this description. Not only did I visit various Hammams and use a very popular one in the city of Fez as a faithful model for what I describe, but I also questioned many Moroccan women about their experiences and what happened to them there. But above all, what makes the Hammam a feminine atmosphere par excellence is its schedule. The territoriality that the women have established in cities where the streets and the cafés tend to be masculine atmospheres. The Hammam is one of the feminine atmospheres par excellence and you have to hear it from the mouths of the women. I could neither let myself invent anything nor rely on the images and descriptions in circulation. Everything had to be firsthand. I am a documentary poet who searches for the most appropriate literary form to communicate these profound realities of longing, where a realist narrative register does not penetrate.

The nucleus of the narrative mechanisms that unfold throughout all five Mogador books is found in this fragment.

In baroque synthesis: there is a reality of feminine atmospheres of desire that needs to be respectfully explored by a man and achieving this is an enormous challenge, in this story a conception of literature as space is put into action, but also as an almost mystical and sensorial quest toward the poetic discovery of the beloved, the luminous body of the beloved, there is an outward display of a subtle abyss of metaphors that sexualize an edifice and a city, a world, there is an intense delayed time where the past and the future coincide: finally there is a narrative toll of a bell, a note that over the course of twenty years will become a quintet. The composition of a corporeal and mystical jubilation.

And, still, when someone reads these pages expecting suspense or a traditional story they might say that there is nothing in them, nothing happens. They are like still water that a hand stirs all of a sudden without managing to penetrate it. But the hand senses something in the water, feels it. Perhaps intensely.

The last reason or unreason, which is really the first, for choosing these pages: the pleasure rereading them produces in me and the hope that they will produce the same in someone else without them even perceiving the complex web that composes the story's fabric.

In Conversation with the Dead

Dialogues in the dark. Tenacious resident of the night, since my first published reflection about the act of writing I've been obsessed with the tacit presence of others in my silences and solitudes. Although I think that I have never really felt alone.

My attention is called to the fact that I have always experienced these visits as breaks from reality. People who are and are not at the same time. Not fantasies but invocations and appearances of words, gestures, sounds, sensations. And their effects on me are totally real.

It is not exactly writers who visit me in the long hours of the night, it is their words, scenes from their lives and works. Gestures and ideas. But also music and disconnected sounds. Right now I hear an ambulance in the distance and before becoming conscious that it is there outside in the street, I am visited by random images of the accidents that I have lived and the ambulances I have had to get into, in reality and in dreams, in films and in novels. The dead writers with whom I speak are like this ambulance. And they are more ghosts than dead. More creations of longing than resuscitated archives.

Chance, unbidden, often invokes completely unexpected presences. My ghosts are multiple and multiform, and in the *collage* that is their bodies there are traces of writers, tongues and faces and hands and sentences and ideas.

Some recur seasonally. Some jump out before my eyes and others wait in the pages for the necessary invocation of a glance. For that reason my library is not a collection of books. It's an assembly of ghosts. The atmosphere of dialogues in the darkness. I don't think of them as dead or living but as present in their words.

Sometimes I prune back my library and the authors who vitally inhabit my sleepless nights are all that's left. But even still there are too many to count. Literally thousands, like the legions of the damned. Mentally I run through my bookshelves, now semi-organized alphabetically. I pause on the poetry of Anna Ajmátova, charged with historical pain. Her striking profile visits me whenever I'm overwhelmed by a situation, showing me her tenacity and poetic gaze. Her lucidity makes her a profound savior. Closer to the sea and to hedonism, the poetry of Eugenio de Andrade, which my beloved sent me from Lisbon, and which I translated enthusiastically into Spanish and published in Spanish before many other authors. Samuel Beckett, the author who taught me in the most precise way how rigor and delirium can turn into art. The author most present in my writing without a doubt and without really seeming to be.

Walter Benjamin, who in his short reflection about his sojourns in Paris spins above all a plural and crystalline fabric, which continues to amaze me. Life's multiple dimensions are always present in him. Roger Caillois, who helps me think of nature as a great aesthetic creator. I'll never forget his stones and insects. He nourishes me with concepts for looking at ancient societies that help us to better understand our own, and when I saw him one night in public discourse with Borges, I understood the way in which all of his work is intensely dialogic. And all art can be that way. San Juan de la Cruz, the unfathomable fire turned into words, who always shows the way to the narrow door of all transcendence. ABC and I pause . . . Desperate to be more concise in my response to this question I shall state that I'm not a reader of a single book or a single author and not even of a few.

A few years ago I published a book titled *Diálogos con mis fantasmas*. It was a gathering of literary presences from a particular time that had provoked me to write several obsessive essays. When I finished it, I realized that all of my essay collections could carry that same title. And that every couple of years a new volume of the same was possible. The essay, in the spirit of Montaigne, is an experiment in which the substance within the person writing mixes, dialogues, with the substances of the world and produces something new and unique. The ghosts or the dead of a writer are our substances in the world before being dead. They are presences.

CODA

You studied with Roland Barthes, and that time in Paris affected you deeply as you explain in the prologue of your book of essays Con la Literatura en el cuerpo. *Can you tell us more about that experience?*

More a master craftsman in his workshop than a professor behind his lectern. The primary and principal teaching of Roland Barthes was not in the content of his courses, not even in his books, but in his approach to teaching, writing, and understanding the world.

He was not just a professor who gave a lecture on a subject that we students could understand and master, rather he was a craftsman who did his work, and we apprentices in his vicinity saw how he worked and tried to do our own best work, always and only learning the trade of a master craftsman. Not inputting or even imitating the content of his teachings, not turning ourselves into his followers, but into craftsmen of the power of the word and modes of realization. Creating instruments: like goldsmiths do using their hands, one should create instruments of thought and writing using one's own body. Concepts and styles that were our own. With one fundamental, three-part question: What is the one thing that only I can do in terms of literary form and thought? What do things mean to me in particular? What is the corporeal footprint that I and no one else can leave behind on the things of this world? Writing, I soon deduced, is a way of being in the world. A very modest and very ambitious trade at the same time.

Roland Barthes gave his seminars in two very distinct forums: the massive class, which was so popular that the attendees arrived hours beforehand to get and hold a seat: a lecture that was transmitted simultaneously in other contiguous rooms. And the *petit seminaire*, where a few of us, no more than ten, formed a space of mutual readership in the presence of Roland Barthes who was another reader in the circle. When he agreed to be my thesis advisor and admitted me as a member of the small seminar he said to me: "You run the risk of getting disillusioned, I'm not a particularly good advisor." And I already knew it. He had written an essay about his small seminar as a small utopist space, a sort of phalanstery. And that text had just seduced me, it made me want to be there. It was not his glory as a fashionable semiologist. Rather the quality of creating spaces where learning followed a unique form. But he did advise me indirectly in the sense of pushing me to accept the enormous challenge all artists and thinkers face when they start out: to be radically yourself.

The power of that instruction in craft, of that necessarily very personal education, multiplied its effect on me because it radiated its exemplary influence into other courses that were key for me during that time period. The next important seminar I took, studying philosophy, was that of Gilles Deleuze. And no less impassioned and formative, that of Jacques Ranciére in the field of the history of ideas and social utopias and that of André Chastel in the field of art history. Each one had a very personal way of living their trade with extreme passion. And between these four masters, more than professors, I had the foundation to construct a personal point of view regarding political life and its masks, social thought, the place of art and the creation of forms, utopias and communitarian practices and hyperindividual creation, the life of ideas, writing, poetry, reading, symbols and their ghosts. Now these are some of my themes, my obsessions. A node of interests and intensities that, I think, is key to what I am as a writer.

A THOUSAND FORESTS

FROM *MOGADOR: THE NAMES OF THE AIR*
[A NOVEL]

Like all the women of Mogador, Fatma frequented the Hammam, which opened its moisture in the morning to female bodies only, reserving the water of its afternoon to lubricate the roughness of male complicity. What was the Hammam in the morning? Secret whirlwind: shout, cake of soap dissolved in water, tangled hair, evaporated fragrant herbs, an orange section in a fountain of pomegranate seeds, mint and hashish on full lips, hasty depilations, sandals of swollen wood, red earth for dyeing hair, a bitten peach, obese flowers, vivid tiles, submerged nakedness moving like the reflection of the moon in the water.

Like the public oven, where every woman brings her kneaded dough and talks with the other women as she waits for her bread to bake, the Hammam is one of the places where the women of Mogador can weave together the fine threads of their complicities. None of the three principal religions on the island has succeeded in extending its prohibitions to the Hammam. No phrase from the Koran, the Talmud, or the Bible may be uttered inside its walls, much less written, and—it is assumed—not even thought. The women are careful always to enter with their right foot and leave with their left, as if having taken only one step between entering and leaving. In this way, they place the Hammam outside of space and time. Consequently, the Hammam has its own laws—those of the complete purification of the body, from which one attempts to remove all sadness, as it is harmful, and to train the body in pleasure, which revitalizes. They are the laws of the oldest form of witchcraft which seeks to stimulate beauty and life by concealing the decay of age.

What is illicit outside is, inside the Hammam, as unsubstantial as a fruit whose peel dissolves in the air and one can no longer distinguish where the fruit begins and ends. The progressive temperatures, the bodies emerging from steam as if from their own element, the voices and their echoes, the infallible massages, the immense fatigue and the drowsy arousal, are some of the thousand happy antechambers through which one who frequents the Hammam will pass on his or her aimless journey. Relaxation and cleanliness are not the first things one seeks in the Hammam, although they may be some of its many consequences.

Fatma knew, as did the other women, that in the afternoon when the sex of its inhabitants changed, the very building of the Hammam was as different from the one she knew as night is to day. The murmur one would hear from the street after midday served notice of the transformations that had taken place. If in the morning the laughter was high-pitched and at times shrill— polished like the points of needles woven into the thicket of voices, shouts wavering between sobbing and song—in the afternoon the waves of laughter would grow rougher, culminating in isolated shouts that loudly exaggerated their manly inflections as if wishing to impress the erection of their presence on the others.

But while the arrogance of the afternoon and the hysteria of the morning are the two rigid extremes that keep the walls of the Hammam taut, its many rooms and fountains let loose, morning and afternoon, the labyrinths that favor the existence of intermediate souls and sexes. Over the entrance to the Hammam, entwined in a fine calligraphy that burned in three colors, an inscription in heavy red letters read:

Enter. This is the house of the body as it came into the world. The house of fire that was water, of water that was fire. Enter. Fall like rain, blaze like straw. May your virtue be the joyful offering in the fountain of the senses. Enter.

That morning, Fatma entered the Hammam resenting the contrast between the overwhelming brilliance outside and the semi-darkness splashed with color from the small stained-glass windows on the ceiling that distributed their dose of sun over the first room. It was a very large room, one of the largest there, with plain whitewashed walls and a row of hooks at eye level where the women left all their garments. There was a high chair by the door from which an obese and vociferous woman watched over everyone's belongings and collected the money each woman paid to begin her passage through the waters.

Suddenly, Fatma saw more than a hundred different pieces of cloth hanging on the walls. There were more fabrics gathered together in these robes, tunics, and veils than in any storehouse in Mogador. Colors and patterns were displayed there that could never to be found side by side—not even in the chests of merchants from the Orient. Each fabric seemed softer than the next and the difference between each was subtle yet distinct, like the blade of a knife. Fatma imagined her fingers would go mad if they had to find their way among those textures without being able to select or reject any of them.

With the same astonishment, she watched the skin of the women taking off these yards of cloth. She would look to see if there was any correspondence between the softness of certain backs and their linens or silks. She imagined that with time and use, cloth and skin placed in contact, performing the same movements, would transmit virtues and defects from one to the other. That woman wearing a torn shawl around her waist revealed a long and conspicuous marking on her stomach. Where did the wound begin? In the cloth? Which came first, the mending or the scar?

Another woman farther off had skin whose color could only have been conceived by a dye-maker who, mixing herbs for several days, could obtain that steely tone glimpsed only in the bricks of a lit oven. When Fatma exposed her belly, laughing at herself, she thought of crushed velvet and slid her open fingers down through the soft, matted hairs to give body to her own black cloth.

As she took off her clothes and felt the sunlight on her body, intensified and colored by the stained-glass skylights, Fatma felt herself touched with delicacy by something that touched alike everyone who entered with her. That light bound her to the other women, dressing her in the same robe and banishing those bothersome angels of modesty who, in contrast to that light, can make even a woman buttressed by cloth feel in need of more veils. Dressed in the colors of the glass, Fatma entered discreetly into the other women's conversation simply by looking at them under the same reflections, and following them at a distance, she entered the second room.

There the windows no longer veiled the women's glances and their skin was returned to its original color. The walls were covered with mosaics painted with geometric friezes and voluptuous strokes that mirrored everywhere the bodies' deepest folds, becoming their infinite echo. No longer hiding bodies but breaking down their existence and multiplying their secrets:

blurring bodies with images of themselves, granting them an extension more subtle than their own shadows. Fatma let her gaze sink into the holes drawn on the wall—holes that were now her own. She wet the waves of her hair in the water of a fountain and the surface of her drenched skin began to gather reflections that had previously shone only in the mosaics.

In that room, the water was not so hot. In the next three rooms the temperature gradually increased until one reached the central room where a large fountain in the middle gushed boiling water. Fatma passed easily through each of those temperatures, knowing they form the ladder leading to the door that finally opens on a region of half-dreams like those she saw for hours at a time from her window each day.

As she entered the central room, she could not help but be struck by the enormous fountain that seemed to flow down from the ceiling in a boiling waterfall, spreading waves of steam throughout the room. Around the fountain was a circle of stone lions, and one had to climb onto them to fill the water buckets. A liquid resembling mercury poured from their throats and coursed through sinuous channels throughout the room, reflecting the naked bodies in its lazy flow. From the lions' anuses came a thick steam, perfumed and tinted.

There were always women playing among the lions, posing obscenely for the others with the stone muzzles and tails, and those who sat serenely on the backs of the lions, soaping their legs. Once the boiling water was on their skin, the steam that rose from them looked, at a distance and against the light, like white flames.

Fatma entered with her eyes half-closed so as to be surprised by the procession of blazing women on lions, muzzles sunk between their legs. They were demons of the obscene and delicate humidity who placed their hands on the stone in a way so smooth and lingering that they revealed how, just a short while earlier, they had placed their hands on the thighs—never so solid—of their lovers.

Around them, several women talked as they soaked themselves; others soaped one another and many made waterfalls of their voices. As she entered, Fatma saw the steamy shadows moving to the rhythm of the fountain, displaying themselves with the same exuberance as the glazed tiles, sliding from one to another as confidently as ocean currents seem to move through the sea, currents she would now join.

In that fluid circle of women who seemed to walk on the steam covering the floor, Fatma forgot her everyday body to enjoy the new properties offered her by a seasoned nakedness. She had moved out of herself as if she had slipped and, as she rose, stood beside her own body. And that slight difference, which obviously only she could perceive, was a wide band over which new joys raced. And if now even her own hands were different and could revive her excitement to the point where she would begin to close her eyes, a short while later that very morning, Kadiya's hands would do the same with even greater skill.

Whereas from the entrance of the Hammam to the room with the great fountain there was a single path on which one was clothed in subtle differences, when one left that profusely overflowing room, concurrent doorways multiplied and one could enter gardens and sunlit springs. They say there are a total of twenty-five rooms in that Hammam, that some are reserved for the powerful and others are segregated spaces: for people with skin diseases, for eunuchs who are still bleeding, for the shamefaced obese, for the uncontrollably violent, for foreigners, for those who refuse to sell their caresses, and for those who can't stand the water and go to the Hammam just to meet other people.

Four gardens were crossed lengthwise by reflecting pools and fountains whose cascades sung in up to twenty-five different tones. One of the rooms had a reflecting pool which was particularly admired because instead of lying on the floor, it lay on a wall on which architect-apprentice-magicians had succeeded in causing an enormous curtain of water to fall from the ceiling to the floor so slowly—practically motionless—that one could see one's own reflection more clearly than on the surface of a standing pool of water. In another room, scenes had been painted on the walls to excite the lusty imagination of anyone who looked at them; or anyone who touched them, since the walls had been made in relief so that the people who adore representations of the burning in the flesh might linger against them.

In another room, the paintings were not merely the blaze: they served as initiation to the fire. They illustrated to passersby the thousand ways to caress the penis with the lips, to envelop the clitoris with the tongue, to suck and lift and bite and caress, in succession or all at once, to fall from bed and get up without having to separate, to shake out obsessive stiffness and to drive away premature softness, to drink again from dry wells and to dry those that trickle down to the knees.

There were rooms dedicated to massage in which the most common was not particularly exciting. It consisted of a robust masseur who linked his arms and legs back to back with those of his victim, the person being massaged lying face down. The masseur drew his body taut as a bow until the joints of the other person cracked. One by one, the masseur collected thirty-two cracks from each patient. After each crack, the fleshy man made a noise with his mouth that sounded like a sheet of paper being torn or a dry kiss, he let out a phrase (whether it was a prayer or a curse no one knew for sure), and shifted his position slightly in search of the next report. In the morning, the masseuses were valued and sought not only for their skillful musculature, but also for the absolute roundness of their bodies. They were like great balls of flesh that absorbed delicate bodies as they rolled along and caused bones to yield the intimidation of their accumulated tension. They also strove to make the joints articulate the sound of a crystal bell that falls and rolls around on a carpet.

There were rooms dedicated to the dyeing of hair and the palm of the hand with a reddish or yellowish earth called *rássul*, which is found only on the outskirts of the city of Fez and is dissolved in rose water or orange blossom water. Eyes were also painted with charred bitter almonds to darken the eyelashes and with kohl to line the eyelids. Fatma preferred to use kohl from the Hammam rather than the merchants in the port, since the kohl from the Hammam was prepared by the women at home, following all the precautions the merchants didn't observe. One had to gather together coral, clove oil, the pits of black olives, a pepper corn from the Sudan, and small kohl pebbles. Most important of all, everything must be ground by seven prepubescent girls or by a woman "who has passed the time when liquids boil in her body," as the *Book of Recipes and Advice of the Women of Mogador* instructs. The ground mixture should be sifted through a coarse cloth and the fine powder that is obtained is dissolved in cat's urine to give a greater shine to the eyes, and is applied with a very thin piece of straw in two lines on the eyelids.

In that same room Berber women displayed their tattoos in their entirety, and brides, their depilations, taking care that the spices, fragrant herbs, and goat's milk poured into the water didn't alter the painful markings on their skin. Beauty achieved through suffering, however slight—but always flaunted—is in Mogador beauty most complete. The display of mutilated flesh, of intense pain glimpsed through makeup, thrives among the women of Mogador with infinite complications. Fatma knew that exuberance well, and since she didn't display the deep tattoos of the other women, it seemed to have little to do with her. But the air of melancholy that gradually came to possess her after that morning would itself become a spontaneous form of displaying pain, of adorning herself with her sadness like an insect that spreads its wings in the afternoon, imitating banana leaves or plum blossoms.

It was still too early that morning for Fatma to display great joy or sadness, and she let a black Egyptian woman named Sofía line her eyes with kohl. This woman knew all the secrets for arresting fertility, sterility, impotency, and other calamities. While she attended to Fatma's eyes, Sofía gave advice to a forty-year-old woman with drooping skin and a flabby waist and spirit. "To hold on to your husband, you will do everything I tell you. Very early in the morning, while he is still sleeping, and shortly before he wakes, repeat in his ear three times: *May heaven burn this forgetfulness from your head, may the floor shake, hurl you, and wake you up deep inside me.* You must do this for eight days without him hearing you while awake, and the first thing you give him to eat in the morning must be a piece of date that has passed the night inside you. But he can't suspect a thing. After a week you will see his passion growing. To keep him from spending it on others, you must steal the sheet that a black woman and man have dampened with their sweat as they made love. Burn it at the foot of your bed. Mix the ashes with rain water that has not been walked upon and apply a little each day to every one of your orifices. If you can't get the sheet dampened by two blacks, you can use the sheet from a prostitute. But in either case, the sheet must be stolen for its ashes to work. The people who dampened it at night can't suspect a thing, before or after. Should anyone else know when and how you do all this, the power of the spell will dissipate."

Fatma was impressed by the docile appearance of the woman who involuntarily nodded her head as she listened, clenching one fist without letting go and touching her throat with the other hand. Fat-ma imagined her undertaking the long and arduous task which Sofía had charged her with, but saw her stopping in anguish before one of the obstacles. The vision of a defeat was on her face, as if the woman herself was sure her future was inhabited by impossibility.

Fatma also imagined her overcoming all the obstacles and being disappointed, having seen no results, asking herself through the passing years at what step, in what movement, in what word of the charm she might have erred.

Fatma was frightened by her desperation, despite having seen the woman in the marketplace besieged by suitors she despised. At that hour of the morning, Fatma could still enjoy the luxury of believing it absurd to persistently desire the love of a person one can't have nearby, while quickly rejecting love that is close at hand.

When Sofía realized that Fatma was growing very tense watching the desperate woman, she hastened to make up her eyes without knowing for whom she was adorning them, and sent Fatma off with a kiss on the forehead.

Fatma was afraid to enter several of the rooms in the Hammam that, at the same time, fascinated her somehow, and as she walked by them, she stood on the threshold watching indecisively. In the snake room, thirty completely toothless and lavishly oiled cobras slithered among hundreds of leather pillows and the naked bodies of those who, morning and afternoon, partook of their privileges. There were those who had their favorites and others who had theirs reserved: snakes that were only taken out of their baskets in the presence of their owners. Fatma dreamed once that she was laughing, entwined in snakes, with the same nervous, high-pitched laugh she had heard other women emit at that unceasing sensation between one's legs. Fatma never dared touch the snakes, although something very powerful attracted her to them. She was horrified by those insistent eyes and those aggressive knots which the snakes allowed to be untied only when hashish smoke was blown on their ears.

But even though Fatma didn't enter that room, caresses bolder than those of ten snakes would leave their infinite mark between her legs and a slipknot, which she didn't yet suspect, was about to tighten around her chest, cutting her breath short, causing her to cast longing glances from her window. Like the sailors longing to see Mogador transformed again into a naked reflection under the water. If the chorus of dragons on the wall could sense sounds long before taking them into their resonant bodies, they would be howling now—like a pack of wolves howling at the moon—to warn Fatma. Kadiya was near.

Translated by Mark Schafer

WORK

1981, *Mitología de un cine en crisis*, Premiá (essay).

1987, *Los nombres del aire*, J. Mortiz (novel).

1987, *Los demonios de la lengua*, J. Mortiz (stories).

1988, *Al filo de las hojas*, Conculta (essay).

1990, *Una introducción a Octavio Paz*, J. Mortiz (essay).

1990, *La inaccessible*, Taller Martín Pescador (poetry).

1991, *Tristeza de la verdad. André Gide regresa de Rusia*, J. Mortiz (essay).

1992, *Ars de cuerpo entero*, UNAM-Ediciones Corunda (essay).

1994, *Cuentos de Mogador*, CNCA (stories).

1995, *Con la Literatura en el cuerpo*, Taurus (essay).

1996, *En los labios del agua*, Alfaguara (novel).

1997, *Diálogos con mis fantasmas*, UNAM (essay).

1997, *Cuatro escritores rituales*, Instituto Mexiquense de Cultura (essay).

1999, *De agua y Aire*, UNAM (book-album).

1999, *De cómo llegó a Mogador la melancholia*, Rocher (stories).

1999, *Aventuras de la mirada*, Isste (essay).

2001, *Los jardines secretos de Mogador*, (novel).

2002, *La huella del grito*, Solar (story).

2005, *Nueve veces el asombro*, Alfaguara (story).

2007, *La mano del fuego*, Alfaguara (novel).

2011, *Elogio del insomnio*, Alfaguara (miscellaneous).

2011, *Decir es desear*, Alfaguara (poetry).

2011, *La página posible*, Aveio (essay).

•

ENGLISH TRANSLATIONS

2001, *Mogador: Names of the Air*, translated by Mark Schafer, City Lights (novel).

2009, *The Secret Gardens of Mogador: Voices of the Earth*, translated by Rhonda Dahl Buchanan, White Pine (novel).

·

AWARDS AND RECOGNITIONS

1987, Premio Xavier Villaurrutia for *Los nombres del aire*.

1988, Guggenheim Fellowship.

1990, Fellowship from Consejo Nacional para la Cultura y las Artes for literary creation.

1991, Premio de Literatura José Fuentes Mares for *Una introducción a Octavio Paz*.

1993, Member of the Sistema Nacional de Creadores de México (renewed in 2002).

1998, Honorary Citizen of Louisville, Kentucky, from the University of Louisville.

1999, Honorary member of the Mu Epsilon chapter of the National Hispanic Society Sigma Delta Pi.

1999, Kentucky Colonel by peticion of University of Louisville.

2000, Three Continents Prize for the French edition of *En los labios del agua*.

2001, Official of the French Order of Arts and Letters.

2002, Honorary Captain of the historic steam engine *The Belle of Louisville*.

2003, Premio Cálamo for *Los jardines secretos de Mogador*.

2005, Gran Orden de Honor Nacional al Mérito Autoral.

2006, Premio a la Excelencia de lo Nuestro awarded by the Fundación México Unido.

2006, Premio Juan Pablos al Mérito Editorial.
2009, Premio Van Deren Coke Achievement.
2012, Premio San Petersburgo for *Los jardines secretos de Mogador.*

JAVIER
MARÍAS
(Spain, 1951)

J avier Marías, the fourth of five brothers, was born in Madrid on September 20, 1951. His father Julián Marías, was an illustrious philosopher, essayist, and educator with a seat in the Real Academia Española. He exercised a notable influence on the intellectual formation of his son and, up until his own entrance into the Real Academia Española, Javier was known as "the young Marías." His mother, Dolores Franco Manera, was a teacher and she died when Javier was twenty-six years old.

His childhood was marked by two events that, since then, have been occasional founts of literary creation. The first: Julianín, his older brother, died when he was three years old (something he alludes to in *Negra espalda del tiempo*). The second was the imprisonment his father endured after a "friend" betrayed him to the authorities of Franco's governement (a similar biography to the father of the protagonist of *Tu rostro mañana*) precipitating the incessant harassment to which he was submitted throughout Franco's regime: he was forbidden from teaching in Spain, which forced him to go do so abroad (Wellesley, Harvard, Yale), where he gave lectures and taught courses. And so it was that Javier Marías spent his first year of life in Massachusetts in the house of the poet Jorge Guillén, the same house whose second story had recently housed Vladimir Nabokov, who would become one of Javier Marías's favorite writers.

During his adolescence he translated and wrote screenplays for his uncle Jesús Franco and his cousin Ricardo, and even appeared as an extra in some of their movies. He also enjoyed the intellectual environment and camaraderie his parents encouraged at home. He got a degree in English Philology at Universidad Complutense de Madrid and moved to Paris, where he immersed himself in his first novel, *Los dominios del lobo*, which he published when he was nineteen. Upon his return to Madrid he met Juan Benet, who he awknowledges as his mentor.

Javier Marías began translating from English to Spanish the authors he wanted to study in greater depth like Hardy, Conrad, Nabokov, Faulkner, Salinger, Stevenson, Browne, and Sterne. In 1979 he won the Premio Nacional de Traducción in Spain for his version of *The Life and Opinions of Tristram Shandy* by Laurence Sterne. Between 1983 and 1985 he taught Spanish literature and translation at Oxford University, taking advantage of that time to frequently travel to London, visit its bookstores, and converse with Guillermo Cabrera Infante and Miriam Gómez.

In 1986 he published his fifth novel *El hombre sentimental.* A strange story of the adulterous romance between a beautiful woman and a young opera singer, which opened with the following epigraph from William Hazlitt: "I think myself into love / And I dream myself out of it." Based on his experiences during his stay at Oxford, Marías wrote the novel *Todas las almas*, published in 1989, an ingenious combination of fragments, essays, photographs, and observations that ruptured and broadened the limits of the conventional novel, a series of mechanisms that, ten years later, he would display even more in the anti-novel *Negra espalda del tiempo.* Since then, Javier Marías has been an assiduous contributor to the written press and his articles often have served as a foundation for books on subjects as diverse as soccer (he's a faithful follower of Real Madrid), film, language, and political reflections.

In 1992, with the publication of *Corazón tan blanco*, Javier Marías expanded his international prestige, supported not only by critics of the novel, but also by its rare success among the reading public. In Germany, the critic Marcel Reich-Ranicki valued his work as "genre hybridism" and lavished the author with praise, which contributed not only to bringing the German public to his work, but to his translation into many other languages. The English translation, *A Heart so White*, carried out by Margaret Jull Costa, was honored with the International IMPAC Dublin Literary Award in 1997. His next novel, *Mañana en la batalla piensa en mí*, in 1994, confirmed him as one of the most important writers of Spanish literature in recent years: the novel won the Premio Fastenrath de la Real Academia Española, the Femina in France, and the Rómulo Gallegos in Venezuela, the first time it was given to a Spanish author.

In 2002 Javier Marías published the first volume of his most ambitious novelistic undertaking to date, *Tu rostro mañana.* The first, *Fiebre y lanza*, followed by *Baile y sueño* (2004), and finishing with *Veneno y sombra y adiós* (2007). The novel develops in an independent way some of the characters previously introduced in *Todas las almas*. This magnum opus of some eleven hundred pages tells the story of a Spanish university professor, involved in the British secret service, who, after going through a divorce goes back to Oxford. His most recent novel, published in 2012, has the title of *Los enamoramientos*, and its English translation, *The Infatuations*, was a finalist for the 2013 National Book Critics Circle Award for Fiction.

Besides being a novelist, translator, and columnist, Javier Marías also holds the title of King of Redonda. The author Jon Wynne-Tyson, who, following a series of chance circumstances had inherited the title of monarch of that miniscule, rocky island in the Caribbean inhabited by birds, was so enchanted by the portrayal of Gawsworth that appeared in *Todas las almas* that he abdicated his throne and ceded the title of King of Redonda to Marías, who then founded a small publishing house with the name of that kingdom. The publishing house awards an annual prize to foreign authors and filmmakers, and over the years, has given honorary titles to various figures of international stature.

THE ACORN

THE TORTURE OF DOCTOR JOHNSON

I think that many, many authors, or maybe not so many, but quite a few of them, and I suppose that I could include myself among them, write novels or realize that we have written a certain novel to include a few paragraphs or even sometimes only a few sentences; ones that by themselves would not stand up properly. And sometimes they might be slightly ridiculous, and they might need another form, maybe it could be a poem, but then a poem is quite a different thing from prose, although of course you can have some poetry in the prose and certainly my prose tries to be rather rhythmical and rather musical and I think I have a strong sense of pace, but certainly sometimes there are a few things that you cannot say just by themselves. It's not something you are absolutely aware of in the beginning, but sometimes you feel it once you have finished a book. In a way you have constructed, you have built a whole architecture, a whole building, just to encompass a few pages or one page, or five pages, or what I usually call in my own novels some lyrical excerpts that you can find now and then, here and there, what in French is called a "*morceau de bravoure*." You have the feeling that the main thing, the very reason for the existence of a particular novel is that one page or those five or ten pages or this paragraph and that one, and this idea and that one. In that sense it is not that you are exactly cheating your reader and as I said before you build a rather complex architecture in order to shelter a few sentences or a few pages, it's not exactly that, it's not that you do that on purpose. Of course you want to tell a story, you do tell it, but there is some moment in which you realize that some fragments or some paragraphs are stronger than the rest somehow, and you feel them that way. And the reason why I have chosen these fragments has to do with that. I realize that I might have chosen others because

590

I think that in most of my novels, or at least in the most recent ones, and by recent ones I mean the ones written since 1983 or 86 perhaps, beginning with *El hombre sentimental*, I think that all of them have, in some way or another, these kinds of salient paragraphs, or outstanding ones.

This excerpt from *Mañana en la batalla piensa en mí* is one of those lyrical passages and at the same time I could say that it is one of the passages I am most proud of because I know that I did something which is not very easy to do and I think I more or less, even if this can sound a bit too boastful, I rather succeeded in achieving what I wanted to achieve. I also realize that it is rare when a reader understands what really happens in this passage. The dying woman, Marta Tellez, is about to become the narrator's lover, but she falls ill. They are half-dressed or half-naked, but they haven't really started and she begins to feel ill and she dies before they have become lovers. And of course there is the little boy, two years old, who is Marta's child and who is asleep in another room. The narrator, after her death, doesn't know what to do with the baby, he thinks that maybe he should try to call Marta's husband who is in London (they are in Madrid); or should he tell someone, should he just leave the baby all alone? He's in a situation that no one would like to be in, in real life. So there comes this moment in which she dies. And the reader has a feeling that they are listening to Marta's voice as she is dying, but it doesn't happen, it's not like that at all. The narrator is the one who is telling the story all the time, from beginning to end, but there is a moment in which he starts to adopt, as it were, the voices of people in danger or people who are about to die: a pilot in a war, someone in the trenches, and these imaginary characters or symbolic characters start speaking in the first person. Then that series of imaginary voices, fictional voices within the fiction that is the novel, give way to a new voice which is Marta's voice as if it were yet another of the fictional voices; it is the imagined voice of Marta in that series of voices. But of course the one who is really speaking is the narrator, Víctor Francés. But I think that the reader has the impression that he or she has really heard Marta while she is dying. So some people say, "wait a minute, what's going on here? This woman is not telling the story, so how is it possible that I am listening to her?" Of course you are not listening to her at all, you are listening to the narrator imagining what she might be thinking at the moment of her death. But I think it's done in a way that it is very soft and subtle so you just accept that it is her own voice. There are no tricks, I don't like to cheat the reader at all, it's very clear, I never want to mix voices, the sort of thing that many writers have done and do, where you never know who is really talking. No, in my novels it is always very clear who is talking, except for maybe one time, but I have done something similar in other books, something which I call *"narración hipotética,"* or "hypothetical narration," when the narrator thinks about what might be going on in someone else's mind. But it is clear that he is imagining it. Most of my novels are written in the first person and one of the things you renounce when you decide to have a narrator in the first person is to know everything. And of course that narrator has always got to justify what he knows or what he heard. That is one of the big losses, although of course you gain other things by using it. And one of the things I have tried to do in some of my novels is not to lose so much when you have a narrator in the first person, but not by means of cheating the reader, no dirty trick as it were, or *"trucos de mala ley,"* as we say in Spanish. So I chose this paragraph because I feel particularly proud of having persuaded the reader that the woman who is not talking, who is just dying in front of the narrator, is really the one communicating and that you are inside her mind.

Then also one of the reasons for choosing this fragment is that I wrote it shortly after my maestro's death, Juan Benet, one of the greatest losses I have had in my lifetime. He was a very good friend, I had met him when I was very young, 17 or 18 and he was some 24 years older than me, and he was really my maestro and a very good friend. He died in 1993, and I think I had already started to write the novel, but I hadn't written this part yet, I wrote it shortly after his death. And so as it happens to anyone when you lose someone very dear, be it a father or a mother or a brother or a very good friend, for a few days at least, or for a few weeks, it is difficult to try to imagine what has happened to the dead person because we are rather dealing with what is happening to us or to the people close to the dead person. And we very easily forget that something has also happened to the dead person. But something happened to that person, too, and I suppose in a way I tried to imagine what might be in the mind of a person who is dying. Maybe this is one of the fragments in my work that I have written in a more passionate way, you could say. Because of course the character in the novel has nothing to do with Juan Benet, who was 65 and a man, and a very different man from this woman in the novel. But somehow I couldn't help having in mind what he might have experienced when he died. And so those are the reasons why I chose this fragment.

As for the short story "When I Was Mortal," it is probably, of the stories I've written, which are not so many, the one I like best, together with the one called "What the Butler Said." The reason for choosing it is because the one telling the story is a ghost, and the point of view of a ghost is a great point of view for telling things. Of course I am talking about literary ghosts, because I don't believe in ghosts or in anything supernatural or preternatural, but certainly I like ghosts in literature and in films as well. The best possible point of view from which to tell a story is when the person who is telling the story, the ghost, is someone who already knows the end of the story, of his own story at least, and it is someone to whom nothing can happen anymore because he or she is already dead. Therefore he can tell the story with a certain amount of calm, which doesn't mean it can't be passionate too. And that's precisely what a ghost can be, someone who knows the whole story, who is not here anymore and whatever is going to happen to him or her has already happened, who in a way is beyond danger, but at the same time is someone who still cares very much about what he left behind. So much so that he comes back and haunts people and tries to have an influence in the lives of the people who are still alive, and the people he cared about, and in that sense he is not a dispassionate narrator, on the contrary. In this short story the one telling the story is a ghost, and he tells something which he considers a real curse, he says "now I know everything, and I also remember everything." That has an echo, of course, of "Funes el memorioso" ("Funes, His Memory"), Borges's story, but here he talks about the time when he was alive, which is a pitiful time because you are not absolutely aware of everything and of course you don't remember everything. And he realizes that some of the things he lived when he was a child first, an adult later, that he thought happened in a particular way, a happier way, were not exactly like that. And of course he recalls his own death, because he didn't know when it happened, but he does now.

One thing I deal with in some of my novels, and in different ways, is the fact that people tend to want to know things and they feel very curious and they want the truth and they want transparency. In a way that's a big mistake. Of course it is something rather difficult to fight against, the willingness to know and of course we cannot help be curious even if sometimes we are also

afraid of what we might come to know. But the tendency is to find out and
to discover and to know more. And in this story you can find that knowing
everything, remembering everything can be a very pitiful thing. People want
to know, but if we knew everything, really, I suppose it would be awful.
People would be killing each other if they knew absolutely everything about
what others think about you. Civilized life would be impossible. But of course
this is not the story itself, this is something behind the story. I have tried in
other books or texts to adopt this ghostly point of view, but on this occasion I
have the ghost himself telling the story and I think it's not bad.

This page from *El hombre sentimental* is the only page in my career in
which you are not totally sure about who is talking. It is easy to imagine who
is talking but it could be either of two different characters. Supposedly it is
the narrator, but it might be someone else as well. It is a very short passage,
but declarations of love are something that we should all avoid nowadays in a
book for sure—I don't mean in life—because it is very easy for it to be ridiculous. The words for that kind of thing are so wasted and so used that it is
really difficult. But I think this is a declaration of love that is not so bad, and
I think it has some merit, or at least should have some credit for being not so
bad. The fact that many readers have felt that these words weren't false and
that they do have meaning, well, maybe that's why I have chosen that fragment. In life even the most used and wasted words can be effective depending
upon the situation, but in literature it is very difficult, and nowadays it must
have special strength. I don't say this excerpt has that, but at least I think it
is acceptable as a declaration of love.

The reason for choosing this last fragment, which is from *Negra espalda
del tiempo*, is because out of all my work, it is the passage that has made me
feel the most moral doubts. I have asked myself "should I write this, should I
put this into somebody else's mind? I have the bad luck that it has come into
my mind, but should I put this into somebody else's mind and make him or
her feel as bad as I am feeling now?" It's not that I thought of suppressing
it, of course not, not so much as that, but I thought that this is a *"putada"* to
make somebody who might not ever think this at all in his lifetime, to make
him think about it, about the idea that nothing ever passes, nothing ever goes
away totally. When children get hurt or are frightened or have a nightmare,
one of the things a mother says to her child is *"ya pasó, ya pasó,"* it's over, it's
finished. You've had a really bad time, but now, in the present, you aren't

having that bad time any more. And those words, "it's over" are very consol-
ing, very healing, as if the present were the thing that counts; it is a consolation to think that that the bad thing or the worst possible thing is over. In
this paragraph the idea is that no, it isn't like that, things aren't always over.
Things that happened are always happening, they are still happening and
they shall always happen. There is an echo of Macbeth here: "it seems as if
our yesterdays were all under the earth, trying to surface." I think the fragment is not bad and it has some force, and it is convincing in a way because
generally the idea would be no, it's true that when things are over, things are
better. Or you can bear what has happened because it is already past, and the
past is always more bearable than the present. So to put in somebody else's
mind the idea that no, watch out, because it's not like that, is not a very nice
thing to do to potential readers.

In Conversation with the Dead

In my case the writer I have most in mind is undeniably obvious and explicit
in many of my books: Shakespeare. I have taken many titles from him for
my works: *Mañana en la batalla piensa en mí, Corazón tan blanco, Cuando fui
mortal,* and *La negra espalda del tiempo,* which is not exactly a quote, but it
comes from what he says in *The Tempest* about the abysm, and of course some
fragments of works by him are also mentioned openly in my books, fragments
from *Richard III* and *Macbeth,* and of course *The Tempest* and from *Henry IV*
and *Henry V.*

And of course Cervantes, although in the case of Cervantes he comes to
me directly in the Spanish language, but also indirectly in the English language because I did translate *Tristam Shandy* about 30 years ago, and it was a
hard task and a long one, and Sterne was so influenced by Cervantes in that
novel that in a way I would say that perhaps it is much more Cervantine than
any Spanish novel of the eighteenth or nineteenth centuries. And of course
by translating that book when I was young I learned so much about writing
and about the use of time in the novel, that I also have a rather permanent
dialogue as it were with Sterne himself and with Cervantes as well. Of course
there are many others, the authors I have translated into Spanish, because
translation is one of the best possible exercises for a writer. If you know two

languages and you can translate, I think that's the best way to learn how to write. If I had a creative writing school, which I would not, but if I did, I would only have students who speak at least two languages and make them translate. Because you happen to be not only a privileged reader, but a privileged writer if you can renounce your own style, if you have one, and adopt someone else's—someone who is much better than you, always if you are translating classics at least—and if you can rewrite that in your own language in an acceptable way, let alone if it is in a very good way, you are sharpening your instruments and your writing will improve tremendously. I translated poetry by Nabokov and Faulkner, John Ashbery, Wallace Stevens, Stevenson, Auden, Thomas Browne, Isak Dinesen, Yeats.

Of course translating well is not enough, you must have some ability for invention and some talent and a few other things, but as far as the instrument goes, that is the best possible school. Therefore, those writers I just mentioned influenced me because I did translate them, they are always very much on my mind, and I have adopted in my own writing sometimes solutions that I have found for them in Spanish. Sometimes in translation you cannot always have an absolute equivalent, but you can add something with which you compensate for what you miss. And sometimes I have even used small things; I remember having used something from Nabokov, in one of his poems he talks about the "mellow moon"; which I translated as "*la luna pulposa*." Whenever I have used that expression in Spanish, I realize that I am in conversation with *my* Nabokov. So I have many authors in mind. Funnily enough, there are more poets who I have more conversations with when writing, and that is something that has not been pointed out very often. When critics talk about evident influences, sometimes I think, "but I have never read that author," but they always link you with other novelists, they never think of poets and I think that one of my strongest influences can be found in the poets, which is why in *Tu rostro mañana* there are quotations from Eliot, Rilke, Machado, and Ashbery.

A THOUSAND FORESTS

FROM *TOMORROW IN THE BATTLE THINK ON ME*
[A NOVEL]

But tonight they did not sleep, possibly none of them did, at least not well, not straight through, not as they would hope to, the mother, ill and half-naked, lying on the bed watched over by a man whom she knew only superficially, the child with the covers half off (he had got into bed on his own and I didn't dare rearrange the miniature sheets and blankets and tuck him in properly), and the father, who knows, he would have had supper with someone or other; after hanging up and looking thoughtful—lightly scratching one temple with her forefinger—and a touch envious (she may have had company, but she was still stuck on Conde de la Cimera as she was every night), all Marta had said was: "He told me he'd just had a fantastic meal at an Indian restaurant, the Bombay Brasserie. Do you know it?" Yes, I did know it, I liked it a lot, I had dined in its vast colonial-style rooms on a couple of occasions, a pianist in a dinner jacket sits in the foyer, and there are respectful waiters and maîtres d'hotel, and huge ceiling fans winter and summer, it's a very theatrical place, rather expensive by English standards, but not prohibitively so, a place for friends to meet and celebrate or for business meetings, rather than for intimate, romantic suppers, unless you want to impress an inexperienced young woman or a girl from the working classes, someone likely to feel slightly overwhelmed by the setting and to get absurdly drunk on Indian beer, someone you won't have to take to any intermediate place before hailing a taxi with tip-up seats and going back to your hotel or your flat, someone with whom there will be no need to speak after the hot, spicy supper, you can merely take her face in your hands and kiss her, undress her, touch her, framing that bought, fragile head in your hands in that gesture so reminiscent of both coronation and strangulation. Marta's illness was making me think morbid thoughts and although I was breathing easily and felt better standing in the doorway of the boy's bedroom, watching the aeroplanes in the shadows and vaguely remembering my own remote past, I thought that I really should go back in to the other bedroom, to see how she was and to try and help her, perhaps take off her clothes, this time in order to put her to bed and cover her up and evoke the sleep which, with luck, might have overtaken her during my brief absence, and then I would leave.

That wasn't how it was. When I went back into the room again, she looked up at me with her dull, clenched eyes, she was still hunched and un-moving, the only change being that now she was hiding her nakedness with her arms as if she were ashamed or cold. "Do you want to get under the covers? You'll get cold like that," I said. "No, please don't move me, don't move me an inch," she said, adding at once: "Where were you?" "I went to the bathroom. You're not getting any better, you know, we ought to do some-thing, I'm going to call an ambulance." But she still insisted that she did not want to be moved or bothered or distracted ("No, don't do anything yet, don't do anything, just wait"), nor did she want voices or movement around her, as if she were so full of foreboding that she preferred everything about her to be in a state of utter paralysis and preferred to remain in the situation and pos-ture that at least allowed her to go on living rather than risk any variation, however minimal, that might upset the temporary and precarious stability— her already frightening stillness—that was filling her with panic. That is the effect panic has, which is why it is so often the downfall of those who experi-ence it, for it makes them believe that they are somehow safe inside the evil or the danger. The soldier who stays in his trench barely breathing, scarcely moving, even though he knows that the trench will soon come under attack; the pedestrian who feels unable to run away when he hears footsteps behind him at dead of night along a dark, deserted street; the prostitute who doesn't call for help after getting into a car whose doors lock automatically, and real-izes that she should never have got in beside that man with the large hands (perhaps she doesn't ask for help because she doesn't believe she has a right to it); the foreigner who sees the tree split in two by lightning and falling toward him, but doesn't move out of the way, he merely observes its slow fall on to the broad avenue; the man who watches another man walk over to his table with a knife in his hand and doesn't move or defend himself because he believes deep down that this cannot really be happening to him and that the knife will not plunge into his belly, the knife cannot be destined for his skin and his guts; or the pilot who watched as the enemy fighter managed to tuck in behind him, but made no last attempt to escape from the enemy's sights by some feat of acrobatics, certain that, although everything was in the other man's favor, he would, nonetheless, miss the target because this time he was the target. "Tomorrow in the battle think on me, and fall thy edgeless sword." Marta must be conscious of every second, mentally counting each one as it passed, aware of the continuity which gives us not only life, but the sense of being alive, the thing that makes us think and say to ourselves: "I'm still thinking or I'm still speaking or I'm still reading or I'm still watching a film and therefore I must be alive; I turn the page of a newspaper or take another sip of my beer or try another clue in the crossword, I'm still looking at things, noticing details—a Japanese man, an air hostess—and that means that the plane in which I'm travelling has not yet fallen from the skies, I'm smoking a cigarette and it's the same one I was smoking a few seconds ago and I know that I will manage to finish it and light the next one, thus everything continues and I can do nothing about it, since I'm not in a mood to kill myself nor do I want to, nor am I going to; this man with the large hands is stroking my throat, he's not pressing that hard yet: even though he's stroking me more roughly now, hurting me a bit, I can still feel his hard, clumsy fingers on my cheekbones and on my temples, my poor temples—his fingers are like piano keys; and I can still hear the steps of that person in the shadows waiting to mug me, but perhaps I'm wrong and they're footsteps of some inoffensive person who simply can't walk any faster and therefore overtake me, perhaps I should give him the chance to do so and take out my glasses and pause and look in a shop window, but then I might stop hearing them, and what saves me is the fact that I can still hear those footsteps; and I'm still here in my trench with my bayonet fixed, the bayonet I will soon have to use if I don't want to be run through by that of my enemy: but not yet, and as long as it is not yet, the trench hides and protects me, even though we're in open country and I can feel the cold air on my ears not quite covered by my helmet; and that knife that approaches me in someone else's hand has still not reached its destination and I'm still sitting at my table and nothing has yet been torn or pierced, and, contrary to appearances, I will still take another sip of beer, and another and another; since that tree has not yet fallen and won't fall even though it's been snapped in two and is falling, it won't fall on me, its branches won't slice off my head, it's not possible, I'm just a visitor to this city, I simply happened to be walking along this avenue, I might so easily not have done so; and I can still see the world from on high, from my Supermarine Spitfire, and I still have no sense of descent and weight and vertigo, of falling and gravity and mass which I will have when the Messerschmitt at my back, who has me in his sights, opens fire on me and hits home: but not yet, not yet, and as long as it is not yet, I can go on thinking about the battle and looking at the landscape and making plans for the future; and I, poor Marta, can still see the glare from the television that continues to broadcast and the warmth of this man who has lain down beside me again and keeps me company. As long as he is by my side, I won't die: let him stay here and do nothing, I don't want him to talk or to phone anyone, I don't want anything to change, just let him warm me a little and hold me, I need to be still in order to die, if each second is identical to the previous second it makes no sense that I should be the one to change, that the lights should still be lit here and in the street and that the television should still be broadcasting—an old Fred MacMurray film—while I lie dying. I can't cease to exist while everything and everyone remains here and alive and while, on the screen, another story follows its course. It doesn't make sense that my skirts should remain alive on that chair if I'm not going to put them on again, or that my books should continue to breathe on the shelves if I'm not going to look at them anymore, my earrings and necklaces and rings waiting in their box for their turn which will never come; the new toothbrush that I bought just this afternoon will have to be thrown away because I've already used it now, and all the little objects that one collects throughout one's life will be thrown away one by one or perhaps shared out, and there are so many of them, it's unbelievable how many things each of us owns, how much stuff we accumulate in our homes, that's why no one ever makes an inventory of their possessions, not unless they're going to make a will, that is, not unless they're already contemplating those objects' imminent neglect and redundancy. I haven't made a will, I haven't got much to leave and I've never given much thought to death, which it seems does come and it comes in a single moment that upends and touches everything, what was useful and formed part of someone's history becomes, in that one moment, useless and devoid of history, from now on, nobody will know why or how or when that picture or that dress was bought or who gave me that brooch, where and from whom that bag or that scarf came, what journey or what absence brought it, if it was a reward for waiting or a message from some new conquest or intended to ease a guilty conscience; everything that had meaning and history loses it in a single moment and my belongings lie there inert, suddenly incapable of revealing their past and their origins; and someone will make a pile of them and, before bundling them up or perhaps putting them in plastic bags, my sisters or my women friends might decide to keep something as a souvenir or a spoil, or to hang on to a particular brooch so that my son can give it to some woman when he's grown up, a woman who has probably not even been born yet. And there'll be other things that no one will want because they are only of use to me: my tweezers, or my opened bottle of cologne, my underwear and my dressing gown and my sponge, my shoes and the wicker chairs that Eduardo hates, my lotions and medicines, my sunglasses, my notebooks and index cards and my cuttings and all the books that only I read, my collection of shells and my old records, the doll I've kept since I was a child, my toy lion, they might even have to pay someone to take them away, there are no longer eager, obliging, rag-and-bone men as there were in my childhood, they wouldn't turn their noses up at anything and would drive through the streets holding up the traffic, car drivers then were still prepared to slow down for their mule-drawn carts, it seems incredible that I should have seen that, not so very long ago, I'm still young and it wasn't that long ago, the carts that grew to impossible heights as they picked things up and loaded them on until the carts were as tall as one of those open-topped double deckers you see in London, except that here the buses were blue and drove on the right; and the pile of things grew higher, the swaying of the cart drawn by a single, weary mule became more pronounced—a rocking motion—and it seemed that all that plundered detritus—defunct fridges and cardboard boxes and crates, a rolled-up bedside rug and a sagging, broken-down chair—was constantly on the point of toppling over, unseating the gypsy girl who invariably crowned the pile, acting like a counterbalance, or as if she were an emblem of Our Lady of rag-and-bone men, a rather grubby girl, often blonde, sitting with her back to the load, with her legs dangling over the edge of the cart, and from her perch or peak, as we overtook her, and we, in turn, clutching our files and chewing our gum, watched her from the top deck of the buses that took us to school in the morning and back home in the afternoon.

We regarded each other with mutual envy, the adventurous life and the life of timetables, the outdoor life and the easy life, and I always wondered how she managed to avoid the branches of the trees that stuck out over the pavements and knocked against the high windows as if in protest at our speed, as if wanting to reach through the windows and scratch us: she had no protection and was alone, perched up high, suspended in the air, but I imagine that her cart moved slowly enough to give her time to see them and to duck down, or to grasp them and hold them back with one grimy hand that protruded from the long sleeve of a torn, woolen, zip-up cardigan. It isn't just the miniscule history of objects that will disappear in that single moment, it's also everything I know and have learned, all my memories and everything I've ever seen—the double-decker bus and the rag-and-bone men's carts and the gypsy girl and the thousand and one things that passed before my eyes and are of no importance to anyone else—my memories which, like so many of my belongings, are only of use to me and become useless if I die, what disappears is not only who I am but who I have been, not only me, poor Marta, but my whole memory, a ragged, discontinuous, never-completed, ever-changing scrap of fabric, but, at the same time, woven with such patience and such extreme care, undulating and variable as my shot-silk skirts, fragile as my silk blouses that tear so easily, I haven't worn those skirts for ages, I got tired of them, and it's odd that this should all happen in a moment, why this moment and not another, why not the previous moment or the next one, why today, this month, this week, a Tuesday in January or a Sunday in September, unpleasant months and days about which one has no choice, what decides that what was in motion should just stop, without the intervention of one's will, or perhaps one's will does intervene by simply stepping aside, perhaps it suddenly grows tired and, by its withdrawal, brings our death, not wanting to want any more, not wanting anything, not even to get better, not even to leave behind the illness and the pain in which it finds shelter, for want of all the other things that illness and pain have driven out or perhaps usurped, because as long as they are there, you can still say not yet, not yet, and you can still go on thinking and you can still go on saying goodbye. Goodbye laughter and goodbye scorn. I will never see you again, nor will you see me. And goodbye ardour and goodbye memories."

I obeyed, I waited, I did nothing and I phoned no one, I just returned to my place on the bed, which was not really my place, though it was mine that night, I lay down by her side again and then, without turning round and without looking at me, she said: "Hold me, hold me, please, hold me," meaning that she wanted me to put my arms around her, so I did, I put my arms around her from behind, my shirt was still unbuttoned and my chest came into contact with her hot, smooth skin, my arms went around her arms, covering them, four hands and four arms now in a double embrace, and that was clearly still not enough, while the film on TV proceeded soundlessly, in silence, oblivious to us, I thought that one day I would have to see it properly, in black and white. She had said "please," our vocabulary is so deeply embedded in us that we never forget our manners, we never, for a moment, relinquish our language and our way of speaking, not even in time of desperation or in moments of anger, whatever happens, even when we are dying. I remained like that for a while, lying on her bed with my arms around her as I had not planned to and yet, at the same time, as I had known I would, it was what I had been waiting for from the moment I entered the apartment and from before then, ever since we arranged to meet and she asked or suggested that we should meet at her place. This was something else, though, a different, unexpected kind of embrace, and now I was certain of what until then I had not even allowed myself to think, or to know that I was thinking: I knew that this was not something that would pass and I thought that it might well be final, I knew that it was not due to regret or depression or fear and that it was imminent: I thought—she's dying in my arms; I thought that and, suddenly, I had no hopes of ever leaving her, as if she had infected me with her desire for immobility and stillness, or perhaps with her desire for death, not yet, not yet, but then again, I can't take any more, I can't take it. And it may well be that she couldn't take it anymore, that she couldn't stand it, because a few minutes later—one, two, three, or four—I heard her say something else, she said: "Oh God, the child" and she made a sudden, light movement, almost certainly imperceptible to anyone watching us, but I noticed it because I was so close to her, it was like an impulse from her brain that her body only registered as the faintest flicker, a cold, fleeting reflex, as if it were the tremor, not entirely physical, that you experience in dreams when you think you're falling and gravity and mass—a plane crashing, a body leaping from a bridge into the river—as if, just at that moment, Marta had felt an impulse to get up and go and find the boy, but had only managed it in her thoughts, in that tremor. And after another minute—and five; or six—I noticed that she was lying very still, even though she was already still, that is, she lay even stiller and I noticed the change in her temperature and I no longer felt the tension in her body, pressed against me, as if she were pushing back hard, as if she wanted to find refuge inside my body, to flee from what her own body was suffering: an inhuman transformation, an unknown state of mind (the mystery): she was pressing her back against my chest and her bottom against my belly and the back of her thighs against the front of mine, the bloody, muddy back of her neck against my throat and her left cheek against my right cheek, jaw against jaw, and my temples, her temples, my poor temples and her poor temples, her arms beneath mine as if one embrace were not enough, and even the soles of her bare feet against my shoes, resting on them, she ran her stockings on my shoelaces—her dark stockings that came to mid-thigh and which I had not removed because I liked that old-fashioned image—all her energies thrown back and against me, invading me, we were glued together like Siamese twins who had been born joined the whole length of our bodies, so that we would never see each other except out of the corner of one eye, she with her back to me, pushing, pushing, almost crushing me, until all that stopped and she lay still or stiller, there was no pressure of any kind, not even that of leaning against me, and instead I felt the sweat on my back, as if a pair of supernatural hands had embraced me from the front while I was embracing her, and had rested on my shirt leaving yellowish, watery marks on it, leaving the cloth stuck to my skin. I knew at once that she had died, but I spoke to her and I said: "Marta," and I said her name again, adding: "Can you hear me?" and then I said to myself: "She's dead," I said, "this woman has died and I'm here and I saw it and I could do nothing to stop it, and now it's too late to phone anyone, too late for anyone to share what I saw." And although I said that to myself and I knew it to be true, I felt in no hurry to move away or to withdraw the embrace that she had requested, because I found it or, rather, the contact with her recumbent, averted, half-naked body pleasant and the mere fact that she had died did not instantly change that: she was still there, her dead body identical to her living body, only more peaceful, quieter and perhaps softer, no longer tormented, but in repose, and I could see again out of the corner of my eye her long lashes and her half-open mouth that were still the same, identical, her tangled eyelashes and her infinite mouth that had chatted and eaten and drunk, and smiled and laughed and smoked, that had kissed me and was still kissable. For how long? "We are both still here, in the same position and occupying the same space, I can still feel her; nothing has changed and yet everything has changed, I know that and I cannot grasp it. I don't know why I am alive and she is dead, I don't know what either of those words means anymore. I no longer have any clear understanding of those two terms." And only after some seconds—or possibly minutes, one, two, or three—I carefully removed myself from her, as if I did not want to wake her or as if I might hurt her by moving away, and had I spoken to someone—someone who would have been a witness there with me—I would have done so in a low voice or in a conspiratorial whisper, born of the respect that the mystery always imposes on us if, that is, there is no grief or tears, because if there is, there is no silence, or else it comes only later. "Tomorrow in the battle think on me, and fall thy edgeless sword: despair and die."

Translated by Margaret Jull Costa

•

"When I Was Mortal"
from *When I Was Mortal*

I often used to pretend I believed in ghosts, and I did so blithely, but now that I am myself a ghost, I understand why, traditionally, they are depicted as mournful creatures who stubbornly return to the places they knew when they were mortal. For they do return. Very rarely are they or we noticed, the houses we lived in have changed and the people who live in them do not even know of our past existence, they cannot even imagine it: like children, these men and women believe that the world began with their birth, and they never wonder if, on the ground they tread, others once trod with lighter steps or with fateful footfalls, if between the walls that shelter them others heard whispers or laughter, or if someone once read a letter out loud, or strangled the person he most loved. It's absurd that, for the living, space should endure while time is erased, when space is, in fact, the depository of time, albeit a silent one, telling no tales. It's absurd that life would be like that for the living, because what comes afterward is its polar opposite and we are entirely unprepared for it. For now time does not pass, elapse or flow, it perpetuates itself simultaneously and in every detail, though to speak of "now" is perhaps a fallacy. That is the second worst thing, the details, because anything that we experienced or that made even the slightest impact on us when we were mortal reappears with the awful concomitant that now everything has weight and meaning: the words spoken lightly, the mechanical gestures, the accumulated afternoons of childhood parade past singly, one after the other, the effort of a whole lifetime—establishing routines that level out both days and nights—turns out to have been pointless, and each day and night is recalled with excessive clarity and singularity and with a degree of reality incongruous with our present state which knows nothing now of touch. Everything is concrete and excessive, and the razor edge of repetition becomes a torment, because the curse consists in remembering *everything*, the minutes of each hour of each day lived through, the minutes and hours and days of tedium and work and joy, of study and grief and humiliation and sleep, as well as those of waiting, which formed the greater part.

But, as I have already said, that is only the second worst thing, there is something far more wounding, which is that now I not only remember what I saw and heard and knew when I was mortal, but I remember it in its entirety, that is, including what I did not see or know or hear, even things that were beyond my grasp, but which affected me or those who were important to me, and which possibly had a hand in shaping me. You discover the full magnitude of what you only intuited while alive, all the more as you become an adult, I can't say older because I never reached old age: that you only know a fragment of what happens or recounting what has happened to you up until a particular date, you do not have sufficient information, you do not know impulses, you have no knowledge of what is hidden: the people closest to us seem like actors suddenly stepping out in front of a theater curtain, and we have no idea what they were doing only a second earlier, when they were not there before us. Perhaps they appear disguised as Othello or as Hamlet and yet the previous moment they were smoking an impossible, anachronistic cigarette in the wings and glancing impatiently at the watch which they have now removed in order to seem to be someone else. Likewise, we know nothing about the events at which we were not present and the conversations we did not hear, those that took place behind our back and mentioned us or criticized us or judged us and condemned us. Life is compassionate, all lives are, at least that is the norm, which is why we consider as wicked those people who do not cover up or hide or lie, those who tell everything that they know and hear, as well as what they do and think. We call them cruel. And it is in that cruel state that I find myself now.

I see myself, for example, as a child about to fall asleep in my bed on countless nights of a childhood that was satisfactory or without surprises, with my bedroom door ajar so that I could see the light until sleep overcame me, being lulled by the voices of my father and my mother and a guest at supper or some late arrival, who was almost always Dr. Arranz, a pleasant man who smiled a lot and spoke in a low voice and who, to my delight, would arrive just before I went to sleep, in time to come into my room to see how I was, the privilege of an almost daily check-up and the calming hand of the doctor slipping beneath your pajama jacket, the warm and unrepeatable hand that touches you in a way that no one else will ever touch you again throughout your entire life, the nervous child feeling that any anomaly or danger will be detected by that hand and therefore stopped, it is the hand that saves; and the stethoscope dangling from his ears and the cold, salutary touch that your chest shrinks from, and sometimes the handle of an inherited silver spoon engraved with initials placed on the tongue, and which, for a moment, seems about to stick in your throat, a feeling that would give way to relief when I remembered, after the first contact, that it was Arranz holding the spoon in his reassuring, steady hand, mistress of metallic objects, nothing could happen while he was listening to your chest or peering at you with his flashlight fixed on his forehead. After his brief visit and his two or three jokes—sometimes my mother would lean in the doorway waiting until he had finished examining me and making me laugh, and she would laugh too—I would feel even more at ease and would begin to fall asleep listening to their chatter in the nearby lounge, or listening to them listening for a while to the radio or playing a game of cards, at a time when time barely passed, it seems impossible because it's not that long ago, although from then until now enough time has elapsed for me to live and die. I hear the laughter of those who were still young, although I couldn't see them as young then, I can now: my father laughed the least, he was a handsome, taciturn man with a look of permanent melancholy in his eyes, perhaps because he had been a republican and had lost the war, and that is probably something you never recover from, having lost a war against your compatriots and neighbors. He was a kindly man who never got angry with me or my mother and who spent a lot of time at home writing articles and book reviews, which he tended to publish under various pseudonyms in the newspapers, because it was best not to use his own name; or perhaps reading, he was a great francophile, I mainly recall novels by Camus and Simenon. Dr. Arranz was a jollier man, with a lazy, teasing way of talking, inventive and full of unusual turns-of-phrase, the kind of man children idolize because he knows how to do card tricks and comes out with unexpected rhymes and talks to them about soccer—then it was Kopa, Rial, Di Stefan, Puskas and Gento—and he thinks up games that will interest them and awaken their imaginations, except that, in fact, he never has time to stay and play them for real. And my mother, always well-dressed despite the fact that there wasn't much money in the home of one of the war's losers—there wasn't—better dressed than my father because she still had her own father, my grandfather, to buy her clothes, she was slight and cheerful and sometimes looked sadly at her husband, and always looked at me enthusiastically, later, as you get older, not many people look at you like that either. I see this now because I see it all complete, I see that, while I was gradually becoming submerged in sleep, the laughter in the living room never came from my father, and that, on the other hand, he was the only one listening to the radio, an impossible image until very recently, but which is now as clear as the old images which, while I was mortal, gradually grew dimmer, more compressed the longer I lived. I see that on some nights, Dr. Arranz and my mother went out, and now I understand all those references to good tickets, which, in my imagination then, I always thought of as being clipped by an usher at the soccer stadium or at the bullring—those places I never went to—and to which I never gave another thought. On other nights, there were no good tickets and no one mentioned them, or there were rainy nights when there was no question of going for a walk or to the open-air dance, and now I know that then my mother and Dr. Arranz would go into the bedroom when they were sure I had gone to sleep after having been touched on my chest and my stomach by the same hands that would then touch her, hands that were no longer warm, but urgent, the hand of the doctor that calms and probes and persuades and demands; and having been kissed on the cheek or the forehead

by the same lips that would subsequently kiss the easy-going, low voice—thus
silencing it. And whether they went to the theater or to the movies or to a
club or merely went into the next room, my father would listen to the radio
alone while he waited, so as not to hear anything, but also, with the passage
of time and the onset of routine—with the leveling out of nights that always
happens when nights keep repeating themselves—in order to distract himself
for half an hour or three quarters of an hour (doctors are always in such a
hurry), because he inevitably became interested in what he was listening to.
The doctor would leave without saying goodbye to him and my mother would
stay in the bedroom, waiting for my father, she would put on a nightdress and
change the sheets, he never found her there in her pretty skirts and stockings.
I see now the conversation that began that state of affairs, which, for me, was
not a cruel one but a kindly one that lasted my whole life, and, during that
conversation, Dr. Arranz is sporting the sharp little moustache that I noticed
on the faces of lawyers in parliament until the day Franco died, and not only
there, but on soldiers and notaries and bankers and lecturers, on writers and
on countless doctors, not on him though, he was one of the first to get rid of
it. My father and my mother are sitting in the dining room and I still have no
consciousness or memory, I am a child lying in its cradle, I cannot yet walk
or speak and there is no reason why I should ever have found out: she keeps
her eyes lowered all the time and says nothing, he looks first incredulous and
then horrified: horrified and fearful, rather than indignant. And one of the
things that Arranz says is this:

"Look, León, I pass a lot of information on to the police and it never fails;
basically, what I say goes. I've taken a while to get around to you but I know
perfectly well what you got up to in the war, how you gave the nod to the
militiamen on who to take for a ride. But even if that wasn't so, in your case,
I've no need to make anything much up, I just have to stretch the facts a little,
to say that you consigned to the ditch half the people in our neighborhood
wouldn't be that far from the truth, you'd have done the same to me if you
could. More than ten years have passed, but you'd still be hauled up in front
of a firing squad if I told them what I know, and I've no reason to keep quiet
about it. So it's up to you, you can either have a bit of a rough time on my
terms or you can stop having any kind of time at all, neither good nor bad
nor average."

"And what are your terms exactly?"

I see Dr. Arranz gesture with his head in the direction of my silent mother—a gesture that makes of her a thing—whom he also knew during the war and from before, in that same neighborhood that lost so many of its residents.

"I want to screw her. Night after night, until I get tired of it."

Arranz got tired as everyone does of everything, given time. He got tired when I was still at an age when that essential word did not even figure in my vocabulary, nor did I even conceive of its meaning. My mother, on the other hand, was at the age when she was beginning to lose her bloom and to laugh only rarely, while my father began to prosper and to dress better, and to sign with his own name—which was not León—the articles and the reviews that he wrote and to lose the look of melancholy in his clouded eyes; and to go out at night with some good tickets while my mother stayed at home playing solitaire or listening to the radio, or, a little later, watching television, resigned.

All those who have speculated on the afterlife or the continuing existence of the consciousness beyond death—if that is what we are, consciousness—have not taken into account the danger or rather the horror of remembering everything, even what we did not know: knowing everything, everything that concerns us or that involved us either closely or from afar. I see with absolute clarity faces that I passed once in the street, a man I gave money to without even glancing at him, a woman I watched in the subway and whom I haven't thought of since, the features of a postman who delivered some unimportant telegram, the figure of a child I saw on a beach, when I too was a child. I relive the long minutes I spent waiting at airports or those spent lining up outside a museum or watching the waves on a distant beach, or packing my bags and later unpacking them, all the most tedious moments, those that are of no account and which we usually refer to as dead time. I see myself in cities I visited a long time ago, just passing through, with a few free hours to stroll around them and then wipe them from my memory: I see myself in Hamburg and in Manchester, in Basle and in Austin, places I would never have gone to if my work hadn't taken me there. I see myself too in Venice, some time ago, on honeymoon with my wife Luisa, with whom I spent those last few years of peace and contentment, I see myself in the most recent part of my life, even though it is now remote. I'm coming back from a trip and she's waiting for me at the airport, not once, all the time we were married, did she fail to come and meet me, even if I'd only been away for a couple of days, despite the awful traffic and despite all the activities we can so easily do without and which are precisely those that we find most pressing. I'd be so tired that I'd only have the strength to change television channels, the programs are the same everywhere now anyway, while she prepared me a light supper and kept me company, looking bored but patient, knowing that after that initial torpor and the imminent night's rest, I would be fully recovered and that the following day, I would be my usual self, and energetic, jokey person who spoke in a rather low voice, in order to underline the irony that all women love, laughter runs in their veins and, if it's a funny joke, they can't help but laugh, even if they detest the person making the joke. And the following afternoon, once I'd recovered, I used to go and see María, my lover, who used to laugh even more because my jokes were still new to her.

I was always so careful not to give myself away, not to wound and to be kind, I only ever met María at her apartment so that no one would see me out with her anywhere and ask questions later on, or be cruel and tell tales, or simply wait to be introduced. Her apartment was nearby and I spent many afternoons there, though not every afternoon, on the way back to my own apartment, that meant a delay of only half an hour or three quarters of an hour, sometimes a little more, sometimes I would amuse myself looking out of her window, the window of a lover is always more interesting than our own will ever be. I never made a mistake, because mistakes in these matters reveal a sort of lack of consideration, or worse, they are acts of cruelty. I met María once when I was out with Luisa, in a packed movie theater at a première, and my lover took advantage of the crowd to come over to us and to hold my hand for a moment, as she passed by without looking at me, she brushed her familiar thigh against mine and took hold of my hand and stroked it. Luisa could not possibly have seen this or noticed or even suspected the existence of that tenuous, ephemeral, clandestine contact, but even so, I decided not to see María for a couple of weeks, after which time and after my refusing to answer the phone in my office, she called me one afternoon at home, luckily, my wife was out.

"What's wrong?" she said.

"You must never phone me here, you know that."

"I wouldn't phone you there if you'd pick up the phone in your office. I've been waiting a whole fortnight," she said.

And then, making an effort to recover the anger I had felt a fortnight before, I said:

"And I'll never pick up the phone to you again if you ever touch me when Luisa is there. Don't even think of it."

She fell silent.

You forget almost everything in life and remember everything in death, or in this cruel state which is what being a ghost is. But in life I forgot and so I started seeing her again now and then, thanks to that process by which everything becomes indefinitely postponed for a while, and we always believe that there will continue to be a tomorrow in which it will be possible to stop what today and yesterday passes and elapses and flows, what is imperceptibly becoming another routine which, in its way, also levels out our days and our nights until they become unimaginable without all their essential elements, and the nights and the days must be identical, at least in their essence, so that nothing is relinquished or sacrificed by those who want them and those who endure them. Now I remember everything and that's why I remember my death so clearly, or, rather, what I knew of my death when it happened, which was little and, indeed, nothing in comparison with all that I know now, given the constant razor edge of repetition.

I returned from one of my trips exhausted and Luisa didn't fail me, she came to meet me. We didn't talk much in the car, nor while I was mechanically unpacking my suitcase and glancing through the accumulated mail and listening to the messages on the answering machine, that she had kept for my return. I was alarmed when I heard one of them, because I immediately recognized María's voice, she said my name once and was then cut off, and that made my feeling of alarm subside for a moment, the voice of a woman saying my name and then breaking off was of no significance, there was no reason why Luisa should have felt worried if she had heard it. I lay down on the bed in front of the television, changing channels, Luisa brought me some cold meat and a shop-bought dessert, she clearly had neither the time nor the inclination to make me even an omelette. It was still early, but she had turned out the light in the bedroom to help me get to sleep, and there I stayed, drowsy and peaceful, with a vague memory of her caresses, the hand that calms even when it touches your chest distractedly and possibly impatiently.

Then she left the bedroom and I eventually fell asleep with the television on, at the same point I stopped changing channels.

I don't know how much time passed, no, that's not true, since now I know exactly, I enjoyed seventy-three minutes of deep sleep and of dreams that all took place in foreign parts, whence I had once again returned safe and sound. Then I woke up and I saw the bluish light of the television, the light illuminating the foot of the bed, rather than any actual images, because I didn't have time. I see and I saw rushing toward me something black and heavy and doubtless as cold as a stethoscope, but it was violent rather than salutary. It fell once only to be raised again, and in those tenths of a second before it came crashing down a second time, already spattered with blood, I thought that Luisa must be killing me because of that message which has said only my name and then broken off and perhaps there had been many other things that she had erased after listening to them all, leaving only the beginning for me to listen to on my return, a mere foreshadowing of what was killing me. The black thing fell again and this time it killed me, and my last conscious thought was not to put up any resistance, to make no attempt to stop it because it was unstoppable and perhaps too because it didn't seem such a bad death, to die at the hands of the person with whom I had lived in peace and contentment, and without ever hurting each other until, that is, we finally did. It's a tricky word to use, and can easily be misconstrued, but perhaps I came to feel that my death was a just death.

I see this now and I see the whole thing, with an afterward and a before, although the afterward does not, strictly speaking, concern me and is therefore not so painful. But the before is, or rather the rebuttal of what I glimpsed and half-thought between the lowering and the raising and the lowering again of the black thing that finished me off. Now I can see Luisa talking to a man I don't know and who has a moustache like the one Dr. Arranz wore in his day, not a slim moustache, though, but soft and thick and with a few grey hairs. He's middle-aged, as I was and as perhaps Luisa was, although she always seemed young to me, just as my parents or Arranz never did. They are in the living room of an unfamiliar apartment, his apartment, a ramshackle place, full of books and paintings and ornaments, a very mannered apartment. The man is called Manolo Reyna and he has enough money never to have to dirty his hands. It is the afternoon and they are sitting on a sofa, talking in whispers, and at that moment I am visiting María, two weeks before my death on the return from a trip, and that trip has still not begun, they are still making their preparations. The whispers are clearly audible, they have a degree of reality which seems incongruous now, not with my current non-tactile state, but with life itself, in which nothing is ever quite so concrete, in which nothing ever breathes quite so much. There is a moment, though, when Luisa raises her voice, like someone raising their voice to defend themselves or to defend someone else, and what she says is this:

"But he's always been so good to me, I've nothing to reproach him with, and that's what's so difficult."

And Manolo Reyna answers slowly:

"It wouldn't be any easier or any more difficult if he had made your life impossible. When it comes to killing someone, it doesn't matter anymore what they've done, it always seems an extreme response to any kind of behavior."

I see Luisa put her thumb to her mouth and bite it a little, a gesture I've so often seen her make when she's uncertain, or, rather, before making a deci-sion. It's a trivial gesture and it's unseemly that it should also appear in the midst of a conversation we were not party to, the one that takes place behind our backs and mention us or criticizes us or even defends us, or judges us and condemns us to death.

"Well, you kill him, then; you can't expect me to do anything that extreme."

Now I see that the person standing next to my television set—still on—and wielding the black thing is not Luisa, nor even Manolo Reyna with his folkloric name, but someone contracted and paid to do it, to strike me twice on the forehead, the work is assassin, in the war a lot of militiamen were used for such purposes. My assassin hits me twice and does so quite dispassion-ately, and that death no longer seems to me just or appropriate or, of course, compassionate, as life usually is, and as mine was. The black thing is a ham-mer with a wooden shaft and an iron head, a common-or-garden hammer. It belongs in my apartment, I recognize it.

There where time passes and flows, a lot of time has gone by, so much so that no one whom I knew or met or pitied or loved remains. Each one of them, I suppose, will return unnoticed to that space in which forgotten times past accumulate, and they will see only strangers, new men and women who, like children, believe that the world began with their birth and there's no point asking them about our past, erased existence. Now Luisa will remember and will know everything that she did not know in life or at my death. I cannot speak now of nights and days, everything has been leveled out without resort to effort or routine, a routine in which I can say that I knew, above all, peace and contentment: when I was mortal, all that time ago, in that place where there is still time.

Translated by Margaret Jull Costa

•

FROM *THE MAN OF FEELING*
[A NOVEL]

When you die, I will truly mourn you. I will approach your transfigured face to plant desperate kisses on your lips in one last effort, full of arrogance and faith, to return you to the world that has rendered you redundant. I will feel that my own life bears a wound and will consider my own history to have split in two by that final, definitive moment of yours. I will tenderly close your surprised, reluctant eyes and I will watch over your white, mutant body all through the night and into the pointless dawn that will never have known you. I will remove your pillow and the damp sheets. Incapable of conceiving of life without your daily presence and seeing you lying there, lifeless, I will want to rush headlong after you. I will visit your tomb and, alone in the cemetery, having climbed up the steep hill and having looked at you, lovingly, wearily, through the inscribed stone, I will talk to you. I will see my own death foretold in yours, I will look at my own photo and, recognizing myself in your stiff features, I will cease to believe in the reality of your extinction because it gives body and credibility to my own. For no one is capable of imagining his own death.

Translated by Margaret Jull Costa

•

FROM *DARK BACK OF TIME*
[A NOVEL]

It isn't only that it can all happen now, it's that I don't know if in fact anything is really over or lost, at times I have the feeling that all the yesterdays
are throbbing beneath the earth, refusing to disappear entirely, the enormous
cumulation of the known and the unknown, stories told and stories silenced,
recorded events and events that were never told or had no witnesses or were
hidden, a vast mass of words and occurrences, passions, crimes, injustices,
fear, laughter, aspirations and raptures, and above all thoughts: thoughts are
what is most frequently passed on from one group of intruders and usurpers to another, down across the intruding and usurping generations, they are
what survives longest and hardly changes and never concludes, like a permanent tumult beneath the earth's thick crust where the infinite men and
women who passed this way are buried or dispersed, most of them having
spent much of their time in passive, idle, ordinary thoughts, but also in the
more spirited ones that give some impetus to the indolent, weak wheel of the
world, the desires and plots, expectations and rancors, beliefs and chimeras,
pity and secrets and humiliations and quarrels, the revenges that are schemed,
the rejected loves that arrive too late and the loves that never wear out: all are
accompanied by their own thoughts which are experienced as unique by each
newly-arrived reiterative individual who thinks them. But that is not all. The
prestige of the present moment is based on this idea, which mothers hurry
to inculcate as a consolation or subterfuge in their offspring: "that which no
longer is, has never been." Yet we may wonder whether the opposite isn't the
case, whether what has been goes on being indefinitely for the simple reason
that it has been, even if it is only as part of the incessant, frenetic sum total
of deeds and words whose tally no one takes the trouble to keep, even if it is
only more glowing coals or fire for the ever-swelling like infectious diseases
to further increase the "intolerable woe" of Middleton, the suicide. The fact
that something has ceased doesn't seem to be reason or force enough for it
to be erased entirely, still less its effects, and least of all its inertia; the black
cylinder of the zoetrope that belonged to Julianín, my brother, could be spun
in its shaft again and again before it stopped, and even then it could be set
back in motion, the horse and its rider galloping, then trotting, galloping,
then trotting, watched one more time through the slits. Everything lasts too

long, there's no way to finish anything off, each thing that concludes enriches the soil for the following thing or for something else, unexpected and distant, and perhaps that's why we grow so tired as we come to feel that our mothers' precarious response, "It's over now, there, there, it's all over," is by no means true. Nothing is over, nothing is there and nothing is over, and there is nothing that doesn't resemble the slow relay of lights I see from my windows when I'm not sleeping or am already awake and look out at the plaza and the street with its early-rising women and men, their eyes still painted with traces of the dark night, their bodies still imbued with the clean or sweaty sheets that were shared or hogged. Or perhaps the man over there with the loose tie and incipient bluish stubble is heading for those sheets now, more as a matter of convention than out of a genuine desire for sleep, he hasn't been to bed since yesterday. He's waiting for the bus so early or so late, maybe without even enough money for a taxi, and looking at the streetlamps that still belong to the night he's emerging from or hasn't yet left, and in his mind are the many hours during which he had to abandon the bullfighters' serious, ceremonious gambling den, you never know how luck will behave, not even when it gives you signals or resists, and especially when you have to find the money to hold on to the woman who's waiting for you at home, fast asleep and heedless of your efforts and your fears, of which she is the cause. The man watches the streetlamps as the day dawns and gusts of wind blow against the back of his neck and ruffle up his hair, making him look like a musician, and he has no faith that this relay of lights, when it is finally over, will diminish the night which, for him, is not confined to the sphere of bad dreams; he has forty-eight hours to find the money he owes, and he won't find it, no chance, the worst ones aren't the bullfighters, who can often be magnanimous, but the hangers-on and admirers and managers to whom he is in debt, the exploiters of artists are the least scrupulous of all exploiters because they believe themselves to be justified, perhaps they're recouping their losses. The man looks at the streetlights thinking that maybe a knife thrust to the belly is the easiest way to give up the struggle to keep someone who wants to go but hasn't yet left, maybe out of sorrow or because she hasn't found her next handhold, it's a question of time, sorrow is soon used up and rage takes its place, rage paid out with interest; handholds are everywhere, it's only a matter of time until she sees them and tries one out, or until they catch sight of this woman who has been waving a red flag for some time now, calling out to them, and reaching out her arm to grab hold. It's only a matter of time and the knife thrust secures it, that time, and then silence, and put out the light and then put it out. The woman watches the streetlamps while trying to protect her hair from the wind with a kerchief, an old-fashioned image not often seen any more, maybe that's why she's not very skilled at it and, not managing to tie the kerchief in place, she gives up, her hair flying in the wind like a banner. She has left the night behind, and her bed, and she thinks with some uneasiness about the young man still asleep there, he's spent too many mornings there since he stayed on without ever saying he was staying, coming and going while she's at work, leaving and returning whenever he feels like it with no explanations, as if he'd rented out a room and didn't live with anyone, neither asking nor telling; but at night when he comes to bed in the darkness, far too late, he wakes her up like a hungry animal—like a child who can't bear to wait—and tears off her nightgown and gets her sheets sweaty, taking up her time for rest, robbing her of her sleep to keep it for himself. The woman stays awake almost all night, thinking about what's happened in the darkness and wondering if this was the last time, she leaves in the morning weary of her thoughts, fearful that when she comes back after all the hours in the world outside he'll still be there, and fearful, too, that he'll be gone; she fears both things equally and hasn't even tried to tell him to stay or go because it also frightens her to think that he might listen to her, or that he might not, if she were to say one thing or the other, one thing and the other, if she dared. And she doesn't know what to do so she doesn't do anything, she just waits for the bus, chilled, watching the streetlamps hold out against the rising light of the sun as if it had nothing to do with them, during this time when their two territories coexist and do not exclude each other though they do not intermingle either, just as the real does not mix with the fictitious, and in fiction it can never be said, "It's over now, there, there, it's all over," not even as consolation or subterfuge, because nothing has really happened, silly, and in the territory that is not truth's everything goes on happening forever and ever and there the light is not put out now or later, and perhaps it is never put out.

Translated by Esther Allen

WORK

1971, *Los dominos del lobo*, Edhasa (novel).

1973, *Travesía del horizonte*, La Gaya Ciencia (novel).

1978, *El monarca del tiempo*, Anagrama (novel).

1983, *El siglo*, Seix Barral (novel).

1986, *El hombre sentimental*, Alfaguara (novel).

1989, *Todas las almas*, Anagrama (novel).

1989, *Cuentos únicos*, Siruela (biographies).

1992, *Corazón tan blanco*, Anagrama (novel).

1993, *Literatura y fantasma*, Siruela (articles).

1994, *Mañana en la batalla piensa en mí*, Anagrama (novel).

1995, *Vida del fantasma*, Aguilar (articles).

1996, *El hombre que parecía no querer nada*, Espasa-Calpe (anthology).

1996, *Cuando fui mortal*, Alfaguara (stories).

1997, *Miramientos*, Alfaguara (portraits).

1997, *Si yo amaneciera otra vez*, Alfaguara (essay).

1997, *Mano de sombra*, Alfaguara (articles).

1998, *Negra espalda del tiempo*, Alfaguara (novel).

1998, *Mala índole*, Plaza & Janés (story).

1999, *Desde que te ví morir*, Alfaguara (essay).

1999, *Seré amado cuando falte*, Alfaguara (articles).

2000, *Salvajes y sentimentales*, Aguilar (articles).

2001, *A veces un caballero*, Alfaguara (articles).

2002, *Tu rostro mañana 1. Fiebre y lanza*, Alfaguara (novel).

2003, *Harán de mí un criminal*, Alfaguara (articles).

2004, *Tu rostro mañana 2. Baile y sueño*, Alfaguara (novel).

2005, *El oficio de oír llover*, Alfaguara (articles).

2005, *Donde todo ha sucedido: al salir del cine*, Galaxia Gutenberg (articles).

2007, *Tu rostro mañana 3. Veneno y sombra y adiós*, Alfaguara (novel).

2007, *Demasiada nieve alrededor*, Alfaguara (articles).

2008, *Aquella mitad de mi tiempo*, Galaxia Gutenberg (articles).

2009, *Lo que no vengo a decir*, Alfaguara (articles).

2010, *Los villanos de la nación*, Libros del Lince (articles).

2011, *Los enamoramientos*, Alfaguara (novel).

2011, *Ni se les ocurra disparar*, Alfaguara (articles).

2011, "Ven a buscarme," Alfaguara (children's story).

2012, *Lección pasada de moda*, Galaxia Gutenberg (articles).

2012, *Mala índole (cuentos aceptados y aceptables)*, Alfaguara (collected stories).

2013, *Tiempos ridículos*, Alfaguara (articles).

·

ENGLISH TRANSLATIONS

1992, *All Souls*, translated by Margaret Jull Costa, New Directions (novel).

1995, *A Heart So White*, translated by Margaret Jull Costa, New Directions (novel).

1996, *Tomorrow in the Battle Think on Me*, translated by Margaret Jull Costa, New Directions (novel).

1999, *When I Was Mortal*, translated by Margaret Jull Costa, New Directions (stories).

2001, *Dark Back of Time*, translated by Esther Allen, New Directions (novel).

2003, *The Man of Feeling*, translated by Margaret Jull Costa, New Directions (novel).

2004, *Your Face Tomorrow 1: Fever and Spear*, translated by Margaret Jull Costa, New Directions (novel).

2006, *Voyage Along the Horizon*, translated by Kristina Cordero, McSweeney's (novel).

2006, *Written Lives*, translated by Margaret Jull Costa, New Directions (portraits).

2006, *Your Face Tomorrow 2: Dance and Dream*, translated by Margaret Jull Costa, New Directions (novel).

2009, *Your Face Tomorrow 3: Poison, Shadow, and Farewell*, translated by Margaret Jull Costa, New Directions (novel).

2010, *Bad Nature, or With Elvis in Mexico*, translated by Esther Allen, New Directions, (novella).

2010, *While the Women Are Sleeping*, translated by Margaret Jull Costa, New Directions (stories).

2013, *The Infatuations*, Margaret Jull Costa, Knopf (novel).

•

AWARDS AND RECOGNITIONS

1979, Premio Nacional de Traducción for *Tristram Shandy*, by Laurence Sterne.

1989, Premio Ciudad de Barcelona for *Todas las almas*.

1993, Premio de la Crítica for *Corazón tan blanco*.

1993, L'Oeil et la Lettre Prize for *Corazón tan blanco*.

1994, Knight of the Order of Arts and Letters of French Letters.

1995, Premio Rómulo Gallegos for *Mañana en la batalla piensa en mí*.

1995, Premio Fastenrath de la RAE for *Mañana en la batalla piensa en mí*.

1996, Premio Arzobispo Juan de San Clemente for *Mañana en la batalla piensa en mí*.

1996, Femina Étranger Prize in France for *Mañana en la batalla piensa en mí*.

1997, Premio Nelly Sachs for his body of work.

1997, IMPAC International Dublin Literary Award for *Corazón tan blanco*.

1998, Premio Letterario Internazionale Mondello-Cittá di Palermo for *Mañana en la batalla piensa en mí*.

1998, Premio Comunidad de Madrid for artistic creation.

2000, Premio Grinzane Cavour for his body of work.

2000, Premio Ennio Flaiano for *El hombre sentimental*.

2000, Alberto Moravia International Prize for foreign literature.

2003, Premio Nacional de Periodismo Miguel Delibes for the article published in two installments: "El oficio de oír llover" (*El País Semanal*, September 28th) and "Locuacidades ensimismadas" (*El País Semanal*, October 5th).

2003, Premio Salambó for the best book of fiction published in Spain in 2002 for his novel *Tu rostro mañana 1. Fiebre y lanza*.

2008, Premio Alessio.

2008, Member of the Real Academia Española (seat R).

2010, America Award (USA) for his body of work.

2011, Nonino de Literatura Award (Italy).

2011, Austrian State Prize for European Literature for his body of work.

2012, Premio Qué Leer de los Lectores, for *Los enamoramientos*.

2013, Rejected the Premio Nacional de Narrativa en España for *Los enamoramientos*.

2013, Premio Formentor de las Letras.

2013, Finalist for the National Book Critics Circle Award for Fiction for *The Infatuations*.

ABILIO
ESTÉVEZ
(Cuba, 1954)

bilio Estévez was born in 1954 in Marianao, in the province of La Havana, where his father worked as a radiotelegraph operator for the Signals Corp at Columbia military base. He majored in Hispanic Language and Literature at Universidad de La Havana, where he also got a graduate degree in Philosophy. During those university years he met Virgilio Piñera and, although he'd been passionate about books and writing since he was little, it was this encounter that made him think of himself as a writer. Their friendship would last until Piñera's death in 1979.

In 1987, after publishing the book of stories *Juego con Gloria*, Estévez made his debut as a playwright with *La verdadera culpa de Juan Clemente Zenea*, a work that received the Premio de la Crítica Cubana. Two years later, with his first book of poems, *Manual de tentaciones*, he again won the Premio de la Crítica, just like Luís Cernuda in Sevilla. The intense production of those years was combined with his teaching activities: he was a visiting professor of Latin American Literature at the University of Sassari, a playwriting professor in Venezuela, in New York, and advisor to various theater groups.

Although he was already recognized as one of the most important playwrights of his generation, he burst onto the scene of Latin American letters in 1997 with the publication of the novel *Tuyo es el reino*, which earned him the Premio de la Crítica Cubana in 1999 and was translated into English, French, German, Italian, Portuguese, Finnish, Danish, Dutch, Norwegian, and Greek. The French version got him the award for "Best Foreign Book" in the year 2000. Due to his literary restlessness, this novel surprised many with its expressive and structural brilliance: the action, unfolding in 1959 Havana, revolves around characters who sometimes vascillate toward the sordid and other times toward the mythical, along a timeline with occasional surrealist airs, lost in a jungle of words, metaphors, poetry, and dreams. The critics ended up saying: "The first book of the Cuban Abilio Estévez opens new literary paths, like *Paradise* and *One Hundred Years of Solitude*."

Prehaps owing to the great recognition of his first novel, the author, feeling asphyxiated in his country of origin and sick of the sensation of fear that he was unable to get away from, he decided to leave Cuba in 2000, and settled in Barcelona. Although the exile must have been a harsh personal blow, Estévez has also recognized that, in the end, it was a satisfactory process in literary terms, not just because of the access to many authors prohibited on the island, but also because of the broadening of horizons that leaving entailed.

In 2002 he published *Los Palacios distantes*, the second part of the trilogy begun in *Tuyo es el reino*, whose action is again set in Havana, but this time in the twenty-first century. The author makes his home city not just a decadent setting (a city in ruins, dirty and empty) but the near absolute protagonist of a plot with marked political content. The trilogy closed in 2008 with *El navegante dormido*, a much more complicated novel than the previous ones, in which the author builds a puzzle where every piece or character ends up fitting and making sense.

Before completing his trilogy, in 2004 Estévez published *Inventario secreto de La Habana*, perhaps his most singular work. A true love song to a Havana that no longer exists, that melds the personal trajectory of the author within his secret and phantasmagorical city; the nameless inhabitants who populate his days; and the literary myths that have inhabited and celebrated the city: Cernuda, Hemingway, Stevens, etc. A mosaic of memory and fiction, *Inventario secreto de La Habana* encompasses diverse genres (fiction, memoir, and guidebook to a mythified city), and constitutes a vibrant, nostalgic meditation and a magnificent reflection on literature.

In 2010 he published the novel *El bailarín ruso de Montecarlo*, a fiction with a great deal of biographical content whose protagonist, a Cuban "myopic, crippled, and ugly without exaggeration," leaves the island and, after burning his passport, settles in Barcelona, opening up a path to redemption.

His most recent novel, *El año del calypso*, has appeared in 2012 under the Tusquets imprint as part of the collection La Sonrisa Vertical.

THE ACORN

I've chosen this excerpt for three compelling reasons: the first, that I had a hard time writing it, much more than any other section of *El navegante dormido*, a novel to which I feel a particular connection. The material resisted me for some time, and that struggle, far from discouraging me, always excites me and spurs me on. There is a combative part of me that is nourished when I write. The second reason: it is a section that someone I love, my companion, finds moving. The third reason might seem like a *boutade* (and, of course, it is), but it has to do with me, with my own inner Mamina fleeing a great fire, not knowing whether the flight will be worth it, not knowing whether salvation exists or what that even means.

In Conversation with the Dead

I would like nothing more than to withdraw to the peace of a desert, but yes, I have dialogues with the dead. Maybe the word *dialogue*, which sounds so good when Quevedo uses it, is a bit of an overstatement. It's more a monologue, the opposite of what happens with the gods, since the deceased are the ones who speak, and we mere mortals only listen. A few of the dead have been with me for a long time now, Dostoevsky, for example. I can't stop reading and re-reading him. And Marcel Proust, who always produces a feeling of surprise and elation in me. And the great Katherine Anne Porter. And the Sherwood Anderson of *Winesburg, Ohio*. Virgilio Piñeira's language is especially clear, the tone of his voice and the lilt of his witticisms have not been erased from my memory. I hope always to hear the voices of Lezama

Lima, of Juan Carlos Onetti, of Felisberto Hernández, of Juan José Saer, of Alfonso Reyes (all speak well, but this last one does so spectacularly). Then there are the dead who aren't, so I don't mention them here.

CODA

As a writer, how has your exile from Cuba affected you?

My exile from Cuba has been good for me as a writer, so far. As a person, I don't know. The world I lived in was very small, very closed, very provincial, to put it one way. All of a sudden, I discovered that the world was a big, unfamiliar place. I discovered that no one is the center of the universe, that you're just one passion among many, and that everyone has the same problems. This awareness is very important for a writer. There is an element of humility there that has been really useful for me. Beyond that, I've been able to read books that I couldn't before; I didn't have access to many cultures. From this perspective, my exile has suited me. From a personal perspective, it's painful to know that you have to leave a place and won't be able to go back. Or that if you do go back, your return implies a failure of some kind. It's like going home not because you've decided to go home, but because you've decided to die before your time. It's going back to the feeling of being on that island and wanting to travel and not being able to because they keep you from leaving, or make it too difficult; I have to get foreign money and visas, and then there's the reality of coming back and having to ask permission to enter, which can be denied. The feeling that I've lost everything is always with me, the feeling that I couldn't leave my home closed up and ask someone to take care of it while I'm gone, but instead that I abandoned it, and that's a terrible feeling. It's starting over, now, at fifty-five—I've been here for ten years—dealing with problems I should have faced when I was twenty, not now.

The refined and subtle way you construct characters really stands out in your work. Has your experience as a playwright contributed to this?

When I write fiction and create characters—and I really enjoy this process—I imagine the space in which they are moving, the backdrop. I suppose that every writer who plans out a novel sees that space clearly, but I see it in dramatic terms, as though it were in a theater. And I want the reader to hear the sound of their voices the way I hear it. The theater has an incredible immediacy, you are really there, and the feeling this produces is truly magical. I never know, with a novel, what the reader is thinking there, in his solitude, or whether he is reacting. All my novels aim to penetrate, to create a concrete physicality, to ground the reader. What has always attracted me to fiction, over and above theater, is the immense freedom you have when you write a novel. Writing a play there are rules to follow, and these are hard to break. You might want to escape them, but there is a line that can't be ignored. But with the novel I feel free, so I like writing novels much more than writing for the theater.

Will you go back to Cuba one day, or is it already too remote?

It's important to have a certain degree of detachment. I think there's nothing more important than ironic distance and I would love to be able to achieve it. Right now I am writing something that takes place in 1930s Havana, a Havana I never experienced, and that comes from somewhere else—not a place of nostalgia, because I obviously can't be nostalgic about 1930s Havana. All the same, you can't always be thinking about lost paradises; reality is now and there's no need to overdramatize. My mother has been a big help, because I ask her questions and am beginning to gather an image of Marianao, of the neighborhood where I grew up. It demands a lot of documentation and historical investigation, and so I'm building up a sense of detachment this way. I remember that writing the section I chose for this anthology was really hard for me. I had to do an extensive historical investigation into the race war of 1912. The woman's movements are not staged. She had to flee. Though it was difficult, I really enjoyed giving meaning to all that; it was an enjoyable challenge, though it cost me.

A THOUSAND FORESTS

FROM *El navegante dormido* (The Sleeping Mariner)
[a novel]

The Story of Mamina

Full of danger were the roads Mamina had to travel to find refuge at the beach with no name.

It took her sixty-seven days, and the setbacks she faced were even greater in number. Two endless months and a week full of unthinkable violence. Fleeing from one end of the island to the other, from the distant soil of Oriente to arrive, without knowing why, at an unstable and Babylonian Havana.

"My own Stations of the Cross," she would say on those rare occasions her spirits were high, or low, enough for her to talk about her journey. Accompanied by the pain of the dead left behind and under the sign of other massacres, deaths no less personal and terrible for their having been strangers, she reflected and suffered along the brutal roads of an island possessed.

Sixty-seven days amid the disasters and consequences of a race war and, to make things worse, bearing the worst possible letter of passage: her dark skin and her face—beautiful, yes, but that of a colored woman born to slaves, the pained, fugitive face of a daughter of the Mandinga and the Embuyla.

It was 1912. It had been only fourteen years since the Spanish Empire, already in terrible condition, lowered its flag, and ten since, the island having become a precarious state—a timid, intermittently democratic republic—a new flag (created by Teurbe Tolón for Narciso López) was raised from the battlements of El Morro and La Cabaña, alongside that of United States. In only fourteen years of independence, there had already been countless strikes, two wars, and two American interventions, as though the ten years of deaths, machete violence, epidemics, starvation, and internment camps between 1868

and 1878 hadn't been enough, or as though they set the stage for the catastrophe that was, without a doubt, soon to befall the young and afflicted republic.

No one called her Mamina back then, they addressed her by her real, full
name: María de Megara Calcedonia. She and her brother Juan Jacobo had
been lucky enough to be born, respectively, in the relatively happy years of
1886 and 1887, when the Spanish Crown found itself obligated, after a bloody
war which neither side had the distinction of winning completely, to abolish
slavery on the "ever Loyal island of Cuba."

The siblings were born in the mountains near Alto Songo, out between
Dos Amantes and La Maya, in the quarters of the El Calamón coffee plantation, which at that time belonged to a formerly wealthy and still legendary
family of the area, the Pageries, who, as their name suggests, were French
or, rather, of French extraction. From Martinique, the Pagerie family arrived
first at Saint Domingue, and from Saint Domingue, fleeing in terror from
the armies of Toussaint Louverture, they ended up in the mountains of Cuba's
Oriente Province. As their surname also suggests, they were close relatives of
the woman who had been Empress of the French, Josephine de Beauharnais,
who was born, as everyone knows, Tascher de la Pagerie. As such, the owners of El Calamón had that air typical of the Bonaparte nobility, something
between stately and wild, a little coarse, that same affected haughtiness
accented by a surprising touch of insecurity. Not only the stateliness, but also
the wildness, the haughtiness, the affectation and the insecurity were amplified by the distance from that heart shared by every French person known
as Paris, and by the everyday struggle of surviving in a land where even the
most mundane undertaking becomes an event, vacillating between the tragic,
the apocalyptic and, ultimately, the absurd. The Bonaparte nobility felt nobler
there, but also more common, more *parvenu*, if that were possible.

Not very large, El Calamón was by then hardly a coffee plantation at all:
it was more like a country house. It still produced a few hundred pounds of
coffee, but that was not enough to maintain the familiar standard of luxury,
which had not been all that luxurious for some time. The war drastically
reduced production. Most of the family's colored workers had run off to join
the fight, which was as long and bloody as it was disorganized and futile.

No one knows, nor was there ever a need to know, whether they went
to war because of a flash of patriotism or a natural desire for freedom. Or
whether they went in search of adventure, which was also likely, given that

waking up every day hours before the sun and climbing up and down the hillsides gathering coffee beans that would be dried and then taken to the roasters and the mills was not what would generally be called exciting work. It made sense that the mambises should have a greater need of freedom than the whites, and that they should feel more at ease on the battlefield with their machetes raised, riding bareback on stolen horses, than in the strictly governed quarters of a coffee plantation or, far worse, in the cruel ones of a sugar plantation. Those battlefields were not battlefields in the way that the civilized meadows of Mont-Saint-Jean or Austerlitz were; they were all hill, jungle, a harsh and savage scrubland where one caught diseases, fought barefoot, and lived and slept free, enjoying life under the open sky, as it is best enjoyed.

The Pagerie family's moment arrived when a distinguished relative, the son of cousin Hortense, traveled from Bavaria shortly before the Ten Years' War with the intention, instilled in him by his mother, to establish a Second Empire in France; to this end, he married a noblewoman from Granada named Eugénie de Montijo. The Cuban coffee Pageries, generations of whom had been born on the island, saw their chance. By the start of the Ten Years' War, the last stragglers had returned to France and invested in silk production and, thanks to the incredible discoveries of Hilaire de Chardonnet, managed to open a few successful factories in Lyon, Marseilles, and Besançon.

In other words, for nearly the same reasons that drove the colored combatants, most of the Pagerie family installed itself in fine homes in Marseilles, Paris, and Lyon. The only ones to stay behind at El Calamón were the two eldest siblings, Delfina and Julien, who were so much of that place that the only Paris they knew was that of Honoré de Balzac (which, of course, was more Paris than Paris). There were even those who quipped, with a smirk, that the Pageries' white skin was not actually French, but the fortuitous union of the Trocadero and the Port of Calabar. They were too tired, apathetic, or tied to the place to go in search of new adventures, and had Rousseau's theories too deeply ingrained in them to repeat, in unison, that everything was perfect in the moment it left the hands of the Creator but it all came apart in the hands of man. Though they had been born in Cuba, they were also French (there is no reason to see a contradiction in this, though one appears at first glance) and therefore quite cultured; children, albeit backward ones, of the *Encyclopédie* and—because everything has always made it to Cuba late, distorted, and smaller than it started—of the six volumes of the *Cours de philosophie positive* published by Comte in 1842.

And so, in part because they were free thinkers, in part because of the African blood that supposedly ran through their delicate, positivist, imperialist veins, Delfina and Julien were among the first to rid themselves of their slaves. Their favorites, those they loved most, a Mandinga and the daughter of a Galician and an Embuyla, Liduvia and Losanto, parents to María de Megara and Juan Jacobo, stayed with them in the house, bearing the acceptable status of freed persons.

The children grew up on that magnificent coffee plantation in disrepair, which was all the more magnificent for being in disrepair. Delfina and Julien taught them how to read and write in French and Spanish using Madame de Staël's *Corinne*, George Sand's *François le Champi*, alongside Fernán Caballero's *La gaviota* and the Duke of Rivas's *Romances históricos*. They instructed them in certain aspects of drawing and mathematics, as well as in a bit of rudimentary philosophy.

From the time she was a little girl, María de Megara had a remarkable talent for embroidery, sewing, and cooking. Juan Jacobo, for his part, surprised everyone (except his mentor, Julien de la Pagerie) when, at twelve years old, he appeared at dinner one night with a Cremona violin that had belonged to the eldest Pagerie and played, with adequate skill and tolerable taste, seven of Paganini's twenty-four caprices.

Juan Jacobo's fate was determined that night. The fate of the others was sealed, as well. Just after entering adolescence, around the same time that don Tomás Estrada Palma took the presidential seat (also the year of Émile Zola's death), Juan Jacobo ran away to Santiago de Cuba to join a band based in El Caney that played at open-air dances and parties celebrating national holidays and saints' days. A band led by the musician José María Figarola, who was also the president of a society for people of color called the Great Dahomey Academy of Oriente Province, which fell somewhere between the Masons and an Abakua.

Around then, as though life were trying to reveal the hidden connection between events, the Pagerie siblings died. In fact, they did not die, since the verb "to die" suggests something beyond one's will. The Pagerie siblings were found dead on one of the plantation's terraces on the same day in February that Delfina turned sixty-nine. She had been shot several times in the head, he, in the heart. Next to Julien lay the old hunting rifle that they had used to ward off prowlers; she had a piece of rice paper at her side with a letter written on it, in French on one side and Spanish on the other, in which she outlined their shared disinterest in earthly life and their desire to be laid to rest together in the dark soil of El Calamón, under a hundred-year-old Ceiba tree planted by their grandfather, don Philippe-Auguste Tascher de la Pagerie.

The coffee plantation, now in the hands of relatives in Lyon, Marseilles, and Paris, was forgotten.

Like everything in Cuba, its decadence ceased to be such (decadent) and turned into ruin.

The Pagerie family left Liduvia, Losanto, María de Megara, and Juan Jacobo a little wooden house in an enclave near the plantation called La Maya after all the maya bushes that grew (or grow) there, bushes with long, rough leaves like agave, and which were (or are) also known as "mouse pineapple."

Liduvia, Losanto, and María de Megara lived in La Maya, getting enough to eat, even enough for the prudent little extra here and there, from the cultivation of their plot of land, while Juan Jacobo, a good violinist (an excellent violinist, if we take into account where he was from), earned a dignified living in Señor Figarola's band.

It was another member of the band, a well-respected student of the Great Dahomey Academy of Oriente Providence, who fell under María de Megara's spell and, in turn, managed to win her. His name was Serafín Minaya. A mulatto flautist as tall, straight, and strong as a tree, Serafín Minaya was born in Moca, in La Española, to the north of Santo Domingo and moved to Santiago de Cuba with his parents when he was twelve years old. The elder Minayas founded a small factory that made glass bottles they then sold to the Bacardi family, those other immigrants from Sitges who had been distilling the best rum in Santiago de Cuba for forty years.

Serafín Minaya was not only light-skinned and handsome, he was also highly cultured, from a good Dominican family, and had an unusually elegant air (the Minaya elegance, people would say). He became Figerola's right hand man and the partner of a colored politician who owned a prosperous ranch in Belona, near La Maya, and who may have been of Hatian origin, named Pedro Ivonnet.

Serafo was twenty-seven and María de Megara twenty-four on that tenth of June, 1910 (the year not only that Halley's comet passed, but also that Winslow Homer and Mark Twain died), when they stood before a solemn colored notary, smartly dressed in a suit with his hair twisted into tight and slightly greenish knots, who had been hired by the Great Dahomey Academy of Oriente Province.

The newlyweds stayed in La Maya, in a room made from Crabwood planks that Serafo built, with his singular strength and enormous hands, onto Liduvia and Losanto's little house. Colomba Bezana, the daughter of María de Megara and Serafín Minaya, was born there on December 12, 1911.

And they were more or less happy for as long as their happiness lasted, which was more or less two years. Until that night in June 1912 when the race wars broke out and La Maya burned the way makeshift towns made of Crabwood planks, Pipistey trunks, and dried palm fronds can burn. [. . .]

THROUGH THE FOREST

Hours have passed since she fled La Maya and started cutting her way through the brush. She must be far away by now. She knows very well that time is different in the forest, that it is more miserly there. She can't hear the shots anymore. The silence of the forest envelops her, a silence punctuated by whistles and voices. She thinks she can still make out the glow of the fire to the south, close to where she imagines La Maya is, or was, or where whatever is left of it is, if there is anything left at all. Not only can she see the light of the fire, she can also smell the intense odor of the filthy black smoke from the burning underbrush, from the beams and the balsa wood that were probably still smoldering, trees turned to ash and houses into torches, the penetrating odor of wood, and the still more penetrating one of charred bodies. A smell that will stay with her. No matter where she goes, where she hides, or whether a month, a year, or a century has passed.

Her progress is slow. She is barefoot and has to be careful. Besides, she knows well that moving quickly through the forest means moving with great care. The forest is a strange place. Nothing like the rest of the world. There is nothing like it; not plains, nor a valley, nor a gorge, nor a mountain. The forest is a place both sacred and damned. A place where gods can be devils and devils, gods.

She is a woman of color, which means that she *knows*; hers is a knowledge found not in the mind, but rather in the blood. And so even she, who learned to read French from Chateaubriand and Madame de Staël, and Spanish from the Duke of Rivas and Fernán Caballero, knows that there in the forest, in that tangled labyrinth bristling with underbrush, vermin, and weeds, making progress means progressing slowly, and that if you want to disappear without getting lost you need to be fully aware of your physical presence, to be precise, self-possessed, because that is the only way to be deft enough to vanish without losing your way, to become a shadow among the sacred shadows of the forest.

She is carrying a machete, though she could not explain how she got it. Liduvia, her mother, probably slipped it into her hand. She knows that her first reaction was to dress Colomba Bezana and get her out of bed. As soon as she heard the first shots and sensed those first fires, without seeing them and without hearing Liduvia's screams or the stream of curses coming out of Losanto, who was already running up the narrow street hoping to find Juan Jacobo and Serafo, or, to be exact (and he knew it well), to meet his death.

She had known for many nights that war was about to break out. Neither her husband nor her brother could calm her. No matter how much they tried to exude serenity, there was a distinct undercurrent of belligerence, and also of uneasiness, to their words. And, more than in their words, in the way they acted. Their silences spoke louder than their lectures. María de Megara was sure that the worst was about to come.

As soon as the first shot rang out and the first tongues of fire took form, she dressed the girl and lifted her from her bed so quickly that her movements seemed rehearsed. Without realizing it, she had been dressing and lifting out of bed to flee for a long time already.

Then she, too, stepped into the street. Her father was running in the opposite direction from those who were trying to escape. She could sense Liduvia pushing her toward the forest.

The crowd of colored men and women ran in every direction. The flames spread in a way imaginable only in a town as destitute as La Maya, built from Crabwood planks, Pipistey trunks, and dried palm fronds.

It was only when she had made her way into the forest that she realized she had been cutting her path with a machete.

Another bit of good luck: Colomba Bezana did not cry. As though the girl understood, as though she knew that what mattered was advancing with patience, pushing back gnarled branches and sickle bush, and stepping over the roots and puddles with absolute concentration, absolute caution, and making as little noise as possible.

Another law of the forest: ignore the swamp-like terrain. Do not pay attention to the snakes, or to the mosquitoes that appear in swarms. Or to your hunger, or the mixture of exhaustion and hunger: in the end, these are more dangerous than swamps, snakes, or mosquitoes. Above all, do not give in to grief and worry about what you left behind. Now is not the time for that. Nor is it the time to think about those who were trapped in the fire and are now no more than pieces of their own bodies, severed limbs left in the road. Now is the time to look forward and escape. For them, too. Escape means saving Colomba Bezana. And also saving herself, because in order to save the girl she would have to save herself, to give herself over to god, and not just any god, but specifically one named Eleggua, the Holy Child of Atocha, the keeper of roads and of those who flee, the guardian of the forest and the plain.

To the south, the flames swell. Behind her are death and destruction. A war on colored people. An entire town burned because of a war on colored people.

She does not know what lies to the north, and that is its advantage. Better the evil you don't know than the evil you do?

There is another bit of luck that María de Megara should be grateful for: she is strong, solid, and resolute, not only in will, but also in body. Will and body have come together in her, now they are one and the same. María de Megara knows that she has gone into the forest, that she is cutting her way through the brush, that she is staving off hunger, exhaustion, vermin, and swarms of mosquitoes. She knows that the Holy Child of Atocha and Saint Genevieve are guiding her. The forest also knows that she has entered, a colored woman carrying a newborn and a machete who will not be beaten by swamps, sickle bush, vermin, mosquitoes, hunger, or exhaustion.

The June night could not be further removed from the horrors in La Maya. It is a night like any other, beautiful and clear, stirred by a breeze that seems to descend directly from a sky as vast, high, and sparkling as a cupola. Cloudless, white with stars. The forest smells like itself, like grass and wet roots, like soil. The wind carries the scent of the distant smoke, of the war, and the sickly sweet odor of animals decomposing. It does not take much effort to get your bearings. Ursa Minor can easily be made out, and from its tail, the world being the world, it is easy to find the North Star.

If María de Megara is sure of anything, it is where she is headed. Salvation, if there is any to be had, lies to the north. Up toward Mayarí, Jarahueca, Nicaro, or Caimana. Toward the sea she has never set eyes on (and near which she will live for over sixty years). If she were to stray southward, the only thing she would find would be another sea she has never set eyes on and has no desire to, and Santiago de Cuba, a dangerous city that at the moment is probably a hotbed of soldiers, a trap.

Thirty years after slavery was abolished, María de Megara feels like a runaway slave. In this hilly region, the terrain rises and falls suddenly, forming little cliffs. Contrary to what one might think, the climb is easier than the descent. The climb requires more courage, of course; it is a matter of mastering one's body, of stamina. The descent, on the other hand, is a matter of chance during which one is at the mercy of forces that are not easy to control.

She stops when she reaches a clearing. She needs to breathe, calm down, get her bearings. The green glow of the fireflies makes it hard for her to tell the sky from the earth. Colomba Bezana, luckily, remains asleep, silent and unaware of the forest, the war, and of death.

María de Megara again catches sight of the fire in La Maya, there in the distance, standing out against the night sky. The tongues of flame seem to be getting bigger and bigger, as though the fire wanted to be visible from far away. They should be able to see that fire, she thinks, in Bayamo, in Manzanillo, in Guantánamo, for that matter, they must know by now in Cabo Haitiano and Kingston, about the way La Maya burned and how colored folk were dying on the Big Island. She also thinks she hears a thumping in the sickle bush, the sound of a machete. She freezes, hoping to discover who else has risked their life to cross through the forest. Blows to the branches, but it is hard to tell whether they are really the blows of a machete, or from what direction they are coming. It seems as though they are coming from many directions at once. She can't be sure, either, whether the sounds she hears are made by people or animals. Or how many are coming toward her. She leans forward, crouches, and moves as quickly as she can toward the trunk of a Palo Diablo tree. She looks up again, and the night looks even more distant and elevated. Down here there is only the fleeting, green glint of the fireflies.

She decides to leave the Palo Diablo and heads down a dry slope. Her bare feet sink into the ground like the Holy Child of Atocha's staff. She finds a small hut made of palm. It is only barely standing upright, and has no windows or doors. There are holes cut out for windows, and a doorframe, but that is all. All the rest is darkness and silence. The dark of an abandoned hut.

Trying to urge herself on, she says or thinks, "No one lives here." But she stays hidden under an old Hornbeam tree. She wants to be sure there is no one in the hut. If it is empty, they may be able to spend the rest of the night there and wait until the sun sets the following day, because one shouldn't waste energy, and she will need to explore, to find something to eat, a carrot or an avocado, guava, tamarinds, or a mango, something that will restore her faith and her strength. There should be a stream nearby. The area is full of them, it is well irrigated by the water coming down off the sierra. A stream where she can not only quench her thirst and calm her sore feet and skin, sore from so much sweat and exertion, but also something even better: where she can try to forget, to look forward to a change in order to be able to press forward on a journey that is not just any journey.

The darkness inside the hut is even thicker than the darkness in the forest. Though some of the guano has fallen from the roof, the crispness of the breeze and the early light does not seem to enter. There is an unsettling odor of wax and burning wicks. And of dead animals. When her eyes adjust to the dark, María de Megara realizes that there are dead doves on the floor. At the same time, she sees a little table, above which hangs a carving of Christ. It is a crude table, made of rough-hewn cane; the Christ is also coarse, carved without arms by a clumsy knife from what appears to be a Cañandonga branch. She does not know whether the Christ is meant to be colored or whether it is the darkness making it look darker, as though it had been coated with tar. There are several extinguished candles around the Christ. She lays Colomba Bezana at its feet and tries, for her part, to kneel. She cannot. She collapses at the feet of the Christ and closes her eyes. She does not pray, in French or in Spanish; she cannot remember how to pray. She does not cry, either. She is tired. She has enough strength left to sigh and let her eyes fall shut. She is asleep before they have even closed.

She is woken by the sound of a dog barking. She does not know how long she has been asleep. The sun is still not up. Then again, there was always the possibility that the sun had come up several times and set again, and that sleep, the exhaustion of so many days, had kept her from realizing it. She can hear the bark of a dog, and a different barking, not a dog's, that seems to be a human voice. María de Megara folds the Christ into her long, tattered skirt. She wraps it up into a little bundle, which she ties several times. She picks Colomba Bezana up and leaves the hut. The barking, and the other barking, that isn't—the voice, a song or something like a song, can be heard coming from the direction of San Nicolás, San Pedro, or El Pozo. Could it be the voice of a soldier? Probably not, she tells herself, soldiers don't sing.

In any case, she knows that she can't take a chance. There is no time to lose. And so, with the Christ tied into her skirt, Colomba Bezana dressed and in her arms and the machete in her hand, she makes her way again through the forest, through the unending night of the forest, where it seems dawn will never come.

Soon, more quickly than she could have imagined, there is a dog at her side. Dark gray, bony, and as dirty as the forest, with huge paws and teats just as big, a dog without fur or a tail, sniffing her calmly. Five or six guinea hens gather around her. María de Megara stands very still and lets herself be sniffed, trying to stay calm and not show any fear, and says a few friendly words to the animal as though she were talking to a little girl.

Mamina! Someone shouts as they break through the sickle bush, an old man or a child, a small figure as skinny as the dog, carrying a lantern.

The dog turns listlessly toward her master, without any particular interest, seeming to forget about María de Megara, who lowers her machete. The guinea hens also peck their way away from her, slowly. By lowering her machete, María de Megara is trying to say, "Don't hurt me, please, my daughter and I are fleeing from the men, the fire, the war, and death." The old man, or the child, that strange image illuminated by the lantern, looks at her for a few moments that seem endless.

"Are you running away? From La Maya?" he asks without moving his lips, like a ventriloquist.

María de Megara nods, trying to look docile, harmless; she even smiles.

"That's a child there?"

The figure holds up the lantern, and the light spreads thinly, like another rag, toward the bundle of cloth Megara holds in her arms.

"A little girl, my little girl," María de Megara says, trying not to let her fear or her agitation come across in her voice, that is, as much as she can help it, in her fear and agitation.

The old man, or the boy, lifts the hand holding the lantern a bit higher. He moves the other one in a clumsy, shaking motion, as though it were a fan, in what seems to be a signal that María de Megara should follow him. Something in that gesture, something at once protective and comical, makes her obey. As though she had also understood, the dog named Mamina jumps up and heads down a rocky slope, followed by the guinea hens. The old man or the boy follows the dog, the hens. María de Megara, with the girl and the machete, follows them all. But more than anything, she follows the light of the lantern, which turns the hill into a far more docile place.

The slope looks white in the light of the lantern. They follow it down through a copse of trees that smells of soursop, clammy cherries, and hog plum. A current of moist air swirls upward carrying another scent, stronger and more agreeable still: that of burning firewood and coffee.

María de Megara feels a surge of hope.

A path begins at the bottom of the slope and cuts through the Artemisia and the guinea grass. The crispness of the air, the faint sound of water, and the smell of freshly brewed coffee are clearer now, and more invigorating. Finally a small hut, also made of palm planks and so whitewashed it almost glows, appears on the other side of a low ridge. María de Megara believes it to be the work of some god. She doesn't know which one, but thinks it must be one of them, because as soon as they come around the ridge and see the hut, the new day dawns, as it always did, from the direction of Jamaica, and the hut seems to glow even brighter, as though its walls were lit from within, and not by the sun drawn forth by the new day, and reflecting off the calcimine someone had used in an effort to dignify its palm planks.

Mamina barks idly. The hens join others and spread out, pecking the ground. Another old man or another boy, the exact replica of the one that had brought María de Megara there, steps into the doorway of the hut and, without smiling, claps his hands a few times in what seems to be pleasure. Were it not for the girl and the machete, María de Megara would have applauded, too. Since she does not applaud, she smiles. In gratitude, relief, and trust.

Behind this other old man or boy appears a woman—chubby, blond, and rosy-cheeked—who must be more than sixty and who holds out her tiny hands in a gesture of surprise and cheer.

"You're on the run, coming from La Maya," says the woman in a spirited, youthful voice. "Consider yourself lucky. My friend says that the dead are being counted by the thousand."

María de Megara feels a strange sense of well-being as she enters the hut, the floor of which, made of ash and pressed dirt and meticulously swept, seems like slate. Like the walls, the furniture is also made of palm planks. The chairs are sawed-down trunks with details and borders carved into them with care. The ceiling is high and made of guano, and has been decorated with colorful scraps of fabric. The same scraps have been sewn together with coarse thread to make curtains that stand in for partitions and doors.

Setting the machete on the floor, María de Megara holds her little girl tight and sits down in one of the palm trunk chairs. She wants to cry and to sing, to thank the Holy Child of Atocha, the god of those who flee and of those who survive. As though they understood, the two old men or boys sing a strange song that seems to be a psalm, the lyrics of which María de Megara does not understand. When they are done, they stare at her as though she were a supernatural being.

Smiling and singing along, the chubby woman disappears behind one of the colorful curtain doors. When she returns she is surrounded by hens and carries a pitcher of milk.

"Saturnina, that's my name, and these are my sons, Gaspar and Baltasar. Names fit for a pair of sorcerers, and to be honest, I think they are. I have a daughter, Eloína, who's married and has been living in Cauto Cristo for the last two years. My husband, a good man they call Machito, drives a cart. You'll meet him soon, he always comes home for lunch."

The sun comes through the windows with surprising intensity. A yellow, clean, precise sun.

María de Megara feels as though she has been traveling through one long night, as though it has been many days since the last time she saw the sun.

Saturnina takes the child in order to give her milk.

"My poor little girl has been asleep the whole time," María de Megara explains.

"I'll put her down. There are blankets for you, too. You must be exhausted."

"You're right, I am."

Saturnina vanishes with the child. María de Megara unties her skirt, revealing the armless Christ painted with tar that had been hidden there. Saturnina is in the doorway now, looking at her with an expression that she cannot quite understand.

"Your daughter is resting," she says.

"She's good," responds María de Megara, "a good girl. She never cried, she never whined, as though she understood that we had to run."

"Your daughter is resting," Saturnina repeats in a monotone, without disturbing the hens that have gathered around her.

María de Megara shows her the armless Christ.

"I found this in an abandoned hut in the forest."

"That's not an abandoned hut, it's our temple. It's where we go to pray."

María de Megara tries to apologize. Saturnina interrupts and gestures toward the Christ.

"Don't worry, consider it a gift. Machito made it. He'll make another, so there's nothing to worry about. He loves carving wood. It's yours, take the Christ wherever you go, may he always be with you. You've earned it."

María de Megara tries to thank her. The woman interrupts her again.

"Your daughter is resting. Why don't you?"

She shows her to a small, windowless room with blankets piled on the floor.

"Is there a stream anywhere nearby? I need to wash up. I have more dirt on me than a corpse."

Saturnina does not look at her. Her expression is serious and her small hands no longer flutter around, but rather are joined over her stomach.

"Sleep now, child, there will be plenty of time to bathe. There is a stream that won't dry up just because you sleep a few hours, as God wills."

María de Megara obediently throws herself onto the blankets. Her eyes close as soon as she lies down. She begins to dream. A dream in which her body rises above the house and above the forest, and goes off toward the sea. María de Megara, who has never seen the sea, sees it clearly before her.

Strangely, she is not surprised by this, or that she flies over it like a cloud. After that she does not dream. Or if she does dream, she does not know, and will never know, of what.

How long has she been sleeping? If really pressed to answer that question, she would probably say, "years."

Because the room has no windows, it is dark. The sun that filters through the cracks between the palm planks to form irregular lines on the slate-colored floor is a small sun from the west that should be starting to set over toward Holguín. A sun that barely, waveringly illuminates the colored scraps meant to decorate the ceiling.

María de Megara hears voices coming from the living room. It is not a conversation. It sounds more like a prayer, a litany. She sits up, trying not to make any noise. She cautiously pulls the curtain aside. On the tightly packed floor, on a pile of blankets, she sees Colomba Bezana surrounded by white romerillo flowers, silverberry branches, two candles, and five or six guinea hens. Kneeling beside the girl are Saturnina, her two sons and a midget María de Megara has not seen before, whom she imagines must be Machito. She is not worried anymore that they might realize she is there, they already know. She opens her mouth but no sound comes out. She walks to the middle of the room and falls to her knees. She puts out the candles with her fingers.

"Your daughter is resting," says Saturnina.

"With the angels," add the boys or old men who are her sons.

The other miniature old man who is probably Machito nods solemnly and springs to his feet, startling the guinea hens.

MAMINA APPEARS

It had to be Mino. Only he could have found María de Megara. Mino never knew who she was or, rather, who she had been, where she was from, or her real name.

Without the girl or the machete, only the armless Christ tied into her skirt, she walked for days not knowing where to go, unsure whether there was anywhere to go or not, and not caring either way.

In those days Mino was a strapping twenty-year-old, all muscle and vigor. He had gone with Doctor Reefy to the cays north of Camagüey in a comfortable sloop, sailing through what has always been known as the Canal Viejo de Bahamas. He found the young colored woman on a beach, the name of which they never knew, either. There on the bluff, she looked like what she, in a way, was: the survivor of a shipwreck. She looked out at the horizon as though the help she was waiting for might appear there.

And that is how it happened, because Mino saw a body laid out on the bluff and called out to the captain. They anchored as close to the shore as they could. The boy rowed the dinghy in to the beach and approached the young woman, whose eyes were open but looked at nothing. To see the truth—that she was a beautiful woman—you really had to want to see it: she was emaciated and wore that expression between drowsiness and anger that comes with hunger and one's bewilderment at not being able to do anything about it.

When she saw Mino, she had two reactions. First, of reaching out her hands in supplication, and second, of pulling in her arms to protect her face and throwing herself backward, ready to defend herself, like an animal used to being abused.

Mino smiled as gently as he could. Though he was a big young man, and all muscle, he could be extraordinarily gentle with women. He talked to her, found the right words and gestures, the friendliest tones of voice, and he calmed her down. He rubbed her feet, which were caked with a crust as hard as stone. When she lowered her arms and closed her eyes, he picked her up and carried her to the boat. He rowed back, smiling the whole time, just as gently. When he reached the sloop, the doctor and the captain lifted her onboard with just as much care. She opened her expressionless eyes and made a face. It was hard to tell whether she was trying to smile, or whether she was about to cry. Everyone there knew how bad the times were, that war had broken out. Everyone there knew the hell from which the woman had escaped. The doctor touched her forehead, which was soaked with sweat, stroked her coarse, dirty hair and, holding her chin in his hand, asked:

"What is your name?"

Either María de Megara was afraid, or she did not know the answer. She remained silent for a few moments, her eyes shining.

The gentleman repeated the question.

And then, as though by some miracle, she remembered the dog from the forest.

"Mamina," she said, lowering her eyes, "is my name. The only one I have."

"Surname?"

"Colored folk don't have those, Sir."

María de Megara probably thought, "If I'm going to start a new life, shouldn't I begin with a new name? And what difference is there between a Christian on the run and a dog from the forest?"

Translated by Heather Cleary

WORK

1987, *Juego con Gloria*, Letras Cubanas (stories).

1987, *La verdadera culpa de Juan Clemente Zenea*, Unión (play).

1989, *Manual de las tentaciones. Prosas poéticas*, Letras Cubanas (prose poems).

1993, *Perla marina*, Ediciones de la revista Tablas (play).

1995, *Santa Cecilia*, Revista Unión (play).

1997, *Un sueño feliz*, Tusquets (stories).

1998, *El horizonte y otros regresos*, Tusquets (stories).

2002, *Los palacios distantes*, Tusquets (novel).

2004, *Ceremonias para actores desesperados*, Tusquets (includes the plays *Santa Cecilia*, *Freddie*, and *El enano en la botella*).

2004, *Inventario secreto de La Habana*, Tusquets (novel).

2008, *El navegante dormido*, Tusquets (novel).

2010, *El bailarín ruso de Montecarlo*, Tusquets (novel).

2013, *El año del calypso*, Tusquets (novel)

2013, *Un sueño feliz. La noche*, Editorial Folium (play)

.

ENGLISH TRANSLATIONS

2000, *Thine is the Kingdom*, translated by David L. Frye, Arcade Publishing (novel).

2004, *Distant Palaces*, translated by David L. Frye, Arcade Publishing (novel).

AWARDS AND RECOGNITIONS

1984, Premio José Antonio Ramos de la Unión de Escritores y Artistas de Cuba for *La verdadera culpa de Juan Clemente Zenea*.

1987, Premio de la Crítica Cubana for the best play published in book form for *La verdadera culpa de Juan Clemente Zenea*.

1989, Premio Luis Cernuda for *Manual de las tentaciones*.

1989, Premio de la Crítica Cubana for *Manual de las tentaciones*.

1991, Premio de la Crítica especializada for staging in *Un sueño feliz*, La Habana.

1991, Premio Santiago Pita for the best theatrical text presented at the Festival de Teatro de La Habana for *La verdadera culpa de Juan Clemente Zenea*.

1994, Premio Teatral Tirso de Molina, awarded by the Instituto de Cooperación Iberoamericana de Madrid, for *La noche*.

1999, Premio de la Crítica Cubana for *Tuyo es el reino*.

2000, Premio for Best Foreign Book in France for *Tuyo es el reino*.

2001, Premio Rine Leal for the best text presented at Festival de Pequeño Formato de Miami for the monologue *El enano en la botella*.

2002, Premio Libro del Año de *La Vanguardia* for *Los palacios distantes*.

2003, Premio for best text at Festival del Monólogo de Cienfuegos for *El enano en la botella*.

2012, Ecole Normale Superieure dedicated a symposium to his work.

2013, Homage to his work was held in the University of Sevilla.

ANTONIO

MUÑOZ

MOLINA

(Spain, 1956)

Antonio Muñoz Molina was born in January of 1956 in Úbeda, Jaén, into the bosom of a family dedicated to agriculture and that, during Franco's dictatorship, and not just because of their republican convictions, had to face all kinds of difficulties.

Of his siblings, only Antonio went to university. In Madrid he studied Journalism and later, in Granada, Art History. He lived there until 1994 and all that time he wrote opinion articles and columns in the *Diario Ideal* and the *Diario de Granada*. Many of those texts constituted his first books: *El Robinson urbano*, in 1984 and *Diario del Nautilus*, in 1986.

He started writing his first novel when Franco died. Finishing it, however, took him ten years. In 1986, when *Beatus Ille* was published, critics read it with great enthusiasm; it won the Premio Ícaro and many readers made their own the city of Mágina, the imaginary world that Muñoz Molina created as an evocation of his city of origin Úbeda.

In *Invierno en Lisboa*, he completely lived up to all the hopes that had been hung on this writer who drank equally from Spanish realism and from authors like Onetti, whose collected stories he wrote the prologue for in 1994. The story, which transpires in a dense atmosphere, is faithful to the noir aesthetic and centers on Santiago Biralbo, a jazz pianist, and his encounters with a mysterious art collector. The novel received the prestigious Premio de la Crítica and the Premio Nacional de Narrativa. In 1991, José A. Zorrilla directed the film adaptation, in which Eusebio Poncela and Dizzy Gillespie participated.

His next novel, *Beltenebros*, in whose setting you can breathe in '70s Madrid, recounts the adventures of a Brit who travels to Spain to assassinate a member of the Communist Party. It was also adapted for film, this time by Pilar Miró.

With a more intimate tone, in *El jinete polaco* (which won the Premio Nacional de Narrativa), Muñoz Molina returned to Mágina, to the heart of a pair of lovers who try to make sense of their lives. *Plenilunio* (1997), on the other hand, although it also adopts elements of pop culture, is the story of a serial killer, whose plot is structured according to modern narrative strategies on top of which stand the Francoist past and its consequences.

Expressing his conviction that to know the past is to understand the present, in 2001 Muñoz Molina published *Sefarad* ("Spain" in Hebrew). The novel pretends to be a historical memoir of displacement in twentieth-century Europe, a metaphor that makes reference to the expulsion of the Jews from Spain and Portugal in the sixteenth century. The tale is organized into seventeen stories in which fictional characters overlap with personalities of real renown like Primo Levi, Franz Kafka, and Walter Benjamin. In 2004, the English translation by Margaret Sayers Peden won the PEN/Book-of-the-month Club Award.

Antonio Muñoz Molina was named a member of the Real Academia Española de la Lengua when he was only thirty-nine. Between 2004 and 2006, the year he published *El viento de la Luna*, he was director of the Cervantes Institute in New York, the city where he spends most of his time when he's not in Madrid. Married to the journalist and novelist Elvira Lindo, in 2007 he received an honorary doctorate from Universidad de Jaén. *La noche de los tiempos*, published in 2009, is his most recent novel.

THE ACORN

I think this fragment from *El jinete polaco* is representative of my writing, of the different interests I have been working with throughout my career. In the first place, I wanted to give shape to an oral tradition and this novel is made up of a great number of different stories that I heard when I was a child. I was continuously listening to stories told by my parents, my grandparents, stories about the family, about the civil war, and in my education as a writer, these types of stories were far more important than books because at the time books were very difficult to come by. So when you think of what made you a writer, maybe this oral tradition I became acquainted with so early in my life was a decisive element in my education. The world was full of stories, and that is why there are so many voices in this novel. And the first part of the book is called "The Kingdom of Voices," because it was a world made up of voices, of different voices telling and interweaving stories.

The second fragment is from *Sefarad* and one of the points of this book is the shifting condition of the self. You believe you are someone, you believe you have an identity, a personal fixed identity, and then you might find out, to your own suffering, that your identity has been decided upon by others. That is what happened to many Jews in Europe. Some of them didn't think of themselves as Jews because either they had converted, or they had simply become secular or didn't practice their religious customs. But when the racial laws came along, they were forced to become Jews. So they found that their personal identities meant nothing in the face of this decision by a political power to turn them into something different. And that is what totalitarian societies do, they try to shift your identity into something different. For example in Spain, after the war, there was something called the "anti-España," and it meant that if you were a Republican, or a Socialist or a Communist or whatever, you were not considered Spanish. Like in the case of the Spanish Jews, they were living in what we now call Spain, for 1,000 years and then overnight they were no longer Spaniards. They were not a recognizable minority in the middle of the country, they were not foreigners living among the natives, they were the natives. They spoke the language, they shared traditions, though some of them followed a different religion. But then, from one day to the next, they became foreigners. And all this has to do with something that is very important in the book, which is the second point; your ability to transcend your personal identity in order to identify with others. This has two different meanings, one that is political and the other literary. The only way for you to write a book, or to read a book, is to partially become someone else, to put yourself in someone else's shoes. That's what writing does, I mean writing is not about telling what you are, about explaining your personal self, writing is very often about trying to find out, or to guess, what other people are thinking, what other lives are like. So this is a kind of moral displacement: in order to read or to write, you have to give up your cherished self and to try to somehow become someone else. And this has two different consequences: first, you must be ready to become someone else because you might be forced to become someone else. Or you may choose to become someone else, you may choose to reinvent yourself. In this book, displacement and exile are not always sad, because sometimes people choose to become someone else. And this flies in the face of all these identity politics, where you have to abide by a forced identity. What I defend is the right to reinvent yourself, and that's actually a very American thing. You may choose to stay loyal to your forbears and your traditions, but you must also have the right to choose to become someone else, to betray this origin, to travel abroad and become someone else. And that explains where the title of this section comes from: "You Are." You are very different things, you are not one single thing, and you can be very different things throughout your life. So it's a kind of celebration of this personal diversity. But then it also has to do with politics in a sense. In a democracy, the only way to accomplish a truly democratic system is to put yourself in other people's shoes, to accept that other people are exactly like you. It sounds like common sense or a platitude, but it takes a great deal of effort to accomplish this because people tend to establish this frontier between "us" and "them"; many regimes, political systems, are based upon this difference. "Us" the righteous, and "them" the enemy. So deciding to make this trip to what is other, to recognize in the other the full right to be as they are, it is quite a revolutionary accomplishment, it is a mental revolution.

Many people, when this book came out, asked me, "why are you, who are not a Jew, writing about the Jews?" And I asked them, "why do I have to be a Jew?" The whole point is that you are able to identify yourself with the experiences of others. That's why in this book there are many stories about people in exile, people from Germany, from Latin America, Jews from Spain, the whole gamut of displacement, exile, and change. And in each and every case I made the personal effort to put myself in that situation, to try to learn what it feels like, which is quite different from writing an essay or a history book. In history you don't have to identify with the other, and you don't have to accept the possibility that your destiny might be similar to the other person's because you tend to feel safe. You read a story about the Holocaust, or about how people suffered in the thirties, and this is something that happened to people very far from you, remote from you, things that appear to be completely absent from your life. But the fact is that many people find out that their lives change very quickly and you can easily become the other. Either because you are forced into exile, or because there is suddenly a new border in your country, or because you become sick, or you fall in love and you decide to change your whole life forever. So this empathy is the key to the book, and to this particular section.

In Conversation with the Dead

It changes with time, because suddenly to your regret, or to your shame, you discover someone who you should have read very early on but hadn't. It happened to me last winter: for the first time in my life, I read *Under the Volcano* by Malcolm Lowry. A friend of mine told me "but why are you so sincere about it?" because I wrote about the discovery in the newspaper, and I guess a writer is always supposed to be "rereading," never admitting to reading a novel for the first time, no. The fact is that it was overwhelming and instantly became a big influence on me. So it is always shifting, although of course you have the usual suspects; Cervantes, Borges, Primo Levi, Bellow. Bellow is very important for me. Maybe Roth was more important in the recent past, and I am reconsidering my connection to his work now. Last year I also read for the first time *To the Lighthouse* by Virginia Woolf, and it was so astonishing, I was so surprised by the beauty and originality of this book. The shape of the novel, and the quality of the writing line by line, the staccato rhythm, the way she punctuates things ta ta ta. So rather than offering a list of the writers I cherish, I prefer to stress the fact that I am always learning and on the lookout for new influences.

V. S. Naipaul, for example, is so good. In a country where writing for the newspapers is writing whatever comes to your mind without paying any attention to the accuracy of things, to find someone who writes with this level of precision, this love of being accurate, paying such close attention to the details. Here if you write for a newspaper you are allowed to write garbage, and it shows in the quality of the newspapers. Then you see this man going places and paying such close, careful attention to things and not allowing himself to be misled by his preconceptions, this is someone who is willing to take anything that comes about because very often he is aware that what he is writing goes against the grain, goes against the accepted opinion. Nevertheless he says what he feels he has to say. He is a bit of a monster, but there is also an important lesson that is to be learned from him; this calling, this job you are doing has to be done in the most serious way. There is no alibi for being slack or being half good or not for being as good as you possibly can be.

CODA

How are you influenced by the fact that you live between worlds and languages, in New York and Madrid?

I think one of the main points in my writing is the fact that I have lived not only in different places but in different times. And this experience is very common among people in my generation, and the idea of displacement is becoming even more common. I was born in a rural, backward society in the late '50s in the middle of a dictatorship in an interior, very poor province. It was not only backward, it had been sent to the past because of historical events. When I was younger, I thought that the world I was born into was something that had stayed motionless for centuries. And then I realized that this seemingly unchanged landscape was not a landscape, but the result of terrible political and historical events—the Spanish Civil War. And the war meant that the natural development of the country was arrested for years, something that has to do on the deepest personal level with how I felt about my father. When I was younger, I thought that my father was bound to the agricultural tradition, that he belonged to a kind of anthropological, timeless space. And then I came to realize that my father, when he was a teenager, was as eager as I was to have a new life, a different life, an education, but it was made impossible by the war. So this is the difference: he was not part of an unchanging cultural landscape, he was the result of a major disruption of development. I learned when my father was much older that he had dreamed of becoming an engineer, and it came as quite a surprise to me. Once I found a picture of him when he was six in 1934, and to my astonishment he was at the beach with his parents! This peasant who I had always imagined lived this completely traditional life had gone to the beach with his mother and father in the early 1930s! So I realized that there was a misunderstanding here, things had gone backward because of the war, not because tradition had always existed that way, where the wheat was still harvested with sickles.

Change began to arrive in Spain in the early '60s, but mainly to the coastal regions, Madrid and Barcelona. But I was born in this backward world, I started in this peasant, dictatorial place, and as a young man I had to adjust to living in a democracy, in a fully developed country, and I began to travel abroad. This is something that goes beyond my own personal experience, I share it with many people in my generation who lived through it to a greater or lesser degree. They were born into this peasant society, and they went on to become very different things. So either because they immigrated to Barcelona or to Madrid or France to find a job, or for whatever reasons, we all suffered and experienced this double life. We belonged to two different worlds, in two different times, and we have memories that seem to go far, far back into the distance of time, farther than our own age. Some of the memories that I write about in *El jinete polaco* seem much older than what could be my experience, because my childhood was spent in a remote time, so there was a sort of acceleration of time.

And now I suspect that there is an even newer world coming along, and that I am starting to belong to the past. When I was a teenager, I was obsessed with the idea that something else far more important was happening elsewhere, like Rimbaud's poem, life was going on in some other place. For example, pop music. You are in Úbeda in the late '60s, surrounded by this peasant society, and you turn on the radio and listen to songs in English and you didn't understand a word, but nevertheless you were thrilled by it, you were aware that this meant a huge change, a very important change was taking place somewhere else and you wanted to become a part of this change. That's how I started studying English, I wanted to know what the songs were about. I bought myself a dictionary and started to translate songs word by word.

I was 19 when Franco died, so I came of age at the time of the arrival of democracy in Spain. I have very clear memories of the dictatorship and of having the feeling that I was a foreigner in my own country; as a Republican in the Spanish sense, as a leftist, you were a kind of born foreigner because you were not part of things, you didn't fit in. So you have a very early and very keen sense of not belonging. On top of that, if you belonged to the working class and were studying on scholarship, it was difficult. At the university my feeling was that I didn't belong in the same way as many other students did because they took for granted their right to an education. In my case, I had to get the best possible grades to keep the scholarship. I had an acute feeling of the weakness of my position, a permanent anxiety of my status. So I wasn't allowed to take anything for granted, and it influenced my overview of things because when you don't take things for granted you are far more able to identify with people who are displaced or who suddenly find themselves as foreigners. Spain was so isolated that the first time I went abroad I got a passport for three weeks because I was within the military age, and I might have been called to go into the army at any moment, so they wouldn't grant a passport for a longer period. And you had to get a certificate of good behavior from the police and another from the parish priest! So coming from Spain, everything abroad was so different, so thrilling and at the same time so menacing because it was such a different world. I remember the first time I traveled was to Rome, and it was so amazing to see a huge rally by people on the left, carrying their red flags, and the police sitting by not doing anything. It was so shocking to me.

And now, you can see a shift in the meaning of the word culture. When I was younger, culture was something you acquired, you got yourself a culture, or you cultivated yourself, in the same way you got an education, and it was a part of this inventing yourself. Culture was something that allowed you to set yourself free from your place of birth, from the conditions you were born into. But now culture has become something that you are born into. You say that you belong to the "Catalan or Andalusian or Gay" culture. You belong to it, you have it, and you stick to it. But I belong to the old school . . . I gave a lecture once in New York that was titled "Don Quixote or the Art of Becoming." It came from something that I read in Bellow, in which he says that there are two kinds of people, the "be-ers" and the "becomers." The "be-ers" are all for being something, and you are it 100% and you belong to it. And Bellow said he felt himself to be a "becomer," you are a process, you are not a given, you are not something static. So I try to be a "becomer."

A THOUSAND FORESTS

FROM *EL JINETE POLACO* (THE POLISH HORSEMAN)
[A NOVEL]

The city's lost voices, stubborn witnesses, neglected, nameless, those who spoke up and who kept silent, those who dedicated years to remembrance or to hatred, who chose dereliction and obscurity: death notices posted in the shop windows along Plaza General Orduña and Calle Nueva where bored old men play dominos and converse under the television's racket in the retirement hall, or perch along Cava's wasted gardens taking in the sun, trampling shards of broken bottles and plastic syringes underfoot, snoozing next to the brazier in cafés full of chairs covered in synthetic upholstery, or shuffling along the lugubrious passageways of the asylum, the memory of departed voices, the expressionless faces of the living dead.

Voices, anonymous faces, figures frozen in time, faces of the dead, of executioners, of innocents, of victims: Inspector Florencio Pérez never solved a single crime, never obtained a single confession or dared to publish his poetry under his own name; Lieutenant Chamorro, a graduate of Barcelona's Popular School of Warfare, held captive fourteen years for aiding the military uprising, freed for twenty-two days of liberty and imprisoned once again thanks to a cockamamie scheme hatched the second he was released, to take a squad of shotgun-toting Libertarians to the mountains of Mágina to assassinate El Generalíssimo, who was there hunting deer or attending a spiritual retreat with military chaplains; Manuel García, a sapper for the Assault Guard, convicted of insurrection when he showed up at the Hospital de Santiago following procedure a few unfortunate minutes after the yellow and red flag had been raised over the building; blind Domingo González, a fugitive of Mágina in May of 1937, whose life was spared by one of the men searching for him, who motioned to the other militiamen to go ahead, move on, the loft is clear, instead of running him through with the prongs of his manure-covered pitch fork when he found him hiding in a stack of hay: later as a judge dressed in wig and toga, he coolly signed death sentences showing clemency to no one, not even his ex-friend and countryman, Lieutenant Chamorro: a ruthless judge and retired coronel, the misanthropic horseman returned to Mágina and took up residence in the house where old Justo Solano had lived in the Plaza de San Lorenzo and was blinded one day after being shot twice in the eyes with salt, condemned to spend the rest of his days terrified that the perpetrator would fulfill his threat of coming back in the darkness to murder him; Ramiro Retratista, a photographer and gloomy man in love with a dead woman, voluntary exile to Mágina, late-in-life castaway in Plaza de España, Madrid, where he took portraits of poor newlyweds on their honeymoon, couples from the provinces standing arm in arm and smiling in front of the statues of Don Quixote and Sancho Panza. And Lorencito Quesada, a celebrated reporter and veteran clerk of *El Sistema Métrico*, Mágina's doyen of the press corps, of radio and television, a willing though failed biographer of the eminent men of Mágina and its region, *Singladura*'s correspondent, investigator of police mysteries and the supernatural, of telepathic powers and the visits of messengers from other worlds to the Guadalquivir valley, author of a five-part series titled *The Enigma of the Walled-In Woman* or *The Mystery of the House of Towers*, titles so evocative it took a while to choose between them, an unnecessary decision anyway since following weeks of feverish work and insomnia, the director of *Singladura* rejected the thirty pages and they never saw publication. It was Lorencito Quesada who discovered the former Inspector and later Deputy Superintendent Florencio Pérez's memoirs, and wanted to reveal them to the world, or to Mágina, and whose enthusiasm knew neither discouragement nor triumph since he struggled unsuccessfully to raise the money and sponsorship to get them published. Likely, he remained the only person in the whole city who was aware of or suspected the retired policeman's literary vocation, this man who had spent his whole life composing verses under a pseudonym, entering nearly all the provincial contests to receive some laurel every now and again, which he never collected in person due to his lack of nerve or excessive embarrassment, or a biting fear of ridicule that grew worse as the years went by, so that on his deathbed he had been tempted to burn his body of work, all of it so meticulously typewritten on the backsides of official forms, following what Virgil did or had ordered someone else to do for him. He had abstained from writing prose until he retired since he considered it a lesser genre, as he later confessed to Lorencito Quesada, but when left without much to keep him busy, without the daily distractions of work, he was overcome by a mounting sense of indolence and melancholy, and so embarked on the narration of his memoirs which may not have sparked the desire to live, per se, but at least it intensified a superstitious fear of death, since what he now truly dreaded was the idea of passing before he was able to finish writing his life story. A widower, he lived with his daughter and her husband, a local video club magnate who scorned him openly, and he had two sons, one was an inspector in Madrid, and the other, the youngest of the three, had been preparing for the seminary as a boy when he inexplicably lost his way; he became the lead singer of a rock band and let his hair grow to his shoulders. When it came time for the Deputy Superintendent to retire, he waited in vain for an emotional homage on the part of his former subordinates, or at least the gift of a commemorative plaque. Lorencito Quesada, always so attentive to detail, dedicated an article to him in *Singladura*, for which he wrote a letter of lachrymose gratitude. He tucked the clipping away in a blue notebook, and shut himself away in the closet-like space to which he was consigned by daughter and son-in-law, with a secondhand typewriter and a package of unused ID requests he had pinched from the police station, not without feeling a slight pang of shame. He began writing in earnest, and realized with astonishment and despair that not much had actually happened in his life. He thought he would be faced with a daunting task, but it soon proved rather trivial, and by the end of the first year, he had narrated the entire seventy years of his life, so the morning came when after sitting at his typewriter for twenty minutes, his memoir in writing caught up with the exact same moment he was living, so after a brief pause, pensive, he went back over his notes of the past few days, placed another sheet of paper in the carriage and calmly began narrating his memoirs of the following day, feeling a bit peculiar at first, and then like a fraud, as if he were cheating a little at a game of solitaire, but he continued writing ever more self-assuredly and even contentedly, telling the story of his youngest son's return to the fold, the black sheep of the family and the bane of his old age, who came home repentant, with short hair, dressed in a tie and begging forgiveness after having lived several years in a commune in Ibiza, and then he described a trip to Madrid where he went back to the same boardinghouse he used to stay in before the war, and how he rowed a boat in Retiro Park and ate grilled shrimp in the Taberna del Abuelo, and offered thanks to the Christ of Medinaceli for the return of his prodigal son: by the time he died, in early June, his memoir had already begun telling the story of the first days of Christmas next, when Mágina's Cultural and Recreational Society was preparing an homage at the Ideal Cinema to celebrate his golden anniversary, wed as he was to both literature and police work.

The farther the manuscript ventured into the future and the fib, the more luxurious the details became, in contrast to the true events, which were told hastily and with an air of disenchanted brusqueness: the discovery of the incorruptible woman took up a mere half a page and offered no shocking exposés, perhaps because the inspector had forgotten the particulars, or as Lorencito literarily suspected, there must be powerful, covert interests that had sworn him to secrecy and that were still in effect even forty years after the fact. Even then, in the early years of his career, the Inspector wore the same self-absorbed expression of sadness and painstaking arrogance that can be seen in the photos taken by Ramiro Retratista, and that never changed even through his old age. "Look at him," Nadia says, remembering him almost fondly, though it's been 18 years since she saw him for the first and only time, an old, crestfallen policeman who refused to accept the ignominy of retirement. She takes the photograph out and shows it to Manuel, who stands behind her in silence, embracing her softly, his two hands beginning to probe under her blouse. "He never changed," Nadia remarks, his face as coarse as cardboard and his hairline that plunged to the middle of his forehead, mane slicked back with pomade though a few stiff, rebellious tufts stuck out over a double arch of black eyebrows and features that were soft and square with a plump, droopy lower lip from which hung a perpetual, unlit hand-rolled cigarette. His jawline was shadowed though he shaved twice a day; he had an impossible face, she thought painfully, almost as impossible as his name, Florencio Pérez Tallante, a name as disastrous for a policeman as for a poet, a ruined, tombstone of a name. Ramiro Retratista photographed him in the same spot where Nadia had seen him years later, nearly the same pose, sitting behind a desk under a crucifix, a picture of Jesus Our Father and a portrait of Franco, a telephone on his right, inkstand on his left, hand on his chin like the effigy of a thinking man. Sitting bored in his office near the clock tower on Plaza General Orduña, he had just begun tapping out syllables with his fingers, when a guard burst through the door to report that a seemingly cracked woman had reported the appearance of an unidentified cadaver, surely a prisoner of the reds who had been buried alive after being persecuted in the vile basement of some clandestine *cheka*. Inspector Florencio Pérez was a believer in proactive measures, so as a preliminary precaution, he ordered the immediate arrest of the incriminating woman, without having seen her or having heard what she had to say. But as the guard was leaving to carry out his orders, which the inspector considered had been delivered in an admirably curt and decisive way, the door to the office burst open and in came a housekeeper, raising her right arm in a cantankerous *viva-España*, shaking the keys that hung from a ring at her hip as raucously as a prison chain. "I was going to alert the priest in San Lorenzo," she said excitedly, not allowing the inspector the slightest opening to drill her with a tirade of indignation, "but then I remembered there isn't one, so I said to myself, Gabriela, bring it to the pound, they have more authority."

The fact that in Mágina they called the police station the dog pound sunk Inspector Florencio Pérez into a state of near mortification: that a scruffy woman wearing a threadbare cloak over her shoulders, a ring of keys and stinking rubber boots would sneak into his very own office at this peaceful hour of the morning, which he usually consecrated to the sweetness of not doing a single thing while counting out his iambic pentameters, that she should raise her voice at him, and lack the proper fear for his authority, making use of the word "dog pound," carried him straight to the brink of cardiac arrest. He pounded his fist on the desk half-heartedly, the only virtue of which was to flip over the ashtray and spill its contents over the pages in the dossiers—where the inspector often hid drafts of poems—and didn't contribute in any way to elevating the opinion he had of himself. He wasn't made for this job, he lacked the character for it, he often confessed to his childhood friend, Lieutenant Chamorro, whom it was his painful duty to detain from time to time. "Ma'am," he said, rising, brushing away the ashes that had soiled his pants and lapels, much like don Antonio Machado, "get a hold of yourself or I'll lock you up for contempt and throw the key into a well." "That's precisely what they did to her," the housekeeper said, whose fetid breath stank of rubber and sewer, like her boots, "they shut her away in a dungeon and didn't have to throw away the key since they mortared the door shut so she'd never get out again." "Come on, that's not true," the guard murmured humanitarianly, but not so quietly that the inspector couldn't hear him: "You'll speak when you're spoken to, Murciano," he said severely, "go on outside and wait for my orders." The guard had a peasant's face and lacked the deportment that goes with a uniform, which was so big for him that when he stood at attention the gray three-quarter jacket hung pitifully over his meager body like a bathrobe. "So you don't want me to apprehend this woman as a detainee?" "You're not to apprehend anything, Murciano," the inspector said, irritated that his subordinate was appropriating his cherished formulas of official lingo, "go on, you're getting on my nerves. I'll let you know what to do when I've proceeded with the interrogation." "So you're not going to lock me in the dog pound?" The housekeeper moved closer to the inspector again, her hands pressed together as if in prayer, as if she were about to fall to her knees: "Like I said myself, you have the face of a good man, just like a little boy." "Madam!" The inspector stood up, realizing yet again that he wasn't nearly as tall as he imagined when in the throes of these fleeting moments of euphoria, and the second wallop of his fist sent a sharp pain through his hand when it came down on the metal edge of a paperweight that represented the basilica of Montserrat. He weighed it mechanically, considering with trepidation how practically any object could be used as a murder weapon. "Sit down," he returned the paperweight to the desk, "be quiet and don't say another word until I ask you to, and do me the favor of showing me the respect I'm due."

But it was no use, he thought, nobody ever respected him, not delinquents, not his subordinates, no one, not even his children, who had handed his memoirs over to Lorencito Quesada when he died without even copping a little peek, like musty old paper handed over to the rag picker. To calm his nerves, the inspector rolled a clumsy cigarette while peering out the balcony window, running his tongue along the glued edge of the rice paper, contemplating General Orduña's statue, to whom this very morning he'd begun dedicating a sonnet. *The immortal bronze of your heroic deeds,*" he murmured wincingly, but didn't give up, *"The bronze of time immortal, hero's gains.*" The fingers of his left hand drummed the glass as he counted out the syllables, completely absorbed, so anxious over the rhyme's difficulty that it took him a while to realize that the housekeeper was standing behind him, still running at the mouth without being asked, without a hint of respect for his authority:

". . . a brunette, yes siree, but with big blue eyes, looked as if she were frightened, like someone who just froze up, can't see or recognize anything, her hair's parted down the middle, like in the olden days, with bows and curls, a black dress and low neckline, black or dark blue, or purple, it's dark in the niche so I couldn't see too well, I didn't want to open the space any wider or touch anything till it's secured, she's wearing a medal around her neck, I did notice that, I think it's Jesus Our Father . . ."

"Glorious thunder riding through the Spains," the inspector decided, without seeing or hearing the housekeeper, *"eternal fire of courage heal our pains."* "She's more or less like you, just a little thing, though she's well-built, but like I said, I couldn't see her too well, and she's like sitting on a chair, I didn't even want to peek inside, I was so afraid of ruining something, shouldn't touch a dead person until the coroner arrives, I know that much, of course she's not laid out, doesn't even seem dead, how could she be, her skin is as soft as a peach, although pale, like wax, yeah, that's it, maybe because these ladies, from what I heard, used to drink vinegar . . ." *"Sing his song of valor, sacred quatrains!"* the inspector nearly squealed with elation, shuffling back to his desk to jot the words down in the margin of an official letter, not wanting to forget such a rotund pentameter, acting as though in fact he were taking down the details of the housekeeper's declaration. An hour later, faced with the unlikelihood of returning to the silent perusal of his absurd words rhyming with "ains," seeing as though he couldn't persuade the housekeeper to keep even a loosely chronological order to her narrative, Inspector Florencio Pérez briskly rang several bells, held two quick telephone conversations and hung the receiver up with just the right amount of gravitas, before he put on his raincoat and hat and ordered one of the cars in the station's flotilla to take him as quickly as possible to the site where the incident had transpired, according to what was later written in his report, the composition of which cost him more sleepless nights than the first stanza of the sonnet to General Orduña, to which he added a verse in the basement of the House of Towers that ended with *"spidery curtains,"* thanks to the many webs he had to brush from his face and hands with infinite repugnance while proceeding with the detailed ocular inspection of what his report called the scene of the crime, not because he was sure one had actually been committed, but to scrupulously avoid repeating *"the site where the incident had transpired"* after only four lines.

In his memoirs, Inspector Pérez recorded the names of the witnesses who had accompanied him to the basement where the incorruptible woman had appeared: the doctor, don Mercurio and his coachman Julián, the forensic pathologist Galindo, Medinilla the court clerk, who years later went on to direct an opulent paralegal agency and became the labor union's parliamentary representative, the guard Murciano, the pig-headed housekeeper, and last but not least Ramiro Retratista, the photographer, and his assistant Matías, struck deaf and dumb after spending a whole day buried under the rubble of a house that had collapsed during shell fire. To the Inspector's mortification, the group unanimously acknowledged don Mercurio's authority with a nod of their heads as soon as he arrived, and whom nobody had called on by the way, and stopped paying attention to the Inspector, as if he didn't even exist, as if he weren't the one who held the highest rank at that moment in time in the House of Towers. "It's a remarkable case of mummification," the forensic pathologist said after the housekeeper closed the doors to the street and the neighbors' voices mingled with the confusion of a flock of pigeons. "I don't think it's more remarkable than me," said don Mercurio, standing next to the Inspector but acting as if he hadn't seen him, distractedly admiring the marble columns and unstable arches of the courtyard: "You must understand that at my age one becomes very familiar with mummies." "According to the vestments in which she's attired, I would say she's been isolated behind the wall for some sixty or seventy years." When desperate, Inspector Florencio Pérez always fell back on using a dab of the scientific to restore his faltering clout. "Sixty years?" the housekeeper shouted as if scolding a blasphemy, with a threatening shake of her keys. "Sixty centuries is more like it, when the house was first built. She was probably kidnapped and held by the Moors . . ." "Don't say such ridiculous things, madam," Medinilla, the court clerk and informer for the secret police said, brandishing his open folder and pen before her, pretending to take notes, "I'm recording everything right here in my notebook, and then it sticks."

They dodged broken statues as they walked, and mounds of rubble overgrown with nettles and hedge mustard, until they arrived at a vaulted hollow beneath a marble stairway, where their voices and footsteps took on the resonance of a crypt. "Be careful on the stairs," the housekeeper said, "they're treacherous." The Inspector descended first, carrying a powerful lantern with chrome grooves, and nobody spoke a word, not even the housekeeper, as they continued through cellars and passageways that led to other identical cellars, full of large pieces of furniture like catafalques and the rotted carcasses of baroque carriages. The housekeeper crossed herself with a pious scribble when the lantern finally lit up the niche that had been opened by a mason, and everyone except don Mercurio kept their distance, watching as the circle of light made the shadows creep along the wall, in the middle of which, like a wax figure set into a niche, or an Egyptian statue majestically devoted to an unknown deity, hands draped across her lap, dressed in the fashion of the Second Empire, the nape of her neck lightly resting against a high-backed chair, the incorruptible woman stared out into the void with her blue eyes sparkling like glass in the lantern light. There was nothing frightening about her, she seemed naturally poised, as if instead of being holed up behind a wall for seventy years, she had just settled into her chamber room to gracefully receive her closest friends, who are waiting respectfully to be called upon to approach, one at a time.

Like a surgeon preparing for a difficult operation, don Mercurio requested his glasses, his case, and the light, without even turning around. Julián stood beside him attentively, instantly obeying every gesture of his hands, leaning forward to get a closer look at the woman while obliging the others to keep their distance from don Mercurio. Julián was now holding the lantern that Inspector Florencio Pérez had handed over in such a docile way that even he considered it privately unforgiveable, and the others were engulfed by the darkness for more than a minute before the housekeeper could light her own gas lamp, the sole illuminated figure of the dead woman, glowing and whitish, with her dusty hair shining about her face like a swathe of black gauze, while the fainthearted shadows whose breathing could be heard in the darkness brushed one against the other unnoticed, and the tiny, hunched silhouette of don Mercurio moved slowly before the floodlit niche, drawing quick gestures of liturgy and conjuring with outstretched fingers, grazing the mummy's face without touching it, until a finger got tangled in one of the ringlets at her temple and raised a tenuous cloud of dust that made both the doctor and his assistant cough.

"Observe, Julián," don Mercurio said, "this young woman didn't resist enclosure. Could she have been drugged before they built the wall, and when she finally came to, died so immediately that she didn't even have time to panic? Examine the phalanges of her fingers—don Mercurio removed his pince-nez and held a tiny though very strong magnifying glass up to the yellow basket of his left eye—anyone who has been buried alive displays certain standard signs when exhumed. Broken nails, broken phalanges, and extremities bent into unnatural positions. Eyes wide open, gaping jaws that have been dislocated from their screams of terror. But not in the case of this woman or this girl, no. Observe her position: complete tranquility. The singular atmospheric conditions of the crypt worked a feat of wonder and a miracle visited this poor woman. It's infrequent, but not exceptional, as archeologists and ecclesiastical authorities well know. What do you think, Julián?" Don Mercurio's wisdom at times produced such a shock of felicity in the coachman that it verged on a weepy ephiphany: "What else can I think but that you're an eminence, don Mercurio." "Don't grovel, Julián, I already have a foot on the edge of the great mystery and the vanities of this world no longer move me. Proof, Julián, 'facts' as the English say." "Careful, don Mercurio," Julián said looking sideways at the others, "there are those among us who are party to the Axis powers." Don Mercurio brought the lens closer to the dead woman's pupil, like an ophthalmologist doing an eye exam. "I've been an Allied-o-phile for a quarter century, Julián. You wouldn't want me to become party to the Kaiser now, but a step away from the grave?" "There is no Kaiser anymore, don Mercurio," said the clerk, who had moved in closer, following the informant's cautionary instinct, "now it's the Führer who rules in Germany."

"Now there's a difference for you," the doctor said, not bothering to turn around. He called for Julián to bring the lantern a little closer, he had brushed the mummy's cheek with his right index finger and was rubbing the pad slowly and delicately against his thumb to register the exact texture of the dust, subtle as a butterfly's wings. It was like grazing the marble of a statue or the surface of a canvas he was afraid of damaging with the touch of his finger, or the closeness of his breath. He cleaned the medal shining in the dead woman's décolletage with the edge of his handkerchief and blew softly on the tiny glass that protected the sepia tinted image of Christ wearing a crown of thorns. He then took a few steps backward, eyes fixed on the woman the whole time, and handed the magnifying glass back to Julián, who scrupulously returned it to its spot in the case, and after rubbing his eyes he adjusted his pince-nez back onto his hooked nose, and suddenly appeared much older and frailer than a moment earlier, as if a sudden fatigue accentuated the hunch on his back or threatened to make him swoon. Julián, who was a good judge of his moods and the alarming fluctuations of his health, handed the lamp to the Inspector and set the case down on the ground, discreetly edging closer to him, as he had done so many times before, to support this body as light as a rag doll's to avoid its collapse, afraid that if he let don Mercurio slip to the ground he just might fall apart completely. But the doctor groped about discreetly in search of his coachman's arm, and locked his right hand around it with the strength of pure determination, chin raised high not a second later, as if squeezing that arm had imbued him with the vigor of its pulse. He put on his hat and confronted the inquisitive, somewhat frightened stares of the others with the same mocking gallantry as ever.

"It is my opinion," he said, "with due reserve for what my venerable colleague here has to say, who is, after all, responsible for drawing up the official dictum of the scene, that it would be wise not to move the body. As you speculated with such relevance, my dear Inspector, this young woman has been behind these walls some seventy years. I know as much because, disgracefully, I still remember how the women of good families dressed when I was young. Who can say she won't disintegrate into dust if we try to move her, no matter how carefully it's done? I imagine you're aware, Inspector, of the late Egyptologist Mr. Carter's work, whom I had the honor of meeting many years ago in Madrid. Mummies perfectly conserved for over four millennia can be irreparably damaged because of too much light, a brusque change in temperature or even a slight humidity in the air."

Inspector Florencio Pérez would have liked to say something, but a feeling of gratitude toward don Mercurio for his attention and toward Howard Carter, whose work he ignored, but whose death suddenly seemed an irreparable tragedy, choked him up so much he was afraid that the knot in his throat would make his voice sound flutey. "I saw a film about this," he heard Medinilla the clerk say at his side. "*The Curse of the Mummy*. But it was Boris Karloff." "I suggest, then," don Mercurio said without as much as a glance in the clerk's direction, "that we call a photographer, seal off the cellar, and seek the advice of experts for the good of science, since it can no longer be done for the good of this young woman, and I figure she no longer cares that we've interrupted her eternal rest." "Amen," the housekeeper said reverently. The Inspector, who had been chiseling out a brand new pentameter ("*pale her face from beyond the grave*"), released from humiliation thanks to don Mercurio's polite consideration, decided it was time he took the initiative, since it was, in fact, his duty. "Murciano," he said in a cordial yet firm tone, "do me the favor of fetching Ramiro. And tell him not to forget the magnesium." "Yes sir." Murciano saluted. "Should I tell the Macanca to beat it?" "And not to come back," the housekeeper added quickly. "If you're referring to the morgue's hearse," the Inspector appreciated the opportunity to demonstrate to don Mercurio his command of the language, "you can tell the driver that we no longer require his services at the present time." "You said it. The cemetery is for the dead, this is a Christian house." The housekeeper was talking so close to the Inspector's face that she sprayed him copiously with her saliva. "As for you, madam," euphoric, calm, almost drunk with authority and self-confidence, the Inspector wiped his chin with his hankie and looked straight into the housekeeper's eyes, "you will do me the favor of leaving me alone with these gentlemen." "Confidential," the clerk said, in a slightly operatic air of braggadocio, "*top secret.*"

Julián accompanied the housekeeper and Muricano out, and came back with the lamp. The light first fell by surprise on don Mercurio's face, who again seemed to have aged considerably over these few hours, and he began to suspect that the doctor knew something he was hiding from the others, there was a heaviness he had never discerned in him before, a sort of abdication of his steely will and private abandonment to the disappointment of death. "He knows who she is and won't tell anyone, he knew her when she was alive and they were both young." But he was afraid to consider such a thing, it forced him to grasp how inconceivably old don Mercurio was and the depths of experience and horror he must keep concealed in his memory after three quarters of a century living so close to pain, misery and agony on a daily basis, having witnessed so many wars and attended to the birth and then the disgrace and death of so many men and women who no longer exist, violet faces breaking into lament in a deluge of blood and guts spilling from screaming women with their knees apart, unmoving faces, recently purged by death on a pillow still smelling of sweat and fear and useless medicines. For don Mercurio, he thought, the living and the dead must be like corresponding shadows, simulations of youth and beauty and vigor, gangrened in deafness by decay and under perpetual threat by the knife-stroke of affliction: he himself, Julián, and the forensic pathologist and the Inspector and the court clerk, were undoubtedly at a greater distance from don Mercurio than that woman who died seventy years ago, and the present moment they all breathed must have seemed like an illusion to him or a theater of shadows like those projected by the lantern and gas lamp, a future so far removed from his youth that even if he wanted to, he could never grant it the genuine texture of reality.

That's how the official police photographer, Ramiro Retratista, saw them when he arrived: five motionless shadows beside a niche that was lit by a gas lamp on the floor, less real and persistent in his imagination than the face and stare of that woman whose posthumous photograph he showed Commander Galaz over thirty years later as proof that he hadn't made up the story of her discovery. They called for me, he said, as they always did when a cadaver showed up, since he took photographs of the living as well as the dead, so he had packed his camera in the saddle of his German motorcycle, used sign language with his deaf and dumb assistant to order him into the sidecar with the tripod in his arms, and took off in his aviator glasses in the direction of the House of Towers, and when they finally guided him into the cellar and he asked expeditiously where the dead person was, he heard the unpleasant voice of Medinilla the clerk say: "It's not a dead person. It's a cadaver in a state of mummification."

But it can't be a mummy, Ramiro Retratista thought when he looked at her face close up, as his assistant unfolded the tripod and set up the magnesium bulbs, she was a very young woman, though a little old-fashioned, look for yourself, he told Commander Galaz, holding up the photograph with hands that already trembled from age, she was very calm, very beautiful, with wide cheekbones and open eyes, her hair was held back in chignons and sausage curls, her cheeks almost seemed blushed, very softly, like in a hand-painted portrait, and her dead eyes looked at me like no living woman's ever had, because their eyes never saw him, women never actually look at the portrait-ist, he explained, they're always thinking about the gentleman the picture will be sent to with an elegant dedication, tender or passionate, it depends. He looked closer at her face, and thought she looked robust and shapely, two adjectives he had once read in a novel, and then lowered his eyes shyly and respectfully to her neck, which seemed made out of wax, and his eyes saw the medal with the pious image and for a split second he thought he witnessed some essential cataleptic breath. He, Ramiro, alone dared to hold the medal in his fingers, hoping to go unnoticed as he did, and turned it over to find that instead of a religious stamp on the other side, there was the photo of a very young man, with a moustache and goatee, like Gustavo Adolfo Bécquer, he told Commander Galaz. He also saw the edge of what looked like a piece of paper that had been folded many times, lodged where her breasts pressed against her décolletage. He moved back a little, staring into those eyes that were like pale glass frosted with dust, riveted steadfastly on him, and corrected the placement of the flashbulbs, moving his own hands almost as quickly as his assistant moved his, with whom he held silent though lavish diatribes, and hid his head beneath the camera's black felt curtain, making it look like don Mercurio's hump, and just as he was about to press the ancient pear-shaped trigger, seeing the image of the dead woman turned upside down, he felt as though he'd been rendered weightless and turned on end too, and suddenly stricken with grief, he wished the magnesium flash might somehow spark her pupils with its brightness and bring her to life, at least for the tenths of a second it lasted before going out.

Translated by Valerie Miles

•

FROM *SEPHARAD*
[A NOVEL]

You are not an isolated person and do not have an isolated story, and neither your face nor your profession nor the other circumstances of your past or present life are cast in stone. The past shifts and reforms, and mirrors are unpredictable. Every morning you wake up thinking you are the same person you were the night before, recognizing an identical face in the mirror, but sometimes in your sleep you've been disoriented by cruel shards of sadness or ancient passions that cast a muddy, somber light on the dawn, and the face is different, changed by time, like a seashell ground by the sand and the pounding and salt of the sea. Even as you lie perfectly motionless, you are shifting, and the chemistry that constitutes your imagination and consciousness is altered infinitesimally every moment. Whole scenes and perspectives from the distant past fan out, open and close like the straight lines of olive groves or plowed furrows seen from the window of a racing train. For a few seconds, a taste or a smell or some music on the radio or the sound of a name turn you into the person you were thirty or forty years ago. You are a frightened child on his first day of school, or a round-faced young man with shy eyes and the shadow of a mustache on his upper lip, and when you look in the mirror you are a man over forty whose black hair is beginning to be shot with gray, whose face holds no traces of your boyhood, though a sort of unfading youth accompanies you as an adult, through work and marriage, your obligations and secret dreams and responsibility for your children. You are every one of the different people you have been, the ones you imagined you would be, the ones you never were, and the ones you hoped to become and now are thankful you didn't.

And your room is different, the city or the countryside you see from the window, the house you live in, the street where you walk, all of it growing more distant, disappearing as quickly as it's seen through the glass, there one moment, gone forever. Cities where it seemed you would live forever but left, never to return, cities where you spent a few days only to preserve them in memory like a clutter of old postcards in bitter colors. Or cities that are little more than their beautiful names, divested of substance by the passing of time: Tangiers, Copenhagen, Hamburg, Washington DC, Baltimore, Göttingen, Montevideo. You are who you were when you walked through them, sinking into the anonymity they offered you.

Perhaps what changes least, through so many places and times, is the room you take refuge in, the room that according to Pascal one should never leave if one is to avoid disaster. "Being alone in a room is perhaps a necessary condition of life," Franz Kafka wrote Milena. There is a computer in it instead of a typewriter, but my room today is much like any of the many rooms I've lived in throughout my life, my lives, like the first one I had when I was sixteen, with a wood table and a balcony that overlooked the valley of the Guadalquivir and the blue horizon of the Mágina Sierra. I would lock myself in to be alone with my typewriter, my records, my notebooks, my books, feeling both isolated and protected. The balcony allowed me to look out upon the vastness of the world, the world I wanted to run to as soon as I could, because my refuge, like almost all refuges, was also a prison, and the only window I wanted to look through was the one on the night train that would carry me far away.

Laura García Lorca, who was born in New York and spoke a careful and proper Spanish that sometimes had a trace of English, showed me her Uncle Federico's room in Granada, in Huerta de San Vicente, the last he had, the room he would leave one July day in 1936, looking for a refuge he wouldn't find. All human miseries derive from not being able to sit quietly in a room alone. I saw Lorca's room, and I wanted to live sometime in a room like that. The white walls, the floor of large flat stones like the ones in my boyhood home, the wood table, the austere but comfortable bed of white-painted iron, the large balcony open to the Vega, to the sweep of groves dotted with white houses, to the bluish or mauve silhouette of the sierra with its snowy peaks tinted rose in the sunset. I remember van Gogh's room in Arles, just as sheltering and austere, but with its beautiful geometry already twisted by anguish, the room that opened onto a landscape as meridional as the Vega of Granada and that contained only the bare necessities of life, yet it, too, failed to save the man who took refuge there from horror.

I wonder what the room in Amsterdam was like where Baruch Spinoza, a descendant of Jews expelled from Spain and later Portugal, he himself expelled from the Jewish community, edited his lucid philosophical treatises and polished the lenses from which he earned a livelihood. I imagine it with a window that lets in a clear gray light like that in the paintings of Vermeer, whose rooms warmly protect their self-absorbed inhabitants from inclement weather but always contain reminders of the expanse of the outside world: a map of the Indies or Asia, a letter from a distant spot, pearls found in the Indian Ocean. One Vermeer woman reads a letter, another one gazes seriously and absently at the light falling through the window, and perhaps she is waiting for a letter. Closed in his room, perhaps the only place he is not stateless, Spinoza shapes the curve of a lens that will allow him to see things so small they cannot be seen by the naked eye. With no aid other than his intelligence he wants to encompass the order and substance of the universe, the laws of nature and human morality, the rigorous mystery of a God that is not that of his elders, who have disavowed that is not that of his elders, who have disavowed him and excommunicated him from the congregation, but neither is it the God of the Christians, who might well burn him at the stake if he lived in a country less tolerant than Holland. In a letter to Milena, Kafka forgets for a moment who he's addressing and writes to himself: *You are, after all, completely Jewish, and you know what fear is.*

Then Primo Levi in his bourgeois apartment in Turin comes to mind, the house where he was born and died, throwing himself, or accidentally falling, into the stairwell. He lived there all his life except for the two years between 1943 and 1945. Before September of 1943, when he was arrested by the Fascist militia, Levi had left his safe room in Turin to join the Resistance, carrying with him a small pistol he scarcely knew how to use and in fact never fired. He had been a good student, earning a degree in chemistry with excellent grades, profiting from what he learned in the laboratories and lecture halls, as well as from literature, which for him always had the obligation to be as clear and precise as science. A young man, slim, studious, with glasses, educated in a renowned bourgeois family in a cultured city, hardworking, austere, accustomed from childhood to a serene life, in harmony with the world, without the least shadow of the difference that would separate him from others, since in Italy, and even more in Turin, a Jew, in the eyes of society and his own, was a citizen like any other, especially if he came from a secular family that didn't speak Hebrew or follow religious practices. His ancestors had emigrated from Spain in 1492. He left the room in which he had been born, and as he walked out the door he was probably struck by the thought that he might not come back, and when he did come back two years later, thin as a ghost, having survived hell, he must have felt that in truth he was dead, a ghost returning to an untouched house, the same door, his room in which nothing had changed during his absence, in which there would have been no change had he died, had he not been spared the cadavers' mudpit in the concentration camp.

"What is the minimal portion of country, what dose of roots or hearth that a human being requires?" Jean Améry asked himself, remembering his flight from Austria in 1938, perhaps the night of March 15, on the express train that left Vienna at 11:15 for Prague, his troubled, clandestine journey across European borders toward the provisional refuge of Antwerp, where he knew the endless insecurity of exiled Jews, the native's hostility toward foreigners, humiliation from the police and officials who examine papers and certify or deny permits and make you come back the next day and the next and who look at the refugee as someone suspected of a crime. The worst is to be stripped of the nationality you thought was yours inalienably. You need at least a house in which you can feel safe, Améry says, a room that you can't be dragged from in the middle of the night, that you don't have to run from as fast as you can when you hear police whistles and footsteps on the stairs.

You have always lived in the same house and the same room and walked the same streets to your office, where you work from eight to three Monday through Friday, yet you are also constantly running and can't find asylum anywhere. You cross borders at night along smugglers' routes, travel with false papers on a train, and stay awake while the other passengers snore at your side. You fear that the footsteps coming down the corridor toward you are those of a policeman. At the border, uniformed men who study your papers may motion you to one side, and then the other travelers, who have their passports in order and are not afraid, look at you with relief, because the misfortune that has befallen you has left them unscathed, and they begin to see in your face signs of guilt, of crime, a mark that cannot be seen and yet cannot be erased, an indelible stain that is not in your appearance but is in your blood, the blood of a Jew or of a sick man who knows he will be driven out of his condition if discovered. Confined in a sanatorium for tuberculosis, Kafka remembers the anti-Semitic remarks another patient made at the dining table, and writes a letter sharpened by insomnia and fever: *The insecure situation of the Jews explains perfectly why they believe that they are permitted to possess only what they can cling to with their hands or teeth, and that only such possession gives them the right to live.*

In the room of a hotel in Port-Bou, Walter Benjamin took his own life because there was no road left to take as he fled from the Germans. Two identities were offered to Jean Améry when he was stopped by the Gestapo, when he was interrogated and then tortured by the SS: enemy or victim. He could be a German, an army deserter, in which case he would be tried and shot as a traitor, or he could be a Jew, in which case he would be sent to a death camp. He was arrested in May 1943, in Brussels, where under the name of Hans Mayer he and his small group of German-speaking resisters printed leaflets and distributed them at night near the barracks of the Wehrmacht, risking their lives on the futile hope that the conscience of some German soldier would be moved by reading them. Primo Levi armed himself only a

few months later with the small pistol he didn't know how to use, no more a
threat to the Third Reich than Améry's leaflets. Neither man was a practicing
Jew; Levi thought of himself as Italian, Améry as nothing but Austrian. But
when arrested, both declared themselves Jews and joined the ranks of victims
condemned not by their acts or their words, not for distributing pamphlets or
plunging into the forest without warm clothes or boots and with no weapon
but a ridiculous little pistol, but for the simple fact of having been born.

You are the person who after the morning of September 19, 1941, must
go outside wearing a Star of David on your chest, visibly displayed, printed
in black on a yellow rectangle, like the Jews in medieval cities, but now with
all dins of regulations regarding size and placement, explained in detail in
the decree, which also lists the punishments awaiting the person who does
not wear the star when he goes out or tries to obscure it by covering it, for
example, with a briefcase or shopping bag or even with an arm holding an
umbrella. In the Warsaw Ghetto, the star was blue, the armband white.

You are anyone and no one, the person you invent or remember and the person others invent or remember, those who knew you in the past, in another
city and another life, and retain a frozen image of what you were then, like
a forgotten photograph that surprises and repels when you see it years later.
You are the person who imagined futures that now seem puerile, the person
so much in love with women you can't remember now, and the person you
sometimes were whom no one else knew. You are what others, right now,
somewhere, are saying about you, and what someone who never met you is
telling of what he has been told. You change your room, your city, your life,
but shadows and doubles of you continue to inhabit the places you left behind.
As a boy you ran along the street imagining you were galloping your pony,
and you were both the rider spurring on your mount with film-cowboy yells
and the galloping horse, and also the boy who saw that horse and rider in
a movie, and the one who the next day excitedly told about the movie to
friends who didn't see it, and you are the boy who with shining eyes listens
to another tell stories, the boy who asks for just one more story so his mother
won't leave and turn out the light, the mother who finishes telling the story
to her son and sees in his eyes all the nervous enthusiasm of imagination, the
desire to hear more, to prevent the loving voice from falling silent or the room
from turning dark, when it will be invaded by dark fears.

You change your life, room, face, city, love, but something persists that has been inside you for as long as you can remember, before you learned to reason, it is the marrow of what you are, of what has never been extinguished, like a live coal hidden beneath the ashes of last night's fire. You are uprootedness and foreignness, not being completely in any one place, not sharing the certainty of belonging that seems so natural and easy in others, taking it for granted like the firm ground beneath their feet. You are the guest who may not have been invited, the tenant who may be ejected, the little fat kid among the bullies in the schoolyard, the one flat-footed soldier in the garrison, the effeminate man among the macho, the model student who is dying inside of loneliness and embarrassment, the husband who looks at women out of the corner of his eye as he strolls arm in arm with his wife on a Sunday afternoon in his provincial city, the temporary employee who never is given a contract, the black Moroccan who leaps from a smuggler's boat onto a beach in Cádiz and moves inland by night, soaked to the bone, freezing, dodging the spotlights of the Guardia Civil. You are the Spanish Republican who crosses the French border in February 1939 and is treated like a dog or someone with the plague and sent to a camp on a rugged seacoast, imprisoned in a sinister geometry of barracks and barbed wire, the natural geometry and geography of Europe during those years—from the infamous beaches of Argelès-sur-Mer, where Spanish Republicans are herded like cattle, to the farthest reaches of Siberia, from which Margarete Buber-Neumann returned only to be sent not to freedom but to the German camp of Ravensbrück.

You don't know who you would be if you found yourself expelled from your home and country; arrested by a patrol of the Gestapo as you distribute leaflets one dawn in the street in Brussels and are hanged from a hook, held by handcuffs behind your back so that as the chain goes up and your feet lift from the ground, you hear the sound of your shoulder joints as they are dislocated; locked in a cattle car in which you spend five whole days traveling with forty-five other people, and night and day you hear the crying of a nursing baby whose mother cannot feed it, and you lick the ice that forms in the cracks between the planks of the car because in those five days and nights there is no food or water for you, and when finally the door is opened on an icy night, you see the light reflecting the name of a station you never heard of before: Auschwitz. "No one knows whether he will be cowardly or brave when his time comes," my friend José Luis Pinillos told me. In a remote life, when he was a youth of twenty-two, he fought in a German uniform on the Leningrad front; when you see the enemy coming toward you, you don't know if you will jump toward him or freeze, white as death, literally shitting your pants. "I am not the person I was then, and I am very far from the ideas that took me there, but there is one thing I know and am pleased to have found out: I wasn't a coward when the bullets began whistling. But I am also alive, and others died, brave men and cowards both, and many nights when I can't sleep I remember them, they come back to ask me not to forget them, to tell the world that they lived."

You don't know what you could have been, what you might be, but you know what in one way or another you have always been, visibly or secretly, in reality and in daydreams, although perhaps not in the eyes of others. And what if you truly were what others perceive and not what you imagine your-self to be, just as you aren't the person you see in the mirror? Hans Mayer, Austrian nationalist, blond, blue-eyed, son of a Catholic mother, himself an agnostic, a lover of literature and philosophy, and who dressed on festival days in the lederhosen, suspenders, and knee socks of folkloric garb, real-ized that he was a Jew not because his father was Jewish, not because of any physical trait or custom or religious belief, but because others so decreed, and the indelible proof of it was the prison number tattooed on his forearm. In his room in Prague, in his parents' home, in the office of his company that insured labor-related accidents, in the rooms of the sanatoriums, in the hotel room in the border city of Gmünd where he awaited Milena's arrival, Kafka invented the perfect guilty party before Hitler and Stalin: Josef K., the man who is sentenced not because he's done anything or stands out for any reason, but because he has been found guilty, and he can't defend himself because he doesn't know what he is accused of, and when his execution comes, instead of rebelling he tamely submits and even feels ashamed.

You can wake up one morning at the unpleasant hour of the working man and discover with less surprise than mortification that you've been transformed into an enormous insect. You can go to your usual café believing that nothing has changed, and learn from the newspaper that you are not the person you thought you were and no longer safe from shame and persecution. You can go to your doctor's office believing you will live forever, and leave a half hour later knowing that a gulf separates you from others, even though no one sees it yet in your face, that you carry inside you the shadow that waits invisible for all. You are the physician waiting in the dusk of your office for the patient to whom you must tell the truth, and you dread the moment of his arrival and the necessary, neutral words. But most of all you are the patient still unaware, who walks calmly down a familiar street, taking his time because he's early for the appointment, leafing through the newspaper that he just bought and that will be left forgotten on a table in the waiting room, a newspaper with a date like any other in the calendar but a date that marks the borderline, the end of one life and the beginning of another, two lives, two that could not be more different.

You climb the stairway with the newspaper under your arm. You almost forgot the appointment, even thought of canceling it, the examination and the simple blood test, it all seemed so silly. You push the door of the doctor's office and give your name to the nurse. You make yourself comfortable on a sofa in the waiting room and look at your watch, not knowing that it is marking the last minutes of vigor and health. You look at your watch, cross your legs, open a newspaper in the doctor's office or in a café in Vienna in November 1935, when a news article will drive you out of your routine and out of your country and make you a stranger forever. A guest in a hotel, you woke up one night with a fit of coughing and spat blood. The newspaper tells of the laws of racial purity newly promulgated in Nuremberg, and you read that you are a Jew and destined to extermination. The smiling nurse appears in the doorway of the waiting room and tells you that the doctor is ready to see you. Gregor Samsa awoke one morning and found himself transformed. Sometimes in the streets of the city I thought was mine, I passed impoverished Jews, émigrés from the East, in their long, greasy overcoats and black hats, with sweaty curls at their temples, and felt repelled, glad that in no way did I resemble those obstinately archaic figures who moved through the spacious streets of Vienna as they had the villages they had left in Poland, Yugoslavia, or Ukraine. No one would stop me from walking into a park or a café, or print crude caricatures of me in the yellow press. But now I am as marked as they. The healthy, blond man reading his newspaper in a café in Vienna one Sunday morning, dressed in lederhosen and knee socks and Tyrolean suspenders, in the eyes of the waiter who has served him so often will soon be as repulsive as the poor Orthodox Jew whom men in brown shirts and red armbands humiliate for sport, and he will travel with him in a cattle car and end up exactly the same way, a walking cadaver slipping in the mud of the death camps, wearing the same striped uniform and cap, sharing the same darkness and panic in the gas chamber. The doctor runs his fingers over a white seashell, strokes the mouse of the computer, seeking in your file the symptoms that confirm the diagnosis, the sentence, the word neither of you utters. When you go back outside, your eyes are at first dazzled by the sun. The passing men and women are strangers. You walk through the city that no longer is yours, and it is with less surprise than shame that you discover, what a bitter awakening, that you are a giant insect. You move through a sinister nightmare, though the places are everyday places and the light is that of a sunny morning in Madrid. You walk along a familiar sidewalk in Berlin, over glass from shop windows shattered during the night, and smell the gasoline that fired the stores of your Jewish neighbors. Later you will remember the headlines, the photograph of Hitler, the chancellor, on a stage in Nuremberg, gesticulating before a panoply of flags and eagles, the large letters that announced your fate, that identified you as the carrier of a plague. You are Jean Améry viewing a landscape of meadows and trees through the window of the car in which you are being taken to the barracks of the Gestapo. You are Eugenia Ginzburg listening for the last time to the sound her door makes as it closes, the house she will never return to. You are Margarete Buber-Neumann, who sees the illuminated sphere of a clock in the early dawn of Moscow, a few minutes before the van in which she is being driven enters the darkness of the prison. You are Franz Kafka discovering with amazement that the warm liquid you are vomiting is blood.

Translated by Margaret Sayers Peden

WORK

1984, *El Robinson urbano*, Rafael Juárez (articles).

1986, *Beatus Ille*, Seix Barral (novel).

1985, *Dairio del Nautilus*, Diputación de Granada (articles).

1987, *El invierno en Lisboa*, Seix Barral (novel).

1988, *Las otras vidas*, Mondadori (stories).

1989, *Beltenebros*, Seix Barral (novel).

1991, *Córdoba de los Omeyas*, Planeta (essay).

1991, *El jinete polaco*, Planeta (novel).

1992, *Los misterios de Madrid*, Seix Barral (novel).

1992, *La verdad de la ficción*, Renacimiento (essay).

1993, *¿Por qué no es útil la literatura?*, Hiperión (essay that appeared published along with another by Luis García Montero).

1993, *Nada del otro mundo*, Espasa-Calpe (stories).

1994, "El dueño del secreto," Ollero & Ramos (story).

1995, *Ardor guerrero*, Alfaguara (novel).

1995, *Las apariencias*, Alfaguara (essay).

1996, *La huerta del Edén. Escritos y diatribas sobre Andalucía*, Ollero & Ramos (essay).

1996, *Destierro y destiempo: Dos discursos de ingreso en la Academia* (acceptance speech in the Real Academia Española published along with the ficticious speech of Max Aub).

1997, *Plenilunio*, Alfaguara (novel).

1997, *Escrito en un instante*, Calima (essay).

1998, *La colina de los sacrificios*, Ollero & Ramos (novel).

1998, *Pura alegría*, Alfaguara (novel).

1999, *En ausencia de Blanca*, Círculo de Lectores (novel).

2000, *Unas gafas de Pla*, Aguilar (articles).

2001, *Sefarad*, Alfaguara (novel).
2002, *La vida por delante*, Alfaguara (articles).
2004, *Ventanas de Maniatan*, Seix Barral (reports).
2006, *El viento de la Luna*, Seix Barral (novel).
2007, *Días de diario*, Seix Barral (diary).
2009, *La noche de los tiempos*, Seix Barral (novel).
2013, *Todo lo que era sólido*, Seix Barral (essays).

•

ENGLISH TRANSLATIONS

1993, *Prince of Shadows*, translated by Peter Bush, Quartet Books (novel).
1999, *Winter in Lisbon*, translated by Sonia Soto, Granta (novel).
2003, *Sepharad*, translated by Margaret Sayers Peden, Harcourt (novel).
2006, *In Her Absence*, translated by Esther Allen, Other Press (novel).
2008, *A Manuscript of Ashes*, translated by Edith Grossman, Harcourt (novel).
2013, *In the Night of Time*, translated by Edith Grossman, Harcourt (novel).

•

AWARDS AND RECOGNITIONS

1986, Premio Ícaro de Literatura for *Beatus Ille*.
1988, Premio Nacional de Narrativa for *El invierno en Lisboa*.
1988, Premio de la Crítica for *El invierno en Lisboa*.
1991, Premio Planeta for *El jinete polaco*.
1992, Premio Nacional de Narrativa for *El jinete polaco*.
1995, Member of Real Academia Española (seat U).
1997, Premio Euskadi de Plata.

1998, Prix Femina Étranger for the best foreign work published in France for *Plenilunio*.

1998, Premio Elle for *Plenilunio*.

1998, Premio Crisol for *Plenilunio*.

2003, Premio Mariano de Cavia for his article "Lecciones de septiembre."

2003, Premio González-Ruano for his article "Los herederos."

2005, Premio Quijote for *Ventanas de Manhattan*.

2007, Honorary Doctorate from Universidad de Jaén.

2010, Premio Luis de Góngora y Argote for the best literary career.

2010, Doctor Honoris Causa, Brandeis University.

2011, Premio Averroes de Oro Ciudad de Córdoba.

2012, Prix Mediterranée Etranger for *La noche de los tiempos*.

2013, Jerusalem Prize.

2013, Prince of Asturias Prize for Literature.

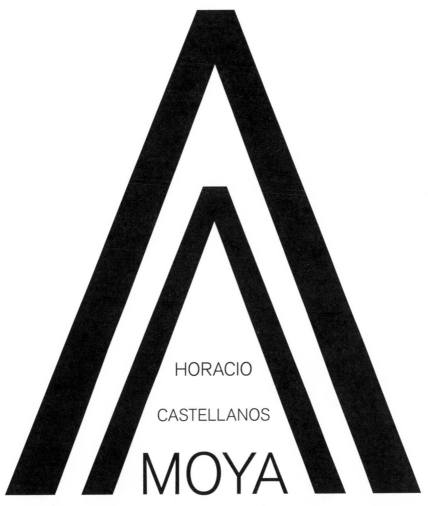

HORACIO

CASTELLANOS

MOYA

(El Salvador, 1957)

For many years Horacio Castellanos has lived outside of his country for political reasons. He was born in November 1957 in Tegucigalpa, Honduras, but he passed his childhood and adolescence in El Salvador, where his family came from. He's always felt himself and identified himself as a Salvadoran man and writer, a sense of national identity that has nourished many of his stories and novels.

In 1976 he enrolled in a Literature program, but three years later, owing to the climate of social upheaval being breathed in the city and the halls of the faculty, he opted to leave the country and move for a while to Toronto. At the time he was twenty years old and had a great desire to write.

He went back the next year and left again twelve months later. This time he went to San José, Costa Rica, where he worked as a proofreader at a university publisher, until in 1981 he moved to Mexico City, where he would live for ten years.

Despite the distance, Castellanos Moya closely followed the civil war that was unfolding in his country and, while in Mexico, he dedicated himself to journalism. He worked at SALPRESS (Salvadoran Press Agency Salpress) and was a correspondent, political analyst, and editor at the Agencia Latino-americana de Servicios Especiales de Información. He was also a columnist for the Mexican City newspapers *El día* and *Excelsior* and for the Hispanic magazine *La Opinión*, out of Los Angeles, California.

His journalistic work did not keep him from, at the same time, begininning to compose an original and provocative body of narrative work that with the passage of books and time did just enough to sustain him. In 1989, he published *La diáspora*, a novel centered on the lives of a group of Latin Americans exiled in Mexico (most of them old revolutionary combatants) where some persist in nostolgia and others keep dreaming of continuing to fight for what they believe in.

Winner of the Premio Nacional de Novela en El Salvador, *La diáspora*, beyond its storyline, is far from being a romantic portrayal of exile or defense of armed struggle. In it, on the other hand, Castellanos Moya makes a direct and bruising criticism of the rhetoric of violence, so in vogue during those years of living under fire, and such a part of the national identity. As the writer himself explained: "Violence is part of *salvadoreñidad*. It is a very violent culture, and it permeates the family, the institutions, the State, everything. So violence is expressed in its literature, and not just in mine, but in an array of writing produced in the country."

In May of 1991, in the death rattle of the war, Castellanos Moya went back to El Salvador. He was one of the founders of the weekly *Primera Plana* and he participated actively in the democratic transition, but soon he became disillusioned by the direction the events were going. All that frustration turned into a novel: *El Asco*. Published in 1997, it immediately turned into a cult classic. In it the essential themes of Castellanos Moya's fiction are condensed: crime, the abuses of sectors of the political spectrum, the loss of belief in utopias, in revolutions, an irresistible prose style, refined, and the use of monologue like an homage to the Austrian writer Thomas Bernhard.

In 1998 he moved to Spain and his work, slowly, began to be recognized by readers and critics, among other reasons thanks to a nod given him by Roberto Bolaño, who defined him as "a melancholic who writes as if from the bottom of one of his country's many volcanos." In 2000, he went back to Mexico City, and a year later he was a finalist for the Rómulo Gallegos with the novel *La diabla en el espejo*, which was followed by, among others, *El arma en el hombre*, *Insensatez*, and the stories collected in *Con la congoja de la pasada tormenta*. Between 2004 and 2006 he lived as a writer in exile in Frankfurt and later in Pittsburgh. Currently he teaches writing classes at the University of Iowa and is recognized as one of the most innovative and engaged writers from Central America, as one of its most provocative and original voices. His most recent novel is *La sirvienta y el luchador*.

THE ACORN

The Torture of Doctor Johnson

It seems to me that these pages reflect the absurdity and ridiculousness of desire, and also the complexity of the human psyche, never really content with what it has. I like the correspondence between the earthquake and the anxiety of the character. I also chose this chapter because I greatly enjoyed writing it.

In Conversation with the Dead

My dead are present in the majority of my books, sometimes quite veiled, sometimes less so. My father died when I was thirteen and since then, every now and then, death rings its bells again: friends and cousins murdered in the flower of life, the beloved elderly who die old. It seems that I write not so much to conjure death but to settle scores with her, to pay her for my dead, and also to settle scores with the murderers. The influence of Faulkner is permanent, but for me it is easy to speak literarily with Onetti, for reasons of language, and because he is the Latin American writer I most admire, although he himself said once, with a wink of modesty, that one should not read his work but rather that of Faulkner. Still, recently I have not conversed much with dead writers; instead I have returned to thinkers addicted to the aphorism, like Cioran, Nietzsche, Canetti, Schopenhauer. Perhaps as I get older and I begin to descend the opposite slope I am looking for another type of conversation, more concise and profound. In practical terms, I turn to Sophocles when I am blocked: only he is able to unblock me.

CODA

You have been a big reader of classics. Do you still use the model of Tacitus, through whom—not from a very technical point of view—you discovered your own rhythm?

It's been a long time since I read Tacitus. He was my model for writing, especially with *El arma en el hombre*: clarity and precision, the old formula, which in poetic terms comes from Horace. As Nietzsche said, "one learns to write from the Romans." And I'm not the ideal person to answer if I have found a personal rhythm. I know I don't like to repeat myself: I prefer to enter into new styles, into different forms of approaching stories. I run the risk of coming off as chaotic and impersonal. But there is definitely an intensity that comes from breathing, a way of breathing that expresses itself in my prose, beyond the narrative resources I utilize.

You have had to go into exile several times because of refusing to be silent during wartime. How does a nation, a whole society become toxic?

Death is the great theme of universal literature because it is the great mystery confronting the human species. So much effort to turn ourselves into nothing? I just finished rereading, after many years, *Pedro Páramo* and I continue to be astonished: what more can be said about death? Now okay, there have always been wars and there always will be, in different latitudes. The key is in how these wars end. If the resolution of war is based on false premises, violence persists, like has occurred in various Central American and African countries. And a plague of this nature destroys a society, both materially and spiritually. They are irredeemable countries, where daily crime and terror become aspects of identity. It remains to be seen how the war in Mexico will be resolved, it will affect the entire region.

The persecution of writers in Latin America by political powers seems unending. You have, unfortunately, endured this same persecution. Could you situate it in the context of the assassination of Roque Dalton?

I think the persecution of writers in Latin America has radically changed following the Cold War. They are no longer chased and assassinated for ideology, as they were in that time period. The men in power do not fear fiction or poetry. So now the victims are journalists. Mexico and Colombia are an example: no one goes after writers for what their poems and novels say, but journalists investigating corruption are intimidated or murdered. The assassination of Rogue Dalton at the hands of his own comrades in 1975 was a paradigmatic case of that ideological toxicity. And the death threats I suffered in the mid-nineties were, on the one hand, bad habits from that old time and, on the other hand, a result of my journalist work. The situation is different now, although there continue to be pockets of backwardness, like in Cuba and Venezuela.

You are the prototype of a writer since all writers are in exile, even if only from themselves, but in addition you are actually in exile. Being an expatriate, a foreigner, how has that influenced what you write?

The condition of exile, of nomadism, has always been the lot of Latin American writers. From Rubén Darío to Cabrera Infante, from Asturias to Vargas Llosa, from Fray Servando to José Donoso, from César Vallejo to Juan Gelman, the condition of wandering foreigner has been part of our tradition as writers. How does that situation influence my work? Everyone has their obsessions and these obsessions impose themselves even beyond foreign landscapes, the conditions of extraterritoriality, in which the writer finds himself. Most recently I wrote the novel *La sirvienta y el luchador*, which takes place in San Salvador, in the gray and boring neighborhood of Pittsburgh, during the year of terror (1980), which has nothing to do with the text I wrote. If there is a story to tell, and that story erupts forcefully from inside, what is outside matters little.

A THOUSAND FORESTS

FROM *SENSELESSNESS*

[A NOVEL]

Lying in the bed, the recently possessed body snoring beside me, I was taken by surprise by an idea, an idea that suddenly blinded me, the idea that hell is the mind not the flesh, I became aware of this at that moment, the idea that hell resided in my agitated mind—distraught—and not in the sweating flesh, for in no other way could I explain the fact that there I was in my bed in my apartment in the Engels Building, unable to enjoy the splendor of Fátima's milky-white skin, a skin that in other circumstances would have delighted all my senses, but whose proximity had now plunged me into a state of such dire agitation that I would have given anything for her not to be there, for nothing to have happened between us, for everything to have been just one more of my fantasies. But no, I told myself as I tossed and turned in bed without being able to fall asleep, with anguish gnawing away at the mouth of my stomach, no, that body I had so strongly desired had only made me understand the vulnerability of pleasure, its fragile and crumbling nature, I reproached myself, unable to find a comfortable position that would allow me to fall asleep or even relax, my gaze fixed on the windows whose curtains I had not closed completely and through which midnight and its suspicious sounds entered; that body so desired by everybody had suddenly lost its charm when just one hour before she had asked me point blank if I'd rather she suck it or masturbate me, a question that didn't make any sense considering the fact that we had been kissing and touching each other passionately for only three minutes—a few seconds more, a few seconds less—on the couch in my apartment, and what should have followed, after she already had my member in her hand and I had my middle finger inside her pussy, was to get totally undressed and lick each other all over until we consummated the act of love, instead of her posing that indecent and inappropriate question as to whether I preferred a blow job or a hand job, as if that whole preamble of confessions, caresses, and kisses that had begun in that beer joint Tustepito as evening was falling had been only a ruse to bring on the moment when she could ask me what I preferred, a hand job or a blow job, something I'd expect from a shrewd prostitute showing her price list to a horny client rather than this Spanish beauty whom, according to me, I had seduced with my charm. Who knows what expression she saw on my face, but she immediately explained in no uncertain terms that she didn't plan on fucking me—*damn it!*—that she had a boyfriend whom she loved very much and who would arrive in the country the next morning, a boyfriend she would never be unfaithful to, even though at that very moment she held my member in her hand and was offering to let me choose if she would jerk me off or suck it, she repeated, instead of getting naked and giving herself to me as logic would dictate. I told her to suck it, because it wouldn't have been a good idea to remain aroused and with my balls bursting, such a strain causes pain and makes walking difficult, even though the magical moment had already passed, that instant when the magic of possession rises resplendent had gone to the dogs the moment she asked that indecent question, more typical of a professional than a girl who's been seduced, I thought as I contemplated her with my member in her mouth, sucking, with agitated and slightly arrhythmic movements, which made me worried I would sustain an injury, perhaps the scratch of a canine, so I suggested she calm down, take it more gently, resting my hands on her head, not concentrating too much on the pleasure she was supposedly giving me but rather attempting to figure out what difference it would make as she was reaffirming her fidelity to her boyfriend, who would arrive the following morning and whom I had just found out about, if she had given me a blow job or been penetrated, a difference that was frankly difficult for me to discern, much more so when she tried to talk without taking my member out of her mouth, saying something like "ca-cu-ca-ci," and looking at me worriedly and without diminishing the flurry of her movements she mumbled over and over again in a guttural way "ca-cu-ca-ci," with such concern in her eyes, until I told her that I couldn't understand what she was saying, that she should take my member out of her mouth before talking, which she did immediately and then she clearly repeated what before I had heard only as "ca-cu-ca-ci," which in fact was the question, "Are you happy?" I would be lying if I didn't admit that this situation surpassed all my expectations, for Fátima posed such a question with the vocal intonations of a young whore, just starting out, anxious and eager to please her client, insecure about her ability to employ techniques she had so recently learned. "Ca-cu-ca-ci," I repeated to myself in disbelief while she stuck my member back in her mouth and carried on with her dazzling performance without me being able to fully enjoy such suckling efforts, given the alienation that awkward and unprecedented situation—so much for adjectives—had immersed me in, but without, thank God, my member failing me, in which case I don't know what would have happened. And soon my absence would become unpleasant, my state of withdrawal would succumb to an overwhelming attack on the senses, when she, thoroughly excited by my member in her mouth, finished taking off the garments she was still wearing, including a pair of military boots and thick socks that seemed to me vulgar and unattractive garments to wear under a summer skirt, a fashion shared by most of her European colleagues and that I had assumed was nothing more than a youthful whim without any further consequences, but that at that moment acquired a sinister dimension when an odor issued forth from those military boots that tore my nasal passages to pieces and made me feel the strongest possible revulsion, an odor that undoubtedly permeated her feet, perhaps beautiful and appetizing from afar, but which I didn't even dare to look at because I had thrown my head back against the couch, my eyes closed, my face wearing the enthralled expression of a man overwhelmed by pleasure, when the truth was that the most diverse images and thoughts were racing through my mind, thoughts and images I clung to tenaciously so as not to succumb to the overpowering assault on my nostrils emanating from the odor of Fátima's feet. No other circumstance explained how I could have been unaware of the precise instant she stopped blowing me and in one abrupt movement climbed on top of me, only my total state of distraction made it possible for Fátima to begin to gallop on top of me with my member inside her without my realizing it, because by the time I was able to react she was already being penetrated by my member and the only thing I could do was pull her toward me so I could bury my face in her neck so as to filter out as much as possible the unbearable stench, which by then had permeated the small living room of my apartment and would probably be difficult to remove from the rug where she was digging in her feet to better ride me. Lucky me that my irrigation systems didn't let me down, for flaccidity at that moment would have been the last straw, and while she was well on her way to a state of frenzy and even as I was attempting to use all possible means to press my nostrils against her skin, my mind was bouncing around like a ping-pong ball from her previous absolute refusal to fuck me to her little shouts now presaging orgasm, from the question about my preference for a blow job or a hand job to the unintelligible "ca-cu-ca-ci," from the baneful military boots to the boyfriend who would arrive the following day; a ping-pong ball bouncing with increasing intensity as Fátima approached her orgasm and shouted, "my love," "my dearest love," as if I were the boyfriend she awaited so anxiously, whereas the only circumstance of any urgency for me was to get her off me so I could quickly go and get the air-freshener out of my bathroom. That nature is capricious I understood once she, satiated and breathless, noticed that I was still aroused, an erection that didn't correspond even remotely to my state of mind and in the face of which Fátima decided to stick my member back in her mouth after saying, "Hey, man, aren't you ever going to come?" at which point I reproached myself for not having the courage to push her aside, I hated that obsessive need I had to make a good impression and my fear of hurting someone that prevented me from asking her to stop, from telling her that it had all been a big mistake, that she should relax and go to the bathroom to take a shower while I made the bed, though I really would have preferred to call a taxi that would take her home right away. But I didn't say anything, instead I let her keep at it until I suddenly understood that coming would be the healthiest thing to do, that I should cut the crap, concentrate on the suction she was applying and forget everything else if only to prevent my balls from cramping up and in the hope of recouping some of my losses from that nonsensical night, but it was already too late and after a while she took my wilting member out of her mouth and said she was tired, that we should go to the bedroom and get under the sheets, which I agreed to, since the situation had already spun totally out of control. And she walked in front of me, giving little flirtatious jumps without me sighing for any of her body's undeniable attributes, all obscured by the disagreeable idea that the stench of her feet would permeate my bed and oblige me to ask for a change of sheets ahead of time, my bed that would no longer be what it had been, even less so when she, already lying down, immediately began telling me about the boyfriend she was expecting the following day, a major in

the Uruguayan army stationed in this country as a member of the U.N. forces
overseeing the implementation of the peace accords signed by the government
and the guerrillas, a tender, affectionate guy who at that very moment was
probably packing his bags in a New York hotel room, his heart set on the girl
who the following day would meet him at the airport and who now lay beside
me, naked under the sheets; a military man she affectionately called Jay Cee,
for that was what he liked to be called, Fátima explained to me, even though
his name was Juan Carlos Medina, Major Juan Carlos Medina, to be more
exact, he preferred that she and his friends call him thus, Jay Cee, two initials
that I repeated to myself, without speaking them, on the verge of panic, while
Fátima revealed to me her decision to go live with Jay Cee in a few days, that
the plans had already been made and she would move her belongings from
Pilarica's place to the large and modern apartment Jay Cee had rented in the
city's exclusive Zone 14, a move that—as she herself admitted as she was
curling up in bed—betrayed some of her principles, especially those related to
the poverty and suffering of the indigenous peoples she worked with, and that
would also be somewhat inconvenient given the scarcity of public transporta-
tion in that wealthy neighborhood. But her relationship with Jay Cee was
above and beyond all that, she said, lying face down, the sheet half-covering
her back, he was an incomparable guy, mature, twelve years older than her,
very understanding, so much so that they shared everything that happened in
their lives, including "parallel encounters" as she called them, referring to
their infidelities, because they had spent several periods of time apart, when
he worked at the U.N. headquarters in New York and she traveled into the
highlands, she mumbled sleepily between yawns, though until then, throughout their entire seven-month relationship, only Jay Cee had confessed with
total frankness to one insignificant "parallel encounter," which Fátima had
understood and forgiven, though she had not had anything to confess. You're
not going to tell him about us, I whispered cautiously, for my fear had by now
become too much, knowing that the girl falling asleep beside me was the
fucking property of a soldier, shit, that I was on the verge of sliding away
headlong on a sled of terror and was searching blindly for the tiniest branch
to grab onto, but Fátima barely even turned her head, the palms of her hands
joined under her cheek like a pillow, she told me that of course she would tell
him, that was their agreement, to always tell each other the truth, to always
trust each other totally, and that she hated pretending and lying more than

anything else. I didn't want to turn her over to see for myself, nor argue in favor of silence, but instead I figured this was a joke, her way of making fun of me, even though her tone of voice didn't leave any room for doubt, sooner rather than later she would reveal our relationship to the soldier, and he would react like any cuckolded man, with the same blind rage, but even worse given the fact that we were talking about a soldier accustomed to resolving his problems through the use of arms, and since he wouldn't shoot her, he would shoot me, most probably, or both of us, I told myself as I descended into an expanding maelstrom of paranoia. I was then going to ask Fátima not to be unreasonable, that she shouldn't let her mouth run away with her, to tell the truth sometimes is foolishness itself, even suicidal, as was the case here, when it was obvious the soldier had tangled her up in his web of full confessions for his own sinister reasons, that she would drag my dignity through the mud between her feet and in the most irresponsible way she would put my life in danger; I was about to demand that Fátima not be so naïve, that she use some common sense, when she started snoring shamelessly, curled up in a little ball, serene in her deep sleep, untouched by my anguish, leaving me in a suffocating state of internal agitation, right on the verge of collapse and the only thing I could think to do was turn off the light and lie down in the bed as stealthily as possible, as if we could thus go unnoticed, as if in this way I could erase once and for all that equivocal night, nothing but torture for me, a night in which the pleasures of the flesh had been but a thin pretext for plunging me into the inferno of the mind, as I already said, because in that semidarkness penetrated by suspicious sounds I understood that I had become the target of that Jay Cee, that it would be effortless for him to kill me and blame my death on the local military thanks to the fact that I was the copyeditor of the one thousand one hundred pages that documented the genocide they had perpetrated against their so-called compatriots, or what was even worse, I thought, tossing and turning in bed, the bloodhounds of army intelligence, already informed about my "parallel encounter" with Jay Cee's girl, would liquidate me and turn my death into a crime of passion, a magnificent three-pronged strike that would allow their act to simultaneously resonate among the priests of the archdiocese, their Spanish colleagues, and the U.N. forces, all of whom were determined in one way or another to cause the army problems. There's no question at all that I was in the grips of the worst of all terrors, as if death were breathing alongside me, as if the snores of sleeping

beauty were the blast of the trumpet announcing the arrival of the black her-
alds, what a thought, for fear distorts everything and I was experiencing
tachycardia, sweating, probably with my blood pressure sky high, absolutely
certain that now I was really in danger. I'd had enough: I stood up, my anxiety gushing out, and went to the living room where I could pace like a prisoner in the tower, that's how I felt, with the death sentence snoring in my bed
and the prospect of a long and sinister night, unless I could gulp down a triple
whisky, a substance I didn't possess, or take a strong dose of Lexotan, the
sedative I was supposed to take 1.5 milligrams of in the morning and a similar dose at night, as the doctor had prescribed several months before, when I
suffered from such episodes after the publication of my article about the first
African president of my country, which forced me into exile, a sedative I
religiously kept at arm's length, not taking the prescribed dosage, afraid as I
am of addictions and knowing that with my compulsive personality I would
have taken it until I'd overdosed. I swallowed two pills of 1.5 milligrams
each, and I sat down to read the long information sheet that came with the
medicine, a glass of water in my hand, determined to distract myself, to no
longer think about the consequences of my relationship with Fátima, to
reduce my anxiety so that I could then go to bed and try to sleep, which—
according to the text I was reading—would happen in no sooner than thirty
minutes, the time it took the pill to take effect, so that while still in the
throes of dejection all I could do was collapse onto the couch, the scene of the
catastrophe, and pick up my notebook from the coffee table and leaf through
it and focus my attention on other voices, other rooms, but as soon as I opened
it I found the last sentence I had written down before leaving the archbishop's
palace, a sentence that perturbed my spirit even further, the sentence, *If I die,*
I know not who will bury me, spoken by an old Quiché man whom the army
had left in the direst possible situation after killing his children, grandchildren, nieces and nephews, and all his other family members, in such an
extremely dire situation that this survivor's last lament in his testimony was,
If I die, I know not who will bury me, the poor old man, a matter I immediately
questioned myself about, a question that landed on my snout like a black
butterfly be cause I didn't have anybody to bury me in case either this Jay Cee
or the specialists of the so-called military intelligence decided to eliminate
me, nobody to take care of my mortal remains if something happened to me,
I thought with sadness, not even the few remaining family members in my

own country, and no one I knew in this foreign country would take care of my bones, I bemoaned in a state of self-pity, perhaps only my buddy Toto had enough affection for me to take up a collection for the funds needed to give me a dignified burial, so my cadaver wouldn't remain in the morgue until it was sold as so much offal to some medical school, I told myself with tears in my eyes, on the verge of despair, because I felt utterly forsaken, not suffering as much as the old indigenous man whose statement had gotten me into such a state of mind, I must admit, but almost as alone and abandoned as him, even though a girl was sleeping in my bed, the intensely desired girl who had possessed me without my getting any pleasure out of it at all and whose imprudence now threatened to push me to my death. I returned to the bedroom to lie down under the sheets, to breathe rhythmically, trying to concentrate on the air coming into and going out of my nostrils, ignoring the stench of Fátima's feet, for I had other worries now, determined as I was to make that ping-pong ball bounce less and less, until I finally fell asleep.

Translated by Katherine Silver

WORK

1978, *Poemas*, Horacio Castellanos Moya (poetry).

1982, *¿Qué signo es usted, niña Berta?*, Guaymuras (stories).

1989, *La diáspora*, UCA (novel).

1993, *El gran masturbador*, Arcoíris (stories).

1993, *Recuento de incertidumbres: cultura y transición en El Salvador*, Tendencias (essay).

1995, *Con la congoja de la pasada tormenta*, Tendencias (stories).

1996, *Baile con serpientes*, Dirrección de Publicaciones (novel).

1997, *El Asco. Thomas Bernhard en San Salvador*, Arcoíres (novel).

2000, *La diabla en el espejo*, Linteo (novel).

2001, *El arma en el hombre*, Tusquets (novel).

2003, *Donde no estén ustedes*, Tusquets (novel).

2004, *Indolencia*, Ediciones del Pensativo (stories).

2004, *Insensatez*, Tusquets (novel).

2006, *Desmoronamiento*, Tusquets (novel).

2008, *Tirana memoria*, Tusquets (novel).

2009, *Con la congoja de la pasada tormenta. Casi todos los cuentos*, Tusquets (stories).

2011, *La sirvienta y el luchador*, Tusquets (novel).

2011, *La metamorfosis del sabueso*, Universidad Diego Portales (essay).

2012, *Baile con serpientes*, Tusquets (novel).

2013, *El sueño del retorno*, Tusquets (novel).

2013, *El arma en el hombre*, Tusquets (novel).

•

AWARDS AND RECOGNITIONS

1988, Premio Nacional de Novela.

2001, Finalist for Premio Rómulo Gallegos for *La diabla en el espejo*.

2009, Northern California Book Award for *Insensatez*.

2010, Selected for the Courrier International Award for *Desmoronamiento*.

EVELIO
ROSERO
(Colombia, 1958)

E velio Rosero belongs to the latest generation of novelists and storytellers to come along after the so-called Latin American *Boom*. Born in Bogotá in March 1958, he spent his childhood in the southern city of Pasto; and in his adolescence he went back to the capital where he would proceed to earn his bachelor's degree. He studied Journalism at Universidad Externado de Colombia. He never finished the program, but he always knew it was his destiny to be a writer. At twenty-one he won his first national story award with "Ausentes."

Since then he has not stopped writing. In thirty years he has published close to twenty books, among them children's literature, a play, long novels, short ones, a volume of poetry, stories, all of which has turned him into one of the most prolific writers of his generation.

Like so many Latin American writers, he lived in Paris for a while and for three years in Barcelona. Being away from his country served to prove that distance feeds melancholy, but not good writing: "I don't write better being far away," as he recognized shortly after returning to Colombia. He lives in Bogotá, tenaciously pursuing his calling of writing without rest, living a life both austere and orderly, like his writing: he moves through the city on his bicycle; he works in a bedroom, in front of a window, from where he can see a lake where grouse swim; in his free time he plays guitar.

Despite his profound style, which draws equally on a vast imagination and reflections on the most latent conflicts, he's not exactly an heir of magic realism nor of the *Boom* of the nineteen seventies. His tact and his books, often inhabited by solitary, misunderstood beings, have helped to create around the writer a halo of *rara avis*. In 2006, Evelio Rosero received the Premio Nacional de Literatura, which signified the recognition of a body of work that strives to understand the loneliness of those desperate characters, unfit for life, often embarking on fruitless voyages that never end. Far from the literary spotlight and trends, Evelio Rosero has always defended literature's duty to social transformation, but he recognizes that the role of fiction goes far beyond that: "The resolution of social and political compromises can be carried out in other kinds of reflective genres: an essay, a history, an analysis, a simple comment. But the Novel with a capital N is the human being, it is life itself."

His extensive oeuvre has been translated into English, German, Greek, and Japanese, among many other languages. His novel *Los ejércitos* won the Premio Tusquets, the ALOA prize in Denmark, awarded by writers and publishers to the best book translated into Danish, and the Independent Foreign Fiction Prize (awarded by the British newspaper, *The Independent*) for Ann McLean's English translation (translator of Julio Cortázar and Carmen Martín Gaite, among others). In it, the author tells a story in which two teachers—Otilia and Ismael—lost in a small town, manage to carry out a life amid the vicissitudes of war without any great trauma. According to the statements of Boyd Tonkin, editor of *The Independent*'s literature section, the novel "not only laments a people's tragedy but celebrates the universal yet always fragile virtues of everyday life and speaks of terrible events with a precision and humanity that win the affection and respect of the reader."

In his most recent novel to be published, *La carroza de Bolívar* (2012), Evelio Rosero continues unveiling his talent as a writer, delving into the world of farce and appearances through a voice as elegant as it is honest.

THE ACORN

A little while ago I had the chance to speak before a group of schoolchildren in Cali. One of the youngest, probably to keep me from talking too much, or because I already had, came up to the stage and handed me one of my books. "Read us a story," he said. Of course, I had no choice but to do just that. It was one of my first children's books, published in '92: *El aprendiz de mago y otros cuentos de miedo*. And the story that presented itself to me when I opened the book at random was, precisely, "Lucía, or, The Pigeons," the piece I've decided to submit as a sample of my best work: a children's story. The reasons behind this choice might seem non-literary, and they are, but not entirely. This is a story written just over twenty years ago, and the whole thing anticipates what I have tried to sketch out in my novels "for adults," especially the two most recent ones, *En el lejero* and *Los ejércitos*. Anyone who knows either of these books will agree. What surprised me the most that afternoon was the realization that a children's story managed to fully capture something that had surrounded and terrified me my whole life: the disappeared, the forced disappearances that have taken place in my country.

A THOUSAND FORESTS

"Lucía, or, The Pigeons"
from *El aprendiz de mago y otros cuentos de miedo*
(The Magician's Apprentice and Other Scary Stories)

One morning we woke up to find that the pigeons had disappeared. The last to have seen them say they flew frantically, violently tracing out strange hieroglyphs in the sky, letters and words and then entire lines, like an infinite poem no one could understand because it was conceived in an unknown alphabet. It had been a chaos of feathers, an icy white drizzle.

And from that moment on we never saw another pigeon in the sky, not a single one.

Lucía and I wondered what could have happened to the pigeons, where they had gone, or who had taken them. The world is different without pigeons, without their little winged bodies crossing its towns like shards of light. We will never forget them.

Watching a pigeon fly was like flying, ourselves, like when you send a kite up in the air and it is carried far, far away and it feels as though you were the kite, up there in the clouds.

Lucía and I thought often about the pigeons, so we wouldn't forget.

"What did pigeons sound like?"

I imagine a pigeon with Lucía's face, her long hair like wings, flying like a smile through the sky. But I don't tell Lucía. I only know that I have thought of Lucía as though she were a pigeon. The last one.

Lucía liked keeping carrier pigeons. She kept them on the roof of her house, and talked to them. She used them to send messages to places around the world and would get messages back from those places, and new messages would come from other parts of the world, brought to Lucía by other carrier pigeons. Now, since there are no pigeons, there are no messages. Not a single message crosses this sky.

The world really had been left without pigeons.

"The pigeons have left this world," Lucía says.

Why didn't I tell her that she was the last one? I don't know.

It is night now and Lucía has just told me that the stars are gone, too, like the pigeons. They just went out, suddenly, the way a candle is extinguished by a breath. There are no more stars in the sky, no matter how much we look and look and our eyes grow heavy with sleep.

The moon has gone, too. What we are looking at is an immense black sheet. The stars and the moon have gone, leaving us without light. What will be next? Nights without stars or the moon are hopeless, they are windowless nights. The moon was a light we had known from birth, and it was gone, and it seemed as though it was us who had gone far away, forever, without saying goodbye.

And the birds, all the birds, went away like the pigeons. The pigeons were only the first.

"Lucía," I think, "you are the last bird." But I don't say it.

Why didn't I tell her?

There are no more guitars, or mirrors. We don't miss the mirrors much, but we do miss the guitars. There used to be a guitar in every house, and sometimes one would play a song. Now there isn't a single guitar in the whole town. What were guitars like? Their groan, their warble, their trill?

Though the disappearance of mirrors did not, the disappearance of cats worried us. "It's heaven for the mice," said Lucía. But the mice had disappeared, too. And all the dogs. The horses vanished, along with their whinnies and their sweaty gallop, and the rabbits, they all disappeared, went up in smoke; we learned that elephants, tigers, and giraffes had disappeared from other parts of the world, and at the same time monkeys, frogs, cows, pencils, paper, light bulbs, windows, colors, tastes, and even dancing alone were slipping from sight, and we suddenly realize we've lost many things, many beings, maybe forever, without knowing when, without even realizing it, as though we had gotten used to having things disappear that had never disappeared before. Strolls in the mountains, stolen kisses, trees, and flowers disappeared the same way. Some people say that watches and wallets have disappeared, and others, that hats have. "Just try and find a hat," they say.

I don't care. I don't care about missing hats or chimneys, churches or walls or the sky.

All I know is that Lucía has disappeared, too.

Lucía disappeared and it's as though the whole world were gone.

She had grown more and more pensive, more solitary; she seemed sick, or distant, or distracted, or tired, or she simply didn't seem like anything. She couldn't stand a life without birds, without the moon.

She went to look for the ones that had gone.

I wanted to look for her; she had to be somewhere. The world is made of places, so I should be able to find her in one of them, even if she's there all alone like before, without the stars and the moon, without her carrier pigeons.

So I started walking. I was so intent on finding her that I forgot to put on my shoes.

The first day I saw a mirage: I thought I had found her, surrounded by pigeons and flowers, with the moon and the stars behind her, and a few hens pecking at a squash; a cat walked noisily across the strings of a guitar, while a black dog chased its tail in an infinite circle. She was wearing a necklace of cherries, and there were irises in her hair. Did she toss me a handkerchief?

When I sprinted toward her with open arms, I ran smack into a tree. Hadn't all the trees disappeared? I wondered. Then I realized that one tree had stayed around, waiting to strike before it disappeared. It was a mischievous tree. After I ran into it, it disappeared completely, like a burst of green laughter.

"Goodbye," I thought hopelessly. "I may never find you."

I saw that the mountains and the grass were disappearing, and every disappearance was a shock, like when you realize there is a ghost under your bed . . . but wait, what ghost? And you look again and the ghost is still there, it hasn't disappeared, it's not a dream; the ghost is still there, but the bed disappears, and the pillows, and you disappear, but the ghost is still there, more real than we are.

I saw that everything was disappearing, that I wasn't there, either. That I had disappeared, that I was the disappeared. But no, I was there. It was the sun that wasn't: I couldn't see myself because the sun's light had disappeared, the whole sun was gone. It was as though the world were gone.

And how am I supposed to find you without the sun, Lucía? How?

"It's going to get colder," said a voice at my side. With a shiver, I realized it was Lucía's.

"Lucía," I said, and repeated her name over and over.

The voices of the world circled around us, hand in hand so as not to get lost.

"Where were you?" I asked.

She told me that she had been looking for me the whole time, and then she found me. She said it just like that:

"I was looking for you the whole time, and then I found you."

"And I found you when I had given up hope," I said.

Lucía and I found one another when the earth was a darkened desert. We held each other and fell asleep and had the same dream: we dreamed that it was all a dream. That we woke up and found the world as it had been, with pigeons, and stars, and guitars. But it was only a dream. In reality, the earth itself had disappeared. The silence was a vast plain and an abyss swirled around it. I reached out and couldn't find Lucía. I thought she had disappeared, too, and got scared, the way you would get scared if this book were to vanish from your hands.

"Lucía!" I shouted, and with that, one last fleeting star, like joy, like destiny, painted the universe with light and Lucía and I could see each other.

Lucía and I could see each other, and we looked at one another.

At least we had not disappeared.

Translated by Heather Cleary

WORK

1981, *El eterno monólogo de Llo*, Testimonio (novel-poem).

1984, *Mateo solo*, Entreletras (novel).

1986, *Juliana los mira*, Anagrama (novel).

1988, *El incendiado*, Planeta (novel).

1989, *Papá es santo y sabio*, Calos Valencia (novel).

1989, *Cuento para matar un perro y otros cuentos*, Carlos Valencia (stories).

1992, *El aprendiz de mago y otros cuentos de miedo*, Cocultura (stories).

1992, *Señor que no conoce la luna*, Planeta (novel).

1998, *Las esquinas más largas*, Editorial Panamericana (urban tales).

1998, *Ahí están pintados*, Editorial Panamericana (children's comedy).

2000, *Cuchilla*, Norma (novel).

2000, *Plutón*, Espasa-Calpe (youth novel).

2001, *Los almuerzos*, Universidad de Antioquia (novel).

2002, *Juega el amor*, Editorial Panamericana (youth novel).

2003, *En el lejero*, Norma (short novel).

2004, *Las lunas de Chía*, Fondo Editorial Universidad Eafit (poetry).

2006, *Los escapados*, Norma (youth novel).

2007, *Los ejércitos*, Tusquets (novel).

2012, *La carroza de Bolívar*, Tusquets (novel).

2013, *En el lejero*, Tusquets (novel).

2014, *Plegaria por un Papa envenenado*, Tusquets (novel)

.

ENGLISH TRANSLATIONS

2009, *The Armies*, translated by Ann McLean, New Directions (novel).

2011, *Good Offices*, translated by Ann McLean and Anna Milsom, New Directions (novel).

·

AWARDS AND RECOGNITIONS

1979, Premio Nacional de Cuento Gobernación del Quindío for "Ausentes."

1982, Premio Iberoamericano de Libro de Cuentos Netzahualcóytl for *El trompetista sin zapatos y otros cuentos para poco antes de dormir.*

1986, Premio Internacional de novela breve La Marcelina for *Papá es santo y sabio.*

1986, Ernesto Sábato Fellowship.

1993, Premio Gómez Valderrama for the best novel published between 1988-1992 for *El incendiado.*

2006, Premio Nacional de Literatura.

2006, Premio Tusquets de Novela for *Los ejércitos.*

2009, Independent Foreign Fiction Prize in recognition of the best book translated into English in the last year for *The Armies.*

2011, ALOA prize (Denmark) for *Los ejércitos.*

2012, Premio Nacional de Literatura for "Revista Libros y Letras."

ACKNOWLEDGEMENTS

This book would not have been possible without the collaboration of many people.

My thanks to Nicholas Bersihand, Juan Pablo Roa, Olga Vives, Sandra Pareja, Gemma Gallardo, Sergi Godia, Will Vanderhyden, Hannah Vose, and Chad W. Post for their work throughout the process of bringing this edition to print.

I am deeply grateful to Andrew Wylie and Sarah Chalfant for their encouragement and for being guides when I needed orientation, and to Tracy Bohan and Kristina Moore for their unwavering support. I would also like to acknowledge the Spain-USA Foundation's belief in the value of this project, especially in the figures of Guillermo Corral and Cristina Ruíz in Washington, and Íñigo Ramírez de Haro in New York.

Most importantly, I would like to thank the writers for their interest in the book when it was nothing more than an idea, for their patience with the ongoing interview process and the generosity of their time.

The book is for Lucas and Aurelio.

Permissions for English Texts

Valerie Miles is a publisher, writer, translator, and the co–founder of *Granta en español*. She is also the co-director of *The New York Review of Books* in its Spanish translation and, in 2013, was voted one of the "Most Influential Professionals in Publishing" by the Buenos Aires Book Fair.